Hiding From the Light

BARBARA ERSKINE

Hiding
From the Light

McArthur & Company
Toronto

This first Canadian edition published in 2003 by
McArthur & Company
322 King Street West, Suite 402
Toronto, ON M5V 1J2

National Library of Canada Cataloguing in Publication

Erskine, Barbara
    Hiding from the light / Barbara Erskine.

    ISBN 1-55278-350-2

    I. Title.

PR6055.R7H53 2003   823'.914   C2003-901758-3

Illustrations by *Rex Nicholls*
Printed in Canada by *Friesens*

The publisher would like to acknowledge the financial support of
the Government of Canada through the Book Publishing Industry
Development Program (BPIDP) and the Canada Council for our
publishing activities.

www.mcarthur-co.com

10 9 8 7 6 5 4 3 2 1

Lighten our darkness, we beseech thee, O Lord; and by thy great mercy defend us from all perils and dangers of this night; for the love of thy only son, our Saviour, Jesus Christ.

The Book of Common Prayer

He who has once seen a ghost is never again as though he had not seen a ghost.

Cardinal John Henry Newman, 1870

God is light, and in him is no darkness at all.

I John 1,5

Note

Matthew Hopkins was, of course, a real man and Manningtree and Mistley are real places. But this story is fiction. The parish about which I write does not exist. Neither does Mike's church, rectory or street. Neither does the lane where Emma lives, nor is there a surgery where I have put one.

The old churchyard appears on maps and in guidebooks, but is now private land. The real church at Mistley does not appear.

Present darkness

LAMMAS

Lightning was flickering over the low Suffolk hills and thunder rumbled in the distance, louder this time. Bill Standing glanced up at the sky where the clouds piled threateningly one on the other, black on purple above the land. He hunched his shoulders and walked on.

He had come out here to think, to clear his head and listen to whatever it was that was battering at his brain, trying to make itself heard. The tide was nearly high, the broad estuary a carpet of white-topped waves hurling themselves inland off the sea. Above his head a gull circled, letting out a wild, mournful cry, then it turned and flew away towards the coming darkness. Bill watched it go through narrowed eyes, feeling the wind on his face. The thunder was louder now and one by one the first heavy drops of rain were beginning to fall. It was early afternoon but it felt like night. Behind him the town was closing down ahead of the storm. He could feel it waiting, watching, bracing itself for what was to come.

His unease was not only caused by the impending storm. There was something else in the air and it scared him – scared him more than anything, in all his eighty-six years, had scared him before.

The old evil there beneath the surface was awakening. It would take very little to set it free. A lightning bolt into the river, a clap of thunder up on the heath, a flash of fire in the furze bushes on the hill and the dark would rise again and envelope the shore, the town, the whole peninsular.

He had known it would happen one day. His father had told him, and his father's father had known it before him. Why

1

now, he didn't know yet, but there was no one left to stop it.

He pulled the collar of his coat up round his ears and looked up at the sky which had grown yet darker. He knew what to do, of course. More or less. But he was an old man, and alone. Were there others out there who could help him? He frowned unhappily, his weather-beaten face wrinkling into deep folds and canyons. If there were, he hadn't seen them yet. What he had seen were signs of trouble, like the blue flames licking from tussock to tussock down on the marsh, fairy sparks, they called them, the sign of danger to come like the black mist hanging on the horizon far out to sea. Darkness long laid to rest was threatening to stir as it had after the Reformation, when the priests who knew how to mediate the dark were overthrown. Hundreds of years before that the evil had come from across the sea; native and Roman gods, and the Christian alike had been vanquished before it as it sucked black energy from this wild, mysterious borderland between sea and shore. For aeons it had lain sleeping, but now he could feel it growing restless. He remembered the words, the ceremonies, to contain it, but did he have the power?

Another clap of thunder echoed over the water and he jumped. It was drifting closer on the wind, circling the town. Lightning flickered behind as well as in front of him now and it was growing darker still, as though the whole world were hiding from the light.

Past darkness

AUTUMN 1644

The room was dark and he could see nothing, but he could hear the creature in the corner, snuffling quietly to itself. He lay quite still in the high bed, staring up towards the tester he could not see, wishing he had not drawn the curtain so close around him. He was sweating profusely, his hands gripping the sheet, holding it tightly up against his chin.

Where was it? He hardly dared blink his eyes. It had moved. He could hear the scrape of claws against the boards.

Don't stir.

Don't even breathe.

It doesn't realise you're here.

If only his heart would stop pounding so loudly against his chest. The animal must be able to hear him, smell the sour fear. Inch by inch he edged up against the pillows away from the sound. There was a crack in the bed curtains now, as the sheet caught against the rough tapestry and he could see a faint line of light from the window shutters. It was nearly dawn.

Sweet Jesu, make it go away.

Another sound from the corner of the room sent a fresh sheen of sweat across his shoulder blades. There was a grunt and the sharp crunch of teeth on bone. Dear Lord, the creature had caught something. It was eating it, there, in his bedroom, taunting him. He could smell blood, smell the rank breath, the rotting teeth, he could almost see its small red, evil, eyes.

How had it got in?

He frowned. He could remember closing the door and sliding the bolt. He could remember barring the shutters. Or had he? He glanced towards the tell-tale strip of pale light. He had felt so ill as he climbed the narrow stairs the night before, the fever once again clamping its sweaty hold over his shoulders. He had fallen on the bed, racked with coughing, too tired even to pull off his bucket-top boots. He remembered that. He moved his foot slightly. No. It was bare. He must have kicked off the soft leather boots and removed his breeches and stockings before crawling under the bed covers.

Outside, the darkness lifted perceptibly. The stars and the quarter moon, hanging low over the hill behind his house, began to fade. The birds were waking. First one tentative call, then another, rang out in the cold garden.

His throat spasmed. He was going to cough again. He mustn't. He mustn't make a sound. He groped blindly for a kerchief, for the sheet, the pillow, anything to smother the noise. If he coughed, the creature would know he was there and turn its attention to him. He could feel the cough building, the tightness in his chest, the agony in his throat. His terror was overwhelming.

As the first cough exploded from him, he heard himself scream. He leaned over towards the bedside table and snatched the dagger that lay there, ready, thrusting it wildly in front of him as the bear turned to stare straight between the bed curtains into his eyes. For a moment they exchanged a long thoughtful glance, then slowly the bear rose to its feet.

Downstairs the maid heard his frantic shouting as she knelt to lay the fire. She glanced up and shook her head. Master Hopkins must be having another of his nightmares. She paused for a moment, listening, then she turned back to the fire.

4

Upstairs, at the first sound of the coughing, the tabby cat dropped her half-eaten mouse and fled from the room, leaving a small pile of bloody entrails in the corner as she leaped for the window, pushed through the unfastened shutters and vanished into the cold dawn.

In the bed, his fear drained away as swiftly as it had come and in its place he felt rage. Rage such as he had never felt before. The women who had caused him to feel such fear would pay and pay dearly for their foul conspiracy. And he knew who they were, for they were on his list. The Devils' List.

Part One

1

The present day

AUGUST

The London air was coppery, metallic on the tongue, heavy with traffic fumes and sunlight. Emma Dickson climbed out of the cab, handed over a note and glanced at her wristwatch, all part of the same flowing movement.

The cabby made a great show of diving into his money bag for change. Mean cow. Only three quid from twenty. She could afford to give him the tip. He glanced at her and in spite of himself his face softened. A bit of all right. Black dress. Gorgeous legs. Slim arms. Nice hair. Good make up. Business lady, but would tart up nicely. He handed her the change. She took it, hesitated, then handed it back. 'OK. You keep it.' She grinned at him as though she were aware of every stage of his thought processes. 'You got me here on time. Just.'

He watched as she turned across the pavement and climbed the steps towards the door. Devonshire Place. An expensive doctor, probably. He found himself hoping, as he pulled away from the kerb, that she wasn't ill.

The shiny black door with gold knocker and nameplate opened to her ring and she disappeared inside, grateful for the coolness of the hall after the blazing heat of the street outside. It was Friday. She had taken the afternoon off to visit the dentist, then she was going home to stand under a cold shower before starting to organise the evening's dinner party.

'Good afternoon, Miss Dickson.' The receptionist opened the door of the waiting room and ushered her in. 'Mr Forbes won't keep you long.'

There was no one else in the large elegant room. Sofas and easy chairs stood somewhat formally round the walls, two huge flower arrangements faced each other at opposite ends of the room and on the large low central table several piles of magazines lay, neatly squared, waiting to beguile her while she waited. Automatically she glanced at her watch. It was hard to relax, to slow down. It had been a hectic morning; she had been on the phone since eight a.m. There had been no time for lunch. For one of the senior fund managers for Spencer Flight, Jordan of Throckmorton Street, there very seldom was. To find she had to wait for her appointment was almost more than she could bear. Taking a deep breath she threw her bag on the largest sofa and picking up a magazine at random she flopped down and kicked off her shoes.

She had to learn to slow down; to relax. She wasn't even sure any more that she was still enjoying the frenetic lifestyle in which up to now she had revelled. With a long slow sigh she stretched out the long legs the taxi driver had so much admired, opened the magazine and glanced at it casually.

She had picked up a copy of *Country Life*. She flipped without much interest through page after page of house advertisements. Mansions and manor houses, even castles, all taken from their best angle, primped, air brushed, seductively enticing. Improbable. But they would all turn out to be someone's dream. Someone who had had the time to stop to consider whether the place they lived was right for them; whether they were happy, whether they should move on.

She turned another page, about to throw down the magazine, then she frowned. She sat up sharply, swung her legs to the floor and sat, staring at the picture in front of her. There were four houses on the page, all in Essex and Suffolk, all smaller than those through which she had been idly leafing. It was the one on the top right hand corner of the page that held her attention. She frowned, looking at it more closely. It was a house she knew.

She read the details with a frown.

15th century listed farmhouse with small commercial herb nursery.
3 bedrooms, 2 reception.
Large farmhouse kitchen.
Garage. Offices. 3 acres.

The house was pretty, colour-washed with exposed beams, an uneven roof, half tiled, half thatched, an oak front door surrounded by the statutory roses. She looked quickly at the other houses on the page. They too were pretty. In fact one was a great deal prettier, but this one was special. Near Manningtree, the details said. North Essex. Minutes from the picturesque River Stour.

It was Liza's.

'Miss Dickson?' It was the second time the receptionist had called her name. 'Mr Forbes is ready for you.'

She jumped almost guiltily. 'I'm sorry, I didn't hear you.' Fumbling inelegantly for her shoes she rose to her feet, still holding the magazine.

'Shall I?' The receptionist held out her hand, ever helpful, ready to replace it on the pile.

Emma shook her head. 'I'm sorry. I need to keep it. This house –' She looked up and saw irritation in the other woman's face. Shrugging, she held it out, then changed her mind. 'Do you mind if I tear out the page? It's a house I know.' She had done it before the woman could object, folding the shiny paper into her handbag and closing the fastener firmly before turning towards the surgery.

The check-up was swift, followed by a change of room, change of chair, brisk polish from the hygienist and she was finished, standing once more on the doorstep staring down the dusty street. Two cabs cruised by in quick succession, glancing at her to see if she was a customer. She saw neither of them. She was still thinking about the cottage which as a child she had known as Liza's.

Summer holidays away from London. Sailing on the Stour. Riding ponies round the paddock. Great-grandpa's pipe. Great-grandma's wonderful cakes. Walking the dogs round the country lanes. There had been all the time in the world, then. Aeons of it. They had walked past Liza's several times each holidays, always very conscious of the cottage behind its hedge and the secrets it was supposed to hold. They had never gone in, never met the old lady who lived there and in her young mind little Emma had started to weave a fantasy about the place, in which that old lady – Liza – had featured as a character in an increasingly complicated fairy story. As an only child she was accustomed to making up stories in which she featured as the heroine, and this one was no

11

exception. Her parents and great-grandparents had no idea about the story and the adventures which were going on in the little girl's head, or the extent to which she missed those holidays when her great-grandparents, too elderly to keep up the big country house, had sold up and moved away. She had never gone back to the area.

She descended the steps into Devonshire Place and turned south, walking slowly, aware of the sun's heat reflecting off the pavement and the house fronts. She was tired and hot and she wanted a cold drink. Reaching Weymouth Street she paused, waiting for the lights to change, then she walked on. The torn page was tucked into the zipped pocket in her bag. There was plenty of time to look at it again when she reached home but she realised suddenly that she couldn't wait that long. The piece of paper was burning a hole in the bag! She stopped in her tracks and fumbled for it. A business man in a dark suit who had been following immediately behind her almost walked into her. He side-stepped past her, stared for a moment and walked on. Two workmen carrying an old sink out of the front door of one of the elegant houses on the corner edged past her and threw the sink into a skip which had been parked against the kerb. She didn't notice the cloud of dust and plaster fragments which flew up as the ancient piece of plumbing crashed into the mess of rubbish. She was staring at the picture. When she did look up again she was ready to find a cab.

'Ma?' She pushed open the door of the small bookshop off the Gloucester Road, immediately spotting her mother standing by the till. The shop was empty but for a woman with two small children. Peggy Dickson raised her hand. She smiled a welcome then turned back to her customers, slotting two books deftly into a bag and handing it to the smallest child. When they finally left the shop she groaned. 'I thought they'd never go. It took that woman twenty-five minutes to choose those books. Those poor little kids, they are going to equate bookshops with boredom, dehydration, the need to pee and starvation, in that order, for the rest of their lives!'

Emma laughed. 'Nonsense, Ma. They were thrilled with their books. That little boy was an academic in the making, if ever I saw one.'

'Maybe.' Peggy sighed with exhaustion. An attractive woman in her early sixties, she resembled her daughter in bone structure alone. Their eyes and hair were quite different – Peggy's hair had once been blonde, whilst her daughter's was dark; the blonde was now the slightest hint highlighted into the smartly cut grey – but the timbre of their voices was similar. Low. Musical. Elegant.

'So, my darling, what on earth are you doing outside that temple to Mammon you call an office?'

Emma smiled. 'I took the afternoon off. It's very quiet at the moment as it's August. Everyone is out of the City. I've been having a check up at the dentist and I'm on my way to Sainsbury's. We've got Piers's boss and his wife coming to supper.' She made a face. 'Then, I hope, a long peaceful weekend! Do you and Dan want to come over for a drink some time?'

Peggy shrugged. 'Can we let you know? I'm working tomorrow – at least till lunchtime. I'll close up if no one comes in, but I don't know what Dan's plans are.'

Emma's father had died in 1977 when she was still a child. Her mother's toyboy lover – only six months younger than Peggy, but neither of them could resist joking about the age difference – was the best thing that had happened in Peggy's life for a long time.

Emma fished in her bag again and produced the page from *Country Life*. 'Ma, the reason I came over was to show you this. Does this house mean anything to you? Do you recognise it?'

Peggy reached for her spectacles and examined the picture closely. 'I don't think so. Why? You're not thinking of buying a country cottage?'

'No.' Emma grimaced. 'Piers would never hear of it. 'No. It's just –' She hesitated and her face grew sombre. 'I saw this at the dentist. Don't you remember? Near where Great-granny lived at Mistley. I'm sure it is.'

Peggy squinted at the page again. 'We did spend a lot of time there when you were little.' She chewed her lip thoughtfully, holding the paper closer to her nose. 'Wait a minute. Perhaps I do remember it now I come to think of it: Liza's. You think it's Liza's? Are you sure, darling? There must be a million cottages that look just like that one. Anyway, it says it's a farmhouse.' She took off her glasses and, putting down the page she surveyed Emma's face, frowning.

Emma nodded. 'I'm pretty sure it is. I loved that house so much I'd recognise it anywhere.'

Peggy nodded. 'I do remember now. You used to peer through the hedge and make up stories about that wonderful old lady who lived there. Liza, presumably. They were lovely times, weren't they. Those holidays seemed to go on forever.'

'Long, sunlit summers.' Emma nodded.

Before Daddy died.

Neither of them voiced that last thought, but both were thinking it.

'Wouldn't it be strange if it was the same house?' Peggy put her glasses back on, squinting. 'It's very pretty. I'm not surprised you're tempted. You are tempted, aren't you?' She looked up and surveyed Emma's face shrewdly.

Emma nodded. Somewhere deep inside an idea had taken root.

'Is this interest a sign you're feeling like settling down at last? Is it possible sweetheart, are you feeling broody?' Peggy surveyed Emma's face for a moment, then she shook her head. 'Well, maybe that's for the best. Not till you're sure about Piers. And you're not. Are you?'

Emma frowned. 'I love Piers, Ma. I wouldn't do anything unless he agreed.'

'No?' Peggy raised an eyebrow. 'He won't agree to this, Em. I can tell you that right now!'

2

Piers stood under the shower for a full five minutes before he stepped out and reached for the towel. He had been expecting Emma to be there when he arrived home from his office but the door had been double-locked, the flat, on the top floor of the converted house at the end of Cornwall Gardens, empty but for two loudly complaining cats. He stopped to give each a brief hello before checking the fridge for dinner party supplies. She couldn't have forgotten that Derek and Sue were coming over, surely. Hadn't she said she was taking the afternoon off? Pulling on some cool trousers and an open-necked shirt he surveyed himself for a second in the mirror in their bedroom, checking out his tall lanky figure, smart haircut, tanned skin – even in casual gear he looked cool and sophisticated – before he went into the living room and glanced round. It was tidy as always, a full array of drinks on the top of the low bookcase in the corner. The pale cream sofas, the linen curtains and the wood floor gave just the right impression. Expensive. Elegant. Comfortable. Two young, well youngish, executives with perfect taste. He walked across to the French doors and reached up to the hiding place behind the curtain for the Chubb key, hanging from its little hook. Unlocking the doors he pulled them open and stepped out onto the roof garden. This was Emma's very own paradise. She had created a little heaven from a sooty expanse between four ugly chimneys. Italian earthenware pots, small trees, roses, honeysuckle, herbs – her special passion – the unexpected riot of colour and sweet scents never failed to take his breath away. Emma's love for gardening and her indelibly green fingers were one of the unexpected sides to her character which he could never quite reconcile with her astute business brain and the sophisticated lifestyle she shared with him. Closely followed by the two cats, he walked over to the wrought-iron table with its matching chairs and opened the large, bleached-linen parasol. Any moment now the sun would have disappeared behind the rooftops, but the parasol perfected the picture of elegance he so enjoyed up here. And on an evening like this where better to be than a rooftop garden?

'Piers?' Emma's voice broke into his thoughts. 'Sorry, darling. I got caught in horrendous queues in Sainsbury's.' She appeared at the French doors looking, as ever, a city animal, elegant and sophisticated and cool – the furthest one could imagine from a busy shopping queue, or a gardener. 'I've got cold meat. Vichyssoise. Ciabatta. Smoked duck. Salmon. Salad. Strawberries and cream. It'll take me five minutes.' She greeted the two cats with a pat on each eager head, joined him under the parasol and held up her own face for a kiss. 'Put the wine in the fridge. When will they be here?'

He felt obscurely irritated suddenly. She knew when they'd be there. Damn it, she had rung up and fixed it with Sue.

'Unzip me?' She turned in his arms just before his kiss landed on target, presenting him with the nape of her neck and the top of a long black zip. 'I called in on Ma. I thought she and Dan might pop over and have a drink tomorrow.' With a quick wriggle of her hips she shed the dress. Under it she was naked but for a pair of the skimpiest bikini briefs.

'Em!' In spite of himself he glanced round, shocked. He would never get used to this side of Emma. Unconventional. Provocative. Always teasing him.

'No one can see! Not unless they've got binoculars and are standing on top of the power station chimneys!' She tapped his lips with her finger. 'Stuffy.'

'I know.' He knew he ought to laugh. But he was cross. He wanted her badly. But there wasn't time. With a groan he ducked into the living room and went to rummage in the wine rack in the corner behind the kitchen door. 'Dry Hills Sauvignon OK?'

'The best! Lovely.' She was still standing naked on the roof.

'Em! They will be here in a minute.'

She glanced over her shoulder at him coqettishly, then she relented. 'OK. I'll jump in the shower. It will take ten seconds to dress.' As she passed him she brought her hands to her hips briefly and gave a quick shimmy. 'Not bad for a thirty-something, eh? And look at the teeth!' She ducked out of reach and ran to the bathroom. In ten minutes rather than seconds she was dressed, her hair brushed, a quick skim of colour on lips and eyelids and she was ready, once again the cool calm City woman, fit partner for a potential director of Evans Waterman, one of the largest City broking houses.

In the event Derek and Sue were half an hour late. By the time they arrived the hors d'oeuvres were laid out on the wrought-iron table, the wine was chilled, the table was laid and the duck and the salad prepared, the duck locked securely away from the enthusiastic attention of the cats.

It was as they moved on to the coffee at the end of the meal that the subject of weekend cottages arose. 'We have a place in Normandy, you know.' Sue leaned back against the sofa cushions and crossed her ankles. 'It would be lovely if you could both come over for a few days.'

Outside, the roof terrace was dark, lit by two shaded lights hidden amongst the flower pots. A gentle breeze wafted the smell of the hot London night into the window. Sue sipped at her coffee. The two cats were asleep on one of the deckchairs outside. 'Have you ever thought of buying somewhere yourselves?'

'No.'

'Yes.'

Piers and Emma spoke at the same moment and they all laughed.

'Sounds like a fundamental difference of opinion,' Derek commented as he reached for his brandy glass. As so often, he found himself wondering how Piers managed to hang on to this lovely spontaneous creature.

'That's because we haven't discussed it yet.' Emma climbed to her feet and went over to pick up her bag which was lying on the side table. 'I saw something today which intrigued me so much, I want to go and see it.' She found the folded page and brought it back to the sofa. 'It's a little farmhouse in Essex.'

'Essex!' Sue hooted. 'Oh, my dear, I think you could do better than that.' She held out her hand for the picture.

'Essex is quite nice, actually,' Derek put in mildly. He raised an eyebrow in his wife's direction. 'The Essex they joke about is in the south of the county, part of the greater London area. But if you go up to the north you have wonderful countryside and lovely villages and towns. Constable country. You're miles and miles from London there. It's very rural.' He held out his hand for the magazine page which Sue had glanced at and dropped dismissively on the coffee table. 'This one, is it?' He tapped the photo. 'It's looks a lovely place. Perfect weekend material. Good sailing up there. Do you sail, Piers?'

Piers had risen to his feet. 'No, I don't,' he said briskly. 'Weekend cottages are not my thing, I'm afraid.' He looked angry. 'Emma knows that. I can think of nothing I would like less than pottering about "doing it myself", mowing grass and being nice to hay-seed neighbours! I hate the country! I was stuck in deep country as a child and I couldn't wait to get away. I can still remember my parents vegetating, telling me to go bird watching, trying to make me interested in nature, for God's sake! I couldn't wait to get away and I will never, never go back!'

There was a moment's intense silence.

'Oh, well!' Emma forced herself to laugh. 'There goes that idea!' She took the cutting from Derek's hand and, folding it, tucked it into her pocket. 'More brandy, anyone?'

Derek and Sue left early – 'It's been a long week, old things, bed for us, I think,' – but it was after midnight by the time Emma and Piers had stacked the dishwasher and carried two more brandies out onto the roof terrace.

'Do you think they enjoyed it at all?' Emma was staring out into the luminosity of the London night.

'Yes, of course they did.'

'They left a bit soon.'

'Like Derek said, they were tired.' He leaned his elbows on the parapet, rolling the glass between his hands. 'Don't worry about it. They have asked us to go to Normandy, don't forget. And while you and Sue were brewing that second pot of coffee he told me it's OK.' He turned to her and she saw the triumph in his face. 'I'm going to be asked to join the board.'

'Oh Piers, I'm so glad. Why didn't you tell me at once?'

'I wanted to wait till we had a glass in our hand. I wanted us to drink to the future. My future and our future.' He held her gaze for a moment. 'And I wanted to tell you when we were on our own because I think we should get married, Em.'

For a moment she didn't move, and he could read the conflicting emotions on her face as clearly as if she were speaking out loud. Elation – that first, at least – worry, doubt, excitement, caution, then that moment which he recognised so well when she withdrew inside herself, her eyes suddenly unfocused as though viewing the future on some mysterious invisible internal screen. He waited. It would only take seconds for her private computation to take place. Until she had done it, he had learned to wait.

He felt a warm pressure against his ankle. Max was circling his feet, purring. He bent to pick the cat up, tickling him under his chin. 'Well?' He glanced at Emma and grinned. 'So far I am not overwhelmed by your enthusiasm.'

She smiled. Reaching forward, she gave him a quick kiss on the lips. 'I love you, P. You know that. And I want to live with you forever and ever.'

'I can feel a "but" coming.'

'No. It's just –' She hesitated, then putting her glass down on the parapet beside him she reached into her pocket. 'When we talked about country cottages earlier, you were pretty damning.' She unfolded the cutting. 'It didn't sound to me as though there was any room for compromise.' She reached out absent-mindedly and rubbed the cat's ears. 'We've never talked about the sort of future that marriage means, P. Kids. Gardens. A life beyond E C 1.'

'And why should we? That's all for the future, surely. Nothing we have to think about yet. In the abstract, yes, I'd like kids one day. If you would.' He raised an eyebrow. 'I've never had any sense that you are hearing the time-clock ticking, Em. My God, that's years off, surely.'

She laughed. 'Not so many. I've reached the dreaded thirties, don't forget.' She reached over for Max, who climbed into her arms and draped himself across her shoulder with a contented purr. 'I want to go and see this cottage. This weekend.'

'Oh, for God's sake!' He snatched the cutting from her hand. 'Em, this is silly. What is it with this place? You know we can't go this weekend. I'm playing squash with David tomorrow. You've asked your mother and Dan over. I've got a report to write. We have a hundred and one things to do.' He moved over to the lamp and held the cutting so he could see it more clearly. 'Three acres. A commercial herb nursery for God's sake, Em. This isn't even a country cottage. It's a business. Look, if you're so keen on the idea of a cottage why don't we go down to Sussex or somewhere and take a look. Or why not France? Now that's an idea. Derek said property there is still a fantastic investment.'

'I don't want it as an investment.' Letting the cat jump to the ground, she threw herself down on one of the cushioned chairs. 'In fact, I don't know that I want it at all.' There was a sudden note of bewilderment in her voice. 'I just want to go and see it. I remember it from when I was a child. It's a cottage I used to dream about. I built a whole fantasy world around it. It means a lot to me, Piers, and if it's on the market . . .' She shrugged. 'Maybe it's meant to be.'

He gave a short laugh. 'Not for me, it isn't. I told you what I think about the country.'

'Well, I want to go and see it at least. As soon as possible. Tomorrow. I'm going to ring the agent first thing.'

'Well, if you do go, you go without me.' He threw the cutting down on her lap. 'The place has probably gone anyway. Did you see the date at the bottom of the page? The magazine was three weeks old.'

3

For a long time Emma lay awake listening to Piers's even breathing. They had tried to patch things up; to paper over the awkwardness; but it hadn't worked. The night seemed to have grown chilly suddenly and going inside they had closed the windows and drifted, apart, towards the bedroom. When Emma had emerged from her long soak in the bath, Piers was sound asleep.

It was impossible not to toss and turn, and after what seemed like an interminable attempt to relax and follow suit Emma got up and walked though into the kitchen. Two alert pairs of eyes watched her from the kitchen table.

'You know you're not supposed to sit there,' she commented half-heartedly, but she made no attempt to move them. Without bothering to turn on the main lights she opened the fridge door. The interior light illuminated the kitchen, filling it with a subdued eerie glow as she poured herself a glass of iced spring water. Slamming the door shut again, she walked on in the semi-darkness into the living room. The faint echoes of the evening were still there. The richness of wine and coffee, of Sue's scent, the sharp aroma of brandy from the glass Piers had put down on the low table as he walked past on his way to bed.

Emma threw herself down on the sofa and closed her eyes. The curtains were open and a faint light seeped into the room outlining the furniture, reflecting flatly from the cut-glass bowl of roses on the table. Two black shadows padded silently from the kitchen and leaped lightly onto the sofa back to sit close to her, like bookends in the silence of the room.

She sighed and closed her eyes.

In her dream it was the year of Our Lord, 1646. The cottage was very small, the rooms dark, but the garden was bright and neat, a riot of colour. She stood by the gate, her back to the church, staring round, and she knew she was smiling. Hollyhocks

21

and mallow crowded the beds with roses and honeysuckle vying for position on the front wall. She could feel the sun hot on her back as she pushed open the gate and walked up the path. She knew she ought to knock, but the front door was open and she ducked inside.

'Liza? Where are you?' She heard her own voice without surprise. 'Liza? I've brought you some pasties from my father's kitchens.' She had a basket on her arm, she realised suddenly, the food inside succulent and still warm beneath a white linen napkin. She put it down on the table and went to the foot of the narrow steep staircase. 'Liza? Are you up there?'

The house was silent. The only sound came from the sudden piping calls of the young swallows in their nests hanging under the untidy thatch.

She ran up the stairs, feeling suddenly anxious, and peered round the room. The small box bed was empty, the patchwork cover neatly spread across it. A coffer chest in the corner was the only other furniture.

'Liza?' She ran downstairs again, very conscious of the emptiness of the house. 'Liza, where are you?'

Outside there wasn't a breath of wind. The heat was overwhelming. Humid. Uncomfortable. The swallows were silent now. Nothing moved. She tiptoed along the path and peered round the corner to the patch where Liza grew some of her herbs. She had thyme there, and rosemary. Vervain. Cinquefoil. St John's Wort. Elecampane. Horehound. A basket lay on the ground nearby and a pair of silver scissors. Emma bent and picked them up. 'Liza?' Her voice sounded strangely muted out here. And it echoed as if coming from a long way away. There was a piece of green ribbon tied around the mulberry tree. She stared at it for a long time, then slowly she turned back towards the gate. From the lane she could see down towards the blue waters of the estuary in the distance. The tide was in. Two boats were sailing in towards the shore. She stopped to watch them for a moment; only when she raised her hand to her face to brush away a tear did she realise she was crying.

When Emma woke, wondering where she was, she found her cheeks still wet with tears. By the time she had fallen asleep again her mind was made up. She would go and see the cottage in the morning and if Piers didn't want to go with her then she would go alone.

22

4

Saturday

Mike Sinclair, dressed in an open-necked shirt and jeans, was standing in the kitchen of his rectory gazing down at the toaster, watching the red elements slowly browning the flabby white slices he had extracted from the bag of Co-op bread his cleaning lady had bought for him two days before. He sighed. He must make time to do his own shopping from time to time. In vain he wrote brown bread on the list, sometimes wholemeal, underlined. White and flabby was what he always got.

The two slices of toast leaped in the air and fell back into their slots. He whisked them out onto a plate and, picking up his mug of coffee carried both over to the table. Butter, still in its paper and already liberally anointed with yesterday's toast crumbs, stood there waiting together with a jar of Oxford Marmalade. He grinned to himself. In spite of the bread it was still his favourite breakfast and it was going to be another glorious day. He had to spend most of it in his study catching up on paperwork and going over his sermon one more time, but it was still very early and there was going to be time for a walk.

He had only been in the parish a few months and he was still feeling his way with both congregation and geography. The best time to explore, he had discovered, was the early morning when the streets and lanes were comparatively empty and he could wander round without being accosted by his parishioners. So, he would allow himself a couple of hours to eat and walk before coming back inside and facing the pile of papers in his study.

Breakfast complete, headlines from the paper which had appeared on his doormat scanned – he had been amused to see when he had first arrived that the lady from the paper shop had assumed he would read the *Telegraph*, so he had gone in to thank her, congratulate her on her business acumen in snaring a new customer and tactfully amended the order to *The Times* – it was time to set out.

The rectory stood back in its garden down a long gravel drive at the end of Church Road. It was not the old rectory, of course – that had burned down a hundred years before – but an old house none the less, acquired by the church in the 1920s as a fit home for a parson and his then large family. It was a big house for one man, but Mike had been enormously pleased to find his new parish was not one of those which had decided a characterless modern bungalow was a fitting habitation for its rector.

It was a pleasant Georgian-fronted building, painted a pale Suffolk pink, the interior probably Elizabethan and heavily beamed. He would try and find out about some of its earlier history one day when he was not so busy. The garden, he had noted sadly, was, apart from a few lovely trees, more or less devoid of interest. It was not very big, which was probably just as well, given the fact that he suspected he would have little time to give to it and there would be no money from either his own pocket or the diocese for a gardener. Wonderfully, he had managed to secure the services of a cleaning lady two mornings a week. Probably not for long. He doubted if he could afford her forever. It had been a shock when he realised just how small in real terms his stipend would be as a country parson. He gazed at the grass. It was as always neatly mown and as always he wondered who on earth had done it. One of the PCC perhaps, choosing a moment when they knew he would be out, or one of the other kind people who had offered him their services when he had first arrived in the parish. Many had offered help. The two food baskets – to stave off starvation, he supposed – which had greeted his arrival, had from time to time been discretely replaced and two ladies had offered to cook him the occasional meal.

He grinned to himself. Several people, including the bishop, had warned him about the ladies. An unmarried, good-looking rector in his early forties – Mike was broad-shouldered, fair-haired, blue-eyed – would be a major target once they had decided amongst themselves that he wasn't gay!

Slamming the door, he headed for the gate. Church Road was,

up here at the top, actually more of a lane. Beyond his house, the church itself sat serenely in its churchyard sheltered by three huge yew trees, a surprisingly rural setting when one considered that Manningtree was actually a small town – the smallest town in England, so someone had told him – and that over the hedge he could see lines of old roofs rising gently up the hillside.

This early, the road was deserted. He strode down it purposefully, passing between houses much like his own, except that where it descended into the centre of the town they were terraced and what gardens they had were hidden by high walls. Down on the corner where Church Road met the High Street the last two houses had been converted into double-fronted shops, but a glance at the roofs showed that they too were as old as the rest of the street. One of them, he had noticed, had been empty since he moved in.

In the High Street he turned east, round the corner and down to the River Stour to walk along the road which bordered the narrow strip of salt marsh and the mudflats which were such a characteristic of the river at this point. He passed a solitary dog walker who acknowledged him with a raised hand and continued on his way. He loved this walk. Strolling along under the sycamores which lined the road to Mistley, the second half of his parish, he followed the pavement which on his right ran parallel to the long wall which once had bounded the great Rigby estates, a feature which had given the road its name, 'The Walls', whilst on his left lay breathtaking views of water, mud and sky. He stopped and stared for several minutes. The tide was out, the river estuary mostly mud, the low Suffolk coast on the far side hidden in the early morning mist. The shore was blue and mauve with sea lavender and tiny yellow-centred asters and as he walked slowly on he became aware of multitudes of birds running about on the mud. He wasn't very good at bird identification but he could recognise a seagull when he saw one, and swans, and what he thought might be oystercatchers, with their smart black-and-white plumage and red bills.

He was heading for the second of the churches in his sprawling parish of Manningtree with Mistley, the one which, he admitted wryly to himself, fascinated him probably far more than it warranted. When he had first arrived he had asked to be shown it several times. He knew of course that it was a ruin, but surely, he had thought, there would be something to see. He knew he was a bit of a romantic, a side of himself he tried sternly to keep under control, but he did feel, quite strongly, that even a ruined church would still have an aura of sanctity about it. Perhaps he would be able to hold the occasional service in the ruins. He had not at the time had the chance to put this idea to anyone locally and perhaps that was just as well. His first few requests to see it had somehow not been heard. And this lack of response had intrigued him. He had investigated its history and found amongst other things that it might have been the burial place of the notorious Witchfinder General. He had of course gone looking for it himself at the first opportunity. What he found had disappointed him, but he had driven past on a rainy day. Today he was on foot and it was a glorious morning and he wanted to see if he could find out why the church had been allowed to fall into decay. Why it had been demolished.

Cutting through the centre of Mistley with its irresistible combination of Victorian industrial buildings, old Maltings and quay, its famous Adam Towers and swan fountain, its lovely houses and cottages, he made his way inland up a short track towards the path across the fields. He loved Mistley. The centre of the village was very small and these days so quiet it was hard to picture it as the bustling town it had once been.

The ruins of the old church lay up a narrow road beyond New Mistley, opposite the lane up which he strolled. Beyond, across the shoulder of the hill, he could see glimpses of the broad estuary, the water brilliant blue beneath the clear sky. There was a wind out there. He could see a white sail tacking out towards the sea, but inland it was very still, and the air was growing hotter. He could smell the wild honeysuckle in the hawthorn hedges, and the hot floury scent of the stubble in the fields.

He paused, looking round. There was still no one about. It was extraordinarily quiet. Turning slowly he found himself wishing suddenly that he had a dog to walk. It would be company on his early-morning strolls. In the distance he could see the huddled roofs of the small hamlet of old Mistley, while behind him sprawled the houses of the new developments. But here, in the fields he was completely alone.

The site of the church was unmarked. All he could see was the brick wall which had surrounded the churchyard. It was almost buried under brambles and nettles now and behind it was what looked like a small orchard or paddock. There was no sign of the church itself at all. Within living memory, so he understood, the tower had still been standing and had been used to conduct funerals, then it had been declared unsafe and demolished. The site had been sold.

On the opposite side of the road was a pink-washed cottage, set back behind a wild tangled hedge. Its windows were dark and bare of curtains. A drunken-looking *For Sale* sign lounged beside the gate.

'Can I help you?'

A stocky, bearded man had appeared in the lane behind him, two black labradors waiting patiently at his heels. The man's eyes were hard with suspicion.

Mike shook his head. 'I was just looking. I wondered if anything remained of the old church.'

'It's long gone.' The man's expression did not invite confidences and Mike found himself biting back his intention of introducing himself.

'A shame,' he said mildly.

'Damn good thing. Evil place! You keep out of there. It's private property.' Whistling to his dogs, the man walked on up the road.

Mike exhaled loudly. Evil? No, how can it be, it's church property, he wanted to shout. Mine! But of course it wasn't true. Not any more. He watched the retreating back for a minute or two, then resumed his inspection of the site. As far as he could see there were no yew trees, no grave stones, no sign at all that there had ever been a church there except for the wall, and, he squinted through the nettles, the twisted remains of a gate lying below what had once been a gatepost deep in the undergrowth.

The wall beyond it, round the corner, had begun to crumble away. Without giving himself time to think Mike pushed his way through the nettles and scrambled over the broken bricks into what had once been the churchyard itself. Branches swung across behind him and within seconds he was totally screened from the road. He smiled to himself. It probably wasn't wise for the rector to be caught trespassing but on the other hand his curiosity had been intensified by the man's aggressive manner.

He moved forward into a patch of sunlight and stared round. He could see signs of old walls now, and a faint rectangular depression in the ground where the church must have stood. The whole area was thickly wooded. As far as he remembered from its description in *The Lost Parish Churches of Essex* it had been a beautiful medieval church with nave, aisle, porch and tower. The village had moved, the population drifting down the hill towards the bustle of the small port on the river's edge, but that did not explain why it had been so completely lost. After all, there were other remote churches around; churches in the centre of a field or a wood and they had not been pulled down. They had been treasured and preserved. The voice of the man in the lane echoed suddenly in his head. 'Evil place!' he had said. Why evil? Was it something to do with Matthew Hopkins and the witches, or was it something else? Something infinitely older? An ancient ash tree shaded the ground and everywhere there were hawthorns and elders, heavy with ripening berries. The grass was kept short, he saw now, by some half-dozen sheep which were grazing on the far side of the trees. It was a beautiful, peaceful place. He took a couple of steps forward and paused. The birds had fallen silent. He shivered as a shadow fell across the ground at his feet.

Why exactly had they demolished the church? And if it was because it had grown dangerous, why had they allowed that to happen? And why had they to all intents and purposes flattened the graveyard? Not a single stone survived upright as far as he could see. And why, on this once-hallowed ground, was there not even one single cross as a memorial to the building that had once stood here?

Slowly he turned. The sun had disappeared behind a single stormy cloud and the warmth of colour had gone out of the morning. Making his way towards the gate he found himself conscious suddenly that someone was watching him. The skin on the back of his neck prickled and he glanced round again. He could see no one.

'Hello?' His voice sounded curiously flat in the silence. 'Is there someone there?'

There was no answer.

By the distant wall the leaves rustled briefly and he swung round. 'Hello?' he called again. The wall was in shadow now, the bricks uneven, covered in moss and ivy. Something moved suddenly and he focused on it carefully. A tiny, mouse-like brown bird was running in and out amongst the ivy. A wren. He watched

28

it for a minute and found he was smiling, his sudden tension defused.

Making his way back to where the gate had been he stared down at the gap in the wall. It had been filled with barbed wire. A rusty chain which had once held the gate closed dangled emptily in space. He fingered it slowly, then climbed back over the wall. Clearly he wasn't the first to do so. He could see the signs now of other feet on the crumbling mortar, bent and broken vegetation, an old footprint set into the mud, long dried and baked in the August sun.

Once in the lane, he turned away from the church and began to walk briskly back towards Mistley. Next time he came up here he would drive up the hill, wear his dog collar and make a few calls. Whilst attending to his parochial duties he could ask a few questions about the church that was no more. He did not even glance at the cottage across the road.

5

Lyndsey Clark had lived in Mistley for five out of her twenty-five years. She knew every inch of this place – the church ruins, the churchyard, Liza's – and regarded them all as her own. She had recognised the rector as soon as he had emerged from the path across the field and she watched curiously to see what he was up to, catching her breath suspiciously as he climbed into the churchyard, creeping forward in the shelter of the hawthorns to see what he was going to do. He shouldn't be here. She shivered violently. He was disturbing the place, she could sense it already, although – she frowned, her head cocked like a dog picking up a scent – not intentionally. He didn't know what he was doing. She shook her head in an anguish of worry suddenly, pushing her short dark hair back off her face.

Leave. Please leave. Quickly. Before you do damage.

Biting her lip, she craned between two branches, her vivid blue eyes focused intently on the figure under the trees.

He was feeling his way. After a while he turned back towards the road, then he stopped and looked straight at her even though she knew he couldn't see her. She was wearing a dark green T-shirt and black jeans which must have blended into the shadows, and yet – she held her breath. Yes, he was a sensitive. That would be dangerous in a man of the church, although in her admittedly somewhat limited experience, those were rare these days.

She heard the wren in the ivy near her, saw him spot the bird and watch it for a moment, smiling to himself, then he was on his way over the wall and out into the lane. He did not even glance in her direction.

Silently she whispered a thank you to the little bird which had taken his attention. It paused, cocked its head in her direction, bobbed a quick acknowledgement and it was gone.

She gave him a minute or two to get well down the lane, then she made her way to the crumbling part of the wall where it was easy to climb in. The atmosphere, usually, thanks largely to her efforts, so placid and dreamlike, was uncomfortable, the air tense and jumpy. She made her way slowly towards a rough patch of grass where lichen and moss had grown over the foundations of the long-fallen wall. It was near here she felt Hopkins most strongly, the man whose evil haunted her life. It wasn't the grave, of course, but too many people had thought it was even after the church was finally demolished, the graveyard destroyed, the land deconsecrated. Especially after it was deconsecrated. Their thoughts, their fears, their excitement and their malice had congealed into a tangible weight of sorrow and fear. Most of the time she could contain it. She knew the ways. Counter spell and spell. Prayer. Binding charms. They all worked if one knew what one was doing; all prevented the reality manifesting from the thought. As long as nothing – no one – upset the balance.

Glancing round to make doubly sure no one was there, she fished in the pocket of her jeans for a small pouch. In it were dried herbs. Herbs gathered from the garden at Liza's. Carefully she scattered the dusty leaves around the inside of the walls before going back to the centre, where she crouched down on the ground and scraped a small hole amongst the grasses with her fingernail. She tucked the pins and the small piece of knotted thread into the soil and covered them, rearranging the grass around the place. In seconds all signs of her intervention had gone. Standing up again she wandered over to a tree stump where for a moment she sat down, the sun on her back. She could hear the bees humming in the flowers nearby. They were calm now, their agitation soothed. If she listened she could hear their gossip, the hive memory, relayed down the years . . .

The garden had been smaller in Cromwell's time, enclosed within
a picket fence, the small neat beds in summer a riot of undiscip-
lined bounty. Fruit and flowers, herbs and vegetables, all crammed
into the spaces between the gravel paths where yet more herbs
had seeded in a riot of colour. Marigold and feverfew, dandelion
and hyssop, thyme and marjoram. Liza made her way slowly
between the rosemary bushes, her basket in her hand, plucking
a sprig here, a leaf there as the sun dried the dew and the plant
oils began to release their scents into the morning air. She woke
at dawn on these summer mornings, glad to lever her aching
bones from her bed. As her body bent and grew frail the pain
became more intense. It was hard to look up now, the curve of
her back was so pronounced. Hard to look at the sky, to see the
sun, to watch the birds fly over. Her knowledge and experience
of remedies and medicines was of little use to her now. Nothing
she did seemed to help. Only the sunshine, with its blessed
warmth shining down on her eased her a little. She crooned a
greeting to the old cat sitting on the path ahead of her and it rose,
coming to rub against her legs, before sitting once more in the
patch of sunlight and lifting a fastidious paw to wash its left ear.

She needed horehound and pennyroyal and thyme for young
Jane Butcher who was near her time. It would be a long and
painful birth if she was any judge. The child in her belly was huge
– the babe taking after its father, John Butcher, a large man whose
two earlier wives had both died in child bed. Why didn't he choose
a woman with broad hips and meaty thighs like his own? Why
did he pick such little child-wives with such narrow bones? She
shook her head sadly. Jane was terribly afraid. And with reason.
Liza passed on amongst her plants. She needed hyssop and black-

32

berry leaves for her neighbour's sore throat and a poultice for Sir Harbottle Grimstone's cowman who had a cut on his hand which was swollen and yellow with undischarged puss. She sighed. They paid well, her customers, and she was happy to help them with their pain, but sometimes she wished there was someone who would help her. Someone to bring her warm soothing possets in the evening, someone to help her change her old woollen gown when the ache in her arms made her cry as she tried to pull it over her head, someone who would take over the garden for her before it ran riot for the last time and took her by the throat and strangled her. She gave a hoarse chuckle at the thought. As long as the plants survived she supposed it was all right. They didn't need to be as neat as they were when she had first planted out her little medicinal garden. And they would probably outlive her. And Sarah came when she could with a basket of food or a warm shawl or a jug of ale. Sarah, daughter of the manor, her suckling child, the little girl who had replaced her own dead baby at her breast. She pulled her small shears out of her pocket and snipped and cut and tugged at the leaves until the basket was overflowing.

The cat had followed her. It stopped near a patch of catnip and threw itself headfirst into the clump, rolling ecstatically amongst the aromatic leaves and she chuckled again.

On a shelf in the cottage she kept the utensils of her trade meticulously neat. Pestle and mortar, bowls, scoops and jugs, all washed and drained and clean. Baskets and bags of dried herbs hung on hooks from the ceiling beams and boxes were stacked carefully on a table in the corner. She set her basket of fresh pickings down on the table and went to check the fire. The iron pot of water hanging over the coals was nearly boiling.

Jane Butcher's medicine first.

She worked on for a long time, conscious that the beam of sunlight coming through the kitchen door was moving steadily across the floor. Soon the sun would move round into the south and her kitchen would be shadowy again and cool. Squinting at the jug in her hand she tried to work faster. Once the sun had gone it was harder to see what she was doing and more and more often the thick black tinctures which came from her pots would spill across the scrubbed oak of her table.

Once she stopped and stared at the door, listening. Had that been someone at the gate? She could hear the high-pitched alarm call of a mother bird telling her young to hide low in the nest – a cry understood and acted on by every other bird in the garden. Perhaps it was the old cat which was causing such consternation. His roll in the catnip might have rejuvenated him enough to stalk a bird but somehow she doubted it. She frowned. Her hearing was still acute even if her eyes were growing dim. In the silence of the garden she could hear menace. Slowly putting down her jug and spoon she hobbled to the door and stood looking out. There was no one to be seen. The lane was empty. There was no sign of the cat. But somewhere something was wrong.

Then she saw him, the man standing half hidden in the shade of the old pear tree in the hedge and she recognised him. It was one of Hopkins's servants. She stared at him for a moment, puzzled. Why was he watching her? Seeing her turn towards him he drew back into the shadows and she saw him clench his fists into the sign against the evil eye before he turned and fled, and in spite of the warmth of the sun across her shoulders and the scents of the herbs around her she suddenly smelled the cold breath of fear.

6

Pulling her MG into the car park near the Co-op Emma crawled slowly between tightly packed rows of cars trying to find a space. 'Better to park there and walk up to the shop,' the house agent had said. 'There's no parking along the High Street here and not much anywhere on a Saturday.'

How right he was. The place was teeming. Someone backed out in front of her and she turned into the space with relief. She was exhausted. It had been a two-hour drive from London – a drive starting with a row with Piers . . .

'I'm sorry. I told you yesterday, I am not going off on some wild goose chase to see a cottage I don't want in a county I don't like on a weekend I want to stay at home!'

He had been furious when she confessed she had rung the agent that morning at nine a.m.

'Yes, you're right. It is Liza's.' The young man's voice had been hoarse, as though he had a bad cold. 'Yes, it is still on the market. There's been a lot of interest, but no one has made a definite offer yet. Yes, you could view it today.'

'Liza's.' She had repeated the name to herself as she hung up. 'Liza's Cottage.'

Will Fortingale, the young man at the estate agent's, did indeed have a bad cold. His nose was red and swollen and he was clutching a large handkerchief as he opened the filing cabinet and pulled out a folder of particulars and a bunch of keys.

'Do you know how to find it?' He withdrew a couple of stapled sheets of A4 and handed them to her.

'It was a long time ago.'

'Right. Well. It's not occupied, so they won't mind you looking round it on your own. You don't want me to go with you?' He glanced up anxiously and she saw the relief in his eyes as she shook her head. He had summed her up as she walked through the door. He could always tell a serious buyer and Emma Dickson wasn't a serious buyer. There was no point in trying too hard with this sale, especially as he was feeling so damn rotten.

She waited whilst he scribbled down some instructions for her, found and photocopied a local map, handed her the keys, then she was out in the street again.

She did not remember Manningtree at all. She stood outside the agent's shop and stared round in delight. It was a pretty town, the centre consisting as far as she could see of little more than the narrow, busy main road in which she was standing with a couple of other streets crossing it at right angles. She squinted at the map in her hand. She was standing on the corner of Church Street. South Street ran parallel with it fifty yards or so along. All were hung with flower baskets – old houses and shops alike decorated with fuchsia and geraniums, lobelia and ivy. She pressed back against the wall as a car swept by and hesitated for a moment, wondering if she should have a cup of coffee somewhere before going on to see the house. She had left home without having any breakfast, and she had been on the road so long she was feeling quite weak. Besides, she was, she realised, suddenly a little apprehensive about finally going inside the house whose keys were clutched in her hand. The whole enterprise had acquired an emotional overload which had begun to alarm her.

She could see a coffee house from where she was standing outside an empty shop, its windows whitewashed, a *For Sale* notice hanging from the jettied storey above the front door. As she stood hesitating the door opened and a man came out. Talking hard and looking over his shoulder back into the shop he cannoned into her violently, nearly knocking her off her feet.

'Oh my God, I'm sorry!' He grabbed her arm and steadied her as she staggered into the gutter, the cottage keys flying out of her hand. 'Oh shit! Let me get those. Have I hurt you? Come and sit down a minute.'

Before she knew it she had been drawn through the door into the empty shop and pushed into a folding canvas chair.

'I'm OK, honestly.' She had finally got her breath back enough to speak.

'No you're not, look at your foot!'

She looked down at her sandalled feet. Below her pink jeans her ankle looked a bit swollen and was already distinctly black. 'It's not as bad as it looks, honestly.' She was overwhelmed and not a little embarrassed by his concern. 'It'll be fine.'

The man who was now kneeling at her feet was tall and wiry, probably like her in his mid-thirties. Dressed in blue jeans and a checked shirt he had short cropped dark hair and a long, rather mournful face. 'It doesn't look fine to me. I am a clot. I never look where I'm going. Colin, do something!'

Emma had not even realised there was someone else in the room. The man who now stood forward was shortish and solidly built with pepper-and-salt hair, perhaps in his mid-forties. He grinned at her peaceably.

'My colleague is always flattening people and I constantly find myself picking them up!' His voice had the unmistakable singsong of the Welsh hills. 'Would you like a doctor, an ambulance, a bandage, a lawyer or a cup of coffee?'

Emma burst out laughing. 'I'll settle for a coffee. That is where I was heading when we bumped into each other.'

'God, that's tactful!' The younger man straightened up. 'Bumped into each other! I completely bulldozed you.'

'You're forgiven!' Emma was rubbing her foot. 'Much as I'm enjoying the sympathy this is not a bruise, you know. It's actually dirt.'

'Off my great clumping shoes.' The younger man looked down at his feet ruefully. 'This place is filthy.'

'I'll fetch us some coffee while Mark looks after you.' The Welshman fished in his pocket for some change. 'We have made an arrangement with the café next door. They will let us bring real cups across here and they have nice home-made cakes and buns.' He winked.

'Are you buying this shop?' Emma looked round for the first time as he disappeared out into the street. The man she now knew as Mark shook his head. 'God, no. In fact I gather the shop is almost unsaleable.' There was another folding chair in the room beside the one in which Emma was seated, and two large metal cases of what looked like cameras and photographic equipment, a heavy coil of cable, two large canvas bags and a spotlight on a tripod. Uneven oak floorboards covered in dusty footmarks and heavily beamed walls and ceiling proclaimed the age of the building. In the far corner a broad flight of stairs led up out of sight. There was an ugly modern counter to one side of them, bare but for a couple of notebooks, two empty coffee cups – presumably from the obliging café next door – pen, light meter and clipboard.

'You're photographers?' Emma waggled her foot experimentally.

'Film. TV.' Mark turned to his briefcase and pulled out a pack of Kleenex. He proffered it hopefully. 'Will this help clean you up? Or there's a loo upstairs.'

'Actually I might go up and wash my hands.' She pulled herself to her feet with a wince.

'Straight up. You can't miss it.' He grinned. It was his lucky day. A beautiful woman, literally, falling at his feet!

Glancing into the upper room from the landing at the top of the stairs she saw that it was large and empty, the windows leaded and dusty. A bluebottle was beating against one of the panes and on the floor below the sill she could see the bodies of several others. She shivered. In spite of the frenzied buzzing of the fly there was a strange stillness in the room which was unnerving.

She found the cloakroom, cleaned off most of the dust, washed her hands and was making her way back towards the empty room when she heard someone walking across the floor towards the staircase. She paused in the doorway, looking round. 'Mark?'

There was no answer. 'Mark, are you there?' The room was empty. The bluebottle was lying on its back on the window sill, spinning feebly in circles. She stepped cautiously into the room. 'Hello? Is there anyone here?'

The silence was intense, as though someone was holding their breath, listening.

'Mark? Colin?' She stared round nervously. 'Who is it? Who's there?'

There was no answer.

Retreating to the top of the stairs she glanced back towards the window and caught her breath in surprise. There was someone there, surely. A stooped figure, staring at her across the pile of boxes in the middle of the floor.

Welcome back.

The words seemed to hang in the air.

For a moment she couldn't move, her eyes locked onto the pale, indistinct face, then a child shouted suddenly in the street below and the moment was over. The figure was gone – a mere trick of the light – the room was empty.

She felt a knot of fear tightening in her chest. Sternly she dismissed it. Hurrying downstairs she limped towards her chair and flung herself down in it, shaken. 'You weren't upstairs just now, were you?'

Mark glanced up from the notebook he was writing in. 'No. Why?'

She shrugged. 'I thought I heard someone up there.' Cautiously she began to rub her ankle.

He scrutinised her face for a moment. 'Really?'

She nodded. 'It was a bit spooky, to be honest!' She gave a small apologetic laugh. 'It was probably my imagination. Did you say you were making a film here?'

Mark nodded. 'A documentary.'

'And what is so special about this place? I mean, I can see it's very old and attractive, but presumably that's not enough to warrant a film?'

Mark shook his head. 'No. Well, as I think you might have guessed, it's part of a series on haunted buildings.' He gave a wry laugh. 'You weren't thinking of buying it, were you?' He nodded towards the keys lying next to her bag. The estate agent's tag was large and obvious.

She shivered ostentatiously. 'Good lord, no. I was on my way to see a country cottage.' She frowned uncertainly. 'Perhaps I'm going mad, but I think I might have seen your ghost up there. A figure, by the window. Does that sound likely?'

Mark stared. 'It's possible. What did it look like?'

'Sort of wan and transparent!'

He grinned. 'Sounds fairly authentic. I'm jealous. I haven't seen a thing yet.'

'It could have been a trick of the light.'

'True.' He was watching her closely.

She raised an eyebrow. 'So, who is this ghost?' And quite suddenly she didn't want to know. She quite desperately didn't want to know. But it was too late. Mark was launching into his story.

'OK, I'll tell you the full sordid tale. This shop is so haunted it has been owned or leased by about a dozen different businesses in the last few years. No one stays long and now its reputation goes before it so it's been on the market for three years.'

'And you're going to film the ghost?' Without realising it Emma had wrapped her arms around herself tightly. She glanced up at the ceiling.

'That's the general idea. We heard about it in a roundabout way through one of our scouts who had worked on *House Detectives* just up the road, and after a bit of research we felt it would fit our series really well. Ah, Colin, sustenance!'

The Welshman had appeared in the doorway with a tray. On it were three large cups of coffee and a plate of cakes. He slid the tray onto the counter. 'If this project takes more than a day or two I'm going to want danger money for cake overload.' He passed Emma the plate. 'Please take the chocolate one because if you don't I will and I mustn't.' He patted his stomach ruefully.

Laughing uneasily, Emma helped herself to a large sticky slice. 'Anything to oblige.' She glanced round the room. The atmosphere was better now. Normal. 'Have you seen it, Colin?'

'It?'

'The ghost.'

'Ah,' Colin glanced at Mark. 'No, not yet. And I'd be grateful if you didn't spread it around why we're here. We've told the café people we're surveyors. Which I suppose, if one were being a little bit disingenuous, one could say was true. They know the story of course, and they'll find out in the end why we're here, but I don't want every bored kid in town tapping on the windows and wailing at the locks the moment it gets dark if I can help it.'

'Have you filmed ghosts before?' In spite of the distraction of the chocolate cake, she couldn't stop herself thinking about the silent upstairs room with its shadowy occupant.

'Yup.' Mark took a bite of coffee and walnut. 'With mixed results and open to all sorts of questions but Col and I were pretty convinced we'd caught something. The last one was up in Lincolnshire.'

'This is a difficult one.' Colin sat down in the other chair. 'The story involves this whole town. It's a very emotive subject. This place is supposed to be haunted by several ghosts, amongst them a guy called Matthew Hopkins. He was Oliver Cromwell's Witchfinder General. One of those all-time villains of history. You must have heard of him? There was a film about him.'

'A bit before her time!' Mark grinned. 'It was a Michael Reeves film. 1968. Our hero was played by Vincent Price, who was fifty-seven years old at the time, although Matthew actually seems to have died before he was twenty-five.' He sucked his breath in through his teeth. 'Well, we all know about historical veracity in films. Perhaps we can do something to put some facts in place. There is enough horror in the truth here, from what I gather.'

'I do remember the film.' Emma frowned. She was feeling uncomfortable again, ever more aware of that upstairs room. 'I must have seen it on TV. I don't know if that was based on fact, but weren't hundreds of poor old women burned at the stake?' She shuddered.

'Ah, well, no.' Mark squatted down on the floor beside one of the bags and drew out a file of papers. 'I'm still researching, but it seems that they weren't burnt at all. They were hanged. And there weren't hundreds of them. More like dozens.'

'Mark is getting all evangelical about this one,' Colin grinned, almost indulgently. 'But that is good. We have to get the facts right. Then whatever story there is here will be all the stronger. Hopkins is supposed to have tortured some of his victims in this building – this shop was part of a much larger house originally. It belonged to the Phillips family and Mary Phillips, who worked with Matthew Hopkins, lived here at some point. She was a really nasty piece of work. She pricked the witches with a vicious spike to find the Devil's mark.'

'Oh, that's awful.' Emma stood up. 'Is that her I saw upstairs?' Suddenly she was shivering violently.

'You saw something?' Colin stared at her. 'A psychic, eh? Bloody hell! And you've only been here two minutes! Well, perhaps we can use you to entice the ghosts out for us.'

'I don't think so!' Emma shuddered. 'No.' She shook her head. 'No, it was my imagination.'

Mark grinned. 'You've gone quite white. There's nothing to be scared of – not in broad daylight.' He raised an eyebrow. 'As you say it was probably a trick of the light. The trouble is, once stories like this one start going round they take off like wildfire, then everyone who sees a shadow thinks it's a ghost, and then it's hard to separate out the objective from the subjective from the downright lies. Although as Colin says, there seems to be so much round here that's quite sinister, almost as though –' He paused and shrugged. 'I don't know. There's a sort of evil ambience about this place. Not just the shop, but this whole area.' He paused thoughtfully. 'Odd, when it's all so pretty. Sorry. Take no notice. We're going to be very objective about this, aren't we, Col? We're conducting interviews over the next week or so and of course we'll be filming in here day and night. It's a good opportunity while the shop is empty. They're arranging yet another short let and once that's under way we won't be able to get in.'

Emma shook her head. 'Well, you certainly have an intriguing job! I suppose this is for the telly?'

'It certainly is.' Mark nodded.

'I shall look forward to seeing it.' She hesitated. 'It feels really spooky up there, whatever it was I saw.'

Mark and Colin exchanged glances. 'I think so,' Mark said quietly.

'I try not to.' Colin grinned affably. 'I don't want my hand shaking while I'm filming.' He paused, his head on one side. 'I don't suppose you fancy being in the film? You could regale us with what you saw just now.'

'I don't think so.'

'OK.' He grinned. 'Worth a try. Here, have some more cake.'

Laughing, she shook her head. 'I must go.' Gathering up her bag and map, she picked up the bunch of keys. 'Thank you for your hospitality. Perhaps if I buy my cottage I'll see you around?'

Mark shrugged. 'Maybe. Good luck with the viewing. I hope it is all you dreamed of.' His gaze followed her to the door. Turning to raise a hand in farewell as she closed it behind her she didn't see the wistful appreciation in his eyes or hear Colin's resigned chuckle. 'Give up, Mark! She's gone.'

7

Emma remembered Mark's final words as she drew up outside the cottage and switched off the car engine. Dozing in the sun behind its curtain of roses it was pink-washed with black beams. Half the roof was thatched, the other half roofed in old lichen-covered tiles and it stood sideways to the lane at its junction with a smaller, narrower road heading off into the country, set well back behind a wall of overgrown garden. She climbed out of the car and for a moment stood still, just staring. It was enchanting.

The gate was broken, the once-black paint peeling off in brittle flakes, looking too frail to touch. She was reaching out to push it open when she became conscious suddenly that someone was watching her. She turned round. A young woman was standing a hundred yards away holding a bicycle, staring at Emma with undisguised hostility. As she saw Emma spot her, she climbed onto the bike and peddled off. Emma shrugged and turned back to the gate. If someone else had wanted to buy the cottage they presumably had had time by now to do something about it. So why should they resent someone looking at the place? Cautiously pushing the gate back on its hinges she let herself into the garden. The flowerbeds were alive with bees and butterflies, a mosaic of bright scented colour. It was the cottage of her childhood memories, her fantasies, of the dream she only hazily recalled. The woman in the lane was already forgotten. Taking a step forward, she stopped again. It was strange. Although as far as she knew she had never set foot inside the gate, she did seem to know it all so well. She knew where each flowerbed lay, beneath the tangle of untended shrubs and weeds, she knew where the pump handle was, to the side of the front door, she remembered the medlar tree and the mulberry and the blackthorn and the pear in the hedge, the apples in the back garden and the circular beds separated with large round lumps of stone and flint.

Shaking her head she sniffed and she realised suddenly to her astonishment that she was crying. Brushing her cheek with the back of her hand she took a few slow paces towards the door. Only then did she realise that she had been so eager to climb out of the car and look at the house that she had left the keys on the passenger seat. Retracing her steps, she found them. There were six on the bunch. Two front door keys, a backdoor key and three shed keys. Selecting the most likely with a shaking hand, she inserted it into the lock. It clicked back easily and she found herself pushing the door open. But she already knew, without having set foot inside, that she was going to buy this house, whatever the cost, financially or emotionally. She couldn't live without it.

In the excitement of the moment she did not give Piers a thought.

The hall was dark. It smelled of rich, sun-warmed wood and dust. She stepped over the pile of circulars and junk mail on the mat and stood, holding her breath.

Welcome home, Emma.

The voice in her head was quiet, but clear. The same voice that she had heard in the shop, surely, but this time it wasn't frightening. It was warm. Enticing. It enfolded her.

She smiled and took a step forward.

I have waited a long time for you to come, my dear.

She frowned. And in spite of herself she shivered. It was her imagination, of course it was, but just for a moment it sounded as though the voice came from outside herself. She glanced round nervously. It was Mark and Colin's fault, with all their talk of ghosts. How silly. There was no one there. No one at all.

This is your house now, Emma. Yours and mine. We're going to live here together, Emma. You'll be happy here, Emma.

The voice was inside her head again, almost as though it were part of her. She took a deep breath and closed her eyes. When she opened them, the voice had gone.

'Is there anyone there?'

Of course there wasn't. How could there be? She was just being foolish.

There were two downstairs living rooms and a largish kitchen, all heavily beamed. The narrow oak staircase led up from the hall to a landing off which there were three bedrooms, one of which, overlooking the front garden and the lane, was by far the nicest and instantly ear-marked by Emma as her own, and a small bath-room which looked as though it had last been modernised forty years ago. The whole place was dusty and shabby, but it exuded a wonderful feeling of peace and happiness. Upstairs the rooms smelled of flowers. It felt like home.

It is home, Emma!

Again, the strange voice in her head. Seductive. Gentle. Insist-ent. Her friend.

'It is, isn't it!' Emma smiled as she discovered she had spoken out loud. 'You're right, whoever you are. This is home!'

She spent the whole afternoon at the cottage wandering round, sitting in first one room then another, exploring the garden, pok-ing around in the outbuildings, totally and completely happy. The gardens were, if she were completely honest with herself, all that she had ever wanted without even knowing that she harboured any such longing at all: sprawling, untidy, packed with flowers and herbs, begging for someone to come and work on them and love them and coax them back into shape. As she stood at the rear of the cottage, surveying the scene, she could feel every fibre of her being aching to get to work, to plunge her hands into the soil, to pick the few remaining roses and bury her face in the soft damask petals. This place had been a nursery. It had been a business. It would be a way of life to whoever bought it. It could be a herb nursery again. It could be a business again, under her ownership.

It was as she glanced at her watch and realised that she would have to leave to catch the agent before he closed that the panic started and the image of the young woman who had glared at her in the lane returned with full force. That woman did not want her to buy the cottage. Why?

Will Fortingale was just about to go home. His secretary had already left and he was tidying away the papers on his desk when Emma opened the door and came in He smiled at her wearily. 'What did you think?'

'I love it.' She put the keys down on the desk.

'You do?' His eyes brightened perceptibly. 'Of course, it's been empty for a long time. It needs a lot doing to it. The last owner ran the nursery but they didn't live in the house. They've got a place up in Bradfield. I think they let the house from time to time to holiday makers, but otherwise it's been empty as you probably realised.' He paused, sizing her up with a quick glance from beneath his eyelashes. Re-assessing her. Well-heeled, but no fool. 'They would probably take a lower offer. It's been on the market a while.'

'Who was Liza?'

He was taken aback by the question. 'I've no idea. Some old biddy who lived there, I suppose. The Simpsons might know. That's the current owners.' He glanced at his watch, torn between wanting to hang on to a potential customer and wanting to lock up and go home.

Emma smiled at him anxiously. 'I'm prepared to put in an offer. Today. Now. You said no one else is interested? But I saw a woman up there watching me.' She closed her eyes and took a deep breath, still embroiled in her inner turmoil. Her hands were shaking. This was madness but she could feel waves of real panic constricting her chest.

Will Fortingale laughed. 'Probably a nosy neighbour. To be honest no one has been up there to look for a couple of weeks. There was a flurry of interest after the ad in *Country Life*, but that fizzled out.' He shrugged. 'It's got too much land for a weekend cottage and not enough for a viable business.' Glancing at her, he raised an eyebrow. 'I presume you want it for the former?'

'No.' Emma spoke without thinking. 'I'd live there per-manently –' She stopped abruptly. That was nonsense. Complete nonsense. How could she live there? Of course it would be a weekend cottage. If that.

She found herself groping for one of the chairs in front of Will's desk. Sitting down, she rubbed her face with her hands. Piers would never agree. She couldn't do this. Not without talking to him. It was madness. Complete madness.

'Are you all right?' Will was watching her carefully. He had recognised some of her feelings at once; he'd seen it all before. The falling in love with a house, the longing, the day-dream-could-happen syndrome. Sitting there opposite him she was within seconds of making some fantasy come true. Usually people hesitated at this point, back-pedalled a bit, played for time. Either they would offer a sum so ludicrously low that there was no chance of it being accepted and their face would be saved, or they would disappear without trace – the dream confronted, acknowl-edged and rejected as impractical.

He walked round to the front of the desk. 'Can I get you a glass of water?' Her face was pasty and white.

She nodded, clenching her hands together and waited as he disappeared into the cupboard at the back of the office which served as a kitchenette and reappeared with a glass and some bottled water.

She drank it greedily and put the empty glass down on his desk. The voice in her head had returned, no longer seductive. This time it was insistent.

You've got to buy it, Emma. You've got to. We've waited too long for this chance. Buy it, Emma!

She took a deep breath. 'I have to have it. I can't explain it. It's completely stupid.' The anguish in her voice was real. What about her job? She loved her job. But did she really enjoy working in the City? Was that going to be her whole life, forever? Until she retired? Was that what she really wanted? Had that voice been her inner self speaking? An inner self who wanted to opt out, to return to that golden time when she was a child, before her father died, when life was full of certainty.

And what about Piers?

She looked near to tears and in spite of himself Will bit his lip in sympathy. 'Why not sleep on it, Miss Dickson? No one else has made an offer.' There he was again, telling her! What was the matter with him? 'You could safely take a day or two to think about it. Maybe go and see it again? Maybe bring someone for a second opinion?' He paused. He did quite badly want her out of the office, he realised suddenly. She was making him feel extremely uncomfortable. Anxiety – even fear – was coming off her in waves.

She was sitting with her eyes shut and for a moment he didn't think she had heard him until he realised that she was staring at him again. 'What sort of offer will they accept?'

He hesitated, toying with the idea of inflating the price, but something made him hold back. He shook his head remorsefully. 'They'd accept fifty K under the asking price. To get rid of it quickly.'

'All right.' Her voice was tightly controlled. 'I'll go for it.' She could afford it. She had her savings and her father's trust money and he would have approved of this, she was sure of it. He had always been an enthusiast.

47

'But you'll want a survey?' Will couldn't cope with this spontaneity. It didn't fit the norm.

'No.' Shaking her head she stood up. She went and stood by the window, gazing out into the street. The empty shop across the road where she had passed her unexpected coffee break that morning was deserted, the front door padlocked. She turned back to Will. 'Ring them. Now. Check they'll accept it.' Her knuckles were white on the edge of his desk. 'And a deposit. They'll want a deposit –'

'Not before Monday, Miss Dickson.' Will found himself seriously worried now. 'Honestly. If you want it, it's yours.' He reached into the file to find the phone number. Glancing up, he indicated the chair. 'Please, sit down again while I phone them.' He smiled at her. 'Relax. I'm sure there won't be a problem.'

8

Saturday lunchtime

'I suggest we do the interviews upstairs.' Colin, having taken the tray back to the coffee shop, was adjusting the lens on his camera. 'The wall up there would be a good background. The herringbone brickwork or whatever it is.'

Joe Thomson, their sound man, had joined them at lunchtime with his daughter Alice who was going to act as production assistant. Joe at forty-two was balding, very tall and thin. His daughter had inherited his height and build. At eighteen she was already as tall as her father. With short cropped hair and studs in eyebrows and nose she appeared far more confident and outgoing than in fact she was. This was her first assignment – a gap job before going up to university. Half of her was determined she would not blow it. The other half was scared stiff.

Colin and Mark had been in Manningtree for two days now, staying at a bed and breakfast in Brook Street, and Joe and Alice had joined them after driving down from London. The first day had been wasted for Colin and Mark when the expected key had not been forthcoming and Stan Barker, the owner, had proved extraordinarily elusive. They had only run him to earth that first evening at the pub, so their first visit to the shop had been perhaps appropriately after dark. The atmosphere had been suitably sinister.

After the visit Mark had slept uneasily and woken early. The second night he had been shocked awake by the sound of someone screaming. Splashing his face in cold water he had stood for several minutes in the bathroom of the bed and breakfast, staring into the mirror before he had tiptoed back to his bedroom. The sound had been part of his dream, he knew that. And yet, somehow it had come from outside him. He climbed back into bed and sat there, with the table light on, huddled beneath the bedcovers fighting sleep. When at last he had dozed off he dreamed he was running down a dark road and there were people chasing him. He could hear them shouting, baying like hounds and growing closer all the time. He was still running, out of breath and drenched in sweat, when his alarm clock woke him.

Mark glanced up at the others from the clipboard. 'I'm going to want the interviews in different settings. Perhaps some outside by the river, or some of the other places associated with Hopkins. Unless the ghosts appear there's basically not much to see here. An empty shop. An empty upstairs. But I'd like to get some shots of that staircase if we can light it properly. I've got three interviews set up for this afternoon, Joe. Barker first. I'm easy where he goes, wherever he feels most comfortable, then we can fit the others round him.'

'You don't think he'll back out at the last moment?' Colin hefted the camera up onto the counter.

'He seemed quite keen.' Mark flipped over the page and made a quick pencil note on his schedule. 'I had a moment of inspiration and told him programmes like this lead to dozens of people trying to buy a property after it's appeared on TV.'

'Not necessarily after a programme like this one!' Colin commented dryly.

'No, well you never know!' Mark glanced at his watch. 'Let's go up and see where it would be best to put him.'

He led the way up the creaking staircase. At the top he stopped, looking into the large upper room. He frowned. Something in there had changed from when he had been in there earlier.

'Problem?' Colin was immediately behind him, Joe and Alice at the rear.

'No.' Mark walked into the room. The last person up here had been Emma. She had seen something. Felt the atmosphere. He stared round thoughtfully. 'Feel anything?'

'Apart from cold?' The others had trooped in behind him. Colin shivered.

'Cold is a start. This is August.'

Colin strode over to the window and glanced down into the street. The window sill was level with his knees and he had to

50

stoop to see out of it. 'We expected bad vibes. What would a haunted house be without them?' Hunkering down he reached for the window latch and pushed the small casement open. 'The room just needs a bit of fresh air. This place has horrendous rising damp and probably dry rot and death-watch beetle and every other scourge that old buildings are heir to. Any of that would be enough to put off a buyer, you know.' He stood up and faced the others. 'Mark?'

Mark was staring at the brick wall. 'I saw something move. There. In front of the wall.' His face had gone white.

They all followed the pointing finger and looked hard at the bricks. The temperature in the room had plummeted. For a moment they stood in total silence, no one daring to move. The traffic noise from the High Street had ceased and the quiet was unnaturally claustrophobic.

'Can't see anything. Shall I go down for the camera?' Colin said quietly. He glanced at Alice. She was gazing at the wall with a slight frown on her face. If she was scared she was hiding it well.

'No.' Mark stepped over beside him. 'No, it's gone, whatever it was.'

Outside a car hooted.

'Probably a spider,' Joe put in firmly. He rearranged his lanky frame, folding his arms nonchalantly.

'Probably.' Turning, Mark stared out of the window, taking a deep breath of the air flooding into the room. A strong smell of traffic fumes rose from the street below, where cars paused to pass each other in the narrow thoroughfare. Suddenly the room felt marginally warmer.

The interview took only twenty minutes from beginning to end. They could tell it was going to be a disaster from the moment Stan Barker walked into the shop.

'I'm not going upstairs.' He stood, uncomfortable in his best suit, just inside the door.

Colin eyed the florid face, the too-tight collar, the jazzy tie, and glanced at Mark with a raised eyebrow.

Mark gave a barely perceptible shrug. 'Perhaps you could stand there, at the bottom of the stairs? I just want to ask you a few questions then we're going to do some shots of the shop itself.'

51

As interviewer-cum-presenter he was going to remain out of shot. If necessary he could get Colin to insert one or two angles of himself later. They always took a few interviewer shots in case.

'So, Mr Barker, how long have your family owned number one Church Street?'

Colin, with the camera, had positioned himself beside him; Joe had pinned a mike to Stan's tie. Stan had the look of a man facing a firing squad.

'My grandfather bought it just after the war.' He hesitated. 'The old house was split into two and turned into shops about the turn of the century, I reckon. The lad as owned this half never come back. His wife wanted shot of the place so it was going for a good price.'

'And what kind of a shop was it then?'

Mark's question seemed to floor him. He hesitated, then he shrugged. 'Butcher. He was a butcher, my granda.'

They were going to have to extricate every word. It was like drawing teeth.

'And what happened next?'

'He weren't well, so he suggested my dad took it over. Well, he didn't want to be a butcher so he said no. They got a man in to manage it. Old Fred Arrow. He only lasted a year.'

Silence. Stan's eyes were riveted to the microphone baffle on top of the camcorder.

'And what happened then?' Mark prompted quietly. Colin moved smoothly to one side, stepping over the trailing cable, changing the angle.

'He said he weren't going to stay another day in the place. Hated it, he did. Said it were haunted. He said he saw Dave Pegram – that's the lad as was killed in the war – standing on the stairs . . .' He broke off and the look he shot over his own shoulder was one of pure terror. Colin smiled. Yes!

'Well, he went and so did the next chap and then another butcher opened up down the street and Da thought he'd pack it in. So he tried to sell the place. No one was interested. Not as a butcher's. Then a woman came along in about 1950. She wanted to run it as a bakery. Fancy cakes and things she sold. She lasted a year – maybe a bit longer, but then she saw Dave as well –'

'When you say she saw Dave,' Mark interrupted smoothly, 'would she have recognised him?'

'No.' Stan shook his head vigorously. 'She weren't local. She'd never met him.'

'But she described him?'

Stan shrugged. 'On the stairs,' she said. 'And upstairs. She had a flat up there, above the shop. There were three rooms in them days and then there's an attic, too. She said he used to walk up and down all night. She'd lie there listening and she could hear him pacing up and down. You might well shiver, young lady!' He addressed Alice suddenly who, dressed in jeans and a skimpy T-shirt had hugged herself with a shudder as she stood nearby with Mark's clipboard clasped importantly to her chest. The goose-pimples on her arms were clearly visible.

Mark sighed. It didn't matter. They could cut that bit.

'I take it she checked there was no one there?'

'She wouldn't go up there. She left. Halfway through the lease, she upped and left. After that there was a whole load of different people. Dress shop. Hardware. Another baker. Bikes. A little tea shop once. None of them stayed.'

'And I understand you asked for the shop to be exorcised?'

Stan looked uncomfortable. 'Stupid business. But nobody would take it on after my Da died, so I got the old rector up here. We reckoned if Dave had never had a proper burial wherever he died, poor bastard, perhaps a few prayers and that would sort him out.'

'And did it?'

The camera moved closer, focusing on Stan's face.

He shook his head. 'No. It wasn't Dave, was it. We'd said the prayers for the wrong bloke. His son turned up in the town one day to see where 'is dad had lived. Turned out he hadn't died at all – or not till years later! He'd gone to Canada with someone else's missus!'

A snort of laughter from Alice broke the tension abruptly. Joe and Colin both glared at her. Mark continued soberly: 'So, what happened after that?'

'Well, we thought maybe the prayers would work anyway, but the noises got worse.' Stan looked down suddenly as though afraid to stare any longer into the camera lens. 'Much worse.'

Mark found his mouth had gone dry. The question he was about to ask died on his lips. There was a long silence. Colin glanced at him with a frown. He stopped filming. 'That's great. Do you want any more, Mark?'

Mark fished in his pocket for a handkerchief and mopped his face with it. 'Yeah. I do. We need to come up to the present. Why you're trying to sell it again now.'

Stan shrugged. He shifted uncomfortably as Joe moved in to adjust the microphone clip and Colin started filming again. 'There's always noises. People walking up and down.'

'And at what point,' Mark took a deep breath, 'did you decide that the house was haunted by Matthew Hopkins, the Witchfinder General?'

Stan stared round wildly. For a moment Mark thought he wasn't going to answer, but he turned back to the camera and speaking fast and confidentially he started on an explanation which sounded, Mark thought suddenly, just a bit too rehearsed.

'Him – the Witchfinder – he's been seen in all sorts of places in the town. And they've seen him up at Hopping Bridge and at the Thorn at Mistley. That's named after him, you know. The Hopping Bridge. So, why not here, too? The worst place is in the Indian across the road. Used to be the Guildhall or some such, that little place where they tried them. The witches. Well, I thought to myself, supposing it's him here. And it was.' He stopped almost triumphantly.

'How do you know it was him?' Mark glanced down at Joe, who had resumed his position slightly behind him, on one knee, second microphone in hand. Joe raised an eyebrow.

''Coz I do. I seen 'im.'

Mark wasn't sure whether the shifty look in the man's eyes was because he was lying or because he was afraid to admit the sighting.

'Can you describe him for us?'

'Tall. Wearing large boots. A pointy sort of hat. And a goatee beard. Everyone as sees 'im says he's got a goatee beard.'

'And he was here in this house?'

'On the stairs. Right behind where I'm standing.'

He turned and they all followed his gaze to the point where the uneven oak risers disappeared around the corner. As Colin focused in carefully and panned the camera across the breadth of the stairs, Alice gave a small whimper.

Mark persevered. 'And was there a historical connection between Matthew Hopkins and this building?'

'He walked the witches here.' Stan folded his arms defiantly.

'Up and down. All night. Didn't let them sleep. In the end they was so muddled they didn't know what they was saying. He'd get a confession out of them, then they'd be packed off to the dungeons in Colchester Castle.'

'What a bastard!' Alice's voice was shrill.

'Cut!' Mark brought his hand down sharply in a chopping motion. 'Alice, one more interruption and you're going home!'

Joe turned to his daughter with a frown. 'Get a grip, Alice. You knew what this job was. Groovy, I believe you said!'

Alice shuffled across to the counter. She was scowling. 'Sorry.'

Mark looked back at Stan. 'So, having decided the building was haunted by Cromwell's witchfinder, you decided to cut your losses and sell it. But no one wants to buy, is that right?'

Stan nodded gloomily. 'Trouble is, the place is falling down. It needs all sorts of repairs. The roof leaks.' He shrugged. 'I can't afford to keep it on. Don't want it. No way. And I need the money. I thought people would like a haunted house. Someone told me there was a market for such like. But, no one has gone for it yet.'

Joe glanced at Mark and winked. So, they had finally got there. The old bugger was making it up. He thought he'd get a better price for the shop if it had a famous ghost. Mark hid his irritation. This wouldn't do a lot for the credibility of the programme.

'Thanks, Stan. I think that's all we need for now.'

'Right.' Stan moved away from the stairs with alacrity. 'I'll leave you to it, then. Just you remember I want you out of here by tomorrow. There's a new tenant moving in Monday.'

'Stan!' Mark called suddenly as the old man moved towards the door. 'What about the other part of the house. The shop next door. Isn't that haunted, too?'

Stan shrugged. 'Never heard that it was. They only walked the witches here, see.' He jerked his thumb towards the stairs. 'Never took them to the nicer side of the house. That's where the family lived. Couldn't hear them scream from that side of the house!'

There was a long silence after he had gone.

Colin eased the heavy camera off his shoulder and put it down with a groan as Alice closed the door behind their interviewee and stood watching him walk out of sight.

'Christ, only one more day! I thought we'd got a week at least,' Mark complained as Joe began to coil up his cables. 'He told me it's going to be an end-of-line discount shop, this and that,

55

probably most of it fallen off the backs of lorries – just till Christmas. You'd think they could give us a bit longer.'

'We can do it.' Colin retrieved the clipboard from Alice. 'If we spend the whole day at it tomorrow – and there's always tonight, of course.' He grinned at her. 'After all, ghosts appear at night, don't they?' He sighed. 'I was more worried about his remarks about ghosts being a selling point. What do you think? Have we wasted the whole afternoon? If he's made all this up, the programme has gone. Damn! If he hadn't said that!'

'We'll cut that bit,' Joe said. He was lighting up a cigarette.

Mark shook his head slowly. 'We'd still know he'd said it.'

'I think he's telling the truth.' Alice hauled herself up onto the counter and sat, swinging her legs. 'That last bit was awful – how they couldn't hear them scream in the other half of the house.'

Mark shrugged. He was inclined to agree with Alice. 'The trouble is, he's after a quick sale. But perhaps it's backfired on him a bit. People like ghosts, but not these particular ghosts. Not to live with. I'm afraid the shop's history, if it's true, will put purchasers off. Still,' he paused and gave a wry grin, 'I suppose when one thinks about it, for our purposes, it could add credibility to the film.' He walked across to Alice. 'Let's see the interview list. We've got two more today. Out and about. I wonder if we should reschedule them and concentrate on this place for now. There's a couple more tomorrow. That's fine. We can do atmosphere here. Then we want corroboration and a few shots of Colchester Castle and its dungeons – you checked for permissions for that, Alice? Good. Then that should about do it. Nice piece. OK, folks. Let's get some film in, of the attic and the first floor. The shadows are moving round a bit now. It'll look a bit more spooky. That's what Emma called it. Spooky. And that was unprompted.' He smiled at the recollection. 'Then we can get some street shots. OK?'

As they busied themselves collecting camera, lights and clipboard a shadow appeared on the staircase by the newel post in the corner where the dusty oak steps disappeared out of sight. Alice glanced round sharply. But it had gone almost as soon as it had appeared.

None of them noticed the sound of footsteps on the dirty boards upstairs.

9

Out at sea the wind had dropped. The waves rose and fell in an uneasy swell, lapping around the Gunfleet Sands. On the shore a man walking his dog in the last of the light along the beach at Frinton stopped and stared at the North Sea. Where, minutes before, he had seen the distant horizon wreathed in a rack of stormy cloud and the waves breaking over the shallows, suddenly he could see nothing. He frowned uneasily. The sky was changing colour as he watched. It was turning a thick dirty yellow. The air was becoming colder and suddenly he could smell deep ocean currents and salt, the smell of northern seas, the smell of the ice floes. The man's dog noticed. It had abandoned its excited sniffing of the weed and shells on the sand and was standing beside him, staring out as he was. It lifted a front paw, pointing, its ears cocked, then glanced up at him, seeking reassurance. The man shrugged his shoulders uneasily. 'Time to go home, boy,' he said quietly. The dog needed no second telling. With an unhappy yelp it turned tail and headed towards the low cliffs and the greensward above. Within minutes the mist had reached the edge of the beach. The cold clammy air lapped at the man's heels. In it he could hear echoes of different places, different times. The distant call of a horn, the shouts of angry men. He turned for a second, terrified; he had imagined it, of course. The smell of the haar, and the swiftness of its arrival, had unnerved him.

Just for an instant he wondered if he could see the curved cruel beak of a boat surging in on the tide. But no, there was nothing there.

As he turned away to follow his dog up the cliff he shivered with fear. The evil was in the mist.

Behind him it swept in along the coast and around into the estuary heading up river towards Mistley and Manningtree. Within minutes the whole peninsular was shrouded in cold, clammy fog.

10

Saturday night

'You have done what?'

Piers stared at Emma with disconcerting intensity.

'I've made an offer. The cottage in Mistley.' She had arrived back home just before ten to find him sitting alone in the roof garden listening to the soft strains of a string quartet, a glass of white wine on the wrought-iron table near him. The cats were asleep on the sofa swing. The hot night was velvet up here, not black, no London night was black. It was bitter, dark orange, scented with traffic fumes and chargrilling from dozens of terraces and rooftops and flowers from the park and the squares and a thousand small expensive gardens. A breath of cold wind trailed past them and was gone, leaving them staring at one another in silence.

Piers sat down and reached for his glass. 'Forgive me, Emma, but I thought I heard you say you had bought a cottage. I must be going mad.'

'You did hear me, Piers.' Her confidence was evaporating fast. She sat down beside him and kicked off her sandals. Her ankle was still slightly swollen. 'You will love it, I promise. I had to make the decision. There was someone else after it.' She rubbed her face with her hands, exhausted after the long drive. 'Can I have some wine?'

'We'd both better have some wine.' Piers's voice was tight with anger. 'Then perhaps you can explain.'

But how could she explain? The certainty. The fear of losing it. The knot of panic-stricken, illogical and desperate emotions which were tearing her apart made no sense to her, either.

'You are out of your mind!' was his terse comment when she had at last finished her rambling account of the day.

'Probably.' She stared after him as he went to lean on the parapet. 'I had to do it, Piers. Don't go on asking me why. I don't understand myself. I know it doesn't make sense. I know I'm mad. It's just –' She paused. 'I knew the house. It was as though I knew every inch inside and out.'

'And you decide to buy every house you've ever visited?'

'No, of course not!'

'Then why this one?'

Emma shook her head 'Because it was home. It was as though I had been there before. Not just in my childhood. I only ever saw the outside then, from the road. I knew every tree, Piers. Every beam in the walls. I can't explain it.' She was trying not to cry. Leaning back in the chair, she stared up at the sky. The silence lengthened.

'I'm going to bed, Em.'

She hadn't realised that Piers had moved away from the wall. He was standing in front of her, looking down at her face. His own was deep in shadow, hiding his anger. 'Where would you get the money from, Em? Have you thought about that?'

'The money is not the problem, Piers. I have my father's trust fund and I will use my own investments. I can afford it. I'm not asking you to contribute.'

'I'm glad to hear it!' He took a deep breath. Several seconds of silence stretched out between them. 'Don't forget that your ma and Dan are coming to lunch tomorrow. Perhaps they can talk some sense into that silly little head, eh?' He stooped and kissed her hair. 'See you in the morning.'

She didn't move. Blinking back tears, she stared up at the sky again. For all the affectionate words she had heard the steely undertone. There would be no compromise over this one. Why had she ever hoped there would?

Sniffing miserably, she staggered to her feet and reached for the wine bottle. The wooden boarding under her bare feet was still warm. She could smell the luminous white flowers of the jasmine growing in the tub near the French doors. A dark shape flitted out of the shadows near her and she heard a loud purr. One of the cats had woken up. Bending, she picked him up and lifted him up onto her shoulder. Her eyes had filled with tears again. Wine glass in hand, she climbed into the swing seat and lay back. In seconds Max was joined on her knees by his sister, Min, cuddled up into the crook of Emma's arm. In ten minutes, Emma was asleep.

As she began to dream first one cat, then the other, slid out of her arms and fled through the scented shadows, in through the French doors and out of sight.

If the old lady's hiding place were discovered, she would die. There would be no escape. She pushed herself further back against the old brick wall and held her breath, aware of her heartbeat thundering in her ears.

'We know you're there, Liza.' The voices were closer now. Women's voices. Soft. Insinuating. 'Come out and talk to us. You know it is what you have to do. It is the will of Christ.'

She put her hands over her ears and pressed hard, fighting to escape their words. If she didn't make a sound. If she stopped breathing. If her heart ceased its infernal din, she would be safe. They would never find her here. Never.

'Liza!' They were closer now. At the gate. 'Liza, why make it harder for yourself? Surrender to us, make your confession before Almighty God. He will be merciful. Come, Liza. We know you're here!' The voices were growing louder, echoing in her head, coming from every side now.

Liza!

Liza!

Liza!

Almighty God will be merciful, Liza . . .

All you have to do is repent Liza . . .

She could feel the sweat, ice cold between her shoulder blades and under her breasts. Her stiff, swollen hands were clenched into tight, white-knuckled balls, her nails cutting deep into her palms.

Come out, Liza!

They were laughing.

Pray, Liza . . .

It's your turn, Liza . . .

With a start Emma sat up, feeling the perspiration cold on her body. She was shaking with fear. It took several seconds before she realised she was still outside on the roof terrace. She staggered to her feet and went to lean on the parapet, staring down towards the patch of darkness which was the garden square, trying to steady herself, aware of the noise of her heartbeat thundering in her ears. It was only a nightmare, for God's sake, sparked off by her row with Piers. Stupid bad dream!

She glanced down at her hands gripping the rail they had added on top of the wall when they moved into the flat. They were shaking. She could actually see them trembling as her fingers clung to the cold metal. With a frown she forced herself to let go and turned towards the French doors.

She stood for a long time under the shower, her face upturned to the sharp drumming of the water, letting it drive out the fear. Then she wrapped herself in a huge towel and went into the kitchen.

'Emma?' Piers found her there an hour later. He turned on the light. 'Come to bed, sweetheart. We'll discuss the cottage in the morning.'

'There's nothing to discuss.' She rubbed her face wearily. 'It's done. The offer is made.'

'And can be withdrawn. You haven't signed anything.'

'No, but –'

'We'll talk about it in the morning, Em. Come on.' He reached for her hand and pulled her to her feet. 'Maybe we can compromise. A cottage might be fun. One day. We could drive around a bit. Get some ideas.'

She sensed a softening of his attitude and glanced at him quickly. 'Do you mean that? You'll think about it?'

'I'll think about it.' Turning off the light, he led her towards the bedroom.

Peggy and Dan were late for lunch. When they followed Emma out onto the roof, Piers was ensconced on the swing seat with a pile of newspapers, the wine already opened, and a half-empty glass beside him on the table.

'Sorry, darling, we couldn't find anywhere to park.' Peggy kissed Emma on the cheek and threw herself down on one of the cushioned chairs. Dan picked up the bottle, checked the ice-cold, clouded glass to see how much was left and began to pour. He was a stout, fresh-faced man with white short-cropped hair and vivid blue eyes. Having retired at fifty from the City, he had spent the last ten years in a new career as a wine importer, specialising in small, select vineyards known only to a very exclusive group of connoisseurs.

'Not bad stuff.' He topped up Piers's glass after he had done the others. 'Good year.'

'I thought so.' Piers folded his paper and put it aside. 'So, how are you both?'

'Good.' Peggy grinned. 'But our news is very boring. I want to hear yours. Did you go and visit the cottage yesterday?' She looked from one to the other expectantly.

Piers scowled. 'So, Em told you about it, did she?'

'Emma rang to say you might go and see it.' Peggy frowned. 'I know she said you wouldn't consider it, Piers, but –'

'She said that too, did she?' Piers stood up. He went to lean on the parapet. 'Perhaps you would like to remind her of the fact, Peggy.'

'Piers!' Emma had followed them out onto the terrace with a bowl of olives in her hand. She shook her head. 'Ma doesn't want to be dragged into this. Nor does Dan.'

'Dragged into what exactly?' Dan sat down on the chair next to

Peggy's. He leaned forward expectantly, his elbows on his knees. 'Come on. Tell me. What's this all about?'

'I went to see a cottage on my own as Piers wouldn't come,' Emma said, passing him an olive. 'And I liked it a lot.'

There was a short silence.

'So, you are going to see it too?' Dan asked cautiously. He was looking at Piers.

'No.' Piers drained his glass. 'And in spite of that fact, in spite of me saying I don't want a cottage at the moment because we're too busy and we can't, actually, afford it, in spite of all that,' he paused for dramatic effect, 'she put in an offer.'

There was a profound pause, then Emma turned to him. 'You may not be able to afford a cottage,' she said quietly, – 'but as I told you last night, I can.' There was a further moment's awkward silence.

'I've got the particulars here.' She stood up and disappeared inside for a moment. When she returned she had a sheaf of estate agent's details in her hand. 'It probably doesn't look that special on paper, but it is.'

'Why don't we all run down there and see it?' Dan drained his glass and held it out to Piers for more as Peggy took the A4 sheets from her daughter and began to read them. 'What about next weekend? It sounds like a fun excursion to me.'

'For you, perhaps.' Filling the glass, Piers put the bottle down and turned to lean over the railing, staring out across the rooftops. 'If Emma wants this place, that's up to her. I don't and I see no point in wasting a day of my life trailing off to see it. If we bought a cottage I would want it to be in Normandy or Brittany. Not, I repeat not, in Essex.'

Emma shrugged. 'So much for mutual discussion.'

He swung round. 'Excuse me? What discussion did you engage in before you made an offer for this place, pray? You went knowing my views. And you decided to buy it knowing my views.' His voice rose slightly.

Dan and Peggy glanced at each other. Peggy leaned forward and touching Emma's arm she frowned and shook her head. 'Let's change the subject,' she said softly. 'I think you two need to talk about this on your own later. Come on, I'll give you a hand in the kitchen.' She led the way in through the doors.

Emma followed slowly. She had picked up the estate agent's

details from the chair upon which her mother had left them. 'I have to have it,' she said as they went through into the kitchen. 'I don't know why.'

Peggy turned. 'You don't know why?' She scanned her daughter's face.

Emma shook her head. 'I made the offer because I was in a complete panic in case I lost it. It's pretty, but not especially so. I've seen prettier. It's not in particularly good condition. The garden is too big for a holiday cottage and Piers hates the idea. I should tear this up –' she waved the papers in front of Peggy's face – 'and forget all about it. Even the estate agent thought I was mad.'

'But?' Peggy's eyes were fixed on her face.

'But! I couldn't be rational about it. From the first moment I saw the ad in *Country Life*, I knew I was going to live there.' She opened the fridge door and brought out a plate covered in foil. 'Mummy, this is weird. I know it more than anyone.'

Peggy frowned thoughtfully. 'You're prepared to risk your relationship with Piers over this house?'

Her daughter nodded. She was near to tears.

'Take a day off next week. I'll come with you. Dan too, if you'll let him. And we'll go and see it again.'

'Tomorrow?' Emma looked up thoughtfully. 'I'll call in sick. I am sick!' She looked round wildly, found a roll of kitchen paper sitting on the draining board, and tearing off a sheet she blew her nose. 'Can you get someone to look after the shop?'

Peggy nodded. 'I'll ring Edward. He's always willing to do a day there for me.' Edward was her next-door neighbour, a retired colonel whose heart had been soundly broken when Dan had arrived on the scene.

'Don't tell Piers,' Emma pleaded suddenly.

'No. I won't.' Peggy sighed. 'But I think you should, Emma. What you and Piers have here is too good to lose, sweetheart. It really is.'

11

Sunday morning

Mike had walked over to the church early. After the early fog it was a glorious day and he could smell new-mown grass from the churchyard where Bill Standing, in his job as groundsman, had been trimming round some of the old graves. A retired professional gardener, Bill liked nothing more than to mow the grass and trim the hedges, training the cascades of rambling roses which grew over the lych gate and across the wall into a glorious patchwork of pink and red. He denied, however, having had anything to do with the mowing in the rectory garden, and had, to Mike's certain knowledge, never set foot inside the church itself. To Mike, this last information had been an amazing piece of news. He didn't understand it at all, especially as the old man seemed so fond of the place. Mike stopped at the gate and raised his hand in greeting. One day he would love to talk at length to the old boy, who, he suspected, was a fount of local knowledge and wisdom, and ask him why he wouldn't go into the church, but so far his attempts to engage Bill in conversation had met with little success.

Bill had been staring down towards the estuary, a worried frown on his face. Mike followed his gaze. There was nothing to see but the bright strip of water and a few wheeling gulls. As Mike watched he shook his head thoughtfully and turned away. The expression on his face was grim. Mike paused and called his name. Bill glanced up, nodded, and turning the mower trundled it off in the opposite direction. Mike shrugged and paused to glance round the churchyard instead. The weathered headstones were mostly illegible now. The salt-laden east winds off the estuary had long ago beaten the inscriptions into indecipherable lichen-crusted anonymity, but there was a quiet warmth in the shelter of an August morning which made it seem a good place to lie in peace.

He opened the gate and walked up the path. The church was already unlocked, one of the churchwardens there before him, making ready for the service. Donald James, who had retired three years before from his position as manager of one of the oldest banks in Colchester, was carrying prayer books through from the vestry and laying them out on the shelf by the door. 'Morning, Rector.' Donald smiled at him. 'Shall we leave the door open and let the sunshine in?'

Mike obligingly pushed the door back as far as it would go. The limed oak with its medieval ironwork groaned slightly as the sunlight hit the grey stone floor.

'That'll be enough books, Donald. I doubt if we'll get very many.' Mike shrugged. 'Pity. But it is the holidays. Several of our regulars are away.' He walked on up the aisle towards the vestry. The small room smelled of books and the old musty hassocks someone had stacked in a corner, rather than throw them away. Mike hesitated in the doorway, then he turned back and walked on towards the chancel. Kneeling on the top step before the altar he gazed up at the cross, composing himself, drawing his thoughts together and, finally, beginning to pray.

Behind him Donald moved quietly between the pews to pick up some fallen rose petals from the carpet beneath the pulpit. He glanced round as a shadow darkened the doorway for a moment and recognising the figure raised a hand in greeting. Judith Sadler was Mike's lay reader. A tall, dark-haired woman in her early forties, she was wearing a severely cut navy trouser suit and a pale-blue shirt with what looked suspiciously like a dog collar. Donald frowned as she headed up the aisle. It would probably not occur to her to leave the rector alone until he had finished praying. Sure enough, she was already speaking when she was several yards from him.

'Good morning, Mike. What a glorious day!' Her voice cut Mike's prayers off in mid-flow. He opened his eyes and sent up a quick last petition. For patience. His predecessor seemed to have thought a great deal of Judith and had recommended her as lay reader very highly. He had not disclosed until later that he had not endorsed Judith's powerful ambition to become a priest herself and that his lack of recommendation had contributed to the Director of Ordinands turning her down for selection, something which Judith was not going to forget or forgive.

Mike rose to his feet and turned with a smile. 'Good morning, Judith.' Ushering her ahead of him towards the vestry so that they could robe in good time he saw out of the corner of his eye that a stranger had entered the church. That was a good sign. He was closely followed by two or three other figures momentarily silhouetted against the bright sunlight. Perhaps he had underestimated the size of the congregation after all.

Several times during the service Mike found himself looking at the unknown man who had seated himself three-quarters of the way down the aisle on the left. He was alone. A youngish man, perhaps in his mid-thirties, he had short cropped hair and a long, lugubrious face. Although he listened intently to Mike's sermon and stood or sat in the right places Mike noticed he took no active part in the service. He did not pray out loud, he did not appear to be singing the hymns and he did not come up to take communion.

Perhaps he was a tourist, curious about the church? He did not have the appearance of an unhappy or troubled soul, but one couldn't always tell. It was not entirely surprising when at the end of the service he saw the man hanging back, obviously hoping for a private word. After Mike had shaken hands with his last parishioners and seen them stroll out into the sunlight, he turned towards the man and they walked slowly together along the side aisle, out of earshot of Donald and Judith.

'Mark Edmunds.' The stranger held out his hand. 'I've been staying up here for a few days. You may have noticed us. We've been filming in one of the shops at the end of the road here.'

Mike shrugged. 'Sorry, I must have missed you. What are you filming?'

'A documentary. About ghosts.'

'Ah.' Mike scanned the other man's face. 'And you want a quote from the church?'

'I wouldn't turn one down if it was offered.' Mark gave a fleeting smile. 'But that's not actually why I'm here.' They had drifted to a standstill beside a memorial to men of the parish who had died in the First World War. 'Presumably you believe in ghosts? That is part of your job, isn't it?' Mark slid his hands into his pockets.

Mike nodded thoughtfully. 'Yes,' he said cautiously. 'I do

believe in them. But I have to admit I have never seen one. And I have never been consulted professionally about one. Do you have a problem?'

Mark shrugged. 'It's daft. We're making a film, as I said, about the old Barker shop. I think the old boy who is trying to sell it is massaging the truth quite a bit, to be honest. But there are masses of stories about things that have happened there. We've filmed some interviews, misty evening scenes, shadows, atmosphere, several hours last night, you know the sort of thing.' He paused, staring up at the neatly cut lettering on the wall plaque, name after name of young men slaughtered for their country.

'And?' Mike put in quietly. 'Something has happened you didn't foresee?'

Mark gave a wry grin. 'Exactly.'

He had left the others in the pub shortly after nine, the night before, pleading a headache, and walked slowly back up the hill towards the bed and breakfast, relieved to be away from the noise and smoke of the public bar where they had found a small round table on which to balance their plates of steak and chips. The two late afternoon interviews had gone well. One had been with a woman who had been employed as a cleaner in the shop some twenty years ago. Her story had been recalled in a voice of calm certainty which had reassured and convinced them all. And her facts had more or less backed up Stan's more lurid tale. She had heard the footsteps on several occasions. She had thought she had seen a figure lurking on the staircase and she had felt uncomfortable going into the shop early in the mornings, especially in the winter when she had had to unlock the door and turn on all the lights, conscious that she was the only person there. The flat had not been used, it appeared, since the flight of the cake-making lady in the fifties. In the end the cleaning lady had given in her notice and had not been back since. They had interviewed her against the backdrop of the river. The second interviewee had not minded doing his bit in the shop itself, but like Stan he declined to go upstairs. He had gone in as an electrician about five years before and had been forced to work most of the day in the upper room, putting in some new wiring. At one point he had turned round and found himself face to face with the man with the goatee beard. The apparition had only lasted seconds but it had been enough. Another electrician had had to be found to complete the job. The language with which he had described his feelings had been fruity to say the least. It had reduced Alice to helpless delighted giggles and made Joe wince. They would have to bleep much of the interview. And now they had left two cameras rolling on long play in the upstairs room.

Mark had strolled on up the hill, feeling better in the fresh air; appreciating the cool soft breeze scented with salt and tar and mud which was blowing up off the river. He let himself into the house, a huge rambling Edwardian pile with masses of rooms for guests and, as they had discovered, the most wonderful full English breakfasts, and climbed the stairs to his room. A shower, an early night and hopefully tomorrow they would find something interesting on the silently rolling film.

He fell asleep almost at once, one arm crooked under the pillow, the other across his face and within minutes he was dreaming. He was running along a narrow road in the dark, the mud squelching under his feet, and he could hear the sound of a horse galloping behind him. He ran faster, gasping for breath, sweat pouring off him. The hedges on either side of the lane were high and he couldn't see where he was going. He blundered into a puddle and then another, desperately trying to keep his feet, aware that the horse was gaining on him fast. Dear God, it was going to catch him. He was searching frantically for a break in the hedge where he could get off the road and hide but the hedges were thorn – the branches were reaching towards him, tearing his clothes, interlaced into an impenetrable wall. He heard a shout behind him. Then another. The crowd were following the horse. He could hear them whistling, baying for his blood, his and that of the woman he was trying to save. He tried to force himself to run faster, but his strength was failing fast. Somehow he had to hide her. Somewhere. There must be somewhere. He could see her beside him now. She was running with him, her hair slipping out of her hood, her long skirts tangling between her legs. She had lost a shoe and she was crying. Then he heard her scream. And it was the same scream he had heard in the shop. In his nightmare suddenly he was there, standing in the middle of the upstairs room, and he was listening to a woman's terrified, agonised scream . . .

Mark had awoken drenched in sweat and panting, and switch-

69

ing on the lamp reached for the wristwatch he had left on the bedside table. It was still barely ten o'clock.

It was a long time before he fell asleep again. This morning when he woke he had found that his first thought had been to find the local clergyman.

Mark took a deep breath and turned back to Mike.

'You know practically every old house round here claims to be haunted either by a witch or by the Witchfinder General?'

Mike raised an eyebrow. 'A slight exaggeration. But I know there are a few such claims. A piece of history like that leaves its mark on a community.'

'And it's good for the tourist trade.'

'Indeed.' Mike glanced at him sideways. 'May I ask what it is that has happened to make you seek me out?'

'Nightmares.' Mark shrugged.

'And you think this would be the domain of the church rather than the doctor?'

Mark ran his hand through his hair. 'I'm not neurotic. I normally sleep like the dead.' He paused and exhaled sharply, eyes closed. 'Not a happy choice of phrase, perhaps. I sleep well. I'm in good health. The only dead which normally give me nightmares are deadlines.' He gave a humourless chuckle. 'It has only happened since we came here. Last night –' he shook his head – 'and the night before, I was running, hiding, trying to hide someone, then, in the dream,' he paused, finding it hard to speak, 'I was upstairs. In the shop. And I heard a scream. I can't get the sound of those screams out of my head.'

Mike felt a small cold shiver tiptoe down his spine. 'Does this fit in with the history of the shop?' he asked gently.

'Maybe. We've been told Hopkins walked some of the witches there.'

'Walked them?'

'Up and down, all night. He practised sleep deprivation. A very effective form of torture. Proper torture was illegal in England, you understand, except where treason was suspected. This was his speciality. No mess. No equipment needed.' He shivered. 'But they wouldn't have screamed. Would they? Not just for walking?'

Mike did not reply immediately. Staring at the ground he absorbed unseeing the gentle colours of the small, stained-glass

70

window thrown onto the grey stone at their feet. 'Would you like to come back to the rectory to discuss this? It's a serious matter and I would really like to take some time to think. And to pray.' He looked up and grinned almost apologetically.

Mark shook his head. 'I can't now.' He glanced at his watch. 'We're filming an interview at one o'clock. I'd better get on. Perhaps some other time?'

Mike nodded. 'Whenever you like. You know where to find me.' He paused. 'Mr Edmunds, before you go, you said you filmed through the night. Was there anything on the film?'

Mark smiled wryly. 'No,' he said. 'Not a thing!'

Mike watched as he made his way to the door and disappeared out into the sunshine.

'So, what was that about?' He hadn't noticed Judith approach. Still wearing her blue scarf and surplice, she was standing only a few feet away, half hidden by one of the pillars.

Mike frowned, suppressing a sudden flash of irritation at the interruption, yet again, of his thoughts. 'Just a short chat. Nothing to worry about.'

He glanced down the church towards the door. 'Donald gone?'

Judith nodded. 'He had to get back. Family duties. Mike, if you're not doing anything would you like to come back to lunch with me? Just pot luck. Salad. Glass of something?' She smiled uncertainly, obviously expecting him to decline, and he felt a sudden wave of pity. He knew Judith was lonely. 'That would be nice. Thanks. I'd love to.'

She lived in a three-bedroomed bungalow in a road of identical houses set in small rectangular plots on the top of the hill behind the town. As Mike climbed out of her car, he looked round at her garden. He had been here many times and knew her life-story intimately. She had lived in this house all her life. Her mother had died when she was at teacher training college and Judith had stayed on to look after her father. His joy had been his garden. From what Mike had heard from others who had known the old man when he was still strong enough to go out and garden, it had been a riot of colour and exuberance in sharp contrast to the grim fifties decor which still adorned the bungalow on the inside. There was little sign of that garden now. Mike could never quite decide whether after the old man's death in 1996 Judith had deliberately rooted out every sign of beauty and grace, or whether it was merely that she was uninterested in gardening and had not noticed the dying roses and the blighted leaves. As each plant died it was cut down and burned and the gap in the soil was rapidly covered by a thatch of chickweed and goose grass.

Mike followed her inside, resigning himself to the statutory small glass of sweet sherry which, he suspected, she bought just for him. She did not drink herself, but would sit and watch him sip from the thimble-shaped glass with an intensity which always made him very uncomfortable.

The table was laid for two. He found himself picturing her returning to the empty house, had he turned down her invitation, and sadly removing one place setting, and he knew that was why he had said yes, as he had said yes every month or so since he had arrived in the parish.

'Judith, you've lived in this place all your life.' He followed her through to the kitchen, a habit which irritated her intensely. She would have preferred him to stay neatly in the lounge until she had the meal on the table in the small dining room. 'Have you come across much interest in the history of the witchfinder?' He leaned on the counter. A couple of bottles of pills stood there, side by side, and he frowned. He hoped she wasn't ill. Tactfully he transferred his gaze to the window and stared out at the back lawn. There were no flowerbeds at all now between the grass and the wooden panel fence. The only remotely decorative item left was a single white plastic-covered washing line.

Judith had turned on the electric element under the pan of potatoes which had been waiting ready-peeled on the stove. 'Matthew Hopkins?' She opened the fridge and brought out some packets of cold meat. 'I think most people know who he was.' Reaching into the drawer for a pair of scissors she sliced the top off each packet in turn and arranged the slices of ham, salami and chicken on a serving dish. 'Why?' She glanced at him sharply.

'I heard he is reputed to haunt various places in the town.'

'Pubs.' She turned back to the fridge for tomatoes and a lettuce in a polythene bag. 'He haunts the pubs.'

Mike grinned. 'That seems strange, given that he was a puritan.'

'Quite.' She threw the lettuce into a bowl in the sink and ran cold water onto it.

'Do you ever teach about him in school?' He took another sip

72

from his sherry and tried to stop himself from wincing as the sticky sweetness hit his tongue.

'I do, actually. I organise a project with Year Fives. I send them off round the place with paper and a pencil and get them to look for a few clues. Then I give them a lesson in more detail. Tell them about the evils of witchcraft. You know the sort of thing. Were you thinking of covering it when you come up to the school?'

'Good Lord, no.' Mike shook his head. 'No, to tell you the truth I was a bit disturbed by something I heard today.'

'That man who spoke to you in church?' Judith turned off the tap and stared at him. 'I knew it. I could see you were worried. He didn't look like the usual type who gets into that sort of thing, not New Agey or grungey particularly.'

Mike frowned. 'No, indeed.'

'What did he say?'

'You know I can't tell you that, Judith.' He smiled to soften the words. 'But it made me think. Wonder. If there are any genuine –' he hesitated, trying to think of a word to describe what he had been told – 'residues of the past.'

'Ghosts?' Judith looked astonished. 'You don't believe in ghosts?'

He frowned. 'Of course I do, Judith.' He paused. 'And so, as a member of the church, should you. You may not be trained to deal with such matters, but you cannot deny their existence.'

He saw a quick flare of colour in her cheeks and bit his lip. He had not meant his words to sound so like a rebuke. 'I agree many so-called ghosts are imagination or whatever, but we cannot deny that such unhappy beings exist.' He put down his glass. 'Would you like me to take this through?' Reaching for the plate of meat her gave her a moment to compose herself.

'I do believe in it,' she said softly. 'And in witchcraft. I just didn't know if you did.'

He swung round. 'I couldn't be a priest of the church unless I believed in such things, Judith.'

'Right.' She tore the lettuce in half. 'Well, that's why I teach them about the Witchfinder General. His methods might have been cruel, but the women he persecuted deserved it. They were evil. I teach all about it to deter the little thugs who are toying with the idea of becoming witches today.'

Mike was standing by the door, plate in hand. He studied her face thoughtfully, trying to hide the shock he had felt at her words. 'Are you saying that there are still witches round here?'

She nodded. 'You'd be surprised how many people there are round here who actually claim to be the descendants of witches. They are proud of it! Oh yes, Mike. There are witches. And ghosts. And ghosts of witches.' She threw the wilting leaves into a wire basket and shook it violently, spattering water around the room. 'I am only amazed it's taken this long for them to start crawling out of the slime and heading your way.'

12

Monday

'Turn right at the signpost. There!' Emma pointed through the windscreen ahead of them. She took a deep breath. 'Supposing I hate it this time when I see it?'

Peggy changed gear and slowed the car. She glanced across at her daughter with a smile. 'You haven't signed anything, Em. You can still withdraw your offer.'

Emma leaned forward as they drove up the lane, squinting in the hot sunlight. It was almost midday and this time it had taken them nearly three hours to negotiate the traffic-clogged roads out of London. Dan had been left behind to mind the shop, the obliging neighbour, after all, unable to help.

Emma found she was holding her breath. 'It's up here on the left. Just round this bend. There.'

Peggy pulled the car off the road and both women climbed stiffly out and stood staring at the cottage. There was a long silence.

'Well?' Emma turned to Peggy at last.

'It's very sweet. I don't know if I remember there being so many roses. That's made it chocolate-boxy.' Peggy took a deep breath. 'And the air is heaven! Have you got the keys?'

Emma reached back through the car window. The keys, which they had picked up on the way past the estate agent, were lying on the glove shelf. Will Fortingale had succumbed to his cold and apparently was spending the day in bed, but his assistant had seemed very happy to let them have them for as long as they wanted them. Grasping them tightly, Emma leaned for a moment on the roof of the car. Her heart was thumping uncomfortably.

Glancing round Peggy saw her and frowned. She put her hand on Emma's shoulder. 'Are you OK, darling?'

Emma nodded. She was biting her lip. 'I wish Piers had come too.'

'I don't think there was a chance in hell of that happening, Em.' Peggy sighed. 'You've got to resign yourself to that. If you buy this place it could be the end of you and Piers.' She scanned her daughter's face. 'You do realise that, don't you?'

Emma shook her head. 'He'll come round. He always does. He's just cross because he didn't think of it himself. And he wanted to consider a place in France. But what's the point of that? If we haven't got a place there, we have a reason to go and stay with Derek and Sue. If we had our own place we'd never see them. He wants to stay with them. So, we shouldn't get a place near them. That all seems very logical to me!'

Peggy shrugged. 'I suppose so. Well, come on. Lead the way.'

Emma paused as they stood in the hall, listening, half wondering if she would hear the strange voice calling to her again, but the house was silent, expectant, as though it, like her, was waiting to hear her mother's verdict.

They spent an hour exploring the cottage and its outbuildings, then they walked out into the garden. 'I have to admit, it is very sweet.' Peggy stared round. 'Idyllic in some ways, but I would have seen you going for something a bit more sophisticated. A bit more modern. And the garden is huge. It's not a very practical idea, darling. You've never done any gardening in your life.'

Emma stared at her. 'Excuse me! What do you call that place on the roof outside the flat?'

'Apart from the roof garden.' Peggy snapped a rose off one of the bushes and sniffed it. 'But that is all in pots!'

Emma shook her head. 'And in the pots is earth. And in the earth are plants. And I have tended every one of those plants for the four years that garden has existed. I designed it. I bought the plants and the pots and I created it! Piers never lifted a finger except to buy the furniture he sits on to watch me tend the garden!'

'Sorry!' Peggy shook her head. 'I stand rebuked. OK. So, you have a huge part of your soul craving to be a gardener. But you are an investment analyst with a totally absorbing job in London. How much time would you have for this garden?'

'I could employ a gardener.' Emma walked out between the beds. The long grass brushed her bare legs and caught at the buckles of her sandals. 'Or I could give up London and come and run this place commercially.' She swung round to face her mother. 'That's what I want to do. I want to garden. I want to tidy it and rescue it and make it thrive again. I want to run it as a business.'

'And Piers?' Peggy scanned her face thoughtfully. 'How does he fit into this plan?'

'He could commute?' Emma paused and suddenly she smiled, her face radiant, full of mischief. 'It's got to work out! Somehow I'll persuade him. Look at it. It's so beautiful! It was meant to be!' She stretched her arms above her head and did a little pirouette. 'We'll sort something out. I know we will. This is my home, Ma. This is where I want to spend the rest of my life!'

13

Monday lunchtime

Lyndsey braked sharply and drew to a halt as she saw the green Peugeot backing out into the lane ahead of her. Her bicycle basket was laden with books and the weight made her wobble slightly as she dismounted. She was close enough to recognise the passenger as the brown-haired woman who had been there on Saturday and she frowned thoughtfully. So, she had brought someone for a second opinion.

'Penny for them!'

She jumped at the voice. A dusty old blue Volvo had coasted to a halt behind her and she was concentrating so hard on the woman in the car, she had failed to hear it. She turned to the balding man at the wheel. 'Hi, Alex. Sorry! I didn't hear you.'

'Just as well I was driving slowly.' He chuckled. He was fond of this gamine young woman with her quirky ways and passionate, vivid personality. 'Are you spying, by any chance?'

She smiled. 'Of course. That woman was here two days ago.'

'It's time someone bought the old place. It'll fall down if they don't.' Alex reached for the handbrake and killing the engine he climbed out. He was a tall man, in his early forties, with the high complexion and bleached eyebrows of the very fair. He had light-blue eyes, their clarity emphasised by a short-sleeved blue polo shirt and cream chinos. He pointed to her load. 'Stick them in the car. I'll run them back for you. It's too hot to bike in this weather, never mind with about a hundred books!'

'I've borrowed them from Oliver Dent. He doesn't mind how many I take as long as I return them.' Lyndsey lovingly ran a hand over the assorted volumes.

Alex opened the door of the car and she passed him the books. 'I didn't know he was a reader,' he said.

'He's got thousands of books. I've just got a job cleaning for him once a week. Poor old boy can't cope up there on his own any more.'

'Well, I hope you've still got time to look after my kids.' Alex stacked the books safely and slammed the door. A quick glance had shown they all appeared to be about plants and flowers.

'You know I have.' She hauled the bike out of the hedge and straddled it. 'You still want me tonight?' She babysat for the Wests two or three evenings a week and sometimes looked after the children after school as well.

He nodded. 'Paula and I are going to supper with someone she's met on the train.' He shrugged with a pained look towards the heavens. 'Networking with knobs on. What did I do to deserve a commuting wife?'

Lyndsey grinned. 'You know you love being a kept man! If Paula didn't make all that lovely money in the City you and the kids wouldn't be able to ponce around in the country having such a good time now, would you!'

'True.' He sighed. 'Not that I'd have chosen redundancy and house husbandry as my preferred career.' There was a moment's silence. His face had grown solemn as he thought of the various failed business ideas, the so-hopefully printed cards, the silent phone at home. In seconds his smile returned. 'Reckon those are rich weekenders, going to buy Liza's? I wonder if they would employ me to run that place for them? The Simpsons had a decent living from that nursery.'

'Not from Liza's they didn't.' Lyndsey glanced fondly towards the cottage. 'That's why they are selling it. Their money came from their garden centre up in Bradfield. Letting this place to holidaymakers was all they did in the end, and even that was too much hassle. Their son doesn't want to take it on now they're retiring and I don't blame him.'

'I suppose so.' Alex sighed. 'Ah well, I must get on. See you tonight.' He grinned. 'I've told Sophie and James you're coming to look after them and I think they're planning mayhem, so be careful!'

Lyndsey raised a hand as he climbed back into the car. 'Not to worry,' she grinned. 'Mayhem is what I do best.'

14

The others were already there when Mark made his way into the shop. He looked round. 'No sign of the new tenant yet?'

'Not a peep.' Colin was eating a toasted teacake, his fingers shiny with butter. 'So there's no one to ask. If we're quick we can get the extra shots we need upstairs and be out of here before they come! All set?' He stopped chewing and stared up at the ceiling with a frown. 'You did check, Joe? It sounds as though there is someone walking about up there.'

They all stared upwards. Alice had gone very pale. Clearly audible, they could hear someone walking slowly across the boards above their heads, the footsteps dragging slightly, one then another board squeaking in sequence as they moved.

Joe gave a soundless whistle. He stubbed out his cigarette in the lid he was using as an ashtray on the counter. 'I just stuck my head in the room. Maybe there was someone up in the attic. Or in the cloakroom. Shall I have another look?' He did not seem too keen.

Mark glanced at the stairs. He recognised an extreme reluctance of his own to climb them. Last night, again, he had had the experience of waking suddenly, his heart thudding, the echo of a woman's scream ringing in his ears. It had for a moment paralysed him with terror as he lay staring up at the ceiling, trying to steady his breathing, aware that he was bathed in sweat and aware too that this time he was too afraid to move, even to reach for the switch on the bedside light.

And now this. He saw Colin watching him, waiting for a decision. 'Are we going up?' Mark shrugged. 'I seem to have a touch of the heebie-jeebies this morning. OK. This is silly. Let's go. We need to see if we can capture a bit of this atmosphere on film.' He took a deep breath.

Colin nodded. 'Want me to go first?' The Welshman raised an

eyebrow, baiting him. The footsteps had stopped. They were all aware of the sound of traffic outside again, almost as though, before, it had not been there.

Mark nodded. He gave a wry grin. 'If you like.'

'OK.' Colin hefted the heavy camera up onto his shoulder.

'I'm not going up.' Alice's voice was shrill. 'I don't think any of us should.'

'Alice.' Joe's tone was half reproach, half mocking. 'Come on. You're not scared, surely? Great big girl like you!'

Alice blushed scarlet. 'No! No, of course not. I think this job sucks.' Tossing the clipboard down onto the counter, she turned towards the door. 'You don't need me, anyway. I'm going for a walk.'

'Alice!' Joe shouted.

'Leave her,' Mark said quietly. 'It's getting to her like it's getting to me. Come on. Let's go up.'

Colin was already halfway up the stairs when the shop door opened. They turned to see a young woman standing in the doorway. With short dark hair and intensely bright blue eyes she reminded Mark of nothing so much as a woodland elf as she hovered on the threshold, gazing at them.

'Can we help you?' Mark turned away from the stairs with something like relief. If the new tenants were arriving they would have to hurry and the sheer number of people on the premises would perhaps do something to help dispel the atmosphere.

Her eyes were enormous. He found himself unable to look away as she took a cautious step inside, leaving the door open behind her. 'What are you doing?'

Behind him Colin retraced his steps and put the heavy camera down on the counter. Mark smiled and stepped forward, holding out his hand. 'Mark Edmunds. We have Mr Barker's permission to be here. I'm sorry. We meant to be finished before you arrived.'

She looked anxious suddenly. 'You were expecting me?'

'Well, we were expecting someone.' Mark dropped his hand as she had ignored it. 'I gather you want to start stocking the shop as soon as possible? If we could have perhaps just an hour more, we could then get out of your hair.' He gave her his most charming smile. It was not returned.

'I am not here to stock the shop.' There was a slight frown

between her eyes. 'I came because you are here to make trouble for us. For all of us who live here.'

Mark glanced at Colin, who raised an eyebrow and gave a mock scowl. 'I can assure you, Miss . . . ?' He paused for her to fill in the name. She ignored the invitation and stood silently, her eyes fixed on his face, obviously waiting for him to continue. He went on, slightly flustered. 'We have no intention of causing anyone any trouble. And we are here, as I said, with the full permission of Stan Barker.'

'Stan told me you are here to film the ghosts.' For the first time her eyes left his face and she glanced past him at the stairs. Mark resisted the urge to turn and follow her gaze.

'We are making a documentary. One of a series about haunted houses,' he said guardedly.

'You have to stop it.' Her voice was stronger suddenly. She rammed her hands down into the pockets of her trousers – tight-fitting jeans, cut off raggedly below the knee which emphasised the slimness of her figure. 'You have to!'

'May I ask why?' he asked gently. 'You said we were here to make trouble. I assure you that is not the case. Programmes like this are usually immensely popular –'

'And stir things up.'

He realised with a jolt that the emotion which was fuelling the brightness of her eyes was anger. 'It will make no difference to you. You and your friends –' she glanced witheringly at Joe and Colin – 'will finish your filming and disappear back to London and never come back here again, and leave us to deal with what you have left behind.'

'I am sorry you should feel like that.' Mark kept his voice even. 'But as I said, the worst you will probably find will happen is an influx of sightseers. I find the locals usually like that. It's good for the economy.'

'I'm not talking about sightseers!' She licked her lips nervously, an infinitesimal darting movement which reminded him of a small reptile. Her tone was dismissive.

'Then what?'

She held his gaze for a moment, then for the first time she seemed to hesitate. 'You are stirring things up,' she repeated.

'What things?' Colin put in.

'The energies . . .' She bit her lip. 'Your interest, the filming,

82

talking about him. It is feeding the energies. I can feel it. The whole town is changing. The atmosphere. The feel of the place. It's centred here. In this shop.'

'Why?' Joe had surreptitiously switched on his mike. The tape was turning.

'This shop – the site – it has always been a centre. So much happened here.'

'*What* happened here?' Joe asked.

'He brought the women here. Some of them. It was the house where Mary Phillips lived.'

'One of the witchfinder's accomplices?' Mark nodded.

The three men glanced up towards the ceiling.

She did not appear to notice. 'Their fear and anger and confusion permeates the walls of this place!' she cried passionately. 'Can't you feel it? No one stays here. No one can bear it. Those women were dragged from their homes, accused, tortured, terrified and killed on the say-so of one man.'

'That surely is what makes the story of the witchfinder so fascinating,' Mark put in slowly. 'The villain is the man who ostensibly was on the side of the right, and the victims are the women who might have possibly been real witches worshipping the Devil, causing all kinds of mischief.'

'They weren't!' She turned on him, her face suddenly hard. 'They were at worst silly old ladies, not knowing what was happening to them. And the ones who did know were guilty of no more than using herbal medicine and the harmless spells that were part of the recipes in those days.'

Mark nodded. 'You would make an excellent contributor to our programme. Why don't you let us film you so that you can put your point of view . . .'

'No!' Her eyes flashed. 'Have you understood nothing I've said? You have to stop the programme. You have to go away and forget all about it.'

'You still haven't told me why.' Mark found the memory of the scream coming back suddenly as he leaned against the counter, watching her. 'If the old ladies were innocent, why should telling their story stir up trouble? Surely they would welcome vindication? And Hopkins himself was a sadistic and violent man by our standards but from what I have read he was sincere in what he believed.'

'He was paid by the head, Mark,' Colin put in softly. 'However sincere, the chap had a good incentive to root out anyone even remotely qualifying for his detection methods.'

'He was not interested in mercy or justice,' the young woman put in. 'And he does not sleep soundly. Neither do his victims. Please, please go away.'

'We are going.' Joe gave her a reassuring smile and folded his arms. 'Today. Don't you worry, love. We'll be out of your hair by teatime and away, and all your energies can calm down again.'

'And you will destroy your film?' She narrowed her eyes.

'We'll think about everything you've said, very carefully,' Mark put in reassuringly. 'I promise.'

She stood for a moment looking at each man in turn, then she turned and ducked out of the doorway. As she hurried away from the shop they heard someone in the street greet her gaily, 'Hi, Lyndsey!' and saw her raise her hand in return.

'Lyndsey,' Mark repeated. 'Remember that. Wow! I wish we'd got that little spiel on tape.'

Joe grinned. 'We did. But whether you can use it is another matter.'

'Good man.' Mark stared thoughtfully after their visitor, then he wandered across and pushed the door shut behind her. 'You know, I'm inclined to agree with her.'

'You mean we should stop?' Colin and Joe stared at him.

Mark shrugged. 'No, not stop. But I think we are stirring things up. I'm even having nightmares about it. Let's get that shot upstairs and then we can pack up. Presumably once we've gone the atmosphere she was talking about – the vibes – will all calm down again!'

15

Monday evening

'No!' Piers was white with anger. 'I will not see it. I will not talk about it. And I will not – ever – go there. If you go ahead with this, as far as I'm concerned we're finished. For Good!'

Emma was leaning on the rail, staring down across the rooftops towards the distant trees of the garden square. A misty pearlescent light was deepening into darkness around them. She said nothing.

'Emma?' Piers's voice softened. 'Please, darling. Think. I love you. I don't want to – *I can't* – live without you.'

Wordlessly she turned towards him and he saw that she was crying. He put his arms around her and gently kissed her on the top of her head. 'I'll make it up to you, I promise.' Her face was buried in his shirt-front, but he felt her nod and he tightened his arms. 'I tell you what. Why don't we arrange a holiday in the autumn? Go somewhere really exciting. Your choice.'

Still silent, she released herself from his grasp. She bent to pick up a cat. 'Have you fed them?' She sniffed into the dark, silky fur.

'Of course I have. Did Peggy not want to come in?'

'No. She was tired. It was a long drive.' Kissing Max's ear, she set him down on the ground again. 'I think I'll have a bath.'

'OK. Why don't I bring you a hot drink in bed later?'

She gave him a faint smile. 'That would be nice. Thanks.'

It was dark when he went inside and closed the French doors behind him. He wandered into the kitchen, wondering what would cheer her up. Tea. Cocoa. Soup. A stiff whisky. 'Em?' he called. The sound of bath water running away had finished ages before. 'Em? What would you like to drink?'

The bedroom was in darkness. 'Emma? Are you awake?' He turned on the lamp in the corner. Emma was lying across the bed, her face buried in the pillow. She was wearing grey silk pyjamas. 'Em?' he whispered. He sat down on the edge of the bed. 'Are you asleep?'

There was no answer.

'Would you like me to bring you something?' He waited for several seconds, then with a sigh he turned off the light and crept out of the room.

On the bed Emma stirred. Hugging the pillow she turned over, her dark hair fanned out across the sheets and, in her sleep, she began once more to cry.

She was late into the office and within seconds of sitting down at her desk, she stood up again. Her hands were shaking and she had the worst headache she could remember.

Emma!

The voice was in her head again.

Emma! Buy it! You've got to, Emma. You have to come back, Emma!

She had awoken late, drenched in perspiration, her bedclothes tied in knots, but her dreams, if she had had any, were gone beyond recall. Piers had already left, after presumably sleeping on the sofa.

'You OK, Emma?' A colleague passing her desk stopped, concerned. 'You look as though you tied one on last night with a vengeance!' He laughed.

She glared at him and turned back to her desk, rifling through a drawer for some paracetemol. Then she picked up the phone. 'Mr Fortingale? It's Emma Dickson. Are you better?' She only remembered just in time to ask. 'I wondered if you had heard back from the Simpsons yet about my offer?' Grasping the receiver with both hands, she stared unseeing at the computer monitor on her desk as she listened to the muffled voice the other end. She nodded slowly. 'Good. Thank you. No, I told you, I don't need a survey. I am instructing my solicitors this morning and as I said, I have nothing to sell. It's a cash transaction and as the house is empty, hopefully it can all go through very fast indeed.' She stood for a long time, listening to the whine on the phone after he had hung up, then gently she tipped the receiver back onto its base.

David Spencer looked up from the report he was studying as Emma appeared in the doorway of his office. She had tapped on the open door then hovered, staring in without seeming to see him.

'Emma?' He rose to his feet. 'Is there a problem?'

She frowned, visibly trying to pull herself together and came in, closing the door behind her. 'I'm giving in my notice, David.' She stood in front of his desk, not meeting his eye. 'I'm leaving London.'

'You are joking!' David ran his hand through thin, greying hair so that the carefully arranged strands rose in disarray around his head. 'You can't – what's happened? For God's sake, sit down. You don't mean it.'

She obeyed him, pulling up a chair, and leaned forward, elbows on his desk, her head in her hands. 'I do mean it, David. I'm sorry. I'll work out my notice, of course.'

'But why?' He resumed his own seat opposite her. His voice was suddenly gentle. 'Are you ill?'

'No.' She shook her head. 'Mad, perhaps.' She gave a small, helpless laugh. 'I'm buying a house in the country and I'm going to work there. I need a break from the City.'

You have to come back, Emma!

The words echoed in her mind for a moment. What was she saying? What was she doing? She was throwing away her career, her relationship, her home, her life. She looked up at David and he noted her pale face and red-rimmed eyes.

'Is this something to do with Piers? Have you two split up?'

'No.' She shrugged. 'Well, yes, I suppose we have. We will. He thinks I'm mad.'

'You are. Look,' he stood up again, 'don't say any more, Emma. Go home. You don't look at all well, if I may say so. Think about this. Take a few days off. Don't do anything you might regret. Please.' He leaned forward across the desk and put his hands over hers. 'You're good at your job, Emma. Don't throw it away.'

He watched her go back to her desk through the glass wall of his office. She picked up her bag and her briefcase, stood for a moment staring down at her desk, then left without a word to either of her colleagues, both of whom looked up and spoke to her as she passed. He frowned. There was something very wrong. He stood for several seconds staring down at his phone, then he picked up the receiver and dialled Piers's direct line.

16

Tuesday afternoon

'Emma?' Piers pushed open the front door and pocketing his keys walked through the small white-painted hall into the living room. 'Are you back?'

The French doors were open and he headed towards them, spotting her at once. She was lying on the swing seat, eyes closed, Max curled in the crook of her arm.

'Hi, old thing. What are you doing home?' He sat down on the edge of a chair near her, incongruous in his city suit and smart black shoes, noting that she too was still dressed in her office clothes.

'I wasn't feeling too good.' She opened her eyes and looked at him. 'What are you doing here yourself?'

'I had a whole lot of reports to check and I kept thinking of this roof garden and a glass of white wine and how awful it was to be stuck in a glass palace in this heat and I thought, I'm going to play hooky!' He smiled and climbed to his feet with a groan. 'I'm going to have a shower and change into something more comfortable. Is there anything I can get you?'

Shaking her head, she closed her eyes again and he watched her for a moment, frowning.

When he came out again some time later she was asleep. Good as his word, he settled down to study the reports, glancing every now and then in her direction as the sun moved round towards the west and the shadow under the canopy where she lay deepened. It was still very hot. He finished a stack of papers, returned them to his briefcase and withdrew another pile. Somewhere below in the busy street he heard the wailing note of a police siren. It sounded for several seconds very close, then rapidly it faded into the distance as the car sped away towards the Cromwell Road.

In her dream Emma stood in the doorway of the cottage, looking round. She was dressed in a black cloak but under it her gown was silk, embroidered with flowers. 'Liza?' Her voice was her own, but the words came out strangely, with a soft country burr and unaccustomed words. 'Liza, where be ye? I've brought ye some butter and some posset.'

She moved forward into the kitchen she knew so well. This small dower house on her father's estate had been given to Liza in her old age as a reward for her care of this wayward young woman and her brother after their mother's death. The fire was lit and a pot of water was hanging over it. She glanced in. It had nearly boiled dry. No herbs. No vegetables. Taking a thick cloth to pad her hands she lifted it off the hook and setting it down at the edge of the hearth she looked round for Liza's cats. There were two, adored and spoiled, which the old woman had reared from kittens over twenty years before while she still lived up at the hall. If she was not careful they would steal the butter before Liza had set eyes on it. There was no sign of them.

The table behind her was strewn with flower heads. Two small boxes of dried herbs stood nearby, both open, both spilled. A knife lay on the floor, the small pestle and mortar beside it. Sarah frowned, a frightened chill suddenly settling over her, cold as the mist that drifted in the lane outside and shrouded the church. 'Liza? Where are you?' The whisper was scarcely audible. She moved to the foot of the stairs and stared up, her foot on the bottom step. For a moment she couldn't force herself to move, then as she put her foot forward the door opened behind her.

'I'm here, my duck.' Liza was standing there, wrapped in a warm woollen cloak against the mist. She stepped into the room and glanced round, smiling as she saws the gifts lying on the table. 'That's kind. I'll enjoy that.'

'Where were you, Liza?' Sarah frowned, still uncomfortable. 'The water was nearly boiled dry and everything is spilled.'

Liza shook her head. 'I ran outside. There was somebody in the lane.' She shrugged. 'Somebody I didn't want to see.'

Behind her a cat appeared in the doorway. It mewed and walked up to her, jumped on the table, asking to be petted. She stroked it absently. 'Sarie, my dear, if anything happened to me, you'd look out for the cats, wouldn't you? See they was fed and had a home?'

'Of course I would.' Sarah caught her hand. 'What is it, Liza? What's wrong? Why are you talking like this?'

Liza shrugged. 'There's folk out there mean mischief, Sarie. Hopkins's men. Someone has been bad-mouthing me to him.'

Sarah let out a little cry of anguish. 'Oh, no! No, Liza. I'd never let that happen. Never. Besides, they would never come for you. Too many people love you.'

Liza gave a toothless grimace. 'Well, that's as maybe.' She put her head on one side. 'You remember all I've taught you, don't you, Sarie? Never forget it. Never.' She shrugged. 'I'll be all right. I'll keep out of their way. But,' she laughed hoarsely, patting the cat again, 'I worry about these two. They were my babies, just like you.'

'Don't, Liza. Don't talk like that!' Sarah clung to her hand. 'No one would hurt you. Or the cats. No one . . .'

91

'No one would hurt the cats! No one!' Emma woke to find she was shouting the words out loud. Piers was bending over her. 'Emma! Emma, it's OK. You've been dreaming!' He was holding her hand.

'The cats!' She sat up staring round. 'Where are the cats?' Suddenly she was crying.

'The cats are fine.' Piers stepped back as she swung her legs to the ground.

'Where? Where are they?'

'Inside. Max was cuddled up with you. Then you began to shout and he was frightened. They're both inside somewhere. Em –?' He watched as she ran across the terrace. She had kicked off her shoes before she lay down and her feet were bare; her hair was dishevelled.

In the living room she stared round. 'Max?' She spotted the cat sitting under the coffee table, his tail swishing from side to side. 'Oh, Max!' She dived on him, trying to scoop him up into her arms, but he turned towards her, hissing. Lashing out at her in a panic he scratched her viciously across her wrist and the back of her hand before diving out of reach into the kitchen.

'Leave him, Em. He's thoroughly frightened. And so are you.' Piers's voice changed suddenly as she threw herself down on the sofa, sobbing. 'What is it, darling? What's the matter?'

She shook her head. 'I don't know! It was the dream. I was so worried something awful was going to happen to them.'

Piers sat down beside her and put his arm round her. 'They are both fine. Just leave him for a moment. You frightened him when you started to shout. Here, I'll get something to put on that scratch. It's bleeding everywhere.'

By the time he had dabbed her wrist with antiseptic and put a sticking plaster over the worst of the laceration, Emma was calm again.

'So, what was the dream about, can you tell me?'

She shrugged. Leaning back against the sofa cushions she closed her eyes. 'That's the silly thing. It's gone.'

Piers paused, watching her. 'Em? Aren't you feeling well? I wondered why you had come home.'

She frowned and put her head forward into her hands for a moment. Then she shrugged. 'My head is spinning. I think I'll go and take a shower, Piers.'

'Perhaps I'd better remind you,' he said quietly, 'or are you just not planning to tell me? You gave in your notice this morning.'

She looked up slowly. 'I hadn't forgotten. How do you know?'

'David rang me. He was really worried. He thinks you're ill. That was why I came home.'

'Well, I'm not ill.'

'Then perhaps, just perhaps, you're off your head.' His voice had become hard.

She stood up, looking curiously vulnerable in her navy suit skirt and silk shirt with her hair dishevelled and her feet bare. 'Perhaps I am.'

The atmosphere was suddenly electric. They were on the brink of shouting at one another, saying things they didn't mean, things that could never be unsaid, and as if sensing it, neither spoke. It was Piers who broke the silence at last. 'I don't want to lose you, Em.'

'No.' She said it so quietly he barely heard her.

'You can't really want to give up your career. All you've worked for.'

'No.'

'You love that job.'

'Yes.'

'Then why? Why, Em?'

She shrugged her shoulders, sniffing. 'I don't know why.'

'What are you planning to do?'

'Run it as a herb nursery.'

Piers stared at her. 'You mean we are still talking about this darn cottage? I don't believe it. You were even having nightmares about it just now. That is what you were shouting about, Emma. You were shouting "Liza" when you scared Max. Please, Emma, you can't do this!'

'I have to.'

'You are prepared to throw everything up, *everything*! To go and live there?'

She nodded.

'Then you are mad. Totally, completely and utterly off your head.'

She gave a watery smile. 'On that at least, we agree. I don't want it to be the end of us, Piers. I really don't.'

'How can it not be? I'm a City person, Emma. My life, my job, my friends are all in the City. I can't . . . I won't commute. And I don't want to spend my weekends somewhere miles out in the country.'

'People do commute from there. It's only –'

'I don't care how long it takes, or how far it is. I don't want to do it. I won't do it.'

'Then it is the end for us.' Her tears had dried and her face was white. 'It has to be. I'm moving down there as soon as the paperwork is done. I'm sorry. I really am. But I have to do it. I have to. It's mine. It's where I belong.'

'You belong here!' Suddenly he was crying.

'No. No, I don't. I don't, Piers. I'm sorry. I'm so sorry.' Tears were pouring down her face, too. Pushing past him she ran towards the door, leaving him staring after her, sobbing like a child.

It was as she was sitting on the bed, cradling her pillow in her arms, having slammed the door on Piers and run to the bedroom, that she realised both the cats were in there already. Pressed tightly together in the five-inch space under the chest of drawers they were staring at her with huge, terrified eyes.

'You're scared,' she murmured at them miserably. 'And I'm scared. I don't know why I'm doing this. I don't understand anything any more. I don't understand anything at all.'

17

Wednesday morning

Flora Gordon was waiting for Emma at Planet Organic. She was already drinking an orange juice. Her wildly frizzy blonde hair was if anything more dishevelled than usual, and she had a pile of shopping bags around her feet as she sat on the high stool at the counter.

'Em?' She slipped down and gave Emma a hug. 'What on earth is the matter? You sounded like hell when you rang me. Why aren't you in the office?' Flora was one of Emma's oldest friends. They had been at school together but after that their paths had diverged, Emma to university and City job, Flora to a career in alternative medicine which had led her to study all over the world before she returned to set up a practice in London.

Emma was fighting back tears, again. 'I've resigned. It looks as though Piers and I are splitting up. I'm moving to the country.'

Flora stared at her for a brief moment, shocked into silence. Then she smiled. 'So? Why on earth are you crying? That's the best news I've heard in years.' She hoisted herself back onto her stool. 'Sweetheart, I know Piers is a dish and I know you thought it was forever, but you and he could never have hit it off for long. You're too different. He's a corporate man; if we are being honest here, a teeny bit stick-in-the-mud; even boring!' She grabbed Emma's hands and hauled her bodily up onto the stool next to her own. 'I know he is sweet and kind and he worships you, but he is stifling you, Em. There's a wonderful free woman in there,' she prodded Emma's chest, 'just screaming to be released.' She leaned forward. 'Where are you going? I hope I can still come and see you often.'

Emma began to smile in spite of herself. She ordered a coffee from the girl behind the counter, then she looked back at Flora and shrugged. 'You're the first person who hasn't told me I'm mad.'

'Of course you're not mad.' Flora put her head to one side and scrutinised Emma's face. 'You've got a lot of friends, Em, people who really love you, but they are on the whole terribly conventional. At least the ones I've met are.' She grimaced. 'None of those colleagues of yours and Piers's see the real you. I was beginning to be frightened that Piers had secretly murdered you and replaced you with a Stepford financial partner!'

Emma laughed out loud. 'I needed to hear that. I've been so torn, Flora. I've been having awful nightmares about the whole thing. I can't tell you how scared I've been. It's such a big step. I'm not really sure why I'm doing it.'

'Because you saw the cage closing?'

Emma stared at her thoughtfully. 'Do you think that was it? I thought it was because I've fallen in love with a cottage up on the north Essex coast where I spent my childhood holidays.'

Flora shook her head. 'We all fall in love with things and do nothing about it.' She giggled. 'Just as well, or Sean Bean would be in my cupboard at home right now, awaiting my pleasure! Em,' she took a deep thoughtful sigh, 'you've actually acted on this impulse of yours, so it must be important. Do you remember, when we were children, we had dreams? We played with the idea of who we would be one day. Everyone does. But when we grow up we forget those dreams. They are still there, but they seem unobtainable. Unrealistic. Best forgotten. You've remembered.' She leaned forward and put her hand over Emma's. 'You've gone back to the scene of your childhood, a childhood when you were wildly happy, and you've been given another chance. There must be a reason for that. Don't throw it away. Don't look back. Go for it!'

Emma was silent for a moment. Outside a car squealed to a halt and they heard an angry exchange of voices from the road followed by the roar of an engine as it sped off again. Two people walked into the shop talking loudly and between them a child started to cry.

'You will come and see me?' Emma bit her lip.

'Try and stop me.' Flora looked at her watch. 'Look, sweetheart,

I've got to go. I've someone coming for a treatment in half an hour. Keep me informed, won't you, and don't you dare forget to give me your new address.' She slipped off her stool and bent to gather up her bags. 'Remember, there's a reason this has happened, Em. Ring me. Keep me posted.' She gave her a hug, blew a kiss and she was gone.

18

Wednesday night

Mike Sinclair woke suddenly and stared round his bedroom. His heart was thudding with fear and he was drenched with sweat. He sat up and reached for the alarm clock by the bed. It had fallen over and he scrabbled for it, disorientated. It was only half past eleven. He had been asleep for less than half an hour. With a groan he walked over to the curtains and threw them back. That huge yellow moon was still there, the light flooding across the garden and into the windows of the house. What had he been dreaming about? It was coming back to him slowly. It was a bear. He had seen a bear padding towards him up the lane. It was a black bear with long curved claws which scraped on the road and huge teeth through which it was slavering, its breath foul, its small red eyes fixed on his face. And he couldn't move. He had not been able to move.

He took a deep breath, staring out of the window, aware suddenly that he was straining his eyes, looking for the bear in the black moon shadows of the garden.

'Come on, Mike. It's only a dream,' he muttered to himself. He went back to the bed and sitting down reached for the switch on the lamp on the bedside table. His old Bible, the one given to him by his grandmother at his confirmation, lay next to it. He picked it up. But the prayer that was running through his mind was that old one: 'From ghoulies and ghosties and long-leggety beasties, and things that go bump in the night, Good Lord, deliver us!' And why not? It said what had to be said. He clasped the Bible to his naked chest. 'Our Father, which art in heaven.' He stopped. A board had creaked on the landing outside his bedroom door. Then he heard something scraping; a rhythmic scrape and click, like the bear's claws. He shook his head and putting down the Bible he strode towards the door. Grabbing the handle he swung it open and stared out into the passage. There was nothing there. 'Hello?' The sound of his voice was shockingly loud in the silence. It was answered by silence. He stepped forward and flicked on the hall light. It shone down on the bare polished boards, the red-fringed runner lying down the centre of the narrowest part of the passage beyond his door, the closed doors leading to unused bedrooms on either side of his and the main staircase with its old black oak banisters and broad polished handrail disappearing into the dark downstairs. He moved to the top of the stairs. 'Is there anyone down there?' His study door was open and he could see the moonlight streaming in across the hall.

Running down the stairs on bare feet, he headed for his study and stopped in the doorway, staring in. The long French windows onto the garden were wide open, revealing wisps of mist curling across the lawn towards the house.

'Damn!' He whispered under his breath. He reached for the light switch. If there were intruders in the house it was his own fault. He remembered pulling the doors closed and reaching automatically to turn the key. At that moment the phone had rung and he had turned away. The conversation with the archdeacon had taken twenty minutes. When it was over he had walked out of the room without checking the doors again.

There were a couple of old walking sticks leaning behind the door – relics of his predecessor's arthritis. He took one up and holding it firmly in his hand he began to search the house. Dining room, living room, kitchen, cellar, four bedrooms, two attic rooms. All were empty and silent. By the time he had finished, every light in the house was blazing. There was no one there.

There would be no more sleep for a while. Swiftly he dressed in jeans and cotton shirt and let himself into the garden. The front gate creaked as he pushed it open, the nameplate showing up clearly in the moonlight. The Rec-ory. The 't' had long gone, to his amusement, though he meant to repaint the black flaking letters one of these days. The road was darker than he expected, the trees blocking the moonlight. This was where the bear had stalked him in his dream. 'Our Father which art in heaven,' he murmured as he stepped into the darkness. 'Hallowed be thy name.' His eyes were growing used to the dark. The road was deserted, the trails of mist dissolving between the trees. There was no bear. Of course there was no bear.

He walked steadily down towards the town centre. There were people around there, drawn as he was by the moonlit night. A group of youths hung around outside the pub. He turned away from them and walked down towards the river. The tide was running, a silver stream between the broad glittering flanks of mud, wraiths of mist hanging, almost invisible, over the water. There were dozens of small boats scattered at anchor, lying at different angles where they had come to rest as the water seeped away. In a while they would refloat, one by one, lifting stickily from the mud, turning gently to lie to their anchors in neat lines, caressed by the incoming glittering tide. He walked slowly, hands in pockets, listening to the contented chattering of ducks roosting on the mud, and the distant whistles of a group of wading birds, almost out of sight, paddling about where the mud turned to silver as the water crept in. A group of people were clustered round a hot dog van parked at the kerb. He could smell the sausages and onions and relish as he approached and his mouth watered involuntarily. He groped in his pockets. No money. Pity, he would have liked a midnight snack. He wished the young people good evening as he passed and was rewarded with a sullen silence. Once he had strolled on he heard a quiet retort addressed to his retreating back. He sighed.

A car was driving slowly up behind him. He ignored it, stopping to stand and stare out across the river. It drew to a halt fifty yards in front of him and backed up until it was almost level. Then it stopped.

'Mike?' Judith leaned across from the driver's seat and wound down the window. 'I thought it was you.'

Damn!

That was the second time he had sworn this evening, this time very much under his breath. 'Judith, what on earth are you doing here?'

'I was going home after having dinner with Ollie Dent. It was so lovely I thought I'd come back by the scenic route.' She opened the door and stepped out. Leaving the car she joined him on the grass, admiring the view. 'Couldn't you sleep?'

He shook his head. 'My early night came to nought, I'm afraid. Nightmares. I dreamed I was being chased by a bear.'

Judith laughed. 'Very Shakespearean! You must have had cheese for supper. That gives one bad dreams. It's a beautiful night to be sleepless, though.' There was a hint of wistfulness in her voice which made Mike glance at her sideways. He knew nothing, he realised, about her private life; he didn't think there was a man around, nor ever had been as long as he had known her, nor a woman, either. She lived alone. She taught at the school and her spare time was devoted to the church.

'How was Ollie?' he asked. Oliver Dent was at least eighty, so he doubted if her relationship with him was more than that of a friend, although one couldn't tell even that these days. His question distracted them both from their thoughts. 'He's better. He's got himself a cleaning lady and it's cheered him up a lot. It's a pity it's Lyndsey Clark, but I suppose even she is better than nothing.'

'Lyndsey Clark?' He was watching the water lapping round a boat lying on the mud near them. 'I don't think I know her.'

'No. You wouldn't.' The tone of Judith's voice sharpened. 'Going back to our conversation about witches the other day: she is one of them. The rector is unlikely to be on her list of close friends.'

'She's a witch?' He turned and stared at her. 'A real one?'

Judith nodded. She scowled. 'The trouble is she's clever. Oliver was telling me all about her. She was all set for a brilliant university career at Cambridge. But that didn't suit her. No doubt they tried to instil some sense into her. So like the silly spoiled child she is at heart, she dropped out. It don't know when she became a witch. Perhaps she was recruited by one of the local covens, but she makes no secret of it. She exudes evil from every pore!' She fell silent for a moment, then she went on. 'She lives by doing odd jobs. She's got a lot of charm; she's very attractive. The men all fall for her left right and centre.' She tightened her lips distastefully. 'So, beware, Mike, dear. If she casts a spell in your direction you could be lost.'

'I'm intrigued.' The boat was surrounded by water now. The tide was creeping silkily towards them across the mud. 'You said before that there was witchcraft round here. Real witchcraft. It worries you in school.'

'From time to time.' Judith shivered. She was wearing a short-sleeved flower-print dress and flat strappy sandals. The warm

101

night air was very still but a raft of small goosepimples showed on her upper arms for a moment. 'It's more a teenage thing. Satanism. But even my kids think it's glamorous. Exciting. There are at least two covens round here, and the kids are in danger of being drawn in.'

'And the church does not provide the glamour or the excitement they crave,' Mike said thoughtfully.

'Absolutely.' Judith shivered again. 'And why should it? It is not an entertainment. It is not meant to be fun.'

'Indeed.' He turned away to hide a wry grin.

'Be careful, Mike.' She glanced at him. 'You're very vulnerable, you know.'

'Am I?' He was genuinely astonished.

'You had to ask me if there were witches round here.' She glanced at him covertly. 'You ought to know, Mike. One can feel it. One can feel the evil. On a night like this, when the moon is full and the mist creeps up the river, there is danger in the air. That man who came to you about the ghosts. He was genuinely afraid or he would not have come to speak to you.'

Mike glanced in spite of himself behind him towards the river. He was silent for a while, his brow furrowed. She was watching him as she let her words sink in.

Eventually he spoke. 'Do you think I should speak to this Lyndsey person?'

'No!' She replied so sharply he took a step back. 'No, Mike. I don't want you going near her.'

'You don't think I'm strong enough to fight her evil?' He sounded reproachful.

'I'm sure you are.' Judith was staring at a young couple wandering along the road towards them. They were arm in arm, every now and then stopping to devour one another's mouths. She shuddered. 'Don't draw her attention, Mike. I'll deal with her. My prayer circle will hold her before the Lord. We'll contain her.'

Mike gave her a quick glance. Why, he wondered silently, did that thought worry him so much?

An hour later Judith, dressed in her cotton pyjamas and powder-blue dressing gown, went into the kitchen. Reaching for one of the pill bottles, she withdrew a single Warfarin tablet and swallowed it with a sip or two of water – something she had done every night since she had had the heart valve operation just before Mike arrived in the parish. Then she padded into her bedroom, where she knelt beside her bed and brought her hands together in prayer as she had done every night since she was a small child. The prayers lasted exactly fifteen minutes and by the end of them she was stiff and shivery, which was strange as the night was so warm. But her bedroom, unheated, even in winter, had always been cold. Climbing to her feet she took off the dressing gown, turned off the light and climbed into the narrow bed. Usually she slept at once, but tonight she was restless. She felt as if she had drunk too much coffee; her pulse was jumpy, her breathing irregular, her eyes refusing to close, searching the bedroom for shapes amongst the shadows cast by the streetlight near the garden gate.

I shall need you to help me, Goodwife Phillips.

The voice came from the figure in the corner of the room.

Judith shrank back against the pillows with a small yelp of fear. Staring, she tried to see him, but the shadows were black where the wardrobe stood between the window and the door.

We have to find every witch in the area. We have to do God's work.

Terrified, Judith nodded. She wasn't Goodwife Phillips. He couldn't be speaking to her.

You enjoyed your work with me, and there is more to do, Mary!

'I am not Mary!' Judith found she had spoken out loud, her voice husky with terror but her indignation at the case of mistaken identity strong. 'You've got the wrong person!'

She was shaking violently.

She lodges in your soul, Judith. You are kindred spirits you and she!

Was that a chuckle she could hear from the corner? As her eyes strained to see the owner of the voice a car turned into the street and the headlights shone for a moment through the thin curtain, lighting up the wall. There was no one there. Of course there was no one there. It was a dream. Desperately she squeezed her eyes shut and pulled her blankets up over her head.

By next morning she had forgotten the whole incident.

19

The huge moon was still lighting up the countryside like daylight as Lyndsey let herself out of her house. The row of three fisherman's clapboard cottages was set in the shadow of the old maltings buildings on the quayside. The deep channel came close to the shore there beyond the dock, and the water was black and moved uneasily beneath the pull of the moon. There was no sound as she paused, glancing across the quay down river towards the broad estuary. Somewhere out there, beyond the strip of water and the shining mud, something old and evil hid, swathed in the cold sea mist. More and more often now she sensed it there waiting, and it terrified her. Was she the only person in the entire peninsular who felt it?

The whole world seemed to be asleep; the cottages on either side of her own were in darkness. Quietly she went back and wheeling her bicycle outside, she clicked the front door closed behind her. No one saw her as she set off along the quay and turned up the narrow road towards the centre of the village.

The site of the old church lay in the moonlight like a bright tapestry, a quilting of light and shadow, black and grey and deep velvet green. As she climbed over the wall she stood for a long time, listening. Somewhere a bird, disturbed by the moonlight, whistled plaintively and fell silent and she could hear the high-pitched squeak of bats as they ducked and dived across the grass.

Sure-footedly she made her way to the centre of the thicket where the north wall of the church had once stood, and kneeling on the dew-wet grass she pulled a night-light from her pocket. She lit the flame and steadied it with cupped hands, waiting for the wax to pool around the stubby wick. A pinch of dried herbs and a few grains of incense which hissed and spat, and quietly she began her prayer to the goddess, muttering under her breath, afraid in the still silence to speak out loud for fear of being overheard. Not that there was anyone to hear. The road was deserted, the houses, out of sight beyond the trees, were in darkness and behind her Liza's Cottage was empty and asleep.

When she had finished she stood for a long time, her senses alert, her eyes scanning the shadows. The place was quiet and still at peace.

Turning at last she walked back to the wall. In the lane she hesitated beside her bicycle, then, after a moment's deep thought she made her way quietly towards the cottage. The *For Sale* sign had gone to be replaced with one which said *sold*. It stood straight and proud, strapped to the gatepost at the end of the holly hedge throwing a black rectangular shadow across the path. Will Fortingale had told her who was buying it. A business woman from London who was so rich she didn't need a mortgage. A weekender. Someone who would probably employ an interior designer and gardeners and change the place out of all recognition. Carefully she let herself into the garden. Out of the moonlight the shadows were very black. The house still seemed to be asleep. Behind the doors and curtainless staring windows she could sense its emptiness and suddenly she was afraid. She stood still, staring round, the tiny short hairs on the back of her neck bristling. 'Liza?' she whispered. 'Liza, are you there?'

No one answered. The moon was sailing higher now, and smaller. In the apple tree by the gate a bird called out in alarm and she saw the small dark shape flit out of sight across the garden.

Making her way between the rose bushes with their burden of overblown, sweet-scented flower-heads, Lyndsey moved silently around the back of the house. The terrace had been extended about thirty years before by the Simpsons. Small moss-covered red bricks had been set in a herringbone design and around the edges of the terrace they had left a dozen or so large old flower pots which still boasted leggy untrimmed lavender and rosemary bushes. The weight of the roses had pulled down the pergola and their scent, rich and sweet in the night air, was almost cloying as she stepped off the terrace and onto the wet grass. She could feel the garden full of eyes, watching her. Small animals and birds, but also other creatures of the night, hidden invisible beings who had made the garden their own. They were worried too, as uncertain as she was about what would happen to this place. 'I'll take care of things, my darlings,' she whispered. She felt them listening, felt them tense suddenly, their attention hers. 'We don't want anyone moving in here, do we? Don't worry. I'll get rid of her. You must help me.'

She glanced up as an owl hooted, and watching its swift silent traverse of the garden, she smiled. 'It'll be child's play for us, won't it. With Liza's help.' She paused, turning round. 'You will help, Liza, won't you? We don't want any newcomer pushing her way in here. This is your place. Yours and mine.'

The Simpsons had lasted eighteen months, so she'd been told, before they moved out of the cottage. Holidaymakers came and went. They didn't seem to bother Liza. After all, there were long periods when the cottage lay empty in between. And since Lyndsey had come back to the village there had been no holiday-makers at all. She had seen to that. She wanted the house empty because the garden was hers; the place, though with such care that no casual observer would see that anyone had been there, where she planted and tended and harvested her herbs.

She had lasted four terms at university. Hateful place. In town. Full of people and cars and noise. Her parents had washed their hands of her when she walked out, her father blustering and indignant, her mother crying. 'Most people would give their right arm to go to Cambridge, Lyn! How can you do this to us? How?'

They had never understood her. Never cared about who she really was, about what was best for her, rather than for them. When Lucy Stebbings, her great-aunt, had died and left her the tiny terraced cottage in Mistley she had taken it as a sign that she was blessed and supported in her bid for total freedom. She moved in and earned a modest living doing odd jobs around the village to subsidise her real work and her passion: her exquisite, detailed paintings and her research into the occult use of herbs which would one day form the core of the witches herb Bible she was planning to write. She had never gone back to her parents' home in Woodbridge. Had never seen her father again. Her mother came over occasionally with food parcels and clothes and clucked around. Lyndsey was barely civil to her. All she wanted was to be left alone.

She shook her head. What had got her thinking about her past suddenly? Liza, probably. Liza wasn't an ancestor. She had had no children who had lived. But Sarah had, and Sarah was an ancestor. Sarah, who was Liza's nursling, Liza's friend and Liza's pupil. Sarah who had ended her days in this cottage, the dower house where she had come to live in her old age and where she had carried on Liza's work.

This cottage should have been Lyndsey's by rights. That it had not belonged to anyone in her family for three hundred years made no difference to her at all. This land, this home, this place, was hers, her natural inheritance, and no one was going to steal it from her.

She shuddered. She could feel her everywhere, the stranger who was buying the house. She too had stood out here beyond the terrace. Her energies were strange. Uneasy. Afraid. She was bringing unhappiness and danger. Suddenly Lyndsey's senses were screaming. This could not be allowed to happen. It would undo all the good she had worked for over the years; unleash everything that she had fought to contain. She was going to re-awaken the evil, allow it in, encourage that mist to drift in from the sea and engulf them all.

The spell was an easy one. First the circle drawn faintly in the grass, her whispered invocation to the guardians of the quarters, her arms raised to the goddess moon as she sailed serenely in the clear, midnight sky.

'Let no one buy this house. Let no one live here. Let no one enter these doors who does not belong. Liza, mother of my mother's race, listen to my prayer and help to guard your home. If anyone should move here, let their stay be short. Let the very doors and walls, ceilings and floors, the spiders, the rats and mice, let them all conspire to drive her out. Let the chimneys smoke and the mildew curl about the walls, let the rot take the boards and the worms the beams.' She paused, pleased with the resonance of the words. Then suddenly she frowned. 'But not so badly that it falls down, of course.' She smiled to herself and shook her head. 'Liza, this is still your home. Your house, your place. Keep this woman out. Haunt her! Scare her! Make her ill. Send her mad. Do not allow her to stay!'

She stared in silence at the moon, feeling its power touching her, feeling her own hatred. Then she frowned. The moon was still a fraction off the full. Perhaps she should return tomorrow when she was at her maximum power and repeat the spell. What had Will told her the woman's name was? Emma. That was it. Emma Dickson. She raised her arms again. 'This house will never

107

be yours, Emma Dickson; you will not thrive here. Don't darken its doors. Don't cross its threshold. Don't touch this garden, which is sacred to Liza's memory.' She felt in the pocket of her jeans. Yes it was still there, the short length of cord she carried with her in case she should have to make a binding spell. Holding it up in both hands, she began to knot it. 'A knot to bind my spell. A knot to keep it well. A knot to hold at bay, the danger that comes by day.' Three knots. The triple seal. Scrabbling with her fingers in the grass at the centre of the circle, she managed to scrape a small hole into which she tucked the cord. She covered it and rearranged the grass. It was done. If Emma Dickson ever moved into this house, she would regret it for the rest of her days.

Part Two

20

End of September

Unable to sleep, Mike had walked out into the icy dawn and was looking across the river. He could see nothing. The previous night's mist had settled into thick fog, blanketing a clammy, viscous tide as it licked towards him across the mud. The silence was intense, heavy and cloying, beating against his eardrums as he narrowed his eyes, trying to see the outline of the old boat lying on the saltings, her ribs bare, her keel rotted and broken.

The atmosphere was eerie and disorientating and he found himself suddenly catching his breath, overwhelmed with fear that there was something out there, hiding just off the shore out of sight. Somewhere across the water he heard the lonely whistle of a bird and he found himself turning round and round, unable now even to see the road, the grass at his feet, the water's edge; totally lost.

He pulled his hands out of his pockets and held them out in front of him, grasping at the air, feeling the icy droplets of fog condensing on his skin. Whatever was out there was evil beyond measure and it was coming closer. He wanted to turn and run, but he seemed incapable of moving. His breath was growing constricted and it was only then that he realised he had been so paralysed with fear that he had been unable to pray.

'Dear Lord, Jesus Christ, be with me.'

His words were muffled by the fog, but he felt comforted.

There was something terribly wrong in the town and others were feeling it too. He frowned. Several times now he had caught sight of Bill staring out towards the river, that look of worried preoccupation on his face as though he were expecting something

111

awful to emerge from the quiet, muddy water. And the atmosphere had been mentioned at the PCC meeting only the night before. Someone had vandalised the church hall, breaking the windows, spraying graffiti on the walls. Telling him about it, Donald James had shaken his head mournfully. Too many things were going wrong. The crime rate in the whole area was soaring. The head teacher at the school was complaining that the children were becoming moody and uncontrollable, joking wryly about it, wondering if it was something in the water. Mike narrowed his eyes, trying to see through the mist. Was there something in the water? Not in the sense the teacher had meant, of course, but something else. Something infinitely more sinister.

It was growing lighter. And suddenly the terrible sense of impending doom seemed to have withdrawn. Suddenly he could see again. The fog was thinning and towards the east he could see a flush of red.

As the sun began to rise through the mist, it was the colour of blood.

21

The house was very quiet. Looking round the small, low-ceilinged living room, Emma added two items to her shopping list: extra-soft cushions for the little sofa she had bought from Peter Jones before she left London, and yet another lamp. In spite of the radiant September sunshine outside, the room was dark. The corners never reflected the light. Shadows seemed to hang there whatever she did to rearrange the lamps she had brought with her.

It was a week since she had moved in, just over six since she had first seen the cottage. In that time the sale had gone through without a hitch, her resignation had been accepted by David Spencer – if reluctantly, and only after her promise that she would continue to supply him from time to time with reports and summaries, that she would stay in Internet touch, and that if or when she changed her mind, she would ring him immediately. Last but not least, she had on that last terrible, miserable day, removed all her possessions, including Max and Min, from what was now Piers's flat.

The cats had at first been astonished and nervous at finding themselves the owners of an entire house and a three-acre area of ground. But the fear was slowly wearing off and now they were intrigued, anxious to explore. She had only let them out for the first time yesterday, all eight paws duly buttered, and they had proceeded cautiously out onto the terrace, sitting close together, the swagger and bravado they had displayed when looking out of the windows all gone. She had watched them fondly, at first afraid they might run away and disappear. She needn't have worried. The first sound of a car in the lane had them bolting back into the kitchen and up the stairs. But it was only minutes after that they were creeping downstairs again, their eagerness to explore and their excitement outweighing their caution.

The furnishing in the house was as yet sparse. Peggy and Dan had come up to see her only three days before, bringing with them a small antique pine table and four chairs for the dining room – soon to be linked to the kitchen by the removal of the lathe and plaster between the studwork – and the oak side-table and the pair of Victorian velvet granny chairs had come from them as well. Upstairs, the bed was new. The Victorian chest of drawers had been her grandmother's, the oak coffer had been Peggy's. But still it didn't feel like home. Thankfully she had not heard the voice again.

She wandered outside. A robin was singing its thready, wistful, autumn song from the collapsed pergola halfway down the garden. That would have to be mended, as would so much of the fencing, the trellises, the gate. The list of work to be done out here was endless, the work to do on the house equally so. She stood still, feeling the sun on her face, breathing in the soft, slightly salty air. She could see down to the widening estuary from her bedroom window and already recognised the fresh cold smell of the mud as the tide crept out leaving the broad dark grey glitter of the river margins exposed.

She perched on the wall for a few moments to get her breath back after her strenuous morning's work on the house. But stopping for too long was dangerous. It was then that the doubts crept in. Her happiness, her sense of absolute rightness, her triumph at finding herself here was not enough all the time, to blot out the worry at what she had done. She had turned her back on a first-class career. She had moved out of the home she loved with the man she adored, and she had spent without a thought a good chunk of her savings and for what? A dream. A fantasy. Even the prospect of doing a bit of freelance work for David didn't entirely comfort her. The income she made from that would never be huge. She glanced up at the window of the back bedroom where her computer sat on a wooden table. Sitting at it she could look out over the garden. That would be her office, if and when she got round to organising it.

Min landed on her lap with a small chirrup of greeting and she bent and kissed the cat's dark head. 'You like it here, don't you, darling,' she whispered. She sighed.

She longed to ring Piers, if only to hear his voice. Glancing back at the kitchen door she could see the phone from here. It was blue, to match the Aga which would be fitted next week. No. What was the point? He would see through her, sense her loneliness and she would rather die than admit she might have made a mistake.

Standing up, she set the cat down on the moss-covered wall and began to walk down the garden path. 'You coming?' She turned and clicked her fingers at Min, who cautiously jumped down and followed her, sniffing at the grass. As Emma watched, the cat paused and began to paw at a bare patch of earth, patting, sniffing, and leaping back, her hair on end.

'What is it, Min? Be careful.' Emma went over to see what she had found.

Lying there, partially exposed, was a knotted length of muddy red cord. Emma picked it up with a frown. She examined it closely. There was something unpleasant about it, although she wasn't quite sure what. 'It's only a piece of string, Min. Here, do you want a game?' She dangled it in front of the cat invitingly. Min backed away and spat.

Emma jumped. 'Sorry! I thought you'd like to play.'

But already Min was trotting back towards the terrace. There, she sat down and began to wash her face. That was enough exploration for one day.

Emma moved on, pushing the string absent-mindedly into her pocket.

The lawn was a matted tangle of knee-high grasses and wild flowers. Two old apple trees, laden with small hard green fruit, stood one on either side of the path and once-symmetrical beds of roses featured beyond them where the pergola had collapsed beneath its riot of blown and dying flowers.

She paused, suddenly uncomfortable. Each time she walked down the garden she stopped here and without quite knowing why, looked round, glancing over her shoulder. She shivered and hurried on. Beyond lay the gate into the herb garden. Beds of herbs, woody and untrimmed, lay around an old boarded barn and behind it there was a poly-tunnel, torn and mildewed, where the young plants had been raised. She loved the barn. It had obviously been the centre of activities when the place was a business and boasted water and electricity that worked, two benches, shelves of pots and broken tools, labels, jam jars, all the stuff which she assumed had not been worth saving.

Two sides of the gardens were enclosed by an old brick wall, some eight feet high. On the third side where she had come in, most of the wall was hidden beneath ivy and wisteria and once-trimmed espaliered pear trees. The shelter the walls gave from the wind created a wonderful fragrant haven. This had once been, she understood, one of the kitchen gardens for the manor house up the road. On the fourth side of the herb garden the wall had almost gone completely, to be replaced by a high untrimmed hedge. Beyond that lay the two-acre paddock – wind-sewn with thistles and ragwort. Wandering between the beds, she snapped off a piece of rosemary and rubbed it between her fingers. Next spring would be the time to start some sort of project here. Until then she would spend her energies on the house itself and on finding her way around the district. Another spontaneous wave of out and out happiness swept over her. At whatever cost, she knew it was right to have come.

When she returned to the kitchen it was with a posy of herbs and roses which she put into a glass and carried through into the living room. Frowning, she glanced round. It was still too dark, even with all the lights on. And there was a strange feeling in the room, as though someone had just walked out of it. She frowned, looking out of the window, but the front garden was empty, the gate closed. There was no one there. She tried to push the sensation aside. Perhaps if she moved the table-lamp closer to the chair and threw another log on the fire the room would cheer up at bit

It was as she was standing there, at the window, that she became conscious suddenly of the piece of red cord in her pocket, nestling against her hip. It felt hot. Unpleasant. With an exclamation of disgust she pulled it out and stared at it, frowning. What on earth was it? She glanced round for Min. The cat had spat at it. Why? She walked over to the fire. Whatever it was, there was only one place for it. As she threw it onto the smouldering logs, the flames hissed and flared almost angrily. In seconds they had devoured it totally. Suddenly the room seemed lighter.

When the phone rang that evening, she was standing at the sink, washing earth from her hands. She had been weeding the old flower pots on the terrace, dragging them into new positions, working out where a garden table and chairs would go.

'Em?' Piers's voice rang in her ear. 'Just checking to see how you're getting on.'

She closed her eyes, fighting the pang of anguish his voice provoked. 'I'm fine. Really happy.' She realised that there were sudden tears trickling down her cheeks. 'You will come down and visit us one day, won't you?' She took a deep breath, steadying her voice with difficulty.

Their parting had been so hard. Nothing had been said to emphasise that this was the end of their relationship, but what else could it be? Piers had not relented. He had helped her pack up sadly, resigned to her going. He had helped her load the cat baskets into the seat beside her, he had kissed her goodbye and waved as she drove away and then – nothing.

She had waited and waited for him to ring, her pride preventing her from being the first to pick up the phone in case she cried.

'The cats are missing you, Piers.'

'Just the cats?'

She couldn't tell if he was smiling or irritated.

'Not just the cats. Me, too.'

There was a moment's silence. 'I'm missing you lots, too. No one's scratching the sofa any more.'

She gave a wistful chuckle. 'You know I tried to stop doing that.'

There was a fractional pause. 'You are sure you're OK?'

'Quite sure. Peggy and Dan are coming down at the weekend with another load of stuff from Waitrose. They seem to think I'm going to starve. Which is silly. There are a couple of lovely food shops here.'

She stood staring out of the kitchen window for a long time after he had rung off. She felt bereft.

Max jumped up onto the window sill beside her and she fondled his chin. 'He said he'd come,' she whispered. 'But I don't think he will.'

The nights were colder now as late summer pitched into autumn and lately they had been very foggy. She switched on an electric fire in her bedroom. Central heating would be necessary at some point soon. She must find a good local man to work on the cottage. The cats were both asleep on her bed and she had locked the doors downstairs. Time enough for night-time excursions when they had grown used to the place and found their way around and she had found someone to put in a cat flap.

Clutching her dressing gown around her, she tiptoed down the landing into the bathroom. It was irredeemably cold, with cracked linoleum on the floor and chipped white enamel fittings. The hot water however came from an electric immersion heater in the linen cupboard which blessedly and unexpectedly worked with enormous enthusiasm. She ran a bath and added some shower gel beneath the taps. Carpet, bathroom fittings, shower, hot towel rail – they were all on her list.

She rubbed steam off the mirror with the corner of a towel and peered at her face. It looked grubby: dust and earth had transferred from hands to nose, hair, eyes, and she was grey with fatigue. She frowned. That did not look like the face of someone living out their dream. She peered closer. For a moment it had not looked like her face at all. Frightened, she glanced behind her. But of course there was no one there.

Exhausted, she slept the moment her head touched the pillow, one cat at her feet, the other in the crook of her elbow. In the bathroom the steam slowly cleared. As the temperature dropped one by one the old oak floorboards creaked, settling into place.

Quietly, Min extricated herself from Emma's sleeping arms and, jumping from the bed to the window sill, sat staring down into the dark garden.

22

The dream was there lying in wait for her. One moment she was drifting in and out of consciousness as she tried to get comfortable on the new unaccustomed mattress, still missing the solid reassuring form of Piers beside her, and the next she was standing, dressed in a long gown and embroidered shawl, in a strange room, by a heavy oak table staring at an open window where someone had called her name.

'Mistress Sarah! Hurry!' The figure at the window looked surreptitiously over his shoulder, clearly afraid. 'Hopkins and his madmen have gone for Liza. You've got to come!'

She felt her stomach turn over with fear.

It was Hal. His father Tom managed the Bennetts' farm. She hurried to the door. 'Hal? Where are you?'

But he had already run away.

Her breath came in short gasps; her mouth was dry with terror. It was only when she could see the thatched roof of the cottage that she slowed down and began to think. Hopkins was a dangerous man. She knew how he worked, setting neighbour against neighbour, encouraging spite, subtly enflaming suspicion and engendering hatred. Anyone who crossed him or questioned his methods was liable to be arrested. Everyone despised him, but with the country at war with itself and everyone afraid, and with him claiming to have Parliament's authority for what he did, there was no one to gainsay him. No one!

Her heart hammering under her ribs, she climbed awkwardly over the fence and tiptoed down the line of the hedge towards the back of the cottage. She could hear shouting. Men and women. They must have come and found Liza somewhere in the garden. Oh please God, let her be all right. There was a rousing cheer. She crept closer. She couldn't see round the corner of the wall. Keeping out of the sight of the windows as best she could, she ran towards the cottage and edged carefully along under cover of the tall hollyhocks, then carefully she peered round. She could see them now, a crowd of men and women in the lane. They were bundling something – someone – into a cart. There was another cheer and they were gone. She could hear the horse's hooves on the mud and stones of the lane and then the laughter and shouting of the crowd who followed behind.

'Wait!' she shouted. No sound came from her mouth. For a moment she found she couldn't move, then she was running towards the gate. On the path she stopped suddenly, looking down. The old cat lay there, its body broken and bloody, its eyes still open as it stared up at the sky. 'Oh no!' Her eyes filled with tears. 'Oh, Liza, no.' She crept down the path into the cottage and stared round. The room was empty. Where was the other cat? Suddenly it was terribly important that she find him. 'Blackie? Blackie, where are you?'

She glanced up the stairs. 'Blackie. Are you there?'

The cat had crawled upstairs to die. It gazed at her from swiftly dimming eyes, its ribs broken, stomach and spleen ruptured, its face smashed, all from the boot of one man. As she knelt beside it and put a gentle hand on its head the pain and fear were already passing. In a minute it was dead.

She looked round, sobbing. 'Liza?' The word was soundless on her lips. 'Liza, why didn't you hide from them?'

Sweet Jesus. She could feel it. She could hear it in the echoes. Evil. Terror. Death.

'Liza!' She was screaming now as she ran down the stairs. 'Liza, come back!'

Her sorrow and fear turning to anger, she ran towards the gate.

There was no sign now of the rabble in the lane. The dust was settling. Nearby a thrush hopped out of the hedge, a snail in its beak, looking for its usual anvil. The stone had been pushed to one side by the scrabbling of a dozen pairs of feet but the bird spotted it at once and began to hammer the shell in quick brutal thumps as she watched.

Sobbing, she made her way home.

'Papa?' There was no answer. 'Papa? Where are you?' Her voice echoed down the oak-panelled corridor.

He was in the great hall, speaking to his steward. 'What is it, Sarah?' Anthony Bennett turned with a frown. His expression softened as he saw his only daughter.

'They have taken Liza. The witchfinder and his rabble have taken Liza, Papa. You have to do something!' She saw her father's steward scowl. John Pepper had worked for the Bennetts for as long as she could remember. She had never liked him.

'It was only a matter of time, mistress. That old woman has cast the evil eye too often for my taste, or anyone else's in the town.'

'That's not true!' Sarah's eyes blazed. 'She has done nothing but good. I remember her making medicines for your family many a time, John Pepper!'

'And my family died, mistress!' The retort had an almost triumphant tone to it.

'They died of marsh ague, not of a curse!' She was indignant.

'And who is to say that? Liza gave them medicines. Maybe they were poisoned.'

'Enough!' Anthony Bennett slammed the book he had been holding down onto the table. 'Leave us please, John. We'll continue our discussion later. Sarah, calm yourself. I fear there is nothing you can do. The law must take its course. I am sure justice will be done.'

'Justice!' Sarah stared at him, white-faced. 'Where was the justice for the others? They had done nothing wrong.'

'If that were true, my darling, they would not have been hanged.' He held out his hand. 'Come and sit by me and we will discuss it, see if there is something we can do.'

She was trembling. 'He will hurt her, Papa. He will force a confession.'

Anthony Bennett frowned. 'Liza is not entirely innocent of

121

whatever charges have been laid against her, Sarah. You and I both know that. Her intentions may have been benign, but her methods have not always been Christian.' He gave a wry smile. 'Have never been Christian, if we are honest! That is, sweet daughter, why your mother first dismissed her from our service. She decided Liza was not a fit nurse for you.'

Sarah's face was burning with indignation. 'But you brought her back, Papa, after Mama died. And she cared for me as her own child. She never harmed me –'

'No. She never harmed any of us. She has been loyal and kind to the Bennett family, which is why I gave her the cottage, and for that reason we will support her and do what we can for her.' He stood up and walked towards the window. His elbow resting against a carved wooden mullion, he stared down into the garden. 'I will speak to our neighbour, Sir Harbottle, who may well end up the judge of the case,' he said slowly. 'Our friendship is severely strained however, as you know, as he is for Parliament and we are for the king. It is not a good time to seek favours.' He turned back to her. 'You must leave this to me, Sarah.' His voice was suddenly stern. 'Do not become involved.' He knew his daughter. For a while, during her short-lived marriage to Robert Paxman, she had settled into blissfully demure matronhood, or so it had seemed to her father. He had sighed with relief. His daughter was safely settled, married to a good, wealthy man. Not gentry, as he would have wished – she had spurned the suitable men whom Anthony had produced for her inspection – but a decent burgess of Colchester who was strong, well-educated, successful and she adored him. The only blight on their five-year marriage had been the emptiness of the nursery. The cradle remained unused, to Robert and Sarah's deep unhappiness, and when Robert had died of the pox Sarah was left wealthy, independent, and alone. Anthony sighed. This was the third time she had ridden over to see him in as many weeks. The loneliness was beginning to wear her down.

He glanced at her face, taking in the heightened colour, the brilliant eyes, the nervously fidgeting fingers. He sighed again. 'I shall call John to escort you home, Sarah. The countryside is still full of soldiers, God help us all, and you shouldn't ride alone. Leave this with me, child. I shall enquire where they have taken her and what is to be done. Don't fret.' He shook his head. He

122

had seen rebellion in her face and he knew the danger she would face if she were to interfere. He had watched Master Hopkins in action over the last year as he travelled the eastern counties. He did not like the man, or his mission.

Sarah stood up and joined him at the window. 'Where will they hold her?'

He shrugged. 'Most probably they'll take her to Colchester and put her in the castle until she can be sent for trial in Chelmsford. He will probably question her at Mistley Thorn or in Manningtree first.'

'No.' It was a moan.

'Maybe he won't bother, or have the time to do that.' He was trying to reassure her. They both knew what questioning meant. Legally it might not be torture, not in the eyes of the law. In the eyes of any sane, God-fearing man or woman it was no less.

'I'm not going to let them kill her, Papa!' The tension in her voice made it shrill.

'Do not interfere, Sarah!' Her father was very stern. The unspoken thought swam into his mind. I have lost a son, only a few months ago, at Naseby, dear God, please don't let me lose a daughter too, in this accursed land where next-door neighbours are at one another's throats and brother fights brother. 'I absolutely forbid it. Your own life would be in danger. They would drag up tales of your childhood in her care. Your name would be sullied by their foul accusations. You must not become involved, do you understand? You must not . . .'

His voice was growing distant. It was echoing in her head. 'Sarah? Sarah, are you listening to me?'

'Yes, Papa.' Sarah was still staring out of the window. She was no longer hearing him, her eyes fixed on the hedge beyond the lawn. 'I have to help Liza somehow. I have to . . . I have to . . .'

Sarah's voice echoed in Emma's head as the dream lightened and dissipated into fragmented sounds and pictures and finally disappeared. When she woke in the early dawn light she was conscious only of a feeling of deep unease. The cats were no longer in the room.

23

Monday October 5th, London

'Take a look, Mark.' Joe pushed the button on the remote and the video started to play. They were silent, Mark half-seated on the corner of the desk, Colin standing by the window.

'There's always noises. People walking up and down.' Stan Barker's voice rang out in the silent room. Then Mark's. 'And at what point did you decide that the house was haunted by Matthew Hopkins, the Witchfinder General?'

'It's good. He comes over better on film than he did in real life.' Mark chuckled.

They all watched for a few moments, then Joe stepped closer to the screen and squatted on his haunches in front of it. 'OK. It's about here. Hang on. Right. Freeze.' The picture stilled and Mark found himself staring at it intently. 'See? There.' Joe reached forward and touched the screen with his finger. Behind Stan Barker's head they could see the staircase leading up out of the shop into the shadows.

'It's too blurred.' Mark tried to fight back the uneasiness that had dogged him ever since Joe had phoned him.

'Wait. I'll play the rest, then wind it back.'

The film sequence resumed. Mark saw Stan wave his arm in the air, gesturing behind him. Then he saw it. A face peering round the corner of the stairs.

'Christ Almighty!' he heard himself exhale loudly. 'Who is that?'

'Quite.' Joe pressed rewind. 'Take another look.'

They viewed the shot three times in silence, then Joe switched off.

'He doesn't appear again?'

'Nope.'

'Why didn't we see this before?'

Joe shrugged. 'It's very blurred. I guess we were all concentrating on Stan when we viewed this material. We put it aside. We did those other shoots. We've been working on other bits of the series. We didn't sit and look – really look – at the film. Col and I spotted this last night. We came up to watch the whole thing through to make a start on it. And there it was.'

Mark stood up and walked over to the window. Joe's small editing room and studio was at the back of his narrow, tall, terraced house in Highgate. They were on the third floor and Colin was still puffing slightly from the climb.

Mark eyed him. 'You're so unfit. Why the hell don't you lose some weight, Col?'

Colin grinned. 'Now, now. You know I have. And I'm a damn sight fitter than old Joe here.' He eyed their host, who was as usual brandishing a half-smoked cigarette. 'When are you going to stop smoking, Joe? It's going to kill you, you know.'

Joe grinned. 'Change the record, Col. Now, Mark, what do you make of the face?'

'It's amazing!' Mark threw himself down in the swivelling chair behind the desk and eloquently wiped the palms of his hands over his denimed thighs. 'And it scares me witless. It's not imagination, is it?'

'Nope.'

'Has Alice seen it?'

'I haven't shown her the tape.'

'Why don't you get her up here and let's see if she spots it.'

'I suppose we could.' Joe pulled a face. He stubbed out his cigarette.

125

'Go on. Give her a yell. She's not squeamish. Don't say any-thing. Just show her the sequence.'

'She'll want to know why. I don't usually ask her opinion.'

'Well, perhaps you should. Now is a good time to start.' Mark levered himself out of the chair and strode over to the door. 'Alice?'

'What?' The voice from somewhere below them sounded distinctly graceless.

'Can you come up a mo'? We want to ask you something.'

He imagined the groan, the toss of the head and grinned to himself. She would come. And sure enough, seconds later he heard the clump of her clogs on the polished wood of the stairs.

'So, what do you lot want?' She was dressed in cropped jeans and a lime-green t-shirt. Mark noted a new stud since he had last seen her. This was above the right eyebrow.

'We're editing the Manningtree film. Remember the interviews in the haunted shop?'

'Mark!' She was scornful. 'It was only six weeks ago!'

'Sorry. It just feels like a long time to us old folk!' He gave Colin a complicit glance. 'OK. So, I want you to take a look at this sequence.' Colin was winding it back again as Joe's daughter sat down on the floor in front of the TV. She crossed her legs. 'So, what are we looking for? The ghost?'

Mark kept his face impassive. 'Look. Then we'll talk.'

Colin began to run the sequence and Alice sat forward, elbows on knees, staring at the screen. 'Boring old bugger!' she muttered. Then she widened her eyes. 'Fucking hell! It *is* the ghost!'

Colin froze the picture. 'What can you see?'

'There's a face, peering down the stairs. Oh, bloody hell!'

'We just wanted to check we weren't imagining it.' Mark could feel a sudden film of sweat across his shoulder blades. 'So, who do you reckon it is?'

'Hard to say.' After her initial reaction, he reckoned she was more interested and excited than scared. 'There's too much shadow to see anything other than the face. It's kind of disembodied.' She gave a delighted chortle.

'OK. Cut the comedy.' Colin ran the sequence back and played it once more. 'Man or woman? What do you reckon?'

'Man.'

'Woman.'

126

Mark and Alice spoke simultaneously.

'Right.' Colin gave a wry shrug. 'What can we agree on?'

'Long nose. Piercing eyes. Sort of brown. Chiaroscuro.' Alice said thoughtfully. 'Kind of Rembrandt figure.'

'No prizes for guessing what you're studying.' Mark walked over to the TV. There was a pencil in his hand and he pointed at the picture. 'See this bit? There. Do you reckon that's part of the figure? A leg perhaps, or a skirt?'

'You can't tell. Not really.' Alice was staring intently at the screen. Then suddenly she turned round. 'Do you realise that he/she/whatever, was watching us?' Her eyes rounded. 'Look. It's not looking at Stan. It's looking straight past him towards you and Dad.'

'That hadn't occurred to me.' Joe looked at Mark. 'I rather wish it hadn't occurred to you, Al.'

'Especially as we are going to have to go back.'

'Go back?' She stared at him. 'Groovy. Can I come?'

Mark laughed. 'If your Dad thinks it's OK. I don't see why not. You're not scared, then?'

'No. 'Course not.' She rose to her feet, graceful in spite of the clogs and deliberately awkward manner. 'I thought the old boy said we couldn't go near the shop once the new tenants had moved in.'

'He did?' Mark pantomimed disbelief. 'Well, I don't suppose we have to ask him. If the new tenants don't mind, then I don't reckon we're going to upset anyone.'

'Are you going to hold a seance?' Alice was heading towards the door.

'Certainly not. This is a serious programme.'

'Seances are serious. I know someone who can do it for you. A medium. She's brilliant!'

'No, thanks.' Mark shook his head tolerantly. 'It's a nice thought, but I don't want to trivialise the programme. No, OK!' He held up his hand. 'A lot of people may think a seance is serious scientific research, but it doesn't fit our remit, I'm afraid. This programme is about tracing the history behind the reputed hauntings as much as anything.'

'And now we've got the coup of the century!' she crowed. 'You wait till I tell my friends.'

'No, Al! I don't want you to tell anyone about this, OK?' Her father looked at her sternly. 'Programme confidentiality, remember. After it's aired, or even, if we decide to use it in the promotion, just before we air the programme, but absolutely not now. We'll be besieged, upstaged, rubbished or someone will run a spoiler if this gets out.'

'And we need to do some more research,' Mark put in quietly. 'I think there may be scope for an hour slot for this one. There is so much history involved. Cromwell. The Civil War. The contemporary attitude to women. Witchcraft and magic. This isn't like the ghost we made a programme about in Nottingham. That was a standard master/servant melodrama.'

'And the ghost failed to appear,' Colin put in.

'They have all failed to appear!' Mark said quietly. 'Up till now.'

They all looked at the TV as though expecting the face to be there even now the screen was blank.

'Shall I book the same bedsits?' Alice enquired as she opened the door. 'Four rooms as before. Yes?'

'When do you want us to go, Mark?' Colin raised an eyebrow.

'Soon. It's got to be soon or I'll be off to uni.' The programme assistant suddenly remembered her mainstream activity.

'I'm afraid it can't be straight away.' Mark had pulled a slim, somewhat battered diary from his hip pocket. 'I've got commitments head to head. Damn. How infuriating.'

'What happens if I've started the course?' Alice was devastated. She screwed up her face. 'Doesn't matter, though. I can call this a project. I've heard everyone skips lectures all the time.'

'They do not.' Her father raised an eyebrow. 'You are going to miss nothing, young lady, not after all the effort you have put in to get there. We'll work something out.'

'And in the meantime, we need to mug up on a bit of history,' Mark put in comfortably. 'I want to know why this man Hopkins had such a personal grudge against witches. I know they say he was in it for the money and he got paid by the head for the witches he caught. But there must have been something else. Col, can you get me a still photo of that face? And see if it will enlarge? I'm afraid it's too shadowy, but you never know.'

'Do you think it's him? Hopkins?' Joe asked, as his daughter clipclopped downstairs in her break-neck footwear.

'God knows.' Mark shuddered. 'This is going to be a fantastic programme. But, you know, there's a part of me that wishes we'd never heard about the ghost shop of Manningtree.' He shrugged. 'I can't think why. It'll be great TV, but –'

'What happens if they won't let us back into the shop?' Colin took the tape out of the video machine and slipped it into its case.

'They've got to.' Mark shrugged again. 'My guess is they'll love the idea. Didn't he say it was going to be a discount shop, short lease? They don't want to buy the place. This will bring in the punters in droves. They've got nothing to lose.'

'The old boy selling it has.'

'Tough. And, damn it, he was the one to tell the story in the first place! If it wasn't for him, we'd never have heard about it. I'll put it to him tactfully. I bet he won't object if the tenants don't.'

'And what about that young woman who came in and warned us off?'

Mark nodded. 'She's one of the reasons we're going back. I want to find our Lyndsey and get her to explain her views on video tape. If I'm not very much mistaken that young lady is going to inject some drama into our story and make it even more exciting than we originally thought, and the voice over is not enough, even if we did have her permission which we don't!'

The other person he wanted to interview was the Reverend Mike Sinclair. To get the church's view on ghosts and witches and, maybe, disembodied faces on shadowed staircases.

24

Tuesday October 6th

She had been there again that morning, the stranger whose face Mike had been unable to get out of his head. She was standing at the water's edge, staring out across the river, her shoulder-length dark hair blowing across her cheeks, her expression contemplative; sad. Once again he had watched her surreptitiously as he took his customary walk along the Walls, glancing back as he stopped to survey the view. After a while she had turned and begun walking slowly towards Mistley, her hands in the pockets of her jacket, her shoulders hunched. He reached the place where, usually, he stopped and he began to retrace his steps, aware that this would bring him face to face with her. He studied her discreetly as they approached one another. She was still lost in thought, sometimes staring down at the pavement at her feet, sometimes looking out across the water. As they drew close together he felt his heart beat a little faster. Ridiculous. Just because she was beautiful. And enigmatic.

As they drew level he nodded to her. 'Good morning,' he said. He smiled.

He thought he saw, just for a second, startled recognition in her eyes and maybe the hint of a smile, then it was gone and he saw her frown.

'Good morning.' Her tone was low and mellow. Already she had passed him. She was walking on. He sighed. Not one of his congregation. Nor ever likely to be, knowing his luck.

The phone call from Mark Edmunds chased all thoughts of her out of his head. Putting down the receiver, he walked across to the window. The leaves on the chestnut by the gate were turning

130

gold now, crisped at the edges, and the conker cases, spiked and fresh green, were beginning to split, showing hints of their rich shiny contents.

He hadn't committed himself to anything beyond meeting Mark when he came up again, which, to Mark's intense frustration, would probably not be for a couple of weeks or so as he had so many commitments in London. If there was to be an interview he told Mark he would need permission from the bishop. He wasn't entirely sure if that were true, but as sure as eggs were eggs if he said anything controversial the bishop would hear about it. He might even see the programme himself and then there would be trouble. Nothing, well almost nothing, he conceded to himself wryly, was as controversial as meddling with the occult and all this talk of witches and ghosts was most definitely doing that. Well, now he had given himself time to think about Mark's request and, before he settled down to do that, the first thing he needed to do was to overcome his very real reluctance to go and see this so-called haunted shop. And – he glanced at his watch – there was no time like the present.

The woman behind the counter was large, florid and did not appear to be particularly benign. She was perched on a high stool and did not look up when he opened the door and walked in. She was engaged in the double delights of eating a large, multi-layered sandwich of which some of the contents were alarmingly brightly coloured and flicking through a back copy of *Hello!* magazine.

Mike studied her dubiously and decided she would probably not be fooled by pretence.

'Good afternoon.' He was wearing his dog collar, which in theory should give him access more or less anywhere. Of course it sometimes had the opposite effect. She looked up and gave him the benefit of a long stare from a pair of startlingly beautiful green eyes.

'Yes?' She spoke with her mouth full in a tone heavy with boredom.

Mike hastily revised what he was going to say in the light of his quick estimation of her IQ. Probably about twenty-five. That would teach him to let himself be influenced by a pair of gorgeous eyes.

'The owner of the shop . . .' May the Lord forgive him a small white lie – after all, permission had been given to Mark, and Mark had asked his opinion . . . 'Has given me permission to have a look upstairs. Would that be OK?'

She shrugged, obviously relieved she wouldn't have to do anything as onerous as take his money. 'Sure.'

He nodded gravely, and turned with some trepidation towards the stairs, leaving her staring after him, the bright eyes suddenly focused, revealing far more intelligence than the quotient with which he had originally allotted her.

Placing a foot on the bottom step, he paused and looked up, his hand firmly on the worn banister rail. It was cold upstairs. Even from here on the ground floor where it was pleasantly warm he could feel the light touch of a draught on his face. He was aware suddenly of the woman's eyes on him; her gaze felt hostile and more intense than was comfortable. It seemed suddenly imperative that he step back, take his hand from the rail, turn to face her. Leave. Instead, he closed his eyes and took a deep breath. As he began to climb he realised that he was praying.

There were fourteen polished oak steps in all, shallow risers, smoothly worn at the centre from four hundred years of climbing and descending feet and it was, he realised – echoing without knowing it the very words Will Fortingale had used in the so-far unsuccessful sale details – a staircase of quality. Not the kind of stair one would expect to find in a down-at-heel shop. The substantial house of which this property had once been a part had been built by a wealthy tradesman of some kind who had not stinted on materials or finish.

At the top Mike stopped. The room was empty save for a heap of half-opened cardboard boxes. Inside them he could see supplies of various kinds of stock for the shop below: end-of-line goods, cheap cooking utensils, children's toys, dusters, coat hangers, cleaning stuff. As he surveyed the room he suddenly realised that his hand was still firmly clasping the newel post at the top of the stairs.

The room was cold, but otherwise unremarkable. He stared round in relief. Relinquishing his hold on the post he stepped onto the floor and moved towards the window, skirting the boxes and avoiding a cascade of shampoo sachets which had fallen from their wrappings.

He shivered. He was right. It was very cold up here. Strangely cold. And the room, at first glance so innocuous, had an odd atmosphere. He paused in his tracks, trying to resist the urge to turn round and look over his shoulder. He was imagining it, of course, as anyone would who had been told a room was haunted.

Taking a deep breath, he walked forward to the window and looked down into the street. He couldn't see much. The road was too narrow and the window-frame too low. It had beautifully carved oak mullions and a broad sill, much stained and scarred, but nevertheless attractive. It was just wide enough and low enough to perch on and he lowered his tall frame into a sitting position. He looked around thoughtfully. His initial unease was abating. The room was just that, a room, old, dusty, untidy, scattered with boxes. He could feel no ghostly presence here. He listened carefully. There were no sounds from downstairs, where the bored shop assistant licked her fingers to help turn the page of her magazine, glanced up once, frowning, to listen for the vicar's footsteps, heard none and promptly forgot him.

Mike sighed. He wasn't sure what he was expecting to happen. A sound? A feeling? An apparition perhaps? Mark Edmunds had obviously seen something which had frightened him, but what? Was it one of the witches? Was it Hopkins himself? Or was it someone else altogether – a previous occupant of the house? Some restless spirit disturbed by the attentions of the television cameras. Or had it merely been their imagination in overdrive?

'I think it's you, Mr Hopkins.' Mike surprised himself by speaking out loud. 'So, where are you?'

He waited, half expecting an answer from the shadows. None came. 'Can you hear me?' He spoke softly, not wanting to draw attention to himself downstairs. 'If you can hear me, why don't you make yourself known?'

Nothing.

'I am a minister of the church. If there is unhappiness here, maybe I can help. I can pray with you.' He scanned the room carefully. Was it slightly colder than before? 'I am here to help bring you peace of mind, so that you can rest.'

He shivered suddenly. There was no doubt about it. The temperature in the room had plummeted and it seemed darker than it had only moments before. He glanced out of the window. The street outside was grey. Wind-tossed leaves cartwheeled down the pavement and he saw a young man, hunched against the cold, pull up his collar as he turned the corner out of sight.

The sound of footsteps beside him was loud, striding across the floor towards him authoritatively, and he spun back to face the room. There was no one to be seen.

'Who's there?' His voice sounded flat and strange in the room, deadened by the cold. He was beginning to feel very frightened.

Silence. But it was not an easy silence. He sensed someone listening; it was almost as though they were standing close beside him.

'Mr Hopkins?' Mike took a deep breath, trying to steady his nerve. 'Is that you?'

Nothing.

'Why don't you show yourself, so we can talk?'

What was that noise? It sounded like a faint laugh. He felt the sweat break out between his shoulder blades. 'Mr Hopkins?'

Whatever – whoever – it was, it was very close. He could almost feel the warm breath on his cheek. His skin crawled. He wanted to move away, but he was trapped there by the window unable to shift either to left or right, whilst in front of him something or someone seemed to be so close he could touch them. Without being able to stop himself he raised his hand and reached out, his fingers clawed.

There was nothing there.

'Mr Hopkins?'

Suddenly it was difficult to breathe.

He found himself gasping, struggling for air, and then he was choking frantically, clutching at his chest. For a moment he thought he was going to die.

Then it was over.

He couldn't move. Still shaking, he tried to compose himself, his eyes closed as the temperature in the room returned to normal. 'Our father, who art in heaven.' His voice came out as a croak.

Somehow he struggled to his feet. He was about to move towards the centre of the room when he caught sight of something moving in the shadows at the top of the staircase, and he was confronted by a pair of vivid green eyes. 'You all right?' The shop assistant was standing watching him. 'I heard you talking.'

Mike nodded, aware that he must be looking as terrible as he felt. He smiled shakily, embarrassed. 'I'm OK. Thank you.'

'Did you want something?' She pronounced it sun-fink.

'No, thank you. I choked on some dust.'

She raised an eyebrow. 'You ghost hunting, like them TV fellas?'

He shrugged. 'Something like that, yes.' He paused. 'Have you seen the ghost?'

She laughed. 'Not likely. I'm out of here before it gets dark.' And turning, she left him to it, clattering downstairs in her high-heeled sandals.

Mike remained where he was for a second. So, she assumed ghosts only came out at night. How wrong she was! With a sigh he followed her down. Whatever there had been up here in the deserted room, it had gone.

She was already back behind her counter as he walked across the shop floor. Halfway across, he stopped suddenly. From upstairs he heard the sound of footsteps echoing clearly on the ceiling above their heads. He glanced at the assistant and saw that the sandwich had been replaced by a KitKat, which she was unwrapping as she watched him. She appeared to have heard nothing. Somehow he managed to move on, to wish her a polite good afternoon, and to head for the door. Closing it behind him with some relief, he stepped out into the street. He did not look back and so did not notice her standing in the doorway, watching him, her eyes fixed unblinkingly on his retreating back. The torn red wrapper of the chocolate bar was still in her hand.

At the corner of South Street he stopped, suddenly over-whelmed by a wave of dizziness and nausea. He was shaking violently, his face burning and he could feel the sweat running down between his shoulder blades as though he had a high temperature, and yet two minutes before he had felt cold. He breathed steadily through his nose, trying to calm the thump of his heart under his ribs. A car stopped next to him to allow a van to drive towards it down the narrow street; the van drew level with him and passed and the car pulled away. He put out his hand to steady himself against the window of the shop on the corner. He was feeling desperately ill. Again he could hardly breathe.

Raising his head almost blindly, he saw two girls walk past, giggling. They were dressed in tiny short skirts that revealed impossibly long legs, lengthened by the thick clumpy soles of their shoes and short-cropped tops, leaving strips of bare skin and tummy buttons exposed although it was cold and windy out here in the street. He saw them glance at him as he propped himself up against the wall of the shop and whisper to each other, then they hurried on, giggling louder than before.

Wantons! Whores!

The words popped into his head from nowhere.

He was appalled. Where had the words come from? He was a tolerant man. He prided himself on his kindness. Still leaning against the wall, he turned to watch the girls as they hurried down the street away from him, dodging the other pedestrians, parting to allow a frail, elderly man to walk between them, regrouping again after he had passed. Normally he would not have given them a second glance. They were not whores. They were schoolgirls!

He closed his eyes for a moment. His momentary fever had passed as quickly as it had come. He straightened up, trying to gather his wits. What on earth was happening to him?

Walking slowly on, he was suddenly overwhelmed with fear. The illness had not been his and neither had the voice inside his head.

Both had belonged to someone else.

25

Every dip and fold in the fields was white with mist; lapping round the trees, curling softly into the ditches, it brought with it a cold silence which was heavy with menace.

Glancing across the road as he drove towards the coast the driver saw the white pall lying across the newly turned stubble and stared. For a moment it looked as though the sea itself had breached the coastline and poured in across the land. In his shock he kept his eyes off the road a moment too long. The blaring hooter of the oncoming delivery van screamed into his consciousness and he tore at the wheel, trying to regain the road. His tyres squealed and ripped up the bank as the vehicle went into a spin. It lost its grip on the tarmac, ploughed through the hedge and into the field, where it finally came to a halt against the lone stag-headed oak which stood on the edge of the mist, the white moisture condensing on the crushed, steaming bonnet and running down the broken windscreen.

There was no sign of the car from the road. The Ford van which had hooted had sped on out of sight towards its destination on the Lawford industrial estate, the driver not even glancing back.

In the field the man sat without moving, his eyes open, staring out of the windscreen at the tree trunk three feet from his face. Wraiths of mist threaded the tree's branches and circled ever thicker around the car. In the silence, what was left of the engine ticked once or twice as it cooled. Behind him a bag of shopping had fallen onto the floor, tossing a box of eggs onto the carpet. A film of egg-white spread slowly in a thin glutinous circle under the seat and began to soak in.

As the man's body slowly cooled, the sky darkened and the fog began to turn black.

At home in his cottage, Bill Standing had watched the mist drift in off the sea and he had felt its menace. It would be content with no less than a man's life today, and nothing and no one was going to be able to appease it until it had fed off a human soul.

26

By late afternoon the heavy mist had turned to rain. It hung across the churchyard as Lyndsey stood beneath the trees watching and listening to the gentle patter of the raindrops on the leaves above her head. Behind her, in the lane, she heard the sound of a car engine, the swish of tyres on the wet road. She ignored it. Huddling into her jacket she tried to concentrate harder, willing herself into the inner silence where she could hear the voices. The car had slowed up and stopped just behind her. With an exclamation of annoyance she turned and peered out through the leaves. The MG had pulled in at Liza's. It was Emma Dickson. Lyndsey's eyes narrowed with resentment as she watched Emma greet Colonel Lawson, who was walking his dogs back up the lane towards his house. Stepping back further into the shelter of the trees, she watched silently as Emma went round and, opening the car boot, pulled out various carrier bags, locked the car, and juggling her purchases fished in her pocket for the front door key. She pushed open the door and Lyndsey saw the two dark brown – almost black – cats jumping round her, standing on their back legs, wanting to see what was in the bags, rubbing against her as she went inside.

She scowled. Why was Emma Dickson still here? Why was the spell not working?

As Emma closed the door, Lyndsey saw her hesitate and glance uneasily across the lane as if she could sense that there was someone watching her. The whole episode had taken no more than three minutes. As a light went on in the downstairs window of the house, Lyndsey turned her back with an angry groan.

'What are you up to this time?'

The voice beside her made her jump out of her skin.

'Alex! Where did you come from?' He was standing on the far side of the wall, watching her. 'And for that matter, what are you doing here? Where's your car?' She rammed her hands deeper into the pockets of her jacket. Rain was running down her hair, plastering it across her forehead. Her blue eyes were furious.

He shrugged amiably. 'I misjudged the weather. I thought I'd take a stroll down here and be back home before it rained. I've been cooped up all day and my head needed clearing.'

'So you thought you'd come and see how Miss Dickson was getting on?'

'No. I had no intention of seeing how anyone was getting on. I only came up here because I'm getting soaked to the skin and it's a shortcut. Besides, the kids will be back from school by now. Bet was collecting them today. I'll have to go and get them from her place.' He paused, eyeing Lyndsey as she moved out of the shelter of the trees and scrambled over the wall, her long legs making easy work of the slippery old red bricks and the tangled brambles as she landed beside him.

'I wouldn't bother with Emma Dickson. She won't stay long.'

He raised an eyebrow. 'What do you mean?' He wished he didn't find this young woman quite so unsettlingly attractive. Those eyes, the urchin-cut hair, the slim figure . . . He moved a pace away from her.

She noticed and smiled to herself. She knew Alex had a soft spot for a pretty face and she knew Paula was well aware of her husband's proclivities. 'I mean she is not going to like it here. She's a townie. She doesn't fit.'

'We're townies, Paula and me.' He shivered. His Barbour jacket was letting in the damp.

'Your wife is.' Lyndsey grinned. 'You've had a good go at going native.'

'But, I know, it will take another twenty years.' He gave a rueful laugh. 'My point is, I have grown to love it here.' She noticed he didn't claim that Paula had. 'Why shouldn't Miss Dickson do so as well?'

'Because she won't.' Lyndsey's eyes narrowed and Alex felt suddenly uneasy. How was it that this girl managed to attract and scare him at the same time?

'Well, I hope you're not going to do anything to upset her,' he said. He sounded pompous and old, even to himself.

'Why should I do that?' She was standing in front of him, her eyes fixed on his.

Because you're a little minx, that's why. He didn't say it, of course. He merely smiled. 'Just make sure you don't.' It was ridiculous that he should be afraid of her. 'I have a feeling you've got something against poor Miss Dickson. She's done nothing to you, after all.'

'Hasn't she?' Lyndsey raised an eyebrow.

'Well, has she?'

'She's bought Liza's.' Her eyes were deliberately challenging.

'Yes, Lyn, someone had to. And you couldn't afford it!' He managed to hang on to the patronising tone. 'Now, I suggest you go home before you catch pneumonia.'

Just for a second he saw the anger which flashed across the blue eyes and he felt another frisson of fear. Stupid. It was gone as soon as he registered it.

'OK, boss.' She gave him that enchanting smile she saved for moments when Paula wasn't around, and turned away to pick her bicycle up out of the hedge.

He watched her ride off. She was trouble, that one. Frighteningly attractive, wild, and potentially dangerous.

27

Emma had seen the end of the exchange when she opened the front door. She had left a packet of screws on the front passenger seat and was ducking out to fetch them. It was too late to turn back. The young woman was peddling off down the lane, but the man was still standing there only a few yards from her gate.

He gave her a friendly smile and walking towards her he held out his hand. 'You must be Emma Dickson? I'm Alex West. I live a couple of miles from here towards Bradfield. How are you settling in?'

She liked the look of him. Solid, calm, thinning red-gold hair, pale-blue eyes and an engaging smile. He radiated slightly diffident charm. And he looked the kind of man you could like – and trust – on sight.

'I'm settling in well.' She smiled at him. She hesitated. 'Look, I know it's a nerve to ask, but as fate has delivered you to my doorstep, I couldn't possibly ask you a huge favour and impose on you for a couple of minutes, could I?' She laughed, embarrassed. 'I pride myself in being totally capable in every way but I desperately need another pair of hands – well, one other hand, actually.'

He smiled. 'I am at your disposal. Two hands.' He held them out. 'What's the problem?'

'I'm trying to fix some hinges in the kitchen. Every time I go to put them on, I need another hand to hold the door. Are you sure you don't mind?'

'Lead on.'

He followed her through the front door, glancing into the room on the right as he did so. She had dumped her parcels from the car in the middle of the floor in there.

'It's in here.' She led the way down the passage. 'I'm redoing the kitchen completely but there's a lovely old dresser in here I want to keep. The doors are falling off and each time I come home I find my cats have levered them open. Look!' They stood surveying the doors in question. Both hung open, dramatically held on by huge old rusty hinges.

Alex bent to scratch Min under her left ear. 'What a lovely cat.'

Min closed her eyes in ecstasy.

'She likes you.' Emma was reassured. She was probably mad to ask a stranger into the house, but Min's instincts were obviously the same as her own. This was a nice man and suddenly she was quite anxious for some solid human company.

'Screwdriver?' Alex had picked up the new hinges and was inspecting them.

'Here.' She indicated three. He selected one and squatted down in front of the dresser door. 'First we must take off the old ones.' It took him only seconds to remove the first screw.

'Who was that woman you were talking to?' Emma took the first bent rusty hinge from him and tossed it into the rubbish bin.

'Lyndsey Clark. She lives down in Mistley. In a cottage on the quay.' Alex rocked back on his heels and looked up at her.

'She comes up here a lot. I've seen her watching me. I've tried to say hello but she pretends she doesn't hear.'

He frowned, trying to force the screwdriver into a burred rusted screw which had twisted to almost nothing. 'You'll get to know her soon enough. I'll introduce you. There, that's got that one out!' He handed her the second hinge.

'How many kids have you got?' She turned away and started to fill the kettle.

'Two. Sophie and James. Six and eight. They go to school in Colchester. My wife commutes up to town each day. She's a commodity broker. As she earns shiploads more than I did, when redundancy reared its ugly head I volunteered to stay at home and be a househusband. Hence having the time to walk around in the rain offering my services to damsels in distress.' He smiled. He was, she noticed, fitting the door very competently without the need for third or fourth hands to hold it in place.

'Don't you get bored?'

He shrugged. 'If I'm honest, yes.'

'I worked in the City. Everyone thought I was mad giving it up and coming down here.'

He tightened the last screw and opened and shut the doors experimentally. Both worked efficiently. Standing up, he put the

143

screwdriver down on the table. 'Everyone round here thought you would be a weekender.' He glanced across at her. 'Anything else need doing while I'm here?'

She laughed. 'Don't tempt me. One of the challenges I'm facing is to be a bit more self-sufficient. I'm looking for someone to do the big jobs, but I've got to learn to do some for myself. If you know a good builder, I could do with his number.'

'I'll have a word with a chap I know. Get him to call round.' Alex paused. 'But I'm always happy to drop in and do any small jobs for you. And, I tell you what. Why don't you come over for a meal? Meet Paula and the kids. We're almost neighbours, so we can impart some of the local gossip to you.'

Her face brightened. 'I'd love that. Would you like some coffee by way of saying thanks for the hinges?' She gestured towards the kettle.

He shook his head. 'No thanks. I do have to get back to the kids.' He headed towards the door. Then he paused. 'You're not thinking of starting up the herb nursery again, are you?'

'I might be.' She followed him down the hall.

'If you do, keep me in mind.' He shrugged. 'I've quite a bit of business experience and willing hands and – as you see – time.'

She watched as he strode out of sight up the lane. A nice man. Friendly. Lonely. At a loose end.

'And he likes cats, Min.' She bent to pick up the animal circling her legs. 'We must be careful, mustn't we.'

The cat nestled in her arms and rubbed its head against her chin.

28

Mike put down the phone. He realised his hand was shaking and, picking up his pen, he stared intently at the heaps of paper on his desk.

'I'll be over in ten minutes,' Judith had said when he had finally decided to ring her. He glanced at his watch, and then at the Bible almost submerged beneath all his correspondence. The screen-saver on the monitor in front of him was swirling silently around, endlessly spinning patterns in front of his eyes. The phone rang. He stared at it for a moment, then leaning forward he turned on the answer machine.

'Lead us not into temptation; but deliver us from evil . . .' he whispered.

The voice in his head in the street outside Barker's shop had not been his. Please God it had not been that of Matthew Hopkins.

Hearing Judith's old Vauxhall on the drive at the front of the house he was at the door to meet her as she climbed out.

'Mike?' She followed him into his study. 'What is it? What's happened?'

'I think I've done something rather stupid.' He sat down at his desk. Putting his head in his hands, he ran his fingers agitatedly through his hair.

She hesitated, then took the chair opposite him.

'I went to the Barker shop this afternoon You know, the shop this TV chap thinks is haunted? He was on the phone to me this morning. Apparently they've only just looked at it properly and he thinks they've caught the ghost on film.' He paused.

'Oh, Mike!' She glanced heavenward, clearly exasperated. 'I did warn you not to get sucked in.'

'I know you did.' He frowned. 'But I wanted to see for myself. So often one hears this kind of story. Rumours start to fly. They feed on themselves. I thought if I could say I had been there, checked it out and found there was nothing, I could help allay the stories before it was too late.'

'And what happened?' She was frowning. 'Don't tell me you saw something.'

'No, I didn't see anything.'

'What then?'

'I felt something. An atmosphere. Cold. That could have been imagination, of course. But then I heard footsteps.' He paused. 'And a voice. Well, not a voice. It was in my head. In the street afterwards. I saw these two girls and . . .' He paused, not quite knowing how to go on. 'I felt judgemental in a way that was completely alien to me. It was as though someone else's views were being broadcast into my brain. And someone else's illness took over my body. Just for a few minutes.' He shuddered. Looking up at her he shook his head. 'I don't quite know how to explain it, but it scared me, Judith, it really did.'

'You've prayed about it, of course.'

He nodded.

'You're probably right and it's your imagination. This kind of story helps to bring in the tourists. Manningtree loves its witches and its witchfinder. It's probably total rubbish and you've done just what they hoped. Picked up on the hysteria. The Witchfinder is part of history. He's not real. Not any more.'

'I thought you said there were still witches here?' He was studying her face.

'Oh, there are, but they are nothing to do with Hopkins.' She leaned forward and put her elbows on his desk. 'Or ghosts. There are two kinds of witch around here. Both evil. Both an affront to Christianity, but nothing to do with the past. Everything to do with modern films and TV.' She shivered. 'Satanists, Mike. Devil worshippers. People who practise child abuse.' She shook her head. 'Vile, vile people. Then you have people who practise what they call Wicca. That's a kind of nature worship. They meet in covens. Evil. Anti-Christian. What they do is horrible. Perverse. Ugly. You'll probably have to deal with all of them in your ministry here, just as you would anywhere. I don't think it's because this is Manningtree, or Essex particularly. Not any more. Don't get sucked in. You didn't really think it was the Witchfinder talking to you, did you?' She gave a short worried laugh. 'Mike, you didn't!'

'No. No, of course I didn't.' He paused. 'Not really. Judith . . .'
He stood up and began pacing up and down the floor, uncomfortable with the vehemence of her outburst. 'Who is the local person to contact about occult phenomena? Is there a deliverance team in place in this diocese who's used to dealing with ghosts and things?'

'Oh, Mike! I don't think you should go down that road.' Her lips narrowed. 'Really. I know there are clergy who get involved with all that; but so many of them are seduced by the glamour and the drama and most of it is just superstitious nonsense. They tend to be high church. Smells and bells. Oh, no way. That would not go down well here, I assure you. The PCC would be appalled. It detracts from the real job. From the Mission.' Her eyes flashed bright with zeal as she pushed back her chair and stood up with him. 'Prayer is all you need, Mike. Why don't we pray now, together?'

Mike turned away. He resumed his favourite position by the window, astonished by the wave of distaste which swept over him; distaste for this woman who believed in nothing and knew everything . . . He took a deep breath. 'Thank you, Judith. That is an excellent idea.'

It was as they finished that she glanced at him thoughtfully. 'Mike, there is someone in the deliverance team you might speak to about all this. John Downing. He's a good man. Very genuine. Sensible. Let me have a word with him. He's an old friend.' She smiled, nodding. 'I'll get him to ring you.'

She was as good as her word. That evening, John Downing phoned.

'Obviously Judith has filled me in as far as she can,' he said after he had introduced himself. 'But I would like to hear the whole story from you.'

He listened without interruption and when Mike had finished there was a moment or two of silence.

'You realise that most of these cases turn out to be anything but genuine hauntings,' he said at last. 'Some of them are hoaxes, of course, but more often they are imagination. Shadows. Spooky houses. The heightened awareness of primed expectation. Even hallucination. Forgive me for asking, but are you on any medication at the moment?'

This was not what Mike had expected and for a moment he

147

saw red. 'Are you implying that I am under the influence of drugs? Perhaps you think I'm a drunk?'

'No, no, Mike.' John Downing's voice was professionally reassuring. 'I have to check these things. It's part of my brief. Just as I have to bring in a psychiatrist to interview you. He is part of the team.'

'A psychiatrist!' Mike's fist almost crushed the phone. 'Now you seem to be implying that I'm mad! What on earth has Judith said to you? I expected support, John, as from one professional to another. I expected you to come and look at this place. To pray with me, not to talk about psychiatrists!'

'And we will come if we feel it is necessary.' John Downing's tone had inadvertently slipped from calming to patronising. 'We are used to handling this kind of case, I assure you. We'll look into it, Mike, and get back to you, OK? And in the mean time I'll pop a few prayers for you in the post. And Mike, don't go back there yourself, OK? Leave it to us.'

Mike slammed down the phone and took a deep breath. If this was Judith's idea of helping, he could do without it. Whatever she had said seemed to have led Downing to assume Mike was an incompetent hysteric!

Angrily he paced up and down his study a few times.

So that was it. He was supposed to leave it to them. Forget it and submit to a psychiatrist's report which would no doubt claim he had imagined the whole thing, or lock him up for being insane!

He threw himself into his chair, tapping his pen against his teeth and it was then the name came to him out of nowhere. Tony Gilchrist.

Mike had met the Gilchrists several years before at a conference before he had taken holy orders himself; he had liked them both enormously and Tony's interest in the deliverance ministry had intrigued him. The man had seemed so genuine, so sane and so humane in his approach to the subject. They had kept in touch sporadically and Ruth had sent him a card with their address when Mike's appointment to his first parish had been announced.

Mike was trying to recall what had happened to bring them to Suffolk. Tony had been involved in a high-profile exorcism up in Lancashire, the kind the church disliked intensely. It had attracted all kinds of media attention, and in the end the bishop had brought pressure to bear. Tony had retired and he and Ruth had moved six months later and disappeared from the news. Mike reached for his address book. Then he picked up the phone.

Tony was in. He too listened without comment to Mike's story. At the end there was a long pause. When he spoke it was one word: 'Fascinating.'

Mike gave a sigh of relief. 'Am I right to be worried?'

'Oh, yes. Don't let anyone kid you these things don't exist, Mike, or that it's your imagination or the pills you took last night for a headache. Go with your instinct. If you're worried, then there is probably something to worry about. Look,' Tony paused at the other end of the line and Mike heard the rustle of pages turning. Obviously a diary. 'Ruth and I are going away for a few days. New grandchild to view and baptise. I won't be away long. When we get back I'll come over. How's that? Just as a friend. For your own sake don't tell your deliverance chappie or let your bishop hear about it – he'll probably have me expurgated before I get near you.' He chuckled. 'Mike, St Patrick's Breastplate. You know the words, of course?'

Mike frowned. '"Christ be with me, Christ within me"?'

'That's the one. Good stuff. It's recommended by the Christian deliverance study group. Make sure you can recite the whole thing – upside down, back to front, in your sleep. Any time. Any place. If you feel threatened, attacked, frightened, even mildly uneasy, surround yourself with those words. Hold the breastplate before your heart, OK? And Downing is right about one thing, keep away from that shop! It sounds as though it is a focal point. And if you can dissuade your TV friend from continuing with his programme, do so. You won't be able to, of course, but try. And don't be interviewed on camera, Mike. Believe me, it leads to all kinds of trouble. I'll come over as soon as I get back and we'll see what can be done. Chances are it will all fizzle out.'

Letting himself into the church later, Mike walked up the aisle. Outside it was growing dark. The building was deep in shadow and he flipped one of the light switches on the bank near the vestry door. The spotlight shone onto the altar, illuminating the cross. It was the wooden cross they left out during the week, the cross they hoped would not be stolen; during services it was replaced by one of engraved brass which looked like gold. The light cast its shadow on the wall and Mike found himself staring at it thoughtfully. He was profoundly relieved to have spoken to

Tony, but there was still something there at the back of his mind which was worrying him. Something hidden in the shadows, lurking deep inside his own brain. With a sigh he knelt down on the step and fixed his eyes on the cross.

'"Christ be with me. Christ within me . . ."'

Above his head, outside in the dark, the rain began to lash against the windows.

29

Tuesday October 13th

FULL MOON

Lyndsey leaned her bike into its usual place in the brambles and switched off the lamp. Staring round she held her breath, listening. It had stopped raining hours before, but the trees were still dripping – she could hear the sound all around her. It emphasised the silence. A cold, clammy mist was lurking in the hollows of the land and clinging to the water.

Across the lane Liza's cottage was in darkness. The houses further up the road were invisible behind the black curtain of trees. Above them, high in the sky, clouds shrouded what witches call the Blood Moon.

Fumbling with the wet metal clip, she managed to remove the bicycle lamp and cautiously she switched it back on. She hadn't expected the night to be so dark. Scrambling over the wall, she crept across the grass, following the narrow beam of light. Everything looked different by torchlight. The contours of the churchyard were more uneven, the trees more angular, the bushes thicker, disembodied in mist. For a minute she lost her bearings completely and she felt a wave of panic sweep over her. She stopped forcing herself to breathe more slowly. She had to be calm. Centred. And strong.

Everything looked strange. The rectangle of greener grass she had convinced herself might be Hopkins's grave was indistinguishable from the rest of the grass around it. She took a step forward, shining the lamp around wildly, unable suddenly to find the right place. She had been here so many times, cast the circle, murmured

151

the binding spell, woven the trap to hold him down, to chain that vengeful sadistic spirit to the earth. It was here. Surely.

Hopkins was one of the reasons she had stayed in Mistley and not given in to her first intention of selling the cottage she had been left. Her careful, painstaking research into witchcraft as the old religion of the mother goddess would have brought him to her notice even if he had not been so infamous locally. But even more than that, this battle was personal, for he had persecuted her own ancestors. She shivered. And his spirit was still prowling the back lanes and fields in the mist. The mist which she feared so much. The mist which carried the scent of blood and the echoes of past evil.

Her toe touched a lump beneath the grass. It was part of the foundations of the demolished church. It was here she sometimes sat, going over the words she was about to recite, murmuring them under her breath, feeling their resonance. Special words; words of power.

There was something about this site that terrified her. It wasn't just that Hopkins might be buried here. It was more than that. It was as though this place was one of those where the evil on which he fed had its origin. There were several places in the neighbourhood like this; she didn't know why, or where that original evil came from, but while the church was here the source of that evil was plugged. She had to admit it, the church had acted as an antidote. The evil was held down, sealed into the earth. The day the last piece of the church was pulled down that seal was broken. She swung her battered leather backsack off her shoulders and set it down in the wet grass. Inside were all the tools she needed: candles, salt, oil, water, in small bottles, a little bowl which stood as her cauldron, the athame, the robe she wore for special ceremonies, the wand she had cut and carved herself from the branch of a hazel tree.

Putting the lamp down, she turned it off. The moon behind the thinning cloud was a dull amber, a colour echoed in the heavens above the estuary where the ports of Harwich and Felixstowe reflected useless wasteful light all night endlessly up into the sky.

Slowly she walked around the spot, laying out her candles and the rest of her tools, preparing the ground. Then when all was ready, she cast the circle. Round she went, again and again, pointing wand and black-handled knife-tip, seeing the light streaming from them, building the wall to keep the spirit of a man locked deep in the ground.

The flames of the night-lights in their little jars flickered in the wind. One blew out and she paused, frowning. She had been conscious only of the sound of her own voice calling out the words of her spell, but now suddenly she was aware of the profound silence around her, broken only by the patter of the rain on the brown and golden leaves of the trees. She shivered and bent to the candle, fumbling with matches from her pocket. Her resolution was wavering. The wall of power was dissolving. She couldn't hold it.

'Help me!' She stood up, her arms outstretched into the darkness. 'Guardian spirits of the four corners, be here. Be strong. Help me hold the circle! Great goddess of the witches help your daughter keep this evil and this man imprisoned!'

She paused, her hands outstretched, her eyes fixed on the sky. The wind which had brought the sharp cold shower had whipped the cloud away from the face of the moon, so that the countryside was lit under its strange copper light.

'Don't let him out to haunt our houses and our roads! Don't let him out to visit our women and bring terror to their lives again. Hold him firm. Bind him here to the earth!' Her voice rang out over the sound of the rain. She stared down at the patch of grass contained in her circle. It was dark, barely lit by the tiny flickering night-lights. There was no sense of power there, no wall to hold him in and within the circle nothing but emptiness.

Her arms dropped to her sides in defeat. He wasn't there. It had all been in vain. He had gone. Escaped. The spirit of the Witchfinder once more prowled the Earth. She had not been able to contain him. He was free.

A gust of wind whipped through the hawthorn trees near her and her candles blew out. She was left in sudden total darkness as the moon once more drew back behind a shroud of thick black cloud.

'No!'

She turned round slowly.

'No! You bastard! You can't have me! You can't have anyone! Not any more!' Her voice had risen to a shriek.

She faced the wind, feeling the cold bite her face. It contained the smell of salt marsh and sea. The branches of the trees were beginning to thrash back and forth, leaves torn away, flying in her face.

She didn't see the figure behind her in the darkness until it was nearly at her side.

30

Earlier the same night

Emma was profoundly asleep. Under her eyelids her eyes moved back and forth, staring into the past. In her dream she was Sarah Paxman again. She was standing outside the Thorn Inn in the centre of Mistley and she was surrounded by crowds. Nearby, at the quayside, a spritsail barge was loading a cargo of sacks of grain and wool. Sailors swarmed up from a flyboat which had just come alongside on the top of the tide. Wheels rattled over the cobbles and the stench of ale from the open door of the inn was overwhelming. She pulled her cloak around her more tightly and beckoned one of the men who had stumbled out of the taproom.

'Master Hopkins, is he here?'

The man stared at her bleary-eyed. 'I reckon.'

'Where?'

'Upstairs.' He jerked his thumb behind him. 'You don't want to go in there, mistress.'

'Oh, indeed I do.' Sarah raised an imperious eyebrow. She

turned and beckoned her maid. 'Follow me, Agnes, and don't say anything.'

Leaving John Pepper with the groom holding their horses, the two women entered the doorway and found the narrow staircase. It led up to a dark corridor. All the doors were closed.

'Master Hopkins?' she called. She managed to keep her voice firm. 'A word, if you please!'

The first door when she flung it open led to a large communal bedroom. It was ill lit and the air was fetid. In the corner the single occupant lay flat on his back on the straw mattress, snoring loudly.

She shuddered and moved on to the next door. This room was a private bedroom, available at a price, for the more discerning customer. It was musty and empty.

'Mistress?' Agnes touched her sleeve. 'See. There.' The girl's voice shook with nerves. She pointed towards one of the doors. A slim line of light showed underneath, clearly visible in the dark passage.

Sarah took a deep breath. She stepped towards it and flung the door open. 'Master Hopkins? I would like a word with you, if you please.'

He was sitting at a wooden table with a goose feather quill in his hand, a young man in his early twenties. His narrow face, already marked by lines down either side of his mouth, was pale of complexion in contrast to the dark beard and hair. His eyes were very bright, his expression watchful. Opposite him sat a plump, fresh-faced, middle-aged woman dressed in black. Sarah bowed to her, unsmiling. 'Mistress Phillips.'

The woman stared back at her, her eyes cold and unblinking. 'Mistress Paxman.'

'You have arrested Liza Clark, Master Hopkins.' Sarah walked to the table and rested her hands on it, leaning towards the young man who had not risen to his feet when she walked in. The candles in the candelabra at his left hand flickered in the draught from the door.

'Indeed we have taken her up.' His voice was quiet; thoughtful. 'What is your interest in the matter?' His quill hovered over the notebook in which he had been writing, as though he were going to take down her words.

The gesture did not frighten her. Her eyes blazed. 'My interest,

Master Hopkins, is that she was my nurse as I am sure you know and she is still my friend. She has no dealings with the Devil, if that is what you claim, and you, mistress,' she turned to Mary Phillips, 'know that full well as you have worked together in delivering children all over this very parish!'

'I should be careful of defending her too passionately, Mistress Paxman.' Hopkins was indeed writing down her name. He dipped the nib in the ink pot and underlined the words twice. 'We might be forced to suspect you of sharing her practices.' He narrowed his eyes, his drawn, pale face perspiring slightly. 'I suggest you go home.'

Sarah met his eyes steadily. 'Not until I have your word that you will release her.'

'Impossible.' His mouth snapped shut on the word like a trap.

'She must have taught you a great deal, Mistress Paxman,' Mary Phillips put in quietly. 'How long did she look after you when you were a child?'

Sarah's mouth went dry. She had not taken her eyes from Hopkins's face. 'She taught me the value of love and loyalty and kindness,' she said slowly.

'But not, I would guess, any good Christian teaching.' He scanned her face for a few more seconds, then he looked down at the notebook in front of him and wrote something next to her name. The very simplicity of the gesture was loaded with threat. 'I do not believe we have seen you in church here, Mistress Paxman.'

Sarah could feel the heat in her face. 'I do not live here any longer, as you well know. My home is in Colchester.'

'But while you visit your father I would expect you to attend service with him.'

'I do not have to explain myself to you, sir,' Sarah retorted hotly. 'If you watch people closely then you will be aware that I have been here only since Monday at noon. And I am here to talk about Liza, not about me. Where is she?'

'She is being held in Manningtree. For questioning.' He paused. 'Then she will be taken before the magistrates.'

'I want to see her.'

'Out of the question.' He looked up. 'Mary will search her for witches marks this afternoon. I do not doubt she will find them. If you do not want to find yourself put to the same test, I suggest

157

you leave Mistley Thorn and go back to Colchester this very day. Do not meddle, mistress. I have a job to do, given me by Parliament. I do not brook any interference.' He put down his pen and at last he stood up. He was not a tall man, shorter than she was by a hand's breadth, but she could feel the strength of his gaze.

She looked from him to Mary Phillips, who had folded her arms, and then back. 'I shall obtain legal representation for her, Master Hopkins.'

'That would be a waste of money, mistress, and a foolish, sentimental act. My powers are total in this matter. I cannot be over-ruled. If the woman is innocent then God will exonerate her. If we find the marks this afternoon and Mary uses her pin to good effect, we shall swim her to make sure. Good morning, mistress.' He bowed.

'You can't. You can't swim her –'

He was walking past her, the notebook under his arm. Pausing, he gave her a final cold look. 'After swimming her, if the Lord finds her guilty we will ask her for a confession which will complete the matter. I feel sure she will confess. In the end.' He gave a thin smile, bowed, and without giving her another glance walked out of the door and down the corridor.

'If I suggest it, Master Hopkins will have you taken up, Mistress Sarah.' Mary Phillips hadn't moved. 'I'll wager a pretty sum I would find witch marks on your person. You went to Liza for a spell to give you a babe, didn't you? Don't think I had forgotten. You asked me as a midwife why your womb didn't quicken from that fancy husband of yours. I couldn't help, so you went to her.'

'You wouldn't help, Mary.' Sarah glared at her, her eyes hard. 'You refused. You wouldn't even examine me.'

'Because England does not need more spoiled royalist brats!' Mary spat the words at her.

'Is that why you asked a fee so exorbitant I could not pay without asking my husband?'

Mary shrugged. 'Whatever. The fact remains that you went to Liza and she gave you a spell.'

'She did not.'

'She gave you a spell and a potion containing the Devil's seed.'

'That is a lie!'

'It's easily proven. If you took the potion you too are a witch, confirmed, enslaved, a harlot of the Devil! Well, Mistress Hoity

158

Toity, we shall see. Witch marks don't bleed from my pin.' She put her hand into the pocket of her gown and produced a long pin set in a handle. 'Shall we try it, Mistress Sarah? Master Hopkins heard of this special test that they use in Scotland. It finds the place the Devil sucks his servants.'

'Don't you touch me!' Sarah whirled away from her, keeping well out of reach. 'You are an evil, cruel woman.'

'I just do my job as Master Hopkins bids me.' Mary held out the pricker at arm's length. 'We'll get to you, my dear, don't you worry. Liza will confess everything and I shall ask her about you especially.'

'She will tell you nothing!' Sarah paused in the doorway.

'Oh, but she will.' Mary gave her a slow, cold smile. 'Believe me, she will. They always do.'

'There is nothing to tell.' Sarah could feel the fear spreading through her body like ice-water.

'So you say. Liza will tell it different. By the time we're finished asking her questions, she will incriminate everyone she has ever known, sweetheart. And you shall be chief amongst them.' Mary thrust the pricker back into her apron pocket. 'I shall enjoy questioning you; finding out where you hide the Devil's tit. In your privy parts, I'll be bound. It's always the best place to look.'

Sarah gasped. Her face was white and for a moment she thought she would faint. Mary took a step forward and Sarah turned. She fled down the stairs, through the taproom and outside to the sound of jeering, beer-soaked voices behind her.

'Mistress Sarah, are you all right?'

Sarah realised suddenly that Agnes had not followed her into Hopkins's room. As she went in, Agnes had fled. The girl had been waiting outside the inn, giggling with a couple of maids from the kitchen.

'Where is Master Hopkins?' Sarah took a deep breath, trying to steady herself.

'He rode off, mistress. Along the river.'

Sarah closed her eyes. She was shaking, she realised, as relief that he had gone swept over her. Shaking and cold with fear.

'We'll ride home, Agnes. Back to Papa's. Call John with the horses.'

'Is it going to be all right, mistress?' Agnes was staring at her. The girl's face was red with excitement, her eyes sparkling. The reason, Sarah realised suddenly, was not unconnected with the two pot boys lounging at the inn door.

'No, Agnes,' she said bitterly. 'It is not going to be all right. I don't know what we are going to do.'

'I don't know what we're going to do!' Emma repeated the words as she opened her eyes and stared round the dark bedroom. 'Oh, God, I don't know what we're going to do!'

She lay still, her heart pounding. She must have been having a nightmare, but whatever it was it had slipped away as she woke, leaving terrible fear behind it. She put out her arm towards Piers, seeking reassurance, and then pulled it back. How stupid to expect to find him there after all this time.

She sat up, shivering. The window was open a crack and she could hear the rain pattering down on the leaves of the honeysuckle on the wall outside her window. The bedroom was cold. There was no sign of the cats. With a groan she pushed her feet out of bed and went to pull on a heavy sweater. Then she went to the window. She pushed back the billowing curtain and was reaching to shut it when she saw a flash of light out in the darkness beyond the garden.

She frowned, staring out. There it was again. Not in the garden, but across the lane in the old churchyard. Someone was moving around in there, carrying a torch. She leaned forward and pushed the sash down a little further to see more clearly. The night air was cold on her face and she could feel the odd drop of rain.

Someone was shouting. She could hear a woman's voice coming from the churchyard. It was anguished, almost screaming. She leaned out even further, straining her eyes in the murky darkness, suddenly afraid. Was someone being attacked out there? Should she call the police?

She shivered violently. The torch light was waving wildly about, and near it she could see a circle of what looked like small flickering candles.

Suddenly making up her mind, she ran down the stairs and pulled on her boots. Taking down her raincoat from a hook in the hall she pulled it on over her pyjamas and sweater and reached for the big torch she kept by the hall phone.

It was cold and damp outside and the mizzle of rain soon found its way down inside her collar as she walked cautiously down the path and let herself out of the gate. Her boots were silent on the wet leaves as she crept through the hedgerow trees towards the churchyard wall. Putting her torch out now she was close and half hidden behind a stunted hawthorn, she peered round. The wind was rising, thrashing the branches in her face, driving the rain into her eyes. It was hard to see. Cautiously she scrambled over the old bricks and crept closer. The dark figure appeared to be walking round in circles; the lights were, as she had guessed, coming from candles on the ground. There seemed to be only one figure there, now she was closer, and she did not seem to be the victim of any sort of attack. She was shouting and gesticulating as she moved round and round in a circle.

There was no doubt what was going on. It was black magic of some sort and Emma fervently, desperately, did not want to be there. It was as she was turning away that a stronger than usual gust of wind blew out the candles, leaving both women in the dark.

Lyndsey's scream as she saw Emma standing near her sent Emma running for the wall. Gripping her torch in her wet hands, she managed to turn it on and the beam of light shone wildly round and up into the sky as she tried to find the gap where she had climbed over.

'Wait!' Lyndsey too had a torch. 'Wait, I have to speak to you!' Knowing the layout of the ground rather better than Emma, she caught up with her easily and grabbed her arm.

'I don't think so!' Emma tried to push her off.

'You were spying on me!'

Rain was streaming down their faces. The hood of Emma's mac had slipped back and her hair trailed wet across her eyes.

'I thought you were in trouble. I heard you scream!' The wind tore the words from her lips. She had recognised Lyndsey now as the young woman she had seen with Alex and the knowledge reassured her. 'Look, this is stupid. Come back to the house out of the rain. We are both getting soaked.'

Lyndsey hesitated. For a moment she turned and stared over her shoulder into the dark, then she gave in. With a nod she turned to follow.

They shed their boots and coats and Lyndsey's robe in the porch and Emma led the way in, heading for the kitchen. 'Let me grab a couple of towels.' She pointed at the kitchen door and turning to the stairs, ran up to the linen cupboard. When she came back down Lyndsey was already in the kitchen, standing by the new Aga. She was now wearing patched jeans and a scarlet sweater.

Grabbing the towel from Emma without a word, she rubbed it over her face and hair. 'If you weren't spying, what were you doing out there?' To Emma's surprise she had a clipped, upper-class accent more suitable to Harvey Nichols than to midnight country churchyards.

'I told you.' Emma was drying herself now. 'I was woken by your screaming. I thought you were being attacked or raped or something.'

'Then why didn't you call the police?' Lyndsey stopped rubbing her hair and stared at her belligerently. 'You didn't, did you?'

'No. I reckoned it would take too long for anyone to come, so I thought I would try and scare them off. I'm sorry. I didn't mean to –' Emma broke off. 'I wasn't spying.'

'But you saw what I was doing.'

'Not really. It was too dark.' Emma refused to meet her eye. 'Were you alone out there?'

Lyndsey nodded. She began to rub again vigorously.

'So, what were you doing?' Emma carefully kept her back turned.

'What you don't know won't hurt you.' Lyndsey threw down her towel. She folded her arms. 'You keep out of that churchyard. It's none of your business, what happens in there.'

Emma frowned. 'If I may say so, I think it is more my business than yours.' She turned round. 'I live right across the road and I don't appreciate being woken in the middle of the night by banshee wails which scare the living daylights out of me!'

Lyndsey's eyes flashed. 'Then why don't you put your head under the pillow? You townies are all the same. You come out into the country and you don't like what you see. You don't

162

understand it. You don't know what you're talking about, but you want to interfere anyway.'

'Hang on a minute . . .' Emma could feel her temper rising.

'No, you hang on. You mind your own business!'

'And let you get on with nice country pursuits. What was it, Lyndsey? Witchcraft? Satanism? I'm supposed to put up with that on my doorstep, am I?'

'That's the point, isn't it!' Lyndsey stormed to the door. 'It's not your doorstep. It's Liza's doorstep. And don't you forget it!' Grabbing at the latch on the door she fumbled for a moment, pulled it open and ran into the hall.

'Look, wait!' Emma called. 'At least let me drive you home. It's a filthy night out there.'

'No, Miss Dickson,' Lyndsey managed to make the name sound like an insult. 'It's not a filthy night. It's a country night!'

Ramming her feet into her boots, she grabbed her jacket and let herself out into the dark, slamming the door behind her.

31

Wednesday October 14ᵗʰ

'Right, kids. Breakfast finished? Teeth next please. Now! Mrs Cox will be here any minute to take you to school.'

Alex presided over the kitchen table like a board meeting. Morning: review the day to come. Evening: discuss the day that's over. Food: each item ticked off and eaten, or if rejected, a reason given. Then, if it was Molly Cox's day to deliver, plates into the dishwasher, shopping list checked, day to himself. If it was his turn, two extra houses to collect three extra children, push the kids into the school door, then a mooch around Colchester, or if there was a collection and tea at going home time organised, a trip further afield. Cambridge or Norwich perhaps. Not London. Not if he could help it. London brought back memories of sitting on the train, shaking with exhaustion; burn out; depression.

Today he was going to ring Emma Dickson and arrange a date for that dinner party to introduce her to Paula.

He paused as he stacked the cereal bowls. Paula hadn't been as pleased as he had hoped when he told her about Emma's arrival. And he was so certain they would get on. Two strong, intelligent women, similar backgrounds, Paula stuck in the country, Emma probably missing the City.

He frowned, recalling Paula's reaction. 'Of course you can ask her over, but I don't suppose it will make a difference to how I feel about this place.' This place meaning Bradfield, Manningtree, Essex, the countryside – anywhere he was – and it frightened him as quite a few of her remarks lately had frightened him. 'When the kids finish at Cambridge House we ought to review the situation, Alex. It's the perfect time to think about the future.' What she meant was: move. And move meant move back to London. He whistled through his teeth, pushing the thought out of his mind and, reaching for the piece of paper on which Emma had scribbled her number, he picked up the phone.

She seemed pleased with the invitation but her manner was a little reserved, which, he discovered, disappointed him. He hesitated as she wrote down his address. Then he came out with it. 'Emma? There's nothing wrong, is there? I haven't offended you in some way?'

She laughed. 'No, of course not. In fact –' she paused and he could picture her frowning, wondering if she should tell him whatever it was that she was worrying about. Clearly she decided she could. Her words shocked him. 'It's about your friend Lyndsey. She and I had a bit of a set to last night.'

He listened without comment while she explained what had happened and in spite of himself he felt a shiver of unease.

'Lyn is a complete clot!' he commented when she had finished. 'Right out of control.' He sighed. 'But she is harmless, Emma. I told you. I wouldn't trust my kids to her otherwise. I think she does consider herself a bit of a witch. Wicca they call it now, don't they? She was probably embarrassed at being caught at it. Look, I'll have a word with her. Don't worry. Whatever she's up to I don't suppose it will do any harm.' He paused. He hoped Emma was convinced, but when she spoke again she still sounded a bit dubious.

'OK, I'll leave it to you. I don't want to make an enemy of her.' There was another infinitesimal silence, then she spoke again. 'Alex, would you think me awfully rude if I asked if I could bring someone with me to supper? My ex.' She gave a small, nervous laugh. 'He might come down for a weekend if there was something exciting laid on.'

He could hear the wistfulness in her tone as she hung up and for a moment he frowned. Poor Emma was obviously finding life in the country more lonely – and more frightening – than she had expected. Picking up his car keys he headed for the door. Young Lyndsey obviously needed a good talking to. And soon.

She was out. He stood on the quay, the wind ruffling what remained of his hair, staring up at her windows, then he knocked at the door again. 'Lyn?' He stooped and opening the letterbox, he called through it.

The house was silent. Crouching low, he peered into the small living room. She had left the curtains closed and the room was dark. He frowned, standing up once more, and turned to face the river. The heavy overnight rain had cleared. Across the water weak rays of sunshine illuminated the low green swell of the Suffolk coast. The tide was neither out nor in. Broad swathes of grey black mud bordered the slow lazy strip of dull water as it crept slowly towards the town.

He sighed. Had she come home last night, or had she gone away and holed up somewhere? There was no way he could tell and no one to ask; he knew she did not talk to her neighbours.

Turning, he walked back up the quay between the cottages, back to the road where he had left his car. Instead of heading up the hill towards home, he decided to drive on into Manningtree to pick up some things from the deli. It was as he drove slowly down the road along the river that he saw the rector standing, hands in pockets, staring out across the water, much as he himself had been doing only minutes before. Alex slowed the car thoughtfully and, decision made, pulled into the kerb.

Mike raised a hand in greeting. Alex was not a parishioner of his but he had seen him occasionally in the town. 'Nice to see the rain has stopped,' he commented as Alex climbed out of the car and joined him.

'Indeed.' Alex rammed his hands into his pockets. 'I wondered if I could have a word, Rector.' He paused, watching a flight of birds making their way low over the water towards the mud banks.

Mike glanced at him, noting the tense shoulders and the anxious frown. 'Of course.'

'I was just speaking to Emma Dickson – I don't know if you've met her yet?' Alex glanced at him quickly, caught the slight shake of the head and went on. 'She's bought Liza's.'

'Ah.' Mike nodded. 'I know where you mean.'

Alex chewed his lip for a moment thoughtfully. 'Do you mind if we walk? I'm not sure whether I should be mentioning this.' He paused again as they turned and fell in step together, walking the way Alex had come.

When Alex showed no inclination to say anything else Mike prompted him gently: 'It is a good place to think, watching the tide go in and out, seeing how the birds follow it.' He paused. 'You live in Bradfield, I believe?'

166

Alex nodded. 'This isn't about me. It's about Emma and Lyndsey Clark.'

'Ah. Lyndsey.' Mike nodded.

'You know her?' Alex finally glanced at him.

'Not personally. Her name has been mentioned to me.'

Alex stopped. He faced Mike almost aggressively. 'In what context?'

Mike shook his head. 'I'm afraid I can't tell you that.'

'She's a witch, is that the context? A stupid, childish, over-dramatic kid who is in danger of getting in over her head.'

Mike scanned his face thoughtfully. 'Have you known Lyndsey long?'

Alex nodded. 'About five years. Since we moved down here from London. But just lately she's changed.' He resumed walking slowly and Mike followed. 'Last night she was up at St Mary's churchyard.' Briefly he recounted Emma's story.

'I suspect Lyndsey would not welcome my interference,' Mike said thoughtfully when Alex had finished. The two men had drifted to a halt again. 'I will pray for her, of course. And for guidance on what to do.' He paused. 'Perhaps in the meantime I should go and visit my new parishioner. Emma Dickson, you said?'

Alex nodded. 'I think the whole episode upset her quite a bit. She's on her own up there and it must have been very, very scary.'

32

Later that afternoon

Mike went to Lyndsey's first, walking down the steep road behind the Maltings. He had always thought this a pretty place. The contrast of the huge dark Maltings, with the row of tiny brightly painted cottages was somehow beguiling. This was not at all the kind of place he would have expected a witch to live. He was, he realised, sufficiently influenced by stereotype to have pictured her hanging out in the middle of some dark uncharted forest, a broomstick leaning beside the door.

The line of cottages lay silent in the late afternoon sun. A cold wind had whipped away the morning's cloud and the bright slanting light was dazzling on the river. Lyndsey's front door was closed, the curtains in the front windows drawn shut. He hesitated, surprised to find himself nervous.

'Christ be with me, Christ within me.' He took a deep breath and raised his hand to the knocker.

There was no answer. Ignoring his very strong urge to turn and flee, he forced himself to knock again. Again the door remained firmly closed. He glanced left and right at the neighbouring cottages. All remained silent, although he suspected he saw the twitch of a curtain in one. He suppressed a wry smile. What would the gossips say, he wondered, at the rector banging on the door of the local witch? Even though he was not wearing his dog collar, they would know who he was. People always did.

Liza's, in contrast, looked far more welcoming. Parking his car next to a dark green MG, he pushed open the gate and paused for a moment, looking up at the front of the cottage. He had passed it often before but perhaps it had been so overgrown he

168

had not noticed it. Now he saw the autumn roses, curtains at the windows, one of which was open and out of which came the strains of 'L'apres midi d'un faune'. He paused in his tracks, listening.

'Can I help you?' She had come round the corner of the building and caught him staring up at the front of her house, lost in thought.

He turned and his mouth dropped open in surprise. It was the woman he had seen several times walking down by the river. Even now, dressed in shabby jeans and a torn shirt and smelling strongly of creosote, she was lovely. For a moment he was struck dumb, then he managed to pull himself together. 'Miss Dickson? I'm Mike Sinclair.' Had she recognised him? He saw her frown slightly, obviously trying to place him. 'We've seen each other down by the river. I think we're both early morning walkers.' He smiled, and then realised suddenly that his clothes – sweater, jacket, chinos, old scuffed shoes, gave no clue then or now as to his calling. 'I'm sorry, I should explain. I'm the rector. I thought I would come and welcome you. See how you are settling in.'

Always acutely sensitive to the way people received the news of who he was, his heart sank as he saw her smile cool slightly. 'I'm afraid I'm not a churchgoer.'

He was disappointed, but not surprised. 'Very few people are these days.'

She relented a little. 'I expect you could do with a cup of tea? Isn't that the traditional greeting for a man of the cloth? If you don't mind crossing the threshold of a non-believer, come in. I must wash my hands. This stuff stinks so badly.' She wrinkled her nose as she led the way indoors and through to the kitchen.' She gestured towards the chair as she went to the sink and reached for some hand cleaner. 'The Aga only arrived a couple of weeks ago and I haven't really entertained anyone yet. You can help me christen it.' She bit her lip. 'Sorry, was that in bad taste?' He saw a flash of mischief in her eyes. 'But it is so handsome I think of it as a friend.'

'Indeed. It's very splendid.' He handed her a towel from the chair-back. 'You seem to have made it very nice in here.'

Christ be with me, Christ within me.

The words came into his head, unbidden. Why? Where from? It was as though someone else had spoken them. He shivered, glancing round the room. It was large – a wall had recently been knocked through into the dining room next door, making a bright, warm, welcoming rectangular space, divided by the oak studs, furnished with an old pine table and dresser, the stone floor scattered with rag rugs. Some of the decoration was unfinished, and he could smell the new paint and plaster.

He found himself eyeing her back view as she turned away to organise the kettle, lifting the lid on the Aga, slopping the water a little so that tiny droplets skittered spitting over the hotplate. Sternly he looked away. He looked down at his hands, clasped on the table in front of him. They were shaking slightly.

He accepted tea and biscuits, then, cautiously, broached the reason for his call. 'I understand you had a midnight encounter with our local witch.' He glanced at her.

'Ah. Who told you? Alex?'

He nodded. 'Also not one of my parishioners. I don't want to interfere, but it can't have been pleasant for you.'

Emma sat down opposite him at the pine table. She had, as he had noticed before, very beautiful, large hazel eyes. Thoughtfully she returned his gaze and for a moment they surveyed each other. Emma looked away first, a touch of colour in her cheeks. 'I think I over-reacted. I feel sorry for her now. It was none of my business. I frightened her as much as she frightened me.'

'You were very brave, going out there on your own.'

'No. Very stupid.' She looked at him again.

'You don't believe in all her mumbo jumbo?' *Christ be with me. Christ within me . . .*

'No.' Emma broke a piece of shortbread in half. She frowned, staring down at the crumbs. 'At least –'

'At least?' he prompted.

'I couldn't see what she was doing.' Emma pushed back her chair and went to look out of the window at the back terrace. 'So I can't really comment. When I accused her, she didn't deny it.' She fell silent for a while. Mike waited. 'She resents me living here. I suppose because I can see the churchyard.' She paused thoughtfully. 'Have you been there?'

He nodded.

'It's spooky, isn't it? Especially at midnight.' She gave a wry laugh.

He was frowning. 'Don't hesitate to ring me if you are ever

170

worried about anything over there. I'm pretty sure she is harmless, but one can never be quite sure, can one. Evil exists, in the most innocent and beautiful of guises.' He looked away, wondering suddenly if she might take his words the wrong way, think he meant her, but she did not appear to have noticed any ambiguity in the statement. She was watching something in the garden.

He stood up, half reluctant, half eager to leave the house with its odd atmosphere and its beautiful owner and saw what she was watching. There was a sleek black cat outside on the terrace. It was sitting staring intently at the base of a pot of lavender. He saw a long elegant paw flash out and retract, holding some tiny rodent. He looked away.

She saw him out and stood for several seconds watching as he walked down the path to the gate, then she disappeared inside and shut the door. He was relieved. For some reason he did not want her to see him duck in amongst the brambles on the far side of the lane and climb over the crumbling wall.

The wet grass soaked the bottom of his trousers as he made his way between the hawthorn trees. Already he could see something on the ground, shining in the low rays of sunlight. In half an hour the sun would have gone down and it would start to grow dark. He walked cautiously towards the glinting reflection in the grass. It was a small cut-glass container holding a candle. He stooped and picked it up and emptying out the rainwater which had filled it in the night he glanced round for more. He couldn't feel anything strange about the place. Or could he? He stared round, listening carefully as though some echo of Lyndsey's strange scream might come to him from the undergrowth. He was remembering his discomfort last time he came here. Perhaps she had been here before, the young witch from Mistley quay.

There were four candle-holders tucked in amongst the undergrowth and three small dishes. One contained a soggy mess of salt, another, he discovered as he cautiously inserted a fingertip and then sniffed it, olive oil. The third was empty. He guessed it had contained water before it had been tipped on its side. Stacking them together on the ground, he considered the other items lying at his feet. A small kitchen knife, a bowl, a knotted cord and a carved stick which he guessed must be her wand. He stared at them, reluctant even to touch them. But it had to be done. They had to be disposed of.

Was that a darker green rectangle in the grass? The sign that this was the site of a grave? He squatted down, staring at the ground. It was cold down there, near the earth, and he shivered violently. Whose grave was it? And was it chance that had made Lyndsey use it as the centre of her magic or had she chosen the place for a reason? Who was buried here?

He stood looking down and immediately he knew the answer to his own question. It was Hopkins. Matthew Hopkins was buried here in this redundant, deconsecrated place. Or did she just think he was? He found himself folding his arms across his chest with a shudder.

'So, Mr Hopkins. Is that what this is all about?' He shook his head slowly. 'Poor, silly girl. Is she out for revenge? Getting even on behalf of those pathetic women you murdered?'

Behind him the sloping rays of the setting sun began to turn crimson as they pierced black swags of cloud on the horizon. The light fractured, as the leaves and branches of the hedges intercepted it, throwing a lattice of shadows at his feet.

Pathetic women?

Murdered?

Or were they evil, daughters of Satan, worshippers at his foul shrine, there to bring the Black Arts to ensnare good Christians? Old women, yes, for the most part. But they had the power. The knowledge. They had known men in their lives, found their weak spots, trapped them with their wiles, sapped their energy, their very life blood. Then they taught their younger sisters. They baptised them with blood, drew back their petticoats to expose their lower limbs and watched while the younger women fornicated with the Devil.

Mike shuddered, unaware that his face had changed, that his eyes, normally kind, slightly myopic, had sharpened and narrowed, that his fingers had angled into angry claws, that his personality had gone and been replaced by that of another man.

Bitches. Whores. Enticing men. Women luring and entrapping men when they were young and beautiful, when they were old, beating and humiliating them. He pictured for a moment one particular old woman, his *grand-maman* dressed in simplest black, her hair hidden beneath a cap of the severest cut, standing over a small, terrified boy. The cane in her hand whistled down over his bony spine and Mike heard the furious words ringing in his head. 'Vile! Horrible boy! Don't ever, ever look at a woman – any woman – again with desire. Do you hear me? Do you? With your lustful thoughts, your lecherous desires, your greed for flesh. I will tell your father! I will tell your *maman*. You are evil. God will punish you!' On and on it went and it wasn't until she had finished that Mike realised that the vicious nagging voice in his head was speaking in French. He flinched at the memory of the cane coming down again and again, feeling the boy's fear and rage. *Sale; petite bête vile; dégoûtant!*

His rage was congealing. Growing. It was turning to hatred; hatred for the entire female race.

When she was at last exhausted and unable to lift the stick any more, she stepped away, leaving him lying sobbing on the ground. He had wet himself.

And the crime for which he was being chastised? He, at the age of eight, had dared to pinch the bottom of one of the maids in his father's rectory and made her giggle.

Mike turned away from the spot where he had been standing and before he knew what was happening he had vomited into the shadows. He reached for his handkerchief, shaking uncontrollably. There was a sheen of sweat across his face. Where in God's name had that come from? It was as though a window had opened in his mind and he had glimpsed someone else's hell. A child's. He took a deep breath, straightening his shoulders, and kicked some mud over the sticky patch.

He prayed for several minutes over the site of the grave, if grave it was, before turning away to gather up Lyndsey's paraphernalia. Loading it all carefully into the boot of his car, he drove back towards the setting sun.

The last streaks of red were showing in the blackening sky as he reached the rectory and he knew what he had to do. The candles, the cord, the salt, the oil, the wand, would be put into the fire, the glass candle-holders smashed and buried with the dishes and her wickedly sharp knife with the curious silver-painted symbols painted on the handle would join them in the ground, its blade snapped in two. They were tainted by the Devil. Only fire and earth, blessed with holy water, could deal with such detritus.

33

Friday, October 16th

The children, neat in their grey school uniforms, were hurrying down the High Street. Each child had a clipboard and a pencil, each a list of questions. Sally Mason lagged behind, keeping an eye on them, wondering if anyone would notice if she took a couple of puffs at a ciggie before she shepherded the children into a group and allowed them to go and sit on the wall overlooking the river to eat their sandwiches and crisps. This was always a popular day out. The Manningtree witch hunt. Normally Judith organised this excursion as a prelude to her virulent anti-witch propaganda lesson next term, but this time she had had to step back from the visit. Something about a specialist's appointment in Colchester. Sally didn't mind. She enjoyed days out of the classroom and this one was easy; it was a small school and the classes were manageable. She had tried to keep the questions simple. Most had been answered when they piled into the tiny museum in the back of the library. Now all they had to do was collect some pub names, find a rowan tree, draw a broomstick – it was still leaning there outside the hardware store, she had checked. After lunch they would walk along the river to Mistley, stand and stare at the Thorn Inn, with its wonderful picture of the Witchfinder on the pub sign, and then at long last they would pile back into the minibus and she could think about going home.

34

Tuesday October 20th

THE MOON IN THE LAST QUARTER

Emma had not been to Colchester Castle before. The man at the little museum in the library at Manningtree had told her to go to the museum there when she had expressed her disappointment that the exhibits about witches over which he presided were aimed more at children than anyone else; he had known nothing about Liza's.

It had been a shock the first time she realised that Liza had not been the old lady she had watched through the hedge as a child. Liza had lived in the cottage in the seventeenth century; a witch, she had been burned at the stake by Matthew Hopkins.

No, not burned. Witches weren't burned in England. That was the first thing she discovered. They were hanged. But not before they had been horribly tortured. Torture as such wasn't allowed in England either; but the single-minded, thorough Hopkins had a series of little refinements with which to torment the suspects he had rounded up. Refinements and tricks. He pricked them with a vicious pin set in a wooden handle. As it was known that the Devil's marks for which he searched the old ladies were insensible to pain, the pin was retractable. When the victim had screamed enough a spring was pressed, the pin slid upwards into the handle and low and behold, the fierce jabbing of the witch pricker produced silence. No pain. Therefore guilt. Case proved.

She followed the signposts down a long flight of stairs towards the castle prison. It was quiet down there, away from the shouts and chattering of the children visiting the Roman exhibits upstairs.

She was the only visitor down here and she could see why. A notice at the top of the stairs suggested the exhibits through the door in the darkness might not be suitable for children.

She stood still at the bottom of the stairs and looked round, half nervous, half expectant. The exhibits were minimal. Disappointingly so. An old wooden stocks stood near the staircase. A small box on the wall held a collection of broken clay pipes and that was it. What was scary about that? Slowly she walked past a series of information boards which told the story of the prison and the people who had passed through its doors and then, there they were. Three panels about witchcraft and the Witchfinder. She read each one carefully, conscious of an increasing sense of anticlimax. They spelt out the minimum of detail about the subject, showed three reproductions of contemporary scenes about witches and their familiars and witches being hanged, and there was a picture of him – a caricature showing him with curly hair and beard, both fair, deep set eyes, aquiline face. Nothing like the man she had seen in her dreams.

Beyond the picture there was a doorway leading into the darkness. She was about to walk in when three girls from one of the school parties upstairs raced down, pushing past her, giggling and shouting, to hover in the doorway staring in. Their shrieks intensified as they pushed each other forward, no one wanting to be first; afraid to go in. Emma stood back and watched, half amused, half irritated, as they dared one another to go through the door. It didn't work. Suddenly all three turned and ran for the stairs. They were going for reinforcements.

Emma took her chance and stepped forward. The notice by the door said, 'On your way in, feel the wood of the door grille worn smooth by the hands of countless prisoners'. She glanced at it and with a shrug put her hands deep into her pockets. Then plucking up her courage, she stepped forward into the strange, all pervasive silence of the darkness beyond the door.

She found herself standing opposite two cells and as she waited in the dark, holding her breath, a low, sinister light appeared in one to reveal a small empty dungeon. The silence was broken as the commentary began.

She forced herself to stay and listen, intensely aware of the weight of the great building over her head, of the dark curved vaults, the bars, the claustrophobia, the pain and the suffering, the terror and despair which permeated every square inch of the walls around her.

At the end of the sequence she walked back towards the exit, numb with horror. It wasn't the screams she had heard – they had been muted, censored – nor the detail which she had seen and heard laid out in those neat, unemotional, easily assimilable chunks. It was the memories it had awakened; memories deep inside herself.

Memories of her dreams.

Memories of the past.

35

Thursday October 22ⁿᵈ

Emma was coming out of the wholefood shop when Mike spotted her on the other side of the road. He had just been to visit the young widow grieving for her husband, lost when the car had left the road and hit the oak tree in the fog, and he was feeling depressed and angry at the waste of yet another young life with so much to give.

'Hi!' He lifted a hand in greeting as Emma turned and saw him. Crossing the road, he fell in step beside her. 'No more midnight disturbances, I hope?'

She shook her head. She was looking pale and tired. 'My latest midnight disturbances are self-generated, I'm afraid. Nightmares.'

'As a result of Lyndsey's activities?' He frowned.

She shrugged. 'Not really. I'm probably just over-tired; doing up a house is the most exhausting job known to man – or woman. There's always that temptation to go on and on, trying to fit in just one more thing. Even watching the builder is tiring!'

He grinned. 'Well, would you let me buy you a coffee as an enforced ten-minute rest?' He indicated the coffee shop two doors down the road. 'I would really appreciate the chance to stop for a breather myself. It's been a bad morning.'

'Bad?' She raised an eyebrow. 'Do vicars have bad mornings?'

Nodding, he opened the door and ushered her inside. 'Oh, indeed they do. We're glorified social workers in some ways, and sometimes things get a bit heart-breaking.'

'I suppose so. I'm afraid if I thought about it at all I assumed that would only apply to inner-city parishes. I kind of pictured you as a cross between those wonderful rural clergymen Francis

Kilvert and Gilbert White – with, after our last encounter, a touch of Father Karras out of *The Exorcist* thrown in!'

Mike let out a roar of laughter. 'I wish! What a wonderful description.' They sat down at a small table in the corner. He nodded to two ladies nearby and shook his head. 'Oh dear. There starts the gossip. I'm sorry, I hope you don't mind being seen in public with me.'

Emma smiled. 'I can live with it. I know so few people round here perhaps I can even qualify as a Mystery Woman. Would it add to your street cred?'

'It certainly would.' He glanced up and held her gaze for a moment. She looked away first.

'So, how long have you been a vicar?' She picked up the menu and opened it.

He grinned. 'Technically, I'm the rector. Different animal.'

'Really?' She gave a disbelieving smile. 'I thought they were the same thing.'

He shook his head. 'Rector is a much more important chap. It's all to do with tithes.' He caught her eye and laughed. 'OK. You're right. They are interchangeable – as is that lovely word parson. And to answer your question, I've only been here a year. This is my first parish. I came to holy orders late in life.'

'Late in life?' She passed the menu on to him. 'I would just like a coffee, please. So, what do you call late in life? You are going to tell me you are a well-preserved seventy next.'

'Not quite!' He pushed back his chair. 'Let me get the coffees, and then I'll tell you all about my strange and devious past.'

'I started as a teacher,' he went on as he sat down again. He had brought two coffees and two flapjacks from the counter. 'That was a bit over-ambitious. I like kids, but not the kind I was encountering. I wanted to teach. To really teach, and all I could do was yell at them and try to keep order. They weren't interested. So I thought I'd do something else; something that made a bit of money, a job in industry. What a revelation that was! I could afford food and even clothes.' He grinned. She liked the way his eyes crinkled at the edges. There was enormous good humour and compassion in his face. He must, she found herself thinking, be very popular with his congregation.

'So, what went wrong? You found God?'

He nodded. 'Oh, God was always there, it's just He started to

179

get a bit pushy and I suddenly realised that was what the teaching had been about. Right instinct. Wrong turning.'

'It must be wonderful to find you have a vocation.' Her voice was wistful suddenly. 'I wonder if I'm about to find mine. As a gardener and a herbalist.' The tone was self-mocking, but he caught the undertone of worry.

'It is frightening to make such a huge change to one's life, isn't it?' He glanced up at her again. 'And lonely.'

It had been a shrewd guess. He saw the pain in her eyes for a moment as she bent her head to her coffee. 'Let's change the subject, Mike. Can I call you Mike, or should I call you "vicar" or "reverend" or something?' She rolled the two words with an attempt at a rural burr.

'Mike will do fine.' He was still watching her face. She was sitting with her back to the window, a slight shadow playing over her features; her hair had tangled in the wind and the cold had touched colour into her cheeks but as he watched he saw her face change before his eyes. The hair was constrained for a moment by a white cap, her eyes narrowed and grew sharp, her wide generous mouth tightened into a snarl. He pushed his chair back sharply, jerking the coffee cups so that they slopped into their saucers.

'Mike? What is it? What's wrong?'

Emma was staring at him, her eyes wide. She was herself again.

He looked away and took a deep breath. 'I'm sorry. I . . . I don't know what happened. I suddenly . . .' He closed his eyes. 'Emma, I'm most frightfully sorry.' He laughed. 'You must think I'm mad!' He shook his head. 'I thought I saw someone beside you.' He didn't mean beside, but he could hardly tell her what he had really seen.

Emma was half smiling, intrigued. 'A ghost?' The idea did not seem to frighten her. 'There seem to be lots of ghosts round here. There is one in the shop next door.'

'Ah.' He paused, glad to change the subject. 'So, you know about that.'

She nodded. 'It's a spooky place. I went in there a couple of days ago to buy some things for the kitchen and it still feels weird.'

'Still?'

'I went in there on the day I first came to view my house. There were some chaps there making a film about the ghost.'

'Mark Edmunds.'

'You know him?'

Mike nodded. 'He wanted me to be in the programme. The church's view.'

'And did you agree?'

He shook his head. 'He's coming up here again, I gather, to do some more filming. But if he asks me again, I'm still going to say no.'

'You should do it. It would make it more interesting to hear what you have to say about it. Do you believe in ghosts?'

Mike looked up and held her gaze for a moment. 'Oh yes,' he said quietly. 'I believe in ghosts.'

Anxiously, she scanned his face. 'That sounded heartfelt.'

'It was.' For a moment he was tempted to tell her what had happened to him in the shop, but he thought better of it. He shrugged. 'Sorry. That's part of the job, too.'

'So, off limits?'

''Fraid so.'

'Being your confidante is quite tricky, isn't it.' Suddenly her eyes were sparkling again. 'What can you talk about? If I'm going to be the femme fatale in your life we've got to talk closely and animatedly about something.' She rested her chin in her hand, tapping her fingernails gently against her teeth. The look was nothing if not provocative. 'You could ask me to do the church flowers.'

His face broke into a smile. 'Unfortunately you would have to go on a waiting list.'

'You're kidding!' She was genuinely astonished.

'No. There are lots of ladies lining up to do the flowers.'

'So, you're in big demand?'

'Of course.'

'Surely you've got a gorgon of a wife to chase us all away?'

'Unfortunately not. Or perhaps, fortunately.' He laughed. 'Actually I do have a gorgon, but she's not wife material.' He paused. 'I shouldn't have said that. Please forget it!'

'Deeply unchristian thought, eh?'

He laughed softly. Tearing his eyes away from her face he reached for his coffee cup. 'Going back to the subject of ghosts, do you mind if I suggest you don't go near that churchyard? I don't think any of us should be there and it worries me.'

'Bad vibes?'

He nodded. 'Exactly.'

'I wasn't planning on going there.'

'Good.' Standing up, he pushed back his chair. 'I'm going to have to go. I've enjoyed our brief encounter, Miss Dickson.'

'Emma, please! After all, I am your mystery woman.'

'Emma.' For a moment he hesitated and she wondered if he were going to shake her hand or kiss her cheek. He did neither. Briefly he touched her shoulder and then he had gone.

36

Friday October 23rd

'Emma, it's gorgeous!' Flora had arrived unannounced, drawing up in her old bright green Volkswagen Beetle as Emma was preparing to go shopping. 'I had no idea it was going to be so pretty.' She was exploring, darting first into the living room, then into the kitchen, examining every corner. She turned and gave Emma a hug, then retrieved her basket from the hall. 'Here. Pressies. I wasn't sure what you were going to need so I brought you lots of stuff!'

There was a pretty pottery oil burner, a Flaming Katy pot plant, a bottle of mead, a ping pong ball for the cats and an electric-blue fringed silk shawl for Emma – or more likely for a chair!

'Why on earth didn't you ring?' Emma was overwhelmed by her friend's enthusiasm.

'Spur of the moment. I had two cancellations, so no work today and I thought, why not! You don't mind, do you?' The huge green eyes were suddenly worried.

'Of course not. It's just . . .' Emma paused. 'Piers is coming down tomorrow.'

Flora grimaced. 'So?'

'So, I can't ask you to stay.'

'Oh, sweetie! I wasn't going to! Besides,' Flora hesitated. 'You never told me it was haunted.'

Emma stared at her.

'You did know?' Flora caught her hand. 'I felt it as soon as I came through the door.'

'Yes.' Emma sank into a chair. 'I did know. I've never seen her, but I know there is someone here.'

'And you're not scared?' Flora scanned her face anxiously.

'No.'

'Good. There's no need.' Flora glanced round the room 'She's pleased you're here.'

Emma smiled. This kind of talk was one of the eccentricities of Flora's that she used to smile at tolerantly. Suddenly it no longer seemed eccentric. On the contrary. It seemed normal. 'I know and I'm glad. I love it here so much.'

Except for the nightmares. She bit her lip. 'How could you tell it was haunted?'

'Same as you, I expect.' Flora grinned. 'Some people can sense these things easily, others –' she leaned forward and punched Emma playfully on the shoulder – 'take longer to get round to it. Right.' She sat down and reaching for her bag, she produced three small bottles of essential oil and a box of matches. 'Here, I wasn't sure if you had any oils left. Let's light the burner. Lavender and Rosemary. And juniper. They give protection. Cleansing. This was a witch's house, yes?' She glanced up for a fraction of a second, then concentrated once more on counting drops of oil onto the water in the burner.

'How did you know that?'

'Didn't you tell me?'

'No.'

Flora shrugged. 'She was a good witch. She must have been. The vibes are nice. Most of them.' She glanced back through the door towards the hall with a slight frown.

Emma raised an eyebrow, half amused, half wary. 'Most? Not all? Is that why you don't want to spend the night?'

For a moment Flora didn't answer. She lit the night-light under the oils and pushed the burner to the centre of the table.

'There is something uncomfortable here, Em. Someone – something – is hovering. It's probably nothing significant.'

She spotted Min on the window sill outside and jumped to her feet. 'Show me the garden, Em. I am so envious of you. I'm tempted to throw up London, you know, and come and help you with your herb garden.'

'Really?' Emma tried to push the thought of something hovering out of her head.

'Really.' Flora followed her out into the garden. 'So, Piers is coming?' She fixed Emma with a disapproving glare. 'Does he come often?'

'The first visit.' Emma shrugged.

'But he's out of your life?'

Emma shook her head. 'Not necessarily. He might like it here.'

'Oh, get real, Em. This is deeply, deeply not Piers.' Flora waved her arms expansively. Then she shivered. 'You know, there is something odd about this place, Em. Someone is watching us, someone impatient for me to leave.'

Emma forced a laugh. 'Stop it. You're scaring me! Listen, come shopping. I've got to buy lots of goodies for the weekend and we'll go to The Crown and grab some lunch. How about that? Take you away from all this atmosphere.'

'She won't like Piers, Em. She won't want him here. You must be careful.' Flora caught her hand.

'Who won't like him? Stop it, Flora.'

Flora shrugged. 'Sorry. I can't help it.' She gave a last glance round and turned back towards the house. 'Right. Shopping it is. And the pub sounds good, too!'

37

Saturday October 24th

Through the open kitchen window Emma could hear the thin melancholy song of the robin sitting on top of the wall of the old wash-house. She paused for a moment in her chores, listening. That was one of the most beautiful and the saddest sounds in nature. It meant goodbye to the summer and the warmth and beauty of the sunshine and the flowers and heralded the start of winter. She found herself shivering in spite of the warmth of the bright room with its Aga. Flora's visit had unsettled her.

She could hardly believe it when Piers had agreed to come. When she phoned him and explained about the dinner invitation from the Wests, she had expected a cold rejection. Instead he had seemed pleased, relieved even, to hear from her and he arrived at half past twelve with flowers, two bottles of wine, a woven tapestry throw from Heals as a housewarming present and two packets of cat treats for the ecstatically purring Max and Min.

'So, how is country life?' He poured them each a glass of wine and sat down at the pine table as she filled saucepans with water and juggled her heavy earthenware dishes between ovens.

'It's good, Piers. I'm enjoying it.' She pushed her hair out of her eyes and accepted a glass from him.

'Any sign of a job?' He raised an eyebrow.

'In the spring. By then I'll have the herb garden ready to roll.'

'I'm looking forward to seeing this.' He took a sip of wine. 'Emma Dickson with soil under her fingernails doling out flower pots at two ninety-nine a pop.'

'I won't starve, Piers.' She glanced at him crossly. 'David is giving me some freelance work. I'm on-line. I get the FT delivered by a boy on a bike from the village every morning. If the plants don't sell, and I feel I'm getting hungry I'll set up as a financial adviser or maybe I'll go and work in a shop or write a book.' She smiled and leaned forward to give his arm a playful punch. 'I will be fine. And you could always come and be a commuter and support me.' She meant it as a joke.

He frowned and looked away, making a sudden fuss of Min who had leaped onto his lap and was crooning as she rubbed her head against his chin.

'Sorry. Didn't mean that last bit. It wasn't supposed to be a serious option.' She took a large gulp of wine.

'Good,' he replied softly. 'Because it isn't an option. Sorry.'

She put on a CD to ease them over the silences as they ate, the soft sad cadences of piano and sax backed from time to time by the thin song of the robin accompanying her soup, homemade bread and cheese and the fresh fruit salad. 'I'm sure we'll have a big meal this evening. So, shall we go and walk by the river? Visit the art gallery? Go and feed the swans?' It was strange having to plan the day, to entertain him, to realise that here, he didn't belong.

They enjoyed their walk. He brought her a pretty dish from the pottery studio on the quay, they strolled along the river towards Manningtree and up into the town, then home. It was seven thirty when they climbed into her car and headed towards Bradfield.

Alex and Paula lived in a modern, ranch-style house at the end of a long gravelled drive. It overlooked open farmland which, in the dark, was bleak and featureless beneath the sweep of their headlights.

Emma pulled the car up near the front door and switched off the engine. She gave Piers a wink. 'Ready?'

'Ready.'

The house was warm and bright and full of music. Alex greeted them cordially and led the way into an open-plan living room at one end of which the table was laid for four. No other guests, then.

'Paula will be down in a sec.' He busied himself getting their drinks. 'And meanwhile meet the sprogs. Come and say hello, kids.'

'Daddy says you've got two cats.' Sophie gazed at Emma earnestly. 'Mummy won't let us have any pets.'

'Now, that's not entirely true, Soph.' Alex frowned. He handed a glass to Emma.

'It is true. I always speak the truth!' The child's expression was very serious. She had a pale, pretty face with huge dark eyes. Long red-blonde hair was held off her forehead by an Alice band. 'I wanted a kitten and a puppy and a pony for my last three birthdays and I didn't get any of them.'

'That's because I know you wouldn't look after them properly and I haven't got the time!' Their mother had appeared in the doorway behind them. 'Hi! I'm Paula.' A slim, elegant thirty-nine year old, Paula West had smartly highlighted short blonde hair and immaculate make up. She was wearing beautifully cut trousers and a powder-blue silk shirt which emphasised the colour of her eyes.

'Daddy would look after them with us,' Sophie pursued her train of thought relentlessly. 'He said he would.'

'He may have said so, but Daddy hasn't got time.' Paula accepted the gin and tonic her husband put in her hand and threw herself down into a chair. 'Please, people, sit.' She raised a glass to them. 'TV now, kids. In the playroom, please.' She shrugged at Emma. 'I know I shouldn't let them, but we get no time to ourselves, otherwise. You did get a video for them, Alex, didn't you?'

'Yes, dear, of course I did.' Alex handed a glass to Piers. 'The kids are fine. They are having a picnic in there.' He winked at his guest.

Mystified by this sign of complicity, Piers nodded wisely. 'I gather you chose the short straw and gave up the City,' he commented.

Alex grimaced. 'I don't know if I really had that much choice at the time. But I don't regret it now. You wouldn't get me going back there for any money.'

'Because you don't have to commute; you don't have to come home exhausted day after day and turn round before it's light next morning to set off back again!' Paula had drained her glass. She held it out to her husband and he took it without comment. He had not, Emma noticed, even touched his own drink. She glanced at Piers and their eyes met. The unmistakable message was, Oh God, it's going to be one of those evenings when the hosts snipe at one another remorselessly and the guests wished they had never come.

188

In fact, it was not that bad. The first gin had revived Paula and once they had moved to the table to eat smoked salmon followed by a crown roast with tiny buttery potatoes and autumn vegetables, she had mellowed enough to compliment her husband on his cooking.

'Of course, the country is better for the kids. It's bound to be.' She had rejected the potatoes, but helped herself to more carrots and broccoli. 'But we can't help wondering if once they move on to the next school it would be better if they were in London.'

'No.' Alex's voice, though quiet, was firm. 'They are fine here; they have friends; they love it here; and yes, they could have pets here. Sophie could have a pony; they could sail. All sorts of things. And they have Lyndsey to take care of them –' He broke off and his eyes flew to Emma's face in mute appeal.

She shrugged imperceptibly, not knowing what to say. It was fairly easy to guess his meaning. Don't tell Paula just how much Lyndsey looks after them; and above all don't tell her that the babysitter is a witch. Especially don't tell her she is a witch who practises black magic in a churchyard at midnight.

She realised suddenly that Piers and Paula were discussing the City. They had discovered friends in common. They had been to the same conferences. In fact, they had probably met before. Their heads drew closer together across the table. Alex reached for the bottle of wine and topped up Emma's glass and then his own. 'Lyn loves the children,' he said softly. 'And they love her.'

'No problem.' Emma took a sip. It was a good wine. 'I caught her at a bad time.' She paused. 'Tell me, is Mike Sinclair a friend of yours?'

Alex put his head to one side. 'More of an acquaintance.' He saw Piers turn to listen and hastened to explain. 'He's the rector down in Manningtree and Mistley. We're in a different parish up here, of course. Not that we go, to be honest.'

'We go at Christmas,' Paula put in.

'You've met him, have you?' Alex asked innocently, turning back to Emma. 'Mike, I mean.'

Emma nodded, squinting into the candlelight. 'I liked him. I told him I wouldn't be one of his flock, but yesterday we met in the village and he bought me a coffee.'

'Good-looking, is he?' Piers challenged.

'Yes, as a matter of fact, he is.'

'And not married, either,' Paula added. 'The ladies of the parish flutter as he walks about.'

The two men guffawed. 'He's probably gay,' Piers put in. 'Clergymen usually are these days, aren't they?'

'No, they're not!' Emma was surprised to hear herself sound quite heated. 'And he didn't seem gay to me. Not at all.'

'So, he obviously made an impression.' It was Paula's turn to laugh. 'I don't blame you. I'm on one of his children's committees when I have time to go and he is a decent man. Very genuine, and no, not gay. But he has got this dreadful lay reader person who follows him everywhere. She never lets another woman near him.' She chortled. 'Sheepdog syndrome. Are you a churchgoer, Piers?'

He shook his head. 'Not my scene, I'm afraid.'

'So you don't believe in ghosts either, then?'

He shook his head again. 'Don't tell me this house is haunted?'

'No.' Paula laughed. 'But yours is. Liza's. You must have heard about the ghost?'

'The house isn't mine, it's Emma's.' Piers put in quietly. 'I am just visiting.'

'Oh.' Paula frowned. 'I'm sorry. I thought you two were an item.'

Emma glanced at Piers. 'Not any more,' she said softly.

'Well, anyway. Emma won't be so alone if she has a ghost, will she?' Paula's voice was over-bright.

'Paulie, no. Not now.' Alex frowned.

'Why not? People love to hear they're living in a haunted house.' Paula stood up and began collecting plates.

'Not necessarily, if they live there alone,' Emma said quietly. She laughed and shook her head, firmly suppressing the memory of Flora's warning only the day before. 'I'm sorry. I didn't mean that to sound so pathetic.'

'It didn't. It sounded heartfelt.' Alex pushed back his chair. 'Don't worry. There is nothing scary in your house. I've always thought it had a lovely warm atmosphere.'

'Considering the ghost was a witch, you mean,' Paula put in, her voice a whispered tremolo. 'But, as Alex says, a really nice witch.'

'Do you know who she was?' Emma asked. She had reached for the remains of her bread roll and was breaking it into tiny pieces.

'Liza of course. Surely someone's told you about her?' Paula called over her shoulder. She had taken the plates into the kitchen and put them down on the counter. She reappeared and began collecting vegetable dishes. 'She was burned at the stake on Manningtree Green.'

'That's not true.' Alex put his hand over Emma's wrist for a second, staying her restless fingers amongst the crumbs.

'I know.' She nodded. 'I have been doing my research. She would have been hanged at Chelmsford after a proper trial.'

'Proper?' Paula was indignant. 'Weren't they tortured?'

Emma nodded. 'They were. But once they appeared before the magistrates everything was done according to the law.' She shrugged.

'Have you seen her?' Piers raised an eyebrow.

Emma shook her head.

'Let me take that roll away.' Alex gently extricated it from her agitated fiddling. 'As I said, that is a happy house and always has been. The ghosts, if there are any, are in Manningtree. They've been filming at the corner shop in Church Street. A TV documentary, I hear. They were talking about it in the deli. The girl who works in the shop says Mike Sinclair went in to exorcise the ghost and came out with his hair standing on end.' He chuckled, distributing fresh plates. 'I forgot to ask him about it. Now, that does sound exciting.'

'And a load of rubbish if you don't mind my saying so,' Piers put in. 'It's wrong to wind people up about ghosts. It scares them.'

'I hope you don't think it scares me!' Emma frowned at him.

'It might. On your own up that lane in the dark. No one for miles. It would scare me.'

'Well, not me. Not if it's a nice ghost.' Emma was indignant.

'Here's pudding.' Paula had reappeared with a huge bowl. It was topped with cream and grated chocolate. 'Trifle. My speciality. Alex does the first courses, I do the pudding.' She produced a spoon. 'Two extra plates, Alex, for the kids. We promised. Now,' she beamed at Emma, 'can I give you some? You must have given up dieting now you're a country girl.'

Emma glanced at her, not sure how to take the remark. Was Paula implying that she was fat? She smiled. 'I'd love some, please.' She studied Paula's face through the glare of the candlelight. There was a brittleness of expression there she recognised all too well. Paula was under immense strain, tired, stressed and, she guessed, very unhappy. Poor Alex. She watched him carry two brimming bowls of trifle out to the children. In a few minutes he was back. 'They're happy.'

'What are they watching?' Emma reached for her spoon.

'*Babe*. For the thousandth time.' He slipped into his chair. 'It's nearly finished. Then it's bedtime. I quite like it if they have a late night. It means we get a bit of peace in the morning. And don't forget, the clocks go back tonight so we get a whole extra hour of bliss.' He chuckled. 'Precious, precious Sunday. If Mike Sinclair realised just how precious he'd stop being surprised that no one goes to church.'

'I don't think he is surprised,' Emma said slowly. She was savouring the sweetness of the trifle. 'When I told him I didn't go, he didn't blink an eye. It must be very disheartening, poor chap.'

'Perhaps he should concentrate on his exorcism techniques and leave honest citizens alone.' That was Piers.

'You could get him to come and exorcise Liza's.' Paula helped herself to another spoonful of trifle. 'Then you won't be scared on dark winter nights.'

'I've already told you, I won't be scared.' Emma frowned.

'Of course you will. You wouldn't be human if you weren't,' Piers put in. 'Then who'll be begging to come back to London?'

There was a moment's silence.

'I won't, Piers,' Emma said softly.

'Ah.' Alex looked from one to the other. 'Do I sense a conflict here? Sorry. Dangerous ground. Shall we change the subject?'

'I can't think why you would want to come and live down here after London,' Paula put in. 'It seems crazy to me. And giving up a good career to grow herbs!'

'Paula, leave it!' There was a clear warning in Alex's voice.

'No! I'm entitled to give my view.' Paula's pale cheeks flushed angrily. 'You know damn well I think we should move back to London. The kids would be happy there. They'd love it. Emma is a fool to give up all that. A complete fool.'

'Thanks a lot!' Emma was indignant.

'Forgive us, Emma. It's none of our business.' Alex was profoundly embarrassed.

'Nevertheless, you are in a position to make informed comment,' Piers put in. 'And Paula is right. If she works in London and commuting doesn't do it for her, then perhaps you should move. No,' he held up his hand as Emma drew breath to interrupt. 'Similarly, Em effectively ended our relationship by moving down here. She knows I think she's mad.' He softened the remark with a smile, reaching out to cover her hand with his own.

She snatched it away. 'I don't think Alex and Paula want to hear about our relationship or lack of it.'

A silence followed, broken only by the ostentatious clatter of spoons on plates. Paula glanced at Alex and then at Emma and frowned, suddenly suspicious. No. Surely not. He wasn't going to fall for Emma, was he? Standing up abruptly she disappeared into the kitchen to fetch coffee.

Emma followed her, arms full of dirty dishes. 'I'm sorry about that. Childish!'

'Don't be silly. The trouble is it's rather shown up the cracks in our own united front,' Paula said coldly. She put on the kettle. 'I'm just going upstairs to the loo.' She did not look pleased when Emma followed her – more out of curiosity than need.

The upstairs of the house was as spacious as the ground floor. Five bedrooms with three bathrooms. Emma was shown into a small guest bathroom generously supplied with exotic soaps and lotions. Having dried her hands, she made her way towards the stairs past the master bedroom where Paula had disappeared. From behind the closed inner door of what must be their hosts' bathroom she heard the sound of violent retching. For a moment she paused, wondering if she should offer help, then suddenly she understood. That was how Paula managed to combine the eating of huge meals and rich exotic trifles with a pencil-thin figure.

When Paula rejoined the others in the drawing room around the open fire she was white and drawn, but otherwise outwardly cheerful as she passed round the cups. Emma had taken a seat on the long, grey-upholstered sofa and was watching Alex feed neatly sawn logs onto the fire. Oozing with resin, they spat furiously as they crackled into the flames.

Glancing up at her hostess, Emma tried to make peace. 'There is a lot about the City I miss, I must admit. The camaraderie. The social life. Even the work!'

'Then why leave?' Paula was standing in front of her proffering the sugar basin.

Emma waved it away. 'It's as if there is something inside me, telling me to do it. A deeper, stronger part of me. Almost some kind of spiritual longing.' She shook her head. 'Don't think I haven't asked myself why – I've lost so much . . .' As her voice trailed into silence her eyes strayed towards Piers, who was standing looking down at the fire, talking to Alex.

Paula frowned. 'It doesn't sound like a very rational decision, if you don't mind me saying so.'

'It wasn't.' Emma shrugged. 'That's the terrible part. It wasn't. But there is no going back.'

38

The same night

With a sigh, Mike stood up and wandered across to stand in his favourite position by the window. While he had been trying to write his sermon it had grown dark outside. A mist lay across the lawn, swirling like damp gauze in the light from the window. He glanced at his watch and was appalled to find it was already well after seven.

Shivering, he pulled the curtains across and turned his back. She was there again, inside his head, the woman who had haunted his dreams the night before; at first he had thought she might be Lyndsey Clark, but she didn't meet the description Alex had given. In fact, she wasn't a twentieth-century woman at all. She was shadowy, there at the edge of his vision, a woman whose hair was concealed by a white cap tied under the chin, who wore a long black dress with a white linen collar. But it wasn't the old woman of his earlier vision. It was a young woman with bright frank hazel eyes and a determined chin, the woman whose face had for a moment overshadowed that of Emma Dickson in the coffee shop down in the town, a woman who could be Emma Dickson except that this was a woman who radiated hatred.

Taking a deep breath, he went back to his desk and stared at the screensaver swirling silently in the corner. The phone was signalling eight missed messages and as he stood there looking at it, it rang again.

'Mike? Are you there yet? I've tried to reach you a couple of times today. I do need to speak to you about the service tomorrow.' He heard the irritation in Judith's voice as he sat down at the desk. His hand had extended almost of its own free will to pick up the receiver. Then it had stopped. The phone fell silent and he sat motionless, staring at it.

He had been like this all day. Shaky, nervous, alternately shivering and hot as though he were coming down with flu. And all day he had been aware of these faces hovering on the periphery of his consciousness. Women. Women in Puritan dress. Voices, echoing in his head.

Putting his elbows on the desk, he clasped his hands and closed his eyes 'Our Father, who art in Heaven.' He stopped. Somewhere upstairs a door had banged. He looked up towards the ceiling. It had been misty when he looked out into the garden. Surely there was no wind?

When the phone rang again a moment later he picked it up without giving himself time to think.

'Mike! At last! I've been trying to reach you.'

'I'm sorry, Judith. I've just got in.' He hoped he would be forgiven the lie. Another lie. 'How can I help you?'

'Tomorrow's service. I said I'd play the organ.'

'Of course. Charles is away.' Mike dragged his mind back to the daily details of running the parish.

'The hymns, Mike.' There was a hint of impatience in her voice. 'You said you'd tell me which ones in case I have to have a brief run through. I'm not that practised.' She laughed.

'And I've given you no time. Judith, I'm so sorry.' He was scrabbling amongst the notes on his desk.

'I thought I would go up to the church now and have a quick go, while there's no one about to hear me. Perhaps you could have a think and meet me there in half an hour or so? I haven't got a key.'

There was another implied reprimand there. She had asked before for her own key. He should have seen that she had one by now.

'I'll be there.' He wasn't sure what he was looking for. There was no list. Not yet. Not until the sermon was written. Not until he had a theme. He sighed. Tomorrow was St Crispin's Day. Was he going to write about the patron saint of shoemakers or should he go for Shakespeare and Henry V? Or both. Surely he could think up something stimulating with that kind of background.

He hung up and glanced at his watch. Half an hour to think,

make a few notes, choose the hymns and walk over to the church with his key.

She was already waiting in the porch when he arrived. 'Judith, I'm so sorry. You should have come on up to the rectory. I am all behind today.' He produced the key from his pocket.

The church was very cold as they switched on the lights. Bill Standing's first job on Sunday mornings as autumn arrived was to come over and go round the back to the boiler house to make sure the heating was on. On the other days of the week it was as cold as a tomb in here.

'Have you got the numbers?' Judith was heading towards the organ, which was up in the side-aisle.

'Here you are. All easy ones.' Mike smiled. 'I took pity on you.'

She glanced at him sharply. 'You sound as though you hadn't given it a thought before I rang you.'

'Not quite true.' Damn it, he didn't need a lecture. 'I had given the theme of my sermon a great deal of thought.' That at least was true, even if he hadn't got much down on paper. 'It is not always easy to select the right subject.'

He watched as she slid onto the seat, unlocked the lid, switched on the pump and lights. 'I'll leave you to it, Judith.'

'I'll drop the key in on my way home.' She was leafing through the music.

There was no way he could say no. All he could do was hope she would put it through the letterbox without disturbing him.

She didn't. Only forty minutes later there was a knock at the door. 'Here you are, Mike.' She was past him and in the hall before he could protest. Dropping the key on the table, she went towards his study. 'So, is the sermon finished?'

'Just about.' He hovered in the doorway behind her. 'In fact, I have to spend the rest of the evening working. I'll go over it again last thing.' He frowned. She had walked over to his desk and was staring openly at the monitor. The coloured screen-saver gave nothing away.

'I've told you before, Mike, you should let me help you with your paperwork.' Her gaze had strayed from the computer to the heaps of letters scattered over his desk. 'You need some secretarial assistance and I would be more than happy to give you a hand.'

He took a deep breath. 'That's kind of you, Judith, but I have a system, believe it or not.' He grinned at her. 'No one else could possibly understand it and I'm very happy to muddle through in my own way.' God preserve him from having her in the house any more than she was already!

She gave a small, disappointed laugh. 'Well, the offer is there.'

'And much appreciated. If I get too behind I'll let you know.' He paused. 'If there's nothing else, Judith, I should get on –'

'You went to see Lyndsey Clark.' She swung round to face him.

'How on earth did you know that?' Mike could feel his impatience growing.

'Her neighbour told me. She saw you. I told you not to go and see her, Mike. I told you to leave her to me.'

Mike frowned. 'Judith, my dear, it is not for you to say who I do or do not see. I welcome your advice, but you must allow me to make my own decisions.' He spoke firmly.

She clicked her tongue against the roof of her mouth, plainly irritated. 'What did she say?'

'As it happens, she was out when I called.'

'So you didn't see her.'

'No.'

'May the Lord be praised.' Judith was standing with her back to his desk now and she folded her arms, effectively barring his way. 'Don't go near her, Mike. I know the girl. When I first came across her I thought she was relatively harmless. Ineffectual. Playing at witchcraft, evil and dangerous though it is. But I was wrong. It is far worse than I feared. She is poison. And she'd never listen to you anyway. The bishop will be horrified to hear you are consorting with people like her.'

Mike felt a surge of his customary distaste. 'The bishop, Judith, will be relieved to hear that I am doing my job, which is trying to help sinners and bring lost souls back to the fold. If he hears about it at all, and there is no reason that he should.'

He was beginning to think some fairly unsaintly thoughts about Judith. The woman's smug humourless face was too confrontational as she stood before him.

But she was smiling at him now, a thoughtful, almost calculating smile. 'Did John Downing get in touch, Mike?'

'He did. We talked it through.'

'And was he helpful?'

Mike met her gaze. He managed to return her smile. 'Indeed

198

he was. He is going to handle the whole thing. He told me not to worry.'

'Good.' She seemed genuinely relieved. 'I was worried about you, Mike.'

He nodded. 'So he said. Now, Judith, I must get on. I'm sorry, but there's a lot to do.'

'And it's nearly nine. Look, if you haven't eaten yet . . . ?' She was masking her aggression well, but her smile did not reach her eyes.

'No, Judith, I'm sorry. I won't have time to eat now.'

He wished he hadn't said the 'now'. She looked first crestfallen and then guilty. But it did the trick. 'I'll leave you, then. Don't forget to change the clocks. I'll see you tomorrow?'

'Tomorrow, Judith. Good night.'

He closed the door behind her and drew the bolt firmly, aware that she could probably hear it sliding into place, and took a deep breath.

John Downing hadn't been in touch again and Mike had no intention of ringing him. Or of confiding in his helpful lay reader. Or the bishop.

And now he really did have a sermon to write!

It was midnight before he printed up the last pages, clipped them together and switched off the computer. With a sigh he headed for the door. The house was in darkness and the central heating had clicked off at eleven, leaving it cold.

Wearily he climbed the stairs and made for his bedroom, thinking about Judith. He foresaw difficulty there. She had been in the parish a long time and obviously had some powerful friends, both in the church and amongst his parishioners. It would not do to alienate her. On the other hand she represented a wing of the church he disliked intensely. Repressive. Old-fashioned and at the same time evangelical. Unforgiving. Joyless.

Puritan. That was the word.

He switched on his bedroom light and walked to the window. The wall of mist outside was thicker than ever now, coming up off the river, pressing against the glass, blanketing any sounds from the road. He stared at it for a moment with a shiver of distaste, then he reached for the curtains and drew them across, shutting out the night. Sally would have loved a night like this.

He turned wistfully towards the bed and drew back the cover. She would have laughed and demanded music and roaring log fires and made gallons of soup and homemade bread. He shook his head sadly. She was probably still demanding all those things, but of another man. Their relationship had survived his abandonment of teaching, but not his resignation from the job in industry and his decision to train for the priesthood. She had never wanted marriage anyway, and she was not prepared to cope with his vocation. 'I would fight another woman for you, Mike. I can't fight God!' she had said, clinging to him, that last day when they had talked it all through like grown-ups. 'I can't do it. There isn't enough room for three of us in this relationship. I know that's a cliché and I know it's small-minded of me. I know it's my fault. I've tried and tried. But I can't do it. And it'll get worse. You'll want a wife who can make jam and dole out sympathy and attend the WI or live in an inner-city parish and pick used needles and condoms off the doorstep. I can't do that, Mike. I never will be able to. Better quit now, before you grow to hate me.'

It had been the right decision. Of course it had. But how he missed her. He sighed. Emma had made the same connections in her mind. The inner city or Gilbert White. He sat down on the bed miserably and he shivered again.

Sally was a harlot. She did not believe in the sacrament of marriage. You did right to put her behind you . . .

The voice in his head was so clear he looked round, expecting to see someone there. He took a deep breath. He was imagining things. He had been sitting in front of the computer for too long.

'Christ be with me, Christ within me,
Christ behind me, Christ before me . . .'

The woman Judith is steadfast in the Lord. She would not suffer a witch to live, a witch like Sarah Paxman . . .

'Stop it!' Mike stood up. 'Who are you?'

His brain was whirling and he closed his eyes. Sounds. Voices. Snatches of speech played in his ears as though he were tuning in to band after band of distant radio transmissions. He spun round, his hands to his head, and before he realised what he was doing he had fallen to his knees, clawing at his scalp as though trying to tear the sounds out of his head. 'Christ be with me. Christ within me – dear God!' He screwed up his eyes and raised his hands towards the ceiling. 'In the name of our Lord, Jesus Christ, STOP!'

Total silence.

Opening his eyes, he stared round the room. It looked absolutely normal.

Shaking, he climbed to his feet and made for the door. Walking unsteadily downstairs to his study, he went over to his desk and sat down, staring unseeing at the pile of papers in front of him, then slowly he reached for his diary. Tony and Ruth Gilchrist's number was written firmly inside the front cover underneath that of John Downing, whom he had no intention of contacting. The couple of times he had tried to ring the Gilchrists before, hoping they were back from their trip to see the new grandchild, there had been no answer. They had presumably decided to extend their stay. Oh God, how he needed to hear Tony's calm, reassuring voice. Please, please, let them be back, and if they were, let them not mind being rung at this hour. He picked up the phone. The bell rang on and on in their empty house and at last he replaced the receiver in despair. They had not even set the answering machine.

He lay in bed for a long time, unable to sleep, his eyes staring up at the ceiling above his head, tracing the faint shadows from the window. The mist had retreated as quickly as it had come, to leave a cold starry night. Frost was on the way. A car drove down the road outside and for a second its headlights shone in onto the wall as it turned the corner of the lane. It drove on and the room was dark once more. Eventually he dozed.

The woman, Sarah, had been to see him again. She had walked into his house in South Street demanding that his servants show her into his presence and she stood there haranguing him about the witch, Liza Clarke. He watched her, listening with only half a mind on what she was saying. The other half was occupied with her. Sarah. Last time she had come to Mistley Thorn she had been decently dressed in black with white collar and cuffs and apron with a hood over her white linen cap. This time she was dressed like the royalist harlot she was; dressed as she so frequently appeared in his dreams. She wore an underskirt of pink poplin, trimmed in velvet ribbon and over it a dress of pale blue wool. There were pearls at her throat and in her ears, and her shoes were high heeled. Over her shoulders she wore a black cloak lined with blue silk.

'You have done nothing to free her, Master Hopkins!' She stepped nearer to him and he smelled lavender and rosewater on her skin. 'Nothing! And after all I asked you! Liza is not a witch.' The chatelaine at her waist chinked softly as she moved. Her hair, beneath the goffered cap, was fair and soft. A stray curl stuck to her forehead. 'You have to let her go. You cannot accuse her!'

'She is already accused, mistress.' He managed to keep his voice steady. He was intensely aware that in her high-heeled shoes she was taller than him. He stepped back, straightening his shoulders, pleased that he had not removed his hat when he came in. The high crown gave him height and presence.

'Have you tortured her? You and Mary Phillips? I have heard what you do to these women!'

'We do the Lord's work, mistress.' He kept his voice steady with difficulty. 'It is our duty before Him to weed out the servants of the Devil.'

'She does not serve the Devil!' Sarah took a step closer, her eyes flashing with anger, and he shrank back. 'She is a God-fearing woman.'

He smiled sourly. 'I hardly think so.' He could feel himself about to cough. He tried to suppress it, failed and turned away, his body racked by spasms of choking. There were flecks of blood on the linen kerchief he pressed to his mouth. 'Please, go, mistress!' There were tears of pain in his eyes he did not intend to let her see. 'Go!'

'I am not going until I have your promise, Master Hopkins!' Her voice was immediately behind him. He could smell the salt-woman scent of her, almost feel the silken rustle of her clothes.

He spun round. 'I said, go! Or do you wish to face arrest yourself, as a conspirator with her in the Devil's work!'

'You wouldn't dare arrest me.' She was so close she had to look down to see into his eyes. 'Your victims, Master Hopkins, are all poor defenceless woman with no one to speak for them. Women who are a drain on the parish. Women who have no family or friends. I have family and friends, Master Hopkins. I have money and property, from my late husband's estate. You would not dare to touch one hair of my head!' Her eyes were fixed on his, unblinking. He could see the soft bloom on her cheeks, the velvet shadows on her skin where her breasts disappeared into her bodice. Her pupils were pinpoints in the hazel irises. 'Let her go, Master Hopkins, let her go.'

Her eyes were changing shape before his gaze. As he watched, fascinated, he realised that the strange smoky colour he found so intriguing was becoming greener. Her hair was darkening, grow-ing straight beneath the cap. But the anger was growing, growing . . . and suddenly he was very afraid.

With a shout of fear, Mike sat up in the darkness, his heart hammering under his ribs. '"Christ be with me, Christ within me" –' It was the same dream. The dream in which he, Mike Sinclair, had somehow slipped into the skin of Matthew Hopkins. Hauling himself out of bed, he staggered over to the window and heaving it up he leant out, taking deep breaths of the ice-cold air. 'Our Father, who art in heaven . . .'

The woman in his dream had been so vivid. So close he could smell her, touch her, hear every rustle of her skirts, and in those last few seconds he realised he had recognised her. She was no longer just a shadow, a ghost from the past.

She was Emma Dickson.

39

Sunday October 25th

END OF BRITISH SUMMER TIME

Emma woke with a start. For a moment she lay disorientated, staring into the darkness. Cautiously she put out a hand and felt the solid warm pressure of Piers next to her. She sighed with relief. She had been afraid after their quarrel that he would somehow disappear in the night. Carefully she wriggled closer, snuggling up against his back, aware of a sudden purr coming from the bedclothes at the foot of the bed. Max or Min was in bed with them. With a happy smile she closed her eyes and in minutes she was asleep again. The dream returned at once.

Sarah had ridden straight back to Liza's cottage. No one had been near it since the old woman had been arrested. She had crept back late in the evening the day after Liza had been taken and laid the two dead cats side by side in the flower bed, covering their bodies with earth and flowers. She gazed down at the tell-tale mound, then sadly she turned aside to pull a few branches from the rosemary bush by the path. She laid them gently over it, then went on into the house. The old lady's possessions had not been touched; no one in the village had dared come in. The pestle and mortar, the jugs, all lay where they had fallen. The herbs had wilted and died, the fire had long been cold ashes; the water in the cauldron had a skim of dust. Sarah's eyes filled with tears as she moved towards the table and trailed her fingers through the crumpled leaves and petals.

'No!' She banged her fists on the table. 'No, I won't let him do it.' She groaned out loud, shaking her fists at the ceiling. 'This cannot be happening. This cannot be allowed to happen!' As she walked round the table her angrily swishing skirts raised a dusty smell of meadowsweet and lavender from the dried strewn herbs on the floor.

'Help me, Liza!' She demanded angrily of the dark corner near the hearth. 'Where are you? Help me!'

There was no answer.

'Liza! Tell me what to do!' She walked over and stared down at the scattering of cold ash. Liza always kept the hearth immaculately swept but now the broom lay on the floor. Near it was Liza's old woven bag. It looked as though it had been trampled deliberately into the dust. She stopped and picked it up, hugging it for a moment to her, careless of the dirt on her gown.

'Mistress, I've been looking for you.'

She jumped as a shadow darkened the door. 'Is that you, John Pepper?'

'Your father bids you return to the house, mistress. He does not think it safe for you to come here.' The man's eyes were everywhere, darting, inquisitive, fearful.

Sarah felt a wave of irritation. 'I have no need of an escort, John.'

'No, Mistress Sarah, but your father thinks it best. There are soldiers abroad everywhere and all sorts with them. Nowhere is safe while this war rages round the land and no one knows who is friend and who is foe.' He scowled as he gave the cottage one further distasteful glance. 'I shall wait outside, mistress, if you must spend further time in here.' She felt a moment of guilt. Since her brother's death she was her father's only child. His anguish when he had heard that news had been so painful she had found it hard to watch, her own terrible grief somehow subordinated to his.

As John Pepper moved away from the door and disappeared from view the sunlight flooded back into the house. She frowned. His loyalty to her and to her father was beyond question but there had been an undertone in his voice she did not care for. Thoughtfully she moved back to the table, staring down at the tools of Liza's trade as herb wife and she shook her head. She had forgotten the war and was thinking back to the days of her childhood when Liza, in a clean neat cap and gown and white apron had helped in the nursery of the Bennett home. 'Listen carefully, my duck.' She could hear Liza's voice now, in her head. 'You're the eldest girl,' the only girl as it turned out, 'and so there are things you should know. Secret things.'

Things she had forgotten. Or had she? When she had set her heart on handsome young Robert Paxman as a husband, she had remembered them then. Liza's husky, seductive whisper in her ear: 'If you want something, my duck, you can have it. Remember that; you can have anything in the whole world if you want it enough and you know the way.' Secretly, half afraid, half excited at the sense of power it gave her, she had risen from her bed as the light of the full moon flooded in at the window and making sure Agnes was still asleep, she had crept out into the garden.

'Mistress, your father will be waiting. He will be worried.' John

Pepper's voice interrupted her thoughts and she jumped guiltily. 'In my view this place should be burned to the ground.' He was just outside, on the path. 'It's imbued with her evil, so it is.'

'That's not true, John!' she rebuked him sharply. 'Liza's not evil. She's just an old woman who has done much good with her medicines. And you were fond of her yourself, not long ago if I remember rightly!' Turning towards the door, she glanced once more round the low-ceilinged cottage room before walking out into the sunshine. It was only after he had pulled the door closed behind her that she realised she was still clutching Liza's old bag.

The crash against the window pane woke Emma with a start in time to see Min jump off the bed and up onto the sill where she sat, chattering angrily into the darkness. Presumably a bird had flown into the glass in the dark. Emma sat up uneasily, aware of the solid sleeping body still warmly bedside her in the bed. It was comforting.

She had been dreaming. She frowned. She had been dreaming about the house as it had been long ago. Even as she struggled to remember she could feel the bright sunshine, the smell of dry herbs hanging from the hooks in the kitchen ceiling, the darkness of the shadows, slipping away. She tried desperately to clutch at them, to fix them in her memory, but they had gone, leaving her full of unease. What was it that she could not recall? What was it that was so unpleasant it swam in her subconscious, leaving nothing but terror?

Piers stirred beside her. 'What is it, Em? Go back to sleep! We've got an extra hour in bed in the morning, remember.'

She lay back against the pillows and stared towards the windows, watching the cat's silhouette against the stars. The mist must have cleared. As she closed her eyes she found herself hoping she would go back to the same dream.

40

It was light when Emma next awoke, and she was screaming.

'Emma! Em, for God's sake, wake up!' Piers was shaking her by the arm. 'Em, what is it? What's wrong? Have you got a pain?'

She stared at him wildly and for a moment she didn't recognise him.

'Emma! Wake up! Em, are you all right?'

'Piers?' She clutched at one of the pillows and held it tightly to her chest. 'Oh, Piers, I had such an awful dream.'

He had climbed out of bed. 'Poor old you.' Coming round to her side he sat down beside her he put his arm round her. 'Hey, you're shaking. Come on, you're all right.' He frowned. 'Em, you're not still having nightmares about this place, are you?'

She shrugged, sniffing. 'It wasn't about this house. Not really.'

'Go on, then.' He stood up and walked over to the window. 'Tell me what it was about.'

She shook her head. 'It's all a jumble. People riding. The chink of harness. The sound of horses' hooves. Men, dressed in black, their faces so angry. So unforgiving. The terrible fear. And power-lessness.' She was sitting up now, still hugging the pillow, and as he watched she began to rock back and forth, tears trickling down her cheeks.

He sighed. 'It is this damned house, isn't it! Even now you're here, it's getting to you.' He paused, expecting her to deny it. She said nothing.

'Come on, Em. We're awake now. Why not get up, have a shower, then we'll have some breakfast. You'll feel better once you're up and about. I'll go and put some coffee on.' He hesitated. 'There's still room for you at home, you know. I'd love you to come back.'

She threw back the bedclothes. 'Piers –'

'I know.' He turned towards the door, heading for the bathroom. 'Thanks, but no thanks, eh?'

'Piers, that's not what I said. It's just that this is my life now –' she called after him, but he had gone.

When she ran downstairs he had been busy. 'Coffee, toast, eggs, sunny side up.' He grinned at her. 'My God, you look awful.'

'Thanks!' She sat down at the table and glared at the plate he put in front of her. 'Did you give the cats their breakfast?'

'Of course.' He sat down and leaning across he put his hand on hers. 'I've been thinking about things while I practised my new-found culinary arts. I can see I'll never winkle you out of here and, you're right we should have a country cottage. And this one would be perfect. Come back to town, Em, and we'll come down here at weekends. David Spencer rang me last week to ask after you. He said your job is still there for you. And you know you're missing it, really.'

'No, Piers. I'm not.'

'Oh, come on. When we talked about it last night at the Wests –'

'We both saw the strain that woman was under. The exhaustion, the stress, the battle to be endlessly on top of everything. You know, Piers, when I first saw this house, I never thought about the job at all. It was irrelevant. It didn't matter to me. Oh, yes, later, of course I thought about it. But not at first. Then, when I did spend those endless hours tearing myself apart about whether to do this or not, it was only because of the money. I could afford to buy the cottage, but could I afford to live here without a job? I'm not a fool. I know it's unlikely that I'll make a living out of herbs. But, do you know, it didn't worry me. And it still doesn't, and you know why? Not because David has given me some work, but because living in London – the lifestyle, the holidays, the restaurants, everything – is so expensive. Stop doing it all and there is no expense. Oh, I'll have electricity, oil, council tax, all that, but it is minuscule compared to what you shell out on your flat and I can grow most of my own food. I still have some of my savings left and part of Daddy's fund. If I'm careful I won't need any more money. And no, I'm not bored. Or lonely.'

Piers stared at her in silence. 'You mean that, don't you?'

'Yes, I do.'

'What about Whiskas? You have two hungry cats to support.'

'I'll cope.'

'And a pension? What about your old age?'

'I'll think of something. Listen, Piers. There is another way. You could come here. Join me?'

'No way. I'm sorry. Oh, Em, I think you're an idiot.' He pushed away his plate, untouched. 'There's not much point in me being here even now, is there? It really is over. Your life is here now and you're not going to compromise.' He stood up.

'Piers? Where are you going?'

'Back to dreadful, expensive London.'

Ten minutes later he was packed and climbing into his car.

'Piers.' She was trying to hold back the tears. 'You can't just go like this. Please. I want us to stay friends at least.'

He paused and came back to stand in front of her. Catching her hands, he stared at her for a moment. 'I hate to see you so unhappy, Em, but I can't do anything about it, can I? You won't let me. Liza's has won. I'll be there for you if you need me, but I'll be in London, and . . .' He hesitated. 'Em, the offer is there now, but it might not always be that way.' He shrugged. 'A man can't wait forever. Kiss the cats for me, sweetheart. And take care.'

Whoever or whatever lived in the house with Emma had not bothered to try and scare Piers away. There had been no point. He was no threat.

The house was unbearably empty after he had gone and there was no sign of the cats, so pulling on her jacket Emma walked down the lane towards the village. The air was cold and blustery and she walked fast, trying to blot out the loneliness and misery which had enveloped her. She wasn't sure what she had expected of Piers, but not the terrible sudden finality of that goodbye.

Walking down past the Maltings towards the Thorn Inn, she stopped to watch the water spouting from the beak of the swan fountain in the middle of its stone basin. Then she wandered down towards the quay.

The mud glistened in the morning light and she watched the choppy waves running up the channel. A few boats still swung to anchor on the tide, but most had been taken out of the water for the winter. She stood, her hands deep in her pockets.

'What are you doing here?' The voice behind her made her jump and she turned to see Lyndsey standing a few feet away with her bicycle.

210

Emma responded to the hostility in her voice with a wave of antagonism. 'So, this is your private patch as well, is it? I thought anyone could walk on the quay.'

'They can.' Lyndsey's face was wary. 'I thought you'd come to look for me.'

'No. Why should I?'

Lyndsey shrugged. 'No reason.'

'You mean because you were so damn rude the other night when I thought you needed rescuing and was willing to risk life and limb to do it?' Emma held her gaze.

Lyndsey flushed. Then she grinned with a small shrug. 'Something like that, I suppose. I'm sorry. I guess we frightened each other.'

'Look, Lyndsey.' Emma sighed. 'I had forgotten that you lived here. Let's start again. Do you want to come and have some tea or something in the café? I'm getting cold and there's no need for us to be enemies, is there?'

Lyndsey shrugged again. It seemed an all-purpose gesture with her, which could mean yes, no or maybe. She leaned the bicycle against the wall and they walked up the narrow street towards the old sail sheds which had been turned into workshops and galleries and boasted a small tea shop.

Sitting by the window looking out across the full expanse of the river, Emma waited for Lyndsey to speak. When she said nothing, she sighed. 'Alex was worried about you.' Far out in the grey, white-topped waves the ribs of an old shipwreck stuck out of the water.

'Alex is always worried about something.'

'He seems to be a very kind man.'

'He is.' Lyndsey looked up at last. 'He's a good friend.'

'He thought you'd disappeared after you ran out in the rain. He thought something might have happened to you. We both did.'

'I went away for a bit, that's all. I needed to think about what had happened.'

Emma studied the other woman's face. She was looking down at the table, idly drawing the teaspoon through the sugar in the earthenware bowl between them.

'Why don't you like me living at Liza's?' she asked gently.

Lyndsey glanced up. 'I have my reasons.'

'I've known the house since I was a child, you know.' Emma went on quietly. 'I wanted it so much I left the man I love to come and live here.'

'That was a stupid thing to do.' Lyndsey's face hardened.

'Yes,' Emma said bleakly. 'Yes, it was.'

'So, why don't you go back to him?'

'I don't know.'

They eyed each other warily. 'I've been having nightmares,' Emma went on, almost to herself. 'About the cottage. In the old days.'

The spoon dropped from Lyndsey's fingers, scattering sugar across the table. 'Sorry, messy!' She brushed the sugar onto the floor.

'I will take care of the house. I do know how special it is,' Emma went on. 'And to be honest I'm not likely to venture into the churchyard. Especially not at night. Especially as it belongs to someone else.' She shivered. 'I really wasn't spying.'

'Good.' Lyndsey narrowed her eyes, staring out of the window across the river towards the wreck. Above it a streak of blue sky had appeared between the torn rags of cloud. 'I have good reasons to be there, and permission.'

'I'm sure you have.' Reasons like black magic. Spells. Emma found she couldn't look Lyndsey in the eyes and ask what she believed and what she did. She looked so normal. Surreptitiously, she crossed her fingers under the table and suddenly she found herself wishing Piers was there too. How he would laugh if she confessed to taking tea with the local witch and how he would mock her if she told him she was scared.

41

Sunday afternoon

As he had half expected on a Sunday, the shop was closed. Stepping out into the street, Mark looked up at the windows. There was no of sign of life. Or anything else. He sighed. He could always go and beg a key off Stan Barker, but he wasn't sure, now he was here, that he wanted to do that. The street was deserted. The brief few moments of sunshine had passed and soon it would begin to grown dark. Retracing his steps, he walked slowly up the High Street, crossed the road and walked back on the other side. Then, still on foot, he headed for Church Street and the rectory.

Mike was once again in front of the computer. He led Mark into the study. 'The only room with a fire,' he apologised, gesturing at one of the worn leather armchairs. 'I hate it when the clocks change. Suddenly winter is on its way with a vengeance and the nights start to get colder.'

'You haven't got to go and take a service or anything?' Mark sat down. 'I forgot Sunday is probably your busiest day.'

Mike shook his head. 'All the services are over. Have you been up to the shop?'

Mark nodded. 'I didn't go in. The place was locked up and somehow I didn't feel I wanted to.' He cleared his throat. 'Have you got a video machine?'

Mike grimaced. 'I'm not quite that out of touch. It's in the sitting room. Through here.'

The room was ice cold. Somewhere in the bowels of the house, the central heating was starting to clank into life but it would be a while before the heat reached this room. Mike drew the curtains across the large darkening windows and switched on the TV.

'It's not long.' Mark slid the video out of its cardboard sleeve. 'Only a few seconds.'

They watched the relevant bit of film three times, then made their way back into the warmth of the study.

'So.' Mark threw himself down in his chair. 'What do you make of it?'

Mike propped himself on the corner of the desk. 'It does look like something, certainly,' he said cautiously. 'I went over there, you know, after we spoke on the phone.'

'And?'

Mike didn't answer for a moment. 'I don't know if there was anything there that I didn't generate from my own imagination.'

'You don't sound very sure.'

'No, well. It's easy to get sucked into this kind of thing. Very easy,' he said slowly. 'There was a sense of evil there. Yes, there was. But it could have come, as I said, from my imagination. Then again, it could have come from Hopkins, or it could have come from the witches. Everyone assumes they were innocent. They might not have been.'

'We're coming back to do some more filming at the end of the week.' Mark shook his head. 'If that was a face on the film, it is potentially very exciting.'

'If.' Mike frowned uneasily. 'It could just be a trick of the light, I suppose.'

'It could be.' Mark did not sound as though he believed it. 'We'll set up again. Same camera position. Same lighting angles. Same shadows, hopefully. See what happens. And I'm getting hold of some more sensitive equipment. We might even try EVP. Electronic voice phenomena. Ever heard of it? It captures ghostly voices outside the normal range of our hearing.' He waited for a moment, watching his host.

Mike had begun to pace up and down the worn carpet. He stopped, frowning thoughtfully. 'I'm sorry, but I don't think you should go back, Mark. Not to try and film again.'

'So, you do believe it.'

'To be honest, I don't know what I believe. But I feel uneasy. Afraid, if you like. If that is a face, it could be anyone. Hopkins. A good witch. An evil witch. I don't believe Hopkins was an intentionally bad man. I think he was sincere in his own way. I

214

think he honestly believed these women were in league with the Devil. But whatever residues are left in that shop are best left alone.'

Mark pulled a face. 'I think Hopkins was a sadistic, vicious misogynist. I think he enjoyed torturing women.'

'No.' Mike shook his head. 'No, he really thought they had congress with Satan. He thought that only repentance and death could save their souls. He did not enjoy hurting them.' He was speaking more vehemently than he had intended. 'He felt the evil that we're feeling; he believed those old women were as guilty as hell.' He wiped his forehead suddenly, astonished to find that he was sweating.

Mark did not appear to have noticed. He exhaled loudly. 'I'm not convinced. 'And I can't believe you are. Not really.' He grinned. 'But, whatever one believes about the old women or Hopkins's motives, surely it's quite possible he is not resting quietly in his grave?'

'It's possible.' Mike sat down opposite him. 'You're not recording this, are you?'

Mark shook his head. 'I wouldn't do that to you.'

'Good. Then I'll be honest with you. I think it's very possible. Too many people are thinking about him. All the time. The town doesn't let him rest. He's in the guide books. He's in the pubs. He's in the museum. You are making a film about him. The local witch is conjuring him in the old churchyard. This is not good news. The trouble is,' he shook his head, 'I'm guilty of it myself. I've picked up on the "vibes",' he waved his fingers in the air to denote inverted commas, 'and I'm having nightmares about the man.'

Mark raised an eyebrow. 'You, too? Then talk to us for the film. I think it's important.'

'Unfortunately I can't. I've been warned that the bishop would take a dim view.'

'Perhaps we could persuade him?'

'I doubt it.'

'Is there anyone else we could get to give the church's side of the picture? I understand there are still exorcists around.'

Mike grinned 'It's called the ministry of deliverance now. And it's a specialist division of the church.'

'So, let me speak to the specialist.'

215

'I'll ask. That's all I can do, I'm afraid. No promises.'

'That's all I want.' Mark stood up and turned to the door. 'I only called in on my way home, actually. I've been up to Ipswich. We're thinking of doing another programme for the series up there. There's a lovely old house in the dock area, very sinister and run down, very photogenic.' He grinned, hesitating. 'Mike, I've got a strange feeling about Barker's shop. It's going to make a fantastic film, but I do want to keep the church involved if I can. Insurance.' He gave a wry laugh. 'None of the other ghosts we've followed up have scared me like this.'

'Then give it up, Mark, please.' Mike had followed him into the hall.

'Sorry. There's too much money invested in this programme already, and it's too good a story. You mention a present day witch – it would be great if we could film her. I'm going to do a lot more research. I'll let you know what I dig up. And if you find out any more about Hopkins I'd be very interested. You are quite knowledgeable about him, aren't you?'

Mike gave a wry grin. 'Oh yes, I'm learning all the time.' He watched Mark stride off across the gravel. 'Only too knowledge-able,' he added grimly under his breath. He closed the door and went back into the study to stand gazing thoughtfully down into the fire.

While he was talking to Mark, his dream had come back to him in astonishing detail. The feelings, the smells, the sounds of the village and the details of the gown of the woman who had come to see him. The pink petticoat, the blue woollen dress, the silk cloak and the woman's face, contorted with anger, the golden flecks in her hazel eyes. Sarah Paxman. But it wasn't Sarah Paxman. It was Emma Dickson.

42

Monday October 26th

'Bugger!'

The whisper in the dark woke Alex from a deep sleep with a start. He groaned. 'What time is it?'

'Half past five and I've just holed my tights.' He heard Paula fumbling and the bedside light came on.

He screwed up his eyes crossly. 'Bloody hell! Isn't it a bit early?'

'I've got an early meeting! It seemed a good idea, with the extra hour.'

Alex groaned again. 'Why don't you get dressed in the bathroom, then? So you can turn on the light and see what you're doing!'

'I do, normally.' She threw the balled tights into the corner. 'Sod it! Where are the new ones.' She was rummaging in a drawer.

'Calm down. There's plenty of time for you to catch the train.'

'That's easy for you to say!' She ripped open the new packaging. 'Don't forget James needs to take his new house shoes and Sophie must find her coloured pencils.' She hauled up the tights and adjusted her narrow black skirt.

'When do I ever forget what the kids need for school?'

'Perhaps when your mind is totally taken up with the beautiful new lady at Liza's,' she said tartly.

He sighed audibly. 'Paula.' They had been quarrelling all the previous day, sniping at each other every time they were out of earshot of the children, mostly about Emma.

Alex had inadvertently started the ball rolling. 'You know, I've been thinking,' he had said as they sat over their coffee with the Sunday papers spread out on the kitchen table between them.

The children were playing quietly for once although it hadn't lasted. 'I'm going to offer to help her get that nursery off the ground. It's the perfect small business opportunity.'

'You haven't got time. You're taking care of the children.'

'The children go to school.' He reached for the review section of the *Sunday Times*. 'And this house does not exactly challenge.'

For some reason she had taken that as an insult. From then on they had batted petty irritations back and forth at each other all day and the atmosphere had not improved when Paula tried to reach Lyndsey on the phone. 'Why doesn't the girl have an answering machine! For God's sake, where is she?'

'I can't help wondering if we don't use Lyn too much,' Alex had put in mildly. 'Why don't we try one of the babysitting circles as back-up?'

'Because I have no intention of sitting other people's kids,' she had retorted, 'and they won't have you because you're a man.'

'OK.' He took a deep breath. 'Well, she is obviously out so we're not going to get her this evening.' They had wanted to go up to the Stour Bay Café for a meal but now they would have to eat at home. Alex offered to go and fetch an Indian, but she curtly refused. In the end they had eaten scampi and chips out of the freezer with the children. Alex watched Paula go upstairs when they had finished and he frowned. When she came back, he was conciliatory. 'Paula, sweetheart. Are you sure you aren't finding all this commuting too much of a strain? We could swap. I could work. I could have a go at getting back into the City . . .'

They both knew it would never happen. And Paula loved her job far too much to give it up.

'Better idea: we could move back to London and I wouldn't have to commute.' She spoke sharply and unguardedly in front of Sophie, who stared at her in horror. 'I don't want to move to London.' The child's eyes filled with tears. 'My best friends are here.'

'And here we'll stay.' Alex reached out to pull her close. 'Don't cry, sweetie. Mummy didn't mean it.'

'Lyn says we'll stay here forever and ever!' Sophie announced defiantly. From the safety of her father's knees, she glared at her mother. 'Lyn says we don't have to do what you say. She says she can make sure we stay here with her. By magic. She promised!'

The shock of her words rendered both parents silent for a moment. Then Paula's tirade had started.

'That girl is obviously turning into a menace! You're right. We are using her too much. We shouldn't have trusted her! How dare she interfere with family decisions. She has no business having a view at all. It is nothing to do with her.'

Sophie's tears had turned to full-blown howls which Alex's hug did nothing to stem, and were then reinforced by James, who on hearing his sister's shrieks ran into the room, headed for his father's knees and started to cry in sympathy. The effect on Paula, faced with the three other members of her family seemingly solidly against her was devastating. Her face crumpled and she had fled the room.

Alex, trying to comfort the children, barely had time to acknowledge the deep warning bell ringing somewhere inside his head.

'I'll try and find someone else to babysit from time to time,' he said later when, with the children comfortably ensconced at the kitchen table painting, he discovered Paula in front of the TV.

'And speak to Lyndsey. Tell her to watch what she says in front of the children. They believe anything at their age.' She did not take her eyes off the screen.

His anxiety was still there. 'I shall certainly do that,' he said thoughtfully. 'They're getting too attached to her. It's my fault. I use her too much to look after them.'

Paula finally tore her eyes away from the programme she was watching. 'I can't blame you for wanting to get out of the house. After all, I do.' She paused. 'But don't go and get involved with Emma Dickson.'

'Oh, Paula, not that again!' He raised his fists heavenward. Couldn't she see that Emma was not a problem? 'What on earth did she say to upset you so much?'

'She did not upset me!'

'It's because she's turned her back on all you hold dear, isn't it? You can't bear to think she's rejected the City.'

'She has also rejected that nice man of hers, if you were paying any attention at all. And she will be looking for a replacement.'

There was a moment's stunned silence, then Alex laughed. 'You can't be serious. Oh, Paula, my love, I'm flattered you should think she'd even look at me, but no –'

'Why?' she interrupted coldly. '*I* looked at you! You think she's too attractive? Too sophisticated? Too young? I doubt if she's even five years younger than me! And I know you. You wouldn't hesitate to look at her!'

'No! No! No!' Whatever he said would be wrong now. He couldn't win. The trouble was, she had identified the wrong target. Attractive as she was, Emma would be no threat to their family. He valued his marriage far too much. The threat, if there was one, was from Lyndsey, and the fact that he would never dare tell his wife that the babysitter he had trusted with their children was a self-professed witch. Oh, she knew about the Wicca, but like him she had thought it totally harmless. Now he was not so sure. Not so sure at all.

Lying back in bed after the sound of Paula's car, on her way to the station to catch the train to London, had died away, Alex relished the silence. In at most half an hour the kids would be waking up and the fraught getting-ready-for-school/breakfast routine would get under way. For an hour he wouldn't even have one second to himself to think, then the rest of the day would stretch ahead of him. Housework. Shopping. But then, he smiled to himself half guiltily, maybe he would pay Emma a visit and test the water regarding a new job.

43

Mike parked his car some distance away from the churchyard and from Emma's cottage and walked up the lane, aware of a certain sense of furtiveness. On his shoulder he carried a black bag, a freebie from a book promotion he had attended once in Canterbury. In it were the items he needed in order to celebrate Holy Communion.

As he passed Liza's he glanced up at the windows, visible in the early morning light just beyond the hedge. Was that one of her cats sitting on the window sill, looking down at him? He looked away hurriedly in case she was there with it and saw him staring.

The place where he could duck into the undergrowth and climb the wall into the churchyard was invisible from her windows. With a quick glance over his shoulder at the road he pushed between the elder and the hawthorn and scrambled over the old bricks. Once inside and out of sight of any passer-by, he paused and looked around. His heart had begun to thud uncertainly under his ribs and he felt his breathing grow shallow and fast. He stared round again, trying to steady himself. He must not show fear. He must not feel fear. If he did he was done for. Useless. Ineffectual. The early-morning light was pale and cold, throwing a dull monochrome across the grass. He found himself wishing fervently that the sun would come up.

Putting down his bag he shivered again, pulling up the collar of his waterproof jacket. Then he rammed his hands into his pockets. The area of ground he was interested in was some twenty-five yards away, half hidden from where he was standing. Perhaps before he went any closer, he would pray.

'Our Father who art in heaven . . .' He whispered the words out loud and stopped. It was as though the world was holding its breath. The rustle of drying autumn leaves ceased as the brisk wind dropped. The gentle confidential murmuring of a small bird

221

in the ivy near him ceased. He could almost feel the beady little eyes on him, watching him closely. 'Hallowed be thy name. Thy kingdom come.' He glanced round again. 'Thy will be done . . .' He stopped. He was sure the temperature had dropped several degrees and he could feel the odd spot of rain on his head. 'As it is in heaven. Forgive us our trespasses, as we forgive . . .' He stopped again. Somewhere near him an owl had hooted, the long quavering call of the night. He caught sight of the shadow on silent wings whisk across the far wall out of sight. What was it Shakespeare said: the bird of night did sit, even at noon-day, hooting and shrieking. Something like that. All right, so it was bad luck to see an owl by day. But night was still very close, lurking in the wooded valleys and under the trees nearby. 'Deliver us from evil. Christ be with me. Christ within me. Christ behind me. Christ before me . . .' Taking a deep breath, he picked up his bag and strode forward to the spot where he imagined Lyndsey to have been standing.

He found a stone, half buried in the mud. It probably came from the fabric of the old church itself. It would do for an altar. Crouching down, he unpacked the bag. Inside was a small Communion set and stole. He put the stole round his neck and opened the little case, taking out the cross and setting it on the stone. Kneeling in front of it on the wet grass, he had to force himself to concentrate. The urge to look over his shoulder was almost unbearable.

Pray. Keep focused.

Quickly, he opened the containers of bread and wine. His hands were shaking. 'I am the resurrection and the life; he who believe in me, though he die yet shall he live . . .' His pulse rate was slowing. The familiar words were giving him strength. Whatever she had done here, this witch with her magic circles and her spells, it was not strong enough to withstand the love and protection of Christ.

When he had finished he stayed where he was, kneeling quietly in the grass for several minutes, then he opened his eyes. The churchyard was still, the shadows gone, the unquiet echoes had died. He looked round, then calmly reassured he set about packing up. When he stood up the knees of his trousers were soaked and muddy, and he had left two small dents in the grass, but the place felt clean, energised. The rite had worked.

Turning away, he slung his bag onto his shoulder and strode towards the wall.

Kill the witch!

The words were so loud he spun round, unsure whether they had been said out loud or whether they were in his own head.

You are a man of God. It is your duty to fight Satan!

Taking a deep breath, he gripped the strap of his bag.

Kill the witch!

'I have blessed this ground in the name of Jesus Christ!' Mike turned round slowly. Lifting his right hand, he made the sign of the cross. 'Let all who lie buried here rest in peace.' He paused, listening. 'From all evil and mischief; from sin, from the crafts and assaults of the Devil; from thy wrath and from everlasting damnation, Good Lord, deliver us.' His voice echoed in the silence with words from the Litany he wasn't even aware he knew by heart. There was no response, and he exhaled loudly, trying to collect himself again.

Forcing himself to walk slowly he crossed the churchyard, climbed the wall and returned to his car where he sat for a moment, his head back against the headrest, his eyes closed. His bag lay on the seat beside him.

The rap on the window nearly made him jump out of his skin. A face was peering at him only a few inches away through the glass.

'You all right, Vicar?'

It was Bill Standing. Mike took a deep breath and wound down the window. 'Hello, Bill. Yes, I'm fine, thanks. Just a bit tired.'

'You look peaky, Vicar, if you don't mind my saying so.' The old man shook his head. 'I thought that the other day when I was tidying round the graves and I saw you and Miss Sadler going into the church together. And I thought it again just now.' Mike was aware of a pair of shrewd eyes fixed on his face. 'You bin up to the old churchyard?'

Mike shrugged. No point in denying it. 'I have, yes.'

'Best not to meddle there unless you know what you're doing.' Bill shoved his hands into his pockets. 'They pulled that old place down for a reason, see. People don't hold with churches round here.'

Mike closed his eyes. When he opened them he didn't look at

223

Bill. 'It's my job to meddle in some things.' He was watching a file of gulls flying in up river against the wind.

'And then again it's not. You mind the living, Vicar. Leave the dead to theyselves.'

'And to you, eh, Bill? Keeping their graves nice and smart.'

Bill shook his head. 'Down at St Michael's maybe, but not up here. Never.'

'Does anyone look after it now?'

Bill shook his head. 'There are sheep in there. They keep the grass down.'

'That's not what I meant and you know it. I'm talking about something else, Bill.'

Bill chewed his lip thoughtfully. 'I know. If there's things need doing, they'll be done,' he said at last. 'Maybe with your help. Maybe not.'

There was a long silence.

Mike sighed. 'Do you know Lyndsey Clark?' he asked at last, cautiously.

'Yes, I knows Lyndsey.' Bill chuckled. 'Silly girl. Playing around with things she don't understand.'

'Then warn her off, will you? Please, warn her off.' Mike reached for the ignition. 'I've got to be going. Do you want a lift?'

The old man shook his head. He stood back and raised his hand. As Mike drove off he peered in the rear-view mirror. The old man was still standing in the road watching him.

44

Emma had pulled off her gardening gloves as she came in to answer the phone, hoping it would be the builder announcing that he was going to come back and finish off replacing some of the floorboards in the room which was supposed to be her study – the room where the computer was swiftly gathering dust as time and again she put off the idea of trying to put some reports together for David. In the background the radio was playing quietly. The kitchen was warm and very peaceful. She threw the gloves down on the table and picked up the receiver.

'Em? It's me!' Peggy's regular phone calls usually began with enquiries about Emma's health and well-being, whether she was eating properly and how the cats were settling in. Today she plunged straight into her conversation; she sounded excited. 'The most extraordinary thing has happened. Are you sitting comfortably?'

'What is it, Ma?' Emma pushed her wind-tangled hair back from her face with the back of her hand. She had been in the shed at the side of the terrace, sorting through the mountains of old clay pots and ancient gardening equipment she had found there. Some of it, she was sure, was old enough to donate to the local museum.

'Ever since you moved in I've been wondering about those holidays we spent at Manningtree with your Dad's grandparents when you were a child. They were such happy times.' There was a fractional silence as her mother gave a small sigh.

'Ma –'

'No, dear. Listen, your Dad never talked much about his own childhood, except that he loved going there too, of course, but I thought I'd sort through some boxes of papers and stuff of his in the attic to see if there was anything from those days, and I found a couple of old albums. They must have belonged to his mother.

Wonderful pictures of her Bennett parents and grandparents. It appears that they lived for generations at a place called Overly Hall, near the farmhouse where they lived when we went up there. It's about a mile from where you are now. Isn't that strange? That he never mentioned it? I'm sure I would have remembered if he had!'

For a moment Emma couldn't speak. 'You mean Dad's family have lived here for hundreds of years?'

'Sounds like it. Have you seen it. Does it still exist?'

'It still exists. It's the local manor house. Someone called Colonel Lawson lives there. I've seen him walking his dogs up the lane.'

'Well, perhaps it helps to explain your love of Liza's. You are a native of the area.' Peggy laughed gaily. 'You ought to go and see it, darling! See if he will show you round.'

'I might. Ma, when are you coming down to see me again?'

There was an unmotherly chortle from the other end of the phone. 'It may not be for a while, Em, I'm sorry. I was hoping to come again soon, but guess what? Dear old Dan wants us to go on holiday. To Mexico! I can't believe it! He won a premium bond, the first win he's had in about forty years and it's enough to take us away for two months! I've found someone to look after the shop. Look, I'll register this parcel of things to you. There are a few letters and two albums, then you'll have them safely, then I'm going shopping!'

Emma could hear the excitement bubbling away behind her mother's voice and she smiled. It was time Peggy had some fun and this sounded the most wonderful fun.

She sat where she was for several minutes after she put the phone down, lost in thought. Her head was reeling with the news. She did belong. Her ancestors had called to her down the centuries and she had heard without knowing why. Overly Hall was a lovely house; she had passed it once or twice on her explorations of the district. It was fifteenth-century, she guessed, gracious, mellow, perhaps the house to which Liza's and Liza's old walled garden had belonged once upon a time.

Almost without realising it she pulled on her coat and boots and she found herself wandering up the lane towards it, drawn by her excitement. It took her fifteen minutes to reach the elegant wrought-iron gates. She stopped and peered in. Two cars stood

226

outside the front door and as she was standing there, wondering if she dared go in and knock, another car drew up behind her. She stood back out of the way, but the driver lowered his window and glared at her. It was Colonel Lawson. 'Can I help you?'

She hesitated. 'I'm sorry. I was just looking. I'm Emma Dickson. I live down the lane at Liza's.'

'I've seen you.' He did not smile.

'I have just found out that my ancestors lived in this house and I couldn't resist strolling up the hill to have a look.' She shrugged.

'Indeed.' His expression did not soften. 'Well, it is not open to the public I'm afraid, so you will have to content yourself with looking from there.' He pressed a remote control on the dashboard of his car and the gates opened; he drove the car in and the gates closed behind him.

Emma was left open-mouthed, standing in the road. She turned away abruptly, hot with embarrassment. He could at least have smiled; have been friendly. She was, after all, a neighbour. So much for the hope that he might ask her in and fête her as a descendant of the family who had once lived in the house.

She stepped away from the gate, then hesitated for one last glance over her shoulder at the wisteria-covered walls, the tall barley-sugar chimneys and the windows with their elegant mullions. It was with a shock of recognition that she realised that in her dreams she had looked out of those same windows; that once, long ago, she had spent her childhood in that house and that it was there that a woman called Liza had cared for her, in the nurseries under the ancient slates.

45

After returning to the rectory from the churchyard, Mike had spent an hour pacing up and down. He had tried to reach Tony on the phone twice but there had been no reply and his two visits to parishioners on the other side of the town had done nothing to distract him. Walking back into the house he listened briefly to a phone message from Judith, decided to ignore it and reached for the whisky bottle; as far as he was concerned, the sun was over the yard arm. He drank a hefty slug and sat down at his desk with a sigh. Where was God when he needed him? Perhaps he should go to the church to pray. It was on days like these that he wondered if his faith was strong enough; had he made a dreadful mistake in joining the church? Reaching for the bottle again, he stared at it for a moment and then pushed it away. He rubbed his face hard with his hands. The trouble was, he was exhausted.

If someone had looked through the window ten minutes later they would have seen the rector fast asleep, his head cushioned on his arms on his desk, an empty glass at his elbow.

Matthew Hopkins slept badly; his phthisic dreams were violent and sudden, full of horror and fear or they were erotic beyond bearing. He was having one of the latter now. He had seen Sarah running towards his house in South Street, her shoes clicking on the rough cobbles, her skirts flying out behind her. In his dream she ran up the stairs, tearing off her cloak, her hair tumbling free of her cap. 'Master Hopkins, where are you?' He heard her throw open one door after another as she ran, searching for him. 'You have to speak to me. We can find a way for you to release Liza; for you to find her innocent!'

He smiled. There were always ways, if one knew how. He was standing in the middle of the room, his arms folded, waiting. When she came in he knew what the bargain would be. And now there she was, in the doorway, staring at him, her eyes alight with challenge.

'So, mistress. What will you offer for Liza's freedom?'

She raised an eyebrow. 'What will you take, Master Hopkins?' She took a step nearer. He could smell the scent of her skin, the rosewater on her hair, hear the faint rustle of her petticoats. He frowned. This was the daughter of a royalist family, beautiful, carefree, dedicated to a life of enjoyment and pleasure. The sorrow in her eyes was only temporary. It came from her brother's, her husband's deaths and her worry for her nurse and friend and, no doubt, coven sister, but it would soon pass and she would revert to type as a worthless hussy. He shuddered imperceptibly at the thought of such delicious, such forbidden fruit.

'Is the price my body, Master Hopkins?' She had moved closer. If he raised a hand he could touch her arm. He could see the faint down on her skin. See the trace of sweet moisture as her tongue ran quickly, eagerly, over her lips. 'Do I have your word that she will go free?'

He couldn't speak. He was fighting his own lust, his longing.

Smiling, she took a step closer. He could see the detail of the pretty ribbon *galants* at her waist and sleeves. Why was the woman not in mourning? Such clothes were an affront to all. Such extravagance. Such lack of prudence and wisdom and purity. He swallowed hard, feeling a constriction in his chest. Now was not the time to cough. He was finding it hard to breathe, but even so, without conscious thought he had reached out towards her, his fingers gently, so gently, touching the silk of her gown above her breasts.

She wore a chemise of the softest lawn and white stockings held up with green garters. 'Do I have your word, Matthew?' Her voice was soft, persuasive as she reached out to stroke his face. No woman had touched him with such gentleness since the day his mother had bathed his wounds after his grandmother had beaten him. On that occasion she had kissed his head and shrugged and told him to keep himself clean and chaste or he would be beaten again, and worse, he would go to hell and then she had turned away from him. His father had not been bothered with the matter; it had been the last day of his childhood.

His longing was unbearable. His loneliness of such aching depths that he could not contemplate a life where it continued. And here was Sarah, with her beautiful hazel eyes, her ripe breasts, her sweet, soft skin, offering him bliss and certain damnation in one sweet night of heaven. He was fighting himself as he stood, his hand on her breast, torn in two by fear and hunger, watching as she stepped away and, her foot on the chair by his table, peeled down first one stocking then the other, tossing her garters onto the table where they came to rest on his open notebook. The chemise slipped easily from her shoulders and fell to her feet, to lie in a warm soft pile on the floor.

She was naked before him.

He stooped and picked up the chemise, holding it to his face, inhaling her scent. It was still not too late. He could still hold back.

'Matthew?' Her whisper was husky, inviting. 'I need a paper with your signature to say Liza can go free.'

He had to move her garters, embroidered ribbons of green silk, to pick up the notebook, the notebook which held his list. The Devil's list. He turned the pages where Liza's name and Sarah's too were written, and when he came to an empty page he tore it out. His hand was shaking as he reached for a pen. She watched him write.

'How will I know you will go through with this?' The lawyer in him was frowning his displeasure, whispering warnings in his ear.

'You have my garters, sir. You may hold them hostage.' She raised her arms to unpin her hair and he saw the heavy weight of it fall down her back.

He groaned, and reaching out his arms he pulled her against him and buried his face in the luxurious chestnut softness, feeling her breasts pressed against the white linen of his shirt.

With a shout of horror, Matthew woke and flung himself across the bed. His fever had returned and he could feel the sweat running down his body. He staggered to his feet, coughing violently, and turned to look at the bed. It was empty. The dream hovered seductively at the corner of his consciousness for a few more moments, then as he fell to his knees it was gone, washed away by tears of bitterness and shame.

Mike woke to find his own face damp, his fists flailing and grasping at the mess of papers beneath his elbows on his desk. He pushed himself upright with a groan.

He remembered every detail of the dream. Both dreams. Oh God, what was happening to him?

Christ be with me. Christ within me.

He went into the kitchen and helped himself to a glass of water, then he walked out of the house. Almost without realising it, he pointed his car towards Liza's.

The house appeared to be empty when he walked up the path and knocked on the door. He stood for a moment, listening to the echoing silence, then he turned to find Emma coming in through the gate behind him.

The sight of her here in the flesh in front of him made him catch his breath. Why in God's name had he come?

'I'll go if you're busy,' he said awkwardly. 'I just thought I would drop in as I was passing.' He had parked his car next to hers in front of the shed she used as a garage.

Kill the witch!

The whisper in his ear was very quiet.

She smiled at him and shrugged. 'No. Come in.' Leading the way into the sitting room, she turned to face him. 'Are you still witch hunting?'

He stopped in his tracks.

A moment's silence stretched out between them. 'What is it, Mike? What's wrong?' The sitting room was cold and dark without sunlight shining through the windows.

What was he doing here? He stared at her, trying to put the picture of her naked, dangling a pair of green silk garters from her fingertips, out of his mind.

'Why did you ask about witches?'

'We were talking about Lyndsey last time we met.'

'Of course.' He smiled at her, in relief. For a moment he had been terrified she could read his mind.

She sat down and turned half away from him, gesturing him towards the sofa. 'How can I help?'

Lowering himself gingerly onto the cushions he leaned forward, his hands clasped on his knees. 'I'm not sure if you can.' The words were unintentionally ironic.

She waited.

He couldn't think what to say next. As the silence lengthened he could see the tension rising inside her. 'Look, Mike. I have had a bad morning. I've just been up to Overly Hall and Colonel Lawson ticked me off for looking in at the gate; just for looking at his house! He made me feel about so high!' She held up her two hands only a couple of inches apart. 'My mother had just rung me to tell me my family used to live there hundreds of years ago. I wanted to see it. I didn't want a tour! Well, yes I did if I'm honest, but he had no need to be so rude! And now you've appeared and you are looking as though I've crawled out from under a stone somewhere. Why have you come?'

He took a deep breath, visibly collecting himself, desperately searching for something to say. 'I just thought you would like to know that I hadn't managed to talk to Lyndsey yet, although I do intend to as soon as possible. I wondered, would you rather I didn't mention your involvement?'

'I'm not involved!' She frowned. The warmth and humour he had displayed when they had coffee together was gone. He looked ill at ease and she found herself reacting to him uncomfortably. 'Please, don't mention me at all. I have seen her. I had a cup of tea with her yesterday, as a matter of fact. We talked. What she does or doesn't do as her religion is really none of my business and with all due respect, I'm not sure it's yours. Being C of E isn't compulsory, is it?'

He looked up and at last he smiled. He did not realise how handsome he looked when the preoccupation had cleared from his face. 'No, of course not.'

She was not to be placated that easily. 'Then I don't see why you should have to get involved, either.'

'Because evil is my business, as well as social work.' He paused. 'I take it there hasn't been any further activity in the churchyard?'

'No, and I told Lyndsey I wouldn't go there again.' She shuddered ostentatiously.

'Do you mind me asking what you think of her?'

Emma shrugged. 'That's hard to say. She's not an easy person to get to know. She's on the defensive all the time and for some reason she sees me as the enemy. I think I shall suspend judgement. You will have to make up your own mind when you meet her.'

He held her gaze for a moment. Her eyes were very beautiful; the eyes he had seen in his dream.

Christ be with me. Christ within me ...

She was smiling now. It was a warm, sexy smile. A smile he found very attractive indeed.

'Mike, it's cold in here.' She had relented suddenly. 'Do you want to come into the kitchen and I'll put on some coffee? It's warmer in there. It's a bit formal in here.' She gave a self-deprecating grimace.

Don't accept. This is a house of evil. There is danger here.

But the voice in his head belonged to someone else. He felt himself tensing with anxiety. This was nonsense. This was a lovely house and Emma was a lovely person.

'Mike?' She was standing up. Her smile had faded and she looked puzzled.

'Sorry!' He leaped to his feet. 'Yes, thank you. That would be nice.'

Christ be with me.

'You said your family came from Overly Hall?' The name was familiar of course. He knew Colonel Lawson. After his first meeting with the man in the lane outside this very house he had called on him and he too had been sent away with a less than hospitable greeting. He was following her into the hall.

She nodded. 'The Bennetts. My father's mother's family.'

Mike stopped in his tracks. 'Bennett?' He repeated. It was barely a whisper.

'That's right.'

Christ be with me. He closed his eyes.

'Mike? Are you coming?' She led the way in. She had left the radio on while she was out and the midday concert was in full swing on Classic FM.

He followed her in and then stopped dead. The two black cats were sitting side by side in front of the Aga. She followed his gaze. 'You don't mind the cats?'

'No, I like cats.' He slid into the chair she indicated on the far side of the round table. 'Usually, that is.' It was odd. These two were regarding him with something that felt like malevolence. He eyed the narrow intelligent faces, the large pricked ears.

The witch has her familiars. They are all evil. Creatures of the Devil, all three.

The voice wouldn't leave him alone.

'I blessed the churchyard this morning.' He dragged his gaze away from the cats to watch her reaching for the kettle.

'I see.' She had her back to him.

'Lyndsey won't like it, of course, but if she is genuinely in touch with Satanic forces, then I have to take action. It is part of my job as a Christian minister.' He swallowed, trying to steady his voice. 'As you say, in our society what she believes is her own affair, but that will not stop me praying for her.'

'I'm glad you didn't expect me to come to your service.'

Why did that not surprise him?

'It wasn't a service as such.' The cats were still sitting watching him. They were making him feel increasingly uneasy. As did the memory of their mistress dressed in a pink silk petticoat and soft revealing gown; the gown which had slipped so easily to her knees . . .

Christ be with me. Please.

She had found the biscuit tin again. There was no plate this time. She just plonked the tin down on the table with the two mugs of coffee.

'Lyndsey will be very angry if she finds out what you've done.'

'I'm sure she will.' He raised an eyebrow. 'Leave that to me. Perhaps I shouldn't have told you, but I wanted to explain in case –' He paused. In case of what? In case his prayers reached her; in case she realised that he sensed evil round her, close, in this pretty, inoffensive house. In case she realised that he suspected so much of the evil came from her?

'In case?' She was waiting for him to finish the sentence.

'In case something happens, I suppose. In case you had seen or heard anything. In case I feel I have to do it again.'

'Perhaps you should have done it at midnight?' She seemed amused, teasing him.

'No. No need for that. Broad daylight is what we want. Sunshine. Evil hides from the light.'

'Then perhaps you should go after it in the dark when it is about.' She raised an eyebrow. 'That would make sense.'

Did she guess how afraid that would make him? He looked up. She was concentrating on the mug between her hands.

'I don't think there is any need for that yet,' he replied softly. 'I'm sure the blessing I did this morning will suffice.' He met her eyes. Beautiful. Enigmatic. Hostile. Like those of her cats. Why hostile? He was surprised to find the thought that she disliked him caused him a wave of something like pain. Perhaps he had got it wrong? Did she like him and dislike his calling? Or was it Sarah who disliked him? He was confused. Normally he was good at judging people. He could sense exactly where they stood on the like/dislike-the-clergy scale and where they stood regarding him personally, but just as his own feelings about her were swinging wildly back and forth, so, it seemed to him, were hers. One minute she seemed to like him, the next, the look she gave him was pure hatred.

Or was that Sarah?

Kill the witch.

He realised his hands were shaking as he clasped them round his mug and he took a deep breath as he raised it to his lips. 'Thank you for that.'

He stood up too quickly. 'I'm afraid I must go. I've got several calls to make.'

She was smiling up at him from those beautiful eyes and before he realised it he had stretched out his hand and put it over hers. 'Goodbye for now, Emma. Take care.'

His last thought, as he left the house, was: that woman is in mortal danger. And so am I.

46

It was several hours later that Lyndsey found Emma stacking pots in the barn. She watched her for a moment in silence before announcing herself from the doorway. Emma jumped visibly.

'Sorry. I didn't mean to startle you.' Lyndsey hauled herself up onto the dusty workbench and sat, her hands clasped round her knees. 'I wanted to talk to you again.' The shadowy old barn with its veiling of spiders' webs and crusted mud was a muted frame for her vivid colouring.

Emma pushed her hair back out of her eyes and surveyed her visitor with a frown.

Lyndsey shrugged. 'Am I in the way?'

'No, you're not in the way.' Finally Emma smiled. 'In fact I'm quite glad of a breather. What can I do for you?'

'I hear the man of God is looking for me?'

'The man of God?' Emma echoed, frowning. 'Oh, you mean Mike?'

'He's been in the churchyard.'

Emma studied her face curiously. 'How do you know?'

'That's easy. I can tell. And he's taken my things. Or someone has. Unless it was you?'

Emma shook her head.

'Then it was him. It must have been. You'll have to find out what he's done with them.'

'Me?'

'I don't know anyone else who talks to him.'

'Alex?' Emma pulled off her gardening gloves and threw them down on the bench.

'Alex hasn't been in the churchyard. Anyway, none of this has anything to do with him.' Lyndsey narrowed her eyes. 'If it hadn't been for you Mr Sinclair wouldn't have interfered in the first place.'

'I suppose not.' Emma seemed less sure of her ground suddenly. 'I'm sorry. He was up here this morning. He's worried about you.'

'I bet he is!' Lyndsey was furious. 'And it's all your fault what with moving here and poking your nose in.'

'Why does my moving here upset you so much?'

'It's because you are stirring things up.' Lyndsey slid off the bench and went to the door where she stood for a moment, staring down the garden. She turned and looked at Emma. 'Waking the past.'

'My nightmares are set in the past.' Emma frowned. 'They are frightening. Violent. I don't always remember them, but sometimes they are about Liza.'

Lyndsey swallowed. Her mouth had gone dry and she took a deep breath, trying to ground herself solidly. Protection. She must not forget her own protection.

Emma came to stand beside her in the doorway, taking in the western sky where a strange orange flush reflected up into the clouds where the sun was getting ready to set.

'My mother rang this morning,' Emma said thoughtfully. 'I never knew it before, but apparently my grandmother's family used to live at Overly Hall.'

Lyndsey turned and stared at her. 'The Bennetts used to live there. My mother's family. They lived at Overly for three hundred years.'

Emma raised an eyebrow. 'My grandmother was Elizabeth Bennett.'

They stared at each other in silence, each searching the other's face for a sign of likeness. Blue eyes met hazel. Dark hair compared to brown. Both were small-boned, of medium height, but there the similarities ended. Lyndsey's sharp features, small chin, high cheekbones, did not remotely resemble Emma's aquiline nose and oval face.

'I suppose that makes us cousins of some sort,' Emma said at last.

Lyndsey wasn't sure how she felt. Her hostility was as strong as ever and yet it did explain a lot. Emma's persistence; her immunity to the spell designed to get rid of her. Perhaps she had sensed it, this blood link between them.

Emma was watching her. 'At least it means I'm not quite so much of an outsider.' She gave a wry smile. 'I was chased away

237

from the hall this morning and I was only looking through the gate!'

'By Lawson?' Lyndsey shrugged. 'He's a funny man. He went a bit odd after his only son died. No one much has been allowed in since then. Don't take it personally. Just keep away from him.' She shrugged again. 'I suppose it explains why you stirred things up. I thought maybe it was those dickheads making a film about Hopkins. But it isn't. It's you.'

'Me?' Emma shivered uneasily. 'I don't understand any of this, but I did meet the film people back in August.'

'Unfortunately they are coming back.' Lyndsey thrust her thumbs into the front pockets of her jeans. She was staring at the far hedge where Max had appeared, tail high and stately, patrolling his new kingdom. 'There have always been cats here,' she put in absent-mindedly.

Emma nodded. 'They love it here. It's heaven for them after London.'

'It would be.' Lyndsey's emphasis did not flatter London.

'Is it Matthew Hopkins's ghost in the shop?' Emma was pursuing her previous line of thought.

Lyndsey shuddered, her whole body reacting instinctively to the name. 'Who else?'

'But not here. Not at Liza's.'

'Of course not here.'

Emma shook her head, thinking of Flora's warnings. 'No, I'd have known if he had haunted this house. I'd have felt something. It is Liza, isn't it?'

Lyndsey looked away. Again the shrug.

'How does the churchyard come in then?' Emma persevered. At last she seemed to be talking to somebody who knew about the past.

'He was buried there.'

'Hopkins?'

Lyndsey nodded. 'It's a strange place. Powerful. Evil. I think I've located his grave there. I had him sealed in. I made a binding spell, but it wasn't strong enough.'

'A spell?' Emma echoed her words. 'A witch's spell?'

'Of course a witch's spell.' Lyndsey gave her a sideways glance. 'So, now you know why it is so important to get my things back. They are consecrated. If he's got them, you've got to get them back for me.' She moved out of the barn and headed up the path round the side of the house towards the gate.

'Consecrated?' Emma followed her. 'Consecrated to what?' She caught Lyndsey's arm. 'Is Mike right? Do you actually worship the Devil?'

Lyndsey wrenched it away. 'No, I don't worship the Devil!' she said furiously. 'Why do people always think that? The Devil belongs to Christianity. They call him Satan. I'm not a Satanist! I'm a witch. I worship the goddess. It's quite different. You of all people should know that if you are of Sarah's blood!'

Her face flushed with anger, she turned and ran to the gate where she grabbed her bicycle from the hedge.

'Wait!' Emma shouted after her. 'Who was Sarah?'

'You'll find out soon enough.' Lyndsey straddled her bike.

'I need to know now,' Emma called, but Lyndsey was already peddling down the lane.

47

Emma stood and watched her go. Sarah was the name that came
to her in her dreams. The woman whose personality was threatening to take her over. The woman who had lived at Overly Hall,
and, she was sure, had lived here at Liza's. She realised suddenly
that she was shaking. The fury and venom with which Lyndsey
had suddenly exploded had frightened her, as had the news that
her volatile visitor was her own cousin. Oh God, that was all she
needed!

She was still standing by the gate when the muddy blue Volvo
pulled to a halt outside.

'Hi.' Alex turned off the engine and climbed out. 'Was that Lyn
I saw peddling hell for leather down the hill?'

Emma stared at him for a moment, trying to pull herself
together. 'It was indeed,' she said at last rather grimly. 'An apt
description as it happens.'

Alex followed her towards the house. 'What's she done now?'

By the time she had recounted the conversation, Alex was
seated in the kitchen with Min on his knees and the kettle was
on the boiling plate once more.

'She scared me, Alex!'

He sighed. 'Ignore her. She has a penchant for the dramatic.'
He kept his own worries about Lyndsey to himself.

'You don't think it's real, then?'

'Witchcraft?' Alex laughed. 'No way. It's an excuse for dancing
round the bonfire in the nuddy!'

Emma smiled. 'So I needn't worry?'

'No. Put it out of your mind. And don't let her think she can
wind you up. I wouldn't put it past her to try and get you out of
here. For some reason she doesn't like you, or anyone else for
that matter, living here. That's what this is all about.'

'It's because it was Liza's house. And Liza was a witch.'

'I don't see what that has to do with it. She clearly doesn't need the house now.'

Emma glanced towards the window. 'No.'

'You don't sound too sure.'

'No.'

Alex took a deep breath. 'You mustn't let it frighten you. Every house round here which is called after a woman is supposed to have belonged to a witch of some sort. There's Kate's up on the Colchester Road and Betty's Corner, down Wix way. They were both supposed to be witches. You know, it might actually be a plus, this witch story. It would bring in the tourists. A potted herb from the witch's garden. In fact what a brilliant name for your business. The Witch's Garden.'

'Hang on.' Emma was half frowning, half smiling. 'Alex, this is jumping the gun a bit.'

'You ought to think about it soon. Time is of the essence.' He grinned. 'After all, everything you stock will have to be grown. You need to be up and ready to run by the early spring. The actual ground needs working. The barns need repair. Where will the shop be? We'll have to identify suppliers. Find stationery, paper bags –'

'Stop!' Emma was laughing. 'I'm not sure Paula would approve of all this.' And nor would Flora if she ever became involved. Suddenly Emma realised that she rather hoped that Flora had meant it when she said she might be interested in joining the venture. The trouble was, she would not be happy to find someone else coming up with all the ideas.

Alex's eager grin had disappeared. 'Paula will come round. Look, I know I get carried away. But I want you to think about it.'

'What on earth would Lyndsey say if we went ahead with something like this?'

'She'd be furious.' He shook his head. 'People tramping all over the place disturbing everything. You reorganising it. Planting new things.' He knew Lyndsey used to make secret visits to the garden. He wasn't sure if she was still doing so, collecting herbs when Emma wasn't around. Probably not.

'And she would put a spell on me?'

I had him sealed in. A binding spell. Lyndsey's voice suddenly echoed in her head. *It wasn't strong enough.*

241

Was that because her spells weren't efficient or because Matthew Hopkins was too strong for her?

Alex was looking thoughtful. 'Do you think I'm wrong? Do you think witches actually do have power?' he asked suddenly. 'Not those poor old ladies in the seventeenth century, but people like Lyn who study Wicca and believe they can actually force people to do things they don't want to do?'

Emma raised an eyebrow. 'Is that what they do?' She thought they had been talking about stopping people doing things they did want to do. Perhaps it was the same thing.

'I used to think it was all about herbs and crystals and stuff. Harmless. Rather attractive, really. Pretty dresses and the frisson of thinking that they dance around naked.' Alex shook his head nostalgically, then he snapped to attention. 'I didn't mean that I think about Lyn like that!'

'No, of course you don't.' Emma was laughing again. 'And I know what you mean. I have a friend in London, Flora, my best friend actually, who is exactly like that. She's an aromatherapist, but she keeps a broomstick in her umbrella stand in her fourth floor flat. And the flat is wonderful. An Aladdin's cave. Crystals. Chimes. Wonderful smells. And her plants love it so much they romp all over the place and grab you by the throat as you go in through the door. But never once, in all the years I've known her, did I suspect she might cast spells in the nude at midnight. Actually . . .' She paused, thinking fast. She may as well forewarn him that other people were interested in this project. 'She would be a good person to talk to about the herb garden. Something else to sell maybe – essential oils and things? She's quite keen to get involved. She could be a consultant, too.'

Alex did not seem worried at the idea. He nodded. He was itching to grope in his pockets for a notebook and pencil but resisted. He didn't want to seem to be trying to take over and he recognised the thoughtful expression on Emma's face. He had sown the seed. Time to let it mature. Glancing at his watch, he pushed his chair back and eased Min off his knees. 'I must go. The kids will be home soon. They have tea with one of Sophie's friends on Mondays and I need to collect them. Can we talk about this again? Soon?'

'Of course.' Emma nodded firmly. She in turn recognised Alex's eagerness. There was a lot of talent and business acumen there, rotting away unused. He could be useful, but she was not about to let him take over.

After he left she pulled on her waxed jacket and let herself out of the back door into the garden. She needed to collect her thoughts. So much had happened today and she was exhausted. She took a deep breath of the cool air and stood staring up at the sky. It would soon be dark. There was still a touch of red in the west, but behind her the cold darkness was rolling in off the North Sea. With a shiver she went to sit on the low wall which bounded the lawn, her hands deep in her pockets for warmth. A few minutes later her eyes had closed.

The dream was waiting for her. In seconds it had overtaken her.

Sarah had tethered the horse at the top of the lane. With a kiss to the soft muzzle and a whisper in its ear to stay quiet in the pitch darkness under the tree she lifted her skirts clear of the ground and hastened down towards the village. The windows of Hopkins's house were shuttered, but to her amazement the front door stood ajar. She pushed it cautiously and peered in. The house was deathly silent. It was in darkness save for a candle burning on the table outside the door to one of the front rooms. The wax had burned low and dripped into fantastic sculptural shapes in the draught from the open door.

'Hello?' Sarah's voice sounded more confident, and far louder than she had expected. 'Master Hopkins, are you there?' Where were his servants? The house was cold, the atmosphere unwelcoming, unpleasant. She shivered, pushing open the door to his closet. She could feel the echoes of his presence in the room. Overwhelming, self-righteous, dark. The notes for the book he was writing were spread all over his desk but he was not there in person. She crept out of the room and stood at the foot of the stairs, looking up. The house was empty. She could sense it and she had no desire to go up and check further. Turning her back on the stairs, she surveyed the hall in the flickering candlelight as if hoping to find a clue as to where he was, and suddenly she knew. Liza had been taken to Mary Phillips's house in Church Street. He was there with her now.

Running down the street, she neither remembered nor cared whether she had closed the door behind her, glad only to be outside, away from the overwhelming unpleasantness of the atmosphere in Hopkins's house. The other houses in the street were mostly shuttered; here and there candlelight spilled out over the cobbles but the place was empty. Listening.

Listening for what?

The High Street was busier. The sound of laughter and loud conversation spilled from the coffee house, and she could see the press of figures through the window. From one of the taverns there came the sound of drunken laughter. Men stood in groups outside the Crown Inn, lanterns burned, a link boy ran before two men on horseback, his torch trailing smoke as they trotted down towards the river and a coach clattered past her up the hill. No one noticed her.

The door of the house on the corner of Church Street was barred. She knocked loudly, aware of faces turning towards her now in the dark from the street behind her.

'Let me in!'

Liza was here. She knew it. She thumped with her fists on the oak panels. 'Let me in!' She could hear feet shuffling along the floor behind the door now. 'Open up. I need to come in!'

The sound of two bolts being drawn back stopped her fists in mid-air and she waited as the door was pulled open a crack. In the shadows the other side of it she could see nothing. 'Let me in! I have to see Master Hopkins!'

The door opened wider and she saw a muffled figure behind it. The woman was carrying an untrimmed candle which flared smokily, showing a pockmarked face and blackened teeth. 'Did he say you could come in?'

'Of course he did,' Sarah snapped. She pushed the door back with the flat of her hand and stepped inside. 'Where is he?'

'Upstairs.' The woman gestured towards the corner with a nod of the head.

The staircase was in darkness but she could see as she looked up, her hand on the newel post at the bottom, a faint shadowy light above her where it turned the corner into the upper room. She could hear voices. Two men talking softly. Then a woman. Not Liza. Gathering her skirts in one hand, she set off determinedly up the stairs.

The room was low-ceilinged, the window shuttered, the only pieces of furniture a table and three chairs. Matthew Hopkins and his assistant John Stearne were seated at the table. On the third chair the old lady was sitting, her arms bound behind her to the chair back, a filthy drool-soaked rag stuffed in her mouth. Her legs were spread-eagled, her skirts pushed up onto her thighs.

'Very well, Mary. I think we know where you will find the Devil's tits.' Hopkins did not look up from the notebook in which he was writing. The old woman moaned with terror.

'Stop!' Sarah threw herself into the room. 'What are you doing?' Her voice trailed away as she saw the vicious spike in Mary Phillips's hand. 'Sweet Jesus, no!'

Mary straightened. 'You have no business here, Sarah Paxman. Leave now!'

'I will not leave. How dare you? How can you behave so cruelly?'

Sarah ran towards Liza and gently pulled down her skirts. Then she reached to pull the gag from the old lady's mouth. 'You have no right.' She spun round to face Hopkins as Liza's dry choking sobs grew louder. 'No right at all.'

'I have every right, mistress.' He narrowed his eyes as the candle flames smoked. 'I have Parliament's commission as their Witchfinder General. Interfering with my business is a crime against the Parliament of this country.' He leaned forward, his small dark eyes suddenly focused on her, seeming to see right through her. Perhaps he was remembering his dream. He wiped his forehead with his sleeve. 'Punishable by death.'

She stepped back, shocked. 'I don't believe you!'

'You would ask to see my commission? You wish to test my resolve to do the job which God has given me? Mary, continue. I need to know the site of the Devil's marks and I need to write down this woman's confession.' He turned back to Sarah. 'Leave

245

now, mistress, or I shall call the guard and have you committed to gaol.'

'You can't.'

'I can.' He stood up at last, and lifting the candlestick nearest him he stepped out from behind the table. 'Guards!' His voice was raw and harsh. Stearne had neither spoken nor moved beyond leaning back, arms folded, squinting up to watch his colleague's face.

'Liza?' Sarah turned towards the old woman in despair. 'What can I do?'

But Mary Phillips had closed in on Liza once more, the pricker in her hand. Dragging back the ragged skirts and forcing the old lady's legs apart, she aimed upwards with vicious force. The first scream tore into the dark silence of the building as a door in the wall behind Hopkins flew open and two men came in.

'The Devil will take you, Matthew Hopkins!' Liza's words were wrenched from the depth of her being. 'He will take you to hell with all your foul conspirators!' She broke into hoarse sobs. 'Tell Satan what goes on here, Sarah! Tell him and call on him for revenge –' Her words ended in another scream as Mary Phillips thrust her pricker once more into the old woman's soft flesh.

Sarah stopped in the doorway and looked back through her tears. Against the lurid light of the candles she saw Mary thrust again. This time there was no scream.

'See, Master Hopkins. We have found a spot where she feels no pain.' A throaty laugh. 'But she is already condemned from her own mouth. Shall we walk her tonight so that we can get a fuller confession? That would be best, I think.' She stood up, flushed with triumph, and threw the long needle set in its wooden handle down on the table in front of him. A smear of blood dripped onto the table top. 'And perhaps then we should swim her, just to be sure.' She paused. 'Shall we test Mistress Sarah here while we have her? It sounds to me as though she is one of them.'

'No.' Sarah stared wildly round the room, from the triumphant stout figure of Mary Phillips with her sweating red face and stained bodice, to Hopkins and Stearne in their neat black suits with white collar and cuffs, and back to the old woman lying trussed in the chair, sobbing as the blood ran down the inside of her thighs. 'No! It's nothing to do with me! I am not one of them. I'm not!'

As she fled down the stairs into the blackness she heard Mary Phillips's words flung after her into the dark of the stairwell. 'No need to run, my dear. I know where to find you! And I know more about your privy parts than most, if you remember, trying to find out why God did not see fit to send you and your man a child. Easy to see why, now. God did not think you a fit and Godly mother!'

Sobbing, Sarah flung herself towards the door, dragged it open and stumbled out into the street.

The wind had died, leaving its scent of mud and salt in the thick mist which had drifted up from the river into the town, swirling round the lanterns hanging outside the inn, its sharp cold dampness mingling on her cheeks with her tears as she turned and ran away down the High Street.

48

Monday, late afternoon

With an exhausted sigh, Paula sat back in her chair and glanced at her watch. Damn! She had missed her usual train. She might as well wait twenty minutes now, before she left the office. Thoughtfully she stared at the screen in front of her. It was displaying the latest figures on the Dow Jones – down six – she squinted at it for a moment without really seeing it, then she reached for the phone. It was thirty seconds before Piers answered. 'Paula? How nice to hear from you. I was going to drop you a line to say thank you for the other night.'

'Piers, are you going to be able to persuade Emma to come back to London?' She had been worrying all day; so much so that she did not realise how abrupt her question might sound.

'I doubt it,' he replied after a second's double-take. His voice had become very dry on the other end of the line. 'We didn't part on very good terms. In fact,' she heard a deep sigh, 'to be honest, I think that was it. Curtains.'

'But she still loves you!' Paula broke off, realising only after she had said it that in fact she knew nothing of the kind. 'At least that is how it seemed to Alex and me. We both felt it was somehow our fault that, well, that you and she were not very happy together on Saturday.' She was chewing the cap of her Swan pen.

Piers gave a polite, humourless laugh. 'Please, don't blame yourselves. Really, don't. It was nothing to do with you. Maybe you polarised us a bit, but that's all. It's that damn house that's to blame. She's obsessed with it.' He remembered his social graces suddenly. 'Oh Lord, I'm sorry. I hope you haven't been worrying about us. That's the last thing either of us would want. I think Em and I have just reached a natural full stop in our relationship. Maybe it just took Liza's to find the weak points and lever us apart. Better now than further down the line.'

'Piers, you mustn't give up on her. You really mustn't.' The cap of Paula's pen rolled off her desk and onto the floor. 'She's going to need you.'

There was a moment's silence. 'That sounds a bit portentous.'

'I know. I don't know why I'm saying it, really.'

Because my husband fancies the socks off her, that's why. And they are alone down there, miles away and you and I are up here in London and can do nothing about it. But it was more than that. Far more. She frowned. Whatever it was – a foreboding, the smallest whisper of a premonition that she was going to lose Alex – had gone. She gave a small, forced laugh. 'Oh well, I tried. Look, Piers, do keep in touch. Perhaps we can catch lunch or something one day?'

As she hung up she glanced at her watch again. Now she would have to run to reach Liverpool Street in time for the next train home.

49

Mark pushed back the pile of books with sigh. He was exhausted and his head was splitting, but the script was coming on well. The more he read about Hopkins, the more fascinating the man became, if only because nobody seemed entirely sure who he was. The sources were full of 'maybes' and 'probables', 'it seems likely that' and 'almost certainly'. Still, he thought, he had enough for his purposes.

The man was a local, born 'probably' in Great Wenham, which was, as far as Mark could see from the map, about eight kilometres as the crow flies from Manningtree. A lot further by road, of course. His father, or at least a James Hopkins, had been the parson there, from – Mark turned to his own scribbled-in note-book – 1612 until 'probably' 1634.

Mark had called in at Great Wenham on his way back from Ipswich. It was just off the A12. There wasn't much there but for the lovely old church set in a wooded valley, peaceful, disturbed only by the sound of birds and the ticking of the clock in the tower. As he walked round it, he found it hard to imagine it as the birthplace of a man who had such demons in his soul. But then again he was reminded of the Brontë household at Haworth. Perhaps the vicarage here too had been crowded, damp, unhealthy. Perhaps the children – Matthew was one of at least four children, 'probably' six – had been given milk from a local farm which had been infected with bovine TB. Perhaps the children were intelligent, creative, repressed, turning in on themselves and developing intense imaginations just as the Brontës had done. But that was where the likeness ended.

Where had Matthew's deeply disturbed personality come from? Somewhere he had found the rather dubious claim that Matthew was 'probably' no more than four foot eleven in height, so perhaps he had suffered from rickets as a child, in common with many people of the period, and perhaps that lack of stature had given him an inferiority complex which contributed to it. His mother, Marie, had been a Huguenot, so almost certainly there was a strict Puritan influence in the family, coming out in one son who became a Presbyterian minister and another, Thomas, who went to live in New England. Was there something else there, in the background? A hatred of women stemming from a difficult relationship with his mother perhaps, or an older woman, a grandmother, even? Mark sighed. Such an idea was intriguing but it could never be proved.

Matthew Hopkins was obviously intelligent and well educated. He himself claimed to have studied in Amsterdam at some point and seemed to have trained in maritime law, maybe in Ipswich, but probably not at university, at least not in England as there seemed to be no record of him having been at Oxford or Cambridge. He certainly seemed to have started his career in maritime insurance, at least until his later more lucrative trade occurred to him, and it was probably the maritime side of his activities which brought him initially to Mistley where there was a flourishing port. While there he had at some point been owner or part-owner of the Thorn Inn – a strange side-line, one would think, for a man who seemed to embrace so whole-heartedly the strict Puritan ethic of his time.

Mark stood up and stretched, wandering over to stand in front of the window. Outside it was dark. His flat looked out over the Regent's Canal and he could see lights reflecting in the water beneath his window. What had possessed the young man to change from insurance to witch hunting at the age of twenty-four? What had turned him to a career which would make his name a byword for cruelty and evil that would echo into the twenty-first century? He shook his head. How had Matthew got them all to go along with him? How had he got himself the authority to do what he did? Mark glanced down at his books. A lot of it apparently was opportunity. England was a torn and bleeding country. By the time of the first trial of witches apprehended by Hopkins in July 1645, the Long Parliament was in its last stages. King Charles the First had been defeated by Cromwell's armies and within four years would be dead. Local law and government was in complete disarray. Add to this the intense religious tension in the air – Catholic versus Anglican, Anglican

251

versus Puritan – and add in on top of that ordinary human nature with a string of failings, superstitions, weaknesses, fears, jealousies, whatever one chose to call them, and they combined into a lethal cocktail. Together with the fact that Essex seemed to have more witches than anywhere else. It would be interesting to fill in some hints as to why. That intense religious conflict; the tradition of magic; the history of the fiercely independent people who lived there, but there would be very little time for philosophical speculation in the film. Just leave it as read that there were more witches in that part of the world, always had been and always would. He chuckled to himself.

Against that background one man, Hopkins, saw his opportunity. Mark sat down and shuffled his notes once more. The general view seemed to be that neither Cromwell nor Parliament had given Matthew Hopkins the position of Witchfinder General. He had no official status at all. He awarded it to himself, and confirmed it himself when he wrote his book *Discoverie of Witches*. He did have powerful friends, though. Sir Harbottle Grimstone, the local Justice, for one. Mark smiled gleefully. What a wonderful name! And once Matthew started styling himself with his new and important title nobody seemed to have contradicted him. His sense of importance and authority fed on themselves. And so the horrors continued.

One thing surprised Mark, though. Matthew had not killed as many witches as Mark had expected. He had thought it was hundreds. He flipped through his books. He would have to get this bit right because what he had found out was going to sound like sacrilege to a great many people. In fact thirty-six women were tried for witchcraft at the Essex Assizes of 1645. Nineteen were executed. Nine died in prison and the rest were still in prison three years later. Only one was acquitted. Thirty-five out of the thirty-six came from within fifteen miles of Manningtree. The thirty-sixth was the one who was acquitted. Mark made some more notes. That came from Macfarlane, who believed that Hopkins probably sincerely felt that his services were needed and that he had found a genuine conspiracy of witches in the area. Including all the rest of the Eastern counties, the total of victims was, according to Hopkins's colleague John Stearne, about two hundred souls – men, women and children.

The other book he was using for his facts was by Ronald Hutton;

his history of witchcraft. Now that was interesting. Mark frowned. He would like to make some comments about the feminist take on witchcraft in the programme. After all, you couldn't talk about witches without women claiming that they had been persecuted merely for being women. He hadn't realised how much feminist historians had exaggerated the numbers of witches executed across Europe, giving the century of witch mania the evocative title of the 'burning times' and claiming it as a male conspiracy against women, when in fact many men had died too. He gave a rueful grin. If he mentioned that, the programme would be slated by female reviewers. But then any reviewers would be better than none. Too many, he feared, would dismiss it as a piece of nonsense. The mention of ghosts always did that. If he wasn't careful they would bring out one of the professional rubbishers of the supernatural to certify him bonkers!

There was another bit he wanted to bring in. The horror. Whether the witches were guilty as charged or not, the methods used to interrogate them were barbaric. Keith Thomas's book *Religion and the Decline of Magic* had bags of good material. He mentioned that Hopkins was very keen on accusations of carnal union with the Devil. That should go in. As should the fact that Hopkins had claimed at the beginning of his campaign that a coven of local witches had conjured up a bear and sent it to kill him.

It was all fascinating. Whatever Matthew Hopkins had or had not done, he had clearly done enough to be remembered and feared to this day in the area which was the centre of operations. The bogeyman of Manningtree.

He sat back in his chair and stretching out his arms, linked them behind his head. Could that be a title for the programme?

Hopkins had moved into Manningtree – there was never a mention of wife or kids, notice – and had lived at some time in South Street and, maybe, at the Thorn Inn. From there he had begun the reign of terror which had made him a very rich man, for he charged a fee, per head, for his witch hunting services.

So what had put a stop to it all? Rationality had kicked in for a start. The good burgesses of nearby Colchester had begun it, as far as Mark could see. Hopkins's career had lasted only two years, then abruptly ended in August 1647 when he disappeared from history. There seemed to be four theories as to what had happened to him. The most mundane and, Mark sighed, tapping his pencil on the keyboard in front of him, sadly the most likely, was that he had died of tuberculosis. That was what his colleague and partner John Stearne had claimed. Then there seemed to be a theory that as the demand for his services dropped off and questions began to be asked about his methods, he might have fled to the American colonies to join his brother in New England, and who knows, restart his witch hunting career over there. There were two rather more intriguing ideas. One, that his neighbours in Mistley and Manningtree, sickened by his activities and suspicious as to how he knew so much about local witchcraft and how he came by his famous Devil's List, swam him as a witch himself and murdered him, or, Mark shook his head thoughtfully, that the Devil claimed him and took him to hell!

An interesting bunch of theories. He spread out four printed sheets of paper and stared at each in turn. Of course if the man had gone to America he would presumably have died there and his ghost would be found flitting round the streets of somewhere like Salem. He had read somewhere that ghosts couldn't cross water – did that include the Atlantic Ocean? Probably!

All the other three theories however were OK as far as the programme was concerned. None of them sounded pleasant. None would have left him lying easy in his grave. Wherever that was.

He had two possibilities so far. The old church at Mistley; as Hopkins's death was in fact noted in the parish registers, it seemed the most likely place, and again, the most mundane. The other was under a patch of especially green grass near the lake where he was supposed to have swum his local victims. That was a starter only because his ghost was supposed to have been seen hovering over it. When they went up there he would film at both sites.

His eye fell on the open notebook by the phone. Mike Sinclair's number was scribbled at the top of the page. His hotline to the church.

He sat back in his chair. When he drove up to Manningtree the day after tomorrow, he would take all this stuff to show Mike. Somehow he had to get him in front of a camera.

When the phone rang he nearly jumped out of his skin. It was Colin. 'All set for another trip to darkest Essex?' The Welsh lilt was always strongest over the phone.

Mark grinned. 'I was just getting my notes together. It's been bloody frustrating having to stay in London when all I wanted to do was get back there. Is Joe lined up?'

'He is. In fact he's got all sorts of ideas for bringing in some special sound stuff. I do hope we can get it into the shop. Have you contacted them?'

'Alice has.' Mark nodded. Outside his small office he could hear the dustcart in the road alongside the canal munching its way through a heap of old cardboard boxes. 'I don't think we'll have a problem. Barker says we can go in if the tenants agree. I think our presence there, with cameras, might in this case work in our favour.' He glanced down at his notes. 'You know, I can't help wondering if something Lyndsey Clark said might not be true: perhaps our presence there was actually feeding the thing. Giving it energy. It likes our interest. It seeks publicity. So, it will appear for us.'

'Wow!' Colin the other end of the phone picked the remains of his doughnut out of the saucer it was lying in and took a large bite. 'It will be wanting an agent and a contract next!' he said with his mouth full. He chuckled.

'Have you got the stills I asked for?'

'Sure thing. And I'm picking up the special camera equipment on Thursday.'

'And Alice still wants to come with Joe?'

'Try and keep her away. She's going to clear it with her tutor, apparently. Joe's not happy but that doesn't cut any ice with her, of course.'

'OK. Well, it seems we're on, then. Joe, Alice and I will go down on Wednesday and you'll join us on Friday, right?'

'Right. Mark, before you go, you have realised the date on Sunday, haven't you.' Colin chuckled again.

Mark frowned. 'Why. Is it significant?'

Colin gave a hollow laugh. 'Might be. It's Halloween!'

50

The same evening

There was still a thin weak thread of ochre light in the sky when
Emma came to. It was very cold and she shuddered uncontrollably
as she found herself still sitting on the wall of her terrace. She
stared round disorientated, aware that her jacket was covered in
a layer of cold dew. She had fallen asleep sitting on the wall.

'Oh, God!' As she remembered the dream her intake of breath
was both a cry of anguish and a prayer. She brought the back of
her hand up to her mouth, pressing the cold skin against her lips
as though by doing that she could stifle her thoughts. The old
woman, her pitifully scrawny legs, the blood, the vile smugness of
the other woman with the sharp spike in her hand and watching it
all, the man at the table with his sharp intelligent eyes and the
neat goatee beard beneath the small mean mouth . . .

Fighting her stiffness, Emma stood up and turned back towards
the house. Behind her in the distance an owl hooted. Pushing
open the kitchen door she glanced at the clock. She must have
been asleep for less than ten minutes and yet so much had happened in the dream. Poor Liza. Liza who had lived in this house.
Lived happily in this house. There was no sense of misery here, no
pain, no anguish. It was a happy house, a house which welcomed
people.

There was a thud on the table next to her as Max jumped up
from the floor. He flirted his tail and narrowed his eyes in greeting.
She could hear the throaty purr which meant he was thinking
about his supper. The moment Min joined him she would be
outnumbered and forced to reach for the cat food.

She went to stand by the Aga, feeling its warmth working its way through to her frozen limbs, as with a cheerful *prrrp* Min popped through the cat flap. No time to think about poor Liza for the next five minutes as she opened the tins, reached for their biscuits and put down their plates, watching as they ate, the two ravenous animals suddenly dainty and refined.

But feeding the cats had been no more than an interlude. The heavy cloying unhappiness of the dream still clung around her like an aura. It had been so real. Too real. There had been nothing in it to reassure her that it had been a dream; the detail, the sensations, and smell – all had been too vivid and the sequence of events too rational to have been a dream.

So what was it?

The cats finished their meal, licked their bowls clean, then swapped places, critically examining one another's dish for over-looked morsels before sitting down one on each side of her in front of the Aga to wash their faces and paws. She smiled indulgently, but it was a smile of habit. Her thoughts were still in that room in Church Street with the pitiful old woman who had once lived in this house, hung her dried herbs from the very same iron hooks in the ceiling beams, stood in this very kitchen to cook up her herbal potions.

Minutes later Emma was heading for the door. She picked up her jacket and her car keys and was on her way to Mistley Quay. There was a light on in the ground-floor room of the cottage and the bicycle was leaning into the ragged box hedge implying that Lyndsey was at home.

The living room was very small, the only furniture a two-seater sofa covered in a scarlet throw, a small Edwardian armchair and a somewhat shabby, large floor cushion. Lyndsey pointed Emma to the chair and herself subsided gracefully onto the cushion in front of the delicate wrought-iron fire place. Emma found herself staring down at the hearth. Three candles, some incense sticks in a small brass pot, a crystal cluster and two or three smooth pebbles from the beach grouped on the opposite side to the coal bucket were the only things in the room she could see which might reflect Lyndsey's calling.

'I had to talk to you.' She shrugged. 'About Liza. How much do you actually know about it all?'

Lyndsey didn't look at her. She was staring into the fire. 'Why do you want to know suddenly?'

257

'I had a dream this afternoon. Another dream.' Emma shrugged uncomfortably. 'It was about her.'

'Describe her.' Lyndsey still didn't look up.

'Elderly. Bad teeth; some missing.' That gaping scream. The agony. The tears. 'She . . .' She hesitated. 'She was being tortured by a woman with a spike who was sticking it into her . . . between her legs . . .' Suddenly she was crying.

Lyndsey shivered. She hugged her knees closer, dropping her head so that her chin rested on them. 'That would be the witch pricker. Round here it was a woman called Mary Phillips. She was amongst other things the local midwife, so she knew a lot about female anatomy. She should have been on the side of kindness, healing, rationality. She herself probably used Liza's herbs to help women with puerperal fever, to clean infected wounds, to help bring down the milk. But she changed sides. For money. She betrayed her calling and her sex!'

There was a long silence, then at last Lyndsey raised her head. She swivelled slightly so she could see Emma's face. 'Shall I tell you the most appalling part of the procedure? Those witch prickers were made so that the spike could be retracted into the handle. When the Witchfinder reckoned they had all had enough fun, Mary would pretend to ram it in, retract the spike and lo and behold she had found one of the Devil's marks, a spot where the woman felt no pain. But how many places did she prick first before deciding to do that?'

'I saw pictures of them in the Castle Museum,' Emma said slowly. 'I went to see. I had to find out what happened.' Her eyes had filled with tears again.

Lyndsey stared at her solemnly for what seemed a long time, then as though making up her mind she stood up and went to the small sideboard in the corner of the room. A bottle stood there with four glasses. She poured a dose into two and handed one to Emma. 'Drink it.'

Emma frowned. 'What is it?'

'Oh, you don't have to worry It's not bat's blood! Actually it's Glenmorangie.' Lyndsey gave a wry smile. 'One of my unwitchly life-aids. Cheers!'

She tipped the whisky down her throat without so much as a splutter and then resumed her place on the cushion. 'OK. Now for the questions. Was he there in your dream? Hopkins?'

Emma nodded.

'Describe him.'

'He was sitting at a table facing them. And me. I came upstairs straight into the room. He was not very tall. Dark hair; pointy beard. Rather baby-faced. Very dapper. Immaculate black suit, broad plain white collar and cuffs. Leather gloves on the table. I didn't notice his shoes. He had a bad cough. He had small, glittery eyes. Dark, I think. Very cold. Distanced from what was going on. He wasn't – at least I don't think he was – enjoying it. It was as though all that, the torture, was beneath him. Nothing to do with him.'

'Oh, it wasn't beneath him. Not beneath him at all. I think you'll find he was enjoying it enormously.' The fire spat and crackled suddenly, a piece of salt-soaked driftwood burning blue and green amongst the lumps of sea-coal. Lyndsey turned back to watch it.

Emma sipped her whisky. 'She begged me to avenge her but he took no notice. They went on with the torture.'

Lyndsey was studying her face thoughtfully. She was pursuing her own train of thought. 'Did you speak to him in your dream?'

'Yes.'

'What did you say?'

'I told him to let her go.'

'And he spoke to you?' Lyndsey was still staring into the fire. Emma saw her tighten her arms around her knees again, resting her chin.

'Yes, he spoke to me. He threatened me. He said he had the Parliament's commission to do what he did. Then they suggested I was a witch, too. If . . . I ran away and left her.'

'You had no choice.' Lyndsey swivelled round to face her at last. 'So, who were you, Emma?'

Emma frowned, thinking. Every detail up to now had been clear. She remembered Mary Phillips looking at her. Remembered the pale eyes, the ruddy, greasy cheeks, the huge rough hands of the woman who when her husband was alive had examined her, pressed her stomach, lifted her skirts and squinted between her legs to give a verdict as to why there was no baby. After two years, still no baby. 'It is God's will,' she had announced at last. 'God does not intend you to breed, Sarah Paxman.' She had gloated. There had been no sympathy there. No understanding. No suggestions.

Unlike Liza. Liza had been gentle. Liza had been sympathetic. Liza had suggestions.

'Well?' Lyndsey's voice cut through her thoughts impatiently. 'Do you know who you were?'

Emma nodded at last. 'Sarah Paxman.' She glanced up at Lyndsey's face and was astonished at the glee she saw there.

'Yes!' Lyndsey scrambled to her feet. 'I knew it!' She went to the dresser and picked up the bottle, then she came and sat on the edge of the sofa, reaching over to pour another half an inch into Emma's glass. 'You've been sent to help me! At first I didn't realise it, but I thought about it again when you told me about being a Bennett and our being cousins. Then I knew.'

'Knew what?' Emma studied her face uneasily.

'I told you. You are here to help me sort him out. Contain him. Sarah Paxman was our ancestor, Emma. She was Sarah Bennett before she married. She was born up at Overly.' Putting down the glass, she slipped onto her knees in front of her and put her hands over Emma's. 'I haven't been able to raise the power on my own. Oh, enough to hold him down when he was weak. That was no problem. I performed monthly rituals in the churchyard over his grave. It held him; kept him helpless. But he grew stronger. At first I blamed you for it because you had moved into Liza's, but that was silly. I didn't understand. Then I found out about all the other things. Do you know about spirits and ghosts? Do you know how they feed on energy?' She searched Emma's face for a moment with her intense blue gaze and then shook her head. 'No, of course you don't. It doesn't matter. I will teach you everything you need to know. The balance has gone. Things have been happening here. One of them is the new priest. The man who has taken my things. He has started to stick his nose in and interfere. He came to the churchyard. At least he has noticed something is going on, which is more than his predecessor did, and I am sure he thinks he is helping but it is quite the reverse. He is adding to the energy. He doesn't know enough about the spirit world. He doesn't understand these things. He is open. Vulnerable. Stupid.' She shook her head. 'Just what we don't need. Hopkins will have him on toast. Then there are those men making a film about Barker's shop. Stupid again. Don't they see what

260

they are doing? They are conjuring him – creating him – begging him to appear. I went and spoke to them, pleaded with them not to go on with it, but no, they wouldn't listen. We're probably going to see that programme on national TV any day now and then he will be able to draw on the energy of millions – *millions* – of people!' She was still clutching Emma's hands. 'We have to get to him first.' She scrambled to her feet. 'You'll have to learn a few things. Quickly, before you get any more involved, but that's all right. I'll teach you –'

'Wait!' Emma extricated her hands and standing up, pushed past her to go and stand in front of the fire. 'Wait, Lyndsey. I can't – I won't get involved in all this!'

Lyndsey's face hardened. 'You are involved.'

'No, I'm not. I've just had a few nightmares. And that's hardly surprising, considering I've moved into a witch's cottage, but that doesn't mean I am going to be drawn into some, what . . . vendetta? The man has been dead for three hundred years!'

'And his spirit does not rest.'

'But he can't hurt anyone. Not now. Why should he?'

'Because he is consumed by hate. And because he cannot be allowed to escape punishment. While he is earthbound he can continue his campaign. He is beyond retribution. To face just punishment he has to move on.'

'Move on where?' Emma was growing more and more confused and uncomfortable.

'To the next plane. The lower astral. Hell, if you prefer.' Lyndsey smiled. 'You've seen the pictures of Hieronymous Bosch? You've read Dante's *Inferno*? You must have. Those are the torments he will face; the torments of the damned; he will face the tortures he inflicted on all those women. He is still fighting it. He is terrified. He knows what will happen to him.'

Emma was edging towards the door. 'Lyndsey, I'm sorry. I can't do this. I don't even want to hear about it . . .'

'Why did you come then?' Lyndsey stared at her, then she took a sudden step back. 'You're not a Christian?'

'No, I'm not. At least,' Emma hesitated, 'I don't know what I am. But I know what I'm not. I'm not a witch. I don't belong to a coven. I don't believe in vendettas.'

'I don't belong to a coven,' Lyndsey put in softly. 'Perhaps it would be better if I did. If I am anything, I am what is called a hedge witch.' She gave a brief, wry grin. 'We have never really had covens in this country. Not in historical times, anyway. I work alone. For good.' She turned away, her shoulders slumped. 'Why did you come and see me, if you don't want to help?'

'I . . .' Emma tried to collect her thoughts. 'I needed to find out what was going on. I was upset by the dream. But I didn't want to join in. I didn't want to get involved.'

'You are involved. I told you. Whether you want it or not. By blood and by choice. You gave up your poncey city life to come here. The house called you back. Liza called you back. And Sarah. Sarah who was our ancestor; your ancestor.' Lyndsey grabbed her arm. 'Don't you understand? You were brought here to help me.'

She's right. You were brought here to send Matthew Hopkins to hell.

The quiet voice in Emma's head cut suddenly through every sound in the room. She put her hands up to her ears, terrified. It was the first time she had heard the voice outside her dreams since she had moved into Liza's.

Lyndsey stood back. 'What is it? What's wrong?'

And you will find him in the last place on earth you think to look . . .

'Emma? What's wrong?' Lyndsey put her hands on her shoulders and gripped tightly, shaking her slightly.

'I don't know. I thought I heard a voice –'

'Protect yourself, Emma. Do you know how to do that? Hold on. I'm here to help you. You'll be safe with me . . .'

'No!' Emma tore herself away from Lyndsey. 'No!' She turned and ran towards the door. Pulling it open, she ran out onto the quay. The night was cloudy, the water black and gently moving on the tide. For a second she stopped, blinded by the dark, then she turned and ran along the front of the cottages to head back up towards the fountain where she had left her car.

With shaking hands, she forced the key into the lock and opened the door, climbed in and pulled it shut behind her.

Lyndsey had not followed her. Standing in the doorway of her cottage she stared out into the darkness, then she lifted her hand and outlined the protective pentagram in the air. The shape hung there, glowing slightly for a moment before it dissipated into a mist and disappeared. Satisfied, Lyndsey closed the door and bolted it. Picking up her glass she resumed her seat in front of the fire and closed her eyes to meditate. Emma was not going to go very far.

She would soon be back. As she sat, cross-legged, weaving her meditation, Lyndsey began to smile.

In the car Emma rushed to get the key into the ignition. The engine didn't respond. As she turned the key again, peering through the windscreen into the dark, the first drops of rain began to fall.

Inside her head the voice laughed softly.

51

Monday night

There had been little time to review the day's chaotic happenings. Mike had had a hospital visit that afternoon, followed by a meeting of the bell fund committee, an interview with a young couple who wanted to marry in the church and two local home visits before he made his way back into the cold, dark rectory at nine o'clock that evening and slammed the door shut behind him. There were ten messages waiting for him on the answer machine. With a sigh he pressed the button and started to listen.

Within minutes the disembodied voices were talking to themselves. Seated at the desk, his head cushioned on his arms, the exhausted rector of St Michael's was fast asleep once more. 'You have no more messages.' The tinny female voice was adamant. Her subsequent silence was followed by a click and a whirr as the machine reset itself. Mike heard nothing of it.

You didn't listen! The voice now hissing in his ear was male and full of scorn. *Open your eyes, man! See what I see! See what they do. Watch them! See the evil everywhere around you!*

Mike sighed sleepily. In some deep recess of his mind he knew he should try to fight; to push the voice away, but it was no use. He was too tired and it was too firmly entrenched inside his head. The eyes through which he saw in his dream were another man's eyes, the brain another man's brain, the thoughts, the education, the beliefs, all belonged to a man who had lived three hundred and fifty years ago; a man who was haunted by bad dreams. A man who was already in hell.

It was standing at the foot of his bed. A great black bear, its jaws slavering blood and spittle, its huge claws reaching out towards him. He screamed, cowering back.

'So, you would try interfering with the Devil's work!' The bear was speaking to him. 'You persecute my servants; you hunt down my followers. But it is all to no avail. I shall win. I shall defeat the followers of Christ.' It shuffled forward and he realised there was someone else in the room with him. It was Mary Phillips with her ugly spike. She was holding it out towards the bear as it turned its beady eyes on her. 'Get thee behind me, Satan!' Her face was greasy with fear and rage.

The bear shuffled closer to them.

'Don't make it angry, Mary.' He glanced at her in terror. 'Don't goad it. Put away that spike . . .' He frowned, and looked again. The white cap was the same, the black dress, the stern, angry mouth, but the woman beside him was not Mary Phillips, it was Judith Sadler, and she was laughing at him, and in her hand he could see the spike. Now it was dripping with blood, which was splashing down her apron, and she had turned towards him.

Mike woke with a shout of fear and found himself sitting at his desk. He had knocked over the mug which held his pencils and pens and they were rolling around onto the floor. The answer machine was still flashing at him. It now showed eleven calls, so the phone must have rung again whilst he was asleep.

He rubbed his face hard with the palms of his hands. His mouth was dry and he was shivering violently.

Christ be with me, Christ within me.

He pushed back the chair and stood up. The curtains at the windows were open and he went to close them, conscious suddenly of eyes staring in out of the dark. After a moment's hesitation he went back to the desk.

The phone rang on and on in Tony and Ruth's house without answer. He held on for several minutes, his knuckles white on the receiver, until at last he put it down. Where on earth were they? He was beginning to be really worried. He was halfway through dialling Judith's number when he stopped and put his finger on the rest to disconnect the call. Judith had been in the dream.

Forcing himself to listen to the eleven messages was a kind of therapy. Three were from Judith, sounding, as always when she could not get hold of him, increasingly irritated. Four were from parishioners, one from the bishop's secretary. One was from the book shop saying the book he had ordered had come in, two cut off without a word and the last was from Don Cunliffe, his spiritual adviser.

He stared at the phone, suspiciously. Had Judith been meddling again? Suggesting to Don that Mike needed counselling? Perhaps he should ring Don. Discuss the dream, the whole Matthew Hopkins thing, with him. He stood up and walked over to the bookcase and back, a path often trodden while he was thinking. Don would take the whole thing out of his hands, notify the bishop's office, contact John Downing and his team, in a purely consultative role of course because he would not believe a word of it, he would forbid Mike to contact Tony and Ruth and recommend he take a holiday.

It would be wrong not to confide his worries to John, but he already knew he would not be doing so. He chewed his lip thoughtfully. The so-called 'help' from the deliverance office had arrived only that morning. A booklet of prayers and a letter from John Downing apologising for not coming back to him sooner, hoping that matters had rectified themselves and asking him to get in touch if he still had any worries. He paused as he walked up and down. It was strange that his spiritual adviser should ring him while he was actually having the dream. Was it Our Lord's way of helping? Something to put his mind at rest?

He found himself looking down into the fireplace. It was a mess of scattered cold ash. The log basket was empty. He considered it for a moment. It would be so nice to have a roaring log fire, to pull up that old leather armchair and maybe pour himself a small glass of whisky. But to fetch the logs he would have to go out of the back door, across the small courtyard between the house and various dilapidated outbuildings, cross the drive and grope in the dark at the huge pile of logs which had been ordered by Donald James in a fit of generous insight which had astonished Mike, but which had unfortunately been delivered and therefore just dumped anywhere, while he was out. The garden at the moment was cold and dark and quite probably crawling with bears. He forced himself to smile, mocking his own cowardice.

When the front door bell rang, jangling through the empty house, he nearly jumped out of his skin.

52

When the car had refused to start, Emma got out, slammed the door, locked it and kicked the tyre nearest her. 'Bastard thing!' She stared round. A group of lads were hanging around outside the Thorn. They had seen her run up from the quay, watched her jump in and slam the door, seen her struggle with the ignition, hit the steering wheel with the flat of her hands and climb out, defeated. One of them jeered. She glared over her shoulder to where the road ran down into the dark alleyway which led back to the quayside cottages. Lyndsey hadn't followed her, but she could feel her still watching her, calling her, exerting what felt like an almost irresistible force to draw her back into the cottage and her web of occult intrigue.

'Need some help, darling?' One of the youths had detached himself from the group. He sauntered over.

'No! Thank you. No need.' She glanced at the stubble-length head of blond hair, the gold earring, the can of lager in his hand. 'I've a friend just round the corner. Thanks all the same.'

It would have been easy to duck back down the dark alleyway to Lyndsey's, but she wasn't sure which she feared most, the scheming witch or the leering example of modern youth. Instinctively she opted for neither. Instead she walked determinedly away from him up the village street. For a moment she thought he was going to follow her, but he contented himself with an inarticulate jeer, the meaning of which was – luckily – hidden in a plethora of glottal stops. She did not look back. It was only as she passed the coldly flood-lit splendour of the twin towers, all that remained of Robert Adam's glorious dream of a church, that she realised she had committed herself to a long cold walk along the edge of the river. Either that or go back and face the boys. Or Lyndsey.

Head down, hands in pockets, she walked quickly, intensely

aware of the broad black expanse of water to her right as it sucked gently at the edge of the salt marsh. Two cars drove past, their headlights reflecting on the wet road, which was the more desolate for its occasional streetlights flickering between the wind-blown branches of the sycamore trees. Glancing behind her nervously she quickened her pace. Ahead of her the lights of Manningtree were bright and welcoming, but she had no idea what she would do when she got there.

Her brain was whirling now. She was running through her brief list of local acquaintances who lived in Manningtree itself. Alex lived several miles away in Bradfield. Will Fortingale, who she had seen once or twice since she had used his services as a house agent, lived with his wife in Brantham, in the other direction, the friendly builder who had knocked the wall through between her kitchen and the little dining room, and put in the cat flap and the bookshelves in her den, and so far failed to finish the floorboards and adored opera, lived in Colchester.

That left Mike Sinclair. As she turned up Quay Street away from the river into the deserted, rain-swept streets he was the only person she could think of who was within walking distance and who might consider it part of his job to rescue ladies in distress; and at least she knew where he lived. She had noticed the rectory once when she had turned up Church Street in the mistaken impression that it would provide a shortcut back to Liza's.

The rectory lay in darkness. The rain was coming down in earnest now, trickling down her neck, soaking her jeans and her jacket as, her hand on the gate, she stared at the house in despair. It had not occurred to her that he might be out. Now, as she pushed open the gate and walked across the gravel towards the house her heart had sunk, and when she rang the bell it was in no expectation of being answered. She didn't ring again. She had already turned away when the door opened behind her.

She almost sobbed with relief as the porch light came on and Mike appeared. He was in his shirtsleeves, looking totally exhausted and for a moment she thought he didn't recognise her. But almost at once his face cleared and he smiled.

'Emma!' He hesitated, the smile vanishing as quickly as it had come to be replaced by a worried frown. 'Is something wrong? Come in.'

She followed him into the long shabby hall and from there into his study. The house, even in comparison to the wet darkness outside, was very cold.

'I'm sorry to disturb you so late.' She realised she was trembling. 'I didn't know who to turn to . . .'

'Wait.' He held up his hand. 'It's freezing in here. I've been out all day, I'm afraid. Let me fetch some logs and put a match to the fire. That would be quicker than waiting for the antiquated heating, and I'll put the kettle on. You look as though you could do with a hot drink. Then you can tell me what you're doing here in the middle of the night.'

She didn't know what courage it took to go out into the dark and stand with his back to the dark misty garden, groping for a few of the least-wet logs from the pile.

Kill the witch. While she's here. The perfect opportunity!

He dropped a log and swore. Christ be with me.

She is your enemy. If you do not kill her, she will kill you!

Christ within me. Christ behind me, Christ before me.

He threw the last log in the basket and hefting it up with a groan, he headed back through the rain towards the house.

He put the basket down by the hearth and then disappeared again into the kitchen, to return five minutes later with a whisky bottle, two glasses, a kettle and a lemon. 'Unless you'd prefer tea?'

Emma shook her head. She shed her wet jacket after he lit the fire – four fire-lighters, she noticed – and pulling a chair close to the flames, she accepted the glass of hot whisky and lemon gratefully.

'I've been a fool!'

'OK. Tell me.' He seemed more composed, once more comfortably within his professional persona.

She glanced at him, reluctant to break Lyndsey's confidence and yet desperately needing to confide. 'I went to see Lyndsey again.' She saw him tense slightly. 'I found out yesterday that we were cousins of some sort.' She gave an uncomfortable little laugh. 'I needed to talk about it.' She sipped from her glass, watching as the fire flared up the chimney, not noticing his expression. He was staring at her, aghast.

I told you she was a witch!

'This is the second whisky I've had this evening. She gave me one too.'

Somehow he managed to control his features. He merely raised an eyebrow. 'You needn't drink it if you don't want to.'

She gave a small laugh. 'I'll hang on to it, thanks.' She looked up. 'What have you done with her magic things? You did take them from the churchyard?'

'Yes, I took them. And I destroyed them.'

'Ah.' She shrugged.

'She could hardly have thought otherwise.'

'Probably not.'

'Did she tell you what she was doing with them?'

Emma hesitated.

'I see. This is part of the confidences you feel you must keep,' he said gently. 'Well, obviously you mustn't tell me anything you don't want to, but on the other hand, remember Lyndsey is playing with fire. I doubt if she understands quite what she has got herself into here.'

Emma smiled ruefully. 'That's more or less what she said about you.'

'Ah, professional rivalry.' He grinned. It suited him. He looked younger, less haggard, almost handsome again in the flickering firelight. 'That doesn't quite explain, though, why you turned up on my doorstep in the middle of the night, unless you came to tell me what she was doing.'

'It's not the middle of the night, Mike.' She glanced at her watch. 'It's not even ten yet.'

'But that is the middle of the night round here.' He laughed. You town folk keep different hours. I'm just a simple country parson, don't forget.'

'Then I'm sorry I disturbed you.' Instead of being amused, suddenly she was irritated again. 'Perhaps you could ring for a taxi for me and I'll get out of your hair.' Draining her glass, she set it down with a thump on the table next to her chair and stood up.

'Hey! Whoa! Don't be silly, sit down!' He raised his hands in surrender. 'I'm sorry; I was joking. Please, Emma, just tell me from the beginning what happened to upset you. Something must have.'

She slumped back into the chair. 'My car broke down.'

He stared. 'So this has nothing to do with Lyndsey?'

'Not really, no. I was scared by some local yokels outside the Thorn. I didn't want to walk past them and I set off in the wrong direction. And I walked and I walked, then it started raining, and well, in the end you were the only person I could think of who I knew. What's so funny?' She glared at him.

Mike was laughing. 'I see. So, you came here *faute de mieux*! Well, I'm pleased you felt you could, and I wouldn't think of getting you a taxi. I'll run you home.' He sat back in his own chair, a shabby comfortable leather armchair which had probably been in the rectory for generations. 'And I thought it was spiritual guidance you were after! So, Lyndsey didn't say or do anything to upset or frighten you?'

'Not really.' She refused to meet his eye. The temptation to tell him the truth, that Lyndsey had been trying to recruit her for a war on the side of the witches, to tell him about her dreams, was very strong, but somehow she couldn't bring herself to do it. She frowned at the flames.

And there was something else; another reason she didn't feel she could tell him. When he smiled, when he was himself, Mike was an attractive man, easy to talk to, to trust. But, from time to time, there was something about him that frightened her. A cold shadow seemed to descend on him and distance him from her. Then he reminded her of her dreams; in fact, though it seemed a preposterous idea, he reminded her of no one so much as the Matthew Hopkins of her nightmare. He didn't look like him in any way, or behave like him, or sound like him and yet, suddenly hanging over him there was a strange cloak of semblance; a miasma. Perhaps it was the churchy atmosphere, the Puritan holier-than-thou image, not that Mike seemed to have that kind of image. Not for a second had he patronised or proselytised her. In fact he had been nothing but kind. Perhaps it was just that he was wrestling with his own demons?

'So, what's the decision?' His voice was very gentle. Persuasive. She jumped. 'Decision?'

'You are obviously embroiled in a deep internal conflict.'

She scowled. 'Very observant of you.'

'Part of the job, I'm afraid. And whatever Lyndsey thinks, I do have a certain amount of experience to draw on.'

'But, as you said, there are confidences I don't think I can break.' She was frowning.

He shrugged. 'Then I shall have to respect that. In the meantime, is there anything I can do?'

271

Kill her!

'Apart from drive me home?'

'Apart from drive you home.'

She stared at the hearth. 'Will you be there if I do need you?'

'Of course.'

'Part of the job?'

'As you say.' He considered her thoughtfully for a moment, his blue eyes intense. 'Please, don't be alone and frightened, Emma. You can ring me at any time, OK?' He reached over towards his desk. 'Let me give you my mobile number. You can always get me unless I'm in church and in that case leave a message and I'll get back to you within the hour.'

'Even at midnight?' She smiled at last, trying to make a joke of it.

He nodded. 'Even at midnight.'

53

Tuesday October 27ᵗʰ

Alex dropped the children off at school early and then drove on to Emma's. It was almost exactly nine o'clock when he knocked on her back door. It was several minutes before she answered. There was a fork in her hand. 'Alex, hi! I'm just feeding the cats.' She was wearing a turquoise silk kimono, her hair wrapped in a towel.

Alex blushed. 'I'm sorry. Am I too early?'

'Too early?' She looked exhausted, he noticed. Her face was pinched and there was a transparency in the skin around her eyes.

'You were still expecting me?' He could not keep the crestfallen note out of his voice. 'To discuss the business?'

Smiling, she stepped back and waved him towards the table. 'Grab yourself some coffee. I've only just made it. I had forgotten, to be honest. I had rather a late night last night.' She scooped some disgusting fishy stuff out of a tin onto two small china plates and put them on the floor. The cats, who had been weaving round her ankles, pounced in obvious delight. She washed the fork and then her hands, sniffing at them fastidiously. 'Ugh, the smell of that stuff is awful, but Max and Min love it.' Grabbing her own mug off the hotplate she came and sat opposite him at the table. 'I was hobnobbing with Mike Sinclair at getting on for midnight. Some gossip is bound to tell you!'

Alex looked up. He raised an eyebrow. 'I see.'

'No, you don't, but it doesn't matter. Alex,' she started, then took a sip of the strong black coffee. 'I've had no chance to think about the herb nursery since I saw you. None at all, to be honest.

273

I've had a lot on my mind, what with one thing and another.'

'Ah, yes. Piers.' He nodded. 'Paula spoke to him yesterday.'

There was a second's total silence. 'She did what?'

'She was a bit upset about the row and everything. Didn't want him to think we were taking sides and getting involved, so she gave him a ring. Sort of asked if there was anything we could do to help you two get back together, you know . . .' He suddenly noticed her expression. 'I'm sorry, Emma. It didn't occur to me – to her – that you would mind.'

'Well, I do mind! I mind a lot!' Emma stood up. 'Would you please tell her to mind her own business.'

Alex bit his lip. 'I suppose it was a bit presumptuous.'

'I'll say.' Emma was furious. 'Look, Alex, if you and I are going to have any hope at all of working together at some future date, there are going to have to be some ground rules. And your wife interfering between Piers and me is absolutely forbidden. Do I make myself clear?'

Alex stood up. He was hot with embarrassment. 'Perfectly. I'm really sorry, Emma. She meant it for the best.'

'No doubt.' Emma was still angry. She took a deep breath. 'I'm sorry, but this morning is not a good time after all. Do you mind if we discuss the herbs another day?'

'Sure.' He tried to hide his disappointment. 'No problem. Give me a ring, OK? Whenever you like.'

As he closed the kitchen door behind him she was still standing by the sink, clutching her coffee mug. She did not even appear to have heard him leave.

He drove back by way of Mistley, intending to drive on to the deli in Manningtree to pick up some of his favourite cheese; comfort food which he knew was forbidden. As he passed the swan fountain, he saw Emma's car parked at the side of the road. Frowning, he slowed down, wondering what it was doing there, and as he did so he caught sight of Lyndsey, dressed in white jeans and a blue Sloppy Jo sweater, coming out of the post office. She was holding a carrier bag. Drawing up behind Emma's car, he got out and called her name.

She stopped.

Alex smiled. 'Are you still on to babysit this afternoon?'

He felt guilty about still using Lyndsey so much, in spite of his own doubts about her activities. It was not as though he really needed her. He adored the kids. He loved their company. And just at the moment he wasn't doing much else. Reading, mooching about. Dreaming up plans for the herb garden.

There was a reason, though; one he would never admit to anyone. He hated being seen to collect the children all the time. He didn't enjoy being the one to go round to other people's houses or standing around with all the mothers waiting for them to come out of school. There were fathers there occasionally, and from time to time a couple of grandfathers, and he doubted if anyone actually noticed or cared why he was available to collect them so often anyway. But *he* knew why. He was a failure, without a job and however much he enjoyed the lifestyle, and kidded himself that it was his choice to be there, that treacherous thought still lurked deep down inside him and probably always would.

Lyndsey had nodded. 'I'll be there. Don't worry.'

'How come Emma's car is here?' He slapped its bonnet.

Lyndsey shrugged. 'Perhaps she's come down to the post office.'

'Obviously not or you would have seen her in there.' Alex studied her face for a moment. 'She's at home, actually.'

'Oh.' Lyndsey was looking innocent.

'But she came to see you yesterday, right?'

'She might have.' Lyndsey slung the white plastic bag over her shoulder. 'I didn't magic her away or turn her into a toad, Alex, if that's what you're thinking.' She glanced at him archly.

'Why did she leave her car behind?'

'Perhaps it wouldn't start.' She gave him an enigmatic grin.

'The rector drove her home in the end,' Alex said.

Her eyes narrowed. 'Are you sure?'

He nodded.

'Stupid cow! I warned her.' She sighed. 'What did she tell him?'

'I've no idea.'

'She must have gone straight round to see him when she left me! How could she be such an idiot!'

'So she did come and see you.'

'Yes, she came!' She was impatient.

'And you said something to upset her.'

Lyndsey did not deny it. She tossed her head angrily. 'No point in standing discussing my business in front of everyone.' Two women had walked past them into the post office. 'You'd better come down to mine!'

She led the way across the road, not bothering to see if he was following her, past the craft workshops where somebody was putting out the sign advertising coffee and homemade cakes, and down the road towards her cottage.

Her door was unlocked; pushing it open she threw her bag down on the sofa. 'OK. What did she say?'

'Very little. Only that she'd been talking to the rector until late.'

Lyndsey sighed again. She stood with her back to the empty fireplace, her hands on her hips. 'I thought she was going to be a friend. I thought she was going to help. Did you know she was a Bennett from Overly?' She glared at him as though it might be his fault. 'She's been sent here for a reason. To help me.'

'Oh, come on, Lyn.' He sat down on the edge of the sofa. In daylight the room was shabby rather than exotic, the candles standing in greasy patches of cold wax, dust clearly visible on some of the surfaces.

'The trouble is, she doesn't understand. She won't trust me. She's afraid and she thinks going to the Christian priest is the thing to do.'

'Perhaps it is, Lyn,' Alex said tentatively. 'For her,' he added hastily.

'Well, it's not.' She drummed her fingers on the wooden mantel shelf.

'Don't involve her, Lyn. If she doesn't understand and she doesn't want to do whatever it is you're planning, leave it, OK?' He waited for some sign that she had taken in what he had said. There was none. 'She's a sophisticated, educated woman, with her own views on life.'

'And I'm not?'

'That's not what I said. But a little chat with you is not going to turn her into a witch overnight.' He was frowning with anxiety. 'Just leave her alone to get on with her own thing. She's not going to harm anyone. Or interfere. She doesn't want to get involved. So forget it!' He had become quite red in the face.

'But that's the point. She is involved.' Lyndsey's hands had gone back into her pockets.

'Why?' He stood up, walked to the door, turned and walked back again. It was only four paces each way.

'Because she's been having nightmares, Alex. About Liza.'

'Oh well, if that's all it is. Anyone moving into Liza's could do

276

that, especially if they find out there is black magic going on in the churchyard about ten feet away on the other side of the hedge!'

'It is not black magic, Alex!' For once she didn't rise to his teasing. 'And it's more than nightmares. Liza is calling to Emma for help. She needs to be avenged. And Sarah is with her.'

'Oh Lord!' Alex ran his fingers through what was left of his hair. 'Who is Sarah, for God's sake?'

Lyndsey hesitated. She had read the account of the trials, studied the period and now, through Emma, she had heard Sarah's actual words.

'She was the woman who vowed revenge.'

'No.' He sat down, shaking his head. 'No, Lyn.' He stood up again 'No, this won't do. Leave it.' He used the voice he normally reserved for Sophie and James.

'I can't leave it, Alex.' Lyndsey was staring down at the floor. 'Emma's in danger.' She looked up and held his gaze. 'You fancy her, don't you?' She gave a bleak smile as he vehemently shook his head. 'Well, whatever, but you want to do what's best for her, obviously. This is serious stuff, Alex. Life and death. Sarah and Hopkins were – are – locked in a duel which is escalating. I've tried to contain it. I did contain it. But now . . .' She shook her head 'It's getting out of hand. Bad things are happening. There seems to be evil in the air everywhere and their feud is somehow feeding off it. I need Emma's help and she needs mine. She's in danger, Alex. Deadly danger.'

Alex said nothing for a moment, then he shrugged. 'Then for what it's worth, I think she was right to go to the rector. If you're right, and I hope to goodness you're not because it sounds like something out of a third-rate melodrama, this is his sort of thing.'

Lyndsey shook her head. 'It's not his sort of thing at all,' she said in despair. 'He wouldn't know where to start.'

54

Tuesday was Mike's day off. His head still throbbing from a sleep-less night, too afraid to close his eyes in case the dreams returned, he dealt with all the phone calls on the machine, recorded his 'I'm not here today, but if you need me urgently I can be contacted on my mobile' message, the mobile having its own message as a second backstop asking for specifics. He had long ago discovered that people's ideas of urgent were random to say the least and that very few of his parishioners appreciated the fact that as his busiest working days were at the weekend, he therefore needed one day a week to himself. He could not however ignore the urgent knock on the door.

It was Ruth and Tony. 'We got your message last night, old boy,' Tony said as they followed him through to the kitchen. 'I am so sorry not to have got back to you sooner.' He shrugged ruefully. 'I was taken ill while we were at my son's and Ruthie here and the children made me stay there being pampered and waited on until I was better. They have now certified me fighting fit, so I thought the best thing was to come straight over.' He had noted at once the dark circles under Mike's eyes, the strain on the younger man's face.

Mike's relief at seeing them was palpable. Tony Gilchrist was a tall, broad-shouldered man in his early seventies. He had a wild shock of white hair, a weather-beaten face, witness to his new-found retirement passion for sailing, intelligent hazel eyes and a firm chin. His recent illness showed in the strain around his eyes and a certain pallor beneath the tan, but his cheerfulness was all encompassing. He was not at first sight at all the epitome of a sympathetic country parson, nor was Ruth the typical parson's wife. Outspoken, tactless at times, always a tower of strength, she was a pretty woman with short wavy grey hair, green-grey eyes and a slim, supple figure, almost as tall as her husband. Her complexion matched his, as did her new-found love of boats. Like him she brushed off Mike's concern about Tony's illness and like him she settled down to listen intently to what Mike had to say.

Mike made coffee and toast as he filled them in with the details of the problem as he saw it. 'I can sense things building up. The atmosphere in the shop was bad.' He shrugged. 'I blessed the churchyard and held a communion service there and I felt it had worked. I don't think the girl, Lyndsey, is particularly evil or indeed skilled at what she is doing.'

'Have you met her?' It was Ruth who asked the question. She was watching his face intently.

He shook his head. 'I only went to her house the once. She wasn't there. Judith Sadler, my lay reader, doesn't seem very keen on my trying to meet her. She says it is sufficient that she and her prayer group deal with Lyndsey.' He gave a wry grin. 'She has practically forbidden me to go and see her. I don't think she rates my skills at dealing with the occult very highly.'

Tony raised an eyebrow. 'You are joking. Your lay reader has tried to tell you what you can or can't do?'

'Tried to.' Mike put a loaded toastrack on the table and turned to the fridge for butter and marmalade. He kept most of his supplies in the huge, aged Electrolux. 'I don't take orders from Judith.'

'Do I detect a certain animosity there?' Tony reached for the sugar bowl.

Mike exhaled. 'She feels she could do my job better than me! I have to confess I don't warm to her. I'm working on that.' He pushed the milk jug across the table. 'She wouldn't approve of you, you're not her kind of person.'

Tony laughed. 'I can imagine.'

Ruth gently moved the sugar bowl out of her husband's reach. 'What is her kind of person?'

'Very low church. Puritan. Unforgiving. Rather grim.'

Ruth raised an eyebrow. 'Poor you.'

'She suits a lot of people round here.'

'Right.' Tony did not appear to have heard the exchange. He eyed Mike thoughtfully. 'Tell me about the nightmares. The voices.'

Mike shrugged. 'Getting worse.'

279

Tony nodded. 'Right. Let's make a plan. Churchyard first, I think. To get an idea of what it's like and check out your disinfecting technique.' He grinned. 'Then you can take us to this shop. From what you've told me, Mike, you and this little witch are actually on the same side. She's trying to deal with this manifestation in her own way. She's a Wiccan, not a Satanist, right?'

Mike shrugged and nodded. 'I assume so.'

'We shouldn't assume anything in this job. OK. Maybe there will be time to pay her a visit. Is there anything in your diary for this morning you can't shift?'

Mike smiled ruefully. 'Only a day of rest.'

'Well, maybe once we've sorted this, you'll be able to get a good night's sleep, my friend.' Outmanoeuvring his wife, he managed to spoon two brimming loads of sugar into his cup. A few slight twinges in the heart department were not about to make him change his lifestyle. There were more important things to worry about.

The churchyard was peaceful in the mellow autumn sunlight. Leading the way to the rectangle of greener grass, Mike stood back beside Ruth and waited, head bowed, as Tony prayed over the grave. Nearby a robin watched, bobbing anxiously amongst the crisped leaves on a hawthorn bush.

'In the name of the Father, Son and Holy Spirit, Amen.' Tony stood in silence for several seconds, then he turned to the others. 'All at peace at the moment, anyway. I doubt if this is the epicentre.' He glanced over his shoulder as if listening intently, then he made the sign of the cross over the grave. 'You know, I doubt if it's even our chap buried here. I sense puzzlement. Righteous indignation. But not evil.' He swung round to face the lane. 'And that, I take it, is Liza's behind the hedge? Idyllic country cottage, with attendant black cat ditto.' He had spotted Min sitting on the wall watching them.

Mike shivered in spite of himself. Ruth noticed. 'You have a problem with the cat, Mike?'

He laughed. 'I shouldn't have. I like cats. But Emma's cats are a bit different. They look just that bit too intelligent. And they don't seem to like me.'

'Burmese, Mike, that's all.' Ruth punched him playfully on the arm. 'At least that one is. Sharp as a razor. Would have no trouble running rings round an old softy like you.'

280

'Do you want to go in and see Emma?' Mike led the way across the rough tussocky ground back towards the lane.

'Not today, I think.' Tony followed him, reaching over to take his wife's hand. 'Let's visit the shop next.' Helping Ruth across the wall, he did not notice the expression on Mike's face. Had he done so he might have been as puzzled as Mike by the curious mixture of anguish and relief which flooded through him as they turned away from Liza's.

The same woman was behind the counter in Barker's Shop. She was still eating and greeted Mike's request for access to the upstairs with the same shrug of indifference. The only change was that today there were two customers in the shop picking their way over the baskets of cheap plastic wares. They ignored the newcomers as Mike led the way to the staircase. At the bottom he stopped. 'Do you want to go up first?'

Tony glanced at him and nodded.

'Are you sure you're up to this, Tony?' Ruth's whisper brought her husband up short.

'I wouldn't do anything I thought was dangerous.' He glanced back at her. 'Or too much for the old ticker, if that's what you're worrying about.' He squeezed her arm.

Ruth nodded and smiled. She watched as Tony set off up the stairs, followed by Mike, then, slowly, she brought up the rear.

Mike held his breath as they climbed, intensely aware of how relieved he was that Tony was in front of him. A breastplate indeed!

At the top of the stairs they stood together and surveyed the room. 'Here?' Tony raised an eyebrow.

Mike nodded. 'The face in the video shot was on the stairs we have just climbed.'

'Right.' Tony put down his bag and drew out his white alb. Pulling it on over his head he knotted the girdle firmly, then he walked slowly across the room and perched himself on the edge of a packing case, facing the window. While Mike and Ruth hovered near the stairs, he closed his eyes. The room was very silent.

Mike tried to pray. There was an overwhelming smell of soap powder today. He could see the huge carton of cheap boxes of the stuff by the wall. A dusting of white had spilled onto the oak floorboards where someone had taken a Stanley knife to the polythene a little too enthusiastically. Underlying that smell was the room's usual atmosphere of old wood and dust, warmed by hundreds of years of sunlight shining in through the small leaded window. It was a pleasant, quiet room, innocuous. Slowly he relaxed. Leaning against the wall, watching Tony's bowed head, he felt himself breathing slowly and deeply, lulled out of his fear.

The scream was sudden and horrible, ringing in his ears. He jumped, staring round the room in terror. Ruth hadn't moved.

Tony turned and looked at him. 'Ah, you heard that?'

Mike nodded. His face was white.

'Heard what?' Ruth looked puzzled.

'Pray for us, my darling.' Tony stood up. 'Hold the room in the light. We have a visitor amongst us.'

Mike stared at Ruth in amazement. To his surprise she merely closed her eyes. He saw her lips move as she began to pray. Tony beckoned him to come and stand beside him.

'Did you hear her scream?' Mike tried to steady his voice.

'I felt rather than heard something.' Tony frowned. 'Mike, I want you to pray. Be strong.'

The temperature was dropping as it had before when Mike was there, and the room seemed to be growing darker.

Mike clenched his fists. 'Christ be with me, Christ within me.'

A wisp of mist curled through the room, licking at the boxes, drifting towards him. Nearby Ruth stood quite still, her eyes still closed, her lips moving almost imperceptibly as she prayed.

'Dear Lord, Jesus Christ, protect us by the power of your name.' Tony's voice rang out, unwavering. 'Send your holy angels to defend us. Strengthen us and keep us safe.'

The mist was fine as gossamer. It hung in the air, hardly moving now, veiling the light from the small leaded panes. Mike could feel the touch of it on the skin of his cheek, the back of his hand, and he shrank back, his eyes widening with horror. It had reached Tony now, and was curling round him, caressing him.

'Our Father –' Tony's voice was still strong. 'Which art in heaven –'

Suddenly he stopped. Mike heard him clear his throat. His hand had gone to his mouth and he seemed to be having trouble drawing breath.

282

'Tony!' Ruth's eyes flew open and she lunged towards him. 'Tony, be strong! In the name of Christ, be strong!'

The mist was drifting past them, turning, spiralling slowly a foot or two above the ground.

Mike tried to move. 'Christ be with us . . .' He couldn't breathe. The mist was encircling him, settling over his face, filling his nose, his mouth, forming a cold film across his eyes. The room seemed to be full of drifting shapes, but he couldn't see clearly. Desperately he tried to take a breath, feeling as if clammy cotton were filling his lungs. His head was beginning to roar and he could feel himself losing consciousness.

And then suddenly it was over. As quickly as it had come, the mist dispersed.

Fighting to catch his breath, Mike sat down on a crate, panting, clawing at his streaming eyes.

'Mike? Are you OK?'

Ruth put her hand on his shoulder. Behind her he could see Tony, his face white. In his hand was a small crucifix.

Mike exhaled loudly. He managed to nod. 'What happened?'

'It attacked you.' Tony moved towards him. 'Whatever it was, an energy, some sort of force, it made a bee-line for you. Mike, I want you to leave us, please. Now. Quickly. Focus your mind on prayer and walk away. Go home. We'll follow you.'

'But what about you?'

'We'll be all right. Please, just do as I ask. Quickly. This shop is a centre of something – that is why it is so haunted. The ghosts too use the energy. For some reason you are a focus. I want to see what happens when you are not here.'

Mike looked questioningly at him for a moment, then at Ruth, who had put her hand on her husband's arm, then he gave a reluctant nod. Turning away he almost ran towards the stairs. *Christ be with me, Christ within me!* Somehow he managed to smile at the woman behind the counter as he headed swiftly across the floor. 'The others will be down shortly.'

She nodded and turned to ring up a sum on the till. It was normal down here, as though nothing at all had happened. Mike heard her flat, bored request for seventy-five pence as he walked out into the street and closed the door behind him.

Taking a deep shuddering breath, he paused to stare up at the windows. There was no sign of life. From the road he could see how dirty the panes of glass were, with a rime of dust and old bleached moss clinging to the corners where in winter the damp would reach further and further into the timber.

Go home, Tony had said. And pray.

Something was going on up there behind those windows. Something which he could not be allowed to witness. Tense with fear and anxiety, he began to walk away.

55

Pushing open the front door, Paula paused and listened. Silence. For a moment she thought the house was empty, then she spotted Alex through the back window. He had been mowing the lawn. She saw his face red with effort, his hands stained green from grass cuttings. The mower blades must have jammed again. Dropping her briefcase and bag she went out. 'Hi there! Guess who has skived off from the office early!'

Alex smiled absent-mindedly. Wiping his forehead with the back of his arm he left an endearing green streak behind as he leaned over to kiss the air about four inches from her cheek. 'Just thought I'd give it the last cut of the year. So, how was the day? It's not like you to walk out.'

'No, well, I was feeling a bit stressed. Where are the kids?'

'Lyndsey's got them. There is some project on at the library. Then they're going to look for driftwood or something.' He opened his mouth as though about to say something and paused.

Paula raised an eyebrow. 'Yes?'

He gave a reluctant shrug. 'We are right to trust her, aren't we?'

There was a moment's silence. 'You were the one telling me she was OK, Alex.' Paula unbuttoned her jacket. She looked out of place in her City clothes and high heels. 'What's happened?'

He shrugged. 'Nothing, really. I'm not worried about the kids. No,' he considered, head on one side. 'No, of course I'm not. Not for one single second. Actually, it's Emma.'

'Emma?' Paula stared, immediately suspicious. 'What has Emma got to do with anything?'

'I saw Lyn this morning. She was coming out of the post office and I stopped to make sure she'd remembered about the kids. She . . .' he hesitated. 'She and Emma had some kind of altercation and –' he paused again. How could he tell her that he was convinced Lyn had put a spell on Emma's car! He shook his head.

285

'She is convinced Emma is in some sort of danger,' he finished awkwardly.

'Danger?' Paula echoed him again. 'For God's sake, what kind of danger?' She turned on her heel and headed back towards the French doors. 'What nonsense! The trouble with Lyn is she lets her imagination run riot. I suppose this is all her witchy rubbish.' She paused and turned round. 'It is rubbish, isn't it?'

Alex nodded. 'Of course it is! No rational person believes in all that. I just don't like the way she's winding Emma up. The trouble is, now she's working up at Oliver Dent's she cycles past Liza's every day. Emma finds it a bit disconcerting. She's putting so much into that cottage.' There was a pause. 'She was very upset, by the way, that you talked to Piers.'

'Upset?' Paula stepped inside with Alex behind her. 'You've seen her today, I gather.'

'Of course. I went up to discuss setting up the herb garden business. There is so much potential up there. Oh, I told her you didn't mean to interfere. After all, we all got on so well at the dinner party it would have been quite normal for you and Piers to be in touch. You have so much in common.' He paused. 'In fact, Piers might have rung you to thank you for the meal.'

'But he didn't.' Paula absent-mindedly headed for the stairs. 'I'll go and change, Alex, OK? Then I want to pop into the village before the shops shut, so if you want to finish the mowing, I'll pick up a bottle of wine for us while I'm out.'

It was only as she pulled on her thick sweater and jeans that she realised that was a stupid thing to say. They had racks of the stuff.

The bottle of red wine was for Emma. Pulling her car in at Liza's, Paula climbed out and stared round. It was an idyllic spot, up a quiet lane, with views over the hedges towards the broad estuary and in the distance to the sea. She sighed, for a moment quite envious.

Emma had just lit a fire in the living room.

'I wanted to apologise.' Paula followed her in and offered the bottle. 'A peace offering. I never meant to upset you by ringing Piers. I really didn't. It was wrong of me and I'm very sorry.'

Emma gestured her towards the sofa. 'Alex shouldn't have told you. I over-reacted. The relationship is a bit dodgy, as you probably gathered.'

Paula grimaced. 'Everyone goes through bad patches.'

'Not this bad.' Emma smiled sadly. 'Alex has been really kind. It's a bit scary when one moves to a new place not knowing anyone.'

'And lonely, I expect.' Paula tightened her lips for a second.

Emma glanced at her. She was still holding the wine bottle and she held it out. 'Shall we open this?' She fetched the corkscrew and two glasses. 'Paula, you don't mind Alex coming over here, do you?'

Paula looked away, embarrassed by her directness. 'Of course not. It's just – oh, you know, he finds it hard to resist beautiful women. I don't mean he has affairs or anything – he doesn't. At least, I don't think so. It's just – oh, hell! I'm not dealing with this very well.'

Emma shook her head. 'You don't have to worry, Paula. He's been kind, but there's no' – Emma shrugged – 'you know, attraction, not on my part, at least.' She handed Paula a glass. 'I still love Piers. I don't know if we can ever work this all out, but I'm not looking for anyone else. Honestly.'

Paula nodded. 'I believe you.'

'I'm glad, because it's true! You should trust Alex more.' The comment came out more harshly than she intended, and she saw Paula's lips purse angrily. She was about to try and soften the remark when the door opened and Max pushed his way in. He stopped and looked enquiringly at Paula, who shrank back into the sofa cushions. 'Oh, God, can you make it go away? I hate cats.'

Emma frowned. 'Of course. Go on, Max, out you go.' She shooed him out and shut the door behind him.

Paula relaxed. She took several sips of the wine. It was too cold and it hadn't breathed but it was nice. It loosened her tongue. She decided to change the subject. 'I gather, while we're all being so very honest and swapping gossip, that Lyndsey Clark has been pestering you.'

'Pestering is a bit strong.' Emma sat down beside the fire, thankful that they were no longer discussing Alex. 'She unnerves me.'

'She's told you she likes to think of herself as a witch?' Paula took another sip. 'It's all nonsense, of course. She enjoys shocking people. Take no notice. Actually, I'm not much better, am I. I know I told you there was a ghost here, but there's no such thing.

All old houses lend themselves to ghost stories.' She glanced round critically as though assessing the potential for ghostly activity in the room. 'You mustn't let me scare you. I don't think I had appreciated that you were living on your own. I thought Piers was here at least some of the time . . .' She sighed and raising her glass, took a large gulp of wine.

Emma was staring at the fire. 'The trouble is, I think I am a bit spooked. I've been having nightmares.'

'Nightmares?'

Emma nodded. 'Horrid ones. Had another last night. It's getting so bad I'm kind of afraid of going to sleep.' She gave a small, self-deprecating laugh.

'Emma, that's awful!' Paula stared at her, for the first time taking in the drawn weariness on the other woman's face. 'Look, have you got a doctor here? If not I'll recommend ours. He's really good. He can give you some sleeping pills. Real knock out bombs. He gave me some and they were brilliant.' She hesitated. 'What are they about, do you mind me asking?'

'My dreams? They are about witches. This place. Death. Torture.'

Paula drew back in distaste. 'That's ghastly.'

'Yes.'

'But it's nothing to do with Lyndsey. Is it?'

Emma shrugged. 'I don't know. There's something odd going on.' She stopped and then went on. 'Lyndsey and I have found out we're cousins.'

'You're joking!' Paula seemed genuinely shocked.

'No.' Emma glanced at the table where the albums and letters sent by her mother were spread out. She had spent the whole morning studying them.

'Well,' Paula went on thoughtfully, 'of course Lyndsey is far more well-heeled than she lets on, isn't she? Rich posh parents. So, I suppose, if I think about it, I'm not all that surprised.'

'She doesn't seem very happy.'

'No.' Paula frowned. 'Although I don't know why. She's terribly good with our kids. They adore her. And she always used to seem happy. Painting. Writing. I think she's working on some kind of book about plants. That's what she was reading at Cambridge. Botany.'

'She must be clever.' Emma was picturing the small dark room, the shabby possessions. She did not remember seeing any books. 'The point I was making, though, about our being cousins. It's actually made quite a difference to me. I don't feel quite so alone, even though we don't get on.' She gave a wry laugh. 'It's tough moving, isn't it? Until the vicar calls.' She meant it as a joke, but somehow the words sounded all wrong.

Paula scanned her face thoughtfully. 'What do you think of him?'

Emma took a deep breath. 'Well, Lyndsey worries him.'

'So she should. That's his job, to worry about witches.' Paula laughed. 'He's quite dishy, don't you think?'

Emma smiled. 'I find him . . .' She paused, looking for the right word. 'Unsettling. Yes, he's good-looking. Very. But he makes me feel uneasy. There's something –' she hesitated again, her eyes fixed on the middle-distance. 'It's tied up with all this. The witches. Liza's. Lyndsey. Ghosts. My nightmares.' Her voice faded to a whisper.

Paula stared at her. She took another quick gulp of wine. 'Do you go to church?'

Emma shook her head.

'Perhaps you should. If you don't like Mike Sinclair, you could always go to our church up here.'

Emma raised an eyebrow. 'I think I shall take a rain check. I am relying on myself rather than divine intervention at the moment.'

Paula drained her glass and stood up. 'Well, if you come from a family of witches, perhaps the church would be better off without you.' She gave a forced smile. 'Who knows how much has rubbed off? OK. I have to go. Just remember, don't rely too much on my husband, because if you do, you and I are not going to get on.'

56

'So, you see, the shop is a centre, though from our walk around the town I'd say this problem spreads over the whole area.' Tony was sitting in the worn leather chair opposite Mike. The answer machine on the desk was blinking again. So far the message count had reached seven. 'My guess is that there are places round here where this sense of evil is strong and those places attract paranormal phenomena. And probably always have.' He frowned. 'Maybe that is what caused the witch mania to focus here in the first place.'

'What do you mean by evil?' Mike stared at him. 'Where did it come from in the first place if not from the witches themselves?'

Tony leaned back in his chair thoughtfully. 'I'll explain. The phenomena disappeared completely after you had gone, you know. We prayed for a while and then left.' He linked his fingers over his stomach. 'I have come across this before in different parts of the country, but never so strongly as here. There are strong energies in the land here, at the edge of the sea. These are natural energies of some sort, which seem to come up out of the ground as a neutral force which can then be harnessed for whatever uses by whoever knows how. They are just there. And people in past times who had the correct esoteric training knew how to use them. The Templars, for instance.' He nodded wisely. 'There are incredible energy sources under their round churches and towers. And the Vikings and Norsemen and Anglo-Saxons harnessed this force too, for their darker northern magic.' He glanced at Mike. 'My guess is that your problem here has roots across the North Sea. But, whoever they were who operated in this area, their magic was strong. They knew how to harness the energy and they used it for what we would call evil purposes; and when they went away they left their evil behind them to swirl in and out with the tides, to drift in and out in the mist and it is still there, to be used by whoever knows how.'

Mike shivered. 'I've seen that mist. And sensed it. It was even there in the shop today.'

Tony nodded.

'And the witches use it?'

'I suspect so. But so can we. We can go to the source of the energy and harness it ourselves in the service of the light.'

'If we know how.' Mike grimaced.

Tony got up and stood in front of the fire. 'If we know how. The energy comes and goes, Mike. I don't know why – perhaps it's something to do with the seasons or the stars or something. But at the moment here, things are bad. People all over the area will be feeling it. They will be unhappy. Jumpy. The crime rate is probably going up. Violence will be escalating beyond the local norm and I'm afraid I have the feeling that you are in some way one of the catalysts, Mike. The shop is acting as some kind of vent hole for the energy at the moment and you are in some way involved. Clergymen often are targets, of course, just because of who they are. I was interested to see if the atmosphere changed after you left. To see if it followed you.'

'It?' Mike felt the short hairs on the back of his neck stir.

'It for now.' Tony nodded thoughtfully. 'It might be an energy, no more than that, or the unpleasant atmosphere itself. Or it might be a he, or a she, or possibly both.'

'Great!' Mike folded his arms across his chest. He shivered. 'And did it follow me?'

Tony smiled. 'On this occasion, no.'

'Thank God for that!'

'Amen.' Tony nodded. 'Now, tell me, who have you told about this, Mike? Have you discussed it with anyone?'

Mike shrugged. 'One or two people, that's all. Judith, of course. A chap called Mark Edmunds. He's one of the TV people making the film. Emma Dickson.' He hesitated. He needed to talk about Emma, but at the same time, for reasons he couldn't quite work out, he was reluctant to do so, even with Tony. 'I get the feeling she knows more about all this than she's told me,' he said cautiously. 'And she knows Lyndsey Clark. She caught her in the act, as it were.'

'Have you discussed all this with your spiritual adviser?'

Mike shook his head.

'Or the bishop's deliverance team?'

Mike grinned. 'I spoke to John Downing and was told to leave it to them. It was also suggested that a psychiatrist might be useful! For me! That is why I came to you, Tony. I'm sure they are excellent chaps, but I want advice.'

Behind them the door opened. Ruth appeared, carrying a tray. She and Tony had called in at the deli on their way back to the rectory and brought with them a wonderful selection of cheeses and pasties plus some organic bread and a four-pack of lager.

'Think of it as grounding,' Tony grinned and reached for one of the cans. 'You've got some hard work ahead of you, Mike. Spiritual work. I would like you to ask the owners of that shop permission to hold a requiem Eucharist up there. But I'm afraid that may just concentrate what is going on elsewhere.' He glanced at Mike, who was licking pâté off his fingers and missed the look. 'In the meantime we must try to defuse the situation. Can you get them to give up on the TV show?'

Mike shook his head. 'I doubt it. I've already asked.'

Tony pursed his lips. 'Right. Then we have a fight on our hands. Even without this extra dimension you must take witchcraft seriously, Mike. The church is very worried about its spread and its popularity. When I was training for the priesthood they used to warn us to be aware that in certain places, and Essex was one of them,' he grinned wryly, 'there might be people who would try to palm the host at Communion so they could sell it to a witch later. We may find we have a widespread problem.' He glanced at his watch. 'Now, Ruthie and I have to go, I'm afraid.' He drained his can of lager. 'I'm going to think and pray and I want you to do the same, and arrange if you can a time for us to hold a service in the shop – ASAP. Pray hard, Mike. The Lord will protect you, you know that, but He will expect you to be strong for yourself as well!'

Mike found himself staring at the empty plates for a long time after they had gone. He picked at a sliver of cheese. The house suddenly felt deserted.

Think and pray, Tony had said.

The church was shady, lit only fitfully by the watery afternoon light filtering through the windows. Walking slowly up to the altar he stared up at the stained glass above his head.

'Dear Lord, as always I need your help and advice. Give me strength and protection against the forces of darkness. Fill this town with your light and your love. Give your strength to those involved – Emma, Mark and his colleagues, Judith, Tony and Ruth, and particularly bless and save Lyndsey from her dalliance with the Devil. Make her understand the danger. Hold her in your love . . .'

Slowly he knelt down. Closing his eyes he whispered the Lord's prayer.

Behind him the church slowly grew darker.

When the door opened with a clank of handle and squeak of hinges, Mike jumped. He paused a moment, realising that the window was now completely dark and, standing up, he turned as a light came on by the door.

'Sorry to interrupt.' It was Mark Edmunds. 'I tried the rectory, so I thought I'd pop in here on the off chance and see if you were in the office, so to speak.'

Mike smiled. 'And you were right. But I was about to go home. How are you?'

'OK. I've been doing some more homework about the Witchfinder and his friends and I wondered if you would be interested in it.'

Mike glanced over his shoulder. Sometimes even he was astounded by the quick response from 'Him upstairs'.

As they strode up the lane side by side through a freshening wind, Mike was considering how to broach the subject of cancelling the film once he got Mark into his study for a serious talk. He was counting without his parishioners, however. As they walked up the drive a figure stepped out from the porch. 'Is that you, Rector?'

Mike recognised the hunched figure of Bill Standing. 'What can I do for you, Bill?'

'I'd like a word, if you please.' Bill glanced at Mark without recognition.

Mark took the hint. 'Why don't I go for a walk, come back when you're free, Mike?'

Bill refused a seat. He stood with his back to the empty fireplace, twisting his cap between his hands. 'There's sommat wrong, Rector.'

Mike frowned. 'What's happened, Bill?'

293

'It's more what's happening. You seen the local paper?'

Mike glanced at a pile of newspapers on a chair nearby. 'I haven't had much time . . .'

'There's been another mugging. This one down by the sailing club.'

'A mugging?' Mike echoed. 'Here?' The crime rate. The violence. Just as Tony had predicted.

Bill nodded. 'And vandals. Worse than usual. I bin watching the papers. Listening in the pub. The balance has gone. You know what the Ward was?' He chuckled.

Mike shook his head.

'Every town and village round these parts had a Ward in the old days. The spirits of the dead and the fairises – fairies, if you like – who protected the place from the evil. They patrolled the old trackways, the rivers and brooks, the crosses, all over the place. They kept watch at night, Rector. Kept the Devil away. Kept him out of the town. No one believes in them now, of course, and they've mostly gone.'

Mike found his mouth had dropped open. He closed it. 'You don't believe this, Bill?' But of course Bill believed it. After everything Tony had said, he believed it himself!

The old man frowned. 'All I know is that there is nothing protecting this place now. The dark is coming in off the sea. The town is going bad. And it's up to you and me, Rector, to put it right. You're going to have to help me after all.'

'I see.' Mike stared at the old man affectionately. Was this 'Him upstairs' again, sending him more help and advice in response to his prayer, or just a coincidence. But then what were coincidences but answers to prayer?

'Young Lyndsey has felt it. She's trying to fight it in her own way, I reckon, but she's playing at it. She thinks it's all to do with Hopkins.'

Oh God, you have sent him to me. Mike took a deep breath. 'And isn't it?'

'Naa!' Bill shook his head. 'It goes back centuries before him. Back to the old days.'

'And what do you think we should do?'

'I don't reckon I know. In the old days the church knew how to deal with these things. I don't reckon your fancy colleges teach you about it any more.'

'Not about the Ward, no.' Tony knew. Perhaps he should bring these two wise old men together.

Bill chewed the inside of his cheek thoughtfully. 'I know about it from my dad, and his dad before him. Cunning folk. Heard of them?'

Mike nodded. 'A bit, yes. Local wise women and men. Witches of sorts?'

'Not witches. They helped people against witches.' Bill was twisting his cap again. 'I tell you one of the things that's happened, Rector, which might have helped set all this off. You know old Spindles, down in Ferry Lane?'

'The house that burned down in the spring?'

Bill nodded. 'They left that ruin right there in the street. No one's pulled it down.'

'They can't. It's a listed building. Once all the insurance stuff is sorted out I expect they will rebuild it.'

'Ah.' Bill scratched his head. 'Well, I reckon some of this bad stuff is coming from there. It was like Liza's, that old place. A witch's house once. On a site where I reckon something bad happened, back in the Dark Ages. Bad on bad, you see? It all built up and exploded into fire. That should have neutralised it. Calmed it down again. They should have finished the job. Pulled it down. Cleared the ground and blessed it. But they didn't.'

Mike was astonished. Was this what should have happened at Barker's? 'You make me feel as though I haven't been doing my job, Bill!'

'Not your fault, Rector.'

'What do you suggest I do?'

'Say your prayers a bit harder, I reckon. Do you have any holy water, like they Romans?'

'Holy water is ordinary water and salt that has been blessed, Bill.'

'Well, chucking some of that around would probably do no harm.'

'Down at Spindles?'

Bill nodded. 'And all round the place while you're at it. At Liza's, there's stuff going on there, and up at old St Mary's – but you've been up there already.' Bill cocked a shrewd eye at him. 'Yes, of course you have. Then there's Barker's shop and one or two others in the High Street, and the Thorn.' He grinned. 'You've got the right idea but I reckon you need to work a bit harder, Rector.'

Closing the door after him, Mike walked thoughtfully back into his study. Outside the evening had brought in a misty darkness which had swallowed Bill's shambling figure almost as soon as he'd stepped out of the range of the porch light. Of Mark there was no sign.

Closed curtains. Roaring fire. Safe. Mike shivered. When someone stood here in his study and started talking about fairies and demons and holy water, he knew things were indeed out of balance. At least he now knew why Bill never stepped over the threshold of the church. A cunning man. He had read somewhere that it was hereditary, hadn't he, and Bill had admitted that was what his father and his father's father called themselves. He had had no idea that such people still existed. But he had had no sense of evil. Whatever gods or spirits Bill served, they were all on the same side.

Sitting down, he leaned towards the fire holding out his hands, suddenly weary. He was remembering when Spindles had burned. It had been a lovely old house, a cottage in a lane running down to the river. The fire investigators had said that the cause had been an electrical fault. The family, luckily, had escaped, although, if he remembered right a family pet had died. A dog? A cat? Locked in one of the rooms. He sighed. Bill was right. Fire was a cleanser. And so was water. But now that they had allowed the evil to come back and gain a hold, they were going to have to work very hard to bring back the light.

Leaning back in his chair, he stared down at the flames licking the bricks at the back of the fireplace. A log split in half with a bang and sparks flew up the chimney into the dark, but as he fell asleep, exhausted, his dream was not of fire but of water.

57

One of the places they swam the witches was the mill pond.
They brought her there that evening and he watched as they
trussed the old lady, forcing her stiff, painful limbs into a cruel
parody of a crouching position, hearing her whimpers – any
strength for screams had long ago gone – seeing her head loll
forward as they lifted her. The old lady was already half dead
with fear and exhaustion and pain. He turned away. So many
women. Aye, and men. A few. So much evil. So little time. The
list was in the pocket of the jacket he wore beneath his cloak.
The list of the Devil's followers, and this woman, Liza, was on
the list.

He turned to watch them lift her, aware that John Stearne had
joined him. He glanced at the other man. 'You have the names
for tomorrow?'

Stearne nodded. They watched as two muscular men swung
the bent, tied-up figure one – two – three – and tossed her out
into the muddy water. A duck took off, quacking its indignation
as it beat the water with flailing wings. The crowd at the edge of
the pond watched in breathless silence as the ripples spread, the
only sign of where the old woman had gone into the water the
rope which had been attached to her waist.

Stearne yawned ostentatiously, a gloved hand over his mouth. 'Any minute now. There!' It was a hiss of triumph as the body bobbed to the surface, floating face down.

The shout from the men and women around them was unanimous as hand over hand, they dragged her towards the bank and up onto the grass. Water, the Lord's servant, had rejected her. She belonged to the Devil.

Walking over to inspect her, Stearne nudged her with his foot. 'Cut the ropes. Is she still alive?' He did not sound particularly interested.

'Aye, she's alive.' They had straightened her up and were dragging her to the cart which had brought her along the river's edge from the village. The movement forced air back into the old woman's lungs and she started to cough painfully. Stearne turned and smiled. 'There you are, Matthew. She'll live long enough to hang,' he said. 'That's all that matters.'

Mike groaned. His head had fallen back against the chair and he woke with a start. He lay still, staring straight in front of him, trying to collect his wits. Jesus Christ! He had been asleep. He had witnessed them swimming a witch. He had stood and watched them do it! Levering himself out of the chair, he paced up and down the room, running his fingers through his hair. The bastard was still in his head! He took a deep breath. Tony was wrong. He was the focus. More than the focus. The host! Desperately he tried to steady the jumping of his heart beneath his ribs. He had to be strong. Prayer would see him through this, as it had seen him through every other crisis in his life. It always had.

So far.

But as he tried to concentrate his mind, he found the words would not come.

58

After the long drive from London Mark was far from upset at the
chance for a walk. As he left the rectory he had glanced at his
watch. He would give Mike an hour with that cantankerous-
looking old man, then come back and perhaps drag him out to
the pub, if you could drag vicars into pubs.

He wasn't sure why he had changed his mind about coming
up with Joe and Alice. Perhaps it was the thought of driving all
that way with a heavy smoker, and Alice's endless gossip; perhaps
it was just impatience, but suddenly he had found it impossible
to sit still at his desk. He had shuffled all his papers and books
into a couple of cardboard boxes, rung the bed & breakfast to see
if he could have his room a day early, and climbed into the car.

Setting off down the hill at a steady fast walk, heading for the
river, he found he was shivering. It was a cold night. Reaching
the strand of salt marsh which ran alongside the road, he stepped
onto the grass and stood staring out across the water, watching
the reflections of the streetlights. Behind, to the left, was the busy
small town, blazing with lights, still full of traffic edging its way
round its right-angle bends and pretty, narrow streets. In front of
him was the head of the estuary. Only half a mile upstream it
would turn into the leisurely winding river so beloved of John
Constable. Here it was dramatically tidal, wild in spite of what
looked like a factory site immediately opposite the spot where he
was standing. East of that stretched the beautiful, gentle Suffolk
shore, invisible in the dark behind the blackly sliding slick of the
tide. It was strange but he had really grown to love this place.

Slowly he began to walk. There was purpose behind the choice
of his route. At the far end of the road, just before it dived up
into Mistley, there was a lake on the far side. Originally a mill
pond, so he had read, then an ornamental lake in the grounds of
Mistley Place, now part of an animal sanctuary, it was bounded

at its northern end by half of the original Adam bridge. The other side of the bridge had gone now, widened out of existence by the road along which he was walking. According to some of the books he had been consulting, this lake might have been one of the places Hopkins swam his witches. It was even called the Hopping Bridge, though the majority of sources felt it was unlikely that it was called after him; after all, it had been built so much later.

A cold wind was blowing across the water into his face as he reached it. Thoughtfully he leaned on the stone balustrade, looking out across the lake. In the mellow light of the streetlamps behind him he could see the willows, the white shapes of swans on the still water. Somewhere out there in the dark someone had set up a ducking stool, according to his book on witchcraft. He shuddered. No doubt it gave an exciting frisson to those who saw it. But it was gossips who were ducked in ducking stools wasn't it, not witches? Witches were thrown in to sink or swim, a primitive throw-back to the pagan belief that the water gods would reject the guilty and accept the good as sacrifice. He pulled up the collar of his jacket against the wind. Imagine the fear of those women, and men. Or were they angry? Did they call on their satanic masters to save them even to the last? He shuddered again. Could he feel that anger here? The fear? Or was it his imagination? He narrowed his eyes, staring out into the dark.

Abruptly he turned away. Whatever it was, he could feel he didn't like it. What he would do was walk on into Mistley, have a pint at the Thorn – Hopkins's own pub – and then go back to see Mike.

Mike and Mark talked until the early hours. Mark's butterfly mind intrigued Mike. The TV man was used to researching subjects, sometimes in some depth and making himself an expert for as long as the research for the programme or the series lasted. He hoovered up facts, unerringly picking up on those which would be of use to him, discarding those which would not fit the scope of whatever it was he was working on at the moment, and at the moment his topic of choice was witches and ghosts. His reading on the subject had been extensive. 'But it's all theory, Mike. Sure, I can feel there is something there. In all the houses we've filmed I've felt something there. But I'm not a fool. I realise it could be my imagination. After all, if one has been told a house is haunted the spook factor goes into overdrive at once, but I've never actually ever seen anything.'

'Until the film.'

'Until the film.'

'And it doesn't worry you that you may be stirring up things which would be best left alone?'

Mark shook his head. 'Look, I appreciate that this worries you, but surely, if there is something there it would be better to find out what,' he said earnestly. 'To see what it is doing; why it's there. Why it isn't resting in peace.' He paused, frowning as he tried to marshal his thoughts. 'From what I've read, a lot of ghosts are sort of drifting mindless shadows. I don't think they are any more than imprints, left in the atmosphere, sort of recorded onto the bricks or the air in some way we don't yet understand, but which probably has a "filmic", if you like, explanation which will soon be easily explained by science. But there are others that produce a definite atmosphere; they have a presence and I think they have a mind. They know they are there and they have a reason to be there. Mostly they are harmless; sad. But some have a far more sinister agenda and in my view they need to be dealt with. I think they're like boils. They need to be brought to a head, lanced, cleansed.' He glanced up at Mike, who was staring thoughtfully into the fire. 'In this case it is the shop itself that is the boil. And that is where you come in. You are a professional who deals with this sort of thing. And what is more, I need someone who can with calm conviction talk about what ghosts are.'

Mike shook his head slowly. 'You are right, of course. But it can't be me. I'm sorry. I can't be on both sides. My job is to counsel and pray and help. If I take part in your programme I am, by your own admission, helping to add stimulus to this thing. I want it sorted. I want these souls put to rest. Returned to God. I want peace to come back to our town.'

'You could say that to camera. All of that.'

'No. I couldn't.' Mike sighed.

'Mike, you must! I need you.'

'No!' Mike stood up and began to pace up and down. 'No, Mark, I'm sorry. Look, please leave it!'

The flash of irritation surprised them both. Mark shrugged. 'OK. I give up. But I think it's a shame. I think it would be helpful. I think it might be just what is needed to bring peace, as you put it, back to the town.' He sighed loudly. 'Have you found out any more about Hopkins?'

'Yes!' Mike turned to face him. 'Yes, I am well aware of what we are dealing with.'

'There is evil here, Mike. Not only a vicious, sadistic man, but women who were real witches. Witches who knew what they were doing. Do you know what started Hopkins on his hunt for the local witches? They had sent a bear to kill him! They started it, Mike. Now, I don't know if it was a real bear, which had escaped from some sort of bear baiting show, or whether it was a demon bear conjured up from the shadows, but he thought it was real!' He stopped abruptly. 'Mike, what is it? What's wrong?'

Mike was staring at him, his eyes wide with horror, his face white. He turned away and walked over to the window. He didn't know if it was a real bear or a demon bear either. And he had seen it, smelled its breath, heard the scrape of its claws, seen the blood lust in its eyes. Drawing back the curtains he stood looking out. He could see nothing. The glass merely threw him back his own reflection.

59

The prayer meeting had gone on longer than usual and Judith brought it to a close smoothly with a final prayer. She glanced round at the ladies with a smile. They had prayed for Lyndsey, shocked to hear she was a practising witch, and they had all prayed for Mike. 'He is a good man,' Judith had said slowly. 'A God-fearing man, but life in a new parish can be hard. Lonely. Is it easy to be led astray. And easy to leave oneself vulnerable to evil influences.' In the pause that followed those words ten pairs of eyes flicked open in astonishment, wondering what she meant. Judith's face was serene, her hands folded over her Bible, her own eyes tightly closed. There was no clue as to what Mike might have done but the implication was clear. Their rector was fallible and needed their prayers.

On the way out, Jane Good, the doctor's wife, paused and touched Judith's arm. 'Mike is lucky to have you there, Judith.'

Judith smiled and nodded. 'To be honest, I don't know what he'd do without me,' she agreed in an undertone. 'But he does his best.' She shrugged. 'Pray for him, Jane.'

She watched the last woman walk towards the road where they had all parked their cars and she closed the door. In half an hour she was on her way for a late supper with Ollie Dent.

The old man had laid out a feast of cold meats and cheeses and some oatcakes and fruit for his guest.

'Young Lyndsey brought them up for me in her bicycle basket, bless her!' He was pouring Judith a small glass of elder flower cordial

'Lyndsey?' She glanced at him. 'Lyndsey Clark?'

It took several minutes to tell him about Lyndsey; several more to persuade the bewildered old man that he should sack her and never allow her into his house again. His protests were overridden with such determination there was nothing he could say. By the time Judith had finished he was too upset to eat or drink and she left him staring at the table, which was still laid out with the lovely food and pretty napkins Lyndsey had brought for his little supper party.

He had grown very fond of Lyndsey, relied on her totally and looked forward to her visits. He didn't know what he was going to do without her. Who was going to talk to him now about books and plants and painting, the way Lyndsey talked to him? Who was going to help him in his little garden, and make him laugh, and bring him news from the village?

Staring down at the untouched plate of oatcakes, he found there were tears in his eyes. It was as though the last ray of sunshine in his life had been taken away.

60

Sarah picked up Liza's old bag and cradled it in her arms, burying her face in the rough weave of the hemp. Inside it, she had found forgotten fragments of dried plants, a small black-handled knife, a piece of red ribbon and several bags of seed. The bag was all she had left of Liza, now that she had been taken away to prison. A tear fell on the rough cord which fastened its neck and angrily she straightened up. Hopkins was not going to kill any more women. Somehow she had to stop him. Somehow she had to make him listen and if he wouldn't listen to reason then she would have to find some other way of reaching him. And reach him she would. Her eyes blazed suddenly.

In her sleep, Emma threw out her arms and groaned. Seconds later she was awake, her heart thudding, adrenaline pouring through her body as she sat up and stared round the dark room. Somewhere outside a fox screamed in the night. Minutes later the sound was answered by an owl.

Wednesday October 28th

'You can go in now, Miss Dickson.' The receptionist beamed at Emma from behind her counter. 'You haven't been here before, have you? Doctor's room is the second on the left. Through there.'

Following her expansively waved directions, Emma found herself shaking hands with a tall red-haired man in his fifties, his infectious smile and warm manner doing nothing to hide the quick acute glance with which he surveyed her as he waved her into a chair.

'So, Miss Dickson, I'm afraid I don't have any notes for you yet, so you are an unknown quantity.' He grinned.

'I've only just moved here, Dr Good.'

'And you're suffering from stress, exhaustion, and a strained back?' He raised an eyebrow humorously.

She laughed. Already she liked this man a lot better than her stressed, abrupt, London physician.

'I haven't strained my back yet. But the rest of it is probably right. The trouble is . . .' She hesitated. After another night of terrifying dreams and hours of lying in bed with the light on, too scared to close her eyes, Emma had decided to take action and visit Paula's doctor. She had no intention of telling the doctor what her dreams were about. She didn't want counselling. What she wanted was sleeping pills.

'Ah.' He sat back, his hands flat on the desk after she had made her request. 'I'm afraid it's not that easy. I don't believe in sleeping pills except as a last resort.'

'This is the last resort.' She frowned.

'You can't sleep, you say. And when you do, you have nightmares. Can you tell me what the nightmares are about?'

Emma shrugged her shoulders. Why not talk about it? Maybe it would help. 'I don't know if you know Liza's? It's up in Old Mistley.'

He shook his head.

'I was told after I moved in that it belonged to a witch.' She gave an embarrassed laugh. 'I didn't think it worried me in any way, if anything it was rather romantic. But I kept dreaming about her. Horrible dreams!'

'I see.' He twiddled his pen thoughtfully. 'You're living alone up there?'

She nodded.

'I can see it could be upsetting. A strange place. A frightening story. No one there with you. The dark silence of the country after the noise of London.'

'It makes me sound pathetic.' Emma shook her head.

'Not at all. Perhaps under the circumstances a few pills might allow you to re-establish a peaceful routine.' He reached for a prescription pad. 'Take these and see how you get on.'

As she shook his hand and turned to leave the room, Emma found herself desperately wanting to confide further, to tell him the whole story, to stay within the safe, reassuring confines of the man's personality. But how could she? He had a waiting room full of patients. He was just a nice man doing his job. To her horror she found there were tears in her eyes as she closed the door, and clutching her prescription, she retraced her steps.

She did not have far to go, however, to find a sympathetic ear. Walking past Barker's shop she glanced in and saw Mark standing talking to the assistant behind the counter. She pushed open the door. 'Hi! Remember me? How's the filming?'

He had been on his way to bring in the coffee so she helped him carry the cups and box of cakes upstairs, where Joe and Alice were arranging a network of mikes. 'Colin is joining us on Friday and we're going to set up some stuff up here to do some filming over Saturday night.' Mark tore open an envelope of sugar and tipped it into his mug. With four of them in the room, the atmosphere was fine. Convivial. Emma perched on one of the crates, watching them, feeling suddenly as though she were amongst old friends.

'I spoke to Mike Sinclair last night,' Mark explained between

307

sips of scalding coffee. 'I still can't persuade him to go on camera but I think he's weakening.'

'What does he think about your ghost?' Emma asked.

'He thinks prayer will sort it. He told me that he and a colleague are going to hold a service up here. Not before Saturday, though.' He grinned.

'So, what is it you're going to do on Saturday night?' She was strangely apprehensive at his words.

'Ah, that's kind of secret.' He gave an apologetic shrug. 'Let's say we need all the ghosts in residence and completely unexorcised. And then, if there is going to be a service later, I want to be there with a camera.'

'Mike would never let you do that.'

'No.' He shook his head ruefully. 'He'll certainly take some persuading. He's a nice chap, but he sticks to his principles. I like him. I find I can talk to him. He must be good at his job.'

'Yes.' Emma stared round the room. 'Yes, he's good. His parishioners seem to adore him.' She paused. 'He rescued me the other night, marooned without a car. He very kindly drove me home.' The car, when she had walked down the hill to look at it yesterday afternoon, had started first go. 'But, I doubt if he'd let you film him exorcising this place.' She shivered. 'It does feel weird, doesn't it.'

'Do you think so?'

'Sort of tense. Expectant.' She recalled Lyndsey's earlier warning. 'Perhaps your ghost likes being on TV. Perhaps it likes being talked about.'

Mark laughed uncomfortably. 'I do hope so.' Without realising it, she had picked up on the one theme that Mike had kept on hammering home to him.

'Did you hear we've got him on film?' Alice finished coiling some spare cable and came over, helping herself to a doughnut. 'It's really cool. Spooky.'

'Aren't you scared?' Emma was feeling more and more uncomfortable in the room, although the others seemed completely at ease.

'No.' Alice was licking jam off her fingers. 'They can't hurt you. Unlike cigarettes.' Her father had lit one up as he perched on the window sill.

'Helps me keep my hand steady on the mike,' Joe replied good-naturedly. 'Right, folks, I don't know about you but I want to do some work. The light's about right now, then we'll go out on location and look for your ducking place, Mark, OK? You don't have to go, love,' he added as Emma made a move.

'Thanks, but I must get home.' Emma suddenly needed to be outside. She felt stifled. Anxious. Every muscle in her body was tight. 'I'll see you around if you're going to be up here a few days.'

Outside she paused, closed her eyes, and took a couple of deep breaths, trying to steady herself. When she opened them she saw Mike walking towards her down the High Street. He was wearing his dog collar, the first time she had seen him in uniform, she realised.

He smiled when he saw her. 'Are you OK? Is the car fixed?'

'We're both fine, thanks.' She was slightly taken aback at how pleased she was to see him. 'Have you come to see Mark and his film crew?'

He glanced up at the window above their heads. 'The haunted shop.' He sighed. 'I thought I'd look in.'

'Expect a bit of pressurising, then. They really want you to be in the film.'

Mike smiled. 'Not a chance.' He hesitated. 'Emma, I feel maybe I didn't help you as much as I could have done on Monday night. You were worried about something . . .'

'No.' she spoke too quickly. 'No, I haven't been sleeping too well to be honest and it's making me jumpy. I keep seeing things in the shadows.' Things like Matthew Hopkins, who looks sometimes out of your eyes? 'I think it's the stress of the move and everything. I've just got some sleeping pills. That'll sort me out.'

Mike looked at her steadily and their eyes met. 'I've had trouble sleeping too,' he said quietly. 'Perhaps it's infectious.'

Emma looked away. 'Dr Good is the man you want, then.'

He laughed. The moment had passed. 'I'll bear that in mind. See you soon, Emma.'

She watched him step inside the shop out of sight, and once again she found she was shivering.

61

Wednesday afternoon

Lyndsey had walked over to the Gordon-Smiths to collect the children after school. In the new, even more complicated collection timetable Rosalie Gordon-Smith brought the children back from Colchester every Wednesday afternoon. Today she had taken them as well. Alex's car was being serviced, so he had dropped Paula at the station at seven a.m., then driven home in hers. This evening he would fetch her when she rang.

The children danced round Lyndsey, full of excitement about something that had happened that day. 'The fire alarm went and we all had to go out into the playground.'

'And was it a real fire?' Lyndsey took each child by the hand as they waited to cross the road. They loved coming back to her cottage to wait for Alex or Paula to collect them. It was the highlight of the week.

'Sort of.' Sophie looked up at her eagerly. 'Someone set fire to a wastepaper basket in the staff room. My friend Becky said one of the teachers must have put a cigarette in there.'

'My goodness.' Lyndsey led them down the steep road. 'I should think that teacher will be in big trouble!' She pushed open the front door.

'What's in your shopping bag, Lyn? Is there something to eat?' James pounced as Lyndsey put the bag down on the sofa.

'Don't touch!' Her shout was too late. The little boy had dived into it, tipping various packets onto the floor.

'Ow!' His eyes filled with tears as he held up a bleeding hand. 'Lyn, there's a knife in there!'

'I know, James. That's why I told you not to touch. Damn,

now it's no use!' She grabbed the boy's wrist. 'Come into the kitchen and I'll wash it. I wish you kids would mind your own business!'

'I'm sorry, Lyn,' James was taken aback. Neither of them had seen her so cross before. 'I didn't mean to.'

'No.' She took a deep breath. 'No, I know you didn't.'

'Can I have some of your magic ointment?'

'Yes, of course you can.' She cleaned the wound, applied the salve and slapped on a large sticking plaster. 'There you are. Good as new.'

'Lyn.' Sophie had been collecting all the parcels. 'He didn't break it.' She held out the knife which had cut its way through its paper wrapping. 'Look. It will still work. It's a very pretty knife.'

Lyndsey took it from her. She had found the small ebony-handled knife in the antique shop in Manningtree that afternoon. It was to replace her athame, her witch's knife, the one that Mike had taken. 'Yes, sweetheart, I know it will still work.' Would it? Even cleansed, the blood energy would still be on it. She put it out of reach on top the cupboard. 'OK, kids. There are some teacakes in there somewhere. Shall we toast them on a long fork in front of the fire? Your dad will be here soon, so we'd better get going.'

Alex arrived just before six and found two contented buttery children sitting with Lyndsey by the fire as she read to them from Harry Potter. It always astonished him that they were prepared to stay for a single second in a house without a television, never mind for a couple of hours or so, but without fail Lyndsey seemed to be able to keep them busy. And happy. He did not know, nor did anyone, that the children were allowed upstairs into Lyndsey's studio. She had knocked the cottage's two bedrooms into one glorious bright living space where her easel stood by the north-facing window overlooking the estuary; a large table was covered in paints and coloured pastels and the plants she drew; and one whole wall was lined with bookshelves. Her bed was a single divan, in the corner, covered in a bright patchwork quilt. In this room there was no dust; no shadow. This was Lyndsey's kingdom and her life. And no one but James and Sophie, who each had their own sketchbook and paint box, was allowed there.

Downstairs, James climbed out of the chair and greeted Alex,

311

hand outstretched. 'Look, Daddy! I cut myself on Lyn's special knife!'

Alex found himself staring at the large pink sticky-plaster on the palm of his son's hand. There were several long seconds of silence. He raised his eyes to Lyndsey's face.

'It's all right, Daddy.' James sensed an uncomfortable atmosphere and was puzzled. 'Look, this is Lyn's magic ointment. She put it on and it made it better.' Running through into the kitchen, he grabbed the small ceramic jar off the draining board. Pulling out the cork, he waved it under his father's nose. Alex was aware of some bright green greasy substance. It did not smell particularly nice.

'Lyn . . .'

'It's OK, Alex.' She anticipated his question. 'It's herbal. Marigold. It'll heal quickly and cleanly.'

'But how did he get hold of the knife in the first place?' Alex frowned.

'It was in Lyn's bag.' James, ever helpful interrupted again. 'It's OK. Lyn's put it out of reach so we can't touch it. But my blood made it dirty.' He looked extraordinarily sorrowful.

Lyndsey pursed her lips. 'I'm sorry, Alex. It never occurred to me the little tykes would rifle through my bag.' She could see Alex frowning. Read his thoughts. Sense his unease. 'I would never willingly hurt them, Alex. You know that,' she said softly. 'I adore Sophie and James. I would do anything to keep them safe.'

'Daddy?' Sophie was tired of being side-lined. 'We've saved you a teacake.' She proffered a jammy, buttery plate. 'I toasted it myself.'

Alex smiled. 'As long as you don't tell Mummy. You know she doesn't like me eating butter.'

The atmosphere relaxed. The children disappeared to collect their things and put on their coats. Alex looked back towards Lyndsey. 'I do trust you, Lyn, but you must keep your stuff to yourself, OK? I don't want the kids involved, even by implication.'

She nodded. 'I know.'

'And I don't want you reading those books to them, either.' He nodded towards Harry Potter. 'There's enough witchcraft around here already and I don't think Paula would approve. Anyway, they're too young!'

She shrugged. 'OK, if you say so.'

'And, while we are on the subject, I want you to leave Emma out of your witchy activities, please. You've upset her quite a lot.'

'If I've upset her, Alex, it's because I was trying to warn her that she's in danger, as you know. The kids are nothing to do with it, you don't have to worry about that. But Emma is different. She's moved into Liza's. She is a part of it all, by choice. Her blood, her ancestors, brought her here. Because she doesn't understand yet, she's vulnerable. If she doesn't take care, this will destroy her.'

Alex stared. 'What will destroy her?' He was talking very quietly, not wanting the children to hear.

'Hopkins. His spirit never rested. He pursued his vile cruelty on into the next world, but that did not suit him. It wasn't enough. So he returned. The people here –' She waved her arm to encompass the village around them and the town itself. 'They think about him. They talk about him. Their children learn about him. I saw a school group today with clipboards and notebooks in the town, doing a project on him! They shudder and listen and laugh. Some of them laugh, Alex! And they say how glad they are it was all so long ago, not realising that every time they say his name, he gets stronger.'

Alex's usually friendly, gentle face had assumed a strange overlay of distaste. 'Oh, come on Lyn. That's all in your imagination!'

'No, it's not!' She thumped the table with her fist, an exclamation of irritation bursting from her. 'Listen to me, Alex. It is real. He is real. Ask that film man at Barker's shop. Ask Emma. They will tell you. Yes, Emma knows. She doesn't understand what is happening, but she knows. Make no mistake.' She sighed. 'Please, Alex, if you have any influence over her tell her what I've said. I shall warn her again but if it comes from you as well maybe she'll listen. Oh!' Again the frustration, another thump. 'Why can't people see what is in front of their eyes! Why are they so brainwashed by modern stupid science they have lost touch with every scrap of instinct, intuition, common sense! That's why I gave up at university! There was no acknowledgement that plants, that anything, had a soul; a spirit. They didn't understand! Emma can feel it. See it. Hear it! I know she can. But still she denies the evidence of her own senses. And that will prove a disaster.'

313

Alex sighed. Her passion was frightening him. And, he realised grudgingly, she had him half convinced as well.

'Look, I will talk to Emma, but I don't want to scare her –'

'She is scared, Alex! What she needs are weapons. The tools to fight the bastards!'

Alex glanced up at the cupboard at which James had pointed. 'Like your special knife?'

'Yes, like my special knife.'

Alex raised his eyebrows. 'I will talk to her, Lyn.'

'Good. Do that.' She saw two enquiring small faces in the doorway and she turned away, pushing her hands into the pockets of her jeans. 'The kids are ready.'

'So I see.' Alex held out his arms and they ran to him.

'Don't forget, Alex, will you?'

Lyndsey stood on the doorstep and watched as they walked away along the quay.

Her last words were whipped away on the wind.

62

Wednesday evening

The plan was that she would ring Alex from the train so he could come and fetch her. Paula pulled out her mobile as the train rattled towards Manningtree. In the office she had found herself staring out of the window as it grew dark, seeing the streaks of red in the wind-swept sky, seeing the dark clouds streaming across a horizon bisected by a forest of high-rise buildings and suddenly, unexpectedly, and not for the first time, she was overwhelmed by claustrophobia. She wanted to go home. She wanted to walk by the river. She wanted to be out of this stifling air-conditioned, stressful place. It was days like this when suddenly she wondered if she were mad working all day everyday while Alex stayed at home. Other days of course she knew exactly why. She adored the work, the people, the buzz. You didn't get that in the country.

She phoned the house, listening crossly to the tone ringing on unanswered, then she phoned Alex's mobile. It was switched off. Frowning, she tried again as the train pulled in at the station. He wasn't expecting her yet, of course. She was so much earlier than usual but supposing he had forgotten he was supposed to come and fetch her? Supposing he was round at Emma's again? She frowned. After her long talk with Emma she had decided that on the whole she didn't like her. The woman was self-centred and weird. The trouble was, she was also very attractive. There was no denying that. But surely Alex had got the message? No, he wouldn't be there. He was supposed to be collecting the children and he would never forget that. He was just a bit vague sometimes. She smiled to herself fondly, as so often torn between her envy of the way he had adapted to the necessity of living at home after his career collapsed, her frustration that he seemed content to live life now at so much slower a pace and her incipient jealousy about what he might be up to while she was not there to keep an eye on him.

She only hoped that whatever he was doing, he had remembered to collect the car from the garage that afternoon so that tomorrow they would be back to their usual routine; she hated being dependent on anyone else because this was exactly the sort of thing that could happen. There was nothing for it. She would have to start walking. There was no way she was going to hang around at the station for hours and she was not about to waste money on a taxi.

Slinging her briefcase over her shoulder, she headed down through Lawford, walking slowly along the road past the industrial estate. There were dozens of other people pouring off the train and out of the station too, but slowly they passed her until she was alone, walking more and more slowly, hoping at every step that her mobile would ring or she would see Alex's car heading towards her down the road. She couldn't walk all the way to Bradfield. The best she could do was to head into Manningtree itself and wait at the pub until he made contact.

As the road went under the railway arch she stopped, her arms aching from the weight of the briefcase and her feet sore from her town heels, and fished out her mobile again. There was still no reply, and there didn't seem much point in leaving a message.

'Damn!' Where was he? How did he think she was going to get back without a lift? She glanced at her watch and realised suddenly that he was probably not back from fetching the kids from Lyndsey's. Wearily, she hefted her case up again.

It was only minutes later that the streetlights went out.

Paula stopped and stared round her, shocked and disorientated. Not just the streetlights, but every light had vanished. The houses behind the hedges on the far side of the road, the factories on the industrial estate which ran alongside the river on her left. Everywhere. The sudden total darkness was unnerving and with it came silence. The mist was drifting across the road in front of her, bringing the cold salt smell of the mudflats. She shuddered. This autumn seemed to have been particularly foggy and she hated it. She listened. It was coincidence, surely, that there were no cars on the road which only moments before had been quite

316

busy. That there were no footsteps on the pavement. It was as though suddenly she was the only person in the world. Strangely frightened, she took a tentative step or two forward. She had lost her bearings totally. Panic swept over her. She clutched her briefcase to her chest, turning round and round.

Then to her enormous relief she saw lights in the distance. The car headlights drew closer, slicing through the mist, and she could see the road again, see where she was, the pavement, the trees in the arc of light. The car slowed beside her. A window lowered.

'Mrs West? I thought it was you. Do you want a lift?'

Paula couldn't see the face. Didn't recognise the voice.

'I'm Judith Sadler. I teach at the local school. Do you remember, we met last Christmas?' The door nearest her opened invitingly.

Paula sighed audibly with relief. 'What's happened to the lights?' she asked as she climbed in and reached for the seatbelt, her briefcase leaning against her knees.

'Power cut. I heard it on the radio. It covers miles, apparently.' Judith drew away from the kerb. 'Has your car broken down?'

Leaning her head back against the headrest with another sigh, Paula explained.

Judith raised an eyebrow. 'Why not come back to my place? You can wait there in comfort until your husband collects you.'

'Could I really?' Paula was grateful, still unnerved by the sudden total darkness; the unexpected fear.

Judith had a large torch on the hall table just inside the door. With the help of its beam she located a box of white candles under the sink, and the kettle which she set on the gas. 'There. That's better.' The house was warm, the candlelight comforting. Paula watched as the other woman made the tea, suppressing the unworthy thought that she would have vastly preferred a large gin and tonic.

'You are lucky having a husband who is prepared to look after your children.' Judith counted four Rich Tea biscuits from a packet and put them on a plate.

'He's a saint,' Paula agreed with more sincerity than she had intended.

'Does he collect them from school every day?'

Paula helped herself to a biscuit. 'No, we have a horrendously complicated system of school runs. Most of the time it works. Today, for instance, the mother of one of James's friends takes them back to her house in Mistley. Lyn collects them on foot and takes them back to her cottage, then Alex collects them from there at six.'

'Lyn?' Judith paused as she was pouring out the tea. Her face in the candlelight was deeply shadowed.

'Lyndsey Clark. She does quite a bit of child-minding for us.'

'I see.' Setting down the pot, Judith put the two cups and the plate of biscuits on the tray. 'Perhaps we should go through and sit in the lounge. It would be more comfortable.' She added the candlestick to the tray. The flickering light illuminated the plate, which now had only three biscuits. Judith stared at it, frowned, and put the tray back down. Fetching the packet she took out another biscuit, carefully added it to the plate and picked up the tray again. Paula was mortified.

They sat down in the lounge, Paula on the sofa, Judith on the chair opposite, the candlelight for all its softening shadows showing up the formality of the room and its cold lack of comfort. Paula perched on the edge of the seat, already regretting that she had agreed to come. She looked around for her briefcase and realised she had left it in the hall. 'Perhaps I should just try Alex again. My mobile is in my case . . .'

'In a minute.' Judith's voice was peremptory. 'First, I feel I have to say something.' She leaned forward, her elbows on her knees. She was frowning. Paula raised an eyebrow as she leaned back in the sofa and waited.

Her hostess pursed her lips solemnly. 'You must understand, I wouldn't say this unless I was truly worried. I would never interfere in anyone's business normally.'

Paula stared at her suspiciously. What on earth was the woman getting at? She waited, her eyes fixed on Judith's face.

It came out at last. 'Do you realise what Lyndsey Clark is?' Judith paused.

'I beg your pardon?'

'She is a witch!' Judith gave an ostentatious shiver.

'Oh, I know she likes to think she is a – what do they call it? A Wiccan.' Paula laughed. 'It's nothing. Fairy tales. She's playing silly games to shock people. It's not real.'

'Oh, Mrs West, you're so wrong!' Judith was indignant. 'My dear, please don't be fooled! The girl is very persuasive. She is very plausible, but the fact remains that the person you are entrusting your children to, worships the Devil. She is involved in the satanic. Have you not heard about satanic ritual?'

Paula went white. For a moment she could not speak. 'You are surely not suggesting that Lyn is involved in that sort of thing?' She was aghast. 'With men?'

Judith shrugged. 'They are all involved in the most unspeakable things.' She shook her head. 'I knew you hadn't realised. I just knew it! Your husband is such a sweet man, it would never occur to him to question her. Even the rector thought she was fairly harmless. I soon put him right on that score. If I had my way people like that should not be allowed to live in decent society. I didn't realise she was looking after your children; had I known that, I would have spoken to you before! After all, I'm the person nominated by the P.C.C. to check up on people who work with children in our parish.' She gave another shudder. 'This is the way it starts – the way they always work. At first they seem completely innocuous and gain people's confidence. Then they move in on the children.'

Slowly Paula shook her head. 'I can't believe what you're saying. She's always so sweet with the children. They adore her.'

'Of course. She has to gain their trust.'

'No. No, I can't believe it!'

'Listen.' Judith edged further forward on her chair. 'I shouldn't be telling you this, because the rector spoke to me in confidence, but now he has realised what is going on, he is very worried about it. About the whole area, not just Lyndsey. She is part of something far bigger. He asked me to pray about it.'

Paula studied her face. She did not like this woman at all, she realised suddenly. She was a smug, sanctimonious cow. But was she right?

'God will show us the way to get her out of the community,' Judith went on. She leaned back and folded her arms. 'And she'll soon start to get the message if no one will employ her. She did housework for old Ollie Dent. I've had a word with him and she won't be going up there any more. If you sack her too that will be a start.'

Paula reached absent-mindedly for her forgotten teacup. 'It seems awfully hard.'

'But necessary. After all, if she begins to see the error of her ways there may yet be hope to save her soul.'

The tea was cold. Paula made a face and put it down. 'Are you sure about all this?'

'Of course I'm sure.' Judith stood up 'Are you prepared to take risks with your children?'

'No, of course not.'

'Then how can you hesitate?'

Paula stood up, too. 'I'll talk to Alex. Tonight. In fact I must ring him or he will be wondering where I am.' She turned towards the hall. Behind her Judith smiled. She was doing God's work. He would be pleased with her.

63

As long as he kept busy, it was all right. Mike had had wall to wall appointments all day, finishing up with tea in an old people's home. It was getting dark when at last he made his farewells, gently unclasped a frail blue-veined hand from his own and made his way out to the car. Sitting in the car park, staring out of the windscreen, it was several minutes before he reached for the keys in the ignition. During those minutes he had been fighting the longing to turn his back on Manningtree and drive across the Stour into Suffolk, to Tony and Ruth's. It had been hovering all day, the thing at the back of his mind. It was like a great black bird, a shadow at the edge of his vision waiting to pounce. His head was heavy; he felt as though he were jet lagged; all he wanted was to curl up in bed and sleep and yet he was afraid. Afraid of being alone. Afraid of being forced to do something he didn't want to do. Especially afraid of his dreams. Taking a deep breath, he fired the engine and let in the clutch. The car slid out of the narrow parking space, hesitated at the entrance gate and resolutely – reluctantly – turned back towards Manningtree.

His bedroom had never seemed more welcoming. It was warm, the central heating for once on and functioning, the light by the bed throwing mellow shadows across his pillows, the rose-pink curtains, chosen presumably by his predecessor's wife, closed against the unexpectedly frosty night air. He had brought up a glass of whisky and his Bible. He planned to sleep with the light on.

Before he climbed into bed he pulled back the curtain a few inches and peered out into the dark. The night was peaceful. Above the line of trees he could see stars; the wind had dropped. For the moment at least there was no fog. Letting the curtain fall into place, he turned back into the room. The trouble was, the shadow he feared so much wasn't outside. It was here inside his own head.

The words of the prayers came, weaving their comfort around his heart, but there was something missing. 'Deliver us from evil.' He stared round the room. 'For thine is the kingdom.' He held his breath. The room around him seemed to be doing the same. 'The power and the glory.' He could do this. He could withstand the attack. His faith was strong. Christ was with him. With Christ on his side how could he fail?

You are right. The Lord is with us!

The voice in his head was clear.

I fight evil in the name of the blood and bones of Christ.

'No!' Mike shook his head. 'We are not on the same side!' He realised that he had spoken out loud. His fingers tightened around his Bible. 'Jesus Christ is merciful. You are not!' He looked around the room again. Silence. He held his breath. Pray. That was what Tony said. Fill your head with prayer. Leave no gaps, no nooks or crannies where he can lodge. 'Why me?' That was stupid, asking a question. Mike closed his eyes and bowed his head, resting it on his interlaced fingers.

Because you are a man of God.

The voice was soft now, less strident.

You needs must fight the Devil, Michael! Destroy the witches!

Mike's eyes flew open. He scrambled to his feet, clutching the Bible to his chest.

You asked me in, Michael!

The voice seemed to be fading.

'Christ be with me, Christ within me,
Christ behind me, Christ before me,
Christ beside me, Christ to win me,
Christ to comfort and restore me . . .' Mike intoned under his breath. Don't argue. Don't enter a discussion. Pray.

At eleven o'clock the old boiler down in the cellars clanked to its appointed stop. The house began to grow cold. Mike's eyes were closing. Each time his head nodded forward he jerked awake and began to pray again. As the cold grew more intense he pulled a blanket off the bed and wrapped it round his shoulders, allowing, just for a moment, the silence in the room to surround him. Nothing. All was quiet.

'Thank you, Lord, for your protection. Stay with me now.

Lighten my darkness, I beseech thee, O Lord, and by thy great mercy defend me from all perils and dangers of this night; for the love of thy only Son, our Saviour, Jesus Christ . . .' The gaps between his whispered words grew longer. At some time after one a.m. his head nodded forward and he slept.

James Butcher was standing in front of Matthew Hopkins's table. The huge man in crumpled, bloodstained clothes, was twisting his cap between his meaty fingers, his face contorted with tears.

'My Jane has died because of you! The only chance she had was Liza's medicine and you took Liza away! You've killed my wife!'

Hopkins frowned, trying to place this man who had forced his way upstairs. 'I am sorry to hear your wife has died, but Liza could not have helped her. Would you have wanted the Devil's hand on her?' He stared up coldly.

Tears were streaming down the man's face. 'She was in travail three days. Three days! She died screaming! Screaming in agony as she bled to death. She died and the baby, too.' Butcher shook his head piteously, his mouth slack. He wiped the back of his hand across his eyes.

'It was God's will.' Matthew was indifferent. 'Leave us. There is nothing to be done. Go home and bury your wife and let it be the end of the matter.' He glanced towards the door, where someone else was hurrying up from the street below.

It was Sarah.

'So, Master Hopkins, are you pleased with the results of your justice?' She leaned forward across his table, her hazel eyes flashing as Butcher shambled blindly out of the room, sobbing. She

323

had regained her courage; her desperation had given her strength. 'What else will you do? How many more people must die? How many more tests will you inflict?'

He looked up and met her gaze, confident that John Stearne, standing in the corner of the room near the window, would escort her to the door. 'I do God's work, mistress.' He was too tired to argue today. The visit of John Butcher and the weakness from the fever had left him drained. 'Beware, lest you too are accused of serving Satan.'

'Where is she now? Where have you taken Liza?'

'To Colchester.' He sighed. 'She will be held in the dungeons there under the castle until she is taken to Chelmsford to the assize, after which she will assuredly hang.'

'Is this lady,' John Stearne's voice broke in quietly, 'not on your list, Matthew?' He stepped forward. Taller, older than his colleague, his face set in deep weary lines, he stood in front of her and looked her up and down, then he turned to Matthew and stabbed at the notebook on the table in front of him with his forefinger.

In the draught from the open door, the candle in its black iron holder trailed smoke across the table and Matthew coughed.

'Search down the names,' Stearne went on. 'I know you wrote Mistress Paxman's down there, Matthew.' He looked Sarah up and down again. 'Her brazenness and her care for this witch betray her each time we see her as one of Satan's sisterhood.'

This time Sarah stood her ground. 'You talk nonsense, Master Stearne. My husband's friends in Colchester tell me they do not believe in your list. They do not believe that women like Liza are witches. What has she ever done to you, Master Hopkins? She is a good, kind, gentle soul who worked to alleviate the suffering of her neighbours. People like poor little Jane Butcher.'

'She is one of the coven, mistress, who met near my house and conjured Satan's creature, the bear, to torment me!' Hopkins snapped back at her. His eyes were watering in the candle-smoke. So far he had found no evidence for the existence of covens anywhere in the region, but perhaps this woman would at last lead him to them. 'Do not speak to me of evidence. There is ample evidence. The woman had two familiars. Cats.' He shuddered. 'And she has confessed. She has confessed everything. And even if she hadn't, and there was no evidence, I need none. If her name is on the list, that is evidence enough! I have Parliament's commission.'

He leaned back in his chair. His face was damp with sweat. Livid patches on his cheeks betrayed the fever lurking in his bones. 'Her name is there.' He picked up his quill and scratched it across the page, underlining a name. 'As is yours, Mistress Paxman.'

Why was she not afraid of him any more? Last time she had backed away, scared of his threats. Now she held his gaze steadily. Confident. He shivered. Were those Satan's eyes looking out of that pretty face? Had she had carnal knowledge of the Devil himself? Taking a deep breath he summoned up the strength to stand, aware that with his tall crowned hat still firmly in place on his head he was taller than her. Just.

'Get thee behind me, Satan!' Fixing his eyes on hers he glared at her, his voice echoing around the room.

Mike started awake with a groan and his Bible fell to the floor from his lap. He stared round. She had gone. The room was empty.

64

'Where on earth have you been?' Alex looked up as Paula came in. 'Why didn't you ring me?'

She dropped her handbag and briefcase on the carpet. 'I tried. There was no answer. I got a lift with Judith Sadler and I went back to her place for some tea. She drove me home in the end. Where are the kids, Alex?'

'Watching telly in the den.' He frowned. 'I'm sorry, I must have forgotten to switch on the mobile. You look all in.'

'I feel it.' She threw herself down on the sofa. 'Were they with Lyndsey this afternoon?'

'You know they were.'

'And they're all right?'

'Of course.' His eyes slid away from hers and he hesitated.

Paula sat forward. 'Oh God, what's wrong? What did she do to them?'

'She didn't do anything. James cut himself on a knife. But he's fine. She put some of her spooky green ointment on and bandaged . . . Paula?'

'James!'

He watched dumbfounded as she ran into the den, grabbed the little boy by the hand and dragged him off to the downstairs cloakroom. There she pulled off the plaster, ignoring James's wails of protest, and proceeded to scrub his hand.

His cries turned to shrieks of agony as the nailbrush she had seized tore into the open wound.

'Hey! Paula! Whoa! What's happened?' Alex followed her into the tiny room and took the brush out of her hand. 'Come on, Jamie, let's find you some proper antiseptic ointment in a tube and a nice new plaster.' He glared at her. 'What the hell was that all about?'

She was shaking. 'Do you know what she puts in that ointment, Alex?'

'Marigolds. She told me.' He patted James's hand dry with some loo paper off the roll and rummaged in the medicine cabinet on the wall, coming out with some TCP ointment and a box of children's brightly coloured plasters.

'Fat from dead babies!' Paula was shaking.

Alex and James stared at her, both shocked into silence. Then both spoke at once. 'Yuk!' James held his hand out as far away from himself as he could.

'Crap!' Alex glared at her. 'Paula, are you listening to yourself? Here, old chap.' He put his arm around James's shoulders, aware that Sophie had followed them and was listening wide-eyed in the doorway. 'You're fine. I don't know where Mummy got that funny idea, do you?' He patted James on the back and gave him a little push. 'Back to the telly, both of you.'

They went, but he saw the nervous way James clutched at his sister's hand, something he hadn't seen him do for a year at least. As they disappeared silently through the door, Alex turned to his wife. 'What in God's name is the matter with you?'

'I had to get the stuff off him, Alex.' Paula ran the taps in the basin and reached for the soap again.

'The stuff, Paula, was marigold ointment. It's made with herbs and Vaseline.'

'Not Vaseline.' She glanced in the mirror in front of them and held his gaze. 'Judith told me.'

'Oh, for goodness sake!' Alex was exasperated. 'You don't believe her?'

'She's with the church, Alex. She's a lay reader. She teaches at the local primary. She's not going to make up things like that.'

'Oh, excuse me!' Alex's voice rose in anger. 'And where does Lyn get these dead babies?'

'Sacrifice.' Paula's voice came out in a broken whisper. 'Satanic rituals.' She scrubbed harder.

'And you think Lyndsey – our Lyn – is involved in that kind of stuff?' He stared at her, aghast. 'Even if I believed that it happened at all, which I don't, and nor does anyone else if you remember all the enquiries that went on about it, how in the world could you believe that she would take part in something like that?'

'Judith has proof, Alex. I know it sounds crazy but she wasn't just making it up.'

'What kind of proof?' He leaned over and turning off the taps took the soap and nailbrush out of her hands. 'Dry them,' he commanded. He handed her the towel. 'Now, come into the kitchen where we can talk without the kids overhearing us.' He glanced over towards the door where he could hear the TV on quietly. Striding over, he glanced in. The children were sitting side by side on the sofa, uncharacteristically quiet, their eyes fixed on the screen. 'Come on.' He caught Paula's wrist and dragged her into the hall. In the kitchen he closed the door.

'You must never let them see her again.' Paula sat down at the table and put her head in her hands. 'Never. I'm not going to the office tomorrow. I'm going to see the rector and then the police.'

'Paula!' Alex was standing over her, appalled. 'You will do no such thing. Do you hear me? Listen to yourself! You are a rational, sensible woman. This is the twenty-first century! People do not, I repeat, do not kill babies and render them down to make fat to put in ointments. Especially not gentle herbal ointments to make other children better!'

'But Judith said –'

'Judith Sadler is clearly a credulous fool,' Alex put in firmly. 'If you are going to have a word with anyone I think it should be the head teacher at the school who is clearly harbouring a dangerous lunatic.' He sat down opposite her. 'Paula, think. This is Lyndsey we are talking about. Our gentle, sweet Lyndsey. We both knew she dabbles in Wicca. She probably does a few spells. She plays with herbs and crystals. For all I know she dances round the fields naked. She is not a witch. Not the kind of witch you are thinking about. She is not a Satanist. And she loves our children. She loves them, Paula!'

328

'She let James cut himself.'

'That was an accident. And you saw for yourself it was not a bad cut.'

'Even so.' She took a deep breath. 'I don't want her anywhere near them again, Alex.' She looked up. 'Not ever. You'll have to find someone else to look after them.'

65

As it grew dark, the mist had drifted once again, in across the mud and up the hill towards Lawford. It was moving imperceptibly in around the houses on the Seaview estate. The gate of number twenty-eight hung off its post. The front garden was full of waist-high grass and weeds, liberally sewn with crushed beercans and torn fast-food boxes.

Behind the front door, two men dragged a third to the bottom of the stairs and pulled open the door to the cupboard that held the meters. Their victim sagged, half conscious, his face a soggy mess of blood and bone as they pushed him in.

His assailants had sensed the evil in the mist. They thrived on it and inexorably it was taking them over. Common sense, humanity, had long ago left them. They did not know why they acted as they did or what this young man had done to annoy them. What they felt now was blood lust.

In a short while the red veil of the Berserker would be drawn across their eyes and their victim would be dead.

66

Thursday October 29th

Paula got up early as usual. Neither she nor Alex mentioned the previous night's quarrel when he climbed out of bed after her and, pulling on his dressing gown, went downstairs to make her some coffee. He kissed her and waved her off in her reclaimed car, meticulously keeping her to her usual timetable, and as she did not once mention taking the day off or going to see Mike, he assumed with enormous relief that she had cooled off overnight and changed her mind.

He was at Emma's by nine. This time she did not seem surprised to see him. He accepted a mug of coffee and threw himself down on a chair at her table without being asked. 'Paula and I had the most God-awful row last night.'

'Ah.' Emma sat down opposite him.

He glanced up at her; she too was looking very tired, he realised. There was strain showing round her eyes. 'Do you mind if I talk?'

She smiled. 'Feel free. Although I'm not too good in the advice department.'

'It was about Lyndsey. Have you met a woman called Judith Sadler?' She looked blank and shook her head so he went on. 'Pure poison. She works for Mike Sinclair at the church in some capacity or other, as well as at the local school.' He took a deep, shuddering breath. 'Wait till you hear what she said to Paula!'

Emma listened with increasing disbelief. 'And Paula believed her?' she said at last.

He nodded.

'Poor old Lyndsey.' Emma stood up and went to fetch the coffee pot from the Aga. She poured them each a refill. 'I admit I think

331

Lyn is a bit odd, but killing babies? No way! Never! That's dotty. I can't believe anyone would believe that.' She sat down again. 'Paula was up here on Tuesday night. She didn't seem worried about the children then.'

'Paula was up here?'

Emma nodded. 'Warning me off her handsome husband.' She grinned.

Alex's mouth dropped open. 'Oh God, Emma, I'm sorry.'

'Don't be. I told her I was still too hung up on Piers to be thinking of stealing other people's men.' She leaned forward and patted his hand. 'I'm pretty sure she was convinced.'

'That's a very naughty smile!' Alex was struck suddenly by how pretty she was when she lightened up, and how sad she had been looking until that moment. She was fanciable; Paula was right. Very.

'OK. Now we've got that out of the way,' she went on, taking another sip of coffee, 'what do you think we should do?'

'Warn Lyn?' Alex frowned. 'Paula doesn't want her going near the kids ever again. They'll be inconsolable. They adore her.'

'That's tough.'

Alex nodded. 'Do you think I should speak to Mike? Paula was threatening to rampage round there. She was even talking about going to the police.' He frowned.

'I doubt if the police would take her seriously.' Emma folded her arms. 'But Mike is already deeply concerned about Lyn. You say this other woman works for him?'

'Yes.'

'She shouldn't spread vicious gossip like that. It's very wrong. And dangerous.'

'That's what I thought.'

'It's buying into this whole witch thing.' Emma looked thoughtful. 'You should talk to Mike.' She stared down into her coffee. 'He seems a very genuine man.' She paused.

'Can I hear a but coming?' Alex asked.

She shrugged. 'I can't make up my mind about him. I like him a lot.' She stopped again, obviously surprised at herself. 'But at the same time he makes me cross.'

'A paradox.' He grinned. 'Perhaps you're just cross because he's a vicar. Waste of a good man.'

She laughed. 'You could be right at that. But he's not gay.'

'No chance. Word is, he was engaged. I'm not sure, but I think the church got between him and his fiancée so when he first came here he was a bit lonely. But in spite of that, so far he's managed to escape all female clutches.'

'Perhaps that's why there's this strange antagonism between us,' she said slowly. 'As I said, he makes me feel cross and uncomfortable when we see each other. I can't think why. And when he sees me coming, I get the impression he looks dead scared!' And sometimes dangerous.

'Either he fancies you rotten, or he thinks you're one of the witchy folk.' Alex gave a grim smile. 'Perhaps it's both! That would explain it. He sees you as temptation and he suspects you bat for the Devil's team!'

'Alex!' She was indignant.

'Sorry. OK, let's get back to the problem in hand. Paula and Lyn. What shall I do?'

'You can't force Paula to go on letting Lyn look after your children, Alex. Not if she feels that strongly about it.'

'So, I'd better go down and tell Lyn the bad news.'

'And warn her about the gossip this woman is spreading about her. That is really scary.' She shook her head thoughtfully. 'The funny thing is that I'm beginning to like Lyndsey. She's odd and different and takes no prisoners but there is something very likeable about her. I'd hate her to be hurt.'

'She said much the same about you, strangely enough. She thinks you're in some sort of danger.'

Emma shrugged. 'She told me.'

'Do you know why?'

'Something to do with my nightmares and Liza's ghosts.' The smile did not quite reach her eyes as she looked away from him towards the window. He followed her gaze. She had potted up a whole lot of small herb plants and put them along the window sill, using some of the old handmade pots she had found in the barn. They looked lovely and he could smell the aromatic scents from where he was sitting.

'Perhaps that is something you should talk to Mike about. If you two are still talking,' he said at last.

'I already have.' She shrugged. 'Yes, we're still talking. The trouble is, I'm afraid it just confirmed his opinion of me. Mad, probably bad, and dangerous to know!'

67

When Mike opened the door to Paula at eight a.m. that morning, he was unshaven and haggard. 'I wasn't expecting anyone this early,' he apologised as he led her into his study. 'Please, sit down.' He gestured her towards the armchair and went over to his desk. She was clearly dressed for the office. Charcoal suit, blue blouse, immaculate tights and shoes, discreet earrings.

'I had a long talk with Judith Sadler last night.' Paula wasted no time. She briskly relayed the gist of the conversation and what had happened at home afterwards. 'So, what are you going to do?'

Mike groaned inwardly. He did not need this. Not on top of the appalling night he had just experienced. 'Judith is a very sincere woman, Paula. But she can be less than tactful at times.'

'I mean, what are you going to do about Lyndsey? If this is true she can't be allowed to go on living amongst decent people!'

'If it is true. Which I very much doubt.' Mike sighed. 'As I said, Judith is very sincere but her zeal can sometimes be a bit overpowering. I'm afraid I agree with your husband. At worst Lyndsey is worshipping pagan gods in her own way. Bad enough from a Christian viewpoint, I agree, but under no circumstances do I suspect her of child abuse or performing Satanic rituals. I shall speak to Judith. She has no business even thinking such things, never mind spreading gossip about them. That is unforgivable.'

Paula frowned. 'I don't think you're taking this seriously enough.'

'I assure you, I am taking it very seriously indeed.'

Listen to the woman. She is a sincere Christian. Do as she says and send to arrest the witch!

Mike felt the sweat break out on his forehead. He wiped it with the back of his hand. 'If that's all, Paula, forgive me, but I have rather a full diary this morning.'

She stood up. 'I think this should go further. If you're not going to do anything, I shall speak to the bishop.'

'That's your prerogative.' Mike stood up too. 'But I beg you, don't be hasty. These things so easily get out of hand.'

'They are already out of hand!' Paula flashed back. 'The whole point is to make sure things get no worse. To stop the damage. To put it right. To get her out of your parish!'

He followed her to the front door. 'I shall consult my colleagues about this, I assure you, and I shall speak to Judith and to Lyndsey herself if she will allow me to. Please, let it rest there for the time being.' He held out his hand as a way of finishing the conversation. She shook it firmly and turned away, but the set of her lips and the angry crunch of her footsteps on the gravel as she walked over to her car did not reassure him. She was not going to leave it there, that was obvious.

He closed the door behind her with a sigh and leaned against it, his eyes closed. His head was thudding like a steam hammer. His eyes felt as though they had been abraded with sandpaper and he was so tired he wondered if he would fall asleep where he stood.

The doctor listened sympathetically. 'Just a bad habit, you say? The sleepless nights, bad dreams . . .'

This was the fifth person this week. He frowned. No doubt the rector too would be reluctant to tell him what the dreams were about. Insomnia was probably one of the most common complaints for which he treated people, but to dread going to sleep. To fight sleep. Then to ask for pills to bring a sleep too deep for dreams. That was unusual.

'The pills won't necessarily stop the dreams. Nightmares are in all probability the result of some deep anxiety. An unresolved problem.' James Good cocked an eyebrow at his patient. 'You know that as well as I do, Mike. Anxieties need to be brought out into the open.'

Not this one, mate. Mike nodded, keeping his reply to himself.

'And a change of scene might help. I know how busy you chaps are. No time for yourselves. Any chance of going away for a few days to break the pattern?' He should have suggested that to all the others, too. He sighed. What on earth was happening? The whole of Manningtree seemed to be restless. Uncomfortable.

Wearily, Mike stood up. 'I might just be able to grab a couple of days. I'll see what I can do. That does sound like good advice.' Oh, how good. To get out of the town and maybe – witches can't cross water? – go and see Tony over the river, in Suffolk.

But before that, see Lyndsey Clark.

The windows in her cottage were open. He stood for a moment on the quay staring at it, trying to feel the atmosphere, calming himself, praying before he walked up to the door and knocked. The door swung open.

Peering inside, he found himself looking straight into the small front room. Facing north, it was dark, but it was far from gloomy. He noted flowers, the crystals sparkling on the hearth, the coloured rugs. He had to admit it did not feel evil in any way he expected.

Christ be with me, Christ within me.

He knocked again, louder this time. 'Miss Clark? Lyndsey?'

Silence.

But something had happened to the atmosphere. He felt it tense. It was as though the whole house were listening.

He stepped back a little. 'Lyndsey?' He could feel the emptiness now. She wasn't there. There was no point in waiting.

'What you doing here, then, Rector?' The voice behind him made him jump out of his skin.

'Bill!'

'Young Lyndsey not there?'

'No.'

'You thought about what I said?'

Mike nodded.

'You said your prayers up at Spindles?'

'I'm afraid I haven't had time.'

Bill shook his head ruefully. 'You need to make time for that one, Rector. Can't you feel it?'

Mike gave a weary shrug. 'Yes, I can feel it, Bill. There is something.'

'And it's getting worse by the day. The whole town is beginning to suffer. It's getting tense. Waiting. The bad times are coming in again. There's been another murder, you know. Up on the Seaview Estate. That's the second. They say it's drugs, but it's not just that. You want to do something about it, Rector, before November Eve.'

'Before – ?' Mike fell silent. 'I'm doing this all wrong, aren't I, Bill? I've been trained to go by the book.'

'Books has their place.' They had begun walking down the quay. Stopping at its edge, both men stared out across the river. Sunlight was reflecting off the water, leaving dazzling patches of ripples. The mist had gone for the time being. 'But there are things that have to be done. The old folk don't care any more. The young don't know how. So, like I said before, I reckon it's up to you and me, Rector. You need to bless the boundaries, bless the site. Clear out the darkness. Then do it for the whole town as well and it will spread over the whole peninsular. There's old evil lurking here.' A flight of dunlin danced over the top of the water, wheeling and swooping in the cold, clear wind.

Mike felt a shiver tiptoe across his skin. 'And you think that, far from being behind all this, Lyndsey is working to fight it too?'

'I reckon. But she doesn't know how any more than you do, Rector!' He chuckled.

To his astonishment Mike heard himself asking, 'Couldn't you do it, Bill?'

Bill shrugged. 'I can do some. But this is strong stuff. It needs the church.'

'Would you come with me? Summon the Ward? Show me where I need to pray?'

Slowly, Bill nodded. 'I reckon that would be best. You and I need to stand together on November Eve, Rector. And perhaps young Lyndsey, too. That's when the trouble will be worst. Always is. We'll pray today. And we'll stand shoulder to shoulder with the Ward come the dark.'

68

Emma was climbing back into her car when Mike turned in at the rectory gate. She waited for him by the front door. 'I had just given up. I'm sorry, this is probably a bad time to come and see you.'

'Not at all.' He was reaching into his pocket for the keys. 'Come in.'

She glanced at him as he unlocked the door. He looked very tired and he did not seem all that pleased to see her. Puzzled and not a little subdued but not surprised by his reaction to the sight of her, she followed him inside. 'I needed to talk to you.' Just in case he thought it was a social call.

'Fine.' He led the way into his study. Flooded by the morning sunlight, it was warm and bright.

She felt suddenly nervous. 'You said you'd be there if I needed you.'

'And I meant it.'

The whore is trying to talk her way into your heart, my friend.

The sudden voice in his head made Mike jump. 'Shit!'

Emma stared at him, shocked and surprised. 'Are you all right?'

'Yes, I'm sorry!' There at last was the boyish grin which she liked so much, the anguished Puritan side to him gone. 'A touch of migraine.' He paused, closing his eyes to apologise silently for the lie. 'I took your advice. I've just been up to get some pills from the doc.'

'I'm sorry, I didn't realise you weren't well. Listen, you don't need me here.' She backed towards the door. 'We can always talk another time –'

'No, Emma, don't go.' He took a deep breath. 'Sit down.'

She sat.

'Now, please. Tell me.'

'Partly it's Lyndsey.'

'Ah!' He sighed. 'So much these days seems to come back to Lyndsey. Whom I have not yet met!'

Emma gave a wry smile. 'Nor will you if she sees you first! The thing is, there is more to it all than Lyndsey.' She took another breath, as though she were finding it difficult to breathe. 'I got my sleeping pills the other day because, as I said, I couldn't sleep. That's not quite the whole truth. The thing is, when I do sleep, as I think I told you, I have terrible nightmares. I thought the pills might help, make me sleep more deeply or something, but they don't. The dreams, the horrors, are still there. Now I don't dare take the pills. I don't want to sleep. Not ever again.' She looked down at her hands and he suspected it was so that he would not see that her eyes were full of tears.

He didn't say anything immediately. When she glanced up she saw he was frowning. 'The nightmares are horrible – frightening,' she went on hesitantly, forcing herself to continue. 'It's the house. Lyndsey. All of it. I keep dreaming about the old lady who lived there.'

'Liza.' Mike said the word almost to himself and she was astonished to see a spasm of something like pain cross his face.

'Yes, poor Liza.'

He looked up at her. 'I know you don't come to church, Emma, but do you pray?'

She was taken aback by the question. 'I suppose we all pray sometimes, even if we don't believe there's anyone there.'

'It's a step in the right direction if you can pretend.' He gave a wry smile. 'It's worth keeping your options open. Words are powerful, Emma. Prayer, even if you think it's superstitious nonsense, works.'

The woman is a witch. Ask her, rather, if she believes in the Devil!

Mike put his hand to his head. He went on, with an effort: 'There is a prayer one can use, if you like. I'll write it out for you. St Patrick's breastplate. Recite it before you go to bed, like a mantra. Picture the love of Christ around you. You may not believe in him, but luckily he does believe in you.' A ghost of the boyish grin crossed his face.

'And you think it will work?' She eyed him quizzically.

'It'll work.'

'Does it work for you?'

He looked up to find her shrewd gaze fixed on his face.

339

'It works, Emma.'

'It just seems too easy. Say a prayer and everything will be all right. A bit simplistic. Sorry.'

'It's a start.'

'And do I keep taking the tablets as well?'

Again the smile. 'Ah, now that is not my department!'

'But dreams are?'

'Bad dreams are.' He glanced away from her. 'Can you tell me about them?'

She hesitated. 'I've told you. Witches. What happened to them.' She bit her lip.

Mike closed his eyes. Suddenly he couldn't look at her any longer.

'It's terrible, Mike. And they won't go away. It's as if –' She paused. 'It's as if they are trying to tell me something. Make me do something. And I don't know what it is . . .' Her voice trailed into silence.

He walked over to the window. Were those wisps of mist drifting through the trees near the gate, or had someone lit a bonfire? He pushed the window open and the autumnal smell of burning leaves reached his nostrils.

Beware, my friend. The whore is hoping to seduce you.

Rubbing his face hard with the palms of his hands, he pulled the window shut with a bang.

'I'm sorry, Mike. I expect there are things you need to do.' She was looking uncomfortable. 'I've taken up enough of your time.'

'I wish I could help more.' He risked a glance. 'We are the best interpreters of our own dreams because we understand the language of our own souls. Perhaps you should try and translate the dream in terms of problems in your life at the moment.'

'No, Mike!' She headed for the door. 'Thank you, but I don't need Freud or Jung or any psycho-babble to interpret these dreams. They are real.'

Lyndsey was waiting for her at Liza's, sitting on the wall of the terrace with Max looking smug on her knee.

'You've been to see the rector. After all I said!'

Emma was astonished. 'How on earth did you know?'

'I know things.' Lyndsey stood up after carefully decanting a reluctant Max onto the wall next to her. 'You must not go near him.'

'Now, look –'

'Listen.' Lyndsey grabbed her wrist. 'He is in league with Hopkins.'

Emma gaped at her for a few seconds. 'Lyndsey, you are out of your mind!'

'No, I'm not. He's being overshadowed.' Letting go of her, Lyndsey turned away and thumped her hands together in frustration. 'Oh, why will no one believe me! I can see him. *See* him, Emma! Hopkins! He has got inside the rector's head. He is trying to make the rector do things for him. Listen.' She spun round to face Emma again. 'You didn't tell him anything?'

'I don't know what this great secret is that you are afraid I am going to tell him! I told him I was having bad dreams. About Liza.' Emma's hand closed around the small card in her pocket on which Mike had copied his prayer. It was one she vaguely remembered from her childhood. They must have used it at school.

She met Lyndsey's gaze and then turned away, wondering suddenly if Alex had told her yet that she would no longer be allowed near his children. She suspected not.

Changing her mind about going into the house, she stepped away from the door. 'Do you fancy a walk? I've got a bit of a headache and I'd love some fresh air.

Lyndsey shrugged. 'OK, if you want.'

They set off up the lane and then cut through the hedge following a footpath along the edge of the field. Beside them the hawthorn and wild rose bushes were heavy with scarlet berries interspersed with the juicy black fruits of bramble and dogwood. Every few steps they took disturbed the birds feeding greedily in amongst branches still green with leaves, only slowly now crisping and turning to autumn colour. Already the wind had begun to strip them from the trees to lie flabby and dying on the path at their feet. Torn cloud raced across the sky, trailing shadows across the newly ploughed furrows.

'Promise you will be careful, Emma.' Lyndsey was strolling beside her. 'The rector will do you harm if you let him. He may not want to, but he may not be able to stop himself. Please believe me.'

'How can you possibly say that?' Emma stopped, suddenly angry. 'He's a good man. And you have never even met him. He told me so.'

'I've seen him. I've watched him. I've seen Hopkins hovering near him, overshadowing him!' Lyndsey stopped suddenly in her tracks with an exclamation of distress. 'Oh, no. Look!'

Emma, almost too shocked and angry at her words about Mike to register the other woman's sudden change of mood, followed her gaze automatically, for a moment not recognising what it was they were looking at. Lying in the nettles at the edge of the path was a small dead kitten. The two women stood gazing down at it. Lyndsey squatted down and stroked it gently. 'Some bastard has shot it. Look.' She pointed at the pellet holes in the side of its head. 'Who could do that? Who could shoot a kitten?' Her voice shook.

Emma was speechless with horror. 'That's awful.' She knelt down on one knee and touched the small ginger face with her fingertip. The kitten was stiff and cold. 'It must have been a mistake. No one would do it on purpose, surely.'

'What sort of mistake?' There were tears running down Lyndsey's cheeks. 'You mean they thought it was a fox? A fox cub? No. They must have been able to see what it was. It's all part of this awful dark hatred that is taking us over.' She bit back a sob. 'We have to bury it.'

They found a couple of sticks and scraped a hole in the soft mud of the bank below the hedge. Gently Lyndsey lifted the kitten. She dropped a kiss on its head and laid it gently in the shallow grave.

'Wait, I'll get some flowers.' Emma too was weeping now. Wiping her eyes, she wandered away on her own a few paces and picked some of the forget-me-nots and little scarlet pimpernel she had noticed growing amongst the stubble at the edge of the field. Returning, she saw Lyndsey was whispering a prayer and she waited quietly, her eyes closed, for her to finish.

'Ready.' Lyndsey looked up.

Emma stepped forward and gently laid the flowers on and around the kitten, then they scraped the soil back over the soft ginger fur. Lyndsey scattered some hips and haws over the place and finally a layer of leaves. 'It's a sign,' she said sadly. 'The balance is going so fast now, even the innocent are being drawn in.'

Emma was biting back her tears again. The small pretty animal had got to her. What it had been doing out in the fields she didn't know. Perhaps it was part of a feral litter out on its first exciting hunt by itself. Perhaps it was a treasured pet, lost all by itself in the dark, seeing a human coming and recognising him as a friend, running towards him squeaking with excitement, because all the humans it had met before had loved it and petted it. They stood for a moment in silence, staring down, then of one accord they turned and began to retrace their steps.

When they reached the gate at Liza's, Lyndsey stopped. 'I think I'll go on home.' She shrugged. 'We're obviously both softies when it comes to cats.'

Emma nodded.

'Remember what I said about Mike Sinclair, Emma. For your own sake.' Lyndsey put her hand on Emma's arm. 'Please.'

Emma said nothing. She watched as Lyndsey walked off down the lane, then she turned and went indoors.

She had dialled Piers's office number before she realised what she was doing. He listened to the story about the kitten and she almost felt the shrug as he replied, 'You wanted to live in the country, Em. They shoot things in the country.'

'But not cats!'

'Hopefully not often.' There was a pause. They were both thinking about Max and Min.

'Please, Piers, can you come down this weekend?'

There was another longer pause. 'I'm not sure, Em. I can't promise, I'm afraid. You've got friends there, haven't you, if you need someone to talk to?'

'You know I have.' She frowned. 'But Piers –'

'Look, I'll try, Em, OK? I'll let you know.' He had hung up before she could even reply.

Miserably, she picked up Max and hugged him tightly. 'Please, Max, take care,' she whispered. 'Don't go out in the fields.'

69

'Mike?' It was the bishop. 'What is all this I hear? Judith tells me you've been in touch with John Downing.'

Mike found his hand clutching his phone receiver unnecessarily hard. 'I did have a word with him a little while ago, yes.'

'She said you'd been working too hard, and not getting enough rest. That's not going to help anyone, old chap. You've got to take care of yourself, you know.'

'I'm fine, Bishop.' Mike tried to keep his exasperation out of his voice.

'Of course you are. Mike, Judith has suggested you take a few days away and I agree with her. You obviously need a break. She's willing to cover for you and take over anything that needs to be done, so there won't be a problem.'

'How thoughtful,' Mike said dryly. He took a deep breath.

'I want you to go today, Mike. Drop everything and go somewhere away from the parish where you can relax completely. Get some sleep. Some fresh air.'

'I get plenty of fresh air in Manningtree, Bishop,' Mike retorted. 'It's by the river.'

'Of course it is.' The bishop hastily rephrased his suggestion. 'What I meant was, a change of air. It's all arranged. I want you out of that rectory by teatime!'

'I can't go, Bishop.' Mike frowned. 'Not just like that. Next week, perhaps.'

'Today, Mike.' The benign voice held a hint of steel.

'Bishop, Halloween is coming up.' Mike knew he sounded desperate. 'There are things I have to do. Things I've promised to do.'

There was a pause. 'Of course. Witches. Judith said you were worried about witches. Mike, you've been told to leave all that to John Downing. All the more reason to be out of that parish until it is all over. Now, no arguments. I shall expect to hear from Judith that you have gone by tonight.'

70

Judith arrived half an hour later. Mike led her into his study and they sat down.

'Mike –!' She leaned forward earnestly, ready to speak, but he raised his hand.

'Before you say anything, Judith, may I ask why you went behind my back and rang the bishop?'

'Because I think you're working too hard, Mike. You need a rest.' She smiled benignly.

'I may need sleep, Judith. I do not need to be packed out of the parish without any notice!'

'Oh, come on, Mike, it's not like that.' She sat forward again. 'Before you say anything else, I should tell you that I have dealt with Lyndsey Clark. So, that's one thing less for you to worry about. It won't be long before she gets the message.'

'What message is that, Judith?' He leaned back in his chair.

'That we don't want her kind round here. That if she knows what is good for her she will leave.'

'I thought you said that your prayer circle could contain her? What changed your mind, Judith?'

'I was wrong, Mike. Very wrong.' She pursed her lips. 'I have evidence that she is far, far more dangerous than even I expected.'

Mike frowned. 'Evidence?' he asked mildly.

She nodded vigorously.

'And are you going to share it with me?'

'Better not, Mike.' She gave a sly smile. 'This is women's stuff.'

Looking up, he caught her expression as she gazed down at him. For a brief second it appeared to hold nothing but contempt. He took a deep breath. 'And because of this "women's stuff" you have seen to it that she loses any jobs she might have so that she can't stay here?'

'I've had a word with the Wests, yes. And Ollie Dent.' Judith looked smug.

Mike clenched his fists. She had certainly been busy. Sometimes Christian forgiveness was hard. More than anything he wanted to wipe that self-satisfied look off her face.

'Judge not and ye shall not be judged, Judith,' he said softly. 'Did you not think that prayer was enough? That Our Lord would be able to deal with this situation without your help?'

'You're not telling me you condone what she has been doing?' Her large brown eyes were suddenly a picture of innocence.

'I am telling you that it is not our place to be judge and jury. That we should not behold the mote in our brother or sister's eye because we might possibly have a great big plank in our own. And I am saying that to suggest that she has taken part in satanic rituals and that the Wests' children are in danger is unforgivable. You do not have a shred of proof.' His voice had risen angrily.

'How do you know?' She stood up and walked up to his desk. 'It is only unforgivable if it is untrue.' Leaning on the desk, she brought her face close to his. 'Why are you so sure she is innocent?' she hissed suddenly. 'Why? Perhaps she has been weaving spells around you as she has around the woman living up at Liza's.'

'Emma?' Mike was looking at her. Her face was very close. Too close. For a moment he didn't recognise the Judith he knew.

'I saw them just now walking in the fields. Talking. Whispering secrets. Close as that.' She thrust her crossed fingers into his face.

Mike could not disguise his feeling of distaste. 'Emma is well aware of Lyndsey's beliefs. And we are both quite capable of taking care of ourselves, Judith. Thank you.'

'Are you?' She held his gaze with eyes that were as hard as stone. 'When the bishop phoned me back last night he was very shocked that you hadn't told him everything yourself.' There was triumph in her voice. 'He wondered if you were really settling in properly, if you felt you couldn't go to him straight away if anything was worrying you. I told him I thought everything was all right, we were coping, but you had had to have a word with his deliverance team.'

'Judith, it was not your place to speak to him!' He stood up, unable suddenly to contain his anger.

'Someone had to, Mike.' She put her hand on his as he leaned

347

forward, his braced fingers splayed on the cluttered desk in front of him.

He shuddered, and straightening, he pulled his hand away sharply. She did not appear to notice.

'I told the bishop how hard you had been working. How wonderfully you have been coping with such a large scattered parish. How I felt you deserved a short break to recharge your batteries.' She smiled. 'I told him there was nothing happening that I couldn't deal with. If there is anyone you need to see over the next couple of days or so, you can postpone your visit to them or I will do it for you. I will take the service on Sunday. It's evensong, so that's no problem. You needn't do anything or tell anyone. I will do it all.'

'But, Judith –'

'No buts, Mike.' She smiled. 'It's all arranged. Bishop's orders. All you have to do is pack a bag and head for the hills.'

She walked over to the window and gazed out into the garden. 'I'll even stay here, if it will help. I know you wouldn't want to leave the rectory empty.'

This woman will help us, Michael. Much like Mary Phillips, to whose soul she has given refuge, she is one of the army of the Lord.

The voice was soft and insidious inside his head.

She will uncover the ungodly and see that they are punished. But it is better that you stay. Yours is the hand that holds the sword of the righteous.

'No!' Mike smacked the desk in front of him. 'Get out! Do you hear me, get out!'

Judith stepped back, alarmed. 'Mike –'

'Not you!' Mike was staring at her, but he did not see her. Just for a second he thought he had seen another face, a man's face, a wispy figure so close to him it was like his own shadow. He wiped his face on his forearm and took a deep breath. 'You're right, Judith. I need to get away. Go somewhere he can't find me.'

'Who?' Judith had lost her confident demeanour. Suddenly she seemed unsure of herself.

Mike was breathing quickly, clenching and unclenching his fists. He had forgotten Judith was there. He had forgotten everything in the struggle to regain control of his mind. He could beat this. He was strong. He would not panic, would not give Hopkins the chance to get anywhere near him.

'Mike? Is it your head? Shall I call a doctor?'

He heard her voice in the distance seconds before it was drowned by the roaring in his ears and then the explosion.

For a moment he didn't know what had happened. He stood stunned, aware only that he was standing amidst a shower of glass, then he looked at Judith. She was chalk-white. 'What is it? What's happened?' he asked. 'Are you OK?'

'It's the monitor, Mike. The monitor on your computer.'

They stared at the smoking wreck of what had once been a fourteen-inch screen on the corner of his desk. A curl of smoke drifted across the room, accompanied by the acrid smell of burning plastic.

Mike shook his head. The voice had gone. The room was very quiet.

He looked back at her and somehow he managed to smile. 'It is definitely time I took a holiday!'

71

Friday October 30th

The answer phone picked up Mark's call to the rectory. He frowned. Away until Monday? He couldn't do this. He was counting on having Mike there on Saturday, at least at the beginning. Not all night, perhaps, not after what Mike had said, but there, at least for a comment. He left a terse message informing Mike that whether he was there or not, they would be filming in the shop all night, tomorrow, thirty-first of October. Then, slamming down the receiver he sat back on the bed in his small room at Mrs Prescott's B&B and rapped the end of his biro against his teeth. If he was going to go ahead with this project, he was going to have to do it properly. This was the perfect time to inject more suspense. Being quite cynical about it, and putting his conscience to one side, he had to wind up the locals! If not Mike, then Lyndsey. He frowned. All very well, but how to find her?

He leaned forward and picked up the phone again. Mrs Prescott's, more of a hotel than a B&B really, had all the facilities including inter-bedroom communication. 'Allie? A bit of research for you.' Smiling, he wondered how long it would take her. In the meantime he had better get back to the shop and help Joe and Colin set up for the final and hopefully climactic shoot.

Alice had not moved from her bed where she had been leafing through a copy of the *Essex Magazine*. Throwing it down, she reached into the drawer of her bedside table for the local phone book and began to search for the Clarks. And Clarkes. There were over two pages of them. She groaned. She would have to go through every one to find those who lived in Mistley and Man-ningtree, and possibly then widen the search to the outlying area. It took her a while to copy down a selection of addresses but finally she had done it and had clumped down the stairs to consult Mrs Prescott about taxis. After all, this was on expenses.

The taxi driver, with perhaps an ulterior motive, suggested the furthest address first. And they struck gold. The woman who answered the door at the end of a neat flower-bordered path, a member of Judith's prayer circle, was furiously indignant that Alice should consider for one instant that she should have any-thing at all to do with 'that godless witch', who lived, apparently, on Mistley Quay. Alice spied out the land, saw that Lyndsey's door was open, returned to the taxi with a thumbs up and paid him off. Even she could see that Mark would not pay for the man to wait and it was not far to walk back to the B&B when one thought about it.

She wasn't sure what her brief was. Mark had only said 'find her', but Alice was not averse to doing a bit of investigating on her own and Lyndsey intrigued her. Slinging her bag, complete with mini tape recorder, notebooks and pencil on her shoulder, she wandered back down towards the quay.

There was no reply when she knocked on the open door. Peer-ing in, she knocked again then, unabashed, stepped inside. 'Hi, Lyndsey!' She was calling loud enough to be heard upstairs. 'You there?'

There was no response. She took a few steps further in, staring round. The sun, shining in obliquely through the narrow south-facing kitchen window, hit the mirror just inside the front door and its light ricocheted back into the room, highlighting the deep lush colours of the throws, the bright paintings of flowers, the crystals and candles, a bowl of late honeysuckle.

'Cool.' Alice's outbreath of admiration was totally sincere.

'Who are you?' The sharp question made her jump. Lyndsey had appeared at the top of the staircase. She had been working in her studio. Running down, she confronted the intruder with a look of extreme anger. 'What the hell are you doing here? Who said you could come in?'

'Hey! Whoa, sorry!' Alice raised her hands in surrender. 'I knocked and shouted. I knew you must be here somewhere or you wouldn't have left your door open. If you don't want people

351

coming in, you ought to lock it, you know.' She threw herself down on the sofa uninvited. 'This is a great pad!'

'Thank you.' Lyndsey was tight-lipped. 'May I ask who you are and what you want?'

'I'm Alice. I'm with the film crew up at Barker's.'

There was a short silence.

'I see.' Lyndsey sighed.

'We wondered if you would like to be on the programme.'

'I want nothing to do with it.' Lyndsey folded her arms.

'Is it true you're a witch?' Alice sat forward on her seat. 'Can you cast spells on people?'

'Look, I'm busy.' Sighing, Lyndsey walked over to the front door and stood beside it. 'I would like you to leave.'

'Sure, I'm going.' Alice didn't move. She smiled in the most beguiling way she knew. 'I'd really like to know. Mark thinks you can help us a lot. We really need someone who knows what they're doing.'

'That I can well believe.' Lyndsey was still unimpressed.

'We're setting up an overnight shot in the shop. Time-lapse cameras and stuff. Everyone is pretty sure that the ghost will appear. Mark is trying to get the rector to come. He's threatening to exorcise the place, but we're not going to let him before we've done the shoot. Then we want to film the exorcism to see what happens. It would be really cool to get you on the film too. A spokesperson for the dark side!' Her eyes were shining.

'I do not represent the dark side.' Lyndsey was losing patience fast.

'Then you're a white witch?'

'Look, Alice –'

'Please, tell me. I want to know.' Alice leaned forward and picked up the chunk of rose quartz sitting on the small table beside the sofa. 'Do you use this in your spells?'

'No, I don't. I make models of people and stick pins into them!' Lyndsey regretted saying it as soon as the words were out of her mouth. 'I'm sorry. I was joking. It's just, I'm really busy right now.' Upstairs on the table by the window a delicate watercolour of autumn honeysuckle and spindle berries was drying on the thick creamy paper even as she spoke. 'Look, you have to tell your director or producer or whatever he is, that he mustn't go on with this film. He is playing with fire, do you understand?'

'You must come and tell him yourself. He won't listen to me.' Alice paused. Then she put her head a little to one side as a thought struck her. 'You do know we've filmed the ghost, don't you?'

Lyndsey stared at her. Her eyes narrowed. 'Filmed it?'

Alice nodded. 'Really. A face in the shadows on the staircase. They'll show it to you if you come down to the shop.' She could swear Lyndsey had gone pale. For the first time she seemed uncertain. She was staring at Alice, but Alice had the feeling she wasn't actually seeing her.

Alice wondered suddenly if she should have said anything. Mark would be furious if she had jumped the gun in some way. 'Look, you'd better not talk about this to anyone. I'm not supposed to have told you.'

'I'm not surprised.' Lyndsey looked grim.

'So, will you come? To the shop.'

Lyndsey hesitated.

'It's really cool. We're filming on Halloween. That's dodgy, isn't it?' Alice looked pathetically eager.

'Yes, it's dodgy.' Lyndsey sighed. 'I suppose he chose the date deliberately?'

'Of course.' Alice gave an evil smile. 'What better?'

'What better indeed!'

'So, will you come?'

'I'll have to think about it. I might come down and speak to him later.'

'Great!' Alice stood up. 'It's going to be a fantastic programme. He wants to put you up against the reverend.'

Lyndsey frowned. 'I'm not being put up against anyone.'

Hastily retracting, Alice shrugged. 'Not literally. He doesn't expect you both to fight or anything. He just wants both points of view. I'll tell him you'll be there later, yeah?'

Lyndsey was staring into space.

'That OK?' Alice repeated.

A shadow had appeared in the doorway and Alice shrank back. 'You at home, Lyndsey?' Bill Standing stepped into the room.

Lyndsey glanced at him, then back at Alice. 'Are you still here?'

'I'm sorry. I'm on my way.' Alice gazed with interest at the newcomer. He was in his eighties, she guessed. Stooped, with a weather-beaten face and wild, wispy white hair. Brilliant. A warlock! He had shrewd, pale-blue eyes which scrutinised her briefly and without recognition as she stepped past him.

'Later, then?' she repeated defiantly over her shoulder, and she stepped out into the daylight.

72

'There's things you and me need to talk about, girl.' Bill waited until Alice was out of sight before turning to Lyndsey. He gave her a long slow look as though confirming something in his own mind. 'It's 'bout St Mary's and what you've been doing up there. You've been messing about with things, girl. If you're going to join in this battle you've got to do it properly, see?'

Lyndsey went to the front door and closed it, then she turned back to face him. 'What are you talking about?'

'You knows as well as I do. That witchy stuff of yours.'

Lyndsey glared at him. 'I doubt if it's your business.'

'It's my business all right. You've been trying to keep Hopkins in his bed, right?'

Lyndsey surveyed him silently.

'Well, you're going about it all wrong,' he went on. 'You are just going to antagonise him. You're not strong enough to do this on your own, girl.'

'Of course I'm strong enough. Wicca is immensely powerful!'

'Wicca?' He snorted with disgust. 'That's American, right?'

She scowled at him. 'Wicca has ancient roots in this country. It's nothing to do with America.' She folded her arms. 'If they practise it, it's because they've learned it from us. It's the one religion this country has given to the rest of the world!'

'It still doesn't make you strong enough to cope with this on your own, girl.'

'So, you're offering help?'

''Course I am. And you needs my help fast. It's Hollantide come Sunday.'

Lyndsey raised an eyebrow. 'Hollantide?'

'Halloween. November Eve. All Saints. All Souls. He'll be stirring then, and others with him.'

'I know that!' She looked cross.

'Well, all your fancy spells and such are not going to tie down anyone as wants to walk. You need the old ways. The real old ways!' He narrowed his eyes.

'And you can tell me?' Suddenly she was watchful.

'If I've a mind. There's things should be done.'

'Why don't you do them, then?'

'I'm doing them. I went out yesterday and burnt simson round the village. You know what that is? That's what they call groundsel. That fumigates the place against evil. I sent the smoke all over. And I've spoken to the rector.'

'The rector?' Lyndsey was disgusted. 'What's he got to do with it?'

'Everything, and don't you forget it, girl. We got to work together on this.'

'Oh, no.' She folded her arms. 'I don't think so! Besides, I'm perfectly strong enough. I know exactly what I'm doing!'

'I don't think you do. A little bit of humility from you wouldn't go amiss, girl. None of us can do this on our own. Can't you see how much danger there is out there?' He waved his arm behind him. 'That mist, it just hangs there, waiting, like a black curtain. It's got such strength in it; such evil!' He shivered and pushed his hands into his pockets. 'I can show you some stuff, same as I'm showing the rector. Stuff as will hold it and bring the light back.'

Lyndsey scowled. 'I told you, I don't need help. You do your thing and I'll do mine. Besides, this is a women's thing. Hopkins has to be dealt with by women.'

Bill gave an exclamation of impatience. 'This isn't just about Hopkins, girl! It goes far deeper than that. If we don't go to the root, we'll never get rid of it. Never. You can't just dance about up at that churchyard going all iddy biddy "women's things" 'bout it. Listen to me, girl!'

'No! Listen to me! I want you to go. *Now*!' Lyndsey's face had darkened. 'How dare you! This is my business. This is Liza's business.'

'You needs the Ward, girl. We've got to reawaken the Ward.'

'I need no one! I can deal with this in my own way. And I will.' Reaching past him she dragged open the door. Outside, tendrils of mist drifted up the quay. 'I'd like you to leave.'

Bill shook his head. 'Do you know what the Ward is?'

'No. And I don't want to.'

'See, you know nothing. Like I said, I reckon they iddy biddy spells of yours are all American. They don't have anything to do with real life in a real place like this, or maybe you need to learn to do them properly. Look,' he was getting impatient. 'You need me, girl, as much as I need you. You, me and the rector. We're the only ones as knows what's going on here.'

'Don't mention him in the same breath as me!' Lyndsey's face was growing red. 'I don't need him. And I don't need you. Now go!'

'Lyndsey, girl –'

'Go!' she screamed at him suddenly. 'Get out! I don't want to hear any more. I know what I'm doing.' She pushed him so violently, he staggered backwards.

In a moment he was outside. As she banged the door behind him he found himself staring across the river. The Suffolk shore was out of sight now, veiled in dark, soft fog.

73

Police Constable John Furness was finally going off duty. With a deep sigh of exhaustion he stepped out of the police station and stood looking up and down the road. A clammy white mist was drifting up from the river, dark against the trees in the garden opposite. He shivered. It had been one hell of a day. What was happening to the world? To this town? This was a nice place. Usually. So why was it suddenly so full of violence? What had made that woman, today, start hitting her child in the Co-op? Screaming and screaming, she had behaved as though she were possessed by some evil demon. And the old boy up near the sailing club. Why had he decided to pick up an axe, walk solemnly down the middle of the road and sink it into one of the boats drawn up on the beach? When John Furness had arrested him, axe still in his hand, the bloke had stared at the axe as though he had never seen it before. Then he had laughed. Laughed! 'You're not going to believe this, young man,' he had said. 'It was the voices. The voices in the mist. They told me to do it.'

They'd called Dr Good to that one. The old boy was carted off to the funny farm, crying, asking for his axe back, saying he had to finish the job.

Walking over to his car, John Furness glanced up. The mist was growing thicker. He could feel it soaking into his clothes, hear it dripping from the trees; he was breathing it in, icy, cold, smelling strongly of the sea.

Fumbling in his pocket for the car key he pulled it out and aimed it at the lock. His hands were cold and he dropped it into a pile of wet leaves and suddenly the rage was upon him, too. Swearing and shouting, he kicked the car, then he kicked the leaves. The key flew towards the fence, but he didn't see it. Already the red veil had descended over his eyes and all he could see was the fog and the blood and all he could hear was the rush of the sea in his ears.

74

The old herb beds were still there under the weeds. Emma stopped to rest her back, the fork thrust into the dark rich earth. Near her the robin watched from its perch on a lump of flint. She groaned softly. Her head was thumping. Two cups of coffee had done nothing to push away the effect of the sleeping pills and she felt drugged, ill and exhausted. She surveyed the ground in front of her. The herb garden had been laid out in two sections. This area consisted of six narrow parallel beds, presumably stock beds. She had found old leggy plants of hyssop and lavender, sage and rosemary and, almost throttled by the weeds, old springy cushions of threadbare thyme. Then there was the more ornamental, central garden which must until fairly recently have contained a wide variety of more unusual herbs. Some were still growing strongly and could be rescued from the sea of grass and weeds. Others had long ago been overwhelmed and would have to be replaced. There was a third area, a bit behind the rest of the garden, where she had found the most unusual herbs of all: monkshood, henbane, deadly nightshade, cinquefoil, hemlock. Witch's herbs.

You want to cut those back hard. Liza would have.

The voice was tetchy, clearly irritated by her tentative efforts.

Emma shook her head. She glanced round. There was no one there. 'Go away!' She knew she was going mad. She had to be.

The fork fell sideways into the mud and Emma jumped. She put her hand to her head.

We got better things to do than work in the garden.

The voice in Emma's head was strong. Determined. Emma closed her eyes.

We know what we've got to do, don't we, Em!

Emma put her muddy hands to her face. 'Stop it!'

Oh, come on. You and I've got things to do. Someone to see.

'No.' Emma was shaking her head from side to side. The robin watched her curiously from bright eyes, ready to fly at any moment. There was no sign of the cats.

You know where we've got to go. What we've got to do!

It was the sleeping pills. They must have made her psychotic. She was having an episode. Her mouth was dry, her lips sore, her eyes red and gritty. Either the tablets or the lack of sleep was depriving her of her reason.

We know where he lives, don't we, Em? The voice was confidential now. *We can find him easily. He thought he had escaped.* The voice was laughing quietly. *But I told him I'd find him. And you're going to help me!*

Suddenly the robin took flight, crying its alarm. Emma looked up. Min had appeared between the hedges at the top of the garden. She sat down, watching Emma with great intensity. Behind her, in the dark shady places at the edge of the narrow strip of woodland, the scarlet berries of cuckoo pint stood out like lamps.

Emma shoved her hands into her pockets with a shiver, staring round. The garden was empty; the voice in her head had gone. To her dismay she found there were tears trickling down her cheeks. Suddenly remembering, she groped for the piece of card with the rector's prayer. She couldn't find it and realised in dismay that it was in her other jacket.

You've got friends, haven't you? She remembered Piers's words as she walked into the kitchen and kicked off her boots. Did she? Were they real friends or had she been here such a short time they didn't count? Not when it came down to it. They had been kind, Mike and Alex, but that was just because they were nice people. Paula didn't seem to like her at all. And Lyndsey? Was Lyndsey a friend? She wasn't sure. Washing the mud off her hands, she sniffed and, tearing a piece of kitchen towel from the roll on the wall, blew her nose, trying to stop her tears. She stared at the white pot of sleeping pills on the worktop near the empty milk pan. Last night she had made herself the warm milky drink prescribed by the doctor, taken the pills and gone upstairs to bed. She had gone to sleep at once, but the dreams had returned with renewed force. Muddled. Violent. By three o'clock she was awake, befuddled by the drugs, wrapped in her dressing gown, sitting at the kitchen table with another mug of milk in front of her. At about half past four she had fallen asleep again where she sat, her head cradled in her arms, to be awoken as it grew light with Sarah's insistent voice in her head.

Emma, get ready. We have to find him, Emma. The time is right. He's here.

Emma sniffed. Picking up the saucepan, which had been standing on the side since the early hours, she put it into the sink and ran some water in on top of the skim of scorched milk.

Emma! The voice was peevish. *Why won't you listen to me, Emma?*

'Go away!' Emma turned off the tap. She reached across to the radio sitting on the window sill next to the pots of herbs and moved it to the table, turning it on. A woman was talking, her voice carefully modulated, interested. An interviewer cut in with a question, the woman paused, rephrased her words, carried on. Emma didn't have a clue what they were talking about.

Emma!

'No!' She took a deep breath and reached for the phone. A bland message greeted her, followed by a beep.

'Alex? It's Emma. I'm sorry to bother you –' She broke off, trying to steady her voice. 'Look, I wonder, if you're there, if you could come over? Please. I need to talk to you.' To someone. The tears threatened to take over and she hung up, embarrassed. Stupid. What would he think? If only Flora had rung back when she had asked her to come again and stay this time. But she had gone away on a course somewhere and wouldn't be back for two weeks. And Piers. Piers hadn't rung back either and she wasn't going to ring him again. And it would be ages before her mother came home. Miserably, she wandered over and surveyed the view from the kitchen window. The sky was clouding over. Rags of windblown cloud were piling in from the west. The apple trees were whipping disconsolately around, leaves scattering amongst wasp-eaten windfalls. She didn't want to go out again. But she had to go somewhere. Where Sarah would leave her alone.

Without giving herself time to think any more, she reached for her car keys and headed for the door.

Driving through the town, she noticed the door to Barker's shop open. Two men were carrying something inside and she recognised one of them as Colin. She found a parking place and walked back. 'Hi!' Their van was parked with two wheels on the pavement and Joe was lifting out a betacam as she stopped beside him. 'Hi!' His grin was friendly. 'Come for tea and cakes?'

She managed to laugh. 'Is it that obvious? OK, you've twisted my arm, but only if you let me go and fetch them this time.'

'You're on. Mark's upstairs.'

The scene upstairs was even more chaotic than usual. A mass of cables were being linked into a network covering every part of the room. Emma set down the food on top of a box containing cartons of soap powder. They were still working around the shop's stock. 'So, how are you, all?' She hoped she didn't look too white and pathetic. She had seen Joe glancing at her surreptitiously as she put down the cardboard box she was using as a tray.

'OK!' Mark paused in his work and set down the clipboard he had been scrutinising. 'You don't happen to know where Mike Sinclair has gone, do you?'

Emma shrugged. 'Isn't he at the rectory?'

'Apparently not. I want him in on this.'

'Does he approve?' She glanced round uncomfortably. Something had changed in the atmosphere of the room.

'Nope. He thinks we're asking for trouble.'

'Which we are.' Colin's comment was not quite sotto voce enough.

Mark raised an eyebrow. 'Trouble is what we're looking for, but only in a sense. I'm unhappy with some of this myself but I'm a journalist and I'm looking for good TV. We can't let the chance go by just because we might upset a ghost.'

'You're upsetting more than a ghost, Mark.' Emma shook her head. 'The whole place has changed. Can't you feel it?'

He stood still, his eyes on the ceiling as if listening intently. 'I don't think so.'

'I can.' Colin grimaced. He helped himself to a cake out of her box.

'Have you seen our ghost?' Joe came and perched on the carton near her. 'Have a look on the screen there. Col? Show her.'

Emma found herself watching a small loop of film. It showed the shadowy staircase, then clearly a face.

'Liza!' Emma's mouth went dry. 'Oh, God, it's Liza!' She squatted down in front of the small screen, watching as the flickering sequence ran again and again.

'How do you know that, girl?' Colin's cake was suspended on its way to his mouth. He stared at her.

Emma shrugged. 'I just know.' She stared at the screen, seeing the fear, the pain, in that shadowy ill-defined hint, then she glanced towards the top of the stairs where the figure must have been standing. 'He tortured her here in this room and her ghost is still screaming, hundreds of years later.'

And we are going to punish him!

The voice in her head was so loud she was sure the others must have heard it.

You and I, Emma, are going to send his soul to the torments of the damned.

'Emma? Are you OK?' Joe switched off the loop. She was staring sightlessly at the screen, her face chalk-white and strained.

We know where to find him, Emma. We know where he is hiding.

She put her hands to her ears. 'Leave me alone!'

'Emma? What's wrong?' Worried, Mark came over to her. He put his hand on her shoulder.

She jumped as if he had slapped her. 'I'm sorry.' Closing her eyes for a moment she tried to pull herself together. 'Migraine.'

'Really?' He did not sound as though he believed her.

She stood up miserably. 'I think I'd better go home.'

'Would you like me to drive you back?' Mark was genuinely concerned.

She shook her head. 'I'm fine. I just need some fresh air.'

'Are you sure?'

She nodded. 'Good luck with the filming.'

Mark grinned. 'I was about to ask you if you'd like to say something for us. That little spiel just now would be good on camera. We thought maybe the face was Hopkins. You say it was one of the witches. Just as good. Just as interesting.' He paused, eyeing her carefully. 'Especially if you tell us how you can be so sure.'

She stared at him blankly, then slowly she shook her head. 'I don't think so, Mark. I'm sorry.'

She had to get out of the shop. She had to get into the fresh air and she realised as she ran down the stairs that she had to see Mike Sinclair.

She only realised how much when she drove up to the rectory and saw that his car was missing. Three times she rang the bell. There was no answer and it was only then she remembered what Mark had said. Mike wasn't there. But, of course, she had the number of his mobile.

75

Piers was sitting on the sofa listening to the chink of plates coming from his kitchen. Playing hooky for the afternoon, he had just listened to his messages. Glancing towards the door he hesitated, then, reassured that no one could hear, he dialled Emma's number, frowning. There was no reply so, after a moment's thought, he dialled another, this time in London. Paula was still in her office.

She listened intently. 'It sounds as though she's missing you,' she said at last after he had described to her Emma's tearful message about the dead kitten she and Lyndsey had found.

'It's because she knows I'll understand how she feels about cats. Any cats.' He gave a wry grin.

'It's more than that, Piers.' Paula became suddenly very intense. 'There are things going on down there which are getting to us all. Lyndsey is not good news, Piers. If Emma has made friends with her you must warn her off. I tried. This woman is a really bad influence. Evil. A Devil worshipper!'

'I beg your pardon?' Piers could not contain his cynical amusement.

'You may laugh, but I am serious. Emma would be better well away from Mistley, for her own sake. See if you can't persuade her to come back to London, Piers, please.'

There was a short pause. 'Are you sure there isn't something else worrying you, Paula?' His voice was dry suddenly. 'An attractive woman down there in the country not a stone's throw away and with whom your husband seems to have formed a close relationship, for instance?'

'Don't be silly!' Paula snapped. 'That's nonsense.'

Piers glanced towards the door to the kitchen. He sighed. Fond though he still was of Emma, always would be, he assured himself silently, there were other women in the world. Women who came without hang-ups, complications and Essex herb nurseries!

'I was only joking, Paula, I'm sorry,' he said quietly. 'Look, I'll keep trying to get hold of Emma and check she's OK, but if you and Alex get a chance to keep an eye on her I would be grateful. She'd never admit in a million years that she was lonely or worried, but I get the feeling something might be wrong and I'm afraid I can't just drop everything and drive all that way. She's got to learn to move on and manage without me. Her choice.'

As he put the phone down he felt a twinge of guilt but it soon passed. There was after all nothing he could do, whatever her problem was. Not from so far away.

Standing up, he wandered towards the kitchen and pushed open the door. 'Is there anything I can do to help?' he asked. The phone call was forgotten.

76

Mike had dumped his bag on the bed of the B&B and headed straight back out. The house where he had found his overnight accommodation was in a small side road just off the main Alde- burgh street. It was a tiny cottage with, he suspected, only two or possibly three bedrooms at most. His, though small, was comfortable, attractive in a nautical sea-faring motif sort of way and very quiet.

He had often headed for this lovely part of the Suffolk coast in the past when he needed to clear his head or work something through to ease his soul. He would walk for miles, breathing the cold clean air, listening to the crash of the sea on the shingle, watching the opaque sandy swell on the horizon, or, turning inland follow the river up towards Snape where the endless beds of reeds rustled timelessly in the wind off the sea. It was strange, he realised, as he walked down onto the beach, how he never seemed to come here in the summer. Crowded beaches, blue seas and quietly moving tides did not appeal to him. He loved the elemental challenge of autumnal gales and winter storms, or the biting east winds of the spring. He looked north up the beach to where the brooding menace of the Sizewell nuclear power station lurked in the distance, a constant reminder of man's ability to threaten and compromise his environment, and resolutely he turned away from it and walked slowly southwards down the beach. He hadn't come to think this time. He had come to cleanse body and mind in the fresh salt wind, to exhaust himself and to sleep.

His walk took him several miles in a wide loop which brought him back to the B&B as it grew dark. There was no sign of his hostess, who had given him a key and a list of the best places nearby to dine, so he luxuriated in a hot bath and at half past seven wandered up the road to the pub where he ordered a half-bottle of wine and some of the best fish pie he had ever tasted.

It was still early when he made his way back to the cottage, which lay in total darkness. Letting himself in he switched on the lights and glanced round. It had finally dawned on him that not only was he the only guest, but that his hostess must live elsewhere. This place was just for tenants, which was why she had offered him the use of the kitchen. She would, she had promised, be there to cook him breakfast and they had agreed on nine o'clock After that she had left and he was on his own.

He walked into the kitchen, wondering whether to make himself a hot drink, decided he was too tired and turning off the lights climbed the stairs to his bedroom.

He had left his mobile on the table near the window. Glancing at it, he felt a pang of guilt. It had been switched off for most of the day. Supposing someone had tried to get hold of him? The guilt did not last long. He would check his messages in the morning. There was nothing he could do till then, anyway.

Amongst other things he should have contacted Bill. The shock of the monitor exploding had put the thought completely out of his head, and of course the old man wasn't on the phone. He bit his lip, worried. But in moments the worry was gone. What could he do from here? He had to hope that Bill would cope on his own. Almost certainly he could.

As he climbed into bed and reached to turn off the bedside lamp, he was aware that he could hear the rhythmic rattle of the waves on the beach in the distance. It was his last waking thought. Too tired even to pray, he was asleep in seconds.

'The date of the assize is fixed. There will be ten women facing charges of witchcraft. Your evidence will condemn them all.' John

Stearne was standing over him as he sat at his table writing. 'We will make good money from ridding the world of these women, Matthew.'

Matthew looked up wearily and nodded. 'But always there are more. The Devil's battalions appear to be infinite, John.' His eyes narrowed. 'And Sarah Paxman is next. The Devil values her. She learned well from old Liza and she is dangerous, John. She is rich. She has connections who will query her involvement with Satan. Who will speak for her.' He coughed violently, reaching into his pocket for a handkerchief. It was already stained with blood. 'And it is Sarah Paxman who pursues me with evil spirits.' His eyes narrowed. 'I thought that the bear with bloodied claws and jaws that drool foul poisons was sent by the other women. Elizabeth Gooding. Anne Leech. But they are gone and still it comes after me. She has sent it to pursue me, John. It comes from her.' He coughed again.

'You must look to your health, Matthew.' Stearne frowned. 'Do you have medicine?'

Hopkins nodded. 'Apothecary Buxton in Colchester has given me a distillation to soothe the cough. I will be well again soon.' He glanced up and smiled coldly. 'There is a pleasing irony in the fact that it was old Liza's syrup which soothed me best. I trust she has left her receipt with some God-fearing person who can make it as she did. I would watch her hang with more pleasure if I could be sure of that.'

Stearne grimaced. 'The physicians would take issue with you, Matthew. Their mixtures are the more powerful and do not involve the use of spells.'

Both men looked down at the notebook on the table. Hopkins stabbed the page with his finger. 'Sarah Paxman is next, John. We must take her up without delay. I can feel her familiars watching me.' He shuddered. 'She is evil beyond measure. Worse than the others.' He glanced up at his companion. 'The woman haunts my dreams, John. She does not let me sleep . . .'

Mike awoke suddenly and lay still, staring up at the ceiling. His heart was thudding unsteadily and his throat was sore. He had been dreaming again. He knew the symptoms. But the dream had gone, evaporating into the ether without so much as an echo. He sat up, staring towards the window. He could still hear the sea, but the sound of the waves was gentler now. More distant. The tide must have turned. Desperately he started to pray.

77

Trapped in the office by meetings and phone calls, Paula had missed the train. And the one after that. She was tired and cross by the time she reached the house and furious to find Sophie alone in the kitchen eating biscuits.

'Where is your father?' Paula dropped her briefcase and went straight to the fridge for the white wine.

'Jamie's been sick.' Sophie reached for another biscuit. 'I haven't had any supper.'

Paula was pouring out the wine, her back to the child. She turned round, frowning. 'Has Daddy called the doctor?'

Sophie shrugged. 'He had a row with Lyn. They were shouting at each other and Lyn cried.' The little girl frowned. 'Jamie cried, too. Then when we got home he was sick.'

Paula scowled. 'You were at Lyndsey's house?'

Sophie nodded. 'She collected us from Sally's. Daddy said he forgot we weren't supposed to go to Lyn's any more. Why, Mummy?' She turned an angry wide-eyed gaze on her mother. 'Why can't we? Jamie and me, we love Lyn!'

Paula drained her glass. 'I'm sorry, darling. I'm afraid Lyn hasn't time to look after you any more. She's too busy.'

'She said she could. She was really cross. She said, did Daddy think she would turn us into toads or something, and then Jamie was sick and it was green.'

'Oh, dear God!' Paula stared at her. 'She wouldn't! Surely she wouldn't!' For a moment she stood stock still, too shocked to move, then, slamming the empty glass down on the table, she turned and ran out of the kitchen. Sophie, sensing trouble, stayed where she was and reached for another biscuit.

Paula found Alex in Jamie's bedroom. The little boy, his face very white, was lying in his bed in his pyjamas. There was an ominously large bowl on the floor by the bed, blessedly empty.

'What in God's name is going on?' Paula was furious.

'I did what you asked.' Alex looked at her, his face as white as his son's. 'I went and collected them and told her we didn't need her services any more. It did not go down very well.'

'And you had to do it in front of the children?' Paula was beside herself with anger.

'What else could I do? I knew if you found out I had left them there you would go apeshit!' He stood up. 'Enough, Paula. We will discuss this later. Jamie needs to sleep.'

The little boy gave a whimper and reached out to clutch his father's hand. 'Don't go.'

Paula tightened her lips. 'I'll go and change. We'll talk later.'

Wearing jeans and a loose sweater, she was in the kitchen again ten minutes later. Putting on some water to boil an egg for Sophie, she was reaching for the wine bottle again when she noticed the light on the telephone blinking. Leaning over she stabbed at the button.

'Alex, it's Emma. I'm sorry to bother you . . .' The disembodied voice broke tearfully.

Paula scowled. She listened to the message and then pressed the delete button.

When Alex appeared she rounded on him. 'So, your girlfriend summoned you, did she? Did you go?'

'Girlfriend?' Alex frowned. He found a glass and helped himself to the last of the wine. Paula had been cutting toast soldiers for Sophie and he took one off the plate, licking the butter off his fingers.

'Emma Dickson.'

He sighed. 'Oh, Paula, for god's sake! I don't know what you're talking about.'

'Her message on the answer phone.'

'I didn't hear any messages.' He threw himself down on the chair. 'I was more than occupied with Jamie puking all over the place. What did Emma say?'

Paula pulled the egg out of the water with a spoon, dropped it into an egg cup and pushed it in front of Sophie.

'She wanted you to go and see her. All weeping and lonely.'

'Oh, shit!' Alex glanced at his watch. 'What time did she ring?'

'I have no idea. And you are not going now.'

'No,' he frowned. 'No, of course not. It's much too late. But perhaps I ought to ring her?'

'Leave it, Alex.' Paula glared at him. 'There are more important matters to discuss. As soon as Sophie is in bed.'

He looked up, frowning. Then he nodded slowly. 'Lyn. Of course.'

'Were you out of your mind to sack her in front of the kids?' Paula resumed the quarrel as soon as Sophie's light had been turned out. Jamie was long since fast asleep.

'I'm sorry. I suppose it was stupid. But what was I to do? She was expecting to pick them up tomorrow. Are you sure we're doing the right thing, Paula? I can't believe she would ever hurt them. She adores them.'

'Judith was certain. She and her prayer circle are praying for us, Alex. For our children. To keep them safe.'

'This is all nonsense, Paula. You must realise that. Nonsense.'

'Is it? Think about it, Alex. You sack her and immediately Jamie is sick. Supposing she did that. Just a little spell, to warn us what she can do!'

'No!' He shook his head violently. 'No. Absolutely, no!'

She was silent and Alex sat down. He sighed. 'She was really upset, Paula. Ollie Dent has sacked her, too. Judith spoke to him, apparently. She has lost both her jobs. Is that what we really want?'

Paula shrugged. 'What other people do is none of our business, but I am not prepared to risk my children. Are you?' She sat forward, staring at him.

'Of course not.'

'Then why are we arguing?' She sighed dramatically, throwing herself back in the chair. 'I know. I'm sorry. I started it. I was just so frantic when I saw Jamie.'

'He's OK, Paula. Just a bit over-excited. He'll be fine.'

'I hope so.'

It occurred to neither of them – then – to pray.

78

It was growing dark as Emma climbed out of the car and walked up the path to the house. Miserably, she slotted the key into the lock and pushed open the door.

'Min? Maxie?' she called.

There was no answering chirrup from the cats.

She walked through into the kitchen and glanced automatically at the phone. The light was steady; unblinking. No one had called.

She stood for several moments staring at the darkening garden, then she turned back to the phone. Piers did not answer. She waited for the message. 'Piers, it's Em.' Her voice sounded strange in the empty kitchen. 'Please call me. I need to talk to you. Soon.' She hung up, glancing at her watch. Of course, he wouldn't be back from the office yet. It felt much later than it was because it was growing dark. Unbolting the back door she slipped out onto the terrace and called the cats again. There was no answer and after a moment she went back inside, bolting the door behind her nervously. She felt terribly alone. And scared.

At least the Aga hadn't forsaken her. She walked over to it and savoured its solid warmth for a moment before lifting the lid of the hot plate and putting the kettle onto it. Then she dialled Alex's number.

Paula picked up the phone. Her voice was sharp. 'Yes, he got your message. No doubt he'll have a word with you next week sometime.'

'Next week?' Emma echoed. 'Is he there? Could I have a word with him now?'

'No, you couldn't.' Paula sounded even sharper. 'He's tired and he's busy with the children. It's really not convenient, Emma, I'm sorry.'

Emma put down the phone. She bit her lip, hurt. Oh God, there must be someone she could talk to. This time she dialled the rectory – of course, he wasn't there. But there was always his mobile. He had said she could ring him any time. He had meant it, too. Surely he had. The phone was switched off. 'Leave your name and number,' the message recited and she did. Somehow she knew he would not call her back that night.

She made a pot of tea and drew the curtains against the darkness, wondering where Max and Min had got to. It would soon be their supper time. They would certainly appear then, and keep her company.

The house was quiet. Too quiet, and she was very conscious of the dark silent garden outside. Walking over to the radio she switched it on, glad of the sudden chorus of voices which flooded the room.

Touring the whole house, she turned on all the lights and drew the curtains, checking each room in case the cats had got themselves stuck somewhere. They were nowhere to be seen.

Nor were they there when half an hour later she looked at her watch and reached automatically for their bowls.

'Max? Minni? Supper!' She banged a fork against the tin. 'Come on you two.'

There was no sign of them. 'Max? Min?' Her voice sharpened in anxiety. She unbolted and opened the back door again. It was cold outside. A spattering of rain blew into her face as she tried to see into the darkness. Stepping out, she walked over to the edge of the terrace, straining her eyes to focus across the garden. 'Max? Min?' The wind was rising now, blowing away her words. It was sharp with salt and mud, a sudden reminder that winter was on its way. From the fields beyond the hedge, she heard the short sharp scream of a fox. Shivering, she turned back inside and closing the door behind her she bolted it once more. They would come in when they were ready. Perhaps they had killed a rabbit and were even now gloating over their own private do-it-yourself supper in one of the sheds or in the barn.

The music ended and someone began to read the news. She listened with half an ear.

Emma!

She frowned, shaking her head slightly. If the cats didn't want their supper, the next thing on the agenda was a drink. She glanced down at the neat wine rack, newly stocked with carefully selected bottles of Shiraz and Merlot and Sauvignon. She didn't feel like wine. Wine was a convivial drink; a drink to savour with friends. She reached into the cupboard for the bottle of malt.

Emma!

She paused, staring round. On the radio they were previewing the evening's programmes. Leaning across the table, she turned up the volume, then she added some water to the Scotch.

Emma!

'Oh, stop it!' She took a gulp from the glass. 'Stop it! Stop it! Stop it!'

She stared at the Aga, frowning. The kitchen, normally warm and cosy, suddenly seemed unnaturally cold. She took another swig from her glass. Her mouth was dry and she realised she was beginning to feel rather sick.

'Max? Min? Where are you?'

The atmosphere felt strange. There was a tenseness in the air which was palpable.

Almost automatically she reached for the phone – her lifeline. But who could she ring? Not Alex. Not Mike. Not Piers.

Lyndsey.

Lyndsey would know what to do. Putting down her glass, she reached for the phone book and with shaking hands she began to turn the pages. It took a long time to find it, but at last she spotted the number against Lyn's address, and punching it in she put the receiver to her ear.

The number rang on and on. Biting her lip, she looked round the room. Surely it was growing darker and colder by the second? 'Lyndsey. Answer. Please.' As the phone rang on she pictured Lyndsey's little house, the small front room, the warm coals on the fire, the crystals, the flowers, and suddenly she slammed down the receiver. She wasn't there. Flora, then. Even if she was far away in London, Flora's voice would cheer her up. She dialled the number and waited. Flora's answer phone was typically forthcoming: 'I'm away for a few days. If you're a burglar my neighbour's rottweiler will get you, so don't bother coming round. If you're an aromatherapy client I'll see you in a couple of weeks as arranged. Anyone else, leave a message. Bye!'

Emma smiled wanly. No Flora then, either. There was no one to help her. Not anywhere.

Emma? We're friends. I'm going to help you, and you are going to help me, Emma.

'No.' Emma shook her head.

Emma, we have to do it. We have to punish him.

The voice was no longer inside her head. It was there, with her in the room.

'Go away!' Emma put her hands over her ears.

We know how to find him, Emma.

'I don't know what you're talking about!' She shook her head miserably. She walked across to the Aga and stood, gripping the towel rail. Automatically she glanced at the temperature gauge on the front. It was up to its full heat, so why did she feel so cold?

Turning her back on it, she went over to the table and reaching for the radio, she turned up the volume as loud as it would go.

You have to hear me, Emma. Listen. The voice was back inside her head. *We have to kill him. Don't you see? We have to make him suffer as Liza suffered. We have to drag Hopkins down to Hell, Emma. And now we can reach him. We can reach him through Mike, Emma.* The voice went on and on. *You can help me reach him, Emma. We have to kill Mike, Emma, then once he is dead, Hopkins will be in our power and we can send him to Hell!*

79

Saturday October 31ˢᵗ

HALLOWEEN

The next morning, Jamie was as right as rain.

'I'm hungry, Daddy!' He bounced into his parents' bedroom at seven o'clock. Alex groaned. There was no sound from Paula. Reluctantly Alex dragged himself out of bed, ducked into the shower, pulled on his favourite gardening clothes – old threadbare cords and faded checked shirt and a cable-knit sweater – and he headed down to the kitchen. By the time he had inhaled his first cup of coffee, he felt wide awake. He gave the children their breakfast and settled down for a few minutes with the morning paper.

'God, you all sound cheerful.' Paula appeared, still in her night-shirt. She reached for the coffee. 'Any news?'

'Pages.' Alex groaned.

'What are we doing today, Mummy?' Sophie slipped out of her own place and went to lean against her mother's knees as Paula collapsed into a chair.

'Nothing, if I have anything to do with it.' Paula groaned again.

'Can we go and see Sally? Can we, Daddy?' Sophie's face was eager. 'Jamie's better and they said we could go again. They said we could ride their pony.'

Alex glanced at Paula and raised an eyebrow. She shrugged. 'Would you take them? If I collect them at lunchtime?'

'Of course.' He smiled. 'OK, kids. Teeth. Make beds. ETD ten minutes!'

*   *   *

It was after he had dropped the children off and seen them scamper eagerly away towards the paddock behind their friend's house, each clutching a windfall apple for the grossly fat pony, that he remembered Paula telling him that Emma had phoned the night before. Pulling the car up in the lane he thought for a minute, then he reversed into a gateway and turned the Volvo, heading back towards Liza's.

The cottage was half-hidden in the mist which lay like a milky blanket across the fields and gardens. He pulled into the lay-by behind Emma's car and climbed out. The doors and windows of the house were closed, the curtains still drawn. He rang the front door bell and waited. There was no reply. He rang again, glancing at his watch. It was still early but he could hear music coming from inside. Perhaps she was already out working in the gardens. He made his way round the side of the house to the terrace and knocked at the kitchen door. The sound of the radio was really loud here. There was still no reply, so he tried the handle. The door was locked. He frowned, knocking again, harder this time, and called out, 'Emma? Are you there?' Perhaps she couldn't hear him because of the music.

A blackbird flew out of the old apple tree in the garden behind him, pinking a warning.

'Emma?'

He moved from the door to the window, and shading his eyes against the reflections, he peered in. The kitchen appeared to be empty. Frowning, he leaned closer, squinting to focus his eyes over the pots of herbs along the window sill. The lights were on. The radio was on the table – he could see the two red lights on the top.

'Emma!' He tapped at the glass and suddenly he saw her. She was sitting on the floor in the corner of the room, her arms wrapped around her knees, her head pressed into them tightly.

'Emma? My God, Emma, what's wrong?' He banged the glass harder. 'Emma. Can you hear me?'

She was moving. He saw her slowly raise her head and stare blankly around her as though she had just awoken from a deep sleep.

'Emma!' he yelled. He rapped on the glass again. 'Open the door! Emma, the door is locked. Can you hear me? Over here? Open the door!'

Damn the music. She couldn't hear him.

Then at last she was looking towards him. He saw her frown. Slowly she released the grip on her knees and straightened her legs. Then, agonisingly slowly, she began to struggle to her feet. For several seconds she stood leaning against the wall, then she took two steps towards the door, staggering, her hand to her head.

'That's it. Come on, Emma. Three more steps and you're there.' He peered through the glass anxiously.

She was leaning against the table now, taking deep breaths, then she was moving again.

Stepping back from the window he hurried back to the door. He could hear her trying the handle from the inside.

'Emma, it's bolted. Pull back the bolt.' His mouth was against the wood.

At last he heard the rasp of iron and finally the door opened. She stood staring at him. 'Alex?' The word was drowned by the blast of music which had hit him.

'It's OK. I'm here now.' He put his arm round her and gently pushed her back into the room. Two strides across the floor to the radio and he had switched it off. Blessed silence flowed around them.

'Max? Min? Where are they?' Emma's eyes had filled with tears.

'I don't know.' Alex pushed her into one of the chairs, then he turned to the Aga. 'You need coffee. What is it? Did you drink too much?' He had spotted the whisky bottle on the worktop.

She shrugged. 'Sarah was here. She wouldn't leave me alone. I tried to ring you.' Her eyes filled with tears again. 'No one came, and the cats are missing.'

'I'm sure the cats are fine.' He reached into the fridge for the jar of coffee. 'I expect they ran off because of the noise. They'll be back soon.'

'Noise?' She was squinting at him.

'The radio. You had it turned up full volume.'

'Did I?' She put her hand to her head again.

'Listen, Em.' Alex was watching her anxiously. 'I wonder if I should call the doctor to look at you. How much did you drink last night?'

She stared at the bottle, her brow furrowed as though trying to focus. 'Not much.'

'Presumably Sarah drank with you?' He was pouring hot water into the jug. 'Who is she, anyway?'

Emma started to laugh. 'Sarah doesn't drink. No, not a drop.' She shook her head slowly from side to side. 'She wants me to kill someone.' She looked up at Alex pleadingly. 'She wouldn't go away.'

'Then maybe I should call the police.' He turned and stared at her, trying to hide his shock.

'No.' Suddenly her laughter had become shrill. 'Not the police. She's in my head, Alex. In here!' She thumped her temple with the palm of her hand. 'She won't leave me alone.'

'OK.' He pushed a cup of black coffee in her direction. 'Just hang on a minute. I'm going to ring the surgery.' Picking up the phone, he walked out of the room with it to be out of earshot. The receptionist passed him on to Dr Good, who was standing beside her.

'As it happens I'll be passing the door,' he said after he had listened to Alex's description of what had happened. 'We don't have a surgery on Saturday. Normally I would suggest you take her to A & E, but if you hang on with her I'll be there in about half an hour. She came to see me only last week so I'd like to take another look at her.'

By the time he arrived, Emma had drunk two cups of coffee and was looking marginally better. There was still no sign of Max or Min.

James Good went with her into the sitting room while Alex waited in the kitchen. Ten minutes later the phone rang. Alex paused to give Emma the chance to pick it up in the next room. When she didn't, he lifted the receiver. It was Piers.

'Emma left a couple of messages. She sounded anxious.' His tone of voice was slightly hostile.

'The doctor is with her,' Alex explained quietly. 'She doesn't seem to be very well.'

'But you are there to look after her?'

'Well, I am at the moment –'

'So, I needn't have worried,' Piers snapped.

'I'm sure she'd like to speak to you,' Alex replied cautiously. Shit! Paula's meddling had antagonised Piers. 'Look, I was only passing. She left a message for me sometime yesterday so I dropped in. It was lucky, because I found her –'

'And she's OK?' There was a moment's silence the other end of the line and Alex heard a woman's voice in the distance. 'Hang on, I'm coming!' Piers was talking to her. Then he was speaking back into the phone. 'Look, tell Em I rang. I'll be in touch.'

'She'd like to speak to you, Piers. If you hold on –'

'I can't. I'm busy. I'll give her a ring tomorrow.' Before Alex could reply he had hung up.

Alex scowled. Poor Emma. She must have rung everyone she knew last night and no one had come to help her. No one at all.

In the living room, James Good had listened carefully to Emma's story.

'I'm going mad, aren't I?' She looked at him desperately. 'I'm paranoid or schizoid or something. You're going to say I should be locked up!'

He smiled. 'No, I was thinking how strange that someone else had come to see me with similar symptoms only yesterday. Nightmares seem to be endemic round here at the moment.' He sat back in his chair and stared at her thoughtfully. 'Is it possible you could go and stay with someone for a few days? Right away from here. A complete change of scene and some company is my preferred prescription.'

She bit her lip. 'I suppose I could go back to London for a short stay. Piers, my ex, said I could go back any time.' It was ages since he had said it. She wondered suddenly if he would still mean it.

'Then now is the time.' James Good smiled at her gently. 'I'll prescribe some mild tranquillisers for you, but on the whole I think a change of scene would do the trick.'

'I'm not being possessed, then?' She fixed her eyes on his.

He shook his head with a smile. 'I don't believe in possession. I do believe in obsession. Too much worry about your move. Too much worry about the history of your house. A lively imagination. A sensitive, highly intelligent woman who is suddenly on her own when she is used to living with someone else. That is a recipe for symptoms like yours if ever I heard them.' He leaned forward and reached into his bag for a prescription pad. 'I don't want you to be alone in this house again for several nights. Can you arrange that?'

She nodded.

'Excellent. Then come and see me in about a week's time and

381

we'll see how you're getting on.' He stood up. 'I must go.' Reaching out, he shook her hand. 'This is a lovely cottage, Emma. You are going to be very happy here. Just give yourself time to adjust.'

80

Saturday morning

'You've got to help me, Tony!' Mike drove up to the tiny cottage on the waterfront at Pin Mill shortly after eleven o'clock and Ruth had pointed down towards the foreshore where Tony was doing something to his boat. 'I spent last night at Aldeburgh, thinking. Thinking was not enough.'

Tony was standing in the mud, dressed in shorts and sandshoes, a thick sweater keeping him warm against the wind. His white hair was blowing wildly as he turned to face Mike, who was gingerly standing on the edge of the hard. He grinned.

'Hang on, I'll come up. Can't have you getting muddy. Come on. Straight into the pub,' he added as he joined Mike. 'Let's have a beer.' They sat at a table in the bar, looking out across the water. Nearby the open fire crackled in the hearth. The room was cheerfully full and noisy. A child appeared from the restaurant area next door, chose a game of dominoes from the pile of pub games on the table near them and disappeared again. At the feet of an old man standing near them a portly spaniel lay down with an audible sigh. It was obviously preparing for a long stay.

'You've been thinking, you say?' Tony said at last as they took their first sip from their glasses. He leaned back in the high-backed settle. 'Not praying?'

Mike frowned. 'Thinking,' he repeated firmly.

'OK. What about?'

'Emma Dickson.'

Tony raised an eyebrow. 'Not the answer I expected.'

'Not the one I expected to give.' Mike shrugged. 'Look, Tony, I don't know what is happening. I keep dreaming about her. But

I'm not me. In the dreams I am another man. Hopkins, a man who is reviled; feared; universally disliked!' He shook his head wearily. 'He is lodged somewhere in my brain and he is having a battle of wits with this woman, Sarah. Only Sarah is Emma.' He bit his lip, gazing into the distance. Out on the river the sun, finally breaking through the racing cloud, glittered for a moment on the water, then in a moment it was gone again. On one of the house-boats moored against the wooded shore, someone turned on a pump. A gush of white frothy water began to pour out into the river.

Tony took a sip from his glass and wiped his mouth with the back of his hand. 'Tell me about Emma.'

'She seems to be a decent woman. A widow –'

'Emma?' Tony prompted.

Mike shook his head. He took a deep breath. 'Sorry. No. Emma is not a widow. She's in a relationship I think, but it's breaking up. He lives in London. She hates London.' He sighed again.

'And what is she like as a person?' Tony prompted gently.

'Charming. A bit lost, I think, moving to the country on her own. She's not even quite sure why she's done it. She's friendly. Intelligent. Very pleasant.'

'Attractive?'

Mike smiled. 'Yes, attractive.'

'A churchgoer?'

He shook his head.

'Does that upset you?'

'It saddens me, obviously.'

'Obviously?'

'Well, it's my job to hope for a bigger flock.'

'Amongst your flock, do you find any of those ladies attractive?'

Mike gave a rueful grin. 'I suppose not in the same way.'

'Is it possible, do you think, that you might even resent the fact that Miss Dickson is not a churchgoer?'

'No, of course I don't.'

'Are you sure, Mike? Be honest with yourself. You lost a fiancée didn't you, when you entered the church. You could be forgiven for wondering if attractive women are somehow beyond your reach now that you are a priest.'

Mike drank some beer. 'This is some deep psychological ploy to suggest that if Emma is not available I am going to equate her with a witch to justify the fact that I can't have her.'

Tony put his head on one side. 'Yes, I suppose it is in a way. It would be comforting, wouldn't it, to equate her with an archetype. She obviously isn't a hook-nosed old hag in a pointed hat, but, to take another equally valid archetype, she could be the beautiful evil seductress. And you are further distancing her by seeing her through the eyes of another man.'

Mike drained his glass. 'So Hopkins isn't an external spirit of some sort? You are saying I have invented him as a psychological device? But what about the ghosts? What about Barker's shop? Or is this over and above all that?'

'It's possible.' Tony stood up and picked up Mike's glass. 'Let me buy you another half while you think about it.'

Mike contemplated what Tony had said, but his mind was a blank. Where was the voice now? The intrusive, opinionated, pious, judgemental voice? It wasn't there. He sighed, strangely content. Was that because Tony was right? It was all in his imagination, his way of protecting himself against the knowledge that he found Emma very attractive, and that she was not for him?

Tony reappeared. He put the two glasses down and produced two packets of dry roasted peanuts from his pocket before he took his seat. 'Now, for the other scenario. Supposing you are being possessed by the spirit of Matthew Hopkins.'

Mike frowned.

'He has wormed his way into your psyche, perhaps at your unwitting invitation, and he is using you for his own vengeful purposes. His battle is with someone called Sarah. Perhaps it has nothing to do with Emma. Perhaps your mind is giving Sarah Emma's face. Perhaps –' he paused thoughtfully – 'Emma is actually involved in some way. She is, I think you told me, living in the house of one of Hopkins's victims. She is a relative of a modern-day witch. She was drawn to the area in some mysterious way she does not even understand herself.' He tore open his packet of peanuts and tossed a couple into his mouth.

'So, what do you think is the truth?' Mike's unease had returned.

Tony turned towards him. His face was very serious. 'You tell me.'

'I can't.'

'You can. Search your heart. And pray. Mike, you are a man of God. You have every weapon in the arsenal on your side.' The kind, understanding friend had gone. Tony's face was stern. 'If this possession is real, Mike, you can only defeat it if you are strong. I can't exorcise you. I can't do it for you. The bishop, the archdeacon, the whole company of the apostles can't do it for you. And remember, Hopkins thinks he is on the side of the angels as well. He will be praying. He is wondering why he is in hell. And, if he is here on earth now, he may not technically be in hell but he is not resting in peace. He is blaming someone. He is blaming someone called Sarah.'

Mike hadn't touched his own beer. With a sigh he stood and picking it up, he walked outside where he stood watching the river. A fishing boat was motoring down the centre of the channel. He could just hear the faint purr of the engine above the sound of the gulls wheeling behind it. On the far shore Orwell Park School sprawled elegantly amongst its green playing fields.

Tony sat, quietly drinking, watching him through the window. It was a full ten minutes before Mike returned to the table.

'I think the possession is real,' he said quietly. 'Too much has been happening. To others as well as myself. To Emma. To Lyndsey. To Barker's shop. To the town. Bill Standing, my groundsman at the church, who calls himself a cunning man, a man of the old faith, Tony, told me to pray round the town. He had to tell me how to do my job. He is convinced the dark is rising, as he put it – old, ancient evil – and he thinks I am not trained to fight it.'

Tony raised an eyebrow. 'And do you feel you are not trained to fight it?'

Mike shrugged. Then for the first time he smiled. 'I feel as though I'm doing a crash course. Maybe you could come and meet Bill, see what you think . . .'

Tony shook his head. 'God believes you can do it, Mike, or he would not have sent you there. It's that simple.' He drained his glass. 'Come on, drink up. Ruth was cooking a huge casserole when I left. There will be mountains of food and I want you to eat well, then rest, then this evening I am going to take you somewhere special. It's a place I go to when I need spiritual refreshment. I want us to spend the night there in prayer and meditation and then tomorrow you can go back to your parish ready to do battle with the saints beside you.' He raised an eyebrow. 'Do you realise that it is Halloween today, Mike?'

Mike nodded.

'Never forget something like that. Your Bill Standing is right to worry. On days like today the dark is very close. You must pray for your parish tonight, Mike. And pray for Emma and for Lyndsey and even for Hopkins himself.'

81

Lyndsey had forgotten about Alice. Bill's long and detailed crash course on the 'stuff that really worked', and the shock of finding herself suddenly unemployed, had wiped the girl's visit completely from her mind. After a night spent walking up and down, meditating, dozing wrapped in a warm rug, and finally sleeping the sleep of the totally exhausted, she awoke on Saturday morning aware of only one thing. It was Halloween, Samhain, the time when spirits of the dead were close at hand and mindful of returning to visit the living, and all around her she could feel the tension, the presence of the other planes. Tonight she would enact a ritual, alone at home, then she would go up to the churchyard, but before any of that she had to try and stop these idiot people summoning Hopkins and his unfortunate victims back to the scene of some of their last encounters on this earth.

Dressed for battle in jeans, a scarlet sweater and a black fleece she stepped out of the house and locked the door behind her. It was not something she normally did but she was well aware that some of the locals knew she was a witch. They might decide today was a day to break in and wreak havoc in her home.

It took her twenty minutes to walk along the river. It was a windy, murky day. The water and mud were a uniform grey, as was the sky which was heavy with cloud except in the distance where it was torn into ragged strips, allowing a few pale smears of blue. Flecks of rain spattered the road as she walked. The swans that always congregated at the edge of the river on the far side of the Hopping Bridge were standing around disconsolately. One or two stared at her as she passed. None moved.

The shop was open. Several customers were browsing amongst the shelves as she opened the door and went in. She stood still for a moment, aware of nothing but the atmosphere. It was cold. Alert. Anticipatory. Walking over to the stairs, she looked up.

'Can I help you?' The woman in charge of the shop appeared suddenly at her elbow. 'That's private.'

'I've come to see the film people.' Lyndsey stared at her.

The latter quailed visibly. 'There's only one of them up there.'

'One is enough.' Lyndsey put her foot on the stairs. Then she stopped and closing her eyes she took a deep breath. She was filled with dread; sick; sweating. She couldn't move. More than anything she desperately wanted to run away.

'Are you going up or what?' The woman was watching her suspiciously now.

Lyndsey nodded. Hand on the oak banister, she found she had to pull herself physically up the stairs.

Colin was up there, thoughtfully looping a cable round his hand. He glanced up.

'Ah, Alice said you might look in. Excellent. Good to see you, girl.'

Lyndsey looked round. She was finding it hard to breathe. 'Where is the other man? The one I spoke to before.'

'He'll be here in a second. It's a big day for us. There is a lot to set up.'

'No, don't set anything up. You have to stop.' Lyndsey took a few more steps into the room. She shivered. 'There must be no more of this. You are encouraging Hopkins to manifest. It mustn't happen.'

Colin raised an eyebrow. 'I know Mark wants to talk to you about this.'

She folded her arms. 'Do you realise what day this is?'

He nodded. 'Halloween. Best day of the year for interviewing ghosts, so I'm told.' He grinned, then reached for a camera tripod.

She glared at him. 'If you think that, you are complete fools. This is not some game! This is deadly serious.'

Behind her Mark had appeared at the top of the stairs. He was listening, a frown on his face. 'I'm glad you've come.'

She swung round. 'Your colleague seems to find this amusing.'

'No. No, he doesn't.' Mark stepped forward. 'Believe me, we take this extremely seriously. And to prove it, I want you to allow us to interview you so that your views are made clear to everyone. The rector feels the same and to a certain extent I agree with you both.' He was watching her closely. 'I am trying to persuade him to appear as well. I really would value your contribution.'

'You want to make a joke of me and my views, don't you?' Lyndsey's voice suddenly rose in pitch. 'Here's the local witch! Let's pillory her.'

'No! No, I don't –'

Mark's denial was interrupted by a shriek from the bottom of the stairs. 'Lyn? It's Lyn. I can hear her!' There was a rattle of small feet on the oak steps and Jamie appeared with Sophie in hot pursuit. 'Lyn, we were buying frisbees with Mummy!' Jamie had a luminous green disc in his hand. 'We heard you! Look, this is mine!'

'Children, come down!' Paula's voice echoed up the stairs. Ten seconds later she appeared. She stared round the room and as her gaze fell on Lyndsey, her mouth tightened grimly. 'Sophie, James, come on down. We have to get home.'

'It was your idea, I suppose? To sack me?' Lyndsey faced Paula across a polythene-wrapped carton of plastic kitchen tools. Her frustration and anger had reached boiling point.

'Yes, but Alex agreed with me.' Paula's voice was flat. 'You are a practising witch, Lyndsey. I don't think it right for you to take care of my children.'

'You knew about it, I've never made a secret of it,' Lyndsey retorted.

James, with a glance at his mother, edged towards Lyndsey and groped for her hand. She put an arm around his shoulders.

'That was before I realised what you do.' Paula strode towards them and grabbing Jamie by the wrist, pulled him away. Jamie let out a wail of protest.

'And what is it I do that is so bad?' Lyndsey shouted. 'Tell me.'

'Satanic ritual. Using children. Murdering babies!' Paula screamed back. 'That's what you do! You let me think you were just playing with herbs and flowers, and all the time you were a murdering, vicious bitch! I trusted you with my babies!' She grabbed both the children, pulling them against her tightly. 'I trusted you!'

'Hey! Ladies, please!' Mark stepped forward, hands raised. Neither woman took any notice of him.

'I'm not a Satanist!' Lyndsey shouted. 'How can you think it? No one murders babies. How many babies are missing? How many times have the police been round searching for murdered babies? How can you say such a foul, vicious thing! For God's sake, Paula.'

She stepped forward and Paula shrank back. 'Don't come hear us. Keep away!'

Both Jamie and Sophie were crying now. The shop assistant had appeared on the stairs, her eyes huge as she took in the scene. Behind her another woman, presumably a customer, was peering round her shoulder.

'Come on, cool it now!' Colin walked over to Lyndsey and put a hand on her arm. 'Please, I think you should leave and take those kids away now,' he addressed Paula. 'You're frightening them.'

'*I'm* frightening them!' Paula echoed furiously.

'Yes, you are.' Colin's voice was very firm.

Lyndsey, her eyes narrowed, advanced on Paula again. 'If I had wanted to put a spell on your children, Paula, believe me I would have done it. Like that!' She clicked her finger and thumb together over Jamie's head. He shrank back with a little scream.

'But you already have, haven't you? You made him sick!' Paula was incandescent with rage. 'You little bitch!' As she pulled the children closer to her, Mark had retreated to the window. He was staring round the room, suddenly distracted, ignoring the others, aware of a change in the surrounding atmosphere over and above the tension caused by the two shouting women. The temperature had plummeted.

'Shit!' he murmured under his breath. 'Colin, I think we may have a visitor.'

Colin caught the tone of his voice. His hand dropped from Lyndsey's arm. She was still looking at Paula. 'You stupid, stupid woman!' She addressed her with icy scorn. 'Have you any idea of what you have done?' She was looking at the two terrified children.

'Lyndsey!' Mark barely breathed her name but she picked up on the fear in his voice and froze, turning to face him.

'What is it?'

'Can't you feel it?'

Lyndsey stiffened. 'Has Emma ever been here?' she asked suddenly, her voice raw.

Mark frowned, puzzled. He nodded. 'She said the face of the ghost was Liza's,' he said softly.

For a moment the room was silent, then Paula let out a groan. She turned towards the stairs. 'I knew it! Oh, God Almighty, I knew it. You are all in it. Come on, Soph. James. Quickly! Out of my way!' She shoved past the shop assistant and headed down the stairs, towing the protesting, crying children behind her. The assistant, after another quick frightened glance round the room, turned to follow her. As they disappeared they heard Sophie's voice, shrill and indignant: 'I want a witch's hat, Mummy, so we can do trick or treat . . .'

Lyndsey, Mark and Colin were left alone. None of them heard Sophie's words; none of them gave the stairs a second glance. Whatever had happened, had happened in the room with them. Lyndsey straightened her shoulders. She moved away from the stacked cartons and stood still in an empty patch of floor and waited, holding her breath.

Colin glanced at Mark. He raised an eyebrow. The glance meant, shall I switch on a camera? Mark nodded. He was watching Lyndsey intently.

Silently Colin stepped over to one of the cameras and switched it on.

'There is someone here,' Lyndsey said softly. 'The anger, that woman's hatred, the children's fear, has given her enough energy to reach us.' She held out her hands. 'Speak to me. I am your friend. Your sister.' Her eyes were fixed in the middle distance, unfocused. She wasn't actually looking at anyone.

Colin and Mark watched quietly, intrigued.

Lyndsey took a step forward. She was smiling. 'I am here to help you. To bring you peace. Show yourself, please. Let me see you.' She glanced round, her hands almost groping at the air in front of her, then suddenly she jerked backwards as though she had been pushed in the chest; Mark saw genuine shock and fear in her face. Almost at once she recovered herself. For a moment she stood still. She looked round at him. 'She's gone.' She frowned uncertainly. 'I thought I could reach her, but she's too angry.' She licked her lips nervously. 'She's so angry!'

'Why is she angry, Lyndsey?' Mark asked softly.

'Why do you think?' She turned on him furiously. 'She was tortured here. By Hopkins. He sent her to her death. She wants revenge!'

Mark glanced at Colin. 'Perhaps we can help her, by giving her a platform.'

Lyndsey stared at him. Then slowly she shook her head. 'You

don't get it, do you? You really don't get it. If you put this on TV you will be releasing something so huge –' She stopped abruptly and took a deep breath. 'Hopkins will come. It is his name that will rebound around the country. He will come and he won't be interested in destroying her. She is already destroyed. He will turn his attention to every other woman in the country! Don't you see?'

Mark blinked. For a moment he had believed her. He had felt the fear, but she was losing it. '*Every* woman?' he repeated. He couldn't keep the scepticism out of his voice.

'Every woman!' She was almost shouting again. 'Look around you! The women of his day were a different species. Now we are all witches in his eyes! All of us. Witches in his sense of the word. Creatures to fear. To suppress!' She grabbed him by the shoulders. 'Call it off. Stop it! Don't let it happen.' Whirling round, she made a dive towards the camcorder placed on the floor near a heap of flattened cardboard boxes.

Just in time Colin saw what she was doing and caught her arm, swinging her off balance. 'That's enough, Lyndsey! We've taken your point,' he said firmly. 'We'll think about it, but that's it. You don't damage our equipment. I don't want to have to call the police. Out now, please. I'd like you to leave.' He was guiding her towards the stairs. 'We'll keep everything you've said in mind, I promise you.'

'Fools! Stupid, stupid fools!' Lyndsey wrenched her arm away from him. For a moment he thought she was going to come back and have another go, but with a furious sob she turned and ran down the stairs, leaving Colin and Mark staring at each other across the silent room.

82

The sun was coming out at last, as Alex and Emma stood on the terrace. They had searched the barns and the sheds, calling the cats every few seconds, but there was still no sign of either of them.

Emma was getting anxious. 'I don't understand. They've never done this before. They have stayed so close to home.'

'Don't worry.' Alex was trying to comfort her. 'If it was one of them I'd worry more. If it's both, surely they must have gone off on a spree together. They'll turn up.' He glanced at her. She was looking very pale, her face drawn and unhappy. 'Emma, I'm afraid I'm going to have to go in a minute. Paula will be wondering where I am. Is there anyone I can ring to come and keep you company?'

Emma shrugged. She had not told him about the doctor's prescription. What was the point? 'Alex, you've been so kind. Don't worry. I'm OK on my own. And I'll give Piers a ring. He said he might come down.' She didn't see Alex's sudden grim expression as she was turning towards the kitchen door, and when the phone rang she smiled almost cheerfully 'There you are. That will be him.'

It wasn't. It was Paula. 'Is my husband there? He's turned off his mobile again.' Paula's anger was palpable. 'Put him on, please.'

Emma grimaced. She handed Alex the receiver and went back outside, trying not to listen, judging Paula's anger by the long silences and Alex's ineffectual attempts to interrupt.

At last he switched off the phone, put it down and came outside. She turned to him. 'I'm sorry. My fault. Blame me.'

He shook his head. 'It's not you, it's Lyndsey. They met in the shops somewhere and had a terrible row. I'm going to have to try and calm Paula down – not so easy once she's got herself worked up.'

She was still standing by the gate after waving the Volvo out of sight, reluctant to go back inside the house, when a bicycle appeared round the corner of the lane. It was Lyndsey. She flung the bike down into the grass behind Emma's car and let herself in through the gate. 'We've got to talk.'

Emma led the way round the back. 'Alex was here and Paula rang. I gather you and she had a row?'

'Stupid woman!' Lyndsey's lips tightened angrily. 'But it's not just her, it's everything! I can't do it on my own, Emma. You've *got* to help me.' She walked ahead of Emma into the kitchen and stopped dead. 'What on earth has been happening in here? The atmosphere is dreadful!' She frowned. 'Not just Paula on the phone, it's more than that. Something else has happened. What is it?' She turned accusingly.

Emma, taken off guard by the ferocity of the question, took a step back. Embarrassingly, her eyes filled with tears and she brushed them away furiously. 'I just had a bad night. Nightmares. I'm so tired!' She bit her lip. 'And now Max and Min have disappeared.'

Lyndsey took a deep breath, visibly trying to calm herself down. 'OK. Let's tackle this bit by bit,' she said more gently. 'If I was a cat, I wouldn't be here now. Not with all this going on. Don't worry about them, they'll come back. Your nightmares are linked to all the rest of it. If we sort it all out, they will go away. As for Alex and Paula . . .' Her eyes hardened. 'They're not friends of mine any more. It's up to you if you still think of Alex as a friend, but Paula – you do know that she hates you, don't you? She's jealous of you. And she hates it that you know me.' She gave a quick smile. 'You go and wait outside. I'm going to start by putting your kitchen right.'

Emma frowned uncertainly. 'Putting it right?'

Reaching over, Lyndsey gave Emma a brief hug. 'Call it Feng Shui if that makes you feel better. Installing good vibes. Then the cats can come home.' She gave Emma a push towards the door.

It was fifteen minutes by the time Lyndsey came and found her in the barn. She was smiling. 'There. Come on back now. I've even made us some coffee.' Lyndsey's unexpected camaraderie was disconcerting.

'The cats . . . ?'

Lyn shook her head. 'Not yet. But they'll come.'

Emma followed her back and just inside the door she stopped, staring round. The room did indeed feel different. It was warm again and almost sparkling; it felt welcoming and happy and safe.

Emma sat down. 'Whatever you've done, thank you. It does feel better.'

'Good. Now for the rest.' Lyndsey sat down opposite her. 'You've got to help me. I can't do it alone.'

'The rest?' Emma eyed her uneasily.

'You've been into Barker's shop. Where they are filming.'

Emma nodded. 'It was Liza's face on their film.'

'They told me.' Lyndsey paused. 'But they aren't going to leave it at that. I've been trying to stop them. Tonight is Halloween and they've got it into their heads to try and film the ghost. Their intention, their longing for it to appear, together with thousands of men and women and children dressing up as witches and ghouls and ghosts, will conjure Liza into being almost certainly, but more than that, it is Hopkins they want. Hopkins they are after. And it is Hopkins they will get. I've tried to stop them. They don't understand. They think I'm mad. Our only hope is to intercept him.'

'Intercept Matthew Hopkins?' Emma's eyes rounded.

'He must not be given the chance to appear. We have to bind him.'

'Oh, Lyndsey, no.' Emma shook her head. 'You know I don't want to be part of this. I really don't.'

'You have to.' Lyndsey grabbed her wrist. Her charm was gone and her eyes were hard. 'There's no one else.'

'No, Lyn. I can't. I won't. I don't want to get involved.'

'You are involved. You are one of us.'

'No, I'm not.' She wasn't sure what 'one of us' meant. She started to tremble again. 'Please, Lyn. I want you to go.'

'No chance. This is too important.'

'No, Lyn. No!' Emma was backing away from her. 'Please. I can't think straight. My head aches. I just want to go to sleep.' She threw herself down in a chair.

'Later. You can sleep all you want later. For now, you have to listen to me. Between us, we can do this. Sarah can do it!'

Emma froze. 'What do you mean?'

Lyndsey held her gaze. 'Oh, come on, Emma. The sooner you face what is happening here, the sooner we can do something about it.' She stood up and walked briskly up and down the kitchen floor a couple of times. 'Sarah Paxman is inside your head, right? You dream about her more and more. You hear her voice. She's telling you what she wants you to do – isn't she?' She sat down, facing Emma across the table.

Emma sighed heavily. She didn't want to hear all this again.

'She wants to get even with Hopkins. She has pursued him backwards and forwards through time and space and now she's tracked him down here, where it all started.' She sat down. 'This is all part of a much bigger picture, Emma. Things have happened on the other planes, other worlds, to do with ancient Anglo-Saxon evil which is helping all this to happen. Hopkins didn't live in this part of the world by accident. He was drawn here. There are huge build-ups of supernatural energy all over East Anglia, which the Germanic invaders knew how to channel. There is a cunning man in the town – Bill Standing – and he has told me all about it, how it works, why it is so powerful.'

'Why doesn't he help you, then?' Emma said weakly.

'He is. He is doing a lot. As is . . .' Lyndsey hesitated. 'Apparently the rector is helping, though I can't think how. In my view he'll make it even more dangerous with Hopkins trying to possess him but Bill says this is so great it needs us all. That's as maybe. I know I can't do it alone, but if we work together, you and I, we don't need them. You are strong, Emma. With your help we can do this!'

'But I'm not a witch,' Emma put in quietly.

'No?' Lyndsey smiled. 'Not formally, perhaps. It doesn't matter. I can teach you what to do. You're a woman, that's all that matters.' She smiled. 'The other two are men, of course. They don't realise that this is about far more than mere techniques. This is personal. You saw what Hopkins did to those women. He may not have done it himself, but he watched and he made notes. What sort of sick bastard does that make him? This is you and me, Emma. And Sarah. No one else can do it.'

'Lyn –'

'Say yes, Emma. You have to. Only you can do it.'

'But –'

'Say yes, Emma! This is for Liza. For Liza, Emma!'

Emma stared up into her eyes. For a moment she couldn't move, then slowly, almost without realising it, she nodded. 'All right,' she said. 'I'll help.'

83

The shop assistant stuck her head around the corner of the stairs at half past five exactly. 'I'm off. You know you've got to lock up when you go?' She stared round the room at the network of cables, the hanging microphones, the cameras carefully positioned on their tripods.

Mark stepped forward and took the proffered keys from her. 'Thanks, Jackie.' He smiled. 'Can you slip the lock on the shop door as you go out? We don't want any local kids coming in with witchy hats on!'

'Sure.' She shrugged. 'You're not staying here all night, are you?'

Mark shook his head. 'No fear. Once we've finished setting up we're off. We'll come back tomorrow and take all this stuff away.' A thought struck him. 'You haven't suddenly started opening on Sundays, have you?'

She shook her head.

'Good, then we won't disturb you. We'll stick the keys through the café letterbox as arranged, OK? So on Monday you can collect them.' He gave her a winning smile but already she was turning away, running down the stairs, her footwear of choice today the more silent trainer, he noted. He waited to hear her leave. The lights went out one by one in the shop downstairs, the door opened, then banged shut, and he listened for the click of the latch before he turned back to the others. 'OK, gang. It's all ours.'

Alice was wearing a black sweater with a large cross suspended round her neck. Her father also favoured sober colours. Mark was wearing a flamboyant red shirt and ancient cords. All were dusty.

Colin and Joe were testing camera angles near the stairs. 'This is the place we know she's going to appear so we want it covered from every angle.' Colin consulted the notes. They had brought in the full ghost hunting kit: 36-ml infra-red base night shot cameras which would cover the light spectrum in which ghosts might appear. Joe had produced an oscilloscope to register any and all noises and would be measuring electro-magnetic fields and looking for extremely low frequency hits on the remote audio lab – tape-recorded onto the hard drive of the sophisticated little piece of kit he had carefully set up in one corner close to the staircase. Mark checked the position of the last two cameras and nodded. 'Just about ready, I think.'

Colin put down his clipboard. 'Do we want some other stuff in shot, Mark? For contrast?' He lifted a box of brightly coloured balloon pumps. 'What about this? Visual irony. Bring on the clowns. That sort of thing.' He put it down with a bang in front of camera number one.

Mark moved back to squint through the viewfinder. 'Too distracting. We can cut in shots of that sort of stuff if we want to, later.' He paused, looking at the window. 'It's very quiet out there.'

Colin chuckled. 'Nervous?'

'Scared, more like.' Mark shrugged. 'Scared something will happen. Scared it won't.'

'Our Lyndsey put the wind up you good and proper, didn't she?'

'A bit.' Mark sat down on an empty crate. 'She has a way with words, that woman. I just wish she would say it to camera. We can't use that stuff you got earlier without her permission.'

'I could go and interview her.' Alice folded her arms and pursed her lips to show her disapproval as her father reached for a cigarette. 'She might talk to me. After all, I got her to come here.'

'True.' Mark glanced at Joe. 'I guess it doesn't matter where the interview takes place. In fact –' He paused to think. 'I wonder if it's worth you taking the small videocam. It's down in my car. It would be fantastic if she let you film her. Go for it, Alice. See what you can do. Sound only is fine if she won't let you film. We can cut it in over something else. A few shots of her dancing round the bonfire tonight would be even better. Or, failing all else, I suppose permission to use some of the voiceover we got this afternoon.'

'Can I take the car, Dad, as you've all got the van?' Alice knew exactly when she could push her luck.

He nodded. 'OK. Dent it and you're dead meat. Understood?'

399

'Understood.' She glanced round the room. 'I'm quite glad to get out of here, actually.'

'I know what you mean.' Joe stood back, surveying his handiwork. 'I'm pleased we're not staying all night. A few hours in the pub are what my nerves tell me I need. See you, kid. Good luck.' But she had already gone.

Mark walked across to the window and looked out into the dark. He shivered. 'I keep on thinking it's getting colder in here. I wonder if Jackie turned off the heating downstairs.'

Colin and Joe both looked at him. 'Time to go, mate!' Colin said darkly. 'I do not intend to be here if something happens.'

'*When* something happens.' Mark raised an eyebrow. He shivered. 'Everything ready?'

'Just about.' Colin adjusted a camera a millimetre or so to the left.

Mark stood up. The atmosphere was thickening perceptibly. He stared round the room one last time. 'OK. Let's go. Cameras roll.' He paused 'It's all yours, ghosts. Now is your chance to make your mark on posterity. Appear on camera tonight and the whole world will see you.' He looked round again. Joe had picked up his jacket and was shrugging it on. Colin had gathered up his old leather satchel, pushing in his glasses, notebook, pen and a spare length of cable, swinging it onto his shoulder. Silently the three men made their way to the stairs and started down. Mark came last. At the top he turned and surveyed the scene. By the window where he had been standing a thin wisp of mist drifted across the floor. He frowned.

'Did you put out your cigarette?' he called to Joe. He already knew the answer. Whatever he could see, it wasn't smoke. Not yet. Nor was that tiny ball of light dancing across the wall opposite him. A reflected headlight? No.

Suddenly he could not stand still a moment longer and turning, he raced down the stairs after the others. Whatever happened in that room tonight, he intended to be as far away as possible.

84

A group of children were standing at the corner of the street. All wore masks and black pointed hats. Most wore cloaks of black or green nylon. One of them held a lantern. Giggling, they turned up South Street and headed for the first house with lights in the windows. Suddenly silent, the humour gone, they gathered round the door and the tallest child, a boy, beat on the wood with his fist. There was no answer. He knocked again, louder, menacingly, aware of the growing impatience in the group clustered round him. As yet, no one had answered their knock. In the house the lights went off suddenly. He hesitated, uncertain what to do.

'Come on, Ray. We'll try next door.' The girl beside him tugged at his sleeve nervously.

'I'll try once more. We know there's someone there.' Ray was not to be put off. Under his mask he stuck out his chin. If they didn't answer he was going to spray a rude word on their front door. Raising his fist, he hammered again.

The door opened slowly beneath his fusillade of blows. Inside all was dark. For a moment nothing happened. They waited, expectant, then suddenly, from the depths of the hall, a huge yellow face appeared, floating. Disembodied.

Ray screamed, and pushing the others out of his way he ran. In seconds the others had followed him.

85

Saturday evening

One by one the women had arrived at the rectory, several in cars, two on bicycles and two on foot. By the time Paula got there, there were eleven seated in the sitting room. Judith showed Paula in and pointed her to the remaining seat on an upright chair against the wall near the window.

'Ladies, I want to introduce Paula West to those of you who don't know her, a newcomer to our prayer circle.' She smiled at Paula, who nodded uncomfortably towards the others. She recognised several of the faces. They were all women whom she saw at weekends at the shops or on the train; some had children at the local school. There were three complete strangers, but Judith made no attempt to introduce each one. She had already taken a stance with her back to the empty fireplace, a Bible in her hand.

'Paula has joined us tonight, ladies, because she had first-hand experience of the witch we have found in our midst. She was tricked into allowing Lyndsey Clark to look after her children and in so doing put them in terrible danger.'

There was a slight frisson in the room. Paula felt all the eyes fixed on her. She could feel the heat rising in her face. She wasn't sure if they blamed her or sympathised, but it was not a comfortable feeling. She gave Judith a quick glance, not sure if she was supposed to say anything. Judith had her eyes closed, the Bible now clasped across her chest.

'Dear Lord, be with us here today, present at our prayer circle.' Judith's voice was very strong. 'And keep us safe on this most dangerous and dark of nights.'

Paula glanced round. Every woman there had her eyes closed. Their faces were solemn, concerned. Solid. Paula closed her own eyes.

They prayed for about twenty minutes, Judith extemporising fluently, including prayers specifically for Paula and Alex, Sophie and James. Then she recited prayers from the old prayer book and the new, before she drew them all together with the Lord's prayer. She had scarcely finished when she opened her eyes and scanned the room. 'Right. What are we going to do?'

'Tell the police.' The comment came from a tall, thin wispy woman with thick glasses. 'She should be arrested.'

'They'll never arrest her without proof,' her neighbour put in quietly. 'Is there any proof, Mrs West? Or is it all hearsay?'

Paula felt her cheeks colour again. 'I have to say Lyndsey has always been kind to my children,' she said carefully. Why was she suddenly feeling disloyal? 'I didn't know anything about Lyndsey's reputation until Judith here told me.'

'You knew she was a witch,' Judith put in sharply.

'Yes, but I didn't take it seriously.' Paula frowned. 'I had no idea she was into satanic ritual. None at all.'

There was a small gasp from amongst the women seated round the room. 'I mean, I thought it was a joke. I didn't think there were such things as witches. Not proper ones. The moment I knew about her, I sent my husband to tell her we no longer needed her services.'

'Why send your husband, Mrs West?' The question came from a short plump woman with dark hair, dyed a shade too intense for her colouring.

'Because it was convenient,' Paula retorted. 'I wasn't afraid of her, if that's what you're implying.'

'There would be no shame in it, Paula, if you were,' put in a third woman. Paula recognised her as an assistant at the bank in the High Street. 'We should all be afraid before Satan.'

'Until we call on the Lord to fight him,' Judith put in. 'And that is what Paula has done. That is why she is here.' She sat down at last, the Bible still clutched tightly to her chest. 'I have made the first move in the Lord's name. I told Lyndsey's other employer what she is and he has also sacked her. Now all we need to do is see that she finds our community is not a comfortable place for her and her kind.'

'That's it. Drive her out.' The bank assistant folded her arms smugly and there was a general murmur of approval.

'That doesn't sound very Christian,' Paula said, troubled. 'Shouldn't we try to win back her soul or something?'

Judith nodded slowly. 'Paula is right. We should not hound Lyndsey out without giving her the chance to repent.'

Banking executive snorted. 'Her sort never repent. They are arrogant and ignorant.'

'Lyndsey's not ignorant,' Paula interrupted. 'She got in to Cambridge.'

'You sound as though you are on her side –'

'I'm not taking sides,' Paula snapped. 'If she has done evil she must pay for it, but we must be sure. We are not medieval barbarians!' She wondered suddenly if anyone else had noticed that there were thirteen of them in the room, and hastily pushed the thought away. These women were her new friends. Her allies. They were on her side against evil.

'We will be sure before we do anything, Paula,' Judith said smoothly. 'We will pray.'

'Are there any other witches round here, or is she the only one? Surely they come in covens, don't they?' A new voice spoke from the other side of the room. All the women turned towards a young red-headed girl in a tight green jumper. She looked down, abashed.

'Yes.' Paula had spoken almost without thinking. 'I know of one other witch. She's a friend of Lyndsey's; in fact they are cousins. Emma Dickson. The woman who has moved into Liza's up in Old Mistley,' she explained to those who were looking blank. 'She has two black cats,' she added. 'Or had.' She smiled.

There was a pause as the women processed this news.

'Cats don't necessarily denote witches these days.' The voice of reason came from the seat next to Paula. The stout middle-aged woman with grey hair smiled at her. 'I have three myself.'

'I'm sorry.' Paula shrugged. 'I've fallen into the trap, haven't I, of looking for stereotypes. Although in Emma's case, I think it may be justified.' Did she really believe that? She bit her lip, then she pushed away her doubt. Lyndsey and Emma were often together these days, as far as she could see. Plotting. Who knows, perhaps casting spells. Maybe out of sheer spite Lyndsey was helping Emma to seduce Alex. Maybe at this very moment they were working on a plan to snatch the children. After all, it would take two people to do that. And these women here were acting in the name of God. They would do nothing that wasn't warranted. They would make it all come right.

'You say she "had" two cats?' another voice queried.

Paula nodded. 'They've gone. My husband told me this evening – she asked him to help her search for them. I think we can say that her familiars, if that is what they were, have been removed from the scene.'

'Good.' The banking executive spoke up again. 'I hate cats.' She shuddered. 'Perhaps in that case we should suggest this woman Emma leaves as well?'

One by one the women in the room nodded their agreement.

Paula looked down at her hands. She was trying to hide a smile.

Judith watched quietly. So, Emma Dickson was in the frame, too. Excellent. Mike spent altogether too much time worrying about her. She remembered that Donald James had told her Mike had been seen having coffee with Emma some time ago. At the time she hadn't worried about it. Stupid. She had missed something there. Well, yet again she was going to have to save Mike from his all too human fallibility. She felt strangely elated. By the time he came back she would have sorted it all out. If that didn't convince the church authorities she was the right person to select for clergy training, nothing would. She glanced round the circle again. They were winding themselves up now, the righteous indignation bubbling nicely, their hostility growing. Soon she would have to calm them down, bring them back to heel with a prayer. Tomorrow would be the time to unleash them on Lyndsey and Emma. All Saints Day. Perfect.

86

Alice parked the car carefully by the swan fountain and sat for a moment staring through the windscreen, watching the stream of water cascading from the swan's beak. The whole town was bathed in the warm sweet smell from the Maltings. It was a bit like Horlicks. It was making her feel hungry and she rummaged in the glovebox in a vain attempt to find something to eat. No chocolates, just empty cigarette packets. She closed the flap with a scowl. Soon it would be dark. She shivered. Dusk at Halloween. The best time to interview a witch.

Dragging her heavy shoulderbag with the precious cargo of camcorder and tape recorder, she slid out of the car and locked it. The street was deserted. There was no sign of anyone, even outside the pub where already a pumpkin, hollowed out and carved into a hideous face, glowed in one of the windows. She glanced up at the sign. It showed Matthew Hopkins, almost a cartoon character in his high hat. As she stared at it the sign creaked slightly in the wind.

Taking a deep breath she hurried down the lane which led out onto the quay, then she headed towards Lyndsey's cottage. To her intense disappointment there were no lights on anywhere.

Taking hold of the knocker she let it fall twice, listening as the sound reverberated through the house. Total silence.

'Shit!' She bit her lip. 'Where is she?' This was her chance to do something really good. Something that would make her father sit up and notice her properly.

She frowned. Where would Lyndsey be on Halloween? Of course. How stupid. She wouldn't be at home. She would be out with her coven doing witchy things. With a shiver of excitement, Alice turned and headed back towards the car. There were one or two places she could think of which might fit the bill and one of them was the deserted churchyard.

She parked a good half a mile away, pulling the car up onto the verge and almost into the hedge. It was very quiet up here away from the village. She shivered violently as she zipped up her jacket and slung the canvas bag strap over her shoulder. The wind was tearing her hair back from her face as she walked carefully down the middle of the road. Like an idiot she had forgotten to bring a torch and here in the black canyon between the high rustling hedges it was especially dark.

As she drew near to Liza's she found her steps slowing. There were lights on in the house pouring out through uncurtained windows into the garden. She stopped by the garden gate, then she tiptoed closer, scrambled cautiously up onto the bank to peer carefully through the hedge. At first she could see nothing. She pressed more closely in amongst the scratchy twigs and leaves, pleased that the sound of the wind would hide any noises she was making, and she narrowed her eyes trying to see in at the window. Then, smiling with glee, she began to grope in her bag for the camcorder.

87

Emma faced Lyndsey across the kitchen table. 'I don't think I can do this.'

'You have to. It's the only way.' Lyndsey had been home, taking Emma's car, and returned an hour later with a large canvas bag. In it was her paraphernalia.

'Oh, shit, no!' Emma watched as Lyndsey brought out the knife, wand, bottle of oil, salt, incense. And then black silk robes. Emma touched them nervously. 'Do you always have a spare?'

Lyndsey smiled. 'No, second best. It doesn't matter what one wears. It's just better to be inconspicuous.'

'Inconspicuous!' Emma spluttered. 'What about the pointed hats? The broom sticks? Everyone else will be wearing them tonight!'

'Everyone else will be playing.' Lyndsey's face was grim. She reached across and grabbed Emma's wrists. 'You have to be strong. We have to do this. Now. I'm not waiting for midnight. The tension is growing every second. It must be nipped in the bud.' She paused, surveying Emma's face. 'You can feel it, can't you?'

Emma nodded. Her mouth was dry. She felt light-headed. 'Can we have some coffee before we do anything else? I'm feeling so odd.'

'No, you need to have your wits about you.' Lyndsey dragged her to her feet. 'We start with a cleansing bath, then the robe. Then we'll go across to the churchyard. She gathered up the robes and headed for the door. 'Come on, Emma!'

Emma was still hesitating. 'I'm not sure –'

Diving towards her, Lyndsey grabbed her wrist again. 'Come on! I'm going to get you ready if I have to bath you myself.' Her eyes were glittering with nervous energy as she pulled open the door and dragged Emma out into the hall and towards the stairs. At the top she glanced round. 'Where's the bathroom?'

'There.' Emma nodded towards the door.

'Right. You go first. Strip. Quick bath or shower with these.' She thrust a small sachet of dried herbs into Emma's hand. 'Then the robe. Naked underneath. Brush some of the herbs through your hair or wash it to make sure there is no negativity clinging to you anywhere.' She pointed to Emma's watch. 'No jewellery. Take that off. And the earrings. I wear special ritual jewellery but there's no time to cleanse and consecrate your stuff. Hurry!' Pushing Emma into the bathroom she pulled the door closed behind her.

Emma stood quite still. She was shaking. She dropped the silk robe onto the floor and moving to the window, she drew the curtains against the darkness outside. Almost on autopilot, she stooped and put the plug into the bath, then she turned on the taps. Untying the piece of raffia which held the sachet of herbs closed, she shook them out into the hot water and at once the air filled with a strange bitter-sweet tang. She watched the leaves and stalks swirling about for a moment, then still half in a daze she pulled off her jeans and sweater, bra and pants and, kicking them into the corner, gingerly stepped into the water. Sitting down, she slid along the bath until she was leaning right back, her legs drawn up so that she could duck under the water. Seconds later she had pulled the plug and was climbing out, flakes of leaf clinging to her wet skin as she reached for her towel. Having combed back her hair, she pulled on the black robe. The silk was soft and cold against her skin and for a moment she paused, growing used to the feel of it. She looked at the door, reluctant now to open it; afraid. It was several seconds before she plucked up courage to put her hand on the handle. She found Lyndsey waiting on the landing. Lyndsey surveyed her for a long cool moment, then she nodded. 'Excellent. I'll be two minutes.'

While Lyndsey bathed, Emma wandered into her bedroom. She glanced at the bed, desperately hoping one or other of the cats would be there. There was no sign. The accustomed double cat-shaped depression on the bedspread was missing. She wandered over to the window, glancing through the curtains across the lane. She half expected to see the churchyard full of eerie lights, but there was nothing. It was dark.

'Ready?' The soft voice behind her made her jump. Turning, she surveyed Lyndsey as they stood, face to face. Lyndsey too had wet hair; hers too contained a residue of clinging herbs. Her watch, too, had gone. Around Lyndsey's neck was a silver pentacle on a fine chain and there were silver bangles on her wrists. She gave a tense smile. 'All set?'

Emma nodded. 'What if I can't remember what to do?'

'You will. If you're in doubt about anything, follow me. I'll initiate you first, outside in the garden, then we'll cross the road and bind him down into the grave. It doesn't matter whether he is actually buried there or not. That is the place I have chosen to imprison his soul forever.'

They ran down the stairs. Lyndsey grabbed her boots. 'We can't go barefoot. It would be crazy. Come on. Let's go.' She picked up her woven bag, so like the bag Sarah had treasured as her only memento of Liza. In the larger bag in the kitchen Lyndsey found her torch. Quietly they let themselves out into the dark.

Facing one another on the grass they stood quite still. Emma closed her eyes. She could feel herself shaking all over.

'A woman should really be initiated by a man,' Lyndsey said softly,' but this is an emergency. I don't need to do the whole ceremony. And anyway, you are a witch already by birth and blood. This is just a formality.'

Emma didn't deny it.

Above them a slim, cold, almost new, crescent moon sailed through a sea of silver clouds. Lyndsey dropped the bag on the grass and bent to rummage in it. When she stood up there was a red cord in her hand. Emma caught her breath. 'I found a cord like that in the garden when I first moved in.'

Lyndsey spun round and looked at her. 'Where did you find it?'

'The cat dug it up.' Emma was watching her closely.

Lyndsey laughed. 'I might have known. What did you do with it?'

'I burned it.'

'So you knew what it was?'

'No, I hadn't a clue. I just sensed it was –' She shrugged 'Unpleasant. What was it?'

'A charm. A spell, if you like. To make you go away.' Lyndsey laughed again. 'I couldn't understand why it hadn't worked. But of course, you are a natural witch. You knew what to do, even if you didn't know why. You, and your clever cats.'

Emma watched as Lyndsey laid out the contents of the bag: a small black-handled knife; a box containing three bottles; a carved stick, a small incense burner and a bell. She was breathing through her mouth, concentrating as she put down the box and set the other items on it. Then she lit the incense and four small night-lights in glass pots. 'There,' she murmured. 'Ready.' She turned to Emma. 'Come close to me, here. Kick off your boots first – we're just going to stand on the grass.'

Emma did as she was told, catching her breath as she stepped into the ice-cold dew.

'I'm going to cast the circle.' Lyndsey had the knife in her hand again. 'We always work in a circle.'

Holding the knife high, she seemed to be offering it up towards the heavens, then she dropped her arm, pointing the tip of the blade at the grass about four feet away from them. Slowly she turned, her concentration intense, and before Emma's eyes a strangely flickering light appeared in the darkness, streaming from the knife, depicting a circle on the grass around them.

'Yes.' Lyndsey completed the circle and laid the knife on the box which served as her altar. Oblivious to everything but the circle around them, she picked up each candle in turn and placed them at the four quarters. Then she raised her arms. 'Hail, guardians of the east. Protect us and bless this circle. Hail guardians of the south, hail guardians of the west, hail guardians of the north . . .'

Emma held her breath.

Lyndsey stooped and picked up one of the small flasks. Pulling out the stopper, she passed the bottle three times through the smoke of the incense, then she turned back to Emma. 'Take off your robe.'

Emma took a step back. 'Do I have to?'

'Do it, Emma.' Emma wasn't sure if the voice came from Lyndsey or from the woman inside her head. Slowly she raised her hands to the fastening at the neck of the robe, opened it, pulled it apart and let it slide from her shoulders. Lyndsey tipped the flask onto her fingers.

'I hereby mark thee with the triple sign. With this you are received into the service of the goddess.'

She raised her forefinger towards Emma's face. In the darkness, barely lit by the flickering lights, Emma saw oil glistening on her fingertip. Slowly and carefully Lyndsey drew a small sigil on her forehead. She remoistened her finger and drew a second figure between Emma's breasts, drawing it slowly over the cold, marble-smooth skin, then a third time she repeated the action, this time trailing the oil into her pubic hair. Emma did not move.

'Welcome, sister.' Lyndsey gave a taut smile. She leaned forward and kissed Emma on the lips. 'See, I have a necklace for you. Dedicated and blessed as my gift to you. You must always wear it in the circle and when you are using your gifts and powers.' From the pile of items on her altar, she produced a leather thong. From it hung a small silver pentacle. She placed the thong around Emma's neck. 'There.' She looked suddenly triumphant. 'There is no time to celebrate now. That can come later. I'll close down the circle and we'll go to the churchyard.'

Emma stood still as Lyndsey dissolved the flickering blue light which had surrounded them, packed her things away into the bag and blew out the candles. She turned to Emma at last. 'Aren't you going to put on your robe?'

Emma jumped. 'Of course! I'm freezing.' She stooped and drew it up and over her shoulders, aware of the intense cold and dampness of the silk against her skin. She was still wondering whether the light of the circle had been real or merely her imagination.

'And your boots,' Lyndsey whispered. 'There are brambles where we are going.'

Emma followed her obediently across the garden towards the gate. She felt sick. She should go back now, before it was too late. What she was about to do was mad and probably dangerous. She was already cold – under the thin damp silk her skin shrank from the wind – and she was increasingly afraid.

Ahead of her she saw the beam of Lyndsey's torch on the path. Stop now. Lyndsey wouldn't notice until it was too late. Turn. Run. Go back to the house. Go inside and slam the door and bolt it.

We're waiting for you, Emma!

The voice in her head was right on cue.

It is time, Emma. You are one of us, now.

'Come on.' Lyndsey had stopped. She turned, the torchlight waving wildly for a moment, the beam cutting across the garden, illuminating trees and hedges and wind-torn roses for a fraction of a second before it moved on, taking in Emma's startled eyes,

412

her white face, then it was gone, once more pointing at the ground near her feet.

Somehow they scrambled through the hedge, the brambles tearing at the black silk. Emma heard her robe rip and felt the sudden flow of blood hot on her skin. They climbed the wall, slippery in the dew and sharp under their hands, and then they were in the churchyard. Standing close together, they paused. Lyndsey had switched off the torch. She was breathing hard. Emma could feel the heat radiating off her skin.

'Centre yourself. Get used to the dark,' Lyndsey murmured. 'Can you see anything?'

He's not here!

The voice in Emma's head was clear, slightly sarcastic.

Why are you here? This isn't the place!

'Lyn?' Emma heard her own voice shaking. The wind was rising. 'He's not here. This isn't his grave!'

Lyndsey spun round. 'It's in all the books, and the parish records. I've often wondered if it's really his grave, but it doesn't matter. I've felt him here.' The torch flashed back on. 'Look! There! You can see the rectangle on the grass.'

Emma shook her head. 'Sarah doesn't believe it.' She put her hands to her face. 'She keeps on. She won't let me be. She's in my head. On and on!' She caught her breath with a sob. 'Lyndsey, help me!'

Lyndsey turned off the torch. She dropped the bag on the ground and grabbed Emma by the arms. 'Let her speak!' she commanded. 'Stop fighting her. See what she wants.'

Emma shook her head. 'I can't.'

'You can!' Lyndsey shook her. 'Let go! Step back! Allow her in!'

Emma gave a sob. 'I can't. I don't dare!' She subsided to her knees with a groan. 'Oh, Christ, let me be!'

'Not Christ, Emma! You belong to the goddess now.' Lyndsey knelt beside her. 'Sarah, speak to me! I know you're there. Tell me what to do!' She seized Emma's shoulders, turning her so that they were face to face. 'Sarah? Can you hear me?'

Emma's eyes opened wide. For a moment she didn't move, then she turned and looked at Lyndsey with a frown. 'I can hear you. Why are you shouting at me?' It was Emma's voice, but the tone had changed; the accent had softened into a local burr.

Lyndsey smiled triumphantly. 'Tell me what to do, Sarah. How can I help you?'

Emma frowned. 'We need to get our revenge, don't we.' She smiled. 'On all of them. On Goodwife Phillips. She died in her bed. She shouldn't have done that. She should have died by the pricker she used on so many defenceless old women.' Emma was smiling now. 'I cursed her, but it was too late. She slipped away from me, but now we're strong enough to reach her. You and me and Emma, we can go after her.' Emma laughed softly. 'I curse you, Mary Phillips! I curse your descendants by the blood and those who inherited your mean, sick spirit. I curse you wherever you are. On earth, in hell, or nestling in some poor woman's soul.' There was a short pause. 'That's it. That's where she is, isn't it? She is hiding inside someone's head. Judith!' Another pause. 'That's where she is. She thinks we can't see her there, but we can, can't we, girls! May you die a thousand deaths in agony, by the pricking of the pin, Mary Phillips, just so you know how they felt! And Master Hopkins!' Again Emma laughed, only this time there was no mistaking her for Emma. The face at which Lyndsey was staring had coarsened into hatred and spittle had collected at the corners of her mouth. Emma had gone. 'Now, it's your turn. Your body may lie in the cold earth, but your soul roams, hunting still for women to torment. And you too have found someone to hide you, haven't you?' She laughed again, loudly; coarsely. 'Oh, yes. So easy, wasn't it, to creep into another man's head! But that makes no difference. We can still curse you, can't we. We three, who have met here on hallowed ground on Hallow e'en. We curse you three times over, Matthew Hopkins.' Her voice was rising steadily. 'You will drown in the blood of your own lungs as the women drowned when you swam them, and you will feel the tightening of the noose around your neck and your soul will feel the flames of hell. And the creatures you killed, our familiars, our cats and dogs and small inoffensive pets will follow you and lick your blood and the bear our sisters sent to pursue you will tear the flesh from your bones!'

There was a long pause after she had finished. In the distance there was a rumble of thunder. A wedge of black cloud drifted across the moon and blotted out its sliver of light. Lyndsey glanced away, down the hill towards the river where suddenly it was misty. She was trembling. Impressed and terrified by what she had unleashed in Emma she looked at her, afraid even to speak.

The silence around them stretched on and on, then slowly she could hear the ordinary sounds of the country night coming back. A fox barked somewhere over towards the fields; above the wood an owl called, to be answered in the distance by a long quavering hoot and, at her side suddenly, Emma began to sob. The tension had drained out of her body.

Slowly, Lyndsey reached over and took her hands. They were ice cold.

Sarah had gone.

In the lane by the churchyard wall there was a small click as Alice turned off her camera. Neither woman heard it.

88

Judith woke with a start, her head splitting. She had been dreaming again and the fear was still with her, but she couldn't recall what it was she had been dreaming about. She stretched out and remembered with a shock of guilty excitement that she was sleeping in Mike's bed. She ran her hand over the pillow beside her. She could smell him on the sheets, feel his presence everywhere in the room – far more than in the rest of the house. Pulling the pillow to her, she hugged it against her breasts, burying her face in the crisp white cotton. She would have to change the bed before she left on Monday, before his cleaning lady came. They must never guess, but until then she was alone with her fantasies.

The weekend was going even better than she had hoped. The prayer meeting had ended yesterday with the resolution to meet again on Sunday and if Lyndsey had not left the village by then, they would pay her a visit and make it very clear that if she didn't leave at once, that same night, she would be very, very sorry. She snuggled down further into the bedclothes, reluctant to move. She would go and see Paula West today – was it today yet? She couldn't see the bedside clock without her glasses. She would check out the children, make sure they were safe and uncontaminated, pray over them. There were others she had to see, too. People who had left messages for Mike; people she was perfectly well equipped to deal with herself. It was so stupid; she would make a far better priest than he; better than any man. Why couldn't they see it?

And then there was Emma Dickson; the woman who lived in the witch's house; the woman who had had two black cats. The woman she needed to keep Mike away from, at all costs. She gave a small shiver and hugged the pillow more tightly. How strange that she had never suspected Emma of being a witch, too.

How stupid of her! It was so obvious. She was using her powers to entice Mike; to ensnare the rector, of all people! And he was so weak he hadn't seen through it. Typical man. Seeing the pretty surface. Ignoring women who were true and honest. The trouble was, Judith couldn't be everywhere at once. She couldn't always be watching over him, and she had never really met Emma. Not properly. Well, Paula's revelation had been timely. Emma was now next on her list of people to deal with after Lyndsey. She, too, would be forced out of town.

She frowned and with a groan she turned over. Suddenly her head was aching badly. And she was getting pins and needles in her arms. Perhaps she should have a drink of water. She shifted the pillow, trying to make herself more comfortable. The discomfort was still there. In fact it was spreading. It was in her calves, now; and all the way up her inner thighs. She shifted restlessly, rubbing her hand up and down between her legs. The pain had spread right up inside her; sharp, pricking pains. She winced as she tried to change her position. She was sweating. Her nightdress was growing damp.

Uncomfortably she sat up, throwing aside the pillow, and leaned across, groping for the switch on the bedside light. It was getting hard to breathe and she felt suddenly very faint. Was she having some kind of an asthma attack? An allergic reaction to something? Please God it wasn't to her medication. Her consultant had just reviewed the prescription for her anticoagulant. Made it stronger. She was due to go for a blood test any day now. She couldn't have taken too much, could she? She had only taken one pill, surely?

Her hand missed the switch and knocked the clock to the ground. With it went the glass of water she had brought upstairs with her, and the bottle of pills. She took a deep, gasping breath, aware that her heart was racing uncomfortably, and managed to swing her legs over the side of the bed. Leaning forward she reached for the lamp again and this time she managed it. In the small pool of warm light thrown by the angled shade she stared down at herself in total horror. She was covered in blood.

'Jesus Christ!' The whispered words came out as a gasp, as she reeled forward, crashed into the table and slid to the floor, blood gushing from her nose and mouth and from the open wound on her leg where it had struck the corner of the table by the bed.

As she lost consciousness she remembered for a fraction of a second what she had been dreaming about. She had been hunting witches, stabbing at them with a small, pointed knife, listening to them as they screamed . . .

89

All Hallow's; All Saints

On and off Mike had dozed, exhausted. It had been almost dark when Tony and Ruth and he had arrived at the church and he hadn't a clue where he was. They had walked across a field, watched by the mournful eyes of a dozen cows, and Tony had pushed open a gate in the low flint wall. Inside the small Norman building was all but hidden amongst its quartet of ancient yews and their attendant oaks and rowan trees.

Tony led the way to the door and produced a huge iron key. 'They only hold services a few times a year. No electricity, of course. The village is long gone. I suppose before long they will declare the church redundant.' He sighed. 'This is a special, holy place, Mike. A good place to be on Halloween. A place to pray for you and for your parish.'

They had brought with them candles, rugs for warmth, a thermos of coffee, a Bible and a small Communion set in a worn leather case.

While Tony slipped on his white alb and knotted the girdle around his waist, Mike, a borrowed stole around his neck, lit the two candles on the altar, then he knelt on the step before the wooden cross. Behind him, Tony too was on his knees in a front pew, Ruth a little way behind him, sitting quietly, huddled into her warm coat. Around them the old church settled into the darkness. Mike could smell the dust of ages, the cold damp of the stone, the mustiness of ancient hassocks, mouldy prayer books and above that the sharper note of burning beeswax and, perhaps, so faint it was nothing but a hint in the dark, a four-hundred-year-old memory of gently simmering frankincense, and in his ears the cadences of plainsong echoing faintly amongst the oak hammer-beams.

He stared up at the cross. How strange that in this battle over a Puritan soul he should be hearing echoes of an older faith. Listening intently, he let the peace and comfort of the place settle over him. Then slowly he repeated the words of the collect from Evensong: 'Lighten our darkness, we beseech thee, O Lord; and by thy great mercy defend us from all perils and dangers of this night; for the love of thy only Son, our Saviour, Jesus Christ.'

Hopkins came to him suddenly an hour later. Strong. Certain in his purpose. Angry. And – a little – afraid.

So much evil. So many more names on my list. So little time to find them all.

Mike kept his eyes fixed on the cross. The long candles had burned down enough for their pale ivory smoothness to be marred by a lacy sculpture of drips. He frowned, distracted. Where had those come from? There had been no draught. In the front pew Tony quietly stood up and came to stand behind him. In her own pew Ruth slipped to her knees.

Help me, my friend. Tonight is the night of greatest evil.

Hopkins's voice in his head was growing tense.

She is collecting the members of her coven. They told me there were no covens. I didn't believe them. They were there, hidden. Her imps. Her friends. They are looking for us.

'Our Father, who art in heaven.' Mike raised his voice to try to drown out the other inside his brain. 'Hallowed be thy name –'

She's coming. I feel her near. But her imps: the two cats who feed upon her, they have gone. They have fled.

Hopkins was breathless. A sharp crack of something like laughter exploded in the silence. Mike paused in his prayer. The shadows above him in the high roof flickered. He clenched his fists for a moment, then pressed his hands together, palm to palm, fingertip to fingertip. 'Thy will be done.'

I can feel her. I can see the Devil at her shoulder . . .

'Lord, bless Emma. Hold her in the sure safety of your love. Make her strong this night. Be with her. Don't leave her. Save her, Lord, I beg you.' Mike paused; he was breathing hard. 'Save all your servants from the evil of this night. Encircle my parish with your love. Fight back the heathen dark, fill the land with light.' He waited again. The silence was no longer serene. It was tense. Full of presences. Listening.

Behind him, Tony's voice was steady.

'Lighten our Darkness, O Lord.'

The flames on the candles were flickering wildly.

'Christ be with me, Christ within me –'

Listen to the voice of the whore!

Hopkins was back. Mike couldn't tell if he was inside his brain or at his ear. He could feel hot breath beside him; suddenly the air stank. It was indescribably foul.

You have to kill her, it is the only way. You have to kill her for me, and her companions with her. Together we can do this. Kill the witches!

Mike was sweating profusely. He clenched his fists again, hearing the knuckles crack. 'Tony, help me!'

'Be strong, Mike.' Tony was beside him, his small crucifix in his hand. He raised it high. 'This is the house of God. I command all evil presences to leave this place!' Stiffly he stepped up to the altar. 'Cast him out, Mike. Command him to leave you!'

'Matthew Hopkins, you have allowed yourself to be drawn in by the very Devil you detest! You will not use my body to fight anyone. I will not allow it! Turn to Christ. Throw yourself on His mercy. And in the name of God, Go!' Somehow Mike managed to raised his voice so loud that it echoed round the church.

'Fetch the bread and wine, Mike.' After a few moments' silence Tony's voice came as a whisper.

'Has he gone?' Mike's eyes were fixed on the cross.

'He's gone.' Tony nodded. 'Can't you feel it? You were too strong for him, Mike.'

The candles had spluttered wax across the old woven altar cloth. The flames had steadied, throwing strong double shadows of the cross. All Mike could smell now was wax. He turned, surveying the church. Every corner was dark. Somewhere out there Ruth was praying steadily, but he could see nothing beyond the circle of light where he stood.

The basket packed by Ruth was where they had left it on the ground in front of the choir stalls. He stared at it for several seconds then, shakily, he stepped away from the altar and went to fetch the Communion set. As he picked up the small zipped leather case, his eye was caught by another box tucked into the corner of the basket. Reaching in, he opened it to find a brass thurible, charcoal disks and matches. Beside them was a small screwtop pot. He unscrewed it and sniffed. Incense. Was that where the smell had come from? Not echoes, after all, of times gone by, but traces of more recent struggles in this lonely church. He turned. Tony was standing before the altar, praying steadily.

Mike's hands were still shaking as he placed the charcoal in the base of the burner and lit it, watching the sparks race spitting across the disk. The grains of frankincense melted and bubbled gently as he fitted the lid in place and gently began to swing the censer on its chain, purifying, cleansing, ridding the sanctuary of the smell of evil. As the scented smoke curled into his nostrils he felt himself growing calmer.

Under Tony's eye he unpacked the Communion set, laying out the little cruet and the chalice, then once more he knelt. There, before the altar, he felt stronger than he had felt for a long time.

He did not see the figure behind him. The woman in the long dress, the dark cloak, the woman with madness in her eyes.

And then out of the silence, a second voice was ringing in his head:

So, the man of God, who shelters the rotten soul of Master Hopkins, now it's your turn. His body may lie in the cold earth, but his soul roams, hunting still for women to torment. His soul is here, with you!

The voice was shrill. Insane. Female.

You have found someone to hide you, haven't you, Matthew!

She was laughing.

Oh yes, so easy, wasn't it. To creep into another man's head.

'Tony!' Ruth's scream echoed round the high rafters of the nave.

The old man spun round, the crucifix still clutched in his hand. 'Sweet Jesus, be with us here. Mike!'

Sarah had stepped between them, her hazel eyes wild. *You think to save him?* She was staring at Tony now. *You hide behind the cross of Christ, but it cannot save! Nothing can save you from the servants of Lucifer!*

Tony gasped. For several long seconds he held her gaze, then slowly his knees began to buckle. The crucifix fell from his hand and he collapsed at Mike's feet, clutching his chest.

'Tony!' Ruth's terror-stricken cry of pain was lost as Sarah turned to Mike, her face a cold mask of hate.

I curse you three times over, Matthew Hopkins. You will drown in the blood of your own lungs as the women drowned when you swam them, and you will feel the tightening of the noose and you will feel the flames of Hell!

She thrust her hand against Mike's chest and he staggered back, gasping, paralysed by the force of her fury, unable even to look at Tony. Frantically he ran his finger round the inside of the collar of his shirt, tearing it open. He could feel the sweat running down his back. Feel its arid heat in his eyes. 'Hopkins isn't here!' Somehow he managed to force the words out. 'He has gone! Listen to me! He has gone! Stand away, Sarah Paxman. There is no place for you here, in the house of God! Matthew Hopkins has gone. Christ be with me.'

The smell had returned. It was worse now. It was choking him. He couldn't breathe. She didn't believe him. She still saw Hopkins behind his eyes. She was pointing at him, reinforcing her vicious spell and already he could feel the cough welling up inside him. The cough that belonged to another man in another time. Unable to stop himself, he began to retch, clamping his hands across his mouth. In the candlelight the blood welling out between his fingers was almost black.

He swallowed, terrified, tasting hot, bitter iron filings. 'In the name of Jesus Christ be gone!' His voice echoed up into the vault of the chancel above his head. He wiped his mouth on his sleeve. His heart was thundering in his chest and his breathing was painful; there was a stitching pain under his ribs. The smell of blood filled his nose.

Near him Ruth knelt on the floor, cradling her husband's head. There was nothing Mike could do to help her. Even as he stood there, his lungs filling with blood, the hazel eyes of the beautiful enigmatic wraith fixed on his, he could feel his own world growing dark.

90

It was after midnight. Across the peninsular the mist rolled in out of the cold clammy swelling of the northern seas, its icy fingers curling in between the huts and up the cliffs at Wrabness, drifting between the trees into Stour Wood, crawling along roads, between hedges, across fields. Inside their houses people stirred in their sleep and groaned. In fields and stables horses flattened their ears against their heads, eyes wide with terror; dogs cringed in fear and howled and in the town children cried in the dark.

In Barker's shop all was still. The cameras in the first-floor room made barely a sound, their red lights the only sign that they were switched on.

The first tendrils of ice-cold mist drifted across the room unnoticed by the cameras. They drifted aimlessly for a while, coalesced and grew thicker.

As the first scream rang out in the silence, Joe's sound-activated recorder snapped on. A small light moved across the ceiling and danced in front of the microphone for a moment, then it darted on to hover in front of one of the cameras.

The show had begun.

91

'Come on, Emma. It's over. Let's get you back in the warm.' Lyndsey took Emma's shoulders and turned her gently towards the lane. Tears were pouring down Emma's face and she was shaking violently. For a moment she couldn't move.

'Emma, there's a storm coming. It's going to rain.' Lyndsey took her cold hand and gave it a tug.

A movement in the shadows near them distracted her for a moment. She stared towards it, frowning suspiciously. Then she shrugged. The wind must have disturbed some small creature in the hedge. Turning away, she thought no more about it.

It wasn't until she had Emma wrapped in a towelling bathrobe sitting in a chair drawn up beside the Aga that she tried to speak to her about what had happened. Emma was staring into space. She was still shivering.

Lyndsey knelt in front of her and took her cold hands between her own. 'That was fantastic. Brilliant!' Her eyes were shining with excitement. 'You were amazing!'

Slowly Emma focused her eyes on Lyndsey's face. 'What happened out there?'

'Sarah came through. She cursed the bastard! Wherever he is, whatever happens, however hard he tries to escape, we are going to nail him. He's a dead man!' Releasing Emma's hands, she scrambled to her feet. 'You and I, Sarah's descendants, are going to avenge Liza's death and the death of all those women.'

'What happened to Sarah? Was she hanged too?' Emma huddled into her chair.

Lyndsey shrugged. 'I don't know. Perhaps. Why else is she so full of anger?'

'But she had descendants. Us. In my dream she couldn't have any children.' Her teeth were chattering. 'I don't understand. And if they are both dead, she and Hopkins, why doesn't she deal with him wherever it is they are? Why does she have to come back and do it here?'

'Because they are not in the same place. He is still full of shit!' Lyndsey slammed her fist into the palm of her hand. 'He haunts this place. Not here,' she waved her arm around the kitchen, 'but this whole area. He's using the evil which comes in with the mist. It gives him power. He was frustrated in his ambitions. He didn't do enough damage. He didn't have time to kill all the women he wanted to kill, so he wants to come back and continue his campaign of terror.'

'And Sarah has followed him, by taking residence in my head.' Emma shuddered. It was all becoming clear at last. 'And that's why he's trying to possess Mike, isn't it.'

Lyndsey nodded eagerly. 'That's what I've been warning you about. I knew he was overshadowing him, though I would have thought that the rector would be the last person on earth he would choose! But Mike is a sensitive, I realised that the first time I saw him in the churchyard.'

Emma forced a small smile. 'Who else would he choose but a man of God? Mike has been having the nightmares, too. He must be in torment. He didn't understand what's been happening to him any more than I did.'

Lyndsey laughed. 'Oh, I think you'll find he understands by now.' She frowned. 'It's odd though, because Bill Standing said he was on our side. Bill knows about the evil and the energies, too. Old Norse and Anglo-Saxon magic. Prehistoric practices. Celtic curses. This land is soaked in darkness. That is why this is happening. We have forgotten how to keep it all at bay. And Hopkins has returned, feeding on it, because so many people have called him back. The TV crew. The children in the village. The people who own the pub and want his ghost there to entice in the punters; people who think the whole thing is a joke!'

Emma swallowed. 'But you joined in. You kept on calling him over his grave.'

'To contain him, not to set him free!'

'But that is what you have done. And he has possessed Mike!' She shook her head. 'And now you have made me a witch!'

Lyndsey nodded. 'But a white witch, Emma. Never forget that. You and I are fighting the darkness.'

'And Mike, what does he do?' Emma bit her lip in her anxiety.

'That's up to him. It depends how strong he is.' Lyndsey shrugged carelessly. She grinned suddenly. 'You cursed him fairly effectively.'

'I cursed him?' Emma was appalled.

Lyndsey glanced at her. 'Don't you remember what happened out there? You were – or rather Sarah was – magnificent. I should think Mike Sinclair is feeling pretty ill by now. As would be anyone hosting the spiritual cesspit which was once the Witchfinder. And not just Mike Sinclair, either. You should have heard yourself cursing Mary Phillips and Judith.' She paused. 'Judith, the rector's lick-spittle. She's been trying to destroy me; she deserves everything she gets.' Her eyes narrowed. 'If you were as good as I think, they might even be dead by now!'

'No! No, I don't believe you!' Emma was horrified. She stood up and threw off the rug which Lyndsey had wrapped around her knees. 'I can't take any more of this. Stop it, Lyn! This is all nonsense. Horrible, horrible nonsense. I don't want anything to do with it.'

'Too late. You can't back out now.'

'I can and I will. I want to get out of here. I'm going to go back to London. I'll ring Piers. He'll let me stay with him . . .'

'You can't leave, not now!' Lyndsey stood up, too. Her smile had vanished. 'You have to see this through. You have to!'

'No, Lyn. I can't. I won't. This is sick. Horrible! I want to get away from it all. If I thought for one single second that what you've told me is true – that I could hurt Mike, or Judith –' She stopped, unable even to finish the sentence, and threw herself towards the phone. 'I don't want to be in this house any more. I have to get out of here.' Grabbing the receiver, she punched in Piers's number.

Lyndsey tried to snatch it from her. 'Emma, don't do this!'

'I have to.' Emma turned her back, dodging Lyndsey's flailing hands. 'Leave me alone, Lyn. I don't want to be part of this, I really don't.'

In Piers's flat the phone rang on and on unanswered.

'Piers!' Emma bit back a sob. 'Answer, damn you. Please!'

Lyndsey fell back. She folded her arms. 'He's not there, is he.' She waited in silence as Emma stood, the receiver clamped to her ear.

At last Emma broke the connection. Her back still towards

427

Lyndsey, she redialled. Piers's mobile, this time. The answer service picked up the call. 'Piers, I need you! For God's sake, come. Please. Come soon.' A tear rolled down her cheek. 'Where are you?' Sobbing, she put down the phone. For a moment she stood still, staring down at it.

'You don't need him, Emma.' Lyndsey was leaning against the Aga rail, watching. 'You sounded pathetic! You are an empowered woman. Why should you need a man?'

Emma turned and stared at her. 'Does it occur to you that I might love him?'

Lyndsey shook her head. 'You've grown out of him. You made that decision when you came here. People move on, Emma. There is no point in trying to cling to a relationship that has become hollow. You shouldn't and he probably hasn't. He's probably in bed with another woman at this very moment!'

Emma stared at her. Her shoulders sagged. 'You're probably right.' For a moment she was silent. 'Perhaps I could go and stay with Alex and Paula.' The suggestion was only half-hearted. She did not believe it herself.

'You don't want to stay with anyone!' Lyndsey was growing irritated. 'This is your home. Here. This is where your destiny lies.' She sighed. 'Look, if you're afraid of being here alone, why don't I stay the rest of the night? You should go to bed. You look exhausted. I don't mind sleeping on the sofa. You'll feel stronger after you've had some sleep. Honestly.' She smiled again.

Emma shook her head, defeated. She didn't want Lyndsey there. She was afraid of her, of what Lyndsey had made her do, but there seemed to be no way out. It was easier to give in. Within half an hour both women were upstairs, Lyndsey in the spare room under the thatch, Emma sitting on her bed staring at the dark window panes between the undrawn curtains. She was shivering again.

Of course Lyndsey was right. Piers had gone. He would not be there for her now. She couldn't – shouldn't – call him in the middle of the night. Now that Lyndsey had gone to bed, Emma was thinking straight again. But there was someone she wanted to talk to very badly indeed and that was Mike Sinclair. She had to make sure he was all right. To convince herself that what Lyndsey had said was rubbish. To warn him – convince him – that he was in danger.

And that the danger came from her.

Cautiously, with a glance at the door, she lifted the receiver from the phone by her bed and dialled the rectory. The answer machine had been switched off, but there was no reply. Frowning, she tried his mobile. That at least was on. Sitting on her bed in the darkness she listened to it ring. It was still ringing as she lay back against the pillows, exhausted, the receiver to her ear.

When the call cut off she was already asleep.

92

Sarah woke suddenly and stared up into the darkness at the embroidered tester above her head. Her heart was pounding as she sat up, listening. There it was again. A shout, outside in the grounds of her father's house. Slipping out of bed, she ran to the window and stared out. She could see nothing, but downstairs her father's dogs had begun to bark.

Behind her there was a sudden urgent rapping on the door. 'Mistress Sarah!' It was Agnes. She pushed open the door and came in, a shawl around her thin shoulders, a candle in her hand. 'Quickly! With your father from home we are undefended. John Pepper is downstairs, he said Hopkins is coming up the lane with a whole group of people. They are coming for you!' Her eyes were huge and frightened, the candle throwing black shadows across her face as she stared at Sarah. 'They say you are a witch!'

For a moment, Sarah was so paralysed with terror that she couldn't move.

'Hurry!' Agnes was almost hysterical. 'If you stay here you will be trapped.' She glanced towards the window. 'Here, put on your shoes. And take a thick shawl. Take mine.' She tore it off and wrapped it around her mistress's shoulders. 'There is no time to dress. John is at the back door. He knows somewhere you can hide.'

Bustling and fussing, Agnes ushered her out of the room and down the back staircase into the huge echoing kitchen, empty now, the centre table scrubbed and bare, the dressers and shelves laden with pots and pans neat and ready for the early start, baskets of fruit and vegetables brought in from the storerooms stacked around the walls. The cook and the kitchen maids slept upstairs in the attics, but the sleepy turnspit boy was curled up on the flags by the smouldering fire. He looked up blearily as they passed and then fell back onto his sleeping mat. In another hour they would start baking the bread for the day. When they questioned him later he would remember nothing of who had passed and he was soundly beaten for his lack of memory.

'Here!' Agnes pulled open the door. The night air was cold and fresh after the warm cooking smells of the kitchen.

John Pepper was standing in the darkness with two horses. 'Hurry,' was all he said.

Sarah glanced beyond him across the courtyard to the narrow gateway which led out into the park. 'Where are they?' She was so frightened she could hardly speak.

'They are coming up to the front of the house from the lane.' He bent to take her foot and threw her up into the saddle. 'They know Master Anthony is away with most of his men and they thought they could take us by surprise. He would not dare try to take you in Colchester and he has been planning to catch you these last few weeks, so they say.'

They were in the saddle now and he turned and led the way at a trot across the yard. Behind him Agnes shut the door and bolted it. Within minutes she was in her own bed, the covers pulled up over her head.

John drew his horse to a standstill under the archway and leaned forward, listening. Behind him, Sarah held her breath, steadying her horse with a gentle hand on its neck. They could hear nothing.

'Follow me!' He set the horse at a canter down the hill, and she followed, aware that the white of her nightgown was billowing round her under the heavy grey shawl.

Behind them Hopkins and Stearne, surrounded by a group of some dozen men, had reached the front door of Overly Hall and were beating on it with their staffs. When there was no answer a group, led by Stearne, separated off and ran along the side of the house towards the back. As they came round the corner they spotted the two horses in the distance, the flicker of white from Sarah's gown clearly visible in the moonlight.

'She's gone. She's escaped!' Stearne turned and yelled back at Hopkins. 'This way. We'll cut them off below the hill.'

John Pepper turned in his saddle and looked over his shoulder. 'They've seen us!' He raised his hand and thwacked the horse's flank. 'Faster, mistress, we'll turn up beyond the wood. Don't fear. They won't catch us.'

Sarah leaned forward, crooning in the horse's ear. 'Faster, sweetheart! Faster.' She couldn't breathe. Some of the men behind them were on horses too. They were galloping across the meadow, leaving the crowd on foot far behind, skirting round the shoulder of the hill. Below them the estuary lay, a streak of silver.

'This way!' John leaned over and caught her rein, wrenching the two horses sideways onto the track. 'Here.' Galloping fast, he led the way across a second meadow and into the trees, guiding them into the deep shadows of the wood. There, he pulled his horse back onto its haunches and slid to the ground. Running to her side, he put his hands up to her waist and pulled her off. 'There. Let the horses go. We can't ride in here. They won't find us, if we send the horses home.' Turning Sarah's mare, he pointed its head back towards the house and smacked its rump.

'John, we'd do better on horses. They can't catch us on horses!' Sarah screamed, but it was too late. The two animals were cantering back up the slope into full view. In the distance they heard a shout of triumph. The men had spotted the riderless animals, and had turned at once towards the trees.

'Gone to ground!' She thought she heard the call, echoing round them.

'This way!' John was racing back towards the lane. The high hedges on either side cut out the moonlight and they ran on. Both were gasping for breath. He had her hand now. He was dragging her after him, desperate to find a way through the hedge as the sound of horses behind them grew closer. Sarah slipped, her foot in a puddle, and her shoe flew off. They couldn't stop. He dragged her on, aware of the horse gaining on them, aware of her terror. The horse was nearly upon them, and he heard her

432

scream just as a gap showed for an instant in the high thorn hedge beside them. Pulling her through it, he glanced round and gasped with relief. They were back in the wood. Dodging through the trees, they made their way further and further into the darkness. The warm sweet smell of leaf-mould surrounded them. They could no longer see the moon. Overhead the leaves were a thick canopy against the sky.

'Where are we going? How can you see?' Sarah gasped.

John chuckled. 'A misspent youth poaching your father's game, I fear,' he said quietly. 'Don't speak now, mistress. Just follow as quiet as you can. And if you know any spells to hide us, now is the time to use them.' She thought she caught sight of the whites of his eyes as he flashed her a nervous glance. 'I go in danger of death as much as you, so do as I say.' He had her wrist in his hand now, as he stopped. He seemed to be searching around for something in the dark. Sarah could suddenly hear the sound of shouting again in the distance. The men hunting them had doubled back. They had found the gap in the hedge. The sounds of pursuit were growing closer. 'They are in the wood, John!'

'Shh!' He tugged at her wrist and she stepped after him blindly.

Suddenly he swore. 'We have to cross that clearing in the moonlight. I had forgotten it was so open.' He looked back over his shoulder. 'Hurry, it's all we can do. Once we are over it, there are places to hide a month and none will find us.' Without pausing, he launched himself out into the open, running low and fast, dragging her after him. Behind them there was a shout of triumph, followed by a sharp crack. 'John, they have muskets!' Sarah screamed. She faltered.

His grip was firm and she had no choice but to run with him.

'Run!' He dragged her on.

There was another bang, a spurt of fire from behind him in the dark, and John let out a cry of pain. He dropped her hand, clutching at his shoulder.

'John, you are hit!'

'It is nothing.' His teeth were gritted. 'Come on, we can't stop or all is lost. Only another few yards and we are safe!'

Somehow he made it, forcing himself to run the last few steps, and they were once more in the thick shadow. This time the wood was far denser, the old oaks interspersed with holly and bramble and dark-red dogwoods. He ducked sideways and pulled her with him into the shelter of an old hollow tree. There he collapsed onto the ground. 'I'm done. If they come, you must run alone.'

'They won't find us, John. They have no dogs and they can't see anything in here.' Crouching beside him on the ground, she could smell his blood. Cautiously she reached out in the dark and touched his shoulder. 'You are a brave man, John Pepper. You risked your life to save me.'

'For your father's sake!'

'And for mine! I will remember this, John.' She paused. They could hear the shouting again. The voices were quite close, in the clearing now, but they were growing no closer. The men were casting about, trying to find their trail, searching for the place they had entered the wood. They were coming closer. Beside her she felt John slump lower to the ground. His breathing was coming in short, painful gasps. If their pursuers came any nearer they would hear him.

Nearby an owl hooted. She glanced up. Judging by the sudden attentive silence, the men following them had heard it too. They were trying to read its message. Had it seen the fugitives in the wood? 'Lead them away, sweetheart. Lead them away,' she murmured. In the dark she could not see the suddenly spread wings, the silent flight, the circling, but the men in the clearing saw it swoop low over their heads and with one accord they turned the way the owl had come, plunging into the trees on the far side of the clearing. Within minutes the sound of pursuit had died away into the distance.

'They've gone.' Her voice was barely audible. She reached over and touched his sleeve. There was no answer. 'John?' Gently she nudged him. In the dark she felt him slump forward to the ground at her feet. He was no longer breathing. 'John!' She shook him. 'John, don't die!'

Silence.

She stared round helplessly. Who could she turn to now, what could she do?

Sarie, my dear.

It was Liza's voice. Liza, from her dungeon under Colchester Castle.

You can't do this alone, my Sarie. Avenge me. Avenge us all. And help John Pepper. Call on the Lord Lucifer, Sarie. He will help you.

'Liza?' Sarah had gone cold with fear. Around her the rough, weathered bark of the old oak was a shelter against the breath of icy wind off the estuary.

Gently she touched John's face. It was growing colder every second.

'Lord Lucifer,' she whispered. She paused, sick with fear. 'Help me now and I will serve you for the rest of my life. Save my good servant, John. Save him and make him well again.'

Her hand was on John's cold forehead. He did not stir. She waited, half expectant, half terribly afraid. In the distance the owl hooted again. Nearby a twig cracked sharply. She held her breath. There was someone there. Hardly daring to move, she craned her neck out of their hiding place to look out into the dark. It was lighter now. A glimmer in the sky to the east bled pale shadows into the darkness of the wood. A black-and-white shape moved quickly out of the corner of her vision and again she heard the crack of twigs. It was a badger.

And then they were upon her, materialising out of the mist which had curled in amongst the trees, cold cruel hands pulling her from her hiding place, a pike stabbing at her shoulder, the night loud with shouting and with fear and pain.

93

'He's dead, Mike!'

On her knees, Ruth cradled her husband's head on her lap. She glanced up and for the first time seemed to notice what was happening.

Mike was crouching near the altar, coughing blood, his breath failing as the woman, transparent as glass, stood over him, her eyes blazing hatred.

'Oh, no!' Somehow Ruth managed to stem her tears. 'You bitch! You will not have him as well!' Gently she lifted Tony's head off her knees. She bent down and kissed his forehead, then she climbed to her feet. 'Get rid of Hopkins, Mike. It is Hopkins she is after.' Her voice was gaining strength. 'Push him out! You can do it. Pray now –' She stopped suddenly in mid-sentence. The anguish in her face was transformed. 'Tony is with us.' Her voice was full of awe. 'I can see him. He is holding us in his arms. He is here!' The tears were flowing again. 'He is surrounded by light, Mike. She can't bear the light. She is a creature of the darkness. Push Hopkins away, Mike, and she will go.'

He could hear her only dimly through the roar of blood in his ears. Somehow he looked up, desperately trying to catch his breath, trying to hear what she was saying. Sarah was so close. So strong. She was so beautiful. He struggled to draw another gasping lungful of air and suddenly he too saw Tony. The old man was standing by the altar, his arms outstretched, a glow like sunlight surrounding him. The sight gave Mike a huge surge of hope. He turned back to look at Sarah, wiping the blood and spittle from his chin.

She stepped towards him, her hate a tangible weapon. Before it, Mike could do nothing. Choking, he collapsed onto the altar steps, reaching towards Tony. But he couldn't get close enough. His strength was going. Sarah was still there, between them.

'Why?' he gasped as she bent over him. 'What did Hopkins do to you?'

94

Asleep, Emma dreamed on.

The shouting, the roughness of their hands, the huge frothy gob of spit full in the face terrified her as she felt them grabbing at her wrists, felt the rope snake round them, pulling tight, felt her feet go from under her as they lifted her off the ground.

'Catch the witch! Try the witch! Take her up! Take her to Master Hopkins!'

Someone else bent over John Pepper.

'He's dead!'

The kick to his ribs was vicious. She did not see it. They had wedged a cloth in her mouth to stop her screaming. Another was tied around her eyes. She could not see if Stearne and Hopkins were there or if these men who surrounded her were merely their dogsbodies. Her fear was so intense she could barely breathe. Perhaps she lost consciousness; she was aware of nothing but terror until later, much later, they tore off her blindfold and she found herself sitting in the chair in front of Hopkins's table.

Immaculately dressed, without a speck of mud on him, he was watching her through hooded eyelids. The screaming crowd had gone. Outside the window a thick dark fog swirled up the street.

'So, Sarah. We have you at last.'

Her wrists were still bound. She had lost her shoes and her feet were bare.

He smiled coldly. 'Yours is the last name on my list, I think.'

His notebook was open on the table in front of him, in his hand the quill. He reached towards the inkwell and his hand was shaking.

Sarah moaned. She tried to spit out the gag, but it was tied too tightly. She could barely move.

'Mary?' Hopkins had not looked up. He was still writing in his small meticulous hand. 'Are you ready?'

A figure moved in the corner of the room at the very periphery of Sarah's vision. Mary Phillips stepped forward. She was wearing a clean white apron.

Hopkins still did not look up. 'I fear this young woman is clever. The Devil particularly favours her,' he said, his tone weary, barely interested. 'It will be hard to discover the Devil's tits, Mary. You will probably have to prick every bit of her to find them.'

Sarah groaned. She shrank into the chair, willing herself to disappear as Mary turned and smiled at her.

'Proceed.' Hopkins put down his pen at last. He straightened in his seat and for the first time looked directly into Sarah's eyes. His gaze was triumphant.

Mary Phillips moved to stand in front of Sarah. She put her hand into her pocket and drew out the long pin set in its wooden handle. For several seconds she stood considering, her head to one side, then she reached forward and plunged it into Sarah's thigh through the skirt of her nightgown.

The pain was so intense she nearly fainted, her scream of agony muffled by the gag.

A small patch of blood spread over the white fabric. Mary stared at it, shaking her head. 'We'd better search for it. Seek out the little marks.' She smiled gravely. Then she bent and pulled up the skirt, leaving Sarah as naked as Liza had been. Sarah closed her eyes in terror, aware of Hopkins's eyes on her, greedily taking in every detail of her body, but then she realised he was shaking his head. He had gone pale, sweat breaking out over his forehead. 'Cover her!' His voice was peremptory. He stood up and staggered over to the window, coughing. 'Search her breasts, Mary. That's where you will find them.'

Mary gave him a scornful glance but she grabbed the hem of Sarah's nightgown and yanked it down over her knees. In almost the same movement she reached out and tore the garment to the waist, leaving Sarah's breasts bare.

'Why not test for yourself, Master Hopkins?' she called out. Her voice was insolent.

He shuddered. Turning, he stood staring down at the woman in the chair, his eyes feasting on her white blue-veined breasts, watching her straining against the ropes, unable to move as the vicious spike hovered uncertainly in Mary's hands as she waited, her eyes on Hopkins's face, for his signal. For a moment he hesitated, then he nodded. 'Do it,' he said, his voice muffled in the handkerchief he had clapped to his mouth.

Sarah's shriek of agony was loud even through the gag and he stepped back, somehow shocked by the amount of pain in the sound. He winced and held up his hand as Mary was about to plunge the pin in for a second time.

'Wait.' He took a deep breath. 'To make this stop, Sarah, you have only to confess.' He paused. 'Move the gag, Mary, so we can hear her.'

As they pulled away the rag she found herself retching so much she couldn't speak, and he called for a glass of wine. Carefully, almost solicitously, he held it to her lips, careful not to touch her, shrinking from her breasts where a trail of shockingly scarlet blood ran down into the stained folds of white lawn about her waist.

'So, Sarah, do you confess?'

'Oh yes, I confess!' At last she had found her voice. 'I serve the Lord Lucifer!' She spat the words in his face. 'I am his and always will be now. You have driven me into his arms, Master Hopkins, and I call down all the curses in Hell upon your head, with his blessing. You will die in agony for what you have done to me and if I hang so much the better, for be sure of this: I shall usher your soul into the depths of Hell with my own hands!'

95

Sunday November 1ˢᵗ

Jane Good had pedalled up the lane to the rectory most Sunday mornings since Mike had arrived in Manningtree. Her weekly bike ride brought her past his door and she had taken to dropping in at about nine to have a cup of coffee with him after he got back from celebrating Holy Communion. A shrewd, motherly woman, she had recognised in Mike a man who needed to have someone to talk to, was probably desperately lonely even if he would die rather than admit it, and who found the slightly plump (hence the weekly bike ride) kind, doctor's wife someone in whom he could if needs be confide. In her bicycle basket were a couple of croissants for them to share over their coffee and two back copies of *Country Life*, which she would have to have back from him in due course so she could put them into the waiting room.

Leaning the bike against the wall, she walked up the steps. The front door was unlocked. She pushed it open. 'Mike, are you there?' His car was missing she had noticed, but sometimes he drove it round the back to the kitchen door, and there was another car there, an old Vauxhall, parked under the horse chestnut at the edge of the gravel.

'Mike, it's Jane!'

There was no answer. She walked through to the kitchen and put the paper bag with the croissants and the magazines on the table. There were about a dozen teacups stacked to drain upside down beside the sink. He must have had a meeting of some sort the night before.

'Mike, are you there?'

His study was empty and she stood at the foot of the stairs as she called up. Even if it wasn't a day for an early service he very seldom overslept. Mike was a natural early riser.

'Mike?' she called, more loudly this time. There was something about the silence in the house which was beginning to alarm her.

Cautiously, slightly embarrassed, she started to climb the stairs. She didn't know which was his bedroom, but only one door was closed. The other rooms, behind half-opened doors, were clearly empty.

'Mike?' She tiptoed up to the closed door and knocked. There was no answer. She hesitated, her overwhelming feeling of unease deepening. 'Mike?'

Cautiously she reached for the handle and turned it.

The curtains in Mike's bedroom were still closed, the bedside light on. Judith was lying halfway between the bed and the window. Jane stared at her, for a moment too shocked and appalled to move. The woman's nightdress was soaked with blood. Blood covered her face; she had obviously reached for a box of man-sized tissues, a wad of which was clutched in one hand, the box lying near her face on the carpet.

Jane ran to her and knelt down, reaching gently for the pulse point below the woman's ear. She already knew she was dead from the white face, the cold skin. Sitting back on her heels she took a deep breath, then she glanced round for the phone.

James Good arrived before the police. He found his wife in the cold kitchen, sitting at the empty table. She smiled wanly. 'It's awful, James. She's covered in blood.'

'I can't believe it! Was there any sign of a break in?' He looked up as they heard the crunch of tyres outside.

She shrugged. 'The front door was unlocked.'

'Where's Mike?'

442

'I don't know. I was looking for him.' She followed her husband into the hall as the two police officers pushed open the front door. The doctor greeted them sombrely. 'It looks as though we have a murder on our hands. My wife found her.'

'It's Judith Sadler. She's the lay reader at the church.' Jane had started to shake. 'She's in the rector's bedroom.'

The policemen looked at one another. 'And where is the rector, Mrs Good? Do you know?' one of them asked.

She shrugged. 'He's not here. I haven't seen him.' She stood back and watched as her husband led the way upstairs and the three men disappeared along the landing, then slowly she walked back into the kitchen.

Five minutes later the men returned. She looked up wearily.

'She hasn't been murdered, sweetheart.' James Good dropped a kiss on his wife's head.

'You mean she's alive?' She stared up at him, hardly daring to hope.

He shook his head. 'No, I'm afraid she's dead. There will have to be a post-mortem of course, but I think she took an overdose of the oral anticoagulant she was on. The tablets were beside the bed. She wasn't my patient so we'll have to check with her consultant, but it looks as though she took too many or maybe the prescription was too strong.'

'All that blood?'

He nodded. 'Massive haemorrhaging; epistaxis. And she'd caught her leg on the table. A varicose vein had haemorrhaged as well. There wasn't a part of her that wasn't bleeding, poor woman.'

'Oh, James.' She looked at the police. 'I'm sorry. I saw the blood and I assumed she had been attacked.'

The senior policeman nodded. He was looking pale. 'Easy enough mistake to make, Mrs Good. She looked terrible. I am sorry you had to find her like that.' He drew out his notebook. 'The fact remains, though, that we need to find the rector. The circumstances are rather strange. She was in her nightclothes in his bedroom. Had obviously been in his bed. If he was there when it happened and left her to die, there are questions which need to be answered.'

'You don't mean . . .' She looked from one man to the other. 'You don't think . . . No, that's ridiculous. Mike wasn't having an affair with her. Oh, no, that's impossible!'

'Can you be sure of that, Mrs Good?'

'Well, no.' She subsided into her chair helplessly. 'No, I suppose not.'

'I think I had better have a look round the house and see if we can find any clues as to where he is, don't you?' The senior policeman spoke again. 'Once we have found him, perhaps he will be able to explain what has happened here himself.'

96

As Emma's strength wavered, so for a moment did Sarah's. It was all Ruth needed. All her pain and sorrow coalesced into a moment of strength as she saw her husband's face transfigured by the light. Standing over Mike's slumped body she turned to the shadowy figure before her and raising her hand she made the sign of the cross. Already Sarah was disappearing. In a fraction of a second she had gone.

It was dawn when at last Mike groaned and cautiously began to move. His head was thudding and his mouth tasted vile. Somehow he managed to open his eyes.

'Ruth?'

He could see her sitting huddled on the floor by the altar. Near her Tony was lying on the ground.

For a moment she didn't react to the sound of his voice, then slowly she turned her head. 'Mike?' It was a whisper. Her face was streaked with tears.

He managed to lever himself to his feet. He examined himself, and the floor around him. There was no trace of blood. No physical sign of his fight for life.

He stood for a moment, dazed, then he limped to her side. 'Tony? Have you called an ambulance?'

'No need. He's dead, Mike. A heart attack.' She gave a small, bleak smile.

'Oh, Ruth.' He knelt beside her, looking down at Tony's face. It was serene. He looked as if he were asleep.

'She was too strong for him, Mike. He had a weak heart. We knew that. But I thought he was going to be able to fight it.' Ruth reached out to touch her husband's cold hand. 'I saw him, you know. He helped you. He brought the light of God into the church and it drove them out. I saw Hopkins. I saw him leave. He drifted away like the lost soul he is. He won't return. Or if he does, one day, it won't be to you, my dear friend. You and Tony were too strong for him.'

'And Sarah?'

She shrugged. 'Ah, she is different. She disappeared. I don't know where she's gone. But I am afraid she may be back, Mike.'

Mike glanced round with a shudder. 'Oh, Ruth, I'm so sorry. This is all my fault. If I hadn't called you –'

'It's what Tony would have wanted. He lived to fight evil.' Her face was white and the tears had begun to fall again, but somehow she managed a wan smile. Gently she rested her hand on her husband's hair and stroked it. 'I hoped we would have more time together, but it was not to be. And I've seen him.' She looked up. 'I saw him, Mike.'

The church was growing light.

Mike stood still for a moment, unsure what to do. He shrugged. 'I'd better phone for help.' He went to find his mobile. The screen was blank, the battery flat. With a sigh, he tossed it aside and turned back to her.

'Say a prayer for him.' Ruth reached out for his hand. She had begun to shiver. 'Please.'

He nodded. Kneeling beside Tony's body he began to pray. As the words of blessing and comfort filled the church, the sun sent its first beam of light through the delicate tracery of stone and glass in the tall south window.

97

Paula was doling out cornflakes to Sophie and James when the police car pulled up outside. The excited children were banished into the garden with Alex as Paula was interviewed in the kitchen.

'I understand you attended a meeting at the rectory yesterday evening, Mrs West?'

Paula had gone pale. She nodded. 'Why? Has something happened to Lyndsey?'

'Lyndsey?' The policeman shook his head. 'I don't know anything about a Lyndsey. If you could just answer my question, madam.'

Paula nodded. 'Yes, I was there. There were about twelve of us.' Why not just say thirteen and be done with it?

'May I ask what you were doing?'

She frowned. 'It was a prayer meeting, officer.'

'I see.' He was looking at his notebook. 'In the presence of the rector, Mr Mike Sinclair?'

'No. He's away for a few days. The meeting was arranged by Judith Sadler.'

'I see.' The policeman made a note. 'The rector is away, you say. Do you happen to know where?'

'No, I haven't a clue. You should ask Judith. She would know.'

'I regret to inform you, Mrs West, that Miss Sadler is dead.' He looked up at her, studying her face.

Paula's mouth fell open. 'No. She can't be. She was fine –'

'What time did you leave the rectory, Mrs West?'

'About nine. We all left together, more or less.' She paused. 'What happened? Has there been an accident? Oh, God!' Reaching into the pocket of her trousers she brought out a tissue. She stared down at it as though not knowing what to do with it. 'She wasn't murdered?'

'Why do you ask that?'

'Because you are a policeman,' she snapped. 'And you are inter-rogating me! Why are you here? How did you know I saw her yesterday?'

'There was a list of the ladies who attended the meeting,' he replied calmly. 'They are all being questioned, Mrs West. Cause and time of death have not yet been established for certain, but at present you ladies seem to have been the last people to see her alive.' He stood up, closing the notebook. 'So, I gather you haven't seen the rector for several days?'

'No.' Paula shook her head.

'He is not answering his mobile at the moment. If you do see him, or think of anywhere he might be, will you ring the station?' He was halfway to the door when he paused. 'You assumed some-thing had happened to someone called Lyndsey, Mrs West. Why was that?'

Paula shrugged. 'She was – is – someone we were praying for.' She straightened her shoulders and looked him in the eye. 'She's a witch.'

The policeman's face remained impassive. 'I see, madam. And do you happen to know her other name and her address?'

When he had gone, Paula stood in the hall, lost in thought.

Lyndsey.

Surely not. Things like that didn't happen. Not for real. Did they? Lyndsey wouldn't. Couldn't. Could she? Lyndsey the witch, the servant of the Devil. Judith's enemy. For a moment Paula stayed immobile, deep in thought, then her face hardened. Grab-bing the car keys off the kitchen table, she reached for her jacket and let herself out of the house. When Alex came in from the garden ten minutes later looking for her, there was no sign of her.

98

Emma finally drifted into an uneasy sleep at about five. She had been awakened by her dream and had sat on the edge of her bed, rocking backwards and forwards miserably for an hour, her arms clasped across her breasts before lying down again, hugging the pillow to her as she stared up into the dark. It was nearly ten when a car drew up outside the cottage and the sound of the engine nudged her into wakefulness. Her head ached, her eyes were sore from lack of sleep. Automatically her hand went out to the pillow near her to feel for Min or Max. The pillow was empty.

Sitting up slowly, she pushed her hair back off her face and stared round. The events of the night before were coming back to her. The churchyard.

Lyndsey.

Sarah.

She shivered. Oh God, what had she done?

Staggering to her feet, she limped across to the window and pushed back the curtain. Piers was just opening the gate.

Gasping, she turned away from the window. Searching frantically for her dressing gown and dragging it on, she ran downstairs on bare feet.

She reached the front door as Piers put his hand up to the knocker. 'Oh Piers, thank God!' She threw her arms around his neck.

He kissed her hair lightly. 'Em! How are you? What's wrong? Your call sounded completely panic-stricken.' He pushed her away and stared down at her. 'God, you look awful.'

She rubbed her hands wearily over her face. There was a reserve in him that had never been there before. It chilled her. 'The cats are missing.' She said the first thing that came into her head. 'I haven't seen them for two days, Piers'. Her eyes filled with tears. 'I don't know what to do.'

'You called me here, in tears, to tell me that?' He took a deep breath. 'OK. Of course, that's awful. I take it you've looked everywhere? They haven't got themselves locked in a shed or something?' His arm round her shoulder, he was guiding her towards the kitchen. 'Could they have gone on a spree and got lost? They are still townies at heart, you know.' He gave a wry grin.

She shrugged. Automatically she walked over to the Aga and reached for the kettle. 'I'm sorry I left such a panicky message. I needed to talk to you so much.' The details of the night before were coming back to her now with more and more clarity. 'Where were you?'

He frowned. 'Out. I have a life, Emma.'

'Of course.' She turned her back on him, leaning on the Aga rail, clinging to its warmth. 'You didn't have to come rushing up here.'

'Thanks! Now you tell me. For God's sake, Emma, I left London at eight o'clock this morning and got clocked by God knows how many speed cameras, and you say I didn't have to come.'

'I'm glad you did.' She turned back to him. 'Really glad –' She broke off suddenly in mid-sentence. Lyndsey had appeared in the doorway, her hair rumpled; she was wrapped in Emma's bathrobe. She glanced from Emma to Piers and back, and raised her hands in mock surrender. 'There are things I have to do. I'll come back later, Em, OK?' She smiled, raised a pained eyebrow in Piers's direction and ducked back out of sight. They heard the sound of her footsteps running up the stairs. When she reappeared a few minutes later she was dressed in her jeans and sweater and she was carrying her bag.

'Your resident witch?' Piers's voice was heavy with dislike. 'I recognise her from Paula's description.'

'She stayed over because I was upset.' Emma heard the defensiveness in her own voice and despised herself for it.

'Whatever.' He was dismissive. 'Em, we have to talk. You and I are finished. You know that, don't you? There is no future for us like this. So many miles apart. It can't work. I'm enormously fond of you, always will be.' He wasn't looking at her now. 'And I love the cats, but, that's it. You must look to other people to rely on now. Lyndsey was obviously there for you. The Wests too, no doubt. I can't keep coming up here.' He glanced at her at last.

'I suppose you've found someone else.' She wasn't sure how she felt. Hurt. Lost. But not surprised. Deep down she had known after their last meeting, and parting, that it was over.

He grimaced. 'I might have. It's early days. I don't want to hurt you, Em.' He got up and came to stand beside her. He rested his hand on hers for a moment. 'Look, I'm lying. I could never turn my back on you. You can always count on me. We'll always be friends.' He glanced at her, inviting a response.

She shrugged miserably. 'I hope so.'

'There will be someone else for you, Em. Someone better than me. Someone who loves the country; someone who can grow to love this place.'

She nodded. 'I know.'

'For a start, what about that vicar of yours?' He grinned. 'I rather gathered from Alex West at that dreadful dinner party that he was smitten.'

'Mike?' She stared at him, shocked. 'I don't think so.' The irony in her voice meant nothing to him.

She stared at her feet, her misery intensifying.

'I saw an ambulance and a police car turn up Church Road as I came past,' he went on. 'Has some down and out come to grief on his doorstep?'

Emma froze. She closed her eyes. Inside her head she sensed Sarah's cold amusement and she took a deep, shuddering breath. 'I don't know. Perhaps. I . . . I should ring up. Make sure he's all right.' She could feel herself shaking with fear. But how could she ring? She was an initiated witch. A would-be murderer. A practitioner of the black arts. What was she going to say? Hi, Mike. I tried to kill you last night by black magic. How are you feeling? Why is there an ambulance there? Why the police? Had she succeeded? Oh God! Was he dead?

'Em?' Piers was touching her hand again. 'It won't be him. I'm sure he's OK.' He was frowning. 'Look, why not sit down? You look really rough. I'll make us some coffee before that kettle boils dry and then I'll give you a hand hunting for the cats.' He guided her to a chair and pushed her into it gently. 'You really did have a bad night, didn't you.'

99

On the contrary, I had a good night. A successful night. A triumphant night!

Emma didn't say the words. They weren't hers. But they were drowning out every other thought in her head but one.

Revenge!

He had spared her any more torture. Her confession was too complete, too absolute. Instead he had ordered her to be taken to Colchester Castle and there they had locked her in a cold cell far below the ground.

Liza was not there. She had already been taken to Chelmsford.

Still in her stained, torn nightgown without even a shawl to protect her, Sarah lay on the dirty straw, shivering. She could already feel the rope around her neck. The cold triumph in Hopkins's eyes haunted her, as did the nearness of his body as he had bent over her and almost tenderly given her that last sip of wine.

Her only hope now was the gaoler's boy. Without money she could obtain no food, no candles, not even an old blanket in this stinking, ice-cold hell, but the child was used to running errands for the prisoners and his father turned a blind eye. When the prisoners were without cash, there were no bribes, no possibility of selling them black market goods. If there was a chance that money could be begged, borrowed or stolen from relatives or friends, then it was worth a shot; the boy was sent for.

Normally no one would have spared even a glance for a witch, but this one was different. She was young. Her hands were soft and white, her nails tended – he noticed things like that – and the address she gave him in the town was in a rich quarter. There was a chance she had rich friends.

Sarah Paxman.

The boy repeated her name to himself as he ducked out of the postern gate and disappeared into the darkness of the Colchester Streets. Sarah Paxman. If there was anyone who would stand by her, he would find them and offer to tell them where she was. For a fee.

All around she could hear the screams and groans from other prisoners behind the heavy oak doors. From time to time a hand appeared desperately clutching at the iron grille, illuminated by someone else's candle. Then all would go dark again. She could hear the scurry and squeak of rats along the walls. They found pickings in the filthy straw. As she huddled into the corner, trying to pull the remains of her nightgown around her, they were coming closer all the time.

She didn't know how long she had been there. There was no difference between day and night in the dark, but it was on the second day that the gaoler dragged open the door of her cell and stood there, the lantern swinging from his hand and throwing wild shadows across the walls.

'Come on. Out.' He beckoned her roughly.

Dazed, she stared up at him, afraid.

'Well, do you want to go or not?' His voice was gruff, but the bag of gold in his pocket was soothing his temper unaccountably effectively.

Sarah scrambled to her feet and staggered towards the door. Outside it, in the foul crowded outer prison, was a face she recognised. 'John Pepper?' She stared, unable to believe her eyes. 'I thought you were dead!'

'Miraculously revived by God's good rain,' he replied dryly. 'And as well. If they had thought me alive they would have killed me for sure. But as it was they must have left me lying where I was when they took you, mistress, and I woke to find you gone.' He was staring at her, taking in her bare feet, the torn bloodstained nightgown, which she clutched across her breasts. 'Luckily for you, Mistress Sarah, your father returned home last night. He and your husband's friends here in Colchester raised the money to get you free, and with them John Butcher and some of the folk from Manningtree who have had enough of Master Hopkins and his ways, so it was relatively easy to acquire an order for your release.' An order from the Justice, which had been accompanied by a hefty bribe for the gaoler.

He guided Sarah towards the steep narrow stairs. At the top he glanced at her face, lit by the flames of the flares in the wall near the guard post, and he recoiled. Anger and hatred were stamped on every feature.

She turned to him. 'Hopkins shall pay for this, but first we have to rescue Liza. John, you must ride to Chelmsford. Will you do this for me? Please, for my sake? For my father's sake? Liza served him faithfully in bringing up his children. He would want this. I know it. It is not too late to save her. Then when you have brought her home I will make him pay. I will make him suffer as we have suffered.'

It was the Devil who had saved her. Of that she was in no doubt at all. He had saved her because she had sworn herself to his service.

100

Alice slumped back on the bed in acute disappointment. 'I was so sure I had got something!' The videotapes were blank; the sound recording a rush of indistinguishable noises, a few distant shouts and a faint rumble of thunder.

'Can't be helped, kiddo!' Her father slapped her on the back. 'It was an awfully long shot. Jolly brave of you, though!' He clicked off the video and ejected the tape. 'I am sure we can use some of what you saw, somehow. What do you think, Mark? Could she do some voice-over about it? No names, of course.'

Mark shrugged. 'Maybe.' It was unlikely but he didn't want to disappoint her. 'Now, can we please get on? Let's find out what the shop has to tell us.'

The four of them stood for a moment in the street, staring up at the windows on the first floor as Mark searched his pockets for the keys. He found them at last and stepped forward to the shop doorway. 'Ready?'

Rain streaked down the street, pouring off the roofs and into the gutters. Nearby a drain gurgled like a raging torrent. Pushing open the door, Mark led the way inside. They crowded in behind him and he shut the door.

'OK?' He paused. The others were watching him in silence.

Alice was the first to speak. 'What is that God-awful pong?' She screwed up her face in disgust.

Colin glanced at Mark. 'It smells as though something died in the night. Not good.'

The shop was as it had been when they left it last night. Reasonably tidy.

Mark took a deep breath. He scowled, revolted. 'Smell coming from upstairs, right? Come on. We'd better see what's been going on.' He led the way up, slowing as he turned the corner at the top. One by one they emerged into the room and stood there in stunned silence.

'Was the equipment insured, mate?' Joe was the first to speak. He stepped past Mark and went to pick up the remains of what had once been an expensive betacam. Not only had every piece of recording equipment in the room been smashed, but every box and carton of stock had been emptied and everything that was breakable had been broken. A thin film of soap powder covered the entire room, but the smell was not of soap.

'Turds! It smells of turds!' Alice had her arms pressed against her nose and mouth. 'Oh God! Ugh!'

'Shit!' Mark bent and picked up a microphone baffle. He was not necessarily referring to the smell. Joe touched him on the shoulder and pointed at the wall. The writing was legible. Just:

DAMNED

'Is it blood?' Alice whispered.

Joe shrugged. 'Right colour.' It was a rusty brown.

The door had been double-locked. The windows all seemed to be secure and unbroken. As Mark tentatively tried the window latch he paused, his head cocked to one side. 'Did anyone else hear that?' Above their heads they could all hear now the sound of slow, dragging footsteps.

Alice let out a low moan. 'Dad?'

Joe reached out and put his hand on her arm. 'There's someone in the attic, Mark. Vandals? Thieves?' They were all staring at the ceiling.

'Has anyone got their mobile? Let's get the cops over here.' Colin whispered.

Mark was biting his lip. 'I don't think this is a police matter.' He was trying to keep his voice steady. 'I'll go and look.' Somehow he forced himself to walk towards the small lobby where the cloakroom door was hanging off its hinges. Beside it a narrow staircase, almost ladder-like, led up towards the attic.

'No, Mark!' Alice let out a sob. 'Don't go up there! Let's get out of here. Please.'

'Someone has to look, Alice.' Mark managed to give her a smile. 'Don't worry. I'll be OK.'

'I'm right with you.' Colin was following him. 'Joe, stay with Alice.'

'Anyone got a torch?' Mark stopped at the bottom of the stairs.

Colin turned back. His bag was lying on the floor. Rummaging in it, he pulled out a torch. He tried to switch it on. Nothing. Shaking it, he tried again and swore. 'No luck. Sorry.'

Mark shrugged. As he set his foot on the bottom step, they heard the sound again, a slow dragging noise, as though something or someone was moving slowly across the floor above their heads. Mark felt a moment's absolute terror. For a split second he froze, unable to move a muscle, his fingers clenched white on the rail which ran up the wall alongside the stairs.

'You don't have to go up, Mark,' Colin whispered. 'We can call the police.'

Mark shook his head. Taking a deep breath, he put a foot on the second step. As he shifted his weight onto it the old wood let out an agonised creak. Mark shut his eyes, sweat streaming down his face. He took another step. And another.

Cautiously, holding his breath, he reached the top and surveyed the upper room. A dim suffused light seeped in through a narrow window, high in the angle of the roof. It was enough to see that the attic was empty. Climbing off the ladder and moving a few steps forward into the roof space, he allowed Colin room to step up beside him. Both men looked around.

'Nothing.' Colin shrugged.

'You OK up there?' Joe's voice floated up to them.

'OK.' Mike found his voice. 'There's no one up here.'

'There must be.' Joe sounded puzzled. 'We can still hear it.'

Colin and Mark looked at each other.

'Mark, Col, come down!' Alice's voice was shrill with fear.

Mark turned back to the stairs. 'I think we've made our point,' he murmured at Colin, who nodded. Hastily they both went back.

In the room underneath, Mark looked up. The sound of steps

457

was louder than before. Up and down. Up and down. Over their heads or . . . He paused, looking round.

It was in the room with them.

What would Mike do? He had wanted to pray. To have a service.

'The Lord's prayer!' he said suddenly. 'Say the Lord's prayer!' He stepped into the centre of the room. 'Our Father,' he said loudly, 'Which art in heaven.' He looked at the others. 'Come on. Pray. Surely you know it!'

'Hallowed be thy name . . .' Alice mumbled quickly. They had learned it at school.

'Deliver us from evil!' That was Colin.

The steps had stopped. The room was suddenly silent. All four stared round, holding their breath.

'It's gone.' Mark said at last. They could all feel it. The atmosphere in the room had suddenly changed.

Alice was trembling. 'It can't be that easy!' she said quietly. 'It can't just take a prayer!' She was half incredulous, half cynical.

Mark shook his head. 'No, it's not that easy,' he replied. 'Otherwise there wouldn't ever be a problem.' He was still listening tensely; suspicious. 'Don't ever think it's that easy!'

They all waited, hardly daring to breathe, but the atmosphere in the room was clearing as they stood there. Outside the window a car rattled down the hill, halted at the crossroads, paused and roared off.

Mark walked over to the window. Bending down, he lifted a broken camera onto the sill. Automatically he tried to eject the film cartridge. To his surprise it came out sweetly. He squinted at it. 'Two thirds of this film has been used.'

The others looked at him. 'You mean there might be something on it?'

Mark clicked his tongue against the roof of his mouth. 'Might be. It's worth a look. See if any of the others are the same.'

Two lots of film had been pulled out of their cartridges and left tangled on the floor. The fourth was intact, as were two of the sound tapes. 'All stopped at about the same time.' Joe tucked them into the poacher's pocket in his waxed jacket.

Alice shoved her hands deep into her own pockets. 'I don't like it in here. It feels as though we're being watched.'

'Too right.' Her father scowled. 'Come on, Mark. Let's get out of here. I think the next time we come it should be with the vicar.'

Mark nodded. 'God knows what Stan Barker is going to say. Or Jackie!' He gave a wry chuckle. 'I think you're right. Let's go and see Mike.'

At the foot of the stairs he paused. Then he went over to the counter. There he found a felt-tip and some paper. Scrawling a large NO ENTRY on the sheet of paper he laid it on the bottom step of the staircase. 'No point in her going up and scaring herself silly if she turns up before we've worked out what to do about all this.'

'You think she won't go up?' Colin grinned. 'Put that there and it'll be the first thing she does.'

'And probably the last,' Alice added darkly.

Mark shrugged. 'At least she won't be able to say we didn't warn her. We'll need to come back and film that room as it is. But for now, let's go and see Mike and borrow his VDR.'

As their van swept up the rectory drive they saw Lyndsey standing on the gravel staring up at the house. Coming to a halt beside her, they climbed out. Alice hid behind her father, not sure where to look.

'You've heard, then.' Lyndsey addressed Mark with something like venom. 'I warned you. I warned you the whole thing would get out of hand! You have to take a lot of the blame.'

He frowned, puzzled. 'How on earth do you know?' The bloody grapevine! How could anyone know unless Jackie had gone straight into the shop after they left.

'The whole place knows! Well, it's done now. She's had her revenge!'

'Old Liza, you mean?' Mark shivered. The rain had started again, harder now, and there was ice in it.

Lyndsey didn't appear to notice. 'Not Liza. Sarah!' Lyndsey's eyes were bright. Almost feverish.

'Sarah?' Mark frowned. 'Who is Sarah? Is she the one that trashed our cameras? Were you behind this, Lyndsey? Because if you were, you have done thousands of pounds worth of damage and I will have that money off you – every last penny of it!'

Lyndsey frowned. 'I don't know what you're talking about. Sarah did this!' She gestured towards the house behind her. 'She killed the witchpricker and the man of God!' She smiled. 'You

459

wouldn't listen. I tried for so long to contain it all, but you had to stir it all up. So inevitably it came to a head. Poof! Like that!' She smacked her hands together.

'Killed the man of God?' Mark echoed. His mouth had gone dry. 'What do you mean? Where is Mike?'

'Where's Mike?' She imitated him perfectly. 'I don't know. Seek him in heaven or seek him in hell! He's not here!' She paused and suddenly she turned towards Alice. 'You were there last night, weren't you?'

Alice shrank back. 'I –'

Lyndsey smiled coldly. 'Yes, you were. Enjoyed it, did you? Spying? Did your film come out?' She raised an eyebrow.

'You know it didn't.' From behind the others Alice could manage a degree of defiance. 'You cast a spell on it!'

Lyndsey continued smiling. 'Either that or you were just too useless!'

'Lyndsey.' Mark stepped forward. He grabbed her wrist. 'Where is Mike?'

'Dead.' She glared at him.

'That is not true!'

'Isn't it?' She wrestled her arm free. 'Didn't you see the police car? The ambulance?'

Mark's hands fell to his sides. 'You're serious?'

'I'm serious.' Her eyes held his like gimlets suddenly. 'This is not a game. Not some great film set with a script you can turn back and rewrite. This is your doing!' She shot the accusation at him so sharply he took a step backwards.

'I don't believe you. If you had murdered Mike, they would have arrested you!'

She smiled coldly. 'I didn't murder him. It was Sarah!' She folded her arms. 'And it wasn't your precious Mike she wanted to kill. It was Hopkins.'

'Matthew Hopkins?' Mark shook his head, thoroughly confused.

She laughed. 'Matthew Hopkins. Mary Phillips. Revenge at last.' She narrowed her eyes, then as though tired of the conversation she turned on her heel abruptly and marched towards the gate, where she had left her bicycle leaning against the fence.

They watched in silence as she cycled off without a backward glance.

'Jesus Christ!' Mark murmured under his breath. 'Now what? Do you believe any of that? What exactly was she saying? Has something happened to Mike?'

They all turned to look at the rectory. They didn't have to knock to know that it was empty. The house looked deserted. The curtains upstairs were closed.

'There's one way to find out.' Colin reached into his pocket for his mobile. 'I've got a mate in CID in Chelmsford. I'll see if he knows what the hell is going on.'

101

'They are definitely not here.'

Piers backed out of the lean-to shed behind the old barn and pushed the door shut, giving it an extra shove to make sure the wooden latch had slotted home. Rain was pouring down his jacket and his hair was dripping into his eyes. 'That's the last possibility, Em. We've looked everywhere. Max and Min aren't here.' He glanced at her. 'Em? Are you all right?'

She had her hands to her head, her fingers pressed against her temples. 'We have to find them, Piers. I can't bear it here without them.' She looked up at him, her eyes red-rimmed and shadowed, her forehead creased with pain.

He sighed. 'Let's go back inside. The cats aren't here. There is nowhere else to look.'

'They're dead, Piers. I know they are.' Tears suddenly spilled over onto her cheeks. 'And it's my fault. If I hadn't come here, if I hadn't brought them to Mistley –'

'Wait!' He held up his hands. 'You don't know that. They may have gone off hiking across the fields having the time of their lives. They can smell winter coming, Em. It's the first time they have ever lived in the country, the first time they have ever *seen* the country, and all their instincts have kicked in. They probably thought, OK. Time enough to spend months sitting by the fire, let's go on one last gigantic hunting spree, then we'll go home to Mum and the new Aga and the tin opener.' He put his head on one side, cajoling her.

She gave a feeble attempt at a smile. 'Perhaps you're right.' She led the way back down the wet grass towards the house. 'So what do I do? Give up?'

'You don't give up. You wait.' He sighed. 'What is it, love? Have you got a headache again?' He had seen her this time, her fingers gently pressing her temples as though testing for some indescribable tenderness.

She stopped on the terrace and closing her eyes, she nodded.

'Are you still not sleeping?'

'No,' she whispered.

'Then why not go in and have a lie down.' He hesitated. 'Em, I hate to leave you when you are so down, but –'

'But you're going to!' Suddenly she was furiously angry. 'You don't actually care a hoot, do you, Piers? You come down, you have a cursory look for the cats – in the name of all the gods, why do you plague me like this!' She stopped, shocked. The last few words had come out in a strident country accent, a voice quite unlike her own.

Piers stared at her. 'Oh, I get the message! Go home, townie!'

'No! No, Piers!' She grabbed his arm. 'I didn't mean to say it like that. I didn't mean to say it at all. That's not me speaking.' She had gone white, two specks of violent colour flaring over her cheekbones. 'Please, don't leave me. Come in. Let's talk some more. Have some coffee before you go. Please.'

But already he was pushing her away, trying to prise her fingers from his arm. 'Emma, don't be stupid. Look, I have to be somewhere.' He shrugged. 'I'm on my way to Woodbridge. I'm supposed to be there for lunch.'

She stared at him. 'So, you didn't even come to see me at all!'

'I did come to see you. I wanted to check you're all right.'

'And I'm not all right.'

He hesitated. 'You will be, Em. A good night's sleep and you'll be fine. The cats will come back. I'm sure of it. Look, sweetheart, I'm going to be late.' He was turning away.

'Piers!'

'No, Emma.'

'You can't leave me like this.' She slammed her fists against her face, shaking her head violently. 'It's not me speaking. It's not.'

He stepped away from her. 'I think you need to see someone, Em. You've let all this get to you.' He glanced towards the side of the house where he had spotted a figure moving behind the wet laurel bushes. It was Lyndsey.

She moved towards them slowly.

'Emma? What's wrong?' she called out.

'She's back! She's here, inside my head!' Emma was crying

suddenly. 'You've got to help me. You've got to get rid of her! Please!'

Lyndsey glanced at Piers. 'Did I hear you were off?'

He nodded. 'I hate to leave her like this, but I don't know what to do for the best. I'm expected somewhere –'

'Stay. Please, Piers. Stay.' Emma was suddenly almost hysterical. 'Don't leave me alone with Sarah! She'll make me do things I shall regret. Please, Piers. Please –' Emma stared at him piteously. 'I can feel her, battering at my mind. Oh God, I'm so frightened. I don't know what to do. What's happening to me? Piers, please, help me!'

Lyndsey had reached them. Dropping her bag on the old table on the terrace where it flopped over into the wet, she pushed Piers once in the chest with her right hand. He staggered back, astonished. 'Leave. Now.' She jerked her thumb behind her, towards the gate. 'Emma doesn't need you any more. I can deal with this.'

'I do need him, Lyn.' Emma had subsided onto the damp moss of the old wall bordering the terrace. None of them were taking any notice of the rain. She rocked backwards and forwards slowly, her eyes closed. 'I can't hold her back.'

'Go!' Lyndsey mouthed the word at Piers.

He hesitated, clearly torn.

Lyndsey ignored him. She put her arm round Emma's shoulders and gently coaxed her to her feet. 'Come inside. We need to talk. Come in. To Liza's. Come inside, Sarah.'

'No.' Emma let out a groan. 'Don't do this to me, Lyn. Don't let her come back.'

Piers frowned. 'Look, I don't know what you're playing at –'

'No.' Lyndsey turned on him, her eyes flashing angrily. 'No, you don't. Go.'

He stepped aback 'Em? What do you want me to do?'

Emma screwed up her eyes. She was swaying slightly.

'You want him to go, don't you, Sarah,' Lyndsey murmured.

Emma nodded.

'Tell him then. Tell him to go.'

Emma sighed, almost rocking with exhaustion. 'Go, Piers. Just go. Thanks for coming.' Her words were slurring.

'I'll look after her.' The piercing blue gaze from Lyndsey's eyes almost knocked Piers back on his feet.

'OK.' He threw them each a further worried glance. 'I leave her to you. But you take care of her.'

Lyndsey smiled. 'I will.' She drew Emma towards the kitchen door. 'Now, my dear.' Guiding her through into the kitchen she slammed the door in Piers's face and bolted it, then she helped Emma take off her boots and jacket before leading her through into the living room where she pushed her down onto the sofa. 'You succeeded, Sarah!' Her voice was triumphant. 'You killed them! The witchpricker and the man who employed her!'

'Killed them?' Emma stared at her. Lyndsey seemed to be swimming in a haze. She couldn't focus on her.

'Yes!' Lyndsey's face was triumphant. 'You have such power. This is your destiny. There is so much you can do. So many wrongs you can put right! For a start,' she paused, thinking, then she smiled. 'Oh yes, there are people out there who need to be taught a lesson. To be taught that what we do is real. Paula West is next, I think, don't you?'

Emma's last conscious thought was that Lyndsey had finally gone mad.

Outside, Piers sat for a moment behind the wheel of his car, staring up at the windows of the cottage. He was not at all happy at leaving Emma with that woman. On the other hand Emma had made her choices. If she had said she wanted to come home with him. If she had admitted she hated it here. If she hadn't lost their beloved cats. He frowned, his hands gripping the steering wheel till the knuckles whitened. She had made it clear that her life was heading, for better or for worse, in other directions now. That was that. He should go on to Woodbridge where someone was waiting for him who had made it very clear she was willing to fill Emma's shoes. She was waiting to introduce him to her parents.

He gave a last glance at Liza's, then slowly he let in the clutch and pulled away. He did not look back.

Inside the cottage, Lyndsey was smiling. Sarah had just heard the news her father had hoped to spare her. The story was under way.

102

'I'm so sorry, Sarah.' Anthony Bennett looked down at his daughter gravely. It was only a few days since she had been released but she had lost so much weight in recent weeks, and now her thin face was ravaged with pain and fear as well and he was about to compound her misery. 'They were hanged yesterday at Chelmsford. There was nothing more that could be done to save them.' He glanced at John Pepper, who was standing beside him, his eyes lowered respectfully. 'John was there. He was able to speak to her briefly and pray with her.'

Sarah stared at John Pepper. Her lips had tightened into a thin white line as she struggled to hold back her tears. He did not look at her. She knew her father was lying about John. There would have been no comfort. No prayers. There would have been nothing but terror and confusion as they tied the old lady's wrists and put the noose around her thin neck and pulled the knot tight under her chin. Four of them had died that day, all from the Manningtree area.

'Thank you for telling, me, Papa.' Somehow she managed to keep her face calm; somehow she managed to hide her rage, her misery, her tears, until she had left the room and walked slowly up the staircase towards the nurseries where she had been a child. The nurseries where her children would have played.

She pushed open the door and stood there, seeing the sunbeams slanting in through the small mullioned windows, seeing the carved rocking horse, the wooden cradle, the rag dolls. Seeing Liza, as a young pretty nursemaid as she must have been when she looked after Sarah's own mother; seeing her as a strong clever woman as she was when Sarah was a child. Seeing her as an old gentle nurse, her knotted swollen fingers chopping herbs, blending creams and lotions, tending the sick with gentle kindness. And then she saw the gallows, the four bodies jerking on the end of their ropes, the lifeless stillness as one by one they died in agony. She heard the jeers and torments of the crowds and then the silence as they grew bored and dispersed, leaving only the crows and kites to tend the dead.

'Sweet Liza, tell me what to do.'

She didn't realise she had spoken out loud.

But of course she already knew. She would kill Matthew Hopkins. She would see him swim or sink, his limbs tied, see his body contorted in agony, see him walk until he hallucinated and screamed his own guilt, and then she would see him die in an agony of choking. Slowly she walked out into the middle of the room, feeling the warmth of the sunbeams stroking through the layers of petticoats and skirts which swathed her legs. 'I swear to you, Liza. On the lives of my children yet unborn, I will avenge you.' Slowly she turned round, drinking in the sweet silence of the room. 'I will pursue him until I have revenge. He will not make me afraid. He will not hunt me again. My anger is too great. And my power, from the Lord Lucifer, too strong.'

She smiled wryly to herself. She had sworn on her children yet unborn and she was a widow; a widow who had borne no children.

But already she could see them. See the man who would be her second husband, see the man who with the aid of Liza's spells she would lure to her bed, who would father her children, who would live with her here in this house one day and watch with her their children play in this very room.

But first there was business to attend to. A man must be punished for the evil he had done and she would not rest until his soul was frying in the fires of Hell.

103

Sunday afternoon

'Where have you been?' Alex was in the hall when Paula unlocked the door and came in. She looked exhausted. 'What the
hell is going on?'

'I went to see some of the ladies in the prayer circle.' Paula
pushed past him into the kitchen. 'You know Judith Sadler is
dead, I suppose.'

Alex stared at her. 'No, I didn't know. I don't know anything!
I have been stuck here all day with a sick child.'

'A sick –?' Paula stared at him. 'Oh God, not Jamie again?'
Alex nodded.

'What's wrong with him?' Already she was in the hall, heading
for the stairs.

'I don't know. He's feverish. I put him to bed.'

'Bed?' She turned halfway up the stairs and looked at him 'Has
he eaten anything?'

'No.'

'Oh God, I shouldn't have gone out and left him.' She was
running upstairs now, two at a time.

Jamie's bedroom was dimly lit by a small bedside light. He was lying in bed, half asleep, tossing his head from side to side.

'Sweetheart?' Paula sat down on the bed. 'What is it? What's wrong?'

He didn't answer.

A small figure had appeared in the doorway behind them. Sophie was sucking her thumb. 'It's Lyn,' she said. 'She's cross with you, Mummy. She said she could make Jamie sick, just like that!' She raised her hand in an imitation of the gesture Lyn had made when they had met her in Barker's shop. Her little fingers couldn't make the clicking noise and she tried again.

Paula stared at her in horror. 'It's Lyndsey's revenge,' she muttered. 'She's fighting us. She's going to destroy us. She has just killed Judith and now she's going to hurt me through my children!'

'Now, just a minute!' Alex put his hand on her shoulder. 'That's nonsense, Paula, and you know it. Don't even think such things.'

She was pushing the hair back off Jamie's face with small agitated movements of her hand. The little boy's head was drenched with sweat. 'He's got a high temperature, Alex. You'd better ring the doctor. We've got to cool him down.'

She stood up and headed for the bathroom. 'Go on, call Dr Good.' She was ringing out a facecloth under the cold tap. 'That bitch. I'll see she pays for this. She can't attack my children and get away with it. You wait till I tell the group.' Her voice was shaking with anger.

Sophie began to cry. 'Am I bewitched too, Mummy?' She ran to Paula, clinging to her arm.

Paula looked at Alex. 'You see what you've done?'

'What *I've* done?' Alex frowned. 'Stop frightening them, Paula, for God's sake. Jamie's picked up a bug of some kind, that's all. Nothing more than that.' He headed for the stairs. 'I'll ring Dr Good.'

Paula went back into the bedroom and began to sponge Jamie's face and hands, feeling the heat soaking into the washcloth, soothing the little boy's restlessness. She called Sophie to her. 'Come over here, darling. We have to pray. We have to pray that a great big angel will come down and take Lyn away. She's become a bad person.' Her hands were shaking.

The phone was ringing in their bedroom. She ignored it. She

was praying under her breath as Sophie ran backwards and forwards to the bathroom with fresh, cold facecloths.

When Alex reappeared he was panting slightly from the stairs.
'I've spoken to Dr Good. He says Jamie will be fine. Give him some
Calpol and let him sleep. Bring him into the surgery tomorrow if
you are still worried.'

'He said what?' Paula's eyes narrowed. 'Did you tell him how
ill the poor little boy is?'

'Of course.'

'Did you tell him what is wrong with him?' Paula shook her
head. 'Of course not. You're too bloody diffident, Alex! Go on,
out of my way. You look after him and I'll speak to the doctor.'

Alex and Sophie heard her shrieking down the phone in the
distance. 'My child is bewitched, doctor! Bewitched! You have to
get here now!' She slammed down the phone. Seconds later she
had reappeared. 'He'll come,' she said grimly. 'In the meantime
we are doing the right thing to keep him cool.' She looked up at
Alex. 'The phone rang. Who was it?'

'Piers. He said Emma is in a terrible state. He was up there this
morning and he had to leave her. He's worried.' He didn't mention
that Lyndsey had been there too, apparently.

'Is he.' Paula pursed her lips. 'Tough. We want nothing to do
with Emma. I hope you didn't say you'd go on one of your little
mercy jaunts up there.' She turned and looked at him. 'You did,
didn't you?'

'No, of course I didn't.'

'No. And you're not going to.' Paula was growing rapidly more
agitated. 'That woman is part of it, Alex. She and her cats. They
have bewitched your child, she and Lyndsey. They are evil.
Vicious. They are murderers.' Her voice was rising hysterically.
'They killed Judith, for God's sake!'

'Paula.' Alex put his hand on her shoulder and squeezed it
hard. '*Pas devant les enfants*! Don't say things like that. Just don't.'
He was looking very cross.

She sighed loudly. 'You're a fool, Alex. A complete fool. Can't
you see it? Perhaps they have bewitched you, too. Jesus Christ!
You should hear the others in the group. They want to go out
now and do something about this. They want to get Lyndsey!
Pray! Pray your son lives. Pray your daughter isn't struck down.
Pray you're not!' She grabbed another cold cloth from Sophie

470

who was standing watching her brother with huge frightened eyes. 'You don't realise how powerful she is, Alex. That's the trouble. She has had everyone fooled. Everyone!' She bent to kiss Jamie's forehead.

'Is he better, Mummy?' Sophie's face was wet with tears.

'Yes, darling. I think he's a little better.' Paula reached out and hugged her. 'And the doctor will soon be here. He'll know what to do.'

'If you ask me,' Alex put in, 'this is more Mike Sinclair's department.' He turned at the sound of the doorbell. 'That'll be the doctor. I'll let him in.'

James Good had dropped everything at the surgery to come, leaving two indignant patients waiting. He was far more worried by Paula's hysteria than by the description of Jamie's illness.

'That bitch, Lyndsey Clark, has put a spell on him. She's a witch. A Satanist. Please, doctor, you've got to help us.' Paula dragged him to Jamie's bedside. As he sat down and reached into his case for thermometer and stethoscope she was pulling at his sleeve. 'You know it was Lyndsey who killed Judith Sadler? She bewitched her too. It was a spell.'

James Good looked up at Paula over his glasses. 'Mrs West, I can't believe I'm hearing all this nonsense from you.' His voice was so stern it silenced her for a moment. 'Poor Miss Sadler died from massive haemorrhaging as a result of a reaction to some medication she had been given. I assure you, she was neither murdered nor bewitched. Now, if you would please be quiet, perhaps I can listen to your son's chest!'

Paula watched in silence as the doctor examined Jamie. Only when he put his stethoscope away did she burst out again, her words tumbling over themselves in her anxiety. 'How is he? What is wrong with him? It's is a spell, isn't it?'

'It is not a spell, Mrs West.' He stood up. He glanced at Sophie and beckoned her over, putting a practised hand on her forehead. 'Now, I want you to keep an eye on this young lady for a bit, because this virus is quite infectious, but blessedly short. Jamie will be fine. You've done all the right things. Dozens of kids in the area have caught this – quite a few grown ups too, so you may get it yourselves. Rest. Lots of fluids and Calpol for the fever. OK?'

Paula followed him out of the room. 'It may be a virus, but she made it happen, you know. I saw her do it. She clicked her fingers over Jamie's head and cursed him. Ask Sophie. She saw it, too.'

'Mrs West.' Sighing, James Good turned to face her. 'Please, this is simply not true and you know it.'

'She's in it with Emma Dickson. She's part of the coven.' Paula was not listening.

'Lyndsey is with Emma now.' Alex put in quietly. 'It sounds as if Emma is in a terrible state. Scared. Hysterical even, so her friend Piers said. You couldn't drop by, could you, Doctor? You can see how everyone is wound up.' He glanced at his wife.

'Oh, great!' Paula gave a bitter laugh. 'That's it. Lots of tender loving care for the witches. It would be better if they both caught something and died! Then they'd have a taste of their own medicine!'

'Paula!' Alex was shocked.

James Good looked concerned. 'Emma was hysterical, too?' He was talking to Alex.

'So Piers said. I'd have gone up there myself, but you see how things are here.' His gesture, aimed at his son's bedroom, took in his wife at the same time.

James Good nodded. 'Well, maybe I'll look in on her if I'm up that way later. This weekend I'm the only one on duty and I left a couple of patients at the surgery to come here. I don't normally see people on a Sunday, but this week seems to be exceptional all round.' He didn't sound reproachful. Just tired. He headed towards the door. 'Please try and calm down, Mrs West. Your children are fine. Nobody has been murdered and Lyndsey Clark is a harmless eccentric. This is all a storm in a teacup, I assure you.'

104

As the murky dawn broke across the wet fields and the newly risen sun vanished into the bank of clouds, Mike turned back to the church and made his way past the sleepy cows towards the yew trees still lost in the wet mist. It seemed like hours since he had forced his aching bones to run across the field to Tony's car, climb in and drive up the lane to the nearest cottage to ring for help, but the doctor had come very quickly and arranged for Tony's body to be removed. Then he and Mike had helped Ruth into the doctor's car. By then the shock had kicked in and she was shaking violently, but her sobs were under control again as she turned to Mike by the car door.

'Mike, my dear. I want you to have this.' She groped at the back of her neck and unfastened the chain of her little silver cross. 'I can't believe you don't wear one. Or the alb. She smiled. 'You are a bit of an old Puritan at heart, yourself, aren't you.' She reached up and gave him a kiss on the cheek. 'Stick it on, there's a dear. Wear it for me.' She paused and bit back a sob. 'And for Tony.'

He smiled and bent down so she could reach, fastening the fine chain behind his neck.

'There. Now keep that on, Mike, please. Remember the cross has huge symbolic power. Right across the board. Sometimes we don't have time to pray.'

It was the sign of the cross that had driven Sarah away as she stood over the two fallen men. Her eyes filled with tears again. 'Sometimes there is no time even to say the word Jesus.' She looked very serious for a moment. 'It saved Tony in the past. It saved his soul last night. He is with Our Lord, Mike.'

'I know.' Mike bent and kissed her on the top of the head.

'And be strong, Mike. There is still a fight ahead of you.'

He nodded, very conscious of the lonely mist-shrouded church behind them, tempted to change his mind and go with them. But there were things he had to do in the church before he locked up. And a final prayer to say.

He watched the car pull away and then turned back towards the yew trees.

The candles had long ago burned down and the church smelled only of wood, old mustiness and the faint echo of incense.

Slowly he walked up the aisle and began to gather up their scattered belongings. Ruth's thermos. The small Communion set. Tony's crucifix lying on the ground before the altar. His stole. As Mike folded it up he stared round. There was no sign that a man had died there. No trace of the blood which had poured from his own nose and mouth. His clothes were unsullied. It was as if it had never happened. As if it had all been a dream.

But it was not a dream. Tony had thought they would be safe in a church; had thought they could strengthen their spiritual muscles here in this peaceful place. And instead it had turned into an arena for their battle.

'But an arena where we won!'

Was that Tony's voice in his head? He shrugged. It was true. In a church he was on his own ground, surrounded by the light. But his greatest battle was still before him, he was under no illusion about that. Quietly, he began to pray.

Somehow he had to rid himself permanently of the restless dark soul of Matthew Hopkins, and then he had to deal once and for all with Sarah.

And Emma.

And now he was alone.

105

Mark flicked the windscreen wipers onto fast speed as he turned the car onto the A137 and headed for Colchester. They had loaded the last of the equipment up by four o'clock and Joe and Alice had driven on ahead in the van.

'So, what next?' Colin rested his head against the seat and closed his eyes.

'After filling in the insurance claim?' Mark shrugged. 'At least we got a bit of film.'

The cameras were all consistent. Nothing happened for the first three hours or so, then suddenly at eleven fifty-eight, according to the time marker on the film, things had begun to fly round the room. Within thirty seconds everything had stopped working. There were no ghosts on the surviving film. Most of it had been trashed. What there was showed clearly the first event out of the ordinary – a box of dusters had lifted as far as could be seen, unaided, floated in the air about two feet off the ground, for several seconds, then tipped over and tossed itself against the wall. There was no one to be seen in the room; the action was clear, in the centre of the camera field. Several seconds later they saw first one, then two, then three small round balls of light seemingly dancing in mid-air. Two audio tapes seemed to be intact. When they played them several groans were clearly audible and the some loud crashes. There were other noises that only Alice could hear, the others could make nothing out. They too would be taken back to the AVID editing suite. They would be listening for extremely low-frequency sounds.

It took a long time to remove all the equipment and clear up and restack the room. Their landlady's husband, Ron Prescott, came up trumps with enough paint to remove the paranormal graffiti, once it had been photographed in great detail with a stills camera and shot from every angle with the little hand-held camera which Alice had left in the car. 'They'll never know.' Mark checked the room before they left.

Stan Barker had been adamant when they reported to him what had happened. Move every trace or he would sue. Mark had pleaded and cajoled to no avail. Stan's original enthusiasm for the film had all but gone. If he lost his tenants as a result of Marks's messing around, there would be trouble.

'I'd like to have had that writing tested. Seen if it was blood, and if so, whose.' Colin had been silent for some time as they drove.

Mark gave a grim smile. 'I had the same thought. I scraped off some plaster. It's in a polythene bag in my briefcase.'

Colin glanced across at him. 'Well done.'

'I couldn't be any firmer with him, Col. I didn't want him to pull the rug on the whole project and forbid us to use the film.'

Colin nodded. 'No, you handled him well. It's a pity we've got to be at this meeting tomorrow. I feel there's a lot more to happen down here.'

Mark nodded. He dipped his lights as another car hurtled towards them through the dark, throwing up curtains of water off the road. 'We need the editing suite, though, Col. I want to hear those tapes and see what we've got.' He cursed as his mobile rang.

'Mark? It's Mike Sinclair.' Mike's voice was broadcast round the car from the hands-free phone. He sounded exhausted.

There was a moment's stunned silence. 'Mike?' Mark gripped the steering wheel. 'Are you all right? Where the hell have you been?'

There was a pause the other end of the phone. 'I know. I should have been there to talk to you about the shop. I'm sorry. I had to go away for the weekend. Didn't Judith tell you where I was?'

Mark frowned. 'No, Mike. No one knew where you were.' He paused. 'Where are you now?'

'At the rectory. Someone's been fiddling with my answer phone. Yours is the only message on it. Judith seems to have re-recorded my outgoing message and then turned it off.'

Mark glanced into the mirror and indicated left. He pulled into a gateway at the side of the road and switched off the engine. 'Is there anyone there, Mike?'

'No. It's all shut up. Judith seems to have gone out. Your

476

message sounded so urgent I thought I'd better ring you at once and explain.'

Mark glanced at Colin and raised an eyebrow. 'Mike, you do know what happened to Judith?' he said cautiously.

There was a short pause as Mike registered the tone of his voice. 'No, should I?' His reply was guarded. 'What's been going on?'

Mark was looking at Colin in the dark. Colin shrugged. 'Mike, I'm sure there should be someone there to tell you. Something awful happened. Judith died last night. At first they thought she had been murdered and Lyndsey Clark was claiming to have had something to do with it. We contacted a CID mate of Colin's and it turned out that it was natural causes – or at least a reaction to some drug she was on – so the police lost interest. I gather she had some kind of brain haemorrhage or something. I'm so sorry.'

Mike didn't reply for several seconds. When he spoke his voice was husky with shock. 'I can't quite take this in. Judith is dead? When did this happen?'

'I don't know a whole lot about it. Some time on Saturday night, I think. But listen, Mike, it gets worse. That woman Lyndsey is a complete nutcase. She was telling everyone she had killed Judith and you, too! She said the whole thing was our fault because we had stirred up Hopkins with our interest in the shop. Once your friendly neighbourhood doctor started looking for natural causes for Judith's death, it didn't occur to him to think about black magic, of course. I don't suppose it would have done anyway.' He was speaking very fast. 'It couldn't have been that. Could it? No one knew where you were, Mike. People were wondering if you were dead! We didn't know what to think, and no one had heard from you.'

Mike sighed. 'Judith knew where I had gone. It was her idea that I went away. I assumed she would tell anyone who needed me where I could be reached.' There was a pause. 'This is awful.'

'I know.' Mark was staring through the windscreen into the dark. Beside them a five-barred gate blocked the entrance to a field. Rain was drumming on the windscreen. 'I think Lyndsey has lost it, Mike. She was claiming all sorts of shit. She didn't seem to know who she was. Or who Judith was. And she was ranting on about someone called Sarah.'

'Sarah?' Mike's voice sharpened.

'Yes, Sarah. Lyndsey's bonkers, Mike!'

477

'Where is she now?'

'I've no idea.'

'Did she mention Emma?' Mike's voice was suddenly tight with anxiety. 'No, don't worry, I've got to go, Mark. I'm sorry.'

'Mike?' Mark leaned towards the phone. 'Mike, are you there?'

'He's gone.' Colin whistled. 'The plot thickens, and you didn't even get the chance to tell him about our ghostly visitors.' He paused. 'We're driving in the wrong direction, aren't we.'

Mark nodded. Starting up the engine he engaged first gear and began to turn the car. 'I've got a bad feeling about all this. Mike's on his own down there and no one else knows he's back.'

106

Sarah was staring at John Pepper. 'Matthew Hopkins can't be dead!' she said. 'He can't be!'

John shrugged. He was standing in front of the fireplace in Sarah's Colchester house. 'John Stearne claims he died five days ago of a consumption and is already buried up at Mistley in the churchyard there. Master Stearne came back from Suffolk specially to watch him put in the soil.'

Sarah sat down abruptly. She was white with shock.

'It's good news, mistress.' John eyed her cautiously. 'There's none to hunt you down now.' He gave a wry grin. 'Nor me, for that matter. No one hunts for witches any more. There is more than that to worry about with the war coming closer all the time.'

'But we are not avenged, John. He has escaped me!' She paced up and down the floor a couple of times, the heels of her shoes clicking on the polished boards. 'I don't believe it! He was to have been hunted down and swum. I needed to see him suffer as I

479

suffered. As Liza suffered.' She was growing more and more agitated. 'The people of Manningtree were going to swim him, John. They were going to see him punished! I know it. I was going to go back to my father's house and we were going to find him. I was going to lead them after him.'

She walked over to the window, turned and walked back again. 'He has escaped! It is all pretence. He is not dead! He has fled. He has gone away. We will find him. He can't have gone far.'

'He is dead, mistress.' John was frowning. 'It is time to let him go.'

'I'm not going to let him go!' She turned on him furiously. 'Do you think he has taken ship from Mistley or Harwich? Where would he have gone? To the Low Countries? To the Americas? He has a brother in the Americas. Agnes told me so. Perhaps he has gone there.' Her agitation was growing every second.

John shook his head. 'Let be, mistress. Just be glad you are safe. No one will dare impugn your honour now. No one will suggest that you were involved with Liza. Let be. Please, for your father's sake. Don't worry him more. He has enough to think about with the king a prisoner in Scotland and the country all to pieces. Liza is at rest. Let her lie in peace.'

'She is not at peace, John!' She turned on him angrily. 'How could you think it?'

Once more she paced back and forth across the room. John stepped back. He could feel her wrath and it frightened him. It was coming off her in waves. Suddenly she stopped. She swung to face him. 'I shall find him, John. If not in this world, then the next. I will find him if I have to follow him through hell and back!'

107

Sunday evening

Mike sat staring at his desk for several minutes after he had spoken to Mark, then wearily he rose to his feet. 'God bless you, Judith.' A quick whispered prayer would have to do for now. There were other things he had to deal with and quickly. Picking up his car keys, he headed back for the door. He wished, not for the first time, that Bill had a telephone. But there was no time to fetch him now. Perhaps the old man would sense that he was needed now more than ever.

Lyndsey's house on the quay was in darkness. He stood on the doorstep and knocked loudly, but it was no more than a gesture. He could see – could feel – that she was not there.

Turning his back on the door, he stood still for a moment and watched the dark water, hearing the hiss of rain as the tide inched along the edge of the quay. Then he turned and pulling the collar of his jacket up around his ears, he headed back for the car.

As he drew up outside Liza's, he saw the black outline of a bicycle leaning into the hedge. He climbed out of the car slowly, staring at it, guessing it belonged to Lyndsey. Emma's MG was there too.

He could see some lights on in the cottage behind closed curtains but there was an eerie silence about the place as he opened the gate and walked up the path. The doorbell rang loudly inside the house and he waited, sheltering under the wooden porch as the rain thundered onto the leaves of the trees behind him. He allowed several minutes to pass, strangely reluctant to try again, then he pressed his finger on the bell once more, leaving it there for several seconds. There was still no sound from indoors.

Sighing, he stepped back into the rain and glanced up at the upstairs windows. Emma and Lyndsey were there all right, so why weren't they answering?

His shoes squelching on the soaking grass, he made his way down the side of the house towards the back and stepping onto the terrace, found he could look straight into the kitchen. There was no one there, not even one of her cats. Making his way over the wet moss-covered flagstones, he reached for the doorhandle and turned it. The door opened.

'Emma?' He stepped inside and stood dripping rainwater just inside the kitchen door. There was no answer. He paused for a moment in the middle of the kitchen, listening intently. The house was silent. Frowning, he walked over to the door and pulled it open. The hall was in darkness. Then he heard it – the muffled sound of a voice.

'Emma? Are you there? It's Mike!' He moved towards the door which led into her sitting room and pushed it open.

Emma was sitting on the sofa, and Lyndsey – he presumed it was Lyndsey – was sitting on the floor in front of her, her hands gripping Emma's wrists. The room was in darkness, lit only by a candle standing on the low coffee table.

'Emma?' Mike stepped into the room.

Both women turned to stare at him. Even in the dim candle-light, Mike could see the total blankness on Emma's face. She did not appear to recognise him for a moment, then suddenly she stood up, pushing Lyndsey away from her so hard that Lyndsey fell backwards onto the floor.

'You!' She pointed straight at Mike, her eyes narrowed, her features twisted with fury. 'You killed her. You killed my Liza.

After all I said; after I begged you! After I told you what I would do –'

'Emma!' Stepping towards her, Mike caught her by the shoulders. 'Emma, listen to me!'

'You tortured her and you watched her hang!'

'Emma!' He held her away from him with difficulty and glanced at the other woman. 'What's happened to her?'

Lyndsey smiled. She had picked herself up off the floor and was now seated in the chair opposite them, watching. 'I think you know what's happened!' She leaned back almost casually. 'You are not speaking to Emma.' Lyndsey appeared to be mildly amused. 'You are speaking to Sarah Paxman. Once, a long time ago, she vowed to kill Matthew Hopkins, and now it looks as though, although somehow he seems to have escaped her up to now, finally you are going to give her the chance to do it!'

As Mike transferred his attention to Lyndsey for a fraction of a second, he let his grip on Emma's shoulder slacken and she took the opportunity to wriggle away from him. In seconds she had renewed her attack, her clawed fingers within inches of his eyes. He seized her wrists. 'Emma, listen to me! You are not Sarah Paxman, do you hear me? Sarah is dead!' He pushed her down onto the sofa. 'And I am not Matthew Hopkins! I am not his descendant. I am not the man reborn. He tried to possess me – no –' He pushed her back as she tried to stand up. 'No, listen, Emma. I am not him. He did not succeed. Hopkins is dead. Do you hear me? He's dead! Leave his punishment to God!'

'She can't hear you,' Lyndsey put in calmly.

'What have you done to her?' Mike shouted at her over his shoulder. 'What has happened here? How can I get her back?'

'The past has caught up with you.' Lyndsey folded her arms.

'Oh, for heaven's sake, get real, Lyndsey!' he snapped. 'Have you hypnotised her? Is she drugged? What has happened to her?'

Emma was trying to stand up again and he shoved her back hard with the flat of his hand. 'Emma, listen to me!' He snapped his fingers loudly in front of her nose. Emma did not react.

Lyndsey snorted. 'No, she's not hypnotised. This is not some magic show. You told me to get real. I suggest that is what you should be doing. This is not pretend. This is not a game of trick or treat. This is revenge time. This is when women fight back and you pay for all the blood and the burnings.'

483

'Which shows how much you know about it!' Mike snapped at her. 'Hopkins didn't burn women. That is rubbish!'

'Rubbish?' Lyndsey leaped to her feet. 'You ignorant, stupid man! Don't you know anything? Millions of women were burned. By men!'

Mike was panting now as he struggled to hold Emma at arm's length. 'Judith was right. I'm beginning to realise where are all the trouble is coming from. It's you.'

'Ah. Yes. Judith.' Lyndsey smiled again. 'The witchpricker. I hear she died a thousand deaths and drowned in her own blood. Sarah did that. Sarah, not me. Sarah is a very powerful woman, Mike.' She emphasised his name sarcastically. 'And now it's your turn for her exclusive attention.'

Mike heard a car drive up outside. The reflection of its head-lights were bright for a moment against the curtains, then they died. The engine was cut. Mike breathed a prayer of thanks as he heard the car door bang. When the doorbell rang he shouted as loudly as he could. 'Round the back! Quickly! The kitchen door is open. I need some help here!'

Lyndsey laughed. 'So, your God needs a bit of backup, does he? Sarah, can you hear me?' Her voice sharpened. 'This man needs to die.'

Out of the corner of his eye Mike saw her dive for a bag lying on the rug near the chair where she had been sitting. When she straightened up there was a knife in her hand. The blade caught the candlelight. 'Here, take it, Sarah!' She thrust it at Emma, who with a superhuman wriggle managed to wrench herself away from Mike's grip and reach out to grasp it.

Mike lunged forward and grabbed at her again, knocking her off balance so they fell together against the bookcase. As they wrestled together grimly the doctor's voice cut through the sud-den rattle of falling books. 'Hello? What's going on in here?' The figure in the doorway reached for the lightswitch. Suddenly the room was starkly lit.

Mike blinked. 'James, thank God! Help me. These women are insane!'

He stepped away from Emma who, dazzled, had suddenly stopped fighting him. She stood trembling, the knife still in her hand, staring round the room in bewilderment. 'He's a murderer,' she said slowly. She was frowning. 'Hopkins killed Liza.' Her strength was failing rapidly and suddenly she was crying. The knife fell to the carpet and she threw herself back onto the sofa, snatching up a cushion and burying her face in it. Drawing up her legs, she curled up defensively, her back to them.

Lyndsey glanced at Mike and shrugged. 'She's gone.'

'Who's gone?' James Good stooped and picked up the knife 'Are you OK, Mike?'

'I'm fine.' Mike was out of breath and badly shaken. 'This is your fault!' He turned to Lyndsey. 'Entirely your fault. You have done this.'

Lyndsey was watching silently as James Good sat down on the sofa next to Emma. Gently he reached for her wrist and began to count the pulse.

'I have done nothing,' she said quietly. 'I watch from the sidelines when Sarah comes. I watch and I wait.' She laughed suddenly. 'Emma is a natural. A hereditary witch. Did you know that, Mr Priest? And now she has been initiated. She is one of us. But she barely needed even that. She was ready.'

Mike could feel his anger rising. He wanted to put his hands around Lyndsey's neck and throttle her. 'That is evil nonsense, Lyndsey.'

'No. Not nonsense. Is it, Em? You serve the goddess now, don't you? You tell him.'

Emma shrank back into the sofa. Her pulse beneath the doctor's questioning fingers was faint and much too rapid as she looked up at Mike, and he was horrified to see the terror in her eyes. 'I don't know what's happening to me. Go away, Mike, please. Don't come near me.' She had begun to shake. 'There's something terribly wrong with me. I can't control Sarah. I can't fight her off. I will kill you.' Her words were slurred. She sounded almost drunk.

'Sarah has gone, Emma. Whoever she was.' The doctor put a professionally cool hand on her forehead. 'There is nothing to be afraid of. It was one of your bad dreams. You're OK now.'

'But I killed Judith. I wanted to kill Mike. I had to –'

'And you know that is nonsense.' James Good smiled at her sternly. 'Mike, I think it might be a good thing if you left this to me.'

'But I can't leave her like this.' Mike was watching Emma in anguish.

'She'll be fine when she's had a good night's sleep.' The doctor gave Mike a quick nod. 'We're all a bit stressed and upset, and I think some calm on our own is what we need.'

Mike bit his lip, then he shrugged. 'OK. I'll be at the rectory if you need me.' He glanced at Lyndsey. 'I think you should leave, too.'

Lyndsey nodded. 'Sure. I'm going. Just as soon as Em is settled. Don't worry. She'll be fine.' She smiled at him sweetly.

It was fifteen minutes before the doctor climbed back into his car, satisfied that Emma was calm and that Lyndsey was looking after her. Both women had relaxed once Mike had gone and Lyndsey was warming some milk in a pan in the kitchen as Emma went upstairs to have a bath.

He sat in the car for a while, watching for lights. The one in the sitting room went off. First one then another went on in the two upstairs front bedrooms. Nodding, satisfied that the little bout of hysteria was over, he reached for the ignition key. Then he sat back thoughtfully. He had remembered Paula and her bewitched child. Bewitched by Lyndsey Clark. He frowned. It was all nonsense of course, more hysteria inspired by Judith Sadler's unfortunate death, but still. Was it safe to leave them like this? On the other hand, both women were clearly on their way to bed and Lyndsey had seemed, in the flesh, so sensible.

He had found it hard to understand what all the fuss was about in there. Of course, Lyndsey was an exceptionally attractive young woman. So was Emma. That was probably at the root of Paula's problem. Jealousy. He sighed. He was so, so, tired. It had been an extremely long day. He'd look in on Emma again in the morning and make sure all was well, and then maybe have a word with Mike about the witch mania which seemed to be building in the town.

He had completely forgotten the small ebony-handled knife he had left lying on the coffee table.

Inside the house, Lyndsey was watching from behind the curtains. She saw the doctor climb into his car. She saw him close the door and reach for his seatbelt. But for several minutes nothing happened. The lights did not come on; the engine remained silent. She frowned. He was wondering if he had done the right thing leaving them. She read his mind accurately, but why had he come? What – or who – had called him out? Emma? No, not Emma. Mike, then. The nosy preaching priest who was soft on Emma. Well, she'd fixed that. Now he knew what he was dealing with he wouldn't be back in a hurry.

Outside the headlights suddenly flared and she saw the car back out onto the road. It was still pouring with rain, the deepening puddles splashing up around the wheels as the doctor disappeared back in the direction of his home.

Lyndsey smiled. She turned towards the door.

Emma, wrapped in a bathrobe, was sitting on the edge of the bed. She glanced up wanly as Lyndsey appeared. 'Have you got the milk? I'd better take his tablets.'

'You can have the milk later,' Lyndsey said firmly. 'I've taken it off the hob. And I've put the trancs down the loo. You don't need stuff like that. You have a job to do first, Emma. Once you've done that, you can sleep till kingdom come if you want to.'

'You've flushed my tablets?' Emma was furious. 'You have no right to do that.'

'I have every right.' Lyndsey grabbed her arms. 'Stand up and pull yourself together. Now, where is Sarah?'

'No.' Emma tried to push her away. 'No, Lyndsey. I've had enough. I am not going to do this. It's dangerous and I'm scared! I want you to leave.'

Lyndsey raised her hand and gave Emma a stinging slap on the face. 'Pull yourself together. Stand aside. Let Sarah in!'

'I won't. I won't, Lyndsey. You can't make me. I am not going to hurt Mike.'

'You are going to kill Mike.' Lyndsey hissed the words into her ear. 'Do you hear me? It is the only way. You are going to kill him because Hopkins is inside him. Matthew Hopkins escaped you, Sarah. Do you remember? You waited and waited to have your revenge and he escaped you. Did he flee to America? Or did he die, drowning in his own blood? Or perhaps the people of Manningtree lynched him without you. Did they kill him before you got the chance? Remember how your anger festered, Sarah? Remember how you couldn't be happy, even with your new husband and your children? It was Liza's magic that gave you those children, wasn't it, Sarah. You owed her everything. And you promised her, didn't you Sarah, that you would avenge her one day.'

'But Mike is not Hopkins.' Emma put her hands to her head, clutching at the last shreds of her sanity. 'Mike is not him, Lyn. He's not. And I am not Sarah!' Desperately she turned, and running to the window she flung back the curtains. Scrabbling for the latch, she pushed the window open. 'I am not Sarah!' She cried out. 'I'm not! And I'm not going to let her in.' She was taking huge desperate gulps of cold night air.

Lyndsey smiled coldly. 'I'm sorry, Emma. You have to stop fighting it. You have no choice. Sarah is here.' She paused, raising her hand and pointing. 'Look behind you, Emma. See her waiting? You and she have a job to do. A man is going to die tonight Emma, at your hand, and only then will history be satisfied.'

108

Sunday night

Jane Good had scrubbed the carpet of the rectory bedroom and removed the bedclothes and the rug, but the stains were still unmistakable on the floor in front of the window. Mike stood in the doorway and stared sadly round. She had found fresh bed-clothes and made up the bed, but somehow he doubted if he would sleep in this room again. What on earth had Judith been doing sleeping in his bed anyway? Somehow he preferred not to pursue that thought.

Running downstairs, he went into the study. He had lit the fire there and every light was on. He was still thinking about Emma. He had to rescue her from Lyndsey and soon. At first he had been surprised at how young and innocuous Lyndsey looked, with her gamine hairstyle and her vivid blue eyes. Then he had seen the hatred in those eyes and he had felt himself waver. Somehow she seemed to have won Emma's trust. But James Good would make sure all was well before he left. He would wait till Emma was asleep and Lyndsey was safely on her way.

Wouldn't he?

He walked over to the fire and stood gazing down into it. He could feel Hopkins nearby. In the room. Watchful. So, he hadn't entirely vanquished him during his vigil in the church. He turned and stared round, narrowing his eyes. 'I'm a match for you, my friend. So, don't try it, you hear me?' He reached for Ruth's silver cross which he was wearing under his shirt.

And now suddenly, he knew what he had to do. Somehow he had to give the cross to Emma. Her need was greater by far than his. His prayers were strong. Tony had seen to that. He was

protected. But Emma was vulnerable. A hereditary witch indeed!
He shuddered. Christ watch over her. Christ be with her, Christ
within her . . .

The doorbell made him jump out of his skin.

He let Mark and Colin in and brought them into the study.

'We thought we'd come back and give you some moral support.
And fill you in on what's been happening.' Mark threw himself
down into a chair. 'Col and I are supposed to be in London first
thing tomorrow but this is more important. Things have got right
out of hand, Mike. And I do feel we're a bit responsible. You
warned us. You tried to stop us; that woman Lyndsey came to
the shop twice, trying to stop us as well. She said we were going
to have trouble.'

'And you were both right.' Colin nodded soberly. 'The shop
was trashed, Mike. All our equipment, cameras, film. There was
writing on the wall.' He shuddered. 'In blood.'

'We think,' Mark put in.

'The surviving time-lapse film shows that nothing happened
for a long, long time, then suddenly stuff starts levitating and
flying about the room, then the film goes blank.'

Mike was appalled. He could feel the cold back in the pit of his
stomach. 'No sign of anyone?'

'No sign.'

'So it couldn't have been vandals?'

'The door was locked. The windows weren't broken.'

'What about other people who have the key?'

'A camera was pointing straight at the stairs, Mike! Anyone
coming into that room would have shown up on the film, if only
for a second. There was no one there. No one visible, anyway.'
Mark shuddered.

'I think it's time for your exorcism,' Colin put in quietly. 'Now
that you're back.'

'And I suppose you want to film it?'

'It would be nice. I can get a camera brought down here fast.'

'And we would like your comments, Mike. You have to put
the church's side of it. At the moment the witches are making all
the running.'

Mike heaved a deep sigh. He threw himself down in the chair
facing his desk and put his head in his hands. 'I'd have to consult
the bishop about filming.' He reached for his diary. 'And I'm going

to contact the diocesan deliverance team now.' Their number was pencilled inside the front cover. He dialled, listened, and thumped the receiver down with an unecclesiastical curse. 'Where is everybody tonight! Just when we need them.'

Behind them the fire flickered, licking at the logs. There was a hiss as a drop of rain made its way down the tall chimney. Upstairs a door banged.

Mark and Colin exchanged glances. 'So, what do we do?' Mark asked nervously. 'Presumably they – whoever they are – can't reach us here?'

Mike glanced up at the ceiling. 'They killed Judith here.'

Mark frowned. 'You mean you don't think it was natural causes. Or at least a reaction to her medication? Warfarin, the chaps in the pub thought.' He did not pass on their ribald comments about rats.

'Judith was identified in someone's mind with the woman who was the witch-pricker for Hopkins,' Mike said slowly. He cleared his throat. 'She died of a thousand pricks. She bled to death, murdered by a witch who sought revenge.'

'Shit.' Mark gave a violent shiver. 'You really believe that?'

Mike nodded. 'I think I do.' He coughed.

Again the fire hissed. The flame died for a moment, then flared an angry acidic yellow.

Clearing his throat, Mike reached for the phone again. 'I'll try another number. There's something building up again. I can feel her in my head, searching for him.' He frowned. He was breathing heavily, the sweat standing out on his forehead. Reaching into his pocket he found a handkerchief and dabbed at his face distractedly as the phone rang on unanswered. 'Isn't there a single clergyman at home anywhere this evening?' he asked desperately. He closed his eyes for a moment. *Christ be with me, Christ within me.*

She was there, so close inside his head. He could feel the hatred. Slamming down the receiver, he fought back the paroxysm of coughing he could feel building in his chest.

'Pray with me. We have to hold her off. She's looking for Hopkins.' He could taste the iron in his throat now, feel the blood welling from somewhere inside his lungs. 'Jesus Christ be with us here.' He clamped the handkerchief against his mouth.

Mark took a step towards him. 'Oh, God! Mike! Shall I ring for an ambulance? What do you want us to do?'

491

'An ambulance can't do anything.' Mike coughed again. 'Let's get out of here, to the church. I feel safer there. Why can't I hold her at bay?' He staggered to his feet. 'The key. Where is the key?' He dragged open the top drawer of his desk, scrabbling wildly amongst pencils and paperclips till he found the large iron key. 'In the church I can contain her. She can't get to my lungs. I drove her away in church before. I can do it again. The bitch. She's trying to kill me!'

He grabbed his already wet jacket and forced his arms into the sleeves. Mark and Colin looked at one another, each seeing the fear in the other's eyes before they followed him out of the door into the dark.

The three men ran across the gravel towards the gate and out into the lane, heading for the church which lay in darkness. Mike fumbled for the iron latch on the gate, pushed it open and they ran up the path between the dark yew trees, splashing through the mud. The light was on in the porch, where a forty-watt bulb barely lit the notice which had been Sellotaped to the door:

> *Owing to unavoidable circumstances*
> *there will be no Evensong today.*
> *Sorry for any inconvenience.*

'Oh, God.' Mike looked at the notice. 'Judith was going to take the service. I wonder who put the notice up.' He was scrabbling with the key with shaking hands, trying to fit it into the lock. A trickle of blood ran down his chin.

'Here, let me.' Mark took the key from him and inserted it, pushing the heavy door open. They hurried in and Mark slammed it behind them. 'How do I lock it? There's no keyhole this side.' His voice slid up in a panic.

'Wedge it with something. Wait, I'll get the lights.' Mike was groping his way into the darkness.

Mark reached out and caught Colin's sleeve. They stood without moving.

They heard Mike bang into something and swear under his breath, then suddenly the lights came on in the chancel. Mike had found a dishcloth amongst the flower arranging materials behind a curtain to the side of the main aisle. Mopping his face, he moved up to the altar, fighting back another paroxysm of coughing which racked his body.

'Help me pray.' He half turned to the others. 'Do you know the Lord's prayer?'

Mark and Colin nodded.

'Our Father . . .' Mike knelt in front of the altar, using one hand to prop himself upright. Mark went and stood behind him and after a moment's hesitation Colin did the same. They recited the prayer together.

'She is using some kind of psychic projection. Attacking me by making me imagine I'm someone I'm not.' Mike could barely speak. 'Either that or she really thinks I am possessed by Hopkins. It's him she's attacking. He died of TB.' He coughed painfully.

'Jesus!' Colin said fervently. 'What can we do?'

'Keep praying.' Mike was really struggling to talk now. 'Pray with me. We can defeat this. We can send her packing.' He reached under his shirt for the little cross and held it tightly.

> 'I bind unto myself the Name
> The strong name of the Trinity;
> By invocation of the same,
> The three in One the One in three.'

He paused, collecting himself.

'Sarah Paxman. I charge you in the name of Christ begone. You cannot touch me in the house of God. This is a place of holy sanctuary. You cannot harm any of us three here. My chest is whole and healed in the name of Jesus Christ; and may the soul of Matthew Hopkins be forgiven whatever sins he committed in his lifetime, so that he may rest in peace. I hereby commit him to the mercy and the keeping of Our Lord.' He paused. The church was very silent. His chest was clearing and he felt stronger suddenly. 'Thank you,' he whispered. He took a deep breath. 'And now we pray for the safety and peace of thy daughter, Emma. Remove the spirit of Sarah Paxman from her. Make her strong. Save her from the powers of evil. Take the soul of Sarah –'

'*No!*'

A scream rang out though the church, echoing under the high beams of the chancel.

The three men reeled back, looking round. Mike recovered first. 'Christ be with us, Christ within us. In the name of Christ, Sarah Paxman, begone. I command you, leave this place –'

'No.' The voice was deeper now. Still recognisably female, and somehow all around them in the silence. 'Emma is mine!'

'Lord, grant rest to the soul of your servant, Sarah. Take her and give her peace. Save Emma from her. Hold her in the light.' Mike's voice was gaining strength.

There was a quiet laugh. 'Emma is mine!' The words resonated round the church. 'By her own choice.'

'Emma belongs to God!' Mike stood up. He raised his hands. 'In the name of Our Lord, Jesus Christ, leave her alone!'

109

'I can't reach him. He is fighting me.'

Emma subsided to the floor, exhausted. The voice was still not her own. She ran her fingers over her face wearily and looked up. Then she frowned. 'Lyn?' She stared round, confused.

'It's OK, Emma.' Lyndsey took her hand and dragged her to her feet again. 'We have to go outside. To the churchyard. We can focus the power there better, over the grave. Use all that dark energy from the mist. You can finish him there.'

Emma stared at her, disorientated. 'I don't want to go out. This is not right, Lyn. What have you made me do?' She shook her head.

Lyndsey smiled. 'I did nothing. It was Sarah. She has grown wonderfully strong. She is using both of us. The two women of her blood.' She laughed in delight. 'Come on, you have to get dressed.' She pulled Emma to her feet and reached for her jeans and sweater, scolding and bullying until she was ready. Then she pushed her towards the door.

Emma was too tired, too dazed to argue. Somehow she found herself following Lyndsey down into the hall. Her arms were being forced into her jacket and her feet into her boots. 'Hurry!' Lyndsey's face was animated, her eyes glittering with suppressed excitement. She reached for her bag which had been lying on the side-table. The little ebony-handled knife was still there on the coffee table, where the doctor had dropped it. Picking it up, she carefully tucked it in with the rest of her things. 'I have my tools here. We will perform a ritual over the grave. It will reach him. The final push. We are so nearly there, Em!'

'Where's Mike now?' Emma was staring round. Her eyes were unfocused. She felt drunk. 'He came back. He was here.'

'No, my dear. You went to see him. Here.' Lyndsey tapped her own forehead. 'He's inside your head. But it wasn't him, it was Hopkins, and it wasn't you, was it. You were Sarah.'

'Christ –' Emma was groping for the words. 'Christ be with me –' She broke off with a small cry as Lyndsey turned round and hit her, hard, across the mouth.

'Shut up!' She was furious. 'Don't say another word. You belong to the goddess now. Come on!' She grabbed Emma by the wrist and pulled open the door.

Rain was still pouring down, slanting icily from the north. Lyndsey cursed silently. She had forgotten to bring the torch. Never mind. She had visited the churchyard so often now that she could have found her way over the wall blindfold. Somehow she dragged Emma with her, aware that every second they wasted Emma, the real Emma, was growing stronger and less confused.

'Go on.' She half pushed her, half dragged her over the wall and once they were safely over, caught her hand again, heading between the sodden thistles and brambles. She was breathing hard.

'No. I'm tired.' Emma was reeling. 'Lyn, this is all crazy. What are we doing here? For God's sake. I'm hallucinating.'

Lyndsey gave a grim smile. She was pulling her ritual tools out of the bag. 'Stand here while I cast the circle.' She manhandled Emma into the partial shelter of a tree. 'That's it. Now, don't move.'

'I can feel Sarah!' Emma was shaking her head. 'I wish she'd leave me alone.'

Lyndsey smiled again. 'She will. One more time. That's all it will take. She needs you, Emma. One more time and we will be rid of Hopkins forever. The town will be safe. The whole area will breathe more easily. His ghost and his evil memory will have gone for good. Only you can make it happen. You want to do that, don't you?' She stared hard into Emma's face. In the dark they could barely see one another, but Emma could feel the power of the other woman's personality reaching out towards her.

'I am not going to do it, Lyn.' Her voice was stronger now. 'You can't force me.' She looked up at the sky. To the east the heavy cloud was a strange livid red, reflecting the lights of Felixstowe and Harwich. Beyond it was the dark.

'I won't need to force you, Emma.' Lyndsey turned away. 'She just needs to borrow your body. She is already part of you, Emma. Only this once. That's all it will take.' Quickly she was arranging the small glass candle-holders on the ground. In the lee of her jacket, with her back to the wind, she managed to strike a match but it was no use. She couldn't light the candles. In a second she had given up. What did it matter? She glanced at Emma quickly and swore, the words lost in the wind. Emma was moving off towards the wall, back to the road, stumbling in the darkness. 'No!' Lyndsey grabbed her athame, the black-handled knife, out of the bag. Cast the circle, that's all that was needed. Raise the cone of magic power. The strong, incredible magic power. Then bring Emma back and force her into the centre where she would be trapped. Then, at last, Sarah would fully be able to enter her soul and finish the job she had returned to earth to perform.

110

Bill woke up suddenly and lay quite still, listening to the wind. The rain was lashing at the window of his cottage but that wasn't what had awakened him. He sat up slowly, every sense attuned. There was trouble out there in the night.

Slowly, groaning with the effort, he climbed out of bed and painfully he began to dress. Dragging on his coat and finally his muffler he made his way to the front door and pulled it open. A blast of cold wind rocked him back on his feet, but he gritted his teeth and forced his way out, closing the door firmly behind him.

Best go to the church. He wasn't sure why. He'd never set foot in it before – no need. Not his place. Not his religion – even though he loved the churchyard – but tonight he knew he would make an exception.

He only hoped the rector was there.

111

Alex crept up the stairs and peered round the door of Jamie's bedroom. He was asleep, thumb in mouth. Paula was sprawled in a chair beside him; her head had fallen back and her mouth was slightly open. He watched her for a moment with a mixture of affection and irritation, then he turned towards Sophie's room. The little girl was fast asleep as well, a teddy firmly cradled in her arms. He smiled and tiptoed out, closing the door behind him.

Even in the pouring rain it would take only ten minutes to reach Emma's house. Late though it was, he couldn't rest until he had checked that she was all right.

Grabbing his car keys off the kitchen counter he let himself out into the rain, and with a last quick glance up at his son's bedroom where the pale glow of the night-light barely lit up the small red and blue fire engines on his curtains, he climbed into the Volvo and backed out of the drive.

Turning the car in next to Emma's, the headlights swept across Lyndsey's bicycle which was still lying against the hedge. Alex frowned. He squinted up at the house. Lights were on upstairs and down; to his surprise the front door was standing ajar, a thin wedge of light pouring out onto the path. Clutching his collar up around his chin he pushed the door open, knocking as he did so. 'Emma?'

There was no one downstairs.

He stood at the foot of the narrow staircase, looking up. 'Emma? Are you up there?' It was strange how one could tell when a house was empty just by the feel of the place without having to check each room. But he ran upstairs in case, glancing into each bedroom, noticing that the bathroom beyond its open door was in darkness.

So, where were they? Running down the stairs again he went back into the kitchen and pulled open the back door. The terrace

499

was deserted, silent but for the slapping of the rain onto the old flags. He shut the door and walked back to the front of the house, puzzled. Emma would never have gone out this late, leaving the front door open. Unless, he frowned thoughtfully, Lyndsey was here somewhere too. Pulling the front door fully open, he stood looking down the path towards the road. The churchyard. Would they be there?

'Christ, I hope not,' he murmured fervently as he pulled up his collar again with a shiver. Stepping out onto the path, he made his way towards the gate and headed across the lane.

Squinting into the wind, he wondered if he could make out a movement in the dark. He wasn't sure. For a moment he hesitated, then he heard a shout – almost a scream – from beneath the trees ahead of him.

'Shit!' He began to scramble over the wall, feeling the wet mortar crumble under his shoes. His trouser leg caught on a broken brick and he heard it tear. He slipped, almost tumbled and managed to keep his balance as he regained his feet on the far side.

'Emma!' He managed a slow heavy lope over the wet uneven ground. 'Emma? Lyn? What's going on?' He stumbled on a tussock of knotted grasses and hurried on, like Lyndsey before him cursing the fact that he had no torch.

He could see the them now. Two faint silhouettes in the dark; they appeared to be struggling.

'Emma? Are you OK?' Alex was panting heavily now. 'Lyn? What are you doing? Leave her alone.'

He had reached them now. He grabbed Emma's arm and pulled her to face him. 'Emma? What's going on? Are you all right? Look, this is crazy. It's pouring! For God's sake come inside.'

'Leave her, Alex.' Lyndsey gave him a push. 'Go away. This is none of your business. Sarah, can you hear me?' She had turned back to Emma. 'Sarah, this man is interfering!'

'Too right I'm interfering.' Alex still had hold of Emma's arm. 'You really are bats, Lyn. I'm beginning to think that Paula is right. You genuinely could have hurt Jamie! Leave it. Stop doing this. You've done enough damage.'

'Jamie?' Lyndsey dropped her hold on Emma and turned on him. 'What are you talking about? How dare you come here and interfere. How dare you?' Her eyes were like quicksilver in the darkness. 'You are standing on sacred ground, within the circle. That is sacrilege.'

'Balls!' Alex took a step towards her. 'If you don't stop this, I'm going to call the police.'

'The police?' Suddenly she was laughing. 'You stupid man! You have no idea, have you. No idea at all.'

'Leave him, Lyn.' Emma was suddenly alert. It was as if she had seen Alex for the first time. 'Leave him alone. Let him go. He means nothing to us.'

'No.' Lyndsey shook her head. 'The goddess must have sent him to us for a reason, Sarah, so we will use him. He is just what we need!' Her eyes were glittering. Suddenly her expression had grown dangerous.

Emma smiled enigmatically. 'What is this nonsense about a goddess, Lyndsey? We do not worship a goddess,' she said firmly. 'We worship Satan himself.' She laughed. It was a strange shrill laugh that held no humour.

Lyndsey shook her head. She set her jaw. 'No. The goddess is here with us. She is here. Now! Look! Listen! Obey!'

Turning her back on Alex, she raised her athame into the air, clutching the handle with both hands. 'Blessed goddess, I do this in your name.' She was shouting towards the sky, exultant.

'My God, she's gone mad! Grow up, Lyndsey!' Alex's angry shout was blown away on the wind. He caught at Emma's arm.

She struggled, trying to push him away as Lyndsey turned to face them again. Her face a mask of rage, Lyndsey stared at Alex for a moment, then calmly and without a trace of emotion on her face she brought the knife down with every ounce of strength she possessed into his chest.

For a moment nothing happened. He stood staring at her in astonishment, then releasing Emma's arm, he clutched wildly at the ebony handle sticking out of the front of his jacket. Slowly he fell to his knees as a dark patch of blood appeared on the green waxed cotton.

'Yes!' Lyndsey's hiss of triumph was almost drowned by the roar of the rain on the leaves around them. 'Can you feel it, Sarah? Fresh blood. The energy is incredible! Incredible!' She raised her hands above her head, fingers outstretched, and lifted her face to the storm. 'Now we can do it. We can reach Hopkins. Now the world is ours!'

Emma stood quite still, paralysed with shock.

As Alex slumped forward onto the ground, the last vestiges of control slipped away and Sarah elbowed her way into Emma's mind.

112

'Hopkins has taken refuge with the parson!'

Sarah turned to Lyndsey and beckoned. 'We have to go there. Now.' She did not even glance at Alex, lying on the ground. Heading towards the wall she walked purposefully forward over the wet grass.

Lyndsey followed, scrambling over the wall after her. In the lane she caught her arm. 'Wait. Where are you going?'

'To the parsonage.' Sarah was already striding down the lane. In her mind's eye it was muddy, rutted with cart tracks, already dragging wet at the hem of her gown.

'No. No, we can drive.' Lyndsey, even in her madness was still a child of the twenty-first century. 'Wait, I know where your car keys are. It will take us hours to walk to Manningtree in this rain. Wait here.'

Running up the path to the cottage, she pushed open the door and hunted desperately on the hall table for Emma's keys. They were there, next to her purse. Grabbing them, Lyndsey turned and ran out again, leaving the door wide open, a broad track of light shining down the brick path and across the wet lawn.

She pushed Emma into the passenger's seat and let herself into the driver's side. With shaking hands she managed to insert the keys into the ignition. She was high on adrenaline, barely able to engage the gears, shooting first forward into the hedge, then, cursing, backwards into the road.

Swinging the car round she somehow found the lights and headed down the lane.

The rectory was deserted. Although there were lights on everywhere there was no car and the door was locked. Lyndsey did not even bother to knock. 'Where is he?' She turned to Emma, who had climbed out of the MG and was standing behind her in the rain.

'He has fled to the church.' Emma was not aware that she had spoken. The alien presence in her head had taken her over completely. 'We'll find him there with his lackeys.' She turned and walked towards the gate.

Lyndsey followed, leaving the car engine still running, lights on, illuminating the pouring rain.

They pushed open the gate into the churchyard and paused, looking at the church. Faint light glowed behind the stained-glass windows and Emma nodded. She was smiling. 'They will have locked themselves in,' she commented matter-of-factly.

Lyndsey nodded in agreement. She grinned. 'And I know where Bill Standing hid the key to the north door. I saw him do it.' She chuckled. 'The witches' door! Follow me.'

The old key was under a flower pot next to the spot where an old lead down-pipe disappeared into a gully beside the church wall. The pot was wreathed with weeds and covered in lichen. It had not been moved for a very long time. Grasping the key triumphantly, Lyndsey led the way, groping along the wall of the church in the black shadow of the yews. 'Most churches sealed their north doors,' she murmured over her shoulder. 'But not this place. This church expects witches!'

They came to the door, which was very small, gothic, the pale ancient oak soaked black by the rain, the base overgrown with weeds. If Bill Standing had ever used this as a way into the church, it hadn't been for a very long time.

Cautiously Lyndsey fitted the key into the lock. It didn't move. Gripping the handle with both hands she gritted her teeth, forcing it round, and smiled with satisfaction as she heard the lock grate open.

'Ready, Sarah?' She glanced over her shoulder.

Emma's eyes were blank. She was staring into space. 'Open the door and let me in. I shall deal with him.' Her voice was quite unlike her own.

Lyndsey nodded. Gripping the twisted iron ring which lifted the latch, she turned it and pushed the door as hard as she could. It opened a foot and then stopped, caught by the heavy woven curtain which was drawn across it on the inside. Lyndsey cursed. Reaching in she hooked the curtain aside, and swept it back with a rattle of wooden rings. A cloud of dust descended on them as Emma pushed past her and walked into the church.

Mike was standing on the altar step, flanked by Mark and Colin. They had all heard the door open.

'Emma?' Mike turned, screwing up his eyes to see into the dark body of the church, past the spotlights focused down from the high roof beams onto the altar.

'Emma has gone.' The voice which floated up the chancel towards them was alien to Mark and Colin. Mike had heard it before. In his nightmares. He reached for his cross.

'This is the house of God!' he called. 'Emma, can you hear me?'

'Of course she can't hear you.' Lyndsey was following Emma up the chancel steps. 'She's gone. Sarah was too strong for her. And she's too strong for you. Wherever Hopkins is hiding she'll find him, even if she has to cut out your heart!'

She and Emma were standing at the top of the chancel steps now. Emma was smiling. 'I have waited a long time to catch up with you, Matthew,' she said quietly. Her voice was low and husky.

Mark stepped in front of Mike. 'Matthew is not here, Emma.'

'It's OK, Mark. I can deal with this.' Mike gently pushed him aside. 'Go and fetch help. I need back up from another priest. Ring the bishop's office. The number is on my blotter. Someone must be there by now. And call Dr Good. Have you got a mobile? Hurry.' His eyes hadn't left Emma's face. 'I want you to fight this, Emma. I'm sure you can hear me. Matthew isn't here. Use your psychic eyes. Look. He has gone for good. God has punished him, Emma. Sarah doesn't need to.' He took a step towards her.

It was Lyndsey who laughed. 'Do you really think you can stop her? You're dead!'

Mike didn't even look at her. Beside him Mark recalled that he had left his mobile in the car. Shit! Slowly he tried to edge towards the step, but to reach the open north door, he had to pass Lyndsey and Emma in the narrow aisle between the choir stalls. He edged sideways towards them, aware that they both had their eyes fixed on Mike's face.

Lyndsey gave Emma a small sharp push. 'Go on,' she hissed. 'You've been waiting for this opportunity for three hundred and fifty years!'

'Tell you what, Mike!' Colin suddenly moved forward. 'Why don't I remove this young lady right out of our way!' Stepping down off the altar step he reached for Lyndsey's arm and grabbing her, pulled her almost off her feet.

'Colin, be careful!' Mike's shouted warning came too late as Lyndsey rounded on Colin with a scream of rage, raking her nails down his face. He staggered back and she followed him, belabouring his head with her fists.

Sarah laughed. 'So, it's just us, Matthew.'

'No, Emma. This is Mike.' Mike stepped towards her.

He was completely unprepared for the way she leaped at him, pushing him off balance against the altar. She took the chance to lean across his shoulder, reaching for one of the candlesticks. As she did so, Mike grabbed her wrist. 'Get help, Mark. Now!' Twisting the candlestick out of her hand, he threw it out of reach. Her strength was extraordinary. He was taller than her and normally would have been able to subdue someone her size easily, but the sheer force of her anger was driving him backwards again. Her face was convulsed with fury. It was demonic.

He seized her wrists and just for a moment he managed to hold her still. It was long enough to catch his breath. 'Emma, listen to me! You have to fight this. Jesus is with us. He is here in this church! Listen, Emma. I want you to pray. Can you hear me? Pray!'

Emma stared at him. She didn't recognise him. She didn't even see him. Sarah, inside her head, had suddenly become aware of where she was. 'I despise your church!' She spat on the floor at his feet. But she could feel it: the strength of the place, the sanctity around the altar. While he stayed there he would be able to fight her as he had fought her in that other church. 'I'm not going to stay here a moment longer. If you want to save my soul you will have to follow me. Outside! Away from the house of your God! Then let us see who is strongest!' Turning, she threw herself down the altar step and began to run down the aisle.

'Emma! Wait!' Mike was running after her.

'No!' she screamed. 'No!' Reaching the main door, she wrenched away the chair that Colin had wedged against the handle and fumbling, dragged the door open. Without a thought for his own safety if he left the sanctuary of the altar, just as she intended Mike tore after her.

There were several cars parked outside, and a group of women standing near the porch. He pushed through them, frantically trying to keep Emma in sight. Ducking through the gate, he caught up with her in the road outside and reached out, trying to catch her arm. 'Emma, please, we have to fight this together!'

'No!' She turned on him like a wildcat. 'Leave me alone! If you follow me, I shall kill you! Don't you see?' That was Emma.

'Hopkins is not going to escape me now. I am going to tear your head off, so that I can find him!' That was Sarah.

Mike staggered back, off balance from Emma's push. By the time he had recovered himself, she had gone, running out of sight into the darkness.

113

Paula woke with a start. She stared round the bedroom, which was faintly illuminated by the night-light on Jamie's table, wondering what had woken her so suddenly. Jamie was sound asleep. Gently she put her hand on his forehead. The fever had almost gone.

She stood up, stiff after sleeping in the uncomfortable chair and, glancing at her watch, made her way to the door. It took her only a few minutes to realise Alex was not in the house. Peering through the kitchen window her worst suspicions were confirmed. His car had gone.

The bastard! How could he? He had left her looking after a sick child while he had skipped off and she could guess where. Emma! That scheming bitch had managed to lure him away with her pathetic phone calls and her helpless-little-me act!

Taking a deep breath to calm her anger, she picked up the phone. Her next-door neighbour answered on the first ring. 'Pam, I am sorry it's so late, but can I ask you a great favour? Could you come and sit for half an hour or so? The children are asleep but I need to go out and Alex isn't here.'

Pam chuckled. 'No problem. I'll be over in five minutes. Usual rate?'

Paula gave a dry laugh. 'As many biscuits as you like and your choice of video.' She was waiting in the hall with her coat on when her neighbour appeared.

Alex's car was pulled into Emma's parking spot, tightly wedged against the hedge as though another car had been there when he arrived. There was no sign of Emma's car now, although Lyndsey's bike was there, lying half buried in the hedge. Climbing out, Paula frowned. The door to the house was wide open, light pouring out across the garden.

She ran up the path and went in. 'Alex? Where are you?'

There was no answer. 'Alex?' She pushed open the living room door. It was empty. One by one she looked into every room in the house, then she walked out again, standing in the rain by the gate looking up and down the road. Only two of them could have gone in Emma's car. So someone must be there.

Across there in the darkness lay the churchyard where Lyndsey cast her spells. She shuddered. The bitch! How could she? To target young innocent children! Paula stepped out into the road and walked across. What was it Judith had said? Pray, as if by praying you could build a wall around the evil which would last forever. The evil which lay somewhere out there in the old graveyard. Not quite knowing why she did it, she found herself climbing the wall and walking slowly across the grass. 'Alex?' she called out. 'Alex, are you there?'

The only answer came from the wind howling in the trees.

Alex was already cold. She didn't need to press her fingers against his neck or take his hand in hers to know that he was dead.

It was only when she tried to turn him over to cradle his head on her lap that she found the little knife with its ebony handle in his chest; the front of his jacket was stiff with blood.

She didn't realise that she was crying until she felt her tears scalding her rain-wet cheeks. Rocking back and forth on her knees, she could hear herself howling like an animal in pain. The wind was rising now, carrying the sound away into the trees.

She sat for a long time, cradling her husband's body in her arms, hugging him close as though by sheer willpower she could coax warmth back into his ice-cold veins.

Lyndsey had done this. Lyndsey, whom Alex had befriended. Lyndsey, the witch. Lyndsey the worshipper of Satan. Lyndsey, the killer of babies! She had murdered him. Paula's eyes suddenly flew open. There was no one in the house, so where was Lyndsey now? Where was Emma? Was Emma part of this too?

Her thoughts flew back to the children. Were they safe? What about Jamie, whom Lyndsey had bewitched? Were they all right?

'Don't worry sweetheart, they'll be all right. I'll take care of them. I'll make her pay. I will.' Lifting her husband's head gently from her lap and laying him back onto the grass, Paula scrambled to her feet, trembling. She could barely speak for her sobs. 'I swear it.'

She turned away from him, then she stopped. Tearing off her raincoat she spread it over Alex and tucked it tenderly round his body. 'God bless, my darling. I'll check they are all right, then I'll come back. I won't leave you alone, I promise.' The tears were streaming down her face as she bent and kissed his cold forehead.

She tore the knee of her tights as she climbed over the wall, shredding the skin, but she didn't notice as she ran back to the car. Revving the engine frantically she backed out into the road and turned with spinning wheels towards home.

Pam was waiting for her. 'Paula? What's wrong? What's happened? Oh, my goodness, look at your leg!'

'Are the children all right?' Paula had pushed past her and was already racing up the stairs.

'They're fine. They are both asleep.' Pam followed her, puffing. 'Paula, there was a phone call for you. I was to tell you that the prayer circle are going to meet at the church to pray for Judith. Does that mean anything?' She broke off with a little yelp of fright as Paula stopped in her tracks and spun round.

Her face in the muted landing light was wild with grief. 'Judith? It's too late for Judith! It's too late for prayers! It's up to us now. I'm going to kill the woman who killed Judith! I'm going to kill the woman who killed Alex! Stay here, Pam. Please. Guard them with your life! Don't let anyone in. Anyone. Please.' Pam was still on the landing as Paula hurtled past her downstairs and out into the rain.

Behind her, Sophie had woken up. In her little room beyond Jamie's she began to cry.

There were four cars outside the church. Paula threw herself out of hers and ran to the porch where several other women had just arrived. They were talking excitedly amongst themselves, staring up the road where the rector had disappeared, running as fast as he could after Emma Dickson.

'Where is Lyndsey?' Paula cried. 'She's killed Alex!' Her eyes were wild, her face muddy and there was blood on her skirt.

Forgetting the rector they stared at her, stunned.

'What did you say?' someone asked, their voice tight with shock. 'Alex?'

Paula stared round. The faint porch-light showed up the women's faces, their hair covered by scarves and hats, their coats

510

and jackets being whipped by the wind. These women were her friends. 'He's dead!' she cried. 'Didn't you hear what I said? He's dead and Lyndsey killed him!'

They couldn't seem to understand what she was telling them. They were staring at her, not believing her, not saying anything. 'Alex is dead!' she screamed. 'She stabbed him. I found him, with a knife in his chest. Lyndsey's knife!' Pushing through them, she ran towards the church door and pushed it open.

The women were staring at each other, not sure what to do, and then slowly they followed her in. 'Where is Lyndsey?' Paula screamed. 'The Lord will tell us! He will know!'

Someone had found the main lightswitch and the nave of the church was suddenly bathed in bright light.

Paula stopped, blinking. Lyndsey was there. She was up near the altar and she seemed to be wrestling with the TV men. Mark, forgetting the mobile, had raced back to Colin's aid.

'So!' Paula stopped in her tracks. 'There she is! The Lord be praised! He has found her for us!'

She headed towards Lyndsey, the other women running in her wake.

'You killed my husband. You tried to kill my children.' Violently pushing first Mark, then Colin aside, Paula slammed her fist into Lyndsey's face. Colin, taken off guard, missed his footing and fell heavily back against the wall.

Lyndsey clutched at her face, blood streaming from her nose. Slowly she turned towards Paula. Through the blood, she was smiling. 'Yes, I killed him! He tried to stop us. He interfered. Then the goddess called for a sacrifice. He gave himself to us, Paula. He asked for it.'

'You bitch!' Paula shrieked. 'I can't believe it. You aren't even denying it.' She swung round to face the other women. 'Did you hear that? She isn't even denying it. She's proud of it. She killed Alex and she's pleased with herself!' She dashed the tears out of her eyes with the back of her hand. 'She deserves to die! We should burn her!'

Suddenly the atmosphere was electric. The other women glanced at each other. 'Yeah. Hanging's too good for her!' a voice came from the back of the group clustered on the chancel steps.

'Make her suffer!'

'Kill her!'

'Call the police, someone,' a calmer voice called out of the crowd. 'That's best. Let them take care of this.'

'No!' Paula faced them, trembling uncontrollably. 'This is not a job for the police! This is for us! This is women's business! Get her!' She lunged forward. 'She calls herself a witch. We'll treat her as a witch. We'll swim her like they swam witches in the past. Swim her. Let her know the fear. Let her know the pain!' Grabbing Lyndsey's wrist, she gave it a mighty tug, pulling Lyndsey off her feet. 'Well, what are you waiting for?' she screamed. 'This way!'

'I'm with you, Paula.' A woman stepped out of the crowd. 'The police will probably give her counselling and let her go! They have no idea. This calls for action. This one is up to us. Come on, girls.'

By the time Colin and Mark had caught their breath, Lyndsey had been dragged screaming from the church. They stood staring, numb with shock, listening to the shrill voices of the women as they faded away in the distance. Not all of them had gone. One or two were hanging back, clearly uneasy about what had happened. The sight of them finally galvanised Mark into action. As they headed slowly for the door he ran after them. 'Stop. Think what you're doing! For God's sake, someone call the police,' he called.

One of the women hesitated. She seemed uncertain what to do. Fumbling in her bag she produced a mobile. Mark grabbed it. It took only a second to dial 999, then the two men ran to the door and out into the churchyard in time to see Lyndsey being bundled into the back of one of the cars parked outside. In a matter of seconds all of them had driven away.

'Come on, we've got to follow them!' Mark turned and ran towards the rectory where their own car stood on the gravel. 'If we don't get there fast I dread to think what will happen. Where the hell has Mike gone?'

Behind them the church was suddenly very quiet as the bystanders made for their own cars and drove away. In the doorway Bill Standing was staring at the altar, frowning. He could see the angry red and black energies in the air around the chancel. The church was going to need a spring clean after this. But he needn't go in. Mike would know what to do. He shrugged himself deeper into his coat. Where was Mike? No time to wait for him. There were things to be done elsewhere and it looked as though he was going to have to deal with them alone.

114

'Which way did they go?' Mark was peering through the windscreen wipers at the deserted main street.

'Guess.' Colin shook his head. 'That woman was insane with grief. They'll kill that girl if we don't get there.'

'They talked about swimming her.' Mark drummed his fingers on the wheel. He thought again for a fraction of a second. 'I know. It's worth a try.' He swung the car into the main road and pressed the accelerator to the floor.

'What did she mean, all that about Lyndsey killing her husband?' Colin was leaning forward, his eyes glued to the windscreen. 'You don't believe that, do you?'

Mark shrugged. 'Do you remember last week? That was the woman who came into the shop and screamed at Lyndsey. She had her kids with her.' He turned the car round the corner onto the Walls. 'Oh, shit! I hope I'm right about this. It's our only chance.'

'There are car lights ahead.'

Mark sent the car hurtling along the road and screamed to a halt behind the other vehicles which had drawn up near the Hopping Bridge. They could see at once that his guess had been right. Lyndsey was lying on the roadside with several women bending over her. Even from there they could see she had been tightly trussed, hands to feet.

As Mark leaped from the car, the women lifted her crouched form bodily to the brick balustrade which bordered the pavement.

'Stop!' Mark shouted. 'Don't do anything stupid.'

One woman glanced over her shoulder towards him. She stood back, hesitating. Then another. It was Paula's voice that came to him out of the darkness. 'Do it! Throw her in. If you don't I will!'

They saw her run at Lyndsey and push her hard. They heard Lyndsey scream and then a huge splash from the water beneath.

A flock of ducks rose quacking in panic from the lake and wheeled off into the dark.

Mark reached the balustrade, panting. 'Where is she? Can you see?' He tore off his jacket. Below him the water was very black.

Behind them first one, then another car drew away from the kerb with a scream of wheels and disappeared swiftly into the night.

'There.' Colin was pointing. One of the streetlights amongst the trees behind him cast a faint misty illumination across the water.

Mark jumped into the water feet first. To his surprise he found he could stand up, his feet sliding about in the mud as he groped frantically around him under the water. 'Lyndsey? Can you hear me? Where are you?' He took a step forward, his hands outstretched, sweeping the water in front of him.

'I think I can see her.' Colin had climbed over the wall himself. He hung for a moment from the bridge, then he let himself drop beside Mark. 'Here. Over here.' He waded with difficulty a few steps towards the trees which overhung the bank. 'She's face down.'

Between them they dragged Lyndsey onto the muddy bank. Colin was trying to straighten her cold legs. 'They've tied her wrists to her ankles.'

'They would. They know their history,' Mark said grimly, groping in his pocket. He produced a knife. 'Here, see if you can cut through the rope. Oh, shit! My mobile is soaked.' He had found it in his jacket pocket where it must have been all along. 'No, there's no signal. We need an ambulance fast.'

'Mine's in my briefcase in the car.' Colin had managed to cut Lyndsey's wrists free of the binder twine which had been used to tie her. Gently he straightened her out and tipped her head back. 'She's not breathing. Can you do mouth to mouth?'

'Yes.' Mark knelt down beside her. 'Go and call, Col. Then come back down and give me a hand.'

Paula was standing on the bridge watching them. As Colin climbed up the bank and scrambled over the wall onto the pavement, she stared at him doubtfully. 'She's dead, isn't she?'

'She's not breathing.' Colin ran towards the car.

Paula went after him. 'If she died in the water, that means she was innocent.' She looked bewildered. 'So, why did she die?'

'We don't know she's dead.' Colin pulled open the car door

515

and reached in for his briefcase, scrabbling frantically amongst sheaves of papers. Finding the mobile at last, he stabbed at it with shaking hands. He called the ambulance and then the police again, then he reached into the back for the old rug which lay there. When he climbed out of the car again, Paula was still standing by the bonnet, staring back towards the bridge. She seemed dazed. 'She shouldn't have died.' She seemed to be indignant.

'No, she shouldn't.' Colin walked back to the wall and vaulted over it, sliding down the wet muddy bank to where Mark was working on Lyndsey. 'The ambulance is on its way, Mark,' he said quietly. He bent and tucked the rug around her cold body. 'Do you want me to have a go?'

Mark nodded. He moved back, so that Colin could take his place. 'There hasn't been any response at all,' he said. He was shaking with cold. 'I don't think she's going to make it. Who is up there?'

'Only Paula. The others have vanished.' Colin went down on his knees beside Lyndsey, putting his mouth over hers. Her lips were cold.

'I'll go up and wait for the ambulance.' Mark was shivering violently now. 'I'll find something for you to put on.' Somehow he hauled himself up to the roadway. Paula was standing where Colin had left her. She was crying.

In the distance they could hear an ambulance coming. Paula looked up. 'They'll save her, won't they?'

Mark shrugged. 'Maybe.'

'She shouldn't have died. She was guilty. She killed Alex. It was her knife. Her magic knife!'

He frowned. He was rummaging in the back of the car for a jacket. 'No, Paula. She didn't really kill him. You've imagined it,' he said sternly.

'She did.' Paula looked bewildered. 'I found his body.'

Mark glanced at her.

'You heard her in the church. She didn't deny it. She was proud of it.'

'Where is he, then?'

'At the old churchyard. Her knife is in his chest. He is quite cold.' Her voice slid up hysterically. 'I found him.'

'Christ!' Mark bit his lip. She meant it. He had pulled the jacket out of the car, about to put it on. He had second thoughts and put it round Paula's shoulders instead. 'I can vouch for the fact that Lyndsey had completely lost it, but, whatever has happened, you shouldn't have done this.'

'I had to.' She shook her head weakly. 'I had to. She had bewitched my children.'

The ambulance appeared, its blue light flashing. Mark stepped out into the road and raised his hand. In only a few seconds two paramedics were scrambling down the bank.

They watched the two men working on her, watched them glance at each other and shake their heads, watched them bend down again, listen intently, cover her face with a mask and lift her onto a stretcher.

'She's breathing. We've got a faint pulse!' one of them said as they loaded her into the ambulance.

'Thank God!' Mark was standing on the pavement beside Paula. Gently he put his arm round her shoulders.

'Here.' The driver went back and pulled three foil blankets out of the ambulance. 'Wrap yourselves in these. We don't want anyone dying of hypothermia. No one else hurt? You all OK?'

Mark nodded. 'Just cold.'

'Right.' The driver slammed the door shut and walked round to the front of the ambulance. 'What the hell was going on here?' He looked back at them all as he pulled open the door. Then he shrugged. 'Anyone want to come with her? No? Well, if you called the police, they might not be here for a while. There's trouble in Walton, and there's been a big pile up at the roundabout near Elmstead. The whole area seems to have gone mad tonight. I've never known it like this, not in all my years in the service!'

They watched the ambulance pull away. Mark glanced at Colin. 'There's no point in waiting, then. I'll ring them and tell them not to bother to come. That's probably best.' He glanced at Paula, then back at Mark. 'What shall we do now?' he asked quietly.

Paula had begun to tremble uncontrollably.

Mark opened the back door of the car and he gently pushed her inside and closed it on her, then he walked round to the driver's door.

'Perhaps we should go back and find out what happened to Mike? What a mess!' He glanced at the back seat where Paula was huddled, moaning quietly to herself. 'Do you believe her?' he murmured.

517

Colin nodded. 'Why on earth would she make something like that up? The whole world has gone mad! I reckon anything is possible. Something must have sent her over the edge.'

'Do you think we should go up there and look?'

Colin turned and peered at Paula. 'Did you call an ambulance when you found your husband?'

She frowned. 'I can't remember.'

Mark started the engine. 'I know where it is. It's where Alice took her non-film.' He threw the car into gear. 'We'll drive up there, Paula, and check what's going on, OK?'

'What's the point?' Paula was shivering violently inside her silver paper wrap. 'No one can help him. She killed him. And the water rejected her.' Suddenly she started to laugh. 'You realise that means that God has already found her guilty!'

115

Bill had managed to climb the hill behind the village. The mist was thick up here, now the rain had stopped, the smell of evil very strong, swirling up from the sea.

Not many people knew about this place. Once it had been sacred. Bronze Age men had buried their dead here. In the Iron Age there had been a temple. Then came the gods from the northern lands across the seas. Not necessarily evil. Not then. But powerful, knowing how to release the energies of the land; knowing how to draw in that mist from the sea.

It was hard to summon the Ward. He wasn't sure he could do it. Traditionally they assembled at sundown in every town and village; the spirits, the ghosts, the elves, the fairies of the land, and then they would spread out along the spirit paths to weave the circle of protection which kept the area and its people safe. In most places now, the Ward was long gone, the old ways forgotten, the spiritual, psychic centres of the towns exposed, helpless before the onslaught of so much evil. There were people who still understood. Young Lyndsey had told him that. Fountain people, they called themselves, some of them. But as far as he knew there weren't any round here. Here there were very few any more to understand or care.

Maybe the Ward would consider it ill-mannered for him to invoke them? Maybe they had disappeared from here, too. But when he had visited Spindles and St Mary's churchyard he had sensed them there standing back, watching. And in the gardens at Liza's. And they used to watch over Barker's shop. But nowadays they were wary; shy; unwilling to come forward.

Shivering in his old tweed coat and woollen muffler, he tried to steady his breath, calm his thundering pulse, exhausted after the steep climb. Slowly he raised his hands. 'Help us,' he whispered. He could feel his father's talisman snug against his chest beneath his vest and shirt and heavy sweater, the secret sigils reassuring. Strong. 'Help us. Come forth. Drive out this vile mist . . .'

His voice was weak. They couldn't hear him. With a shiver he looked round. On his own he wasn't strong enough. He needed Mike. From the very start he had sensed that. This wasn't cunning versus Christian. This wasn't the Elder faith against the new. This was good against evil. This was dark against light.

He didn't know the words any more. Perhaps he never did. All he had was an honest heart and the desire to save his town. Perhaps it would be enough? If they were still there. If they were listening. If he could convince them.

116

'Emma, wait!' Mike had run after her up the road, where she turned away from the rectory and passed the next two houses. There the streetlights stopped and the road turned into a country lane. It was very dark and she was hard to see in the distance. 'Emma!' he called again, panting. 'Wait. We have to talk.' She was splashing through puddles, dodging overgrown branches in the hedge, drawing steadily ahead of him until the lane curved away towards the east and he lost sight of her.

He couldn't afford to lose her now. Forcing himself on, he tore up the lane, slipping on the mud where a tractor had gone up the centre of the tarmac leaving a trial of debris behind it. 'Emma!'

He turned the corner and there she was, waiting for him. In the dark he could barely see her face, but she was smiling.

He skidded to a stop, warily. 'Emma, is that you?' He was panting heavily.

She laughed. She was scarcely out of breath. 'Emma has gone. I told you.' She paused, her head a little to one side. 'So, you couldn't resist coming after me, Matthew. You fancied me, didn't you! You wanted me in your bed. And so here you are, to see if you can persuade me to spare you. But you see, it won't work. Not this time. Not ever again.'

Mike was watching her carefully. 'So, Sarah. How do you intend to kill me?' He kept his voice light; unthreatening. 'Tell me, have you a knife? A gun? Or are you going to do it with a spell?'

To his relief he saw the uncertainty in her eyes. She was frowning.

'No spell is strong enough, Sarah. Not now,' he went on, pushing his advantage home. 'He has gone. Gone forever! Do you hear me? I am not Matthew Hopkins. He tried to possess me but I fought him. I will fight him again, if I have to! Leave it,

521

Sarah. God will deal with Matthew. And he has comforted Liza.'

She shook her head. 'Liza wouldn't want to be comforted by God. She worshipped Satan.' Her accent thickened again. 'As I do. And he is more than a match for your God, parson.'

'I don't think so, Sarah.' Mike smiled. 'I believe that love and light can win against hate and darkness every time.' His breathing was steadying now and he was feeling more confident as she continued to stand there talking to him. She had no weapons. There was nothing she could do.

'Emma, I want you to be strong,' he murmured quietly. 'I know you can hear me. We can push this woman out. God is with us here. We can do it. I am going to command her spirit to leave you. Are you ready?' He took a step forward.

She didn't move.

He raised his right hand to make the sign of the cross. 'In the name of God the Father; in the name of God the Son, and in the name of God the Holy Spirit, I command you, Sarah Paxman, to leave this place now. I command you to leave Emma alone and never return.' He managed to make his voice ring out powerfully against the muffling thickness of the mist.

He paused. Somehow he had expected some sign. Some great struggle. But Emma made no sound at all. She continued to stand there staring at him.

The silence lengthened. Then suddenly she laughed. The sound made his skin crawl. 'So, priest! What do you do now? I'm still here!' Her eyes sparkled, almost coquettishly as she tossed her head and turned, striding away from him into the darkness. A little further on, the lane debauched out onto the hillside where the short rabbit-cropped grass was studded with wet furze, and she moved ahead of him out onto the hill at the very edge of his vision, fading in and out of sight as the wisps of mist trailed around her, caressing, drawing her on. Mike stumbled into a rabbit hole and swore quietly under his breath. He mustn't lose sight of her now.

'Emma! Emma, wait!'

Her only reply was another peal of laughter.

Somewhere to the left of him, higher up on the hillside he could see a patch of light. A bonfire? A powerful torch? Emma had turned the other way, instinctively seeking the darkness.

'Emma!'

It was then that he saw the stooped figure, wrapped in coat and muffler, emerge out of the mist.

'Bill? What are you doing here?'

'I am trying to summon the Ward.' Bill straightened his shoulders. 'Where were you, Rector? We needed you at Hollantide! The evil flooded us from every side. Every Devil and demon was there and you chose to go away!'

'I didn't choose to Bill.' Mike stared round anxiously. He could no longer see Emma. 'I had no choice. But I was praying for you.'

'Aye, well. I need you to pray now, too. You and I need to stand shoulder to shoulder, Rector. Do you have your holy water?'

Mike shook his head.

'Then bless this.' The old man held out the wet branch which he had pulled from a tree in the hedge at the bottom of the field. 'And flick it into the mist. With your blessing it will be holy. By tradition it is sacred. It will do the trick. You and I together can summon the Ward, Rector. We can drive out the evil and rescue that young woman's soul while we're about it.'

'Where is she?' Mike was staring into the mist.

'Not far. She's hiding from the light on the hillside there.'

'What is it?' Mike frowned, feeling the beads of moisture condensing on his eyelashes.

'Fairy fire.' Bill chuckled. 'Make no mind, Rector. It's not Christian, but it's strong and it's good. We're on the same side, Rector, remember? It seems to me you don't think you're strong enough for all this, but you are. You can do this.'

Mike glanced at him. He was right. He could do this. His faith was strong enough. He raised his right hand over the branch of rowan in his left and made the sign of the cross.

'Help us, friends!' Bill was calling into the darkness. 'Bless this place. Bless that young woman. Bring the light back to this land!'

Mike could see her now. She was standing still, staring back towards them. In a few quick strides he was at her side. 'Sarah Paxman, I command you to go. In the name of God, of Jesus Christ and of the Light, I command you to go!' He lifted the rowan and flicked it across Emma's shoulders, showering her in ice-cold droplets of water.

She screamed.

523

'No!' Her hands went to her face, clawing at her eyes. 'No! I can't see. I'm blind!'

'Emma, fight. Drive her out.' He stepped towards her. Groping for the chain around his neck, he unfastened it. It took only seconds to hang the little silver cross around her neck. She shrank back, sobbing. Bill joined him. 'Here. Give her this as well.' He dragged the pendant from his own neck and put it over her head to hang next to the cross. Emma subsided onto her knees in the mud, sobbing. 'I can't . . .' She was finding it hard to breathe. 'I can't see.'

'You'll be all right, girl.' Bill put his hand on her shoulder. The two men held their breath, watching Emma carefully, then Bill gave a long contended sigh. 'Rector, look.' He nodded behind them up the hill. A woman was walking away from them into the mist. A woman in a long gown.

Mike's mouth fell open. 'Sarah?' he whispered.

Bill nodded. 'She's gone. Your woman here will be all right now. The Ward will deal with that other one.'

'So it worked? They came?' Mike looked down at the rowan branch in his hand.

'It worked. They came.' Bill chuckled again. I reckon tomorrow we'll find the mist has gone. The sun will come out again.'

Mike sighed. He turned back to Emma and held out a gentle hand. 'Emma?' he said cautiously. 'Can you hear me? Do you remember the little prayer I taught you? I want you to say it. Christ be with me, Christ within me. Say it, Emma.'

She smiled wearily. 'Mike?'

'Say it, Emma. Christ be with me.'

'Christ be with me.' She repeated it faintly. 'Mike, what has happened? Why am I here?' She was looking round in confusion. She put her hands up to her face and pushed the wet hair off her forehead. 'Have I been sleep-walking?'

Mike nodded. He smiled with relief. 'That is exactly what you've been doing, Emma. Come.' He held out his hand. 'I want you to come back down out of the mist.'

She went to him hesitantly, still confused. 'I don't understand –'

'You don't have to.' He put his hand round her shoulders. 'Are you coming, Bill?'

Bill shook his head. 'I reckon I'll stay out here for a bit, Rector. I've got some thank yous to say. I'll follow you down in a minute.'

Mike nodded. Turning back towards the lane, he guided her back over the grass through the mud and onto the road. From there they made their way slowly down towards the church. Somehow it felt right that they should go there.

She followed him without protest as he led her into the porch and through the door. Stepping into the nave, she stopped and stared round, and he saw her frowning.

'It's all right.' He took her hand gently and led her up towards the chancel. 'Do you remember being here before?'

She stopped again. 'I was here with Lyndsey?'

He nodded.

'Where is she?'

'I don't know.' He bent to pick up the candlestick lying on the floor where it had fallen after he had wrestled it from her hand. Setting it on the altar, he replaced its candle and reached for his matches. 'There. That's better. I like candlelight.' He was watching her carefully. Soaked to the skin, her hair straggling round her face, she looked desperately tired and her eyes were full of unhappiness. But they were Emma's eyes. The wild, vicious gaze of Sarah Paxman had gone. She pushed her hands deep into her pockets, shivering, and as though she could stand no longer she suddenly sat down on the kneeler which ran along the altar rails. Mike sat down beside her and after a moment's hesitation he put his arm round her shoulders. Her hair smelled of rain and incense and whatever scent it was she wore – something musky and mysterious. Without thinking he dropped a kiss on the top of her head and she leaned back a little into his arms. 'It's peaceful in here,' she murmured. 'I'm so tired, Mike. I'd like to stay here forever.' She sighed. 'This is a safe place. Sarah doesn't like it here.'

He nodded. 'Safe and quiet. Just us and God.'

She didn't reply and he remained quiet. Was it going to happen to him again? Was his faith going to chase her away before he had even found her?

'She won't come back, will she?' she said quietly.

'Lyndsey?'

'Sarah.'

He shook his head. 'If she does, we'll be ready for her. I don't think she'll come back. I saw her go. Besides, it was Hopkins she was after, not me.'

'Aren't you afraid of me?' She turned and looked up at him.

'No.' He took a deep breath. 'Not any more. I believe in the power of prayer, Emma. In the strength God gives me. I'm actually a bit of a wimp on my own.' He grinned. 'But with those sort of guns behind me, I realise now that I can do anything.'

She gave a small laugh. 'I wish I could believe you.'

'Why not give it a try?'

She didn't reply for a moment but he saw her hand go to the little cross he had hung around her neck. He wondered if she was going to pull it off, but she left it there. 'Can one be unanointed?' she asked thoughtfully. 'I am an anointed witch, and a hereditary witch in my own right, even without Sarah on board.' She wasn't smiling any more.

Mike took a deep breath. 'We can deal with that.'

'I was christened,' she went on, almost absent-mindedly. 'Like all good little middle-class babies, in spite of my witchy blood.'

'Then you're in with a head start.' Mike tightened his arms round her a little. 'Just say the word, and I'll get to work on you.'

'With bell, book and candle?'

'If that is what it takes.'

They both looked up as the latch on the door at the end of the aisle lifted with a sharp click. Mike sighed. He wished those moments with the two of them alone could have gone on forever.

The door opened and a figure appeared in the distance. It was Mark.

Mike stood up and helped Emma to her feet as Mark made his way cautiously up the aisle. 'Is everything all right?' He glanced at Emma.

She nodded. 'Mike escaped my clutches.' She smiled shakily.

'I am glad.' Mark grinned. Then he glanced at Mike, his face serious again. 'I've come from the rectory, Mike. Colin is waiting there with Paula West. Bad news, I'm afraid.' He glanced at Emma. 'Her husband is dead.'

'What?' Mike stared at him.

Emma closed her eyes. She gave a little gasp of misery. 'I was there, wasn't I. I was at the churchyard when he died. I was Sarah. I couldn't help him.' She sank down onto the step again and put her head in her hands. 'Oh, Mike, what have I done?'

'You haven't done anything.'

Mark glanced at her and then at Mike. 'I'm afraid it gets worse.

Mrs West and a group of her friends dragged Lyndsey away. In her confused state she decided that Lyndsey should be swum as a witch. Lyndsey was tied up and thrown into the lake.'

Emma looked up blindly, tears pouring down her face. 'She's not dead!'

'I don't know.' Mark shook his head. 'I don't think so. She's been taken to hospital. We haven't heard how she is.'

'Paula wasn't alone, you say?' Mike put in, appalled. 'There were other women there too?'

Mark nodded. 'They ran away when they saw what Paula intended. Common sense kicked in at the last minute. It was Paula alone who pushed her in. Jane Good is going to take Paula back to her house. She has left her children with a babysitter there. I'm afraid one way or another there is going to be police involvement in this. Luckily Lyndsey confessed to killing Alex West in front of several people, so that will exonerate you, Emma.' He sighed. 'Poor Lyndsey. She seems to have been a very disturbed young woman. And Paula must bear the grief of losing her husband as well as facing whatever charge the police bring.'

'But surely they will understand?' Emma climbed unsteadily to her feet. 'If Lyn killed Alex, Paula can't be held responsible for what she did. And Lyn will be all right. She will, won't she?' She stared from one to the other.

Mark shrugged. 'We must hope so,' he said quietly.

527

117

Jamie and Sophie were fast asleep when Jane Good and Colin let them all into the Wests house with Paula's key. And so was Pam, exhausted by her anxiety after Paula's lightning visit. They woke her gently, told her the tragic news and Pam and Jane put Paula to bed with the help of some sleeping tablets which they found in the bathroom cabinet.

'I'll stay for the rest of the night,' Jane reassured Pam as they came downstairs again. 'If you could help me later, to contact any family who need to know?'

Pam nodded. 'Paula's mother will come. And Alex's –' Her eyes filled with tears. 'I couldn't believe it when she told me before. I can't believe it now.'

'No.' Jane patted her shoulder gently. 'It's always hard to believe when someone dies so needlessly and so suddenly.' She shook her head.

Colin walked Pam to her car and then came back to find Jane sitting on a kitchen stool, nursing a cup of tea. 'There's one for you there.'

'Thanks.'

'I've checked upstairs. They are all asleep.'

'Poor woman.' There was a long silence. Then, 'Jane, I think I should go back to the rectory.'

She nodded. 'Of course. Don't worry, James will be here soon. And the police, I fear. I hope to God they will be lenient with her.'

Colin nodded. Slowly he headed for the door. 'Are you sure you can cope?'

'Of course I can cope,' she said. 'I just hope Paula can when she wakes up.'

118

Bill found Mike and Emma still in the church. For the first time in his life he walked right inside and made his way slowly up the aisle to where they were standing. He glanced from Mike to Emma slowly, and he frowned.

'Bill?' Mike scanned his face anxiously. 'What is it?'

Bill shook his head. 'All is well for now. The Ward have done their bit. The town is asleep and at peace.'

What point in telling them that Sarah was still there? That she was standing behind Emma once again. That in that last moment he had failed them. He was tired. There was no more that he could do. He stared round the church. He had seen Lyndsey, too, hovering in the church porch. A lost soul. Literally. She had died then, in the hospital or in the ambulance or there on the roadside by the lake. Tomorrow the town would hear which.

'Thank you for the amulet.' Emma was smiling at him. She put her hand up and touched the cross and the pendant at her throat. Behind her Sarah shrank back in distaste, her body as wispy as the mist above the sea.

'You take care of it.' Bill nodded slowly. 'Don't take it off. Or that bitty cross, either!' There was a point to hanging all these things on oneself. Not just superstition. Focus. That was it. They helped focus the belief and the protection of millions of people over thousands of years on you. When you needed it.

Mike was strong, he had found the faith he needed. It was up to them now. They would have to fight that one last fight together.

Slowly, Bill turned. 'You should carry holy water with you, Rector. You never know when you will need it,' he said over his shoulder.

'Thanks. Perhaps I will.' He didn't mean it, of course.

'And the rowan. What did you do with it?'

Mike shook his head. 'I threw it away.'

'I see.' Bill had reached the door. 'Good night, Rector. Good night, Miss Emma.'

119

Leaving the locked church in darkness, Mike and Emma went back to the rectory where all the lights were blazing. Colin and Mark had accepted his invitation to stay there for the night. In the morning they would be returning to London with their films, their notes and their plans. The editing suite was booked. What they would make of the documentary now, Mike didn't know, but he accepted the film would still go ahead and that he would probably be in it. The commission, and the funding had long been in place. The media would not stop for tragedy and death. On the contrary.

When the other two had disappeared upstairs to find their bedrooms, Mike flung himself down in a chair across the fire from Emma. A few handfuls of twigs and a couple of logs had warmed the room and brought in an element of cheerfulness.

'Are you sure I can't persuade you to stay too? There's plenty of room.' It was four in the morning.

Emma shook her head. 'I need to go home, Mike.'

He sighed. 'OK. But you are going to have to let me drive you and see you in. You are not going back to a dark empty house on your own.'

As it turned out, the house was far from dark. Every light seemed to be on and the front door was still wide open. Alex's car was parked outside.

'Oh God, Mike!' Emma stared at the old Volvo as they drew up. 'I had forgotten it would still be here.' She glanced nervously across at the churchyard. The overgrown hedge and verge had been trampled flat, the ancient rusted gate dragged open. Police scene-of-crime tape fluttered along the edge of the lane to the tree on the corner, cordoning off the area.

'We can go back to the rectory after we've checked here,' Mike said gently. 'You don't have to stay.'

But she was already climbing out of the car, making her way up the path.

There did not appear to have been any intruders in the house. Mike checked everything, then he locked the back door and slammed the front door shut. He found Emma sitting at the kitchen table, still wearing the jacket which he had solicitously put round her shoulders earlier. She was staring into space.

'Tea?' He reached for the kettle. 'Or would you like something a bit stronger?'

'Something stronger.' She smiled at him bravely and stood up. 'It's here, in the cupboard.' As she pulled out her bottle of whisky she saw the answer machine blinking. Automatically she punched the button.

As Mike reached two glasses down from the shelf and uncorked the bottle they heard Piers's voice ring out round the kitchen. 'Em? I've been trying to reach you all evening. I hope everything is OK and that the cats have turned up.' He paused, obviously trying to find the right words for what he wanted to say next. 'Look, Em, I wanted to tell you this myself before someone else does. I'm sorry to leave it on the machine, but well, I wanted you to know.'

Emma was frowning. Mike passed her a glass.

'Em, look, I know this may seem rather sudden. The thing is, as you suspected, I've met someone. Someone very special. It wasn't working with you and me, was it?' He paused again.

Emma walked away from the machine and sat down.

'She's called Eva.' He was still struggling. 'Em, I asked her to marry me this afternoon and she's said yes. I want you and me to go on being friends. We always will be friends, won't we?' He sounded anxious. Guilty. Upset. 'I'll – I'll talk to you tomorrow. I just didn't want anyone ringing you and letting you know except me. God bless, Em. Talk soon.' The message was cut off.

Emma drained her glass. 'Well,' she said with a sigh. That was all. She stared down at the empty glass and Mike, taking the hint, reached for the bottle.

'I'm so sorry,' he said gently.

She shrugged. 'It was bound to happen. He and I were finished. I just –' She paused. 'I didn't think it would happen so soon.'

532

Mike took a sip from his own glass. It was, he noticed as he caught a glimpse of his wristwatch, nearly five a.m. 'He asked about your cats,' he went on. 'I noticed they weren't around. They haven't come back?'

She shook her head. 'I've looked everywhere.' The tears were close again and she was overwhelmed with exhaustion. She slumped back in her chair.

It was at that moment she heard the voice.

Now is the time, Emma. The perfect time.

She sat up, her fingers rigid on the glass.

Mike frowned. 'What is it?'

'She's here. She's come back, Mike. In my head.'

'She can't have! She's gone!' He was appalled. 'Hold on to the cross, Emma. We'll pray together.' He realised suddenly with a stab of terror that he could see the figure standing behind Emma. The woman was dressed in a long black gown; she wore a white cap and her hair was curled into ringlets round her head. She was staring over Emma's head, straight into his eyes.

'Fight her, Emma.' Mike stood up. 'Don't let her in.'

Emma put her hands to her head. 'I'm too tired, Mike. She's too strong.'

Mike lunged at the figure behind Emma. It disappeared as he raised his hands to its neck. It was Emma who laughed, but when she spoke it was not Emma's voice; it was not Emma's hand which tore off the cross and amulet and tossed them contemptuously onto the table as she stood up.

'Matthew? Where are you? This is where we finally meet again.' She dragged open the drawer in the kitchen table and took out the bread knife.

'Matthew is not here, Sarah.' Mike took a step backwards. 'I told you that. He and I have parted company. We prayed together all Saturday night and he has gone. I am too strong for him, now, Sarah. He is never coming back.'

Sarah's eyes were fixed on his. They were a different colour from Emma's, he realised suddenly. Lighter. Harder.

'It is over, Sarah. It is time to forgive. Innocent people have died, Sarah, because of you. Do you want to add to the total of misery and mayhem that has been caused down the centuries? You can't hurt Matthew Hopkins by killing me.'

His eyes went to the knife she was clasping in her hand.

She was hesitating. Briefly he saw Emma before him again. He saw the puzzled anger in her eyes. He seized the moment. 'Pick up the cross, Emma. Put down the knife and pick up the cross.'

She stared at him blankly.

'Listen to me, Emma. You have to be strong. Christ is with you, Emma. And the Ward. The Ward has taken back the town. The mist has gone.' He hadn't even realised he had said the words. 'You can fight this. Witchcraft is not for you.'

The figure was standing behind Emma again, less substantial now, her eyes like huge dark holes in her face.

Mike lunged forward and twisted the knife out of Emma's hand. 'There!' He threw it into the sink. 'The cross, Emma. Now, fight her! Lord have mercy upon thy servant, Sarah. Teach her forgiveness and love. And forgive her. Loose her from the bonds of evil and anger and free her from her sins. All this I ask in the name of Jesus Christ Our Lord.' He raised his hand and made the sign of the cross again.

There was a moment of total silence as Mike held her gaze and then Sarah lifted her hands as if in surrender. She was separating from Emma, drifting behind her. The last he saw of her was her smile and she had gone.

Emma slumped forward across the table. He was by her side in a second. 'Are you OK?'

She nodded. 'I felt as if I was dying for a moment,' she whispered. 'Every ounce of my energy drained out of my body.' Subsiding into her chair, she closed her eyes.

Mike crouched down beside her and put his arms round her. He rested his head for a moment in her lap. 'She's gone, Emma. Really gone. I don't think she'll be back this time.'

'I could have killed you.' She reached past him and pushed the drawer closed. There were several other knives in there.

He looked up at her and raised an eyebrow. 'I don't think you could. I think you would have overridden her!'

'How can we be sure?' She put her hand on his head and stroked his hair.

'I'm sure.' He smiled.

'And Hopkins?'

He looked up at her. 'I'm sure about him. All this has strengthened my faith, Emma, but it has also taught me not to turn my back on the past, good or evil. Tomorrow I am going out with

Bill Standing again and I am going to learn from him how to make sure the light stays in the town. I can learn from him but he can learn from me as well.'

'And what am I going to do?' She bit her lip. 'I don't think I know how to learn to be a Christian.'

He stood up. 'Ah, but that is my job, too. To teach you.'

'But what if I can't?'

He shrugged. 'I'll have to learn to put up with it.' He took her hands and pulled her to her feet. 'Emma, not so long ago I was thinking of resigning from the church. I've changed my mind. I love my job and I love it here and I have a feeling I have grown to love you.' He made a rueful face. 'And of all of those things, you three are going to be the biggest challenge.'

She smiled wearily. 'I'm not sure how to react to that. Or what you mean by three of us? I'm scared to death by my alter ego, but as far as I know there is only one.'

He laughed. 'I was referring to the cats!'

'Ah.' She smiled sadly. 'If they come back.'

'They'll come back. I have a feeling about it.' He paused. 'You haven't screamed and run out of the room at my suggestion?'

'No.'

'Sleep on it, Emma. We've all the time in the world now to get to know each other properly.'

She nodded. Wearily she stood up and turned to the door. Then she stopped. 'Will you be here when I wake up?' She was anxious suddenly.

He nodded. Walking over to her he put his hands on her shoulders and gently he kissed her forehead. Just for a moment she leaned forward into his arms, her head against his shoulder. Then she drew back. 'Mike, has this declaration anything to do with Piers's message?'

He raised an eyebrow. 'I suppose it made me feel the way might one day be clear?'

'I see.' She nodded. She smiled again and reached up to touch his lips with a fingertip. Then she turned away and began to climb the stairs.

Mike watched her go. He glanced at his watch. It was morning. He should go back to the rectory, but the rectory could wait. He was not leaving Liza's until Emma was up again and he had made sure she was OK.

There was a sharp bang behind him and he jumped. He swung round. A small black figure had appeared through the cat flap. A second later another face appeared, considered him for a moment and pushed in as well.

Mike smiled. 'So, you're back. I'll bet you little blighters knew what was going on. Did you wait until Sarah had gone?'

He reached out and Max walked up to him, stiff-legged. After a moment's suspicious sniffing, he rubbed against Mike's hand.

'Do you think you and I could get to know each other?' he asked softly. He scratched Max's ears. 'I reckon your mistress would authorise some milk and some cat food it she were here.' He turned to the fridge. 'And then I think you two should trot upstairs and snuggle up for a sleep with her. I can't think of anything at the moment which would please her more.'

120

Outside in the dark, Bill Standing was staring down river towards the east. The mist was going. He raised his arms into the wind and, his voice strong and resonant, he began his invocation to the light.

121

November 1ˢᵗ One year later

Daily Telegraph

'Mark Edmunds's much-hyped new series ended last night with an appropriately gory story for Halloween. Filmed in Manningtree in Essex, home of the notorious Witchfinder General, he treated us to atmospheric shots of lovely countryside and a suitably sinister shadowy old house, culminating in a close-up of what he claimed was a ghostly face and then shots of mayhem which made me wonder whether Mark's ghost had been watching too many B movies. This was the best of what has been an intriguing series. It started well, but the ending let it down. I am still not sure I'm convinced.'

Sun

'Cracking stuff. Mark Edmunds's ghosties really got me by the ghoulies!'

The Times

'Mark Edmunds always produces thoughtful, watchable programmes, well researched and beautifully filmed. Last night's, however, tipped over into the sensational and I felt he lost his usual dispassionate objectivity. He demanded too much credulity from his audience. Did he really expect us to believe that the writing on the wall was human blood. He must stick to fact if he wants us to be convinced. A welcome debut for reporter Alice Thomson. I hope we see more of her.'

Guardian

'Containing a range of comments from the locals, from the inane to the thoroughly objective summary from the local rector and his wife, this was a well balanced and exciting attempt to convince that the supernatural exists. But I can't help believing that the full story has not been told even now . . .'

Author's Note

As so often when I finish writing a novel my first instinct is to supply a long bibliography at the end! I shall as usual resist the temptation, and content myself with saying that there are huge numbers of books on the Civil War and even more on the subject of witchcraft, both in history and as a spiritual practice, so that if you want to know more you can read on for ever . . .

Liza and Sarah are fictional characters like all those in the part of the story set in the present day. One of Matthew Hopkins's first victims was an Elizabeth Clark; this is not her – but my Liza is a representative of the many old women upon whom he concentrated the brunt of his attentions.

Hopkins's motivation is endlessly fascinating; he is so universally disliked it is hard to get beyond the initial horror of what he did. But there must have been a reason for his actions. The nightmares and sexual fantasies of a TB sufferer combined with a general growing suspicion of witches and the Puritan ethics of the time seemed as good a place to start looking as any.

Hopkins himself is famous, infamous is perhaps the better word, throughout the eastern counties of England and his name is linked to many a house and pub where stories of his evil deeds linger, but nowhere as much as in the two small towns on the River Stour where he was based.

Legends of the women he burned are legion – although in England witches were hanged. Burning as a punishment in England was reserved for treason and the interestingly named crime of petty treason which was the murder of a husband, so the witches who were burned in East Anglia must have resorted to using their magic arts against their spouses. It was in Scotland and in Europe that the burning times truly earned their name.

As usual I have so many people to thank for their help and advice while I was writing this book.

For my first inspiration I want to thank the group of women in Manningtree who over an excellent lunch at the Stour Bay Café suggested that Hopkins would make a good subject for a novel. And our former rector, The Reverend Chris Harvey who once very gently complained that clergymen always seemed to come to grief in my novels. So, Chris, here is a clergyman who lives to tell the tale, and he's the handsome hero, to boot!

I should like to thank the many people in Manningtree and Mistley who have so patiently answered my questions about their predecessors and their ancestors and their ghosts – and who have begged to remain anonymous! And the charming and without exception kindly witches and Wiccans who have talked about their craft.

Thanks too, to Pat Taylor for her insight and inspiration. To Dr Brian Taylor for keeping medical details roughly within the bounds of possibility. To Phil Rickman for his always wise advice, particularly on the making of TV documentaries. To Peter Edwards for further information on the making of TV documentaries and for knowing what an insurance company actually does when a ghost trashes your cameras!

Over the years I have been lucky enough to know many clergymen who have been inspirational and helpful in the writing of my books, but in particular I would like to thank the Reverend David King for so patiently answering my questions and filling in important background.

Thanks to Nigel Pennick for his last minute masterclass on the Ward. I should make it clear that the rescue and redemption coaxed out of the Ward by Bill Standing in a single short ceremony would, according to Nigel, take at least a hundred years!

Thank you to my son, A. J., who helped enormously with my research and with psychological background information and to my son Jonathan for the title and for his painstaking help with photographing the River Stour and taking as many digital liberties with the scenery as I have in my text.

I should emphasise that any inaccuracies in the research for this book are mine alone.

As always I owe so much to my editorial team – Rachel Hore and Lucy Ferguson – and to my agent Carole Blake.

And one last word: Mistley and Manningtree are lovely places. The mist, if ever it was there, is long gone!